George E. Waring

Waring's book of the farm;

Being a rev. ed. of the Handy-book of husbandry. A guide for farmers

George E. Waring

Waring's book of the farm;
Being a rev. ed. of the Handy-book of husbandry. A guide for farmers

ISBN/EAN: 9783337872908

Printed in Europe, USA, Canada, Australia, Japan

Cover: Foto ©Andreas Hilbeck / pixelio.de

More available books at **www.hansebooks.com**

WARING'S

BOOK OF THE FARM;

BEING A REVISED EDITION OF

THE HANDY-BOOK OF HUSBANDRY.

A GUIDE FOR FARMERS.

CONTAINING PRACTICAL INFORMATION IN REGARD TO BUYING OR LEASING A FARM—WHEN AND WHERE TO BUY—BEGINNING OPERATIONS—KEY-NOTE OF PRACTICAL FARMING—FENCES AND FARM BUILDINGS—FARMING IMPLEMENTS—DRAINAGE AND TILE-MAKING—PLOWING, SUBSOILING, TRENCHING, AND PULVERIZING THE SURFACESOIL—MANURES—ROTATION OF CROPS—ROOT CROPS—FORAGE CROPS—LIVE STOCK, INCLUDING CATTLE, HORSES, SHEEP, SWINE, POULTRY, ETC., WITH WINTER MANAGEMENT, FEEDING, PASTURING, SOILING, ETC. —DIRECTIONS FOR MEDICAL AND SURGICAL TREAT- MENT OF THE SAME—THE DAIRY IN ALL ITS DEPARTMENTS — USEFUL TABLES FOR FARMERS, GARDENERS, ETC., ETC.

By GEORGE E. WARING, Jr.,
OF OGDEN FARM,
CONSULTING ENGINEER FOR SANITARY AND AGRICULTURAL WORKS.

WITH ILLUSTRATIONS.

PHILADELPHIA:
PORTER & COATES,

PREFACE.

I HAVE on my shelves an old book—worm-eaten and time-worn—which professes to teach every art connected with the domestic animals of a hundred years ago, from horses and cattle to goats and fighting-cocks, including their diseases, their habits, and their uses, together with every art belonging to the complete education of a sporting man of the last century;—all written "By a Country Gentleman *from his own experience.*"

Such originality cannot be claimed for the present work; for while none of the operations of the farm are unfamiliar to me, and while I profess to be, by education and experience, a practical farmer, I have tried to tell in its pages not only what I have learned over my work,—which, in the case of any individual, is woefully little,—but also what I have gained from the recorded experience of other farmers, who have been accumulating, little by little for 2000 years and more, the precious sap with which our tree of knowledge is fed.

I have endeavored, too, to look beyond the farmer who has done so much for the unfolding of the riches that Nature, our universal mother, showers upon her industrious sons, and to question, as well, those devoted friends of the farmer, the chemist and the student, who ask from Nature something more than her material gifts, who seek the very cunning of her deft handicraft, who—not satisfied with the fact that she rolls up her bounty from seed-time until harvest—ask how her work is done; how the seed sprouts, the leaf shoots, the blossom unfolds, the fruit ripens; how renewed life and vigor spring from death and decay; how fields are exhausted, and how made fertile; how crops are increased, and kine are grown; how from only air and earth and water such a marvel as man is made to live and move.

I trust that my experience as a farmer has assisted and guided my effort to separate the chaff from the wheat, or at least to select from the teachings of others (whether in the field or in the study) the information that the farmer, as a farmer, will be most benefited by gaining. I have endeavored to forego all theorizing, and to state the leading facts of the art and of the science of farming as plainly and clearly as I could, so that any man who can read at all, and who has ordinary intelligence, may find my statements as free as possible from "hard words," and that he may feel, as he goes along, that it is a brother farmer who is talking to him, and that what he is saying both his reason and his experience lead him to believe worth the telling.

It is now too late in the day for a sensible man to look with anything but profound respect on the invaluable aid rendered to agriculture by the discoveries of science and by the practical application of these discoveries; and if any farmer feels the old carping spirit rising within him, he will, if he be wise, look for a moment at the other side of the question, and consider in what important particulars his own life has been improved by that which he denounces as book-farming,—to which he owes the iron plow, the mowing machine, and probably the house over his head.

This book is intended especially for the use of those practical, working farmers who are willing to believe that, while they have learned much from their own experience, it is not impossible that other farmers (and men in other vocations as well) may have learned something too—something that it may benefit them to learn also; and who are liberal enough to see that the truth and value of a fact is not destroyed by its being printed.

As will be seen by reference to the Table of Contents, a wide range of subjects is discussed: in fact, it has been attempted to write just such a book as a young man leaving another occupation and turning his thoughts to farming would be glad to take for his guide. There is not an important statement in these pages that I do not believe to be reliable, nor a theory advanced that my own experience has not taught me to approve.

Calling especial attention to the third and eighth chapters of the book,—"The Key-Note of Practical Farming," and "Manures,"— the only ones in which the chemistry of farming is much noticed,— it may be said that they are the result of years of study and speculation, kneaded into shape by other years of experience.

It is sad to look back to the days when "Agriculture" was a rosy future with me; when my work was done with the regularity and precision of clock-work by cheap and respectable farm hands; when my crops were all large and my cattle were all fat; when an analysis of my soil, and a chemical ledger-account with each field, kept fertility at the top mark; and when the balance-sheet at the end of the year was always adding to my fortune,—and then to bring my sobered gaze down over the hillside of hard realities that ended in the plain of simple "Farming," of humdrum hard work, dear labor, scant manure, small crops, bad markets, sick animals, and—the least in the world—a sick heart; with "soil analysis" an *ignis fatuus,* and nothing but patience and toil and skill and experience and hard study to take its place.

I make no complaint of the disappointment, for even the harder experiences of life are not without their advantages,—when they are past,—but the hope of turning the steps of other young farmers into pleasanter paths was not the least motive for the writing of this book.

GEO. E. WARING, JR.

Ogden Farm, NEWPORT, R. I., 1877.

LIST OF ILLUSTRATIONS.

BOOK OF THE FARM.

CHAPTER I.

BUYING A FARM,—OR LEASING.

THE very large class of men in America who are either leaving other pursuits to establish themselves in the country, or who, having been brought up on their fathers' farms, are about starting for themselves, find the question of buying a farm to be, for the time, the all-absorbing question of their lives ; and it is very natural that it should be so, for the business is, emphatically, one of a lifetime.

Being, unfortunately, the occupier of leased land, which has so much of another man's affection and interest invested in it, that its purchase is impossible, I can speak with very cordial earnestness on this point ; and I can all the more strongly urge absolute ownership, as of all things almost the most desirable, because I daily feel the uncertainty and unsatisfactoriness of a leasehold tenure.

So much of the man himself, so much of the daily sweat of his face, so much of his hope, and of his anxiety, goes to the ground that he tills ; so many of the associations of his home, with its joys and sorrows, are entwined around every tree and shrub in his dooryard, that I can conceive for him no more dismal thought in life than that, some day, he must pull himself up by the roots, and, further on in his years, must take a fresh start, with all his interest to cultivate anew. Apart from any question of economy or of interest, I would strongly urge every man, who finds it possible for him to do so, and who means to end his days on a farm, to buy his land. Let the farm be smaller than he could hire, and less convenient ; let him go in debt for it if he must, but I deem

him to be a happier man who *owns* a small place, even with a
mortgage for his shadow, than is he who, with better facilities for
his daily occupations, and better conveniences for his daily life, has
hanging before his eyes the fact that some day, when he is older
and less able to commence farming again, he must resign his improvements to his landlord, turn the key on his home, and pitch
his tents in strange fields.

The question of economy, however, cannot be set aside.
There are, I know, many farmers whose aim in life seems to be
to see how much money they can screw out of the land to invest
on bond and mortgage, and the more often they can move and
apply their leeches to fresh cheeks, the more fully they will gratify
their lowest ambition. They save at the spigot of improvement,
and are unconscious of the open bung of exhaustion; in their
way they are happy. But every man who means to take a broader
view of farming, and recognizes the fact that the most substantial
part of the returns of his labor, and of his outlay, consists in
better buildings, better soil, and better stock, will see a sufficient
reason for wishing to become the owner of the fee of his farm.
In the other transactions of life, where the principle holds good
that any thing is worth what it will fetch in the market, business
men invest money with a view to the chances of its return at any
time when they choose to sell. In farming, this principle does
not hold good—at least not with regard to the farm itself.

It is better that the question of selling be not at all considered,
for a valuable farm is always a very difficult thing to sell, and very
rarely brings so much as it is worth. There are persons who
speculate in farms, who buy worn-out land at a low price, and,
after improving it, sell it at a high price. They often make money
by the operation, and they generally do good. They are a useful
class of enterprising men, but they are not the kind of men that I
have in my mind now—men who intend to "follow" farming as a
permanent occupation, who have made up their minds that it is the
thing to do, and who regard it not so much an enterprise as a *living*.
To such, I say, buy your farm judiciously, and, of course, as
cheaply as you can. Make up your mind whether it will suit you,

before you buy, and, having bought it, don't entertain the idea of selling it, nor consider the money you invest in improvements in the light of the selling value they will add to the farm, so much as with reference to the annual return they will bring in convenience, economy, or fertility. In short, consider your farm as a part of yourself, and let it "grow with your growth, and strengthen with your strength;"—you will find your yearly advantage in so doing.

Under all circumstances, make the purchase of a farm a matter of the most careful study. Probably it is the only farm that you will ever buy, and it will have very much to do with your prosperity and your happiness throughout your whole life. If you have been bred a farmer you will be able to decide what you want, and can form an opinion that will be more satisfactory (to yourself at least) than any that you will get from books or from men.

If you have passed your previous life in another occupation, and now mean to make your living by farming, the best advice that any one could give you would be to go and pass a whole year with the best farmer you know. Become a regular "farm hand," with an understanding that you are to be allowed to learn to do all kinds of farm work. "Work away for dear life at *his* farm, "and make him tell you all he knows. Fancy it is *your* money in-"stead of his that buys every ton of manure he expends."* After such an experience, and with the aid of what you can learn from books, you will probably be able to judge for yourself, better than any one else can judge for you, what sort of farm you want.

It is a good plan, (for a man who has an opinion of his own,) to ask the advice or opinion of others pretty freely, not that such opinions are generally worth much, but they are often suggestive of new points to be considered.

I do not propose to say much in the way of *advice* on the subject of farm buying. The variety of tastes to be suited, and the variety of wants to be supplied, are about as numerous as the men themselves who are seeking farms, and, while taste may be in a great measure educated and modified, and while the real

* Talpa.

requirements of all systems of farming might be enumerated and discussed, it would be far beyond the scope of this book to attempt either. There are, however, a few general principles whose application is so universal that they should always be borne in mind, but beyond these I do not deem it practicable to go.

To those who want to buy for a *home* rather than for a *farm*,— who want an ornamental farm, or a sort of agricultural country-seat,—these directions can be of use only in so far as they apply to the strictly agricultural aspects of their case. The very important considerations of beauty, society, and the conveniences of luxurious living must be determined by the light of other considerations than those with which simple farming has to do.

At the same time, every farm must be the home of the farmer's family, and must, (or should,) comprise the influences which are to have the most weight in the development of his own and his wife's characters, and in moulding the habits, the tastes, and the constitutions of his children.

As a man has but one life to live, he should be very careful that he so lives as to get from it the greatest possible amount of health, comfort, cultivation, and ability for usefulness for himself and for his family. This requires a healthy location, a good house, good facilities for education, good neighborhood, and good land. To get all of these is the lot of but few men. Generally, we must be content with only a part of them. Inasmuch as,—after health,— money is not the greatest good, but the means for attaining the greatest good, the quality of the soil is of more importance than any other thing except healthfulness of situation. A hundred bushels of corn or forty bushels of wheat to the acre, will not compensate a man for a houseful of fever and ague, but if they can be had without the disease, they will lead the way to almost every thing else that is needed.

The first thing to be decided is, whether to remain in well-settled parts of the country, or to emigrate to virgin land. In the latter case, the question should be, in how far will large crops and lighter work compensate for the want of good schools, good society, and good home-markets. In the former, in how far will the social, educational, and commercial advantages make up for the poorer quality of the soil. I assume that in either case the consideration of health is the most important of all.

The far West, with its newer and more fertile land, is very tempting to one class of men, and the older-settled parts of the country, with their older civilization and their more dense population, have equal charms for another class. There is much to be said in favor of both; but as the broader culture, and more careless feeding which is practiced on the larger farms of new countries, requires less exact knowledge and less close economy than is indispensable on higher-priced land, the objects of my book will be best attained if I confine my attention to the requirements of the more thorough system of agriculture that small farms make necessary. These are based on universal principles, and the extent to which they may be, or must be, modified, as land grows cheaper, farms larger, labor dearer, and produce less valuable, must be decided by every man for himself.

It is possible to keep fifty cows on a farm of fifty acres. Whether it will *pay* to do so must be decided by the prices of milk and of labor. It would pay to do it near New York City. It certainly would not pay in Western Kansas. Still, a farmer in Kansas could only be benefited by knowing *how* it may be profitably done by the farmer in New York.

While the settlement of wild lands is often a good thing for the settler, and always a good thing for the country, I think that it is often undertaken under a very mistaken notion that it offers the only chance for a man of small capital.

Let us suppose a young man, just married, to have a cash capital of $1,000, (and the same principles will hold good in the case of a smaller or a much larger amount,) with which he purposes to commence farming. He starts life with his own head and hands, the head and hands of his wife, and his $1,000 in money. His object is to so use these advantages as to get out of his life the greatest amount of good. The world lies before him for a choice. He can buy—with a mortgage—five or ten acres on the outskirts of a manufacturing town at the East, or he can have a hundred and sixty acres at the West for the taking. If he is the right sort of man, he may grow rich, with the same amount of labor, during his whole life-time, on either place. Fifty years hence he would have, at the West, a capital farm, well fenced, well watered, with good out-buildings, and with a good house. Probably, he would also have his share of political honor and of social distinction. At the East he would have glass-houses, hot-beds, rich land for vegetables, a house " with all the modern con-veniences," and the most agreeable kind of work for the evening of his life. He would be less likely to achieve personal distinc-tion, but, on the other hand, his wife would have, at least at the commencement, less drudgery, and his children would have better advantages for education near home.

These are the two extremes which are open to him, and his opportunities cover the whole ground between. It is for each man to weigh well the arguments on both sides of the case, and decide for himself,—what no book can tell him,—which path promises the most of what he considers the most desirable.

In choosing a farm in the far West, the considerations which should influence one are rather political and commercial than agricultural. There is so much perfectly good land to be had, that it is much more difficult to decide upon the most desirable location, than it is to find good land in the chosen situation.

Farther east, however, good situations are plenty, while good land is not always to be found, and the more nearly we approach the Atlantic coast, the less easily can we suit ourselves in this respect.

I can say little about the South that ought to have weight in deciding a quiet farmer to go there. The state of society is so unsettled and the prospect of the immediate future is so uncer-tain, while so many Northern men who went there under the most favorable circumstances, and with the most flattering pros-pects at the close of the war, have come home wiser and sadder than when they went, that it seems to me that a prudent person should leave the Southern lands, with their many great advan-tages, for the settlers of some future day.

Supposing the region for the new home to be decided on, and

that it be near one of the larger towns at the East, what are the considerations which should decide us in the selection of the farm?

First.—Avoid a malarious district. There is no curse like fever and ague,—which will bring more misery to a family than any amount of prosperity can overcome, and of which there is far too much both at the East and at the West.

Second.—Choose a small farm,—small, that is, in proportion to your capital. I think no man is wise who at the East goes in debt for more than fifty acres. With plenty of capital, a farmer of good executive ability can hardly have too much land. Any one who has to work himself out of debt, mainly by the labor of his own hands will find fifty acres better than more. His chances will be better with ten acres than with a hundred. So far as one man's work is concerned, especially with small means for the purchase of stock, implements, and manure, the more it is concentrated, the better it will tell in the end, and fifty acres brought to the highest state of cultivation of which the land is susceptible, will produce more at much less cost than will a hundred acres only half so well cultivated.

Third.—Buy a farm that is very much run down and out of repair, rather than a good farm with good improvements which are not exactly what you will require, unless you can get the improvements for much less than it would cost you to replace them. Better pay fifty dollars an acre for a place that fifty dollars more will make exactly right, than a hundred dollars for a place that never will be exactly right.

Fourth.—Remember that to clear up swamps, build stone walls, and dig out rocks and stumps costs much labor, and delays legitimate farm operations. Farmers are not apt to reckon these things at their full cost, because they do not usually pay out money to have them done—forgetting that their own labor, thus spent, might be more advantageously applied to better land. The tile drainage of wet clays may be undertaken with more confidence, because such soils when thoroughly drained are usually the most profitable of all for cultivation. Still, in purchasing land of this sort we should calculate to pay out from thirty to sixty dollars an acre for draining tiles and labor,—an expenditure which not unfrequently comes back in two or three years, from the *increased* production; while the improvement is permanent, and often increases yearly for a long time; yet which does consume capital.

Fifth.—Be sure that the place is adapted to the sort of farming you mean to follow. Do not hope to raise the best fruit on moist, cold land, exposed to the highest winds, nor to raise the best grass on a ground that is too high and dry. If your soil will require heavy manuring, and your system of farming will not produce much manure, you should be near enough to a town to haul out stable manure or other fertilizers without too great cost.

Sixth.—I don't know but that this should follow next after the question of health. Bear in mind the fact that the farm is to be your home. You are a man and your work is out of doors. If you have comfortable lodging, and sufficient shelter, you may get on without being made unhappy by a dismal house. But your wife and your children have equal claims to consideration, and you make a grave mistake if you compel them to live in an uncomfortable or cheerless house, with no pleasant surroundings, and no hope of having them.

Unhappily a very large majority of farmers do make this mistake, and they are rewarded for it by the promptness with which their children run from the old roof-tree as soon as their age and circumstances will allow it, not always, it is true, to better their condition, but always in the hope of a more agreeable life. It will be better for agriculture in America, and, therefore, better for America and for the world, when farmers' children can find no pleasanter place than the home where they were born and when they realize the fact, (for it is a fact,) that the life of a farmer may be as comfortable and as elegant as that of a merchant or a manufacturer. Buy a good farm,—or one that you can afford to make good, in a good situation,—with schools, churches, and society for your family, and you will have a good prospect of a happy life.

Or, if you decide to move to the West, get as many of these advantages as you can, and trust for the rest to the fact that schools, society, and markets are working their way into the newer States with great rapidity. By the time that your children are grown up, it is probable that your new home will be much better surrounded by all of these than would now seem possible.

LEASING.

There has recently been published in London, under the title of "Practice with Science," a series of essays on various agricultural topics. Eighty of its four hundred pages are devoted to the question of leases. There, the farmer who owns his land is an exception. Here, fortunately, the leaseholder is an exception, and an exception so rare that we need not devote much time to the discussion of his position,—one which is generally temporary, inasmuch as he almost always looks forward to the time when he will be able to buy a farm of his own.

The main thing to be said about leases is, that it is for the mutual benefit of both landlord and tenant that they be made as long as possible, in order that the tenant may afford to make such improvements, and to pursue such a course of cultivation as his advantage and the good of the farm may require; that he be allowed every possible facility for good farming, and that he be restrained from any course of cultivation or any sale of crops that will lessen the value of the land for future use.

A lease for a single year at a time, and the privilege of selling hay without returning manure, will usually end in the impoverishment of the farmer, and of the farm too.

2

CHAPTER II.

THE farm is bought, cheaply because it is in a badly run-down condition, but it is only the middle of September, and there is time enough yet to do a good deal in the way of improvement before winter sets in.

The house is pretty good,—a little painting and lime-washing and paper-hanging, will make it cosy enough for a commencement, and it can be patched up so that it will be a snug house, until there is money to make it better. There is too much demand for money on the farm for much to be spent for ornament now.

On the whole, it is not a bad purchase: seventy-five acres of land,—fifty cleared and twenty-five in wood,—two miles from a busy town which gets two-thirds of its food from the West, and most of its butter from the city markets, and which affords a good supply of stable manure. Our end of the town stretches out in a sort of village which has a nice-looking school-house, hardly more than a mile from us. The neighborhood immediately about is good, and the place looks home-like, if the house is an old one. On this score, our young man is quite satisfied, but he has plenty of hard work ahead, a heavy mortgage on his farm, and barely capital enough to work his way to prosperity. It will take a stout heart, a strong arm, and a clear head to bring him through, but it can be done, and I have placed him in this position because his is the lot of most men who marry young and start in life as farmers.

His course must be marked by the most patient industry, but the industry must not be all of the body. Farmers who have gone before him—for thousands of years—have learned a good deal, and what they have learned has been written and printed.   Other farmers are trying experiments, the results of which are as valuable for him as for them. Men in other walks of life have applied their knowledge to finding out how plants grow and what influence is exerted on them by soils and manures.   Their discoveries have been published, and many of them have been approved by practice on farms.   Altogether, this constitutes more knowledge about the operations of the farm than he could gain by experience if he lived ten lives, and spent every day of all of them in the most energetic work on his farm ;—more than he could "think out for himself" if he were to keep up a steady thinking until Doomsday.   And it is, very much of it, knowledge which he, as a farmer, needs to have, just as much as a doctor needs to know what others have learned of medicine.

The best use he can make of a portion of his money is to spend it for agricultural books and papers, and the best use he can make of his leisure time is to spend a fair share of it in reading them. Let his neighbors call him "book farmer," if they will, and let them decry "theories ;" he will work none the less faithfully for any thing he learns out of agricultural books, and in the end he will find that a ton of hay will cost him no more because he knows something of the principles of hay-making, and of the laws which operate in the growth of grass.   The condition of his farm, ten years hence, will be a sufficient answer to those who have ridiculed his habit of reading about farming.

Still, he should read with great caution and with judgment. There is a great deal in agricultural books, and still more in agricultural papers, which is crude and fanciful, and which cannot be successfully applied in practice.   While he should read faithfully, he should make use of what he reads only with great care, and avoid trying, at least on a large scale, any thing which is not actually proven to be suited to his case.

The first of his out-of-door operations should be to make a map of his cleared land, with the division fences, and the location of the buildings.   This map need not be very accurate—what is most necessary is to have something that will serve as a reminder when he is studying over his future operations, in the house in bad weather. It will cost very little to have a surveyor make a diagram of his boundary lines from the description in his deed, and he can pace off the starting-points of his division fences, so as to make a map good enough for his own use.

Very soon after taking possession, he should manage to get in five or six acres of rye. This will never come amiss. If the pastures are backward in the spring, he can cut enough, daily, for a green bite for his animals, and what he does not need to use in this way will be worth, in straw and grain, much more than it will have cost.

Other necessary work, in repairing buildings for temporary use, building up fences where they have fallen down, providing winter food for his stock, and getting ready for winter generally, will occupy his time until cold weather actually sets in. Even if he have ready money for improvements, I would recommend him to be very careful about commencing them at once. He needs at least a whole winter to make up his mind what he really wants, though, if he has swamp land on his place, he can make no mistake in hauling out muck to be composted with the manure as fast as made. As soon as he can decide which field he will put in corn the next year, if he intends to buy manure from stables in the town, he should commence hauling and spread it directly on the sod to be plowed in in early spring. If he is sure of early pasture, he may omit sowing rye, and plow his corn land as early as possible, spreading the manure on the furrow. The crop will probably be better for it, and he will, at least, have that much spring work done beforehand. This fall-plowing should be confined to land which will not be likely to wash, and if the subsoil is an unfertile "blue-pan," great care should be taken not to bring it to the surface. On many soils it is best, late in the fall, to defer the plowing until spring,—enriching the soil as much as possible by top-dressing.

When the winter has really set in, and he has long evenings and stormy days for house-work, he should study his map well and develop a plan for future operations. What to do about buildings, what fences to remove, so as to enlarge his fields, what to rebuild, what land, if any, to drain, what crops to plant, what stock to keep, how to improve the pastures, which meadows to break up, which to top-dress and bring into better mowing condition — these and a hundred other questions will present themselves, and they must all be decided with most careful judgment. Though he do his best, he will make many mistakes, and when, in the spring, he comes to review in the field his winter's work in the house, he will see reasons for changing many of his plans. But, for all that, his plans will have been profitable to him, in many ways, and he will be in a better position to decide on the best course after having made them.

When he really gets at work, in March or April, he will have his hands full, and his head full, too, with the management of each day's operations. Then, his practical experience will come into play, and, tempered by what he has learned by his winter's reading, must carry him through planting, haying, and harvest, as best it may.

It would be too much a work of mere imagination to describe all the labors of the season ; to fancy this field to be drained ; that one to be made smaller ; this larger ; a barn to be built here ; a shed there ; and all that,—I prefer to leave these details to the young man's own discretion, and, (as I cannot write out directions for all farms,) to turn to the discussion of the various principles and operations which all farmers need to know about, so that not only he, but all others, may have, so far as I am able to give it them, a convenient hand-book of their occupation.

CHAPTER III.

THE KEY-NOTE OF GOOD FARMING.

THE teachings of agricultural chemistry and of vegetable physiology are very much less positive now than they were fifteen years ago, concerning many matters of very great importance to the farmer. The old idea of the *practical* value of soil analysis exploded long ago, and it shook the very foundations of " Book Farming."

Still, there are many things that are positively known—proven by simple and unmistakable evidence—that are of practical value, yes, of vital consequence. Many other things we are led to believe are undoubtedly true, and we know are of great importance, but their positive proof lies, thus far, among the hidden processes of nature's workshops, waiting the day when a keener-eyed science than ours shall unfold them. Thus far we can only draw inferences from them—valuable inferences, it is true, but not yet absolute rules.

To enter upon the discussion of these facts and inferences, so as to develop their full influence in agriculture, would compel me to entirely change the purpose of my work. I can only touch upon a few fundamental truths which lie at the root of the great economies of our art.

I desire, at the outset, to disclaim all sympathy with the popular outcry against *theory*, believing that agricultural writers have done much harm by catering to the prejudice on which this outcry is based. *Theory* is a correct statement of the principles by which any effect is produced; it is a recognition of unchangeable laws, and is as necessary to the farmer who grows Indian corn, as it is to the mechanic who makes the mill by which corn is ground.

To *guess* at the cause of any effect, and to imagine that certain laws may be made to act in a way in which it is not proved that they can act, is by no means theory,—it is a mere fancy, and it is this fancy that has been decried under the name of "theory." A knowledge of theory is necessary to real practice, and I desire, so far as my limits and my ability will allow, to justify good practice with theory, and to prove theories by practice, stating the whole case so far as possible, in the plain English of common life, avoiding, wherever practicable, such purely technical terms as are not familiar to farmers.

The first great aim of all farming is to raise the largest possible crops at the least possible cost, and good farming considers any injury to the soil as a part of the cost. The use that is to be made of crops after they are raised, is an important but a secondary consideration. How to raise the crops is the first question, and in answering it we should know what plants are made of, whence their constituent parts come, and how they are put together. The farmer should recognize the fact that he is a manufacturer, whose object it is to make roots, or stems, or leaves, by putting together the raw materials in his store-house, in the most complete, most satisfactory, most workmanlike manner. To do this he should understand his machinery and his material, at least so far as the present state of agricultural knowledge enables him to do so.

In a certain sense the requirements of all cultivated plants are the same. They all need the assistance of the soil, the air, the light and heat of the sun, and water to attain their growth, and they will be more or less perfect in their development according to the completeness with which all of these different agencies are allowed to act.

I have not the space to give such a complete statement of the teachings of chemistry as applied to agriculture as is necessary to a profitable understanding of the more intricate laws of vegetable growth, but there are certain leading principles which chemistry has unfolded, that should be familiar to every farmer, and which, fortunately, may be plainly stated and easily understood.

If a hundred pounds of grass is laid upon a shelf, in a warm room, it wilts and shrivels up, losing much of its weight. This results from the drying out of the water with which its pores are filled. If it is allowed to become rotten, it loses much more of its bulk, its texture is broken up, and it gives off foul odors. In this case it loses a part of its own substance, (not only the water which filled its pores and gave it its natural form, but a part of the very material by which its pores are surrounded,) and, if kept under circumstances favorable to decomposition, it will finally be reduced to a blackened mass, almost a mould, with no indication of its original form, and with not a twentieth part of its original weight. If this small residue is burned, only a handful of ashes will remain of the once luxuriant grass. The same result would come of a like treatment of every plant that grows. Some would be more and some less rapidly reduced by the original decay, while fire, which is only a more active decay, would drive away water, fiber, bark, leaves, and roots, and leave only the ashes behind.

Our grass is destroyed,—where has it gone? The water has "dried up," become vapor, and gone to help make the rains and the dew. The gum and starch, and flesh-forming parts have rotted away, and have floated off as gases into the air whence they originally came, and where they are again on duty, ready to enter the leaves of plants, or, being dissolved by the moisture of the soil, to travel up their roots and again take on a useful form. The woody matters that have burned away have followed the same law, and will follow it again and again as long as growth and decay last. All that remains to us is our poor handful of gray ashes,—this is the only part of our grass that can be supplied by the soil alone, and to the soil we must give it again.

Let us now examine the different sources of plant-food :—

THE SOIL.

A fertile soil contains various proportions of clay and sand, and mixed earthy substances and decayed vegetable matter ; these, together, forming nearly its whole bulk, and acting in a mechanical rather than in a chemical manner upon the growth of plants.

That is, they constitute a porous mass; with a certain power of absorbing moisture from the atmosphere, from rains and from the "water table," * which lies at a greater or less depth below the surface; with a greater or less ability to admit the circulation of air; with a certain power to absorb and retain heat; and with pores between its particles into which roots may penetrate. So far as these qualities are concerned, the most fertile soils are those which are loose in their texture, and neither light enough to become too easily dry, nor so heavy as to be too excessively wet in rainy seasons. Such soils may have a wide range of composition without materially differing in fertility. All that is required is that they contain enough clay to give them a good consistency, and enough marl, or vegetable mould, or sand to prevent their being too stiff. They may contain very little or very much sand, very little or very much vegetable matter, and very little or very much marl. Even the clay may be present in large or small proportion without necessarily making the soil much richer or poorer.

These mechanical ingredients of soils may vary in the following proportions without materially affecting its fertility, providing, of course, that they are so apportioned to each other as to make a mass of the proper consistency.

Organic matter (vegetable mould)...............from 8 ozs. to 70 lbs. in 100 lbs.
Clay.......... .... " 5 lbs " 35 " "
Sand (silicious)........................... " 20 " " 90 " "
Marl (calcareous or limy sand)................. " 5 " " 20 " "

A perfectly fertile soil, out of which the water has been dried, may contain as much as 98 or even 99 per cent. of matters which never enter the roots of ordinarily cultivated plants, and which only perform the mechanical offices set forth above.

Intimately mixed with this mass of material, and, like it, derived from the decomposition of the rocks or from the decay

* By the "water-table" is meant the level of the standing water in the ground—the water which is neither dried up from the surface, nor drained away below, by natural or artificial means. It is nearer to the surface or farther away from it in proportion to the completeness of the drainage, the dryness of the season, and the amount of rain-fall.

of the vegetable matter from which the soil was formed, are from one to three pounds in each one hundred pounds of other substances which go to form the ashes of all cultivated plants, and the fertility or barrenness of any soil which is in good condition in other respects, depends on the presence or absence of these parts. All soils, once fertile, which, without growing more wet, have become unproductive (which have been exhausted) through an improper system of cultivation, have become so in consequence of the removal of the available supply of one or more of this class of ingredients, and their fertility can be restored only by the addition of the missing substance, by the application of some agent like lime or unleached wood ashes, or by deeper plowing, better draining, the use of green crops, or exposure to the action of frost. The first process is a direct return of the materials which have been taken away; the others either bring up similar matters from the unexhausted subsoil, or, by causing the corroding, or the pulverization of coarser particles of the soil, they expose to the action of roots, the same constituents, which had been locked up within them.

The following table gives the names of the most important of these plant-feeding materials, and the proportion which they bear to the whole weight of the soil :—*

Phosphoric acid	1	lb to	4	lbs	in	1000 lbs of soil
Sulphuric "	½	"	3	"	"	" "
Magnesia	5	"	10	"	"	" "
Chlorine	1	"	2	"	"	" "
Soda	3	"	8	"	"	" "
Potash	1	"	20	"	"	" "
In all, from	11½	"	47	"	"	" "

These proportions vary a good deal within certain limits, but they are always exceedingly small. Lime varies very much more widely.

To sum up the case, then, the soil, in a practical point of view, may be regarded as a mass of material, which admits the

* For greater simplicity, I make no account of the *silicates, oxide of iron,* and *oxide of manganese,* and which should be considered in a scientific treatment of the subject; but which are not of great practical importance in this connection.

roots of the plant, and holds it in its position; absorbs the heat, air, and moisture which are required to be about them; and contains in very small quantities, certain materials which are necessary to growth, and which can be supplied only by the soil.

Nitrogen and carbonic acid, which are absorbed by the roots, are necessary constituents of the soil, but as they come originally from the air, I have deemed it best to postpone their consideration.

THE AIR.

The air, like the soil, consists of an immense bulk of materials which, so far as the growth of plants is concerned, have mainly a mechanical action. This immense mass contains *carbonic acid* in the proportion of about one part to twenty-five hundred, and *ammonia* in very much smaller proportion; it also contains very varying amounts of watery vapor. These three substances,—for, although only thin air to our senses, they are as substantial as the soil itself, and can be weighed, and measured, taken apart and put together again with as much accuracy as though they were wood or stone,—are the great sources of the material of which all plants are composed.* All of the plant, whether the smallest grass or the largest tree, is made up of the constituents of *water, carbonic acid*, and *ammonia;* save only the small part that remains as ashes after burning.

One thousand pounds of red clover hay, out of which the water had been dried, contained—

Ash......................	77 lbs.	(from the soil.)
Carbon	474 "	(" carbonic acid.)
Hydrogen	50 "	} (" water.)
Oxygen...................	378 "	
Nitrogen.................	21 "	(" ammonia.)
	1,000 lbs.	

* As in the case of some of the minerals in the soil, I make no account in this connection of nitric acid, nor of the many gaseous results of vegetable and animal decomposition, as I desire to state the leading principles of growth in the simplest form possible. So far as these gases are definitely known to have an influence on vegetation,

These proportions vary somewhat in different analyses, but not
materially. Such of these substances as exist in the air are taken into
the plant by the leaves, or, having been carried to the soil, by rains,
(or added to it by manure, or by the decay of vegetable matter,)
through the roots. The ashes are taken directly from the soil.
The manner in which they are taken, and the sources from which
they are taken most readily, will be discussed hereafter. What I
desire to especially emphasize in this connection is the fact, that
by far the larger part of all plants comes originally from an atmospheric source, and that only a small percentage of their constituent parts is supplied by the mineral portion of the soil.

THE PLANT AND ITS FOOD.

The cultivated plant has two sets of feeding apparatus : the
leaves and green stems, and the roots. The leaves and green
stems absorb *carbonic acid* from the air, and the roots absorb from
the soil the *mineral matters, ammonia*, and *carbonic acid*. Within
the organs of the living plant such changes take place as are
necessary to separate these different compounds, to reject what is
not needed, and to assign to its proper place in the organism each
element that is to be retained. These changes take place without
our aid, are beyond our control, and are therefore, in a practical
point of view, not necessary to be discussed here.

In red clover hay fully ninety per cent.,—and in all other products about the same proportion,—of the *dry* weight consists of
carbon, oxygen, and *hydrogen*, which are always abundantly supplied to the plant by the decomposition of *carbonic acid* and
water. Of the ashes, certain ingredients, as *magnesia, silica,
sulphuric acid, oxide of iron, chlorine, soda*, the *oxide of manganese*, and generally *lime*, are either found in all arable soils in

they need in no way affect the practices of the farmer. The word "ammonia" is used
here (in accordance with a common though not strictly scientific usage) to designate
those nitrogenous compounds which under certain circumstances may assume the form of
ammonia.

such abundant quantities that it is not necessary to add them in manure, or they may be so cheaply and easily obtained that they are of secondary importance in practice.

Therefore, it is chiefly desirable for the farmer to give his attention to the sources from which the plant may derive its three remaining ingredients,—*nitrogen, phosphoric acid,* and *potash.* Without these none of our cultivated plants will attain their full development, and when a soil ceases to produce good crops, (supposing it to be in good mechanical condition,) it is almost always in consequence of a deficiency of one or more of them. I propose therefore to restrict my remarks about agricultural chemistry to a consideration of these three substances,—without a proper management of which no man can be an entirely practical farmer. He raises no crop which does not contain them, he sells no animal or vegetable product which does not take them from his farm, and he has no soil so rich that they, or some of them, need not be returned to it to keep up its fertility. Whatever course of cultivation he pursues, he should never lose sight of these elements, and he should pay no greater heed to the dollars and cents that he receives and pays out than to the NITROGEN, PHOSPHORIC ACID, and POTASH which constitute his real available capital, and whose increase and decrease mark the rise and fall of his true wealth.

Other constituents of his soil are removed in the crops and in the animal products sold, but they are such as are usually contained by the soil in larger quantities, or as may be cheaply procured from other sources, and they are rarely removed to a sufficient extent to cause an impoverishment of the land.

The elements spoken of above, as well as *lime* and other mineral manures, will be more fully treated in the chapter on Manures; but I desire, at the outset of my work, to call especial attention to the characteristics and uses of these three cardinal elements.

NITROGEN.

Nitrogen is an element not only of all plants, but of every part
of the plant.   Root, stem, branch, and leaves, at some period of
their growth, contain it in every minutest part of their structure.
Its quantity, in comparison with the other elements, is extremely
small ; but, in vegetable growth, the importance of any constituent of the tissues is not to be measured by its quantity.   It may
play the smallest possible part in the building up of the plant, but
so much of it as is necessary must be at the right spot at the right
time.   If the sap lacks the atom of nitrogen that is required, all
the other atoms in the sap go for nothing.

It generally forms from 10 to 40 parts of every 1,000 parts of
the dry weight of the whole plant—by far the largest proportion
being lodged in the grain.

The experiments of Boussingault showed that 1,000 lbs. of
each of the following articles contain the amount of nitrogen
stated in the table.   (The substances were thoroughly dried at a
high temperature).

Wheat	23 lbs.
" Straw	4 "
Rye	17 "
" Straw	3 "
Oats	22 "
" Straw	4 "
Peas	42 "
" Straw	23 "
Potatoes	15 "
Beets	17 "
Turnips	17 "
Red Clover hay	21 "

This, like all other tables based on vegetable analysis, is to
be regarded as indicating the general proportion which the different
elements bear to each other, rather than the positive amount of
each.   They vary a little, according to the conditions of growth,
but not very materially.

In the crops, as grown, of course these proportions will vary according to the amount of water they contain : 1,000 lbs. of turnips contain about 900 lbs. of pure water, while 1,000 lbs. of ripe peas contain only about 86 lbs. Therefore, 1,000 lbs. *fresh* peas contain about 39 lbs. of nitrogen, while 1,000 lbs. fresh turnips only contain about 1¾ lbs.

The reason why nitrogen, although forming a so much smaller part of the substance of our crops, is more necessary to be considered by the farmer than the other substances that are derived from the air, is because, while there is a certain amount furnished by natural means,—enough to enable plants to make a tolerable growth,—they are generally benefited by the addition of an increased supply as manure. The other atmospheric elements take care of themselves. The air about the leaves and the water of the sap contain them abundantly, in a form that is always available. With nitrogen the case is different. Although it exists in the atmosphere in the form most useful to vegetation,—that of ammonia and nitric acid,—the plant cannot usually obtain its supply through the leaves, but it must find its way into the soil and enter the roots with the water that goes to form the sap.

Ammonia and nitric acid are the universal sources of the supply of nitrogen to vegetation. Ammonia is a gas formed during the decomposition of vegetable and animal matters. These all contain nitrogen, and when they are destroyed, either by fire or by decay, their nitrogen escapes in the form of ammonia, or as nitric acid. Usually, the original product of all destruction of organic matters containing nitrogen is ammonia, which gives great value to all animal manure, which is one of the manurial ingredients of rain water, and which is the farmer's best assistant in making his land produce the largest crops that with its supply of mineral food, it is capable of growing.

Liebig, speaking of the sources of the nitrogen of plants and of the supply of ammonia, says :—

" We cannot suppose that a plant could attain maturity, even
" in the richest vegetable mould, without the presence of matter
" containing nitrogen, since we know that nitrogen exists in every

" part of the vegetable structure. * * * * * * * We
" have not the slightest reason for believing that the nitrogen of
" the atmosphere takes part in the processes of assimilation of
" plants and animals ; on the contrary, we know that many plants
" emit nitrogen, which is absorbed by their roots, either in a
" gaseous form or in solution in water. But there are, on the
" other hand, numerous facts showing that the formation in plants
" of substances containing nitrogen * * * * takes place in
" proportion to the quantity of this e'ement conveyed to their
" roots in the state of ammonia derived from the putrefaction
" of animal matter. * * * * * * * Let us picture
" to ourselves the condition of a well-cultivated farm, so large
" as to be independent of assistance from other quarters. On
" this extent of land there is a certain quantity of nitrogen con-
" tained both in the corn and fruit which it produces, and in the
" men and animals which feed upon them, and also in their ex-
" crements. We shall suppose this quantity to be known. The
" land is cultivated without the importation of any foreign sub-
" stance containing nitrogen. Now, the products of this farm
" must be exchanged every year for money and other necessaries
" of life—for bodies, therefore, destitute of nitrogen. A certain
" proportion of nitrogen is exported in the shape of corn and
" cattle, and this exportation takes place every year, without the
" smallest compensation ; yet after a given number of years, the
" quantity of nitrogen will be found to have increased. Whence,
" we may ask, comes this increase of nitrogen ? The nitrogen in
" the excrements cannot reproduce itself, and the earth cannot
" yield it. Plants, and consequently animals, must, therefore,
" derive their nitrogen from the atmosphere. * * * * * *
" A generation of a thousand million men is renewed every thirty
" years ; thousands of millions of animals cease to live, and are
" reproduced in a much shorter period. Where is the nitrogen
" contained in them during life ? There is no question which
" can be answered with more positive certainty. All animal bodies
" during their decay yield to the atmosphere their nitrogen in the
" form of ammonia. Even in the bodies buried sixty feet under

" ground, in the church-yard of the *Eglise des Innocens*, at Paris,
" all the nitrogen contained in the adipocere was in the state of
" ammonia. * * * * * * * The nitrogen of putre-
" fied animals is contained in the atmosphere as ammonia, in the
" state of a gas which is capable of entering into combination
" with carbonic acid, and of forming a volatile salt. Ammonia
" in its gaseous form, as well as all its volatile compounds, is of
" extreme solubility in water. Ammonia, therefore, cannot re-
" main long in the atmosphere, as every shower of rain must
" effect its condensation, and convey it to the surface of the
" earth. Hence, also, rain water must at all times contain
" ammonia, though not always in equal quantity. It must con-
" tain more in summer than in spring or winter, because the
" intervals of time between the showers are in summer greater,
" and when several wet days occur, the rain of the first must con-
" tain more of it than that of the second. The rain of a thunder
" storm, after a long protracted drought, ought, for this reason,
" to contain the greatest quantity conveyed to the earth at one
" time. * * * *

"It is worthy of observation that the ammonia contained in
" rain and snow-water possesses an offensive smell of perspira-
" tion and putrefying matter,—a fact which leaves no doubt
" respecting its origin."

To repeat,—while there is a certain amount of ammonia and
nitric acid presented to the roots of plants in a state of nature,
the excessive growth at which good farming aims, can be stimulated
only by the addition of increased supplies, either by the application of manures, or by such a system of cultivation as shall cause
an increased absorption of ammonia from the air.

Nitrogen is not only a necessary element of all plants, it is
even more largely a constituent of the bodies and of the milk of
animals, and it remains an object of the greatest care of the
farmer through the whole course of his operations. He must first
procure it to apply to his growing crops, must next so use it in
his stock feeding as to produce the greatest development of meat,
of milk, or of wool, and then must so economize that which the

3

animal has rejected, in the manure, as to have the largest possible supply for his future crops.

PHOSPHORIC ACID.

Phosphoric acid is, in a certain sense, even more important to the farmer than nitrogen. This latter is supplied in limited amount by natural process,—it is absorbed by the soil directly from the atmosphere, and it is brought down in the water of rains. Phosphoric acid, on the contrary, is a fixed ingredient of the soil, and it is never brought to it by wind and rain. We have, in the soil, a certain amount, and only a very small amount, while of this, the larger part is locked up in the interior of pebbles, or compact clods which no root can penetrate. All that is available to a crop is that which, being on the surface of the particles of the soil is directly within the reach of roots, and of such roots as come in contact with those particles. Probably, when any soil has been exhausted by improper husbandry, it is, in ninety-nine cases out of every hundred, the phosphoric acid that is gone. From Maine to Minnesota the gradual advance of "enterprise,"—that sort of enterprise which, as it passes from east to west, reduces the yield of wheat from 30 to 12 bushels per acre,—has been marked by the taking up of new lands, by the production of good crops for a few years, and of a precarious subsistence for a few more, and by the destruction of the profitable fertility of the soil within the life-time of the second generation,—all through ignorance or disregard of the value of phosphoric acid, and of the limited ability of the most fertile soils to supply it to consecutive crops. It is commonly urged, when phosphoric acid is mentioned, that most farmers do not know what it is, that a very large majority of them never heard of it. Speak of the use of phosphate of lime, (which is valuable mainly on account of its phosphoric acid,) to a man who is unacquainted with it, and he will probably say that it may be a good manure in "some parts," but that he does not know that it would do any good on his land. If he has just settled on new land at the West, he will show you his deep black loam, that " has more richness in it than you can get out in a thousand years." This would be all very well, if it were possible for a farmer to compel his crops to live on the food that he happens to know about, if roots took nothing from the soil that he has not heard of, if plants did not require the same nutriment in "all parts," and if "richness" meant only good color and good tilth.

So long as we were farming the stubborn hillsides of New England, and while our population needed elbow-room, while the Mohawk and Genesee valleys in New York, the Western Reserve and rich river bottoms of Ohio, and the wonderful prairies of the farther West invited the hard-worked farmers of the East to better crops, and an easier life, it was at least excusable that all who could get away should mind the bidding, and go ; and the world is better for their having gone,—richer and more free for the marvelous people and the marvelous opportunities of the North-west. But now, the case is greatly changed. The richest lands of the country have been brought under cultivation—many of them have been, already, ground under its heel. Emigration from the Genesee Valley, or from Illinois, to Kansas or to Colorado, is not excusable, on any agricultural grounds, and it can only do harm if its object is to seek richer lands. Richer than the present lands once were, the new lands cannot be, and any course of cultivation that would keep these from speedily running down would equally renovate the older soils.

In the monthly report of the Department of Agriculture for October, 1867, the editor, in an article headed " Wheat Culture Ruinous," says, " Is proof of impoverishment wanted ? one witness " only is needed,—the soil itself. First thirty bushels per acre, is " the boast of the farmer ; then the yield drops to twenty-five, to " twenty, to fifteen, and finally to ten and eight. Minnesota " claimed twenty-two bushels average, a few years ago, (some of " her enthusiastic friends made it twenty-seven,) but she will " scarcely average, this year, twelve, and will never again make " twenty-two under her present mode of farming. To be sure, " there are excuses. The seasons do not suit as formerly, blight " or rust comes, or the fly invades, but all these things are evi-

" dences of exhaustion, and prey upon the soil in proportion to its
" deterioration.   *   *   *   *   * The average yield of wheat in
" England is stated at twenty-eight bushels per acre, never less
" than twenty-six, unless in a year of unusually bad harvests.
" The average in this country, is less than half of the lowest of
" of these figures.   Why is it? Certainly not because our soil is
" naturally poorer than theirs, neither because our climate is so
" much worse for wheat culture.   It is mainly for want of a
" suitable rotation of crops, of a more careful husbandry of
" resources of fertilization, of a more thorough and careful cul-
" ture."

To show to what extent the element under consideration
enters into the composition of the crops that we raise, and the
various farm products that we sell, attention is asked to the
following table :—

*Amount of Phosphoric Acid contained in 1,000 lbs. of the Ashes of each of the follow-
ing substances :—*

Grain of Wheat (average of six analyses) . . . . 498 lbs.
"   Indian Corn. . . . . 501 "
"   Rye (average of two analyses). 490 "
"   Oats (with shell). . . . . 149 "
"   Buckwheat . . . . 500 "
"   Beans. . . . . 357 "
Hay. . . . . 120 "
Clover. . . . . 63 "
Potatoes. . . . . 113 "
Beets . . . . 60 "
Milk. . . . . 217 "
Bones. . . . . 390 "
Lean Meat (about). . . . . 500 '

It may be true that farmers generally do not know much
about phosphoric acid, but it is equally true that it is high time
they learned.

In England they have got this knowledge to a certain degree—
as we are getting it now,—at great cost,—and they are putting
their knowledge to such eager account that they even ransack
the lat le-fields of Europe for human bones, and quarry the phosphatic rocks of the whole world to replenish their soils. We are

beginning to follow the same course here, and in the older parts of the country phosphates of lime, (good and bad,) meet with ready sale. Still, as a class, we are learning only one-half of what we ought to learn. We should know not only how to get a supply of phosphoric acid for manure, but how to economize what we already have, and how to keep up the available supply in the soil; and I bespeak attention to the further treatment of this subject under the heads of "Manures," "Feeding," and "Rotation of Crops."

POTASH.

What has been said of the importance of phosphoric acid is in a measure true of potash. Fortunately this substance has a name and many characteristics which are familiar to all, and its discussion does not require the use of "new-fangled" names and expressions.

It is second to phosphoric acid in the extent to which it is used by plants, as will be seen by the following table:—

Amount of Potash contained in 1,000 lbs. of the Ashes of the following substances:—

Grain of Wheat (average of six analyses)	237 lbs.
" Indian Corn	250 "
" Rye	220 "
" Oats (with shell)	123 "
" Buckwheat	87 "
" Beans	462 "
Hay	300 "
Clover	161 "
Potatoes	515 "
Beets	390 "
Tobacco leaves	264 "

NOTE.—The proportion of potash varies considerably in growth under different circumstances.

The exhaustion of the tobacco lands of the South, and of the potato fields of western Connecticut, is mainly due to the removal of their potash.

I postpone the further discussion of this subject also to the chapters on "Manures," etc.

Having in the foregoing remarks struck what I believe to be the key-note of the scientific practice of agriculture, and indicated the points which seem to me to be of the most vital importance to every farmer who would regulate his operations, so far as is possible, by what is positively known of the fundamental laws of fertility and growth, I proceed to the consideration of the daily details of his business, the "How to do it" of practical farming; —and I shall, whenever the occasion offers, recommend that the treatment of the soil and its products, of the live stock of the farm, and of manures, be based on what has already been shown to be the very groundwork of true economy in agriculture.

CHAPTER IV.

FENCES AND FARM BUILDINGS.

FENCES.

WHAT fences to have, and how to make them, are questions which may well engage the attention of the new occupier of a farm,—and of the old occupier too, for that matter.

There is a great deal said about the advantage of dispensing entirely with fences, as they do in many parts of Europe,—and it is said with much truth. But, unfortunately, in this respect Europe is not America, and so long as we keep cattle at pasture, and have not pauper children to watch them, so long must we build fences to keep them from encroaching on our neighbor's property, and from straying into our own grain fields.

It will be a happy day for American farmers when they can escape the necessity for building expensive fences, and can bring into their fields, and into clean cultivation, the weedy headlands which are now worse than wasted ; but that day will not come in many a long year, and, for the present, we must content ourselves with making fences as little expensive, and as little of a nuisance, as is possible.

There are whole counties in New England, and probably in southern New York, in which all the farms are not worth so much to-day as it would cost to build the fences within their boundaries; and there are whole townships in which the fields will not average two acres in extent. I think I have seen farms in which they average less than one acre. I know some fences, in Connecticut, which are eight feet wide at the top, the sides being of immense blocks of granite laid to a face, and the center filled with smaller stones.

Under the best management such a fence, with its headlands, will occupy land a rod wide,—or an acre for every half mile. Of course, the reason for building fences such as this is that there are stones to be cleared from the land; but it would be much cheaper to bury the larger stones where they lie, by digging pits under them and dropping them out of reach of the plow, while the smaller ones could be disposed of much more cheaply, and in a way to do good instead of harm, by digging large trenches and making stone drains. It costs less to dig a ditch four feet deep and two feet wide, on an average, and put the stone in them than to lay up a good wall of the same dimensions. In the one case we make quite a serviceable drain, and in the other we encumber the land and obstruct cultivation.

Of course, in our ordinary method of managing a farm, we must have fences around all fields which are to be used entirely or partly for pasture. We must have lawful fences around the whole farm, and must inclose the roads by which cattle are to be driven to pasture. Still, the smallest possible amount of fencing that will accomplish this, we should always seek to have.

Pasture fields should be as large as is consistent with the necessity for giving them occasional rests. The whole pasture land of a farm should be divided into not more than three fields, and two would be better; although, if they are never to be plowed, division fences, which may be standing, will do less harm than on cultivated land.

So far as the arable land of the farm is concerned, I think that the greatest economy of cultivation, and the best results in crops would be secured if it were not divided by fences at all. The only reason why it should be, is, to enable us to pasture mowing lands in the fall, or to use them for pasture after they have ceased to produce paying crops of grass,—neither of which practices are consistent with the best cultivation. A good hay field should never have a hoof upon it, except during the operations of top-dressing, rolling, or harvesting. If it produces a heavy crop of hay, that is enough to ask of it, and any attempt to get more by pasturing animals upon it will lessen its value for future crops, much more than its use as pasture will be worth. If it has ceased to produce good hay, in paying quantities, it should be renewed, either by being brought into cultivation, or otherwise.

In giving this advice, I assume that we have no more land under the plow, and in meadow, than we can properly attend to. If we have, it will probably pay best to turn the excess out to pasture. When we go to the expense of plowing, cultivating, and harvesting, we should so manage as to get the largest possible return for our labor, and that we shall get by raising the largest crops that can be got with a reasonable outlay of money and work. Three tons of hay per acre is within the easy possibilities of any ordinarily good land, if it is properly managed; and it will cost less, and pay better to get it from one acre than from two, to say nothing of its better quality.

This subject will be discussed more fully hereafter, in considering the rotation of crops, and the treatment of grass lands.

If the course suggested above is adopted, it will be best not to have the course of the plow and of the mowing-machine interrupted by fences, and to have no weed-breeding headlands bordering our plowed fields. Even with a board fence, or an iron one, which occupies but little room, we must leave a space of at least four feet on each side that cannot be well cultivated—a total width of a half-rod given up to weeds, or at least wasted from the field, and an annoyance in many ways. The fence and headlands around a square field of five acres will occupy nearly three-quarters of an acre. To this loss add the time spent in turning at the ends of furrows, in plowing and in cultivating, and the trampling of the rows in one case, and of the plowed land in the other, and the expense of keeping fences in repair, and we shall have a formidable sum total of the cost of too many fences.

It would be impossible to establish any universal rule for all farms, and for all farmers, but it may be stated as a good general principle that every farm should have the smallest amount of fencing that will answer the only purpose of fences,—that is, to keep loose animals where they belong.

All that has been said against the inordinate use of fences, does not by any means lessen the importance of making such fences as we do have in the best and most thorough manner. In the first place, boundary fences must be "lawful fences," which have been described, (more forcibly than elegantly,) as "*horse high, built strong, and pig tight.*"

Mr. Todd* says:

"Our civil law, in relation to fences, which appears to be "founded on principles of strictest equity, provides that where land "is inclosed, and lies contiguous, and possessed by two different "owners, each must build and maintain a good lawful fence on "one-half the distance of the entire line between their land. "According to law, A may not build his half of the fence exactly "on the line, neither may B, but each must erect his fence on "his own land as near to the line as he desires, but neighbors "usually erect their fences exactly on the line. * * * * *

"If A refuses to build or maintain one equal half of a line "fence between his land and the land owned by B, by giving A "thirty days' legal notice that he must build or repair his line "fence, and A neglects to do so, B may build or repair such "fence and collect of A the expense of building, the same as for "any other indebtedness.

"If A has land not inclosed, or 'open to the commons,' which "lies contiguous to the land of B, if B desires to have his land "inclosed, he must build all the fence between them. If A should "then inclose his, he cannot hold one-half of the line fence. "He must allow B to remove one-half of the fence, and he (A) "must build a fence in the room of it, or he may purchase one- "half of it. If he refuses to do either, B, the owner of the "fence, may prosecute A, and recover pay for half of the line "fence.

"B may not, in a fit of resentment or frenzy, remove his "division fence, and throw open his own fields to the commons

* Young Farmers' Manual, vol. i., page 285.

" with impunity, unless he gives A ten days' notice of his inten-
" tion to throw open his fields to the commons between Novem-
" ber and April. During the time from April to November, if a
" line fence is removed by B, and A is made to sustain any loss
" by such removal, B is responsible for the damage."

Four feet and six inches is considered a lawful barrier against
any animals, and a fence lower than that is, in the eye of the law,
a sufficient barrier against the smaller animals. The court must
decide whether the trespassing animals were *unruly*, and whether
the fence was sufficient to keep them out if they had not been.

So far as interior fences are concerned, it should be remembered
that a poor fence makes an unruly animal and a good fence an
orderly one. It is better, where horses and cattle are to be kept, to
make all fences four and a half feet high, though a part of this height
may consist of a narrow bank of earth on which the fence is built.

The material of which the fence is to be made must depend
mainly on what is most easily accessible. In heavily wooded, new
countries, capital fences are made of the roots of large trees, torn
from the ground and set up edgewise. Where wood is plenty and
stone scarce, rail fences are generally cheapest, although, in good
lumber districts, board fences, with their greater durability, are
more desirable, while, for general use, about houses, lawns, and
gardens, a picket fence has some great advantages ; and when
there are good stones to be had, nothing can supplant stone walls.
Where nothing is to be had but a fertile soil, that of itself must
furnish the fencing by producing a stout growth of hedge-row.
If the material for the fence must be brought from a distance,
iron wire netting is best to be used.

To discuss the manner of making all kinds of rail, board,
picket, and iron fences, (which offer a very great variety of characteristics, and may be made to suit,) and the growing of hedges,
which is a study by itself, would either swell this volume to a
very undesirable size, or compel the exclusion of other topics
which are of greater importance.*

* Those who seek information on these subjects will find them treated at length in
the "Young Farmers' Manual," and in Warder's " Hedges and Evergreens."

Stone walls and rail fences are the great fences of the country. The latter require very much less skill to build in an enduring manner than the former, and their proper construction is very much easier. In any country where they are much used, they are generally well made, and the different forms of "worm," "post and rail," "stake and rider," etc., are too well understood to need more than a passing notice in a hand-book.

The stone wall, however,—when well made the best of all fences,—is generally built in the most unpractical and uneconomical way possible. Probably the majority of the stone fences in New England commenced their career as a tier of boulders and irregular stones set one above the other, on the surface of the ground, and kept in position by a very nice adjustment of their centers of gravity; and such of them as were without yearly care have ended it as long heaps of rubbish, covered with brambles and elder bushes,—a sort of spontaneous hedge with a stone foundation, flanked by thistles, cockles, iron weed, and golden rod ;— possessing all the disadvantages and performing few of the offices of a fence.

A poor stone wall is the worst fence that can be imagined. It is thrown down by every winter's frost, and must be repaired,— not merely every year, but, worst of all, every *spring*, after the frost is all out of the ground, and when spring work is pressing.

A good stone wall, with a broad base, a sure foundation, plenty of lock-stones, and well capped, is expensive to make, but when made it is made for a life-time. No unruly animal can break it down, no frost can "heave" it, and it need never be touched from one end of the year to the other.

The two great requisites are, a solid and dry foundation and proper construction. More than in the case of almost any thing else there is a good and a bad way to do the work. Two walls may be built with the same stones, on the same ground, and at the same expense, and one be good and the other good for nothing.

The following cut (Fig. 1) shows the cross-section of a wall two and a half feet wide at the base, one and a half at the top, and four and a half feet high, which is hardly worth the stone it contains. It stands on level ground, with no drainage, and no foundation other than a moist soil. Its stones are laid up on the independent principle—all that each one asks of another is a place to rest. The sides are straight and the top level. To all outward appearance, it is perfectly good. But when winter sets in, the freezing ground will raise the whole concern perhaps, an inch, in the air; warm weather comes and thaws out the warm side first, and it settles an inch below the level of the other side; then another frost lifts it up again, and another thaw settles it. A few such rackings topple down a lot of stones against the side of the wall; then comes another frost, and these stones keep in the ground until after the opposite side has thawed, when that goes down, and more stones fall that way, or the wall gets a twist. A few winters of such racking work will finish the wall, and it must be rebuilt.

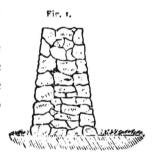

Fig. 1.

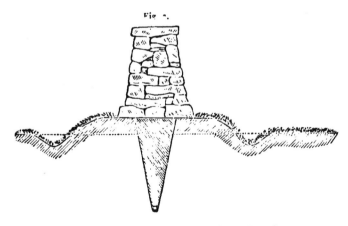

Fig. 2.

Fig. 2 shows the cross-section of a wall built of the same stones laid in the proper manner, on a suitable foundation. The first thing has been to make a sufficient drain (which, for this purpose,

need not be more than two and a half feet deep) to remove the
water of saturation.   Then the earth has been plowed up into a
ridge a foot above the general level of the ground, with a good
water furrow at each side.   On this ridge, after it has had a year
to settle, the foundation course has been laid of the largest stones
well bedded, well " chocked up," and with " broken joints "
wherever the stones were not long enough to reach entirely across
the wall.

If some of the stones are so large as to reach six inches or a foot
beyond the wall on each side, there is no objection to their use
next to the ground.   Above this course the stones should be well
selected and so laid (on their best faces) that all of the smaller
ones shall be bound together by long ones which reach entirely
across the wall, or at least have a good bearing on each side of
the joint between them.   This " locking " is the most important
part of the whole operation, and without it, no wall, even if built
of square blocks of hewn stone, will withstand the movement
against which even the best foundation cannot entirely protect it.
The cap-stones, selected during the building of the wall, should
reach entirely across the top.   They had better be even six inches
too wide than one inch too narrow, and the heavier they are the
better will be their binding effect.

Concerning the face of the wall, it is worthy of remark that,
as a general rule, too much smoothness should not be sought after.
The general line of the face should be true, and the crevices
should be sufficiently well chinked to give each stone a firm support, but the smooth faces of the stones had better be laid *down*
than toward the face, as solidity is of more value than smoothness.
In a park wall a smooth surface is very desirable ; in a farm wall
extra smoothness should be sacrificed to solidity.

If a stone wall is built in the manner last described, the chief
care that will be necessary for its preservation will be to prevent
boys from accepting the invitation which its broad, level top offers
for a run ; if the cap-stones are not disturbed, and if its chinks
are not loosened by climbing, it will not need repairing for many
years.

A very common and a very good substitute for the ridge at the bottom of the wall, is a trench from one to two feet deep, filled with small stones, but even in this case it is better to have an underdrain, directly beneath, or at the side of the wall. If beneath it, with at least six inches of well-rammed earth separating it from the small stones in the trench, lest earth be carried into the drain by surface water and choke it up.

GATES.

Gates are so much better than bars that they ought to be universally used wherever frequent passage with vehicles is necessary. Bars being much simpler, and not liable to get out of order, are sufficiently good for the entrances to pasture-fields, but the time lost in taking them entirely out, when the entrance must be frequently used for wagons, is a sufficient objection to their use in

Fig. 3.

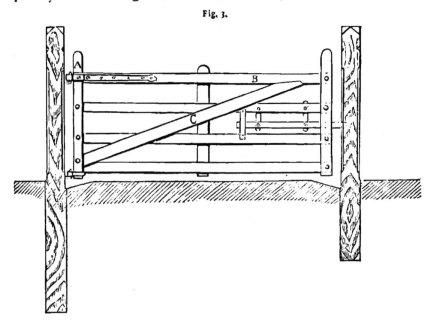

such cases. The difficulty of making a gate that will swing well on its hinges, latch easily, and swing clear of the ground, year after year, is to me one of the mysteries. The tendency of gates to "sag," and of hinge hooks to work loose, seems to defy the wisest mechanical skill and to overturn all our preconceived ideas of the strength of material.

There are gates which are always in order, which close of themselves, and which latch when closed, but they are generally either very new or very expensive. A good, cheap, farm-gate, which will always be in order, is very much needed, and the need has given rise to no end of inventions.

These, however, seem generally to seek to overcome the difficulty by a complication of parts, or by some device which sooner or later fails in practice.

So far as our present experience extends, the simplest gate is the best. Probably as good a form as any is that shown in Fig. 3. Its most important parts are the *heel post*, A, the *arm*, B, and the *strut*, C.

On these we must chiefly depend to prevent sagging. They form together a right-angled triangle, and if made of hard wood, accurately fitted together and well pinned or bolted, will maintain their position as well as any other form. The other parts of the gate should be made as light as possible, and all, except the latch post, D, are as well made of pine as of heavier wood.

The arrangement of the slats and tie-pieces is not very essential. The strap of the upper hinge should run out at least two feet on each side of the arm, and be securely bolted. The hook of the top hinge should pass entirely through the post and be

Fig. 4.

fastened by a nut, the thread being cut far enough down on the hook to enable us to draw it up, little by little, as the front end of the gate settles.

The lower hinge of the gate is better, in all cases, to be made as represented in Fig. 4. This is so arranged that the gate, unless fastened open, will close of itself. It is much better to be obliged to fasten a gate open, in case of need, than to run the risk of its being carelessly left open. The post on which the gate hangs is a very important part of the arrangement. Unless it remains firmly in its perpendicular position, the best gate will work badly.

The best gate-post for farm purposes, is a single long stone, but a good stick of hard wood, set not less than five feet in the ground, and filled around at least for three feet below the surface with small stones, so that the frost can have no effect on it, is good enough—while it lasts. The various devices for holding the post upright by rods, or braces, are of little effect.

The post against which the gate is fastened when shut, it is not so important to have set deeply. It need only be firm enough to withstand the racking to which it will be subjected when a high wind blows directly against the gate. It ought, for this purpose, to be a stout stick or stone, set not less than three and a half feet in the ground, and protected against the action of frost as recommended for the other post.

The gate may be fastened by a hook, a latch, a bolt, or a pin. In either case, the fastening should be about half way between the top and the bottom, so that the force of direct winds will have an equal bearing above and below. If fastened at the top or bottom, the gate would be more racked in heavy blows.

The form of latches are various. That which seems to me the best for farm-gates is shown in Fig 3, which is a bar of hard wood passing easily through two slots in the gate, and hung lightly on the short straps of iron, so that it will swing freely back and forth, hanging naturally in such a position that it will enter a groove in the post (Fig 5), or better, a space between two blocks in front of the post. This space should be at least half an inch wider than the thickness of the bolt, and the blocks should slope off gradually, and be faced with sheet-iron, over which the end of the latch will slip easily. When the gate is closed, this inclined plane or slope forces the latch back, and when it reaches the groove it drops in by its own weight.

Fig. 5.

4

Concerning the dwelling-house, it is not worth while for me to say any thing, except so far as relates to the dairy department, and this will be treated hereafter under its proper head.

Although the dwelling is a very important element of farm economy, the tastes of individuals and their ability to spend money for ornament and for convenience vary so greatly, that even a tolerably full discussion of the architecture of farm dwelling-houses would require very much more space than could here be given to it. In the vicinity of towns there are always architects and builders whose services can be commanded whenever necessary. In the more remote frontier districts, the simpler style of dwelling, which is all that the opportunities of the situation allow, is usually built without the aid of skilled labor, and for temporary purposes only. Barns, sheds, hay-barracks, sheep-folds, poultry-houses, etc., belong more properly to the range of subjects under consideration. The first principle to be observed is, so far as possible, to bring every thing within the same four walls and under the same roof, and to adjust the size of the structure, not so much to the present requirements, as to the future needs of the farm.

In a very large majority of cases, however, it is not practicable to follow this rule. It would require a larger investment at the outset, than most farmers would be able to make, especially in view of the many other necessary expenses which must be defrayed from their usually limited capital. Yet in all cases where such a complete barn as is above referred to cannot be built at once, the possibility of building it at a future day, and the importance of approaching it as nearly as possible at the outset, should be constantly kept in view. A given amount of space can be more cheaply inclosed in one large building, than in several small ones, while the concentration of stock and food under one roof, the greater ease with which barn work may be done in a conveniently arranged large barn, and the much more complete supervision which a farmer is enabled to have over the indoor work of his assistants, are strong arguments in favor of the plan.

Formerly, when hay wagons had to be unloaded entirely by hand, the height of the hay bays of a barn had to be regulated by the height to which it was practicable to pitch hay ; but the rapidly extending use of the horse fork or elevator has done away with this restriction. Hay can now be easily and rapidly raised to any height, and not only may we gain the extra space which the greater height of the bay gives, but a considerably greater capacity in proportion to the height, which comes from the closer packing at the bottom of a high bay.

That it is much more convenient, easier, and cheaper to feed stock in the building in which all of the hay and other fodder is stored, every farmer knows without being told. *How much* easier it is, is only known to those who have spent their lives in foddering cattle in sheds and yards from distant hay barns, from which every forkful of hay must be carried in bundles or on a cart.

Furthermore, the more hay has to be carried about the more it is wasted, and the more liable it is to be injured by bad weather, while the convenience of keeping manure is in exact proportion to the concentration of the stock, under the most favorable circumstances.

I have recently had occasion to give much attention to this question in undertaking the improvement of a worn-out and "run-down" farm of sixty acres,* on which, with sufficient capital at command, I am endeavoring to prove that good farming may be made to pay, where bad farming has been starved out. My aim is to make sixty acres of land which would not, when I took it, support five head of cattle, furnish all the food, winter and summer, that will be required by *fifty* head—except meal and grain for working animals. To do this, I need the best sort of a barn, with every convenience for storing hay, fodder, and roots, for cutting and steaming food, for sheltering animals, in hot

---

* Ogden Farm, near Newport, R. I.

weather and in cold, for keeping all manure made, under cover, from the time when it is dropped until it is carted on to the land, and for "soiling" my animals in summer.

It would not be difficult to make a plan of a barn with more various capacities and more conveniences than that at Ogden Farm for the handling of grain, etc., but it seems to be desirable that recommendations for the construction of farm buildings should be based as far as possible on the personal experience of the writer,—and in my own case I have endeavored to combine every thing that is really essential to convenience and economy. I have prepared drawings of this barn exactly as it is built, and with only such attachments as I purpose having in regular use.

This is in no respect a "fancy" building. It is as plain as a pike-staff, as all farm barns should be, with not a dollar expended anywhere for ornament, and, although it has many of the "modern conveniences," they are all such as I have seen in practical and *profitable* use elsewhere, except in the single item of the railway and car to carry the feed to the heads of the stalls, which is a cheap arrangement that recommends itself, especially where animals are to be "soiled,"—that is, fed on green fodder in their stalls all summer.

The first problem that presented itself was to so arrange the barn that there should be no pitching *up* of any thing—that the hay should be hauled in wagons on to the top floor of the barn, and there stowed away by horse-power; thence thrown down to the feeding floor; and the manure from this to the cellar;—or, in summer, that the corn fodder or other green food should be dumped from a cart directly into the car, by which it will be taken to the cattle.

In short, I wanted a side-hill barn, but had no side-hill to build it on, the land sloping only two feet in a length of one hundred feet.

The barn stands in the middle of an old apple-orchard, about two hundred and twenty feet wide and three hundred feet long, two rows of trees being left all around the space occupied by the barn. The whole is surrounded, except at the entrance end, by a stone wall

Fig. 6.

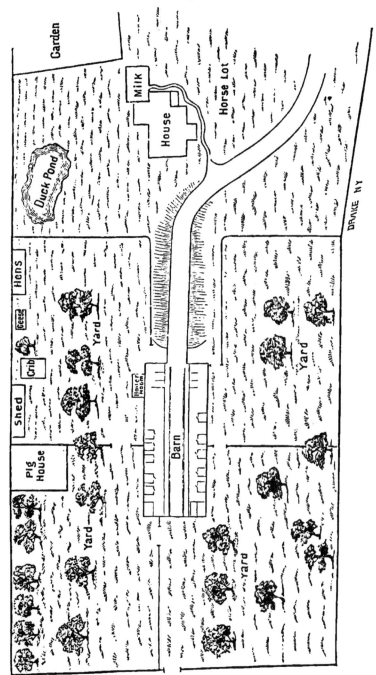

five feet high, and is to be divided, by walls of the same height, into four yards, communicating by gateways. Each yard contains about one-third of an acre, and is to be used as an exercising ground for one-fourth of the stock. The arrangement of the yards and buildings is shown in Fig. 6.

The arrangement of the entrances at the opposite ends by which the different floors are reached is shown in Fig. 7, which represents a sectional view through the barn at the head of the stalls on one side. A perspective view is shown in Fig. 8, which shows the east end and south side of the barn. The north side is exactly the same as the south, except that the stone foundation is carried up to the level of the top floor for better protection against cold north winds. Figs. 9, 9½, and 12 show the arrangement of the cattle, hay, and basement floors.

The cellar was dug out seven feet deep at the east end and five feet deep at the west end, the earth excavated being mainly deposited back of the abutment, making an easily graded road, striking the level of the ground about two hundred feet east of the barn. The descending driveway, by which the cellar is entered from the west, slopes about four feet in a distance of thirty feet, the steepest grade about the barn. The entire basement on each side of the gangway is for the storage of manure, except that portion which is taken off by the root cellar, 22 × 25 feet. The walls are of stone, laid in lime and cement mortar, and the wall about the root cellar is topped out with brick, fitted closely around the floor timbers.

The root cellar is ventilated by a window on the south side, which is also used for shooting in the roots. The gangway is left clear for wagons to be taken in to be loaded with manure. The arrangement of the feeding floor is tolerably well shown in the cut. Its only peculiarities are—(1) A railway which extends from the west end, the entire length of the barn, on which runs a four-wheeled truck, holding in summer a rack large enough to contain a horse cart-load of green fodder, and in winter a large box for cut and steamed food. (2) An open-slatted floor occupying a length of seven feet from about the middle of the line of

Fig. 7.

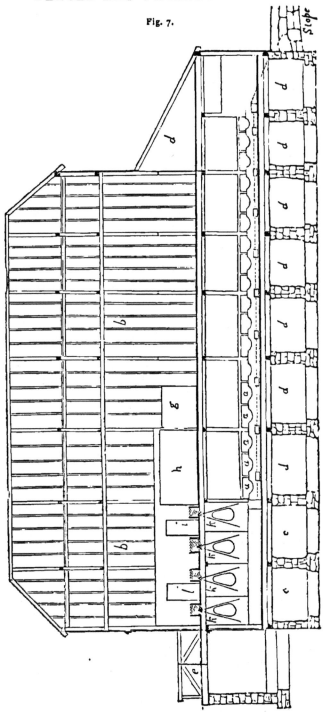

stalls to within five feet of the outer wall. This floor is made of
slats six inches wide, placed one and a half inch apart. This
arrangement gives light to the basement and allows all of the urine
to run through, while the treading of the cattle presses through
most of the dung, the remainder of which is thrown through small
scuttle-holes near the outer wall. So far as I can judge from
over a year's trial, this open floor is excellent, though, had the
timbers been prepared for it, it would have been better to have
had the slats run lengthwise of the barn, as in that case they
would have given an equally good footing if only three inches
wide, and the space for the passage of manure would have been
doubled.

It is intended that all of the horned cattle should feed from the
level on which they stand. Green fodder, or long hay, being
thrown directly on the floor between the front of the stalls and the
elevated border of the railway, the cut feed being given them in
tubs, which may be frequently set out in the sun, or, like the long
fodder, being placed on the floor, which, as it is free from obstructions, can be swept and washed out at pleasure. The cattle are
tied by the neck. Should stanchions be preferred, (and it is an
open question which is best,) they could still be fed in the same
way.

The oxen are fed from mangers inside of their stalls, so that the
gangway between them and the horses, where the food is received from the upper floor, may remain unobstructed. The
two loose boxes on the south side of the barn are of equal size,
with a space of about a foot and a half above the partitions for
ventilation and for the lighting of the inner one, which has no window. The entire floor of these boxes is slatted in the same manner with the floor under the hind quarters of the cattle. A rail
from the division of the stalls to the outer wall, at the center of
each side of the barn, may be used to separate the cattle of each
range of stable into two sections, each having its own door communicating with its own exercising ground. The hay floor, which
is reached by a very easy grade over the embankment and bridge,
has no center posts. The space from the floor to the bottoms

Fig. 8.—Perspective View of Barn, showing the east and south sides.

To face page 56

Fig. 9.

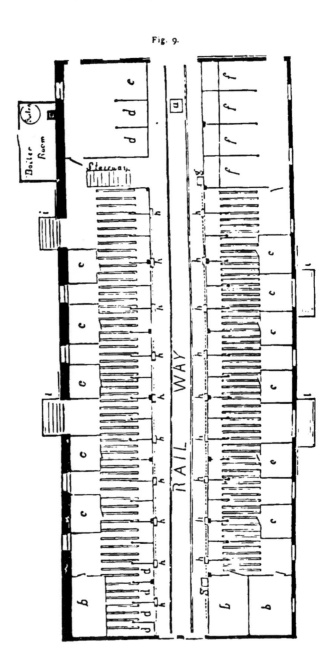

To face page 57.

of the trusses (eighteen feet) is entirely unobstructed, save by the side braces of the three center frames, which were necessary to give stiffness to the building. The feed-room, tool-room, workshop, and chamber are independent structures, seven and a half feet high, with strongly timbered ceilings, capable of holding any weight that it may be necessary to put upon them. The space above the workshop, etc., will be used for storing hay, while that over the feed-room will be used as a receptacle for cut hay, to be taken up from the cutting machine, which stands on the main floor west of the feed-room, by an elevator similar to that used for grain. The capacity of the hay floor will be about one hundred and twenty tons, besides ample space for wagons. The trap-door opposite the door of the chamber corresponds with one between the rail tracks on the floor below. Through these, roots are hoisted from the cellar to the upper floor, where they are cut by a root-slicer. The steam-box, grain and meal bin, etc., are in the feed-room, leaving sufficient space for the mixing of cut food, and its delivery through the trap-door to the rail-car below. A steam-boiler and a small engine for driving the hay-cutter will be erected in a shed north of the ox stalls, against the stone wall which, as already stated, is, on this side of the barn, carried up to the upper floor. Greater safety against fire makes this arrangement advisable. The reasons which have induced me to adopt this method of preparing winter food, and the details of the system will be set forth in the chapter on " Feeding."

One winter's experience with a Prindle steamer and a horse-power hay-cutter has proven both the advantage of this mode of preparing food and the necessity for better means for cutting a large supply, and more abundant steam for cooking.

A self-regulating pumping windmill has been erected over a spring one thousand feet distant, forcing water through a pipe into a tank on the hay-floor, communicating with iron water-troughs, one in front of each pair of cattle stalls, so arranged as to be always supplied with water. This arrangement for supplying water has now been in operation for nine years, and it is in all respects perfectly satisfactory. The windmill is entirely self-regulating, and works steadily and well

Fig. 10.

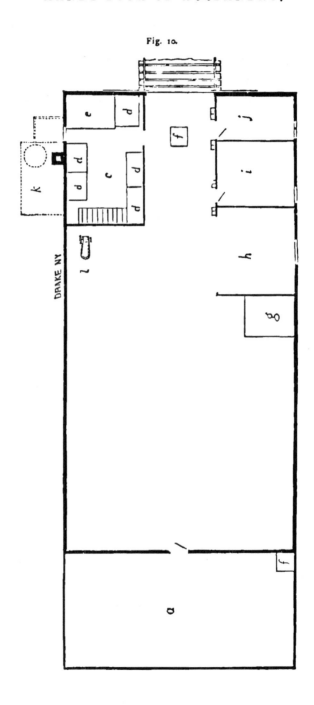

in all winds, having passed uninjured through some of the most severe storms ever known on this coast. A windmill of larger size—sufficient for driving a small grain-mill, thrashing-machine, feed-cutter, etc.—may be erected on the top of a barn.

The ventilation of the barn is by means of a simple covered opening, in the centre of the peak for the hay-floor, and two more active ventilators, one at each end, communicating through wooden funnels, following the slope of the roof on each side, and descending through the hay-floor and the cattle-floor to the cellar. The manure cellar being entirely closed from the outer air, the ventilating pipes can be supplied only by drawing down the foul air of the cattle-room, through the slatted floor. I append herewith the specifications for the carpenter work, which includes the sizes of the timbers.

" All the materials for this building will be furnished by the " owner, and the contractor is to put them together in the most " thorough and workmanlike manner. The work of framing, rais- " ing, and covering, including shingling sides and roof, to be com- " pleted in thirty days from the time that the foundation walls are " ready for the sills.

" On the north side of building and wing the foundation wall will " be carried up to height of under side of second story floor. On " the south and ends the wall will be carried up one foot above the " grade level, and on these there will be an 8×8 sill, the ends " to be carried up to and built into north wall.

" The summer-breasts in this floor will be tenoned into the sill " on the south, and the north ends will rest on an 18-inch buttress. " Each summer-breast will be supported on two piers, as shown on " plan, and will be pinned to the sill. All these sticks will be " 6×8, placed edgewise.

" On the first floor and over piers there will be 6×8 sup- " ports under two-inch flooring.

" Corner posts 6×8, other posts 6×6, and one at every bay.

" The girt will be 6×8 placed edgewise, and the beams of " second story floor will be framed the same as those of first " floor.

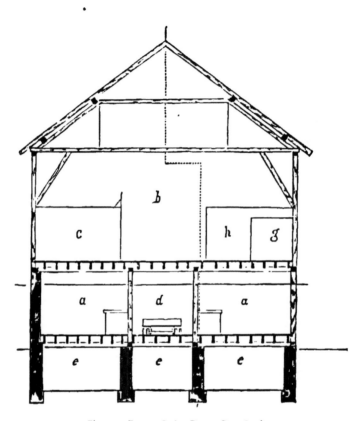

Fig. 11.—Barn at Ogden Farm—Cross-Section.

a a. Cattle Stalls.
  b. Hay-room (capacity of 120 tons).
  c. Feed room in one corner of hay-room.
  d. Passage between cattle.
e e e. Manure cellar—one end of the right-hand space being walled off for roots.
  g. Water tank.
  h. Tool-room, etc., in one corner of hay-room.

" The girt on the north will rest on the wall, and will form the
" sill on that side.

" The plates will be 6 × 6.

" All the posts will be framed as shown in framing plans, and the
" braces 4 × 6 will be tenoned and pinned in a thorough manner.

" The studs 2 × 6, and there will be six in each bay. Those
" in the ends and in the lean-to will be spaced out in the same
" manner. All outer studs will be properly framed.

" The trusses will be framed as shown on section. The tie-
" beams will be 9 × 6, made of three thicknesses bolted together.
" The principals and straining pieces will be 6 × 8. The tie-
" beam will be notched down to the plate and will be kept in
" place by means of an iron strap, secured on each side to the post
" below the plate. The principals and tie-beams will be strapped
" together, as shown on section, and the tie-beam, to crown not
" less than 2 inches, will be supported by means of iron rods, nuts,
" and washers, as shown on section.

" Purlins 6 × 6, and to be notched in jack-rafters, also to be
" notched in, to be 2 × 8. There will be 34 pairs on the main
" roof. Rafters for lean-to will be of same size, and will be spaced
" in the same manner. They will also have braces or collar beams.

" The ridge board will be 2 × 10.

" On the west end of main building to give the necessary
" amount of strength to carry the load, frame a truss above the
" girt on each side, making the girt the tie-beam, and put in 6 × 8
" principals. Frame the whole together properly, strap the princi-
" pals to the girt, and put a suspension rod with nuts and washers
" into each truss.

" Cover exterior of building, roof included, with hemlock
" boards, set window and door frames, and shingle the whole build-
" ing, lean-to included.

" The rafters will project 18 inches beyond the line of the build-
" ing, and the boarding will run up by the rafters till it meets the
" roof boarding.

" All floor joist will be 2 × 12 and 16 inches apart from cen-
" ters. Headers and trimmers for hatchways 3 × 12.

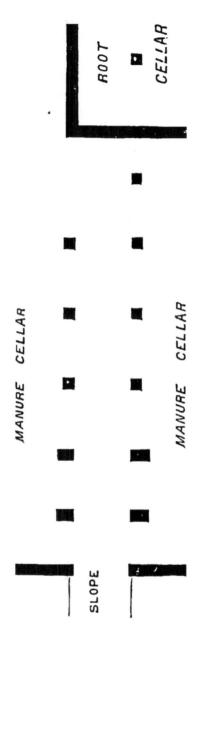

" Make first floor gangway, front half of cow stalls, five feet
" out from the side walls, and floor of horse stable of 2-inch plank
" matched with splines. Cover the rest of first floor with 2×3
" joist one inch apart and spiked down.

" In the stable floor and back of the horses there will be a gutter
" with a pitch to the west, to take the water to the manure pit.

" Cover second story floor with 2-inch plank, matched with
" splines and spiked to floor beams. The flooring to be notched
" for posts and studs, and to fit up close to outer boarding.

" All the windows are to have plain cases. They will be glazed
" with ordinary 8×10 glass. Besides the number of windows
" shown in the plan there will be one of the same size in each peak.

" All doors not otherwise described will be hung with rollers at
" the top, and the frames of sliding doors will be of 2-inch plank.

" Fit up the horse stables with permanent partitions the whole
" height of the story, making the stall divisions of the usual height.
" Close the mangers up at the bottom and in front up to the ceil-
" ing. In the center there will be an opening, horse-collar shape,
" with a cast-iron rim, and the bottom of mangers will be covered
" with sheet zinc.

" From gangway on second floor there will be covered openings
" to let down feed into the mangers.

" Opposite the horse stable there will be an ox stable as shown
" on plan, fitted with a permanent partition, and to have openings
" on gangway for feeding.   .

" On the second floor there will be permanent partitions set and
" ceiled on one side and overhead with $\frac{7}{8}$-inch matched spruce.
" The doors will all be battened, and that to the chamber will have
" a lock and catch.

" The hatches on both floors will be hung on hinges and will
" each have a ring and staple flushed in.

" Over the hatches there will be an eye secured to the ridge-
" board for a fall.

" There will be a bridge to floor of second story, made of
" 8×8 chestnut sleepers, and covered with 3-inch plank.
" On each side of main building there will be eave troughs,

5

"with a pitch from the center to the two ends, and wooden
"spouts to take off the water from the roof, also at end of lean-to.
"All the outside doors have platforms in front as shown in ele-
"vations."

For poultry, animals sick with contagious diseases, and such
uses, small inexpensive buildings have been erected in the yard,
as remote as possible from the barn. The swine are kept
entirely in the manure cellar, being fed through a shoot from
the feeding floor.

The entire cost of this barn, including the digging of the cellar,
materials and labor, and a liberal estimate for the cost of steam
and water-works, and a horse hay-fork, will not exceed $7,500, or
a yearly cost for interest, repairs, and insurance, of $700. It would
be difficult to estimate in figures the yearly *value* of such a barn;
but the perfect protection of all manure made, the sheltering of
fifty animals and of all the implements and vehicles required on
the farm, the saving of the labor of watering stock, the great
economy of such convenient feeding arrangements, the ability of
two men to cut a week's supply of fodder in two hours by the aid
of a steam-engine, the storage of 120 tons of hay, and the reduction of the labor of "soiling" to its very lowest point, must be
worth far more than $700 a year.

The increased value of the manure alone, over that which lies
in an open barn-yard exposed to rain and sun, to "drenching and
bleaching," would go far toward making up the amount, which
is only $14 per annum for each animal accommodated.

The barn is somewhat more expensive in the item of doors an-
windows than it would need to be if soiling were not intended.
For this, it is important to secure the most perfect ventilation in
warm weather, which is accomplished in the case in question by
the use of six doors, five feet wide, one door ten feet wide, ten
single windows, and one double one, and by very thorough ventilation from above.

The doors are all hung from the top on iron rails, and the single
ones close against stout jambs.

Of one thing I am very sure ; many a farmer in this country has detached barns and sheds which could not now be built for $10,000, yet which, from their small size and disconnected location, have much less capacity than the barn at Ogden Farm, and offer few of its conveniences, while they include no provision for the care of manure.

A very good plan for a small barn, "for a farm of fifty acres or less," is given in Thomas's Register of Rural Affairs, vol. iii., p. 129, which is here given with his own description :—

"The plan here given is sufficient for a farm containing fifty "acres under cultivation, and yielding good crops, with general "or mixed husbandry. For special departments of farming, it "must be modified to apply to circumstances.

"Fig. 14 is a plan of the principal floor. Being built on a "moderately descending side-hill, the thrashing floor is easily "accessible through the wide doors on the further side, and the

Fig. 13.—Perspective View.

"wagon, when unloaded, is backed out. These doors should "be each at least five feet wide, so as to give an opening of ten "feet ; and about twelve feet high, to allow ample space to "drive in a load of hay. The door at the other end of the "floor is about five feet wide, and is used for throwing out "straw. A narrow window on each side of this door, and one "with a row of single horizontal lights over the large doors, "keep the floor well lighted, when stormy weather requires the "doors to be shut.

" The bay, on the right, will hold at least one ton of hay for
" every foot of height, or some 20 or 25 in
" all. By marking the feet on one of the
" front posts, the owner may know, at any
" time, with some degree of accuracy, how
" many tons of hay he has in this bay,
" after it has become well settled. The
" upright shaft, V, serves at the same time
" to ventilate the stables below, and for
" throwing down hay directly in front of
" the cow stables. It should be made of
" planed boards inside, that the hay may
" fall freely, and for the same reason it
" should be slightly larger downward. It
" should have a succession of board doors two feet or more
" square, hung on hinges so as to open downward, through the
" openings of which the hay is thrown down for the animals.
" When not in use, these doors should be shut by turning
" upward and buttoning fast. A register should be placed in
" this shaft, to regulate the amount of air in severe weather.
" This may be a horizontal door at the bottom, dropping open on
" hinges, and shut by hooking up closely or partially, on different
" pins.

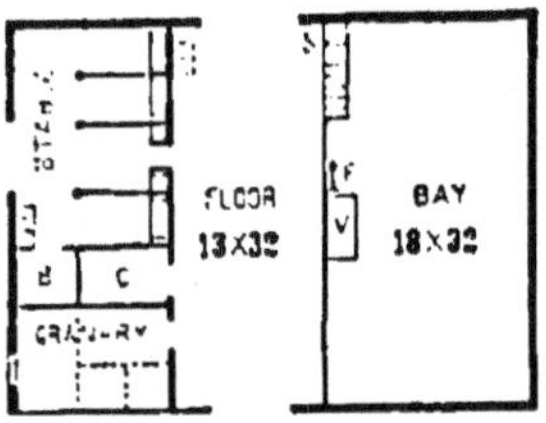

Fig. 14.—Principal Floor.

A. A trap door, for throwing down manure.

B. Closet for harness, saddle, buffalo skins, etc.

C. Tool room.

E. Trap-door for straw and roots.

F. Ladder to bay.

V. Ventilator and hay shoot.

S. Stairs to basement.

" Fig. 15 shows the form of the ventilator at the top of the build-

Fig. 15.

" ing. It is made of
" wood, except the four
" iron rods or bolts at the
" corners, and secures the
" advantages of Emer-
" son's excellent cap,

Fig. 16.

" which causes the air to draw upward at all times when there
" is wind from any quarter. Fig. 16 is a section showing the
" interior.

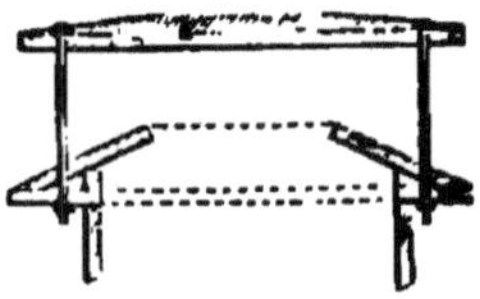

" A fixed ladder, on the line between the bay and the floor,
" enables the attendant to ascend readily at any moment.

" As a basement is usually too damp for horses, a stable large

" enough to hold five is placed on this floor. The middle stall
" will receive two horses to stand abreast ; and being placed
" opposite to the door six feet wide, will readily admit a span in
" harness, for temporary feeding, which is often a great conve-
" nience. A narrow passage from this stall admits the attendant to
" the barn floor. A trap-door at A allows the cleanings of the
" stable to pass at once to the manure heap below.

" These stalls are represented as only four feet wide. Five
" feet would probably be better, making but one narrow stall on
" each side the wide one, and allowing room for four horses in all.
" A door under the girth, at E, allows straw and roots to be dis-
" charged into the root cellar below—the roots being first depos-
" ited there, and then a few feet of straw upon them, protects
" from freezing."

" *The Granary*, 8 by 13 feet, contains three bins which have
" a part of the front boards movable or sliding, so that when all
" are in their place, they may be filled six feet high. They will
" hold, in all, about 350 bushels. The contents of each bin may
" be readily determined by measuring and multiplying the length,
" breadth, and depth, and dividing the number of cubic feet thus
" obtained by 56, and multiplying by 45. The result will be
" bushels. It will, therefore, be most convenient to make each
" bin even feet. A scale should be marked inside, showing the
" number of bushels at any height. Bags may be marked in the
" same way, after trial, with considerable accuracy, and save
" much trouble in measuring, for many purposes, but not for
" buying and selling. A short tube, with a slide to shut it, may
" pass downward from one or more of these bins, so that bags
" placed in a wagon in the shed below, may be easily and rapidly
" filled.

" A bay for unthrashed grain occupies all the space over the
" horse stable, tool room, and granary ; and movable poles or
" platform over each end of the floor also admit a considerable
" quantity besides.

" *The basement*, (Fig. 17.) This needs but little explanation.
" The cows are fed from the passage in front of them, into which

"the hay-shoot discharges, in front of which a door opens to

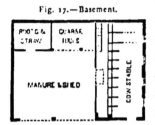

Fig. 17.—Basement.

"the shed, for the ready feeding of an-
"imals outside. The two inner stalls
"shut with gates, and serve for calf-pens
"when needed. Coarse implements, as
"sleds in summer, and wagons and carts
"in winter, may occupy the inclosed space
"adjoining, entered by a common gate."

For the very comprehensive requirements of a farm devoted to "mixed husbandry,"—when live stock, fruit, grain, etc., are each to receive their share of attention,—I have seen no plan for building a barn and sheds that seems so complete as that prepared by Dr. Hexamer for the Agricultural Annual of 1867, and which he describes as follows:—

"EXPLANATION OF GROUND PLAN.—*The Main Building*, "50 × 80 feet, exclusive of the approach, contains 1st. *The* "*Cook-room* for boiling or steaming and preparing feed, which is also "a convenient place for butchering in winter; *a, a*, are boxes, "with inclined floors, for mixing cut feed; *c, c, c, c*, are grain "boxes, connected by shoots with the granary on the floor above, "(see Fig. 20,) and capable of holding a week's supply of meal and "grain; *b* is a water-tank with penstock, or a cistern and pump; "*d* is a caldron; *e*, a hydrant for filling it; *f*, the chimney; *g, g*, "stairs to second story. 2d. *The Root-cellar*, which is divided "into four bins filled through trap-doors from the floor above; "*h, h*, are ventilators running to the roof; next this is the *The* "*Fruit-cellar*, and beyond this *i*, the cider press; *k*, place for "coopering, cleaning barrels, etc.; *m*, a vault under the approach "to the third floor, intended for an ice-house, but which may be "used as a cellar, or very well as an engine-house, detached from "the barn and made fire-proof; *l*, cool cellar for hanging meats; "*n, n, n, n*, descending planes from second story; *o, o*, ascend- "ing planes from cellar.

Fig 18.—The Perspective Elevation.

This is a view from the southwest ; the manure sheds on the south side of the yard, the gates and fences, being omitted to give a better view. The outside is of perpendicular boarding battened ; and the only attempt at ornament is the very heavy window caps, sills, and casings, with simple eaves and gable-brackets.

Fig. 19.—The Ground Plan.

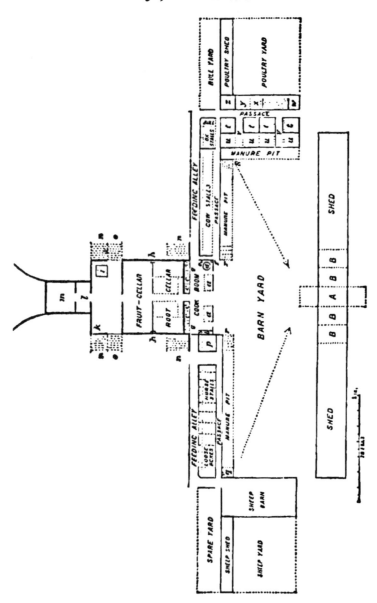

" *The West Wing* is 21 × 100 feet.   The feeding alley 6 feet
" wide.   There are windows on the north side.   The horse-
" stalls are 5 feet wide and 9 feet long, exclusive of mangers,
" which are 2 feet wide.   The loose boxes, for calf-pens, calving
" stalls, etc., are 7½ × 9 feet.   The passage behind the stalls is 4
" feet wide ; *p* is a double stall for a harnessed span, or for use as
" a large loose box.   The manure pit is 8 feet wide and 3 feet
" deep ; and *q* is a privy.

" *The East Wing*, for cows and oxen, is 19 × 100 feet ; feeding
" alley 6 feet.   The platform for cows is arranged for twenty

Fig. 20.—Second Floor.

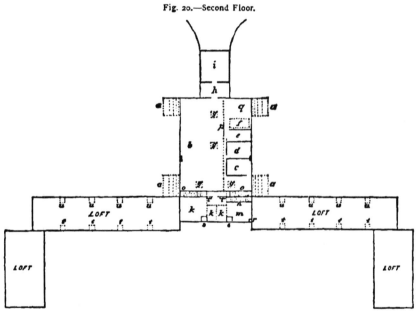

" stalls, 3½ feet wide ; mangers, 2½ feet wide.   The inclined
" platform, from rear of manger to the manure gutter, 5 feet ;
" and the cemented manure gutters are 18 inches wide and 4
" inches deep.   These gutters are on an incline, and discharge
" every 15 feet into the manure pit.   The ox-stalls are 8 feet
" wide for each yoke.   Bull stall, 5 feet wide.   The platforms for
" oxen and bull are six feet long, exclusive of manger ; *r, r,*
" mark descending ways for carts to back down into the manure
" pit, which is bridged at (*S*) for the oxen to pass.

" *The Piggery and Fowl-house* is 25 × 50 feet, and opens directly
" into the yards; *t, t, t, t,* hog pens, 10 × 10 feet; *u, u, u, u,*
" yards; *v, v,* feeding alleys; *W* is the main fowl room, with
" roosts; *x,* laying room, separated from the roosting room by a
" movable partition. The nest-boxes are so arranged along the
" north side, that any one can be pushed into the hatching room
" (*y*) without disturbing the hen; *z* is the room for fattening
" fowls in the autumn, or for any convenient purpose when not so
" used.

" MANURE SHEDS.—The wash of the *Barn-yard* runs in the
" direction of the arrows into the liquid manure cistern (*A*) from
" whence it can be pumped over the compost heaps, *B, B, B, B.*
" The leaders from the barn roofs do not discharge into this
" cistern, but may be turned into the manure pits, when the
" manure gets too dry. The sheds are for carts, wagons, plows,
" etc., also for absorbents and materials for composting to be used
" with the manure.

" EXPLANATION OF SECOND FLOOR PLAN.—*a, a, a, a,* as-
" cending roads; *b,* carriage floor; *c,* tool-room; *d,* workshop;
" *e,* harness room for carriage harness, farm harness is kept in the
" stables behind the horses; *f,* place for horse-power; *g, g, g, g,*
" trap-doors to cellars; *h,* cool room; *i,* ice-house; *k, k, k,* bins
" in granary; *n,* stairs to upper floor; *o, o,* stairs from lower floor;
" *l, l,* feed shoots to grain boxes, (*o,* in Fig. 19;) *m,* sleeping room

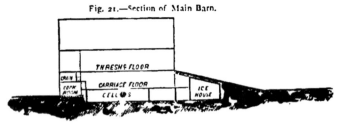

Fig. 21.—Section of Main Barn.

" for a man; if not wanted as such it may be added to the
" granary. The dotted line *p,* is a horizontal shaft, fixed close to
" the ceiling, and moved by steam or by horse-power. This
" works all the machinery used in the barn, the belts running to
" the cellar below, and to the thrashing floor above; *q,* place

" for cider mill over the cider press ; *r*, chimney ; *s, s*, hay-shoots
" from above ; *t, t, t, t*, trap-doors for
" bedding ; *u, u, u, u*, trap-doors for
" hay, stalks, and other fodder. The
" corn floor may be over one of the lofts.

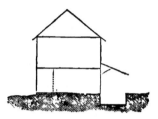

Fig. 22—Section of Wing.

Dr. H. also recounts, as follows, "the
conditions of a good barn," etc. :—

" 1. There should be one head, and
" he should be able to control com-
" pletely everybody and every thing in the whole barn. To
" obtain this, 'Centralization' and one general system are
" necessary. Without this no man can farm with profit, and no
" barn plan is good which is incompatible with a high degree of
" both.

" 2. Arrangements for saving labor as much as possible, in
" taking care of stock and other work. The easiest way should,
" when possible, be the right way.

" 3. Security for fodder, grain, roots, fruit, and all crops.

" 4. Facilities for protecting, and means of making manure.

" 5. Provision for the comfort and health of animals.

  " *a*. Full and direct light in the stables.

  " *b*. Ventilation of stables, cellars, and loft.

  " *c*. Southerly exposure of yards.

" 6. Shelter for all tools and implements.

" 7. Provision for work on rainy and cold days."

Mr. Thomas, in the Register of Rural Affairs, quoted above,
gives the following very useful hints to those who are about
building barns :—

" ESTIMATING THE CAPACITY OF BARNS.

" Very few farmers are aware of the precise amount of shelter
" needed for their crops, but lay their plans of out-buildings from
" vague conjecture or guessing. As a consequence, much of
" their products have to be stacked outside, after their buildings
" have been completed ; and if additions are made, they must of
" necessity be put up at the expense of convenient arrangement.

" A brief example will show how the capacity of the barn may
" be accurately adapted to the size of the farm.

" Suppose, for example, that the farm contains one hundred
" acres, of which ninety are good arable land ; and that one-
" third each are devoted to meadow, pasture, and grain.   Ten
" acres of the latter may be corn, stored in a separate building.
" The meadow should afford two tons per acre, and yield sixty
" tons ; the sown grain, 20 acres, may yield a corresponding bulk
" of straw, or forty tons.   The barn should, therefore, besides
" other matters, have a capacity for one hundred tons, or over
" one ton per acre as an average.   Allowing 500 cubic feet for
" each ton (perhaps 600 would be nearer) it would require a bay
" or mow 40 feet long and 19 feet wide for a ton and a half to
" each foot of depth.   If twenty feet high, it would hold about
" thirty tons.   If the barn were forty feet wide, with eighteen
" feet posts, and eight feet of basement, about forty-five tons
" could be stowed away in a bay reaching from basement to peak.
" Two such bays, or equivalent space, would be required for the
" products of ninety well-cultivated acres.   Such a building is
" much larger than is usually allowed ; and yet without it there
" must be a large waste, as every farmer is aware who stacks his
" hay out ; or a large expenditure of labor in pitching and re-
" pitching sheaves of grain in thrashing.

" In addition to this, as we have already seen, there should be
" ample room for the shelter of domestic animals.   In estimat-
" ing the space required, including feeding alleys, etc., a horse
" should have 75 square feet ; a cow 45 feet ; and sheep about
" 10 square feet each.   The basement of a barn, therefore, 40
" by 75 feet in the clear, will stable 30 cattle and 150 sheep, and
" a row of stalls across one end will afford room for eight horses.
" The thirty acres each of pasture and meadow, and the ten
" acres of corn-fodder, already spoken of, with a portion of grain
" and roots, would probably keep about this number of animals,
" and consequently a barn with a basement of less size than 40
" by 75 would be insufficient for the complete accommodation of
" such a farm in the highest state of cultivation.

" It has formerly been a practice, highly commended by
" writers, and adopted by farmers, to erect a series of small build-
" ings in the form of a hollow square, affording an open space
" within this range, sheltered from severe winds. But later ex-
" perience, corroborated by reason, indicates the superiority of a
" single large building. There is more economy in the materials
" for walls ; more in the construction of roofs—a most expen-
" sive portion of farm structures ; and a saving in the amount of
" labor, in feeding, thrashing, and transferring straw and grain,
" when all are placed more compactly together. The best barns
" are those with three stories ; and nearly three times as much
" accommodation is obtained thus under a single roof, as with the
" old mode of erecting only low and small buildings.

" An important object is to avoid needless labor in the trans-
" fer of the many tons of farm products which occupy a barn.
" This object is better secured by a three-story barn than by any
" other, where a side-hill will admit of its erection. The hay
" and grain are drawn directly to the upper floor, and nearly all
" is pitched downward. If properly arranged, the grain is all
" thrashed on this floor, and both grain and straw go downward
" —the straw to a stack or bay, and the grain through an opening
" into the granary below. Hay is thrown down through shoots
" made for this purpose to the animals below, and oats are drawn
" off through a tube to the horses' manger. The cleanings of
" the horse stables are cast through a trap-door into the manure
" heap in the basement. These are the principal objects gained
" by such an arrangement ; and as the labor of attendance must
" be repeated perpetually, it is very plain how great the saving
" must be over barns with only one floor, where hay, grain,
" manure, etc., have to be carried many feet horizontally, or
" thrown upward.

" HOW TO PLAN A BARN.

" The first thing the farmer should do who is about to erect a
" barn, is to ascertain what accommodation he wants. To

" determine the amount of space, has already been pointed out.
" He should next make a list of the different apartments required,
" which he may select from the following, comprising most of
" the objects usually sought :—

1. Bay or mow for hay.	8. Root cellar.
2. Bay or mow for unthrashed grain.	9. Room for heavy tools and wagons.
3. Bay or mow for straw.	10. Manure sheds.
4. Thrashing floor.	11. Granary.
5. Stables for horses.	12. Harness room.
6. Stables for cattle, and calf pens.	13. Cisterns for rain water.
7. Shelter for sheep.	14. Space for horse-power.

" If these are placed all on one level, care should be taken
" that those parts oftenest used should be nearest of access to
" each other ; and that arrangements be made for drawing with
" a cart or wagon in removing or depositing all heavy substances,
" as hay, grain, and manure. In filling the barn, for example,
" the wagon should go to the very spot where it is unloaded ; the
" cart should pass in the rear of all stalls to carry off manure ;
" and if many animals are fed in stables, the hay should be carted
" to the mangers, instead of doing all these labors by hand.

" If there are two stories in the barn, the basement should con-
" tain,—

1. Stables for cattle.	4. Manure shed.
2. Shelter for sheep.	5. Cistern.
3. Root cellar.	6. Horse-power.
7. Coarse-tool room.	

" The second floor should contain,—

1. Bays for hay and grain.	3. Stables for horses.
2. Thrashing floor,	4. Granary.
5. Harness room.	

" For three stories, these should be so arranged that the base-
" ment may be similar to the two-story plan, and the second
" story should contain,—

1. Bay for hay.	3. Granary.
2. Stables for horses.	4. Harness room.

" The third or upper story,—

1. Thrashing floor.	3. Bays for grain, including space over floor.
2. Continuation of hay bay.	4. Openings to granary below.

" In all cases there should be ventilators, shoots for hay, lad-
" ders to ascend bays, and stairs to reach quickly every part;
" besides which every bin in the granary should be graduated
" like the chemists' assay-glass, so that the owner may by a
" glance at the figures marked inside, see precisely how many
" bushels there are within. A blackboard should be in every
" granary, for marking or calculating ; one in the stable, to
" receive directions from the owner in relation to feeding, or
" keeping accounts of the same ; and a third should face the
" thrashing floor, for recording any results."

So much for barns. I have used all the space that can be devoted to the subject in a work having the wide range which
this has ; yet I have hardly done more than to introduce the
subject in its more important aspect, and have attempted only to
enlist the interest of the reader, and, by showing him what others
have done or described, to induce him, if he have need for a barn
on his own farm, to give the subject, (which is more fully treated
in other publications,) the fullest attention, and to study well the
requirements of his own particular case.

Other farm buildings will be considered in connection with the
particular branches of industry to which they belong: corn-cribs,
with corn culture, for example ; poultry houses with poultry, &c.
In conclusion, I would say that I have found it to be to my own
advantage, and am sure that other farmers would find it to theirs,
to employ a competent architect to make complete plans of the
whole work before commencing operations. It saves material,
saves time, and saves the cost and annoyance of many alterations,
which are sure to suggest themselves during the progress of the
work, unless the details have been previously studied out as they
only can be with the assistance of complete drawings made to a
scale.

BARN-YARDS.

The barn-yard must necessarily be regulated by the character
of the land on which, largely for other considerations, it has been
found necessary to locate the buildings, yet it should have its due
weight in determining the location.

When cattle are kept at pasture, at least during the day-time in summer, it should be a very good reason that induces a farmer to so place his barn that he cannot have the yard on the warmest and sunniest side of it.   Ordinarily the coldest winds of winter blow from the north and northwest, while the warmth of the morning sun in winter falls best into nooks whose lookout is toward the southeast.   Therefore a southeast exposure is usually the best.   If there are to be several buildings, they should be so arranged as to shelter the yard from the north and west.   Shelter from the east is not so important, but if it can be conveniently procured it has a certain advantage if so arranged as to allow the early morning sun to fall in the yard.   A close fence, six or seven feet high, would be better than a high building.   When a shed is to be used, it is a good plan to build the barn on the north side and the shed on the west side of the yard.

The barn-yard ought, always, to have sufficient slope for sur-face drainage, but the wash should be collected in a pit or deep pond hole at one side, and into this, straw, leaves, and muck may be thrown to absorb the liquids reaching it.   If cattle are to be fed in the yard, and are expected to make manure of a large amount of corn-fodder and straw, it is very well to have a nearly level yard, with a slight depression in the center, and to give them a dry footing by a profuse feeding of these materials, of which they will consume the best parts, trampling the refuse under foot.   Such an accumulation properly composted during the summer will make excellent manure for autumn use.

No farmer, however, who has once learned the feeding value of both corn-fodder and straw, when cut and mixed with other food, will continue to waste them under the feet of his animals, unless he is entirely careless of his own interest, or has a superabundance of fodder that he cannot sell to advantage.   By hook or by crook, he will contrive, in some way, to make them available for food.

Whatever plan is pursued the surface of the barn-yard should receive no water, save that which falls directly upon it from the clouds.   Surface gutters should protect it against the flow of water from other ground, and the roofs should be supplied with eave-troughs, discharging into cisterns or outside of the yard.

It will always pay to build a rough shed over that part of the yard which is to contain the pit or hollow for the manure, and the yard drainage,—especially if the droppings of the cattle are daily removed from the rest of the yard and added to a compost under the sheds.

FARM ROADS.

I would not feel justified in recommending that extra men and teams be employed to make substantial farm roads, but there are at least a hundred half days in the year, when the regular force of the farm can be occupied with such work—adding by every hour's work to the permanent future efficiency of the teaming appliances. Any thing which will enable each team, in all future time, to carry a heavier load than is now practicable, or to carry the same load more easily, must add to the permanent money value of the farm.

The foundation of all good roads—at least when any improvement of the natural roadway is necessary,—lies in good drainage. Roads are made soft only by water. Either the subsoil is so badly drained that the water of the surface soil cannot sink into it, or it is so wet that the frost is a long time in leaving it in the spring. So long as the frost remains in the subsoil it forms an effectual barrier to the descent of the water which makes the surface soft. Land on a well-drained subsoil parts with its frost very much earlier in the spring than that on an undrained one does. It is, therefore, of the utmost importance that the subsoil be as dry as it can be made.

Fig. 23.

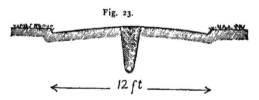

←———— 12 ft ————→

Thorough draining will not make a road always hard, but it will very much lessen the duration of the muddy condition, both when

the frost is coming out of the ground and in times of protracted
rains.   A narrow road, say not more than twelve feet wide, may
be sufficiently drained by a single line of tiles laid under its
center, as shown in Fig. 23 ; but if it is much wider than that it
will be better to lay a drain at or near each side, as shown in Fig.
24.   These drains should not be less than three feet deep.   The
manner of constructing them is given in the chapter on "Drain-

Fig. 24.

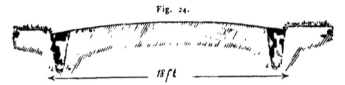

age."   They should be made with the same care and in the same
manner as ordinary land drains, and may often be connected with
the same system.

While a good underdrain, alone, will often very much improve
a good road, it is usually advisable, especially in heavy land, or
on land with a heavy subsoil, to use stones, and if possible gravel,
which will make a road good at all seasons of the year.

As in the case of many other sorts of farm work, there are two
ways of making a stone road, both equally costly, but by no
means equally effectual.   One way is to dig out the road to a
depth of a foot and a half for its whole width, and fill it to within
six inches of the surface with stones carefully laid on their flat
sides, and brought to a uniform face at the top—then to cover
them with gravel or other filling.   If gravel cannot be obtained,
a mixture of broken stones and common earth makes a good

Fig. 25.

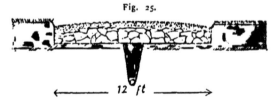

surface.   This sort of road (shown in Fig. 25) is excellent when
first made, but a few years of heavy teaming will "shake it to
pieces."   The jarring caused by heavy teams passing over it will

displace some of the stones in the lower bed, and the gravel from above will work under them. When this disturbance is once commenced it goes on more and more rapidly, until finally some of the stones will have worked their way to the top, some of the gravel will have gone to the bottom, and the road will be really in a worse condition than before the improvement was undertaken—but for *farm* roads the plan is a good one.

A much better and more durable road, made on a modification of what is called the Telford plan, although no more expensive than that just described, is very much more satisfactory and enduring, especially for public highways.

The ground is dug out to a depth of two feet at the sides, and nine or ten inches in the center, but in a curved line, as shown in Fig. 26. The depressions at the sides are solidly packed with

Fig. 26.

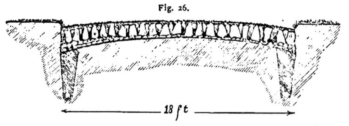

18 ft

small stones to the line of the slope of the surface of the road. Larger stones—as flat ones as can be found—are then set on edge as closely as possible over the whole bed, and "spalls" or "chinking stones," are tightly wedged in between their tops. A heavy iron maul or sledge-hammer is then used to drive in the wedging stones, and to break down the projecting points of the larger stones, until the whole mass is as firm as a floor. Sufficient "crown" should be given to this bed to afford surface drainage, (say 3 inches in an 18-ft. road,) and only so much gravel or earth put upon it as will completely cover the stones, and prevent the wheels being jarred by them. If properly drained and well made, such a road will last a life-time, and will require very little attention to keep it in order.

CHAPTER V.

DRAINAGE.

DRAINING WITH TILES.

To condense within the limits of a few pages even a tolerably complete description of the construction and mode of operation of tile-drains, and to give a clear statment of the theory of under-drainage in general, is no easy task, and it would probably be of little use for me to attempt to do it more satisfactorily than by making the following extracts from what I have already written on the subject.*

The following articles on the subject, which I have at various times furnished for the *Evening Post*, properly bear upon this branch of it:—

WHAT IS UNDERDRAINING?

It is an axiom of good farming that all land should be thoroughly underdrained: underdrained, of course, either naturally or arti-ficially.

There is nothing mysterious either in the operation or in its effect. The ability to plow and plant early in the spring, the perfect germination of seeds, the rapid and luxuriant growth of healthy plants, the ability to plow and otherwise cultivate growing crops,

* 1. An Essay on "Tile Draining," in the American Agricultural Annual for 1867. New York : Orange Judd & Co.

2. "Draining for Profit and Draining for Health," published by the same house. (1867.)

3. A Chapter on "Tile Draining," in the Farmers and Mechanics' Manual. New York : E. B. Treat & Co (1868.)

4. Various Communications to the *American Agriculturist* and to the *New York Evening Post* on the same subject.

and the opportunity for seasonable harvesting and for fall plowing, all depend more upon the condition of the soil as to moisture than on any other single circumstance.

For the purpose óf illustration, we will suppose an acre of land to be inclosed in a water-tight box, its bottom being four feet below the surface, and its sides reaching to the surface, with no outlet at any point. The whole acre lies open to the rain, and the whole depth is saturated by every heavy storm. This acre of land may have the most thorough cultivation of which it is capable, and may be manured as land was never manured yet, and its produce will inevitably be precarious. In very good seasons it may be fair. In wet seasons it will be weak and badly matured, and in dry ones it will be mean and stunted. It will be the first of May instead of the middle of March when we plow it; the plowing will paste together more than it crumbles it; the harrowing will do as much harm as good; the seed will probably rot in the ground and have to be planted a second time; and the growth will be slow except during the short interval (often only a few days) between the conditions of " too wet " and "too dry."

In short, the soil will be putty one-half of the time, and brick the rest of it : " It girns a' the summer and it greets a' the winter." It is such a soil as no man can afford to cultivate at all. Now let us knock the bottom out of our box and see the result. Of course we must assume that it is underlaid by a stratum of gravel or other porous material. The water which has filled the spaces between the particles of the soil, lying there until evaporated at the surface, sinks slowly away and leaves the whole mass pervaded by air, the particles themselves holding by absorption enough water to make them sufficiently moist for the highest fertility, but affording very little for the cooling operation of evaporation at the surface. When a heavy rain falls, the soil may be for a short time saturated (soaked full) with water, and this drives out all of the air it has contained. As the water settles away, after the rain, fresh air follows and embraces every atom with its active fertilizing oxygen, and deposits, in the upper layers, carbonic acid, and ammonia, and all else that makes air impure and soil rich. Indeed, the water itself has washed the air clean, and then on filtering through the loose soil, has deposited, near enough to the surface to be within the reach of roots, all of its impurities.

Seed planted now finds as much moisture as it needs for germination, and only as much ; its rotting in the ground is impossible. And if we will follow all of the processes of growth, and all of the operations of cultivation and harvesting, we shall find that the former are never impeded by too great wetness of the soil, and that the latter may be performed always in good season and with the best effect. Neither are the crops destroyed, or even greatly injured by drought, for if there is one effect of underdraining that is established beyond doubt, it is that it is at least the basis of all those operations by which we most successfully attempt to overcome the effect of drought ; and it is itself the greatest of all preventives of drought.

Instead of being a pest to the farmer, disappointing half of his hopes, and baffling his best skill, this acre of land has become a pliant tool in his hands. So far as it is possible for him to be independent of the changes of the weather, he has become independent of them, and he works with a certainty of the best reward, which changes his occupation from a game of hazard to a work of fair promise.

To answer the question, then, which stands at the head of this article, underdraining is the knocking out of the bottom of the water-tight box in which our soil is incased. If we are the happy occupiers of land through which water settles away as it falls, we have no need of the operation. But if our only (or our chief) outlet is at the surface, with the drying sun and wind for draining tiles, we do need it, and we can never hope for the success to which our seed, our manure and our labor entitles us until we adopt it.

How it is best to do the work depends on soil, situation, price of labor, price of material, and depth of outlet that can be secured.

Stone drains, tile drains, brush drains, board drains, mole plow tracks, and all other conduits for water are proven pretty good, so long as they continue to afford a channel through which the water can run freely. The choice between them is based on the questions of durability, cost, and availability. The only positive rules applicable to all cases are that the drain should be a *covered* one, and not an open ditch, and that it should be, whenever possible, at least three, and better four, feet deep.

FARM DRAINAGE.

While it would hardly be fair to say that farmers are more slow than men of other classes to adopt improvements in the methods of their trade, as hardly any other industry has been, within the same time, so completely revolutionized as has farming, in the single item of hay-making, since the introduction of the mowing machine—still there are some improvements whose practical usefulness, and whose applicability are universally acknowledged, yet which seem to find it hard work to fight their way to general adoption.

The drainage of moist land is one of these. We use the expression *moist land*, because land which is absolutely wet is either drained or let alone, as a matter of course. Every farmer knows that his swamps must either be made dry (or at least only *moist*) or must be left to the bulrushes. The far larger part of our cultivated farms, which come under the designations "late," "naturally cold," "heavy," "sour," "springy," etc.,—the larger part of all our more fertile lands, that is,—are cultivated year after year, under very heavy disadvantages; their half crops, and the extra labor and "catching" work that they entail, being accepted as a sort of doom from which there is no available means of relief.

Almost every farmer of such land is ready to admit that it would be better for being drained, but he has got on so long without it, and draining is such expensive work, that, having no example for its benefits before his eyes, he "gets on" without it to the end of his days.

It does seem hard to believe that on solid upland, that only cost fifty dollars an acre in the first instance, and produces fair crops in fair seasons, it will pay to spend from fifty dollars to one hundred dollars an acre more to make it a little dryer, where more of the same sort can be bought at the original price. But exactly this must be believed before farming can become in America what it already (and by means of drainage) has become in England, and before our farmers can be so successful as they ought to be and as they have the means of becoming.

The cost of draining (and its cost is the great obstacle to its adoption) should be compared, not with the cost of the land, but with the capital on which the yearly cost of labor, seed, and manure is the interest. For instance, the following is a very moderate estimate of the expense of raising an acre of Indian corn, when it is intended to be the first crop of a rotation running through four or five years :—

Plowing	$5 00
Harrowing	1 50
Manure	12 00
Seed	50
Planting	2 00
Cultivation (hoeing, &c.)	7 50
Harvesting	10 00
	$38 50

This is a constant quantity, and is an outlay that must be made on wet land as well as on dry, on cheap land as well as on dear. It is (at seven per cent.) the interest on over $500. That and the $50 paid for the land make the total investment of capital in the operation.

It will be a good crop—a very good one—on such land as we are describing ("naturally cold" land) that yields fifty bushels of corn and two tons of fodder, worth $57 50—or about 10 per cent. on the investment of $550.

By precisely the same manuring and cultivation, on the same land, after thorough underdraining, (say at a cost of $100 per acre, although this is too high,) in a season that would yield the above crop on the undrained land, we should surely get seventy-five bushels of corn and three tons of fodder, worth $86 25, or thirteen and a third per cent. interest on an investment of $650.

This difference of crops, (an increase of fifty per cent.,) costing only the interest on the outlay for draining, which is as permanent as the land itself, is not more than may be expected under average circumstances; yet we have stated only a part of the argument on which the apostles of drainage justly depend for the advancement of their ideas.

Land that remains wet so far into the spring as often to delay the plowing until it is time to plant, may, after being drained, often be plowed in March instead of May; when the seed is planted, it will never be rotted in the ground and call for a new planting, if the water can find its way to the drains below. Weeds, which grow while the land is too clammy to be hoed, and get beyond our control, so that when the ground is dry hoes and horse-hoes have to wage an unequal warfare against them, may, on drained land, be attacked on almost any sunny day and killed with little work; and when the time comes for hauling off the crop, as in spring in hauling on manure, it will not be necessary to wait weeks for the ground to be solid enough for the teams to work, nor will the ground be so much injured in the operation.

In short, work can be done in proper season, done in a proper manner, and done with a definite certainty of a fair return, and with very much less dependence on the weather than when the water of heavy rains has to lie soaking in the soil until dried up by the sun and wind.

It may be objected to the above calculation that it is unfair to capitalize the annual cost of cultivation, manure, etc., because these expenditures come from the yearly income of the farmer, and do not represent the interest on his capital. If this view of the case be taken, it will surely be fair to charge the cost of draining by its annual interest, and not by its gross amount, for it benefits not only the crop of the first year, but of all subsequent years —and often in an increasing degree—while it is subject to no deterioration, but remains as permanent and as safe an investment as is a mortgage on a neighbor's farm.

What is needed is that we have more general information on the subject, more practical examples of the beneficial effects of draining, and cheaper draining tiles. All of these will come slowly at first, but they are coming surely; and they cannot fail to increase in rapid progression, by the very effect of their own influence.

That land should be made damper by being made more dry, that underdraining should be one of the best preventives of the ill effects of drought—this is the apparently anomalous proposition on which one of the strongest arguments in favor of draining is based.

When we see a field baked to the consistence of a brick, gaping open in wide cracks, and covered with a stunted growth of parched and thirsty plants, it seems hard to believe that the simple laying of hollow tiles four feet deep in the dried-up mass would do any thing at all toward the improvement of its condition. For the present season it would not; but for the next it would, and for every season thereafter, and in increasing degree, so long as the tiles continued to act as effective drainage.

The baking and the cracking, and the unfertile condition of the soil are the result of a previous condition of entire saturation. Clay cannot be moulded into bricks, nor can it be dried into lumps, unless it is made soaking wet. Dry or only damp clay, once made fine, can never again be made lumpy unless it is first made thoroughly wet, and is pressed together while in its wet condition. Neither can a considerable heap of pulverized clay, kept covered from the rain, but exposed to sun and air, ever become even apparently dry except within an inch or two of its surface.

Underdraining, if the work is properly done of course, after it has had time to bring the soil for a depth of two or three feet to a thoroughly well-drained condition, will equally prevent it from becoming baked into lumps, or from being, for any considerable depth below the surface, too dry for the purposes of vegetation. In the first place, the water of heavy spring rains, instead of lying soaking in the soil until the rapid drying of summer bakes it into coherent clods, settles away and leaves the clay, within a few hours after the rain-fall ceases and before rapid evaporation commences, too much dried to crack into masses.

Of course, this is only the beginning of the operations of improvement. It is merely the foundation, but on heavy soils it is the necessary foundation, of the processes (natural and artificial) by which the improvement is effected and made permanent. The only direct effects of draining are to prevent the soil from ever being completely saturated for any considerable time, and to remove from below water, which if not so removed would be evaporated from the surface.

The formation of a crust on the surface of the ground is in direct proportion to the quantity of water that is removed by evaporation, and the crust constitutes a barrier against the admission of air in direct proportion to its thickness. Consequently, the larger the quantity of the water that is removed by the drains the smaller is the obstacle offered to the entrance of air.

The more constantly the lower parts of the soil are relieved from excess of water and supplied with air, the more deeply will roots descend, and the more frequently will the air in the lower soil be changed—the easier its communication with the atmosphere.

On these two principles depends the immunity from drought which underdraining helps us to secure. In dry weather the soil gets its moisture from the deposit of dew—on the surface during the night, and on the surfaces of the particles of the lower soil constantly, day and night.

The familiar example of the " sweating " of a cold pitcher that stands in the sun and wind on a hot July day, illustrates the manner in which the dew-laden air of our dryest weather gives up its moisture (greater then than at any other time) to the particles of the cool-shaded lower soil with which it comes in contact. A box of finely pulverized earth, two feet deep, previously dried in an oven—placed in the sun and wind on the dryest and hottest day of summer, would soon become sufficiently moist for the growth of plants, by the deposit of dew among its lower and cooler particles. Let the same earth be saturated with water and closely compressed, and it would, under the same circumstances, be baked and dry throughout its whole depth. No air could enter for the deposit of dew, and, from its compact condition, all of the moisture that it contains would move, by capillary attraction, from particle to particle, to supply the evaporation at the surface, while the crust thus formed on the surface would prevent the free admission of air, even if the lower soil were loose and porous.

It is the same in the field. A heavy clay soil, saturated with water, dries up to a condition that will not admit of the circulation of air. Even if the thin surface-soil, containing much vegetable matter, is loose enough, it is soon heated to such a depth that the little moisture it receives during the cooler parts of the day is dried out by the midday sun, while the compact subsoil is impervious to all atmospheric influence. Plants grow well enough during the weeks that separate the rains of early spring from the heat of midsummer; but when the drought sets in—the roots being only in the surface-soil—for roots will not enter a cold, saturated subsoil—vigorous vegetation ceases, and we accuse Providence of having sent us a scourge for our sins. As well blame Providence for our loss if we neglected to plow and harrow and plant at seed-time, as for loss from neglect to drain away the water that places us at the mercy of the drought.

If we underdrain the land, even without the use of the subsoil plow,—but rather with it,—the early growth will be less precarious and more uniform, and the roots of our crops will push down into the subsoil, where they will find, all through the dryest summer, enough moisture for their uses. For the first year or two, of course, we could only hope to modify our evils, but in time we should find, as the writer has found in his own practice, that if we keep the surface of our underdrained ground well stirred, a six weeks' drought, that lays the whole country side bare, has little power to diminish our crops.

KINDS OF SOIL WHICH ARE BENEFITED BY TILE-DRAINING.

All soils which are so retentive that the water of rains is not (at least during the season of growth,) absorbed as it falls, and carried readily down to a point below the ordinary reach of the roots of crops—say to a depth of at least three feet—will be benefited by draining. With the exception of actual swamps, the soils which derive the greatest advantage, are, of course, those which, during the spring and fall, are completely saturated with water, and during the heat of summer, are baked to a hard crust and broken with fissures ; but all heavy loams, friable soils, which rest on impervious subsoil (or hard pan),—indeed all but sands, and the lighter deep loams and gravels—are very much benefited by such a removal of their excess of water as can be economically effected only by tile-draining.

THE MODE OF ACTION, AND THE EFFECT OF UNDERDRAINS.

A thoroughly underdrained field is one which is underlaid, at suitable intervals, with lines of continuous pipe drains, which admit the water of the soil, and convey it to an outlet, from which it is completely removed. The water which falls upon the surface is at once absorbed, and settles through the ground until it reaches a point where the soil is completely saturated, and raises the general water level ; when this level reaches the floor of the drains, the water enters at the joints and is carried off. That which passes down through the land lying between the drains, bears down upon that which has already accumulated in the soil, and forces it to seek an outlet by rising into the drains.* For example, if a barrel standing on end be filled with earth which is saturated with water, and its bung be removed, the water of satura- tion (that is, all which is not held by attraction *in* the particles of earth) will be removed from so much of the mass as lies above the bottom of the bung-hole. If a bucket of water be now poured upon the top, it will not all run diagonally toward the opening ; it will trickle down to the level of the water remaining in the barrel, and this will rise and run off at the bottom of the orifice. In this manner the water, even below the drainage level, is changed with each addition at the surface. In a barrel filled with coarse pebbles, the water of saturation would maintain a nearly level surface ; if the material were more compact and retentive, a true

* Except from quite near to the drain, it is not probable that the water in the soil runs laterally toward it.

level would be attained only after a considerable time. Toward
the end of the flow the water would stand highest at the points
farthest distant from the outlet.   So, in the land, after a drenching
rain, the water is first removed to the full depth, near the line of
the drain, and that midway between two drains settles much more
slowly, meeting more resistance from below, and for a long time,
will remain some inches higher than the floor of the drain.   The
usual condition of the soil (except in very dry weather) would be
somewhat as represented in the accompanying cut (Fig. 27.)

Fig. 27.

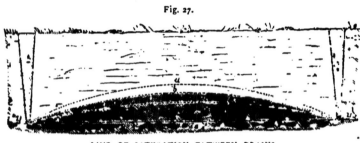

LINE OF SATURATION BETWEEN DRAINS.

The dark shading to the line *b* represents the water of saturation in the soil, which, immediately after a rain has stood at *a*,
and is descending toward *c*.   In time of drought it would in
most soils, descend nearly or quite to the level of the drains, or
even, in severe drought, much lower than this.

To provide for this deviation of the line of saturation, in
practice, drains are placed deeper than would be necessary if the
water sank at once to the level of the drain floor, the depth of
the drains being increased with the increasing distance between
them.

Theoretically, every drop of water which falls on a field
should sink straight down to the level of the drains, and force a
drop of water below that level to rise into the drain and flow
off.   How exactly this is true in nature cannot be known, and is
not material.   Drains made in pursuance of this theory will be
effective for any actual condition.

Any system, which so disposes of the water falling on the land,
produces the following important results :—

1. *It greatly lessens the evil effects of drought.* During the hottest weather there is a great amount of water in the atmosphere which has been evaporated from the earth by heat, and which is held *by heat*, in the form of vapor. When this vapor comes in contact with bodies sufficiently cooler than itself, they take away its heat, and the vapor contracts to the liquid form (condenses) and is at once deposited as dew on the surface of the cooler substance. At night, after a hot summer day, the earth is much cooler than the air, and consequently, as it absorbs heat from the atmosphere and from the watery vapor contained in the air, dew is deposited. The familiar example of a cold pitcher, which seems to *sweat* in hot weather, while it is only absorbing heat from the air, and causing the vapor of the air to be deposited in a liquid form, is an illustration of the action of this law of condensation. In like manner, a knife-blade condenses dew from the breath, by depriving the moisture in the breath of its heat, and thus causing it to assume the liquid form.

So, when the water is removed from the soil, the spaces between its particles (which, before drainage, had been filled with water) are occupied by air, and, to a greater or less extent—owing to the motion of the air above the surface caused by winds, and to the effect of changes of temperature below the surface—this air is constantly changing, and that which enters from above, charged with vapor, gives up its heat and therefore its moisture, both of which are absorbed by the lower and cooler soil. In consequence of this action—especially where the surface of the soil is kept in a loose condition, so as to admit air freely—drained lands withstand drought better than those which are undrained.

2. *It enables the soil to receive a larger supply of the fertilizing gases of the atmosphere, (carbonic acid and ammonia.)* The air always contains more or less of these gases, which, with water, are the chief sources of the materials of which plants are made. When the water which fills the spaces between the particles of the soil is drawn off, air enters and takes its place, and the carbonic acid and ammonia are absorbed, ready to be taken up by the

roots of plants, and to produce beneficial changes in the mineral ingredients of the soil.

The rain which falls, finding the soil in a porous condition, sinks into it, and gives up the gases which it contains, passing out of the drains, nearly pure; while, if the land were already saturated, or had not been made porous by the process of draining, the water would, to a greater or less extent, run off over the surface, and instead of enriching the soil, would carry away some of its more fertile parts.

3. *It warms the lower portions of the soil.* We have already seen (1) that the air which circulates in the soil gives up heat, and it thus elevates the temperature of those parts which are cooler than the atmosphere. The water of rains also, in passing down through the soil, carries with it the heat of the surface, and deposits it, and a portion of the heat which it received from the warm air through which it fell, in the lower and cooler parts of the soil. In hot weather, the water which issues from the mouth of a drain is often ten degrees cooler than that which falls on the surface, and all of its lost heat has been given to the soil.

4. *It lessens the cooling of the soil by evaporation.* This is one of the most important effects of draining. When liquid water becomes vapor, it increases in bulk 1723 times, and it contains 1723 times as much heat. The heat required to evaporate it, is taken from surrounding substances. When water is sprinkled on the floor, it cools the room, because in becoming a vapor (drying) it takes heat from the room. If a wet cloth be placed on the head, and the evaporation of its water assisted by fanning, the head becomes cooler—a portion of its heat being taken to convert the water into the condition of vapor.

The same action takes place in the soil. When the evaporation of its water is rapidly going on, by the aid of the sun and wind, heat is abstracted and the soil becomes cold. If the water of the soil is mainly removed by draining, there is comparatively little to be evaporated, and comparatively little heat is taken away—probably not more than is received from the atmosphere, (3.)

This cooling of the soil, by the evaporation of its water, greatly retards the growth of crops, and the fact that draining lessens evaporation is one of the strongest arguments in favor of its adoption. An idea may be formed of the amount of heat taken from the soil in this way, from the fact that, in midsummer, twenty-five hogsheads of water may be evaporated from a single acre in twelve hours.

5. *It greatly facilitates the chemical action by which the constituents of the soil are prepared for the use of plants, and by which its mechanical texture is improved.* Ordinary soils contain roots and other organic matters, and the various minerals which aid, directly or indirectly, in the nutrition of plants. Before the roots, etc., which have been left in the soil by a previous crop, can become useful to a new growth, they must undergo the process of decay, which is a slow combustion, requiring the action of atmospheric air. In a soil saturated with water, this decay cannot take place. It proceeds most actively in thoroughly drained land, while in land which is often too wet, it is greatly retarded. The mineral constituents of plants can be taken up by roots only in solution of water, which can dissolve them only from the *surfaces* of the particles of the soil, and usually only after they have undergone a chemical change from exposure to the air and moisture. The more freely air is admitted into the soil, the more easily will the coarser particles be disintegrated, thus exposing more surface, and the more readily will the exposed portions be prepared for the dissolving of their fertilizing ingredients. These chemical changes also greatly improve the mechanical condition of the soil, tending to make it more light and friable, and, both from its greater fineness and from the increased amount of its decayed organic matter, to enable it more readily to absorb fertilizing gases (2) from the air and from rains, and to condense the watery vapor of the atmosphere in dry weather, (1.)

6. *It tends to prevent grass-lands from "running out."* The *tillering* of grasses—that process by which they constantly reproduce themselves by offshoots from the crowns of the plants—goes on during the season of growth, as long as the roots can find

7

sufficient nutriment in the soil, unless arrested by their coming in
contact with a cold, wet, uncongenial subsoil. By withdrawing
the moisture which causes this unfavorable condition of the subsoil, we may maintain a full supply of grass plants, as long as we
can keep the soil rich enough to support them.

7. *It deepens the surface soil.* The withdrawal of the water
which, in undrained lands, occupies the subsoil for so great a portion of the growing season, allows the roots of plants to extend
much farther from the surface, and in decay, these roots deposit
carbon (black mould) in the spaces of the lower soil, while the
mineral parts are improved by the action of the air, thus,
gradually, converting the subsoil to the condition of the surface
soil.

8. *It renders soils earlier in the spring, and keeps off the effects of
cold weather longer in the fall,* because the water, which renders
them cold, heavy, and untillable, is earlier removed, and the excess
of water, which produces an unfertile condition on the first
approach of cold weather, is withdrawn.

9. *It prevents the throwing out of grain in winter;* because the
water of rains is at once removed, instead of remaining to throw
up the surface by freezing, as it does by reason of the vertical
position taken by the particles of ice.

10. *It enables us to work much sooner after rains,* inasmuch as
the water will pass down to the level of the drains much sooner
than it will soak away in an undrained, retentive soil, or be
removed by slow evaporation from the surface of the ground.

11. *It prevents land from becoming sour;* because the acids which
result from the decay of organic matter, in the presence of too
much moisture, are not formed in the more healthy decomposition
which takes place in a sufficiently dry and well-aerated soil.

12. *It lessens the formation of a crust on the surface of the soil after
rains in hot weather.* When water, having mineral matters in
solution, is drawn up from the lower soil, it deposits them, at the
point of evaporation, at the surface, often forming a hard crust,
which is a complete shield, to prevent the admission of air with
its fertilizing gases and water vapor. In proportion to the com-

pleteness with which the water of rains is removed from below, do we lessen the evaporation by which this crust is so largely formed.

DRAINING OPERATIONS.

LAYING OUT THE WORK.*

THE OUTLET.—The first important point, in arranging a system of drains, is to seek the lowest suitable point at which an outlet can be obtained. This should be, whenever possible without too great cost, at least four feet (better four and a half feet) below the general level of the land near it, that the drains

Fig. 28.

Outlet, secured with masonry and grating.

may be covered to that depth, even in the lowest part of the land to be drained, though it is sometimes better to place the drains at a less depth for a short distance, than to incur the cost of deepening a ditch on a neighbor's property for a very long distance.

The position and depth of the outlet being established, it

* For want of space, the reasons for adopting the methods herein set forth are not discussed. They are those which experience has shown to be the best.

should be permanently built up with brick or stone, (as represented in Fig. 28,) the work being done solidly, but as rudely as
may be thought proper. The ditch below this outlet must be
of sufficient depth and capacity to keep it always free from obstructions.

MAINS AND SUB-MAINS.—Having procured substantial stakes
about eighteen inches long, stake out the main drain from the
outlet through the principal depression of the land, and if the
ground slope in other directions than toward this depression, or if
there be a broad valley with sloping land at each side, stake
other lines, connecting with the first, and running at the bottom
of the various slopes, or in the middle of the secondary depression, so arranged that they shall have a uniform descent for their
whole distance. The proper arrangement of these collecting
drains requires more skill and experience than any other branch of
the work, as on their disposition depends, in a great measure, the
economy and success of the undertaking.

LATERAL DRAINS.—Having so arranged the mains and sub-
mains that water flowing down the various slopes, in the line of
steepest descent, would reach them without materially changing
its course, stake out parallel lines, forty feet apart (the first line
being twenty feet from the boundary of the land to be drained)
running directly down the slopes in the lines of their steepest
descent, or as nearly so as is consistent with tolerable simplicity
of arrangement, and connecting with the main lines at their feet.
The stakes which indicate the points at which the laterals strike
the main lines, may be marked so as to be easily recognized as
indicating these points, and the original stakes of the main lines
may be taken up and reset at points mid-way between the laterals,
or at shorter distances, if necessary. On the lateral lines, they
should be at uniform distances; on the main lines, they should be
as nearly so as possible.

MAPPING.—Commence at the lower end of the main line and
mark the stakes consecutively A, Aa, Ab, Ac, etc. Then, supposing sub-mains to unite with the main line at stakes b and c,
mark the stakes of these Ab 1, Ab 2, Ab 3, etc ; Ac 1, Ac 2,

Ac 3, etc; and their laterals $\frac{Ab\ 1}{1}$, $\frac{Ab\ 1}{2}$, $\frac{Ab\ 1}{3}$, etc., until the stakes of all the drains are so marked as to be clearly designated. (See map, Fig. 29.)

Fig. 29.

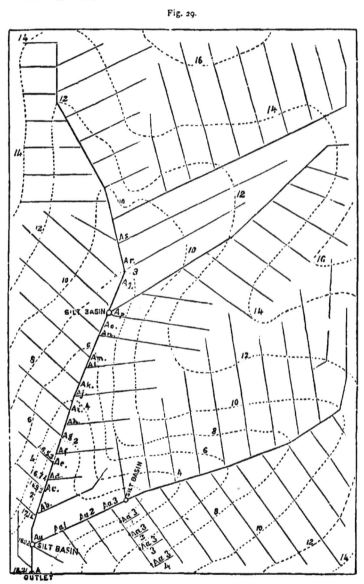

Map of a ten-acre field, showing the conformation of the land; the arrangement of the drains and silt basins; and the method of marking the stakes. Scale 160 feet to 1 inch.

Next, survey the boundaries of the land, and all of the lines, and note the position of each stake on the map, having reference to some permanent landmarks, so that the exact position of any point of the drains may at any future time be found, in order that repairs and alterations may be made without loss of time in hunting for lines whose exact location is forgotten. Such a map of drains, which are entirely hidden, is always satisfactory and often useful.

LEVELS.—Except on land which has a rapid descent, drains should be laid with more accuracy as to the depth than is possible by the aid of the eye alone, and in order to do this, the elevation of the ground at each stake should be measured and recorded. First, drive in a *grade stake* (a peg eight or ten inches long) at the side of each stake, until its top is nearly even with the surface of the ground; then imagine a horizontal plane above the ground, at such height as will be above the highest grade stake of the whole system of drains, and by the aid of a leveling instrument, such as is used by railroad surveyors, ascertain the distance from the imaginary plane, down to the top of each grade stake, and mark it in pencil, near its proper stake on the map. This will give perfect data from which to compute the depth at which the tiles are to be laid, or the *grade* of the drains.

On nearly level land this process is indispensably necessary, while its importance diminishes as the surface inclines more steeply; where the fall is as much as one foot in fifty feet, an ordinary carpenter's level will do sufficiently accurate work, and on steeper slopes the eye is a sufficient guide. Generally, however, the main drains (having less fall) should be very accurately leveled; and the leveling of the whole tract is in all cases satisfactory, and is essential to perfect drainage, while its cost is trifling, as it may be done by the surveyor at the time of mapping the lines.

GRADING.—The proper adjustment of the grades on which the tiles are to be laid, is, by far, the most important question connected with draining. Not only must we make sure that the outlet is lower than the head of the drain; it is necessary that the whole line pursue a well-regulated descent, and equally necessary that *every single tile* be placed at the precise depth required to bring it into line with those above and below it (except when the rate of fall is purposely changed). It has been well said that "*the worst laid tile is the measure of the goodness and permanence of the whole drain,* just as the weakest link of a chain is the measure of its strength."* No tile should be so placed as to offer an impediment to the even flow and velocity of the current which reaches it from the tile above. The fall of a drain should not decrease in velocity as we proceed toward the outlet, lest particles of soil, (technically called *silt,*) which are carried along by the rapid flow, be deposited by the slower current and obstruct the drain. †

Above all, should undulations and irregularities be avoided. Draining is pre-eminently worth doing well, if worth doing at all. The cost of tile, and the labor of digging and refilling the ditches, constitute the chief expense of draining, and it is the most improvident sort of " penny-wisdom" to economize in the item of precision. One ill-laid tile in a main drain may render useless

Fig. 30.

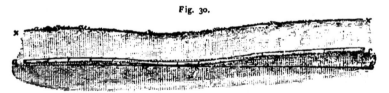

Defective Grade, resulting from Uniform Depth.

five thousand whose outlet lies through it. Drains must not be laid at a *uniform depth* from the surface, but on a straight line of descent at the proper *general depth*. Figure 30 shows a drain in uniform depth, and the line, *a c*, passing through it shows how it deviates from the proper inclination ; at the point *d* the tile would be filled with " dead water," and might soon be obstructed with silt. By aid of the levels taken at the grade stakes, the proper depths to be given at these points may be readily computed and

* Talpa, or the Chronicles of a Clay Farm.

† Under the head of "Silt Basins," will be found directions for managing this change of grade when necessary to be made.

marked on the stakes, and, for the distance at which the rate of fall is unchanged, the line of tiles should be a straight line, lying at the computed distance below those stakes.

The computation may be made as shown below. For illustration we take the first three spaces of the main drain (*A*) on our map (fig. 29).

Note that the *first* column represents the marks on the stakes; the *second* is the measured distance between the stakes; the *third* the total descent of one hundred feet of drain, (eight-tenths of one foot and six-tenths of one foot per one hundred feet;) the *fourth*, the amount of fall, at this rate, from stake to stake; the *sixth*, the recorded grade at each stake. The first figure of the *fifth* represents the recorded grade of the floor of the outlet, (21.71,) and by subtracting from this the fall between *A* and *Aa*, (.34,) we obtain the grade of the drain at the latter stake, (21.37;) subtracting from this the next fall, (.36,) we have the grade at *Ab*, etc.; then, by subtracting the figures in the *sixth* from those in the *fifth*, we have in the *seventh* the depth of cutting at each stake.

FORM OF COMPUTATION FOR DEPTH OF DRAIN BELOW TOPS OF GRADE STAKES.

No. of Stake.	Distance between Stakes.	Fall, (in feet and decimals of a foot.)		Depth below Imaginary Plane.		Depth of Drain.
		Per 100 ft.	Between Stakes.	To the Drain.	To the top of grade stake.	
A.	......	.....	.....	21.71	18 21	3.50
Aa.	42 feet.	0.80	0.34	21.37	18.02	3.35
Ab.	45 feet.	0.80	0 36	21 01	17.14	3.87
Ac.	38 feet.	0.60	0.23	20.78	16.92	3.86

For want of space, in the map on page 101, only such points have been marked with letters and grades as are necessary to illustrate the text.

The least rate of fall which it is prudent to give to a drain, in using ordinary tile, is 2.5 feet in 1,000 feet, or 3 inches in 100 feet, and even this requires very careful work.* A fall of 6 inches in

---

* Some of the drains in the Central Park have a fall of only one inch in one hundred feet, and they work perfectly: but they are large mains, laid with an amount of care and with certain costly precautions, (including very precisely graded wooden floors,) which could hardly be expected in private work.

100 feet is recommended whenever it can be easily obtained—not especially as being more effective, but as requiring less precision and expense.

DIGGING THE DITCHES.—It is not necessary that a ditch for tile-draining should be more than four inches wide at the bottom,—only wide enough to allow the workman to stand with one foot in front of the other,—and if it widens to twenty inches at a height of four feet from the bottom, he will have room enough to work in. Soils which are tolerably retentive

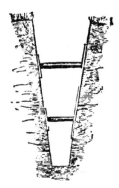

Fig. 31.—Bracing the sides in soft lands.

will stand at this angle during the short time that ditches need remain open. If inclined to cave in, the weaker places may be supported by boards braced against the opposite side. (Fig. 31.)

For four-foot drains, stretch two lines, parallel to each other, twenty inches apart, leaving the stakes at a distance of two or three inches from one side of the inclosed space. Then, with an ordinary spade, cut the lines neatly, remove the surface soil, and throw it on the staked side of the line. Dig the ditch to a depth of three feet, throwing the lower soil on the bank opposite to that on which the surface soil has been placed. Now, take a narrow ditching spade, Fig. 32, four inches wide at the point, and dig down opposite the stakes to the depth marked thereon. The depth may be measured by an instrument similar to that represented in Fig. 33. Having reached this point, set up at each of two or more of the stakes a "boning-rod," seven feet long, Fig. 34, fastening it in place by laying two bits of board across the drain, holding the boning-rod between them, and held in place by stones or earth laid on their ends.

Fig. 32.

Fig. 33.—Measuring Staff.

The line of sight taken across the tops of two of these boning-rods will be exactly seven feet above the line of the bottom of the drain, and a "plumb-rod" (which is a boning-rod with a line and plummet by which to place it perpendicularly) will have its cross-head exactly in a line with those of the boning-rods, when its foot stands on the true line of the bottom of the drain. The ditch may be dug with the narrow spade to within about two inches of the desired depth, and it may then be trimmed to the exact line (with the aid of the plumb-rod) by a finishing scoop, Fig. 35. The position of the laborer in the narrow ditch, and the mode of using the scoop, are shown in Fig. 36.

As the laying of the tile should be commenced at the extreme upper ends of all drains, so that no dirt may be washed into them; and, as the finishing of the bottom should immediately precede the laying of the tile, lest its bottom be made uneven by water flowing over it, the ditches should be first roughly finished to the outlet, (at a little less than the final depth,) for the removal of the water during the work, and the boning-rods should first be set at the upper ends. When the rate of fall does not

Fig. 35.—Finish- Fig. 34.—Boning scoop.   ing Rod.

change, the boning-rods may be set at intervals of from 80 to 120 feet, as the sighting may be accurately done at this distance. Of course, a rod must be set at each point at which the fall changes. The manner of sighting over the boning-rods, and the intermediate plumb-rod, is shown in Fig. 37.

If, by mistake, the bottom is dug out too deeply, the earth with which it is filled up to the proper grade must be beaten solid.

TILES—KINDS AND SIZES.—There are various forms of tiles in use in this country—known as "round," "sole," "horseshoe," etc., but it is not proposed, here, to discuss their comparative merits. Experience, in both public and private works, in

Fig. 36.—Position of Workman and Use of Finishing Scoop.

this country, and the cumulative testimony of English and French engineers, have demonstrated that the only tile which it is economical to use, are the *best* that can be found; and that the

Fig 37.—Sighting by the Boning Rods.

[*A* and *C* are the boning-rods. *B* is the plumb-rod. *A*, *B*, *C*, is the line of sight (7 feet above the grade). *Y*, *V*, is the line of the bottom of the drain, which will be correct when the plumb-rod, standing upon any point of it, has the top of its cross-head in the line of sight, *A*, *B*, *C*.]

best, thus far invented—much the best, is the "pipe and collar," (Fig. 38,)—or round tiles; and these are unhesitatingly recommended for use in all cases. Round tiles of small sizes should not be laid without collars, as the ability to use these with them constitutes their chief advantage. They hold them perfectly in place, prevent the rattling in of loose dirt in laying, and give twice the space for the entrance of water at the joints. A chief advantage of the larger sizes is, that they may be laid on any side and thus made to fit closely, while the shrinking of the top of the sole tiles (from more rapid drying in manufacture) makes it ne-

cessary to trim the ends, to make even a tolerable joint. The
usual sizes of these tiles are 1¼ inch, 2¼ inches, and 3½ inches
in interior diameter. Sections of the 2¼ inch make collars for the
1¼ inch, and sections of the 3½ inch make collars for the 2¼ inch.
The 3½-inch size does not need collars, as it is easily secured in
place, and is only used where the flow of water would be sufficient
to wash out any slight amount of foreign matters that might enter
at the joints. When collars cannot be conveniently procured, an
excellent substitute for them may be cheaply obtained from any
tinsmith, in the form of strips of refuse zinc, galvanized iron,

Fig. 38.—Pipe Tile and Collar, and the same as laid.

or tinplate from 1½ to 2 inches wide. I have had such made by
a tinsmith in Newport, for a cost of 8c. per lb.—averaging perhaps, $3 per thousand. They are easily formed to the shape of
the tile by being bent over a round stick. If used with "sole"
tiles (those having a flat side to stand on) they need be only long
enough to form a saddle over the top.

The sizes of tiles to be used is a question of consequence. In
England, 1-inch pieces are frequently used, but 1¼-inch tiles* are
recommended for the smallest drains. Beyond this limit, the proper size to select is, *the smallest that can convey the water which
will ordinarily reach it after a heavy rain.* The smaller the pipe,
the more concentrated the flow, and, consequently, the more
thoroughly obstructions will be removed, and the occasional
flushing of the pipe, when it is taxed for a few hours to its
utmost capacity, will insure a thorough cleansing. No inconvenience can result from the fact that, on rare occasions, the drain is
unable, for a short time, to discharge all the water that reaches it;

* Taking the difference of friction into consideration, 1¼-inch pipes have fully twice
the discharging capacity of 1-inch pipes.

and if collars are used, there need be no fear of the tile being displaced by the pressure. An idea of the drying capacity of a $1\frac{1}{4}$-inch tile may be gained from observing its *wetting* capacity, by connecting a pipe of this size with a sufficient body of water, at its surface and discharging, over a level dry field, all the water that it will carry. A $1\frac{1}{4}$-inch pipe will remove all the water that would fall on an acre of land in a very heavy rain, in 24 hours—much less time than the water would occupy in getting to the drain in any soil which required draining; and tiles of this size are ample for the draining of 2 acres. In like manner, $2\frac{1}{4}$-inch tile will suffice for 8 acres, and $3\frac{1}{2}$-inch tile for 20 acres. The foregoing estimates are, of course, made on the supposition that only the water which falls on the land, (storm water,) is to be removed. For main drains, when greater capacity is required, two tiles may be laid, (side by side,) or, in such cases, the larger sizes of sole tile may be used, being somewhat cheaper. Where the drains are laid 40 feet apart, about 1,000 tiles per acre will be required, and, in estimating the quantity of tile of the different sizes to be purchased, reference should be had to the foregoing figures : the first 2,000 feet of drain or less requires a collecting drain of $1\frac{1}{4}$-inch tile ; the water from more than 2,000 and less than 7,000 feet may discharge into $2\frac{1}{4}$-inch tile ; and for the outlet of from 7,000 to 20,000 feet, $3\frac{1}{2}$-inch tile may be used. Collars, being more subject to breakage, should be ordered in somewhat larger quantities.

LAYING TILE.—There is a tool made for laying pipes and collars, but it is recommended that they be carefully laid by hand, a process which, though somewhat difficult in narrow ditches, is not impossible, and is much more satisfactory. The tiles, each having a collar passed over the end, should be placed along the side of the ditch, within easy reach of a man standing in the bottom. He commences at the upper end of the ditch, and walks backward as the work proceeds. The first tile is laid

Fig. 39.

Pick for dressing and perforating tile.

with the collar on its lower end, and with a flat stone or bit of broken tile fitted closely against the upper end. The collar is then slipped along until only one-half of its length is under the tile. The next tile has its nose inserted in the unoccupied half of the collar, and one-half of its other collar is drawn forward to receive the next tile—and thus to the lower end of the drain. The trimming of the ends of the tile, and the perforations in the tiles of main drains to admit the laterals, are made with a pick (Fig. 39). To make a hole in the tile, use the pointed end of the pick, chipping around the circumference of the hole until the center-place falls in. Collecting drains should be laid a little deeper than the mouths of the laterals which discharge into them,

Fig. 40.—Lateral Drain entering at Top.

(allowance for this having been made in the original grading,) that these may be admitted at the top of the main. When the lateral and the main are of equal size, the best way to make the connection is to substitute a long pipe in place of the collar, making a hole at the top of this, to admit the lateral, as shown in Figs. 40 and 41.

SILT BASINS.—In new drains there is always some earthy matter (silt) in the water which flows through the pipe,—the looser earth about the joints is carried in, in small quantities, during the early action of the drain. If the fall of the drain is irregular this silt may be carried in suspension in the water, where

Fig. 41.—Sectional View of Joint.

the current is rapid, and deposited in the depressions, or more level parts, where the flow is sluggish, and cause the obstruction of the drain, which is thereby rendered worthless. In ordinary soils, the amount of silt entering at the joints of the drain, will, if the fall be regular, cause no inconvenience, being either all carried out at the mouth of the drain, or deposited throughout its whole length to a depth so slight as to be of little or no consequence. If, on the other hand, it becomes necessary to diminish the fall

in proceeding .oward the outlet, there is danger that the silt,
which was carried by the more rapid stream above, will be
deposited by the slower current and cause a stoppage of the drain.   In the drainage of the Central
Park, this danger was guarded against by the use
of *silt-basins* at all points at which the fall of a
drain (which had not a very steep descent, say
two or three feet in one hundred feet) became
less rapid.   The silt-basin is a vessel (larger
than the tile with which the drain is laid) extending some distance below the grade of the drain.
It has the effect of arresting the movement of the

Fig. 42.

Silt-basin made of six-
inch tile.

water, thus allowing its silt to settle to the bottom, and has sufficient depth to accumulate that which will probably enter it

before the drain commences to
run clear water. For a lateral
drain of small caliber, a very good
silt basin is made by placing a
single six-inch tile on end, sink-
ing it two-thirds of its length
below the floor of the ditch, and
admitting the tiles from above
and below at opposite sides. It
should be covered with a well-
fitting, flat stone, and should
stand on a stone or a board—not
on the earth, (Fig. 42.) For
drains of somewhat larger size
a small chamber of brick-work
may be used, (Fig. 43,) and for
the collection of the mains of
several systems, it is satisfactory
to build a well two feet in
diameter, having a depth of two
feet below the bottom of the out-

Fig. 43.—Square brick silt-basin.

let drain, and reaching the surface, with a good cover which may be kept locked, (Fig. 44.) When large sizes of vitrified earthenware pipes (ten or twelve inches in diameter) can be obtained, they make a very good and cheap silt-basin, answering very well for the collection of several small drains. One of these is shown in Figure 45.

The most perfect deposit of the silt will be secured in those basins which admit and discharge the water on the same level; but a difference of two inches—sufficient to allow the action of the in-coming drains to be seen—is so satisfactory to the eye of a proprietor, that it may well be tolerated in basins which are built to the surface, although the fall tends to keep the water in the basin agitated to its bottom, and somewhat interferes with the deposit of silt. Basins, which can be opened at the surface, should have their outlets protected by coarse wire-cloth or upright grating, to prevent the entrance of rubbish, which may, by accident, reach them.

Fig. 44.—Silt-basin, built to the surface.

The position and size of all underground silt-basins should be carefully noted on the map. In the event of the stoppage of any drain, (which will be indicated by the wetness of the ground), dig down to the first silt-basin below the break, and the cause will generally be found to be the accumulation of silt beyond the capacity of the basin, and, by taking up a few tiles each way from it, until they appear free from deposit, the difficulty may be remedied in far less time than would have been necessary if the silt had been allowed to deposit itself through a long stretch of the drain. If the soil is very "silty," (containing layers of running quicksand,) the ditch immediately over the silt-basin should be left open for a short time after the drain is laid, so that, by simply removing the stone cover, the deposit of silt may be watched and removed, until it ceases to accumulate, when the ditch may be permanently filled in.

FILLING IN THE DITCHES.—As fast as the tiles are laid, they should be securely covered, in order that they may not be broken by stones falling in from the banks; and that their position may not be disturbed by the water running in the ditch.

The best covering to place immediately over the tile, is *the heaviest and stiffest clay* from the ditch, because this compacts more readily than any other material, and allows

Fig. 45.—Silt-basin of vitrified pipe.

less of its finer particles to enter the tile. It is a mistake to suppose that there is the least necessity for placing a porous material next to the tile. Especially should sods, or other covering which contain organic matter, be avoided, as affording a less firm packing around the tile, and, on the decay of the organic parts, furnishing loose particles to enter the joints. Throw in fine clay,—dropping it gently about and over the tiles, until they are well covered, and then fill in to a depth of eighteen inches with clay. This filling should now be trampled down with the feet, and then rammed with a wooden maul (Fig. 46) until quite firm. By this process, the tile will be securely clasped by the clay, and the least possible amount of silt will enter the drain. As to the entrance of the water, the young drainer need give himself no trouble. To use the language of an English farmer, "experience will prove that you can't keep it out, and it is astonishing how soon the water will *learn how* to get in, even if strong clay is rammed tight over

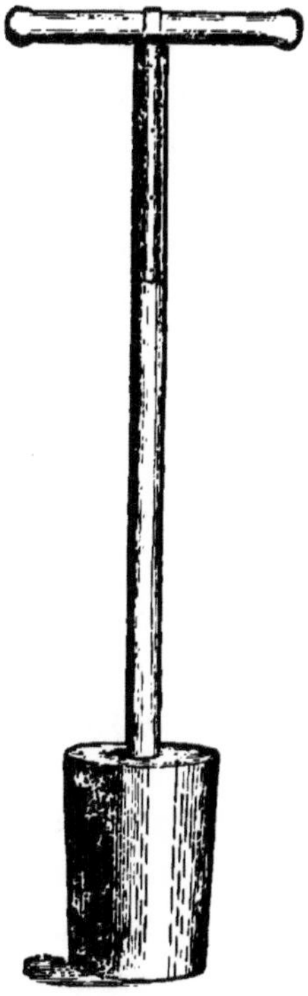

Fig. 46.—Maul for ramming.

8

the pipes." After the ramming is completed, the rest of the ditch may be filled, and it is recommended that the surface soil, which was thrown to one side, be mixed with the subsoil throughout the entire depth.

Full and complete directions for the laying out and making of tile drains, such as would suffice for any farmer contemplating the improvement may be found in books on the subject, whose cost is trifling as compared with the cost of the work, and no one should undertake it without first learning all that is to be learned from books on the subject.

Underdraining should be commenced in the winter time, and very early in the winter. When the ground is locked fast with frost, and when it is impossible to do any out of door work, the farmer has leisure for such a careful study and consideration of the question as is necessary to any successful draining operation; not that the ditches may not be as well dug, and the tiles as well laid without the least previous consideration, but because the work is very expensive, and any slight mistake made in the arrangement of the drains, may result in its being done incompletely, or in its being too costly.

I have, during the past year, drained the whole of Ogden Farm, and, of course, have endeavored to do the work as thoroughly and as cheaply as was possible. The land drained (that which constitutes the farm proper is sixty acres) lies over the crown of a hill, and all but five or six acres of it has sufficient slope for easy drainage, without their being a very great fall in any part of it. The difference of elevation between the highest and the lowest point is about fifty feet; and these points lie about a half a mile distant from each other. While the slope of the land appears to the eye to be absolutely uniform, the taking of accurate levels demonstrated that there were considerable inequalities, and that drains, laid according to the very best judgment, founded on the apparent slope, would not have stood in proper relation to the true slope.

The course pursued was the following: The whole farm was staked off into squares of one hundred and sixty feet each, and levels were taken at all of the points of intersection, showing the elevation of those points above an imaginary plain underlying the whole farm. This was all shown upon the map, and upon the same map contour lines,—or lines of equal elevation,—at differences of level of one foot, were laid on in a different color from the lines marking the squares. In the accompanying map the black lines show the lines defining the squares, and the figures at their intersections show the elevation of the land at that point above the imaginary-level plain. The red lines show the lines of equal elevation along the surface of the land ; of course the line of steepest descent of the land is in all cases at right-angles to these. The blue lines show the location of the drains.

Before a stroke of work was done upon the land, the levels were taken at the intersections of the black lines, and these and the contour lines were drawn upon the map ; and in every instance, in advance of the staking out of the drains upon the ground their location was drawn upon the map and was staked on the ground directly from the map. This insured the locating of each drain in what, not guessing, but actual measurement, showed to be the right place ; and enabled an estimate to be made in advance of the quantity and sizes of tiles required, and of the amount and cost of the work to be done.

By reference to the map it will be seen that the following rules have been adhered to, so far as circumstances would admit :—

First.—Always to run the lateral drains parallel to each other, and down the deepest descent of the land ; in some cases they are not parallel, and in others they run in a direction slightly different from the steepest inclination—the object being always to harmonize those two conflicting requirements so as to produce the best average result.

Second.—To lay no drain on such a course that water running through it would flow more rapidly in the upper than in the lower part of the drain ; it has been necessary in this matter also to deviate somewhat from the rule. This has never been done, however, except where the reduced rate of fall was sufficient to insure so rapid a flow as to carry off any silty matters which might have been carried by the more rapid stream above. For instance, in the extreme southwest corner of the farm it will be seen that the long drains of the main system were not carried directly down to the main drain near its outlet, although such a course would have allowed the size of the tile a little ways back from the outlet to be somewhat reduced. The reason for this was, that the land near the extreme corner is so nearly level that there would have been danger (in carrying the drains at a uniform, depth directly through it) that silt, accumulated in their upper ends, would have been deposited by the sluggish flow near the main, and have caused the obstruction of the tiles. To avoid this, the collecting drain, starting from near the south fence, and running in a northwesterly direction, was made to cut off the longer laterals at the foot of the steepest inclination—the land lying between this collecting drain and the main outlet being furnished with drains of its own, laid upon a uniform though slight fall.

Third.—To make the drains four feet deep and forty feet apart ; this rule has been adhered to as rigidly as possible, though of course, owing to slight inequalities in the surface, it was at times necessary to make the depth a little more or a little less than four feet for a short distance, and it was also necessary, occasionally, as in the field north of the barn, to deviate a little from the parallel line, bringing the drains less than forty feet apart at their lower ends, and making them a little more than forty feet apart at their upper ends. In a few instances drains have been run up between two converging lines so far that they divided a space of less than eighty feet. In such cases these intervening drains were made somewhat less than four feet deep at their upper ends, and the cost of digging was thereby reduced.

The work of draining was commenced in the autumn of 1867, in the extreme northwest corner of the farm. Owing to the early setting in of severe weather, it was possible only to dig the main outlet ditch which runs along the west line, and to complete the northernmost six laterals. As soon as the ground was settled in the spring of 1868, the work was recommenced with vigor, and the severe weather of the month of December found the work entirely finished, with the exception of a few laterals, and the main drain south of the house. These would also have been completed but for a mistake in sending tiles, which made it necessary to delay the work until the ground became frozen, and to hazard the danger that the caving in of the main drain in spring would so choke the laterals which were laid, that they would have to be taken up and remade.

Except for this slight accident the work would have been entirely completed within the time and the cost originally estimated.

As to the effect of the work as shown in the production of better crops, it is hardly possible yet to speak with much certainty. The spring of 1868 was very wet, and it was impossible to get a single field drained in time for it to be planted in season for the best growth. Even if this could have been done, it is not likely that, so soon after the construction of the drains, their action would have been sufficient to produce a very marked effect on the soil. Therefore, the most that can be said at this time is with reference to the condition of the land in the matter of readiness for cultivation, and this can be best illustrated by a reference to the land lying north of the dwelling-house. This land, as will be seen by the contour lines on the map is very much the most level tract on the whole farm. Its subsoil, like the subsoil of the entire farm in fact, is a very compact blue clay, intermixed with gravel and streaks of black oxide of manganese, the whole forming a material of so nearly impermeable a character that, with all my confidence in draining, I fully expected that it would be several years before any very marked result was produced. Hitherto this farm, though beautifully situated on the top of the highest hill in this vicinity, has been so constantly wet, except in seasons of extreme drought, as to have baffled every effort to make it tolerably fertile, and to disappoint, if not to impoverish, every owner and every tenant who has ever had any thing to do with it. It has long been known in the vicinity as "Poverty Farm," and I do not believe that the average estimate

fixed upon it by the best farmers in the township, simply as
agricultural land, would have given it even one-fourth of the
value of an ordinarily good farm. In fact, one of the chief reasons for its purchase was the belief that, while it could be bought
for a low price, thorough underdraining must, in time, make it an
excellent farm ; for its surface soil seems capital, and its subsoil
is such as, after draining and deep cultivation, must become one
of the best.

That this opinion was a correct one is partly demonstrated
already by the experience with the field to which allusion was
made above,—that north of the house. The draining of this land
was commenced about the middle of September, and up to that
time (there having been no decided drought during the season) there
was hardly a day when the water did not stand on its surface, and
at no time, after a heavy rain, could it be comfortably driven over
for two or three weeks. The draining was completed on this
piece by the middle of November. On the 26th it commenced
raining at about 10 A M., and at that time the outlet drain, which
passes under the road east of the farm, was carrying about one-
half inch depth of water in a four-inch pipe. It rained very hard
until 5 P.M. when it cleared off. At sunset this main was running entirely full. At noon on the 27th—the next day—plowing
was commenced on the wettest part of this land, and the ground
was amply dry enough for the operation. At night-fall the tile of
the main was running only about one-quarter full. This shows
that an amount of water which would have prevented our going
upon this land in its undrained state before the next June at the
earliest, found its way *immediately*, even through the compact subsoil, to tile drains lying four feet below the surface, and was
carried away as rapidly as could possibly be desired. The same
rapid removal of water is obtained over the whole farm, and the
hope is yet cherished that its old title of " Poverty Farm" need
never be applied to it again.

The cost of the work of draining 60 acres in the very best
manner has been, I regret to say, a trifle more than $6,000—just
about enough more to pay for two or three accidental interrup-

tions to the work—leaving the actual cost. accidents aside, $100 per acre.

Of course the question is asked, and asked generally, I think, with a good deal of doubt as to the answer, whether this expensive work can possibly pay—whether we shall ever be able to get back a hundred dollars per acre as a result of the beneficial influence of the draining. Suppose we do not. We purchased the farm to have the farm, and not to get back its cost; and we did the draining, not in order that we might pocket the cost of the draining, but in order that the cost might be profitably invested. If the money had not been used in this way it would probably have brought a return of 6 per cent. on a safe investment. It is now invested in the safest possible manner and if the result of this thorough draining of land, otherwise good, does not amount to at least $6 per acre, it will be remarkable. My own impression is that in favorable seasons such acres as are well cultivated will bring a return (ascribable entirely to the draining) of at least $30 each. And in addition to all this there is the satisfaction of knowing that when plowing day comes plowing can be done, and that it will not be, as it hitherto has been, postponed for a month on account of a single heavy rain. Probably the ability to systematize the labor of the farm and carry on its various operations without interruption will, of itself, be worth $6 an acre every year.

I have gone thus particularly into a description of a purely personal operation with the belief that there is no sort of argument which is so effective with readers generally, and especially with agricultural readers, as one that is based on actual experiment; and, in connection with the map, any farmer will be able, from the description given, to form a better idea of how the work of draining may be done, and of its extent and cost, than by any description of a purely hypothetical case.

When the Ogden Farm drainage was commenced the best process for doing the work and the best means were those described in the first edition of my work on draining,* and the system

* "Draining for Profit and Draining for Health." New York, O. Judd & Co. 1867.

of drains on the northwest field of the farm and that lying west
and south of the barnyard was made according to the directions
therein laid down.   By the time this was completed the very important inventions of Mr. C. W. Boynton, in connection with
the manufacture of draining tiles, enabled me to adopt a much
simpler and more satisfactory method, which, in its application to
the rest of the farm, has proven itself to be in many respects a
great improvement.   And I would gladly pay one-half of the cost

Fig. 47.   Fig. 48.

of the original work to have it, also, done in the same manner.
Mr. Boynton's improvement consists, first, in the making of tiles
of the best quality of fire-clay, two feet long ; and second, in the
use of "junction pieces," which are short tiles of the size of the
main, having a branch at the side to which the lateral may be
attached.

The character of these junctions, and the manner in which
they may be used, will be readily understood by reference to the
following description :—

Formerly the best way to admit a lateral drain into a main was
by breaking a hole (with a light sharp-pointed pick) into the side
of one of the tiles of the main, trimming off the end of the lateral
so as to make it fit as closely as practicable.   It was impossible

Fig. 49.

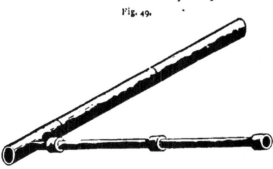

in this way to make
a joint that would
not more or less ob-
struct the flow of the
stream.

Boynton's junc-
tion, however, (Fig.
49,) consisting of a
short tile of the size

of the main, with a piece of the size of the lateral, attached to it
before burning, so smoothly moulded that the stream is in no way

interrupted, and set on at an acute angle, so that the force of the stream flowing from the lateral drain adds to the velocity of the current in the main, entirely obviates this difficulty, which was one of the greatest connected with the old style of work, and makes the drainage of land even less uncertain than before.

Among the minor improvements made by Mr. Boynton, the Bend, (Fig. 50, quarter bend, and Fig. 51, one-eighth bend,) for turning corners in drains, allows the stream to change its course gradually and

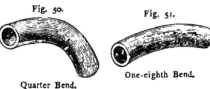

Fig. 50.

Quarter Bend.

Fig. 51.

One-eighth Bend.

smoothly, and with much less retarding effect, than with the angular turn which alone was possible in using straight tiles with beveled ends; the reducing tile, Fig. 52, enables us to change from one size to another in a straight drain without making an abrupt edge in the bore of the drain; and the glazed outlet, Fig. 53, with a grating to exclude vermin, makes an excellent and durable finish at the only point at which they first attack the work.

Fig. 52.

Reducing Tile.

Fig. 53.

Grated Outlets Glazed.

LAND DRAINAGE—DETAILS OF THE WORK.

It is never pleasant to confess errors; but I am convinced, by what I have recently seen, that, in previous writing about drainage, I have been mistaken on one point. That is, in insisting, as a universal rule, that the whole line should be opened from the upper end of the lateral to the lower end of the main, and that the main should be kept open until the tile-laying and covering should be finished in all its laterals. This is frequently, but not always, true,—perhaps it is not even generally so.

I have probably directed the laying of over a hundred miles of tile drains, and I have always tried to approach as nearly as possible to the English practice, as I had seen it described. I have bought sets of English draining-tools, and have read in English agricultural books and papers about the way in which

the work is done. I have seen pictures and diagrams showing every step of the operation, and have had letters from
England (in reply to my questions) telling me precisely what they
do there. I have tried for fifteen years—with scores of Irish
ditchers—to imitate them, and have finally concluded that the
statements made were not true, and that the pictures drawn were
drawn from the imagination. I could in no way get my ditches
dug without having the men tramping on the bottom, and making
more or less mud according to the amount of water,—and this
mud, running toward the main, carried a sure source of obstruction with it. Hence, I have always recommended that the whole
line be opened from one end to the other, before a tile is laid, and
that the tile-laying be commenced at the upper ends of the laterals
and continued *down stream*, so that no muddy water would run
into them, as would be the case if the tiles were laid from the
lower end upward.

I am still convinced that in very wet, soft land, or where the
grade is so slight that great care is necessary to preserve the
uniformity of the fall, this precaution is necessary. But wherever
there is a fall of as much as one foot in a hundred feet, if the
bottom is ordinarily firm, *the best plan will be to reverse the direction*,
and to commence laying at the *lower* end of the drain—putting in
the tile, and covering it up, as fast as the digging progresses.

I am led to this change of opinion by seeing the thing done by
drainers of English education. What I could not understand from
description, nor attain by experiment, is made clear by observation.
*In the digging of ordinary drains the foot of the workman never reaches
to within less than a foot of the bottom of the ditch;* consequently,
there is no trampling of the floor of the drain, and no formation
of mud. What water may ooze out from the land (and, as but
little of the ditch is open at once, the amount is very small) has no
silt in it, and cannot obstruct the tile through which it runs.

I will try to describe the process so that all may understand it.
We will suppose the main drain to be laid and filled in, junction
pieces being placed where the laterals are to come in, and that we
are about to dig and lay a lateral emptying into it.

1 A line is stretched to mark one side of the ditch, and the sod is removed to a spade's depth (15 inches wide) for a length of about two rods, and a ditch is dug about 18 inches deep, with a narrow bottom. 2. A ditching spade, (Fig. 54, *a*,) 20 inches long in the blade, 6 inches wide at the top, and 4 inches wide at the point, —made of steel and kept sharp,—is forced into its whole length, and the earth thrown out. Of course it will be necessary in very hard ground to do some picking, but it is surprising to see

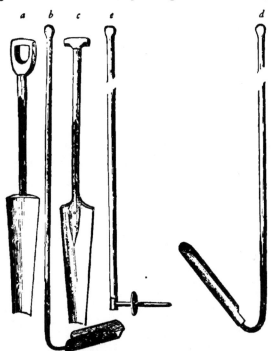

Fig. 54—Tile-draining Implements.

with what ease a man with an iron shank screwed to the sole of his boot will work the sharp point of this spade into an obdurate hard-pan. The loose earth that escaped the spade is removed by a scoop (Fig. 54, *b*) 4 inches wide, which the workman, walking backward, draws toward him until it is full, swinging it out to dump its load on the bank. In this way he gets down 3 feet, and leaves a smooth floor on which he stands. 3. Commencing again at the end next to the main, with a narrower, stronger, and even sharper spade, of the same length or a little less, (Fig. 54, c,) 4½ inches wide at the top and 3 inches at the point, he digs out as nearly as he can, another foot of earth—he facing the main and working back, so that he stands always on the smooth bottom, 3 feet below the surface. When he has dug for a length of 2 or 3 feet, he takes a snipe-bill scoop, (Fig. 54, d,) only 3 inches wide, and using it as he did the broader scoop, removes the loose earth. The round back of this scoop, which is always working a foot below the level on which the operator stands and which performs the offices of a *shovel*, smooths and forms the bottom of the trench, making a much better bed for the tiles than it is possible to get if it has to be walked on, and regulates the grade most perfectly.

4. When the short length of ditch has been nearly all dug out and graded, the branch on the junction piece of the tile is uncovered, and the tile is laid by the use of a "tile-layer," (Fig. 54, e,) operated by a man standing astride the ditch on the banks. The collar is placed on the end of the branch on the upper end of the tile. The implement lowers the tile, (with its collar in place,) and the other end is carefully inserted in the collar on the branch. Then the end of the second tile is inserted into the second collar, and so on until nearly all of the graded ditch is laid.

Fig. 55.—Opening the Ditch and Laying the Tiles.

5. The most clayey part of the subsoil is thrown carefully down on the tile and tramped into its place,—all but the collar end of the last tile being covered,—and the ditch filled at least half-full and pounded.

6. Another rod or two of the ditch is opened, dug out, laid,

and filled in as above described,—the amount opened at any one time not being enough to allow the accumulation of a dangerous quantity of water. If there is any considerable amount of water in the land, or if it is feared that it may rain during the night, the tile is left with a plug of grass or straw, which will prevent the entrance of dirt.

Fig. 55 gives a section of a ditch with the work in its different stages. The tile is shown in section.

And now for the result :—

Last year, after the draining of Ogden Farm was completed, I undertook the drainage of a neighbor's land, employing the same gang of experienced Irish ditchers. The best bargain I could make was for *one dollar per rod* for digging and back-filling (tile laying not included). The *best* men earned $3.50 per day,—the average not more than $2.25. Owing to the lateness of the season, the work was suspended until this year's harvest should be completed.

This year I hired a gang of tile-drainers from Canada, who had English experience. They work precisely as above described. The price paid is 75 cents per rod for digging, back-filling, *and tile-laying* (for the whole work complete, although owing to the *hard-pan*, much picking is required). The best man among them completes seven rods per day, ($5.25,) and the average is fully five rods ($3.75). The amount of earth handled (owing to the narrowness of the ditches) is less than one-half of what it was last year, and the work is done with a neatness and completeness that I have never seen equaled.

What these men are doing others can do as well, and I am satisfied that in simple, heavy clays the whole work of digging and tile-laying can be done for less than 50 cents per rod.

While tiles are much the best, and generally the cheapest material that can be used for making underdrains, there are many parts of the country in which they cannot be obtained, and in all cases they require a direct outlay of money—a process against which many farmers have an aversion. For these reasons, (and sometimes because it is absolutely necessary to get rid of stones which are not needed in making fences,) it is often desirable to make drains with other materials.

STONE DRAINS.

Stone drains, when well built, may last a very long time, but they are not so reliable as tile drains, for the reason that they cannot be so made as to keep the water flowing through them in a smooth current, nor so as to entirely prevent it from flowing over the earth, which it may wash up and deposit where it will obstruct the channel. They are, also, more liable to be reached by water from the surface, running down through fissures in the soil—such water being the best possible destroyer of any drain, stone or tile, on account of the earth it carries with it.

Contrary to the general idea, stone drains are usually much more costly than tile drains; they require a much wider trench to be dug, and refilled, and it frequently costs more than the price of the tiles to lay the stones properly, after they have been deposited at the side of the trench.

Every farmer in a stony region knows how to lay a stone drain, with an "eye," "throat," or "trunk," as the channel for the water is called, but there are two important principles connected with such drains, which are usually not known, or are disregarded.

1. A stone drain should never form a part of a system of which the other part is laid with tiles; because if the stone drain empties into the tile drain it will be very likely to deliver to it so much sand or gravel "silt" as to obstruct it, while if a stone drain is used as an outlet for tile drains, it will greatly lessen their permanent value by its own liability to become closed.

2. No porous material—neither small stones, straw, sods, brush, nor shavings—should be placed on the *top* of the stones forming the channel. It is not from above that any drain should receive its water. The water that is drained away from a saturated soil *always rises into the drain from below.* The amount flowing in from the sides is hardly worth notice, and any that might come

directly down from the surface would be very likely to bring with it matters which would choke the channel—that which rises into the bottom of the drain is as clear as spring water, (is spring water in one sense,) and can only obstruct the drain by washing into heaps the earth that it flows over in its course through the drain.

It is very well to cover the stone-work with the smallest quantity of shavings or leaves that will prevent the earth with which the trench is filled from rattling into the " eye," but this should be immediately covered with the stiffest subsoil at hand, which should be trampled or rammed down so solidly that no streams of water and no vermin can work their way through it. Sods make a very good covering when they are first laid, but they soon decay, and afford the best possible material for obstructing the drain. If small stones are to be used at all they should not be placed over the drain, where they can only do harm ; but below it, where they protect the earth against the action of the stream, and allow the water of saturation to rise freely into the drain.

The different methods of laying stones so as to form a channel are too well understood to need illustration, and the selection of one or another must depend very much upon the character of the stone to be had for the purpose. In every case, they should be so laid that they can neither be undermined by the stream, and made to "cave in," nor be forced out of their places by the weight of the filling above them.

If the chief object is to get rid of a large amount of stone, this may be best accomplished by digging very wide trenches, wide enough to use a plow for loosening the ground to the whole depth, and dumping the stones in from a cart, merely leveling them off within one and a half or two feet of the surface, and packing the heaviest soil over them. In a very large drain of this sort, the water will always find a passage, unless it is so carelessly laid that surface streams flow in.

A very good way to get rid of useless stone walls is to dig a trench at one side of them and throw them in—finishing off the top as above directed.

PLANK, BRUSH, AND POLE DRAINS.

When 2-inch planks or slabs can be cheaply procured, a good drain may be made by cutting the bottom of the ditch so as to leave a shoulder at least three inches on each side as shown in Fig. 56, and lay across—resting on the shoulders—pieces of

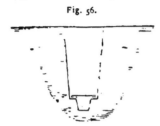
Fig. 56.

plank or slab sawed to the proper length, to reach from one side of the ditch to the other, and fitted as closely as possible at their edges. For the smaller drains— not more than six inches across, between the shoulder, common hemlock boards, one inch thick will suffice, and will last for a long time. In all cases the wood should be thoroughly soaked before laying, so that it will not be necessary to leave joints to allow for swelling. In a clay subsoil, such a drain would last long enough to be economical. In quicksand it would be good for nothing. The grain of the wood must run *across* the ditch.

If a ditch is filled with brush (especially cedar) to its top, commencing at the upper end, and laying the butts toward the mouth of the drain, and the brush then pressed down as closely as possible, and covered with well-compacted earth, it will make a very good " make-shift " drain—so much better than none at all, as to commend itself highly to those who cannot afford to make stone or tile drains.

Small poles laid evenly in the ditch, with just enough fine covering to keep out the loose dirt of the filling will often prove very good.

When either the poles or the brush decay, the earth itself will often preserve the channel for a long time.

CHAPTER VI.

PLOWING, SUBSOILING, AND TRENCHING.

" In ancient times, the sacred plow employed
  The kings and awful fathers of mankind ;
  And some, with whom compared your insect tribes
  Are but the beings of the summer's day,
  Have held the scale of empires, ruled the storm
  Of mighty war, and then with unwearied hand,
  Disdaining little delicacies, seized
  The plow, and greatly independent lived."

                                        THOMSON.

A FEW years ago a " Young Farmer " in England wrote to the
" London Gardeners' Chronicle and Agricultural Gazette," asking
information concerning the " Art of Plowing." The following
was the reply of that very able paper :—

" The niceties of this subject are no longer of the importance
" they once possessed. Well-drained land should be ' smashed
" up'—that is the proper way to treat it. If you want to know
" all the mysteries of the subject, as it used to be practically
" carried out, consult ' Steven's Book of the Farm.' The whole
" vocabulary of this once tedious subject has become obsolete:
" in place of *gathering up, crown and furrow plowing, casting* or
" *yoking,* or *coupling ridges,* casting ridges *with gore furrows,*
" *cleaving down ridges,* with or without gore furrows, plowing
" *two in two out, plowing in breaks,* etc., all that the land now
" needs, in order to efficient cultivation, is, according to Mr.
" Smith, of Woolston, a ' smashing up ;' and it is to land drainage
" as permitting a deeper rough tillage before winter, and to steam
" plows and steam cultivators as enabling it, that the most striking
" lesson of recent experience in land cultivation is due."

9

Plowing has the following objects :—

1. To destroy existing vegetation.

2. To loosen the soil and prepare the seed bed.

3. To allow the lower parts of the surface soil to be prepared for the better use of plants by the action of atmospheric influences.   .

4. To deepen the surface soil.

5. To cover manures, green crops, or dung.

6. By a combination of the foregoing efforts, to admit air and water more freely among the roots of plants.

The first and the fifth of these objects are best attained by such regular turning of the furrows as shall completely invert the soil, or at least as shall turn it over so far that the harrow will leave only the lower soil on the smoothed surface.

The others do not require such nicety of work, and, indeed, they are better accomplished by such treatment, as will more thoroughly break up the furrow.

In plowing grass land, I think that a carefully turned flat furrow, —that is, the laying of the grass side of the furrow-slice flat upon the bottom of the plow track, or turning it completely over like a board,—is conducive to the most rapid rotting of the sod, while it renders it less liable to be torn up by the harrow, which at the same time acts more uniformly on the freshly turned earth.   In turning in green crops, the flat furrow has the same advantage. In plowing in farm-yard manure, however, it is quite as advantageous,—perhaps more so,—to mix it more thoroughly throughout the whole depth of the plowed soil by adopting the lap-furrow.

The chief objections to the flat-furrow system seem to be that, with a given amount of power, the plowing cannot be so deep ; that the sod is less broken up ; and that less air is admitted among the particles of the soil.   These objections are enough to condemn the practice, except for the accomplishment of the two purposes referred to above.   For all but these it is better to plow with lap-furrows, and better still to so crush the furrow in plowing, that it is not turned over in any definite shape ;—simply pulverize it as much as possible, and push it out of the way, to make room for the next bite. As a merely mechanical operation the plowing of pure sand, which it is impossible to turn in a regular furrow, affords the best model, and any arable soil would be improved by being made as fine as sand, so that it would not turn in a regular furrow.

The English use, very extensively, an implement called a grubber, which is a stronger and deeper cultivator, loosening the soil more completely than any plow for a depth of 6 or 8 inches, when drawn by horses. Its teeth project forward like the point of a plow, so that their action is more upward than that of the harrow, while they hold better to the ground.

THE KIND OF PLOW TO BE USED.

A single manufacturer of agricultural implements in New York city advertises over a hundred varieties and sizes of plows, and there are hundreds of other large manufacturers and dealers in the country who would add immensely to the number from which we may select.

In choosing a plow for light land or heavy; for sod or stubble; for shallow work or deep; for sand, clay, gravel, or plastic mould, there are many considerations which should influence us, most of which are familiar to all practical plowmen, and none of which are so well defined that they can be made the basis of any established rule. Lightness of draft and uniformity of work are the great things sought after, and they are very important; but some lightness of draft may be very well sacrificed to completeness of the pulverization of the furrow slice, and uniformity—except in plowing grass land—is of much less consequence than thorough breaking.

In all the investigations that have been made concerning the draft of plows, from the time when President Jefferson submitted to the French Institute his paper on the true shape of the mould-board, and throughout a long course of mathematical philosophizing on the subject, the only thing of universal application that can be said to be established as a *rule*, is, that on ground in which a wheel would not be clogged up, a wheel on the front part of the beam lessens the draft of all plows, and makes them work more easily generally. After the world has been supplied, for three-quarters of a century, with diagrams and formulæ on the direction in which the furrow-slice moves over the mould-board, —all of which prove the advantage of a hollow form, so regulated that a straight edge may be laid across any part of it, at right angles to the line of motion, touching at all points,—there comes a "convex mould-board" plow, (on which a straight edge so placed will touch only at a single point,) which is claimed to be in all ways superior, and which, in my hands, has certainly performed very satisfactorily; and the "cylinder" plow, on which it would touch at only two points.

This is, it must be confessed, a humiliating fact, and it at least shows that science has thus far failed to appreciate all of the resisting forces which come into action in the process of plowing; and it conveys to the farmer the intimation that he should attend even more to the completeness with which a fair expenditure of the force of his team will break up his land than to the ease with which he can do a certain amount of work. It is not quite true that the hardest plowing does the most good; but, as above stated, some heaviness of draft is well compensated for by more complete pulverization.

In making a selection of plows, therefore, we can hope for but little aid from books, and, more than in almost any other department of our work, must depend on practical experience and a judicious observation. Obviously, that plow is the best which will do the work *as it ought to be done* with the least expenditure of force. My own experience has led me to believe that, for light work—not more than seven inches in depth—I get the most complete pulverization that is possible with one pair of horses, from the use of Holbrook's stubble plow, No. 66, or of Allen's cylinder plow, with skim attachment, and for heavy work, with a strong double team, going to a depth of nine or ten inches, from the Ames Plow Company's Eagle, No. 25.

The skim attachment of Allen's cylinder plow cuts off about two or three inches of the land side of the furrow-slice, and folds it over on to the furrow side, thus lessening the weight on the mould-board. It helps to pulverize the furrow, and at least does not *increase* the draft.

Holbrook has a plow with a skim attachment, which is said to be an excellent tool, but I cannot speak from any actual experience with it.

He also makes a "swivel" or "side-hill" plow, which is very highly recommended for plowing on hill-sides, or on level land. By turning the furrow always in the same direction it obviates the necessity for leaving dead furrows.

Among the other plows which I have found by experience to be admirably adapted to all kinds of work, in heavy and in light soils, are Smith's patent cast-steel plows, made by the Collins Co., near Hartford, Conn.

The manufacturers claim for this plow the following advantages:—

"1st. It is the only plow yet produced which will invariably "scour in any soil.

"2d. It is now a well-established fact that it will last from three "to six times longer than any other plow.

"3d. It can easily be demonstrated that it draws lighter than any "other plow cutting the same width and depth of furrow.

"4th. It will plow in the most perfect manner at any desired depth, "between three and twelve inches, which is a third larger range than "is possessed by most other plows, while in difficult soils none other "can be run deeper than six or eight inches.

"5th. The same plow works perfectly not only in stubble and corn "ground, but in timothy and clover sod.

"6th. In every part it is made of the best material, and no "pains are spared to produce a uniformly good and merchantable "article."

The same firm has brought out a plow without handles, with Volkman's "Guide,"—a plow that holds itself to its work, and returns to it when thrown out by stones even better than it could be held and replaced by a plowman. I consider these steel plows one of the greatest improvements that I have adopted. The plough-guide especially is a great labor saver. With its aid, any boy who can drive a team can do good work.

This "Guide" has now been before the public long enough to have worked its way into popular favor, but has failed to do so. It is necessary, therefore, to say that while holding, personally, to any former opinion of its value, I cannot recommend its purchase without stating this fact. As a rule, every new tool that has real practical merit will make its own way. At Ogden Farm, the Volkman Plow Guide has shown itself to be worth having, but it obviously has not that general value that should make it one of the first implements to be bought. The limited capital of the farmer may be better employed in some other way.

Plowing is the fundamental work of cultivation, and very much of the success of all cultivation depends upon its being done when the conditions are such as to produce the best result. No matter how hurried the work may be,—especially in the case of heavy clay soil,—more will be lost than gained by plowing when the land will be puddled and packed by the pressure of the mould-board and of the feet of the team. Light and dry soils may be worked without injury at any time, though even these get a better "weathering" if plowed in the autumn.

The first condition, and by far the most important of all, is to plow *when the soil has only enough moisture in it to make it crumble when moved.* If it is too wet (unless very light land) it will be compacted into clods, which it will take years to break down, and which will do far more harm than the plowing will do good. If it is too dry it will be very hard to plow, and the furrow slice will contain lumps which it will be difficult to make fine. Still, it is better to plow when the land is very dry than when it is very wet.

The second condition is to plow in autumn, or as soon as convenient after the crops are off the ground. Man can, after all, do only a part of the work of cultivation, the most important part is done by nature, and we should aim, so far as possible, to aid her. She works at the processes of pulverization, sweetening, and oxidation* chiefly during the winter and spring.   In the summer she is busy at other things, but in winter she takes hold of every lump of the rough furrow tops, splits its particles apart with her wedges of ice, roughens their edges so that they will never stick together again, turns the black oxide of iron into iron rust, sets free the pent-up plant food, sweetens the acids, and performs such wonders in mechanics and chemistry as man can never hope to equal—wonders which have made the world what it is, and without which its population could not live.

If heavy land is saturated with water in the autumn, and lies soaking all winter, the action of the frost and air can do but little good, and the plowing would surely do harm, but with proper underdrainage—with only so much water in the soil as its particles will absorb within themselves, the spaces between them being filled with air—there is nothing to equal fall plowing— which has the further very great advantage of lessening the hurry and the tax on the strength of the teams in the spring.   One good plowing in the fall is a saving of time in the spring, and does more good than half a dozen plowings without the subsequent weathering to prepare the land for the production of crops.

Spring plowing—except in plowing grass land for corn—should be done as early as is consistent with a proper regard to the state of the land.   It is better not to plow clay land at all than plow it when wet ; but take the first opportunity when it is dry enough, to do as much as possible, not only for the sake of getting so much of the work out of the way, but to give the air as much time as possible to act on the newly turned ground.

HOW TO PLOW.

Plow your land deeply, and " smash it up."   This is the beginning and the end of what is *theoretically* good plowing, without regard to the condition of the soil and subsoil.   If the directions can be followed without injury, they are emphatically the directions that should be followed.   If the land is fallow, and if there

* Rusting.

is nothing in the character of the subsoil to make it objectionable when brought to the surface, we cannot plow it too deeply nor too roughly. If our land will not admit of such treatment now, without injury to present crops, the sooner we can bring it to a condition in which it will, the better for it and for us.

It is now too late in the history of agricultural improvement for it to be worth while, in a treatise like this, to discuss the reasons why deep plowing is advisable, for although the average depth of the furrow-slice in all the United States is certainly not over four inches, there are very few readers of agricultural books who need to be told that the country would be vastly richer, and would get its income with much greater certainty, if the average were eight inches.

I would not recommend that it be attempted to reach the extra depth at once,—if experiment shows that this can safely be done, as it very often will, well and good,—but in many soils the end must be gained gradually. A little of the uncultivated, raw sub-soil must be brought up each autumn, and prepared by the winter's frosts, to be mixed with the surface, or else a long course of sub-soiling and cultivation must first ameliorate the earth that until now has been locked against the circulation of air.

In giving the above figures, by way of illustration, I by no means intend it to be understood that eight inches is my limit of depth. Ten, twelve, sixteen, or twenty inches would not measure my modest desire, on land in which it is possible to sink a plow to so great depth,—for I believe I could make more money from one acre, twenty-four inches deep, than from six acres, four inches deep,—certainly more from a farm of fifty acres, well cultivated and enriched to the depth of twelve inches, than from one hundred acres, six inches deep. I think we should value our land by the cubic feet of good soil it contains, rather than by its superficial feet.

If we are plowing sod land we should lay the furrows uni-formly, and as smoothly as possible, so that the grass may all be covered out of reach of the harrow, and so that there shall be no holes or gaps among the furrows. To do this requires a skill

which is acquired at the plow-stilts, not over books. The best
instructor in plowing is a good team and plow on good land.
The only principle that can be set forth here, with much advantage, is that the plow should be so adjusted that it will almost
"go alone."   The forces and the resistances should be so
balanced that the implement will incline to keep its proper depth
and width, and its erect position.   It should require very little
guiding, except when it meets with accidental irregularities of the
surface or with stones.   All plows have a certain depth at which
they run naturally.   To set them deeper than this necessitates a
constant bearing to the land side on the part of the plowman, and
for deeper work it is better, when practicable, to get a plow that
naturally runs deeper.

The "line of draft" in all plows runs from the point of the
center of resistance (which is near the front of the plow in the
ground) straight to the ring on the ox-yoke or horse-collar, and
the point to which the draft chain is attached, at the end of the
beam, lies exactly in this line.   If the line of draft is lengthened
it rises more gradually from the center of resistance, and the end
of the beam must descend to join it—this lowers the point of the
plow and makes it run deeper.   If it is shortened, it rises more
abruptly, and causes a raising of the beam, and a less depth of cut.
These changes may be made by lengthening or shortening the
draft chain or traces.   The length of the line of draft remaining
the same, if the chain (or whiffletree) is attached to the upper part
of the clevis, the end of the beam goes down until the line of
draft is met by the point to which the attachment is made—and
the plow goes deeper ; if attached to the bottom of the clevis, the
beam must rise until this point meets the line of draft and the
plow runs less deep.

By a movement of the clevis to the left side, the beam is
turned to the right, until the new point of attachment is in the
line of draft, and the plow takes less land.   By moving the clevis
to the right, the plow is thrown to the left, and takes more land.
By throwing the clevis as far as possible to one side, the plow
may be made to work to the right or left, so that a furrow may

be cut close to a fence. In such case, however, the team not being directly in front of their work, pull at a disadvantage.*

The young plowman will have to experiment by altering the length of his traces and by changing the attachment at the clevis, until he finds the proper adjustment of the draft and the right width and depth of the furrow ; after this, if his plow is suited to its work, he will have an easy time of it, in fair land,—among stones and roots his task cannot be made an easy one.

It is better, if possible, to make the necessary alterations by changing the clevis rather than by lengthening the traces or the draft chain,—for the closer the team can be kept to the plow, the more advantageously they will exert their power.

Judiciously used, the roller or wheel is of great advantage, but it should be set up free from the ground until the plow has been exactly adjusted to its work,—then lowered so as to take a very little of the downward pressure, barely enough to keep it revolving. More than this would tend to lift the plow out of its work, or to increase the resistance. Its proper use is to assist in steadying the plow, so that it will not feel the swaying of the line of draft.

Cut the furrows in as nearly a rectangular form as possible, that is, have the land side of the plow perpendicular and the sole flat. No matter how much you break up the slice before you turn it to its place, (and except in plowing sod, the more this is done the better,) you cannot work neatly, unless you keep a good furrow, of uniform height and width, and with a straight land side and bottom.

It is found in practice, that, except for very thin or shallow plowing, the proportion of furrow best adapted to economical working is as seven is to ten,—that is, a furrow seven inches deep should be ten inches wide ; ten and a half inches deep, fifteen inches wide, etc.

---

* These directions apply to plows which turn the furrow to the right, or right-hand plows. For left-hand plows they must be reversed.

PLOWING FROM THE CENTER OF THE FIELD.

About fifteen years ago, at the Farmers' Club, in New York, the question of the "Gee-about system of plowing" was much discussed. I numbered myself among its adherents and advocates, and I have since seen no reason to change my opinion of its merits.

The only difficulty about it is to find the right starting point, and to keep the furrows so uniform in width as to come out even on all sides at the end of the work.

The advantages of the system are manifest :—

First. The soil, instead of being plowed against the fences, where it is of no use, (is rather injurious,) is turned toward the center of the field. Of course this should not be continued to such an extent as to strip the land very far from the fences, but it may be repeated a good many times before the headland will be stripped too far.

Second. The team never treads on the plowed land, which is left as light as the plow turns it, while they work better at the corners from their more solid footing.

Third. There is less heavy handling of the plow at the turnings, and even the plowman has better footing for his hardest work.

Fourth. There are no dead furrows left in the center and toward the corners, as in plowing around from the outside.

To lay out a field for plowing in this way, (see Fig. 57,) take a long pole and measure a certain distance inward from two points on each side, (say three rods,) and set stakes at the points so found, (*a, a, a,* etc.) Then take a position opposite one corner of the field, and set a stake where the lines ranging from the two stakes at each side of you intersect, (*x.*) Set stakes opposite the other corners in the same manner. Next, measure another distance inward from the stakes first placed, and mark the points of their outer section, (*b, b, b,* etc.,) and stake the corners as at *y, y, y, y.* Continue in this way until you have only a small

Fig. 57.

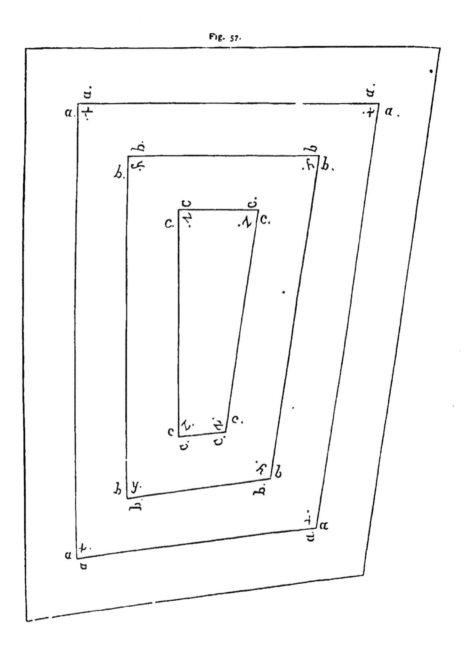

space left between the lines which inclose the center of the field, (c, c, z, etc.)

Commence the work by plowing this small space, commencing at the stakes last set for the first furrow, and throwing the earth *from* the center, as it is difficult, especially in an irregular field, to get evenly started in plowing toward the center. After this piece (which need not contain more than a square rood) has been plowed up, reverse your direction and turn your furrow against the outside of it, and so continue until you reach the boundaries of the field.

The stakes set at a, a, b, b, etc., will be useful as guides, enabling you to so regulate the width of the furrow on the different sides that you will come out even at the end of the work.

I am aware that this plan is open to the objection that it is unusual, but I feel confident that any farmer who will try it will find its adoption easy, and that it has all the advantages claimed for it.

In fields with parallel sides, the center piece may be larger, and be plowed in "lands,"—or in a single land against a back furrow, but this cannot be quite so neatly done in a piece of any other shape, though it is not impossible, after one furrow has been thrown *outward*.

I have concluded to say nothing of the manner of plowing in "lands," "ridge and furrow-plowing," etc., not because the subject is not important, but for the reason that, after a careful search through hundreds of pages that have been published about it, I have failed to find any thing of importance that I had not already learned in practice, and that will not form a part of the very early practical education of any young farmer who needs the knowledge.

There are so many topics which demand attention in a hand-book for general use, that only the more important can claim much space.

On one point, both practical experience and common sense fully agree. That is, that (as was stated under the head of "Fences") the fields should be so arranged as to make the furrows as long as possible. It has been found, by actual trial, that, in plowing a field three hundred yards long, a man and team will do one-third more work than in plowing one one hundred yards long —the difference in time being made up in the more frequent turnings required by the shorter furrows.

In cutting furrows nine inches wide, the time required to plow an acre at the following rates would be—

Going at the rate of 1½ miles per hour............7 hours 20 minutes.
  "   "   " of 1¾ "   "   " ....6 "   30   "
  "   "   " of 2¾ "   "   " ....4 "
  "   "   " of 3½ "   "   " ....3 "   8   "

In this table no allowance is made for turnings.

The distance traveled in plowing an acre is as follows :—

Width of furrow, 8 inches.....................Distance, 12½ miles.
  "   "   9 "   .... "   11   "
  "   "   10 "   .... "   9⁹⁄₁₀ "
  "   "   11 "   .... "   9   "
  "   "   12 "   .... "   8¼   "

SUBSOILING.

By the term subsoiling, is meant any process which loosens the subsoil without bringing it to the surface. In spade work, it is done by throwing the top spit forward, and loosening, without removing the next spit below. In plowing, the loosening effect is produced by following in the furrow of the surface plow with a *subsoil plow*, which passes like a wedge, or like a mole, through the subsoil, allowing it to fall back, in a loosened condition, into its original place.

There are several forms of this implement. That which is best known being a cast-iron plate shaped very much like the land side and projecting point of the common plow. On the right-hand side, in the place of the mould board, there is a rising flange, or inclined plane, which raises the earth on that side about four inches, (with a slight side thrust). As the plow passes through the ground, the loosened subsoil falls off behind. The tool does good work, but requires a heavy team.

A very great improvement on the original form is shown in

Fig. 58, of which the working parts are made entirely of wrought iron and steel. The draft is very much lighter than that of

Fig. 58.

the wing plow, described above, and it is much easier to manage it on stony land.

This is the most deceptive implement used in agriculture. It looks as though it would produce but little effect in a heavy clay subsoil, yet in actual trial it produces more commotion in the ground than any other subsoiler that I have seen used. The total rise given to the earth at the level of the plow foot is hardly more than an inch, but it so completely crushes the soil above it, and for considerable distance on each side, that it leaves the bottom of the furrow raised in a ridge three or four inches high. The action of this foot is both upward and sidewise, the soil being loosened, very much as shown in the shaded portion of Fig. 59.

Fig. 59.

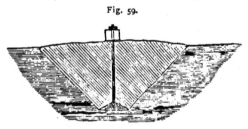

On land that needs draining, subsoiling is of no use, at least its effect is not permanent enough to make it pay; but in a soil that is (either naturally or artificially) well underdrained, I know of no operation connected with the cultivation of the land, except draining itself, that is so beneficial and so lasting in its effect. A well-drained subsoil, that has been once well broken up with a subsoil plow, will never again become so hard and impenetrable to roots as it was before the operation. It opens a way in the lower soil for the deeper entrance of roots, and these are always ready to avail themselves of an opportunity of going down beyond the reach of the drying effect of the sun's rays and of the wind. When the crop is removed, these roots remain and decay in the subsoil, entirely changing its character. The more ready admission that is given to the water of rains and to the circulation of air, hastens the chemical changes in the composition of the subsoil, and these changes, together with the decay of the roots, will in time bring the soil to the condition of that which has been turned by the surface plow, so that, after a very few years, a subsoil which would have impaired the fertility of the field if at once turned up in large quantities, may be brought to the surface as plentifully as is desired. This, in connection with a gradua deepening of the surface furrow, is the best means of making the soil deeper,—of making more soil to the acre.

I must repeat, however, that on wet land, the foregoing effects cannot be expected, at least not in a sufficient degree to make the operation advisable.

The depth of the working of the subsoil plow is regulated by means of a clevis, in the same manner as that of the surface plow, and it may be made to run from six inches to eighteen inches below the bottom of the furrow of the surface plow, according to the character of the subsoil and the strength of the team. As many as eight oxen are sometimes used, and often a single pair will do good work.

The " trick " of the work is to set the plow as deep as it will work without getting beyond the control of the plowman. It has a wonderful tendency to take too deep a hold, as soon as it passes a point at which the team can exercise a lifting force upon it, and it will sometimes get " set " beyond the power of extrication, except by digging. So far as the plowman has any power to prevent it from going too deep, he must keep it out by *lifting* at the stilts. By bearing down, as he would do in the case of the surface plow, he will only drive its wedge-shaped point deeper into the ground.

The steel subsoiler (the one shown in Fig. 58) has other uses besides that of following in the furrow of the surface plow. The smallest size, running six or eight inches deep and drawn by one horse, is a capital cultivator for working between rows of corn or roots, loosening the soil more deeply and more thoroughly than any other implement. It should not, however, be run so near to the rows as to cut off the spreading roots, nor should it be used at all except during the earlier periods of growth.

The larger sizes, running a foot or more deep, at intervals of two feet in width, will loosen up a run-down or hide-bound meadow or pasture, so that a top-dressing and subsequent rolling will often restore its fertility, and postpone the necessity of bringing it into cultivation.

Land that has been plowed in autumn may be better prepared for the planting of the next spring by the use of this tool—crossing the field first in one direction and then in the other—than by the use of the common plow. Of course, the harrow would be as necessary in the one case as in the other.

TRENCHING.

In the Island of Jersey, (in the English Channel,) which has always been noted for its great fertility,—and especially for the large parsnips there grown, which are extensively used in cattle-feeding, and which require a very deep soil,—there has been used for a hundred years what is known as the Great Jersey Trench Plow, which, drawn by six or eight horses, turns the soil to a depth of from one and a half to two feet, the surface soil and the manure being first turned into the bottom of the deep furrow by an ordinary plow drawn by two horses. Neighbors "join teams" for the operation, which is called "The Great Digging."

For the deep cultivation of gardens and small tracts, it is customary to do the work of trenching by hand; the process being to dig a trench about two feet wide, and of the desired depth,

10

throwing the soil all out on one side, then to dig down to the same depth for another two feet, putting the top soil in the bottom of the first trench, and the last digging on the top, thus completely inverting the soil. The manure is either put at the bottom of the trench or mixed evenly through the whole mass. When the last trench has been dug out, the earth thrown from the first trench is wheeled around and used to fill it.

I cannot better close this subject than by saying, for the third time, that no benefit at all adequate to the outlay can be hoped for from either trenching or subsoiling, unless the subsoil is (either naturally or artificially) *well drained.*

PLOWING WITH THREE HORSES ABREAST.

It is generally considered that three horses working abreast exert as much force on a plow as four horses working in pairs, and such experience as I have had in the matter indicates that

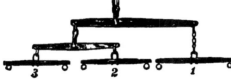

Fig. 60.—Set of Whiffletrees and Eveners for Three Horses.

the opinion is a correct one. There are several methods for gearing such teams. The simplest, and, I think, the best, is by the use of an evener, with a set of double-trees and a single-tree, as shown in Fig. 60.

The reins may be arranged in a triple set, or, with a tractable team, I have usually found it sufficient to tie the three bits together, and to pass a single rein to the outside rings of the bits of the two outside horses. It is especially desirable that one horse should walk in the furrow and the other two on the unplowed land where they have the best footing. This requires the plow to be set far to the furrow.

CHAPTER VII.

PULVERIZING.

Reduce the soil to a powder, or bring it as nearly to that condition as you can. The roots of plants absorb only such matters as are presented to them on the *outsides* of the particles of the soil, and the air, water, and manure which prepare the plant food to be taken up, can only act on such surfaces. A soil may contain enough mineral food for twenty crops, and yet be practically barren, if its food is locked up within impenetrable clods.

As the draining away of the water in which the particles of the soil are immersed, allows roots to travel over wider pasturage, and allows the changing air to do its work of chemical preparation, so the finer pulverization of the particles is conducive to the increasing richness of the land, to the better supply of food, and to the easier seeking of food by the plant.

The great pulverizer in our northern latitudes is frost, to the action of which sufficient reference has been made in the preceding chapter. The tools which we use for the work of pulverization, after the plow and the subsoiler, are the roller, the harrow, the cultivator, the horse-hoe, etc.

THE ROLLER.

The best roller (and the most costly) is made of cast-iron wheels, from twenty to thirty-six inches in diameter, and twelve wide, set close together on an iron axle, on which they revolve independently. From four to six of these wheels (or sections) are used together, and they are provided with a pole and double-trees, and with a box in which stones may be placed if extra weight

is desired.   This roller (Fig. 61) has the great advantage of turning around without disturbing the surface of the soil, as it would
if all in one piece.

Fig. 61.—Field Roller.

A cheaper roller, and one answering a tolerably good purpose,
is made by setting a smoothly shaven log so as to revolve in a
frame similar to the one shown in the cut.

The roller has several important uses.   By passing over the
land after plowing, it settles the furrows so that they will not be
turned over by the harrow, and it gives the best possible crushing
to the top of the slice, grinding it to dust.   After the harrow has cut
the ground (which the plow has inverted in a lumpy condition) into
smaller lumps, the roller passes over it again and crushes these
still smaller.   The more frequently the two operations succeed
each other, the finer the soil will become, especially at the top,
while each rolling presses down to the general level of the surface
such stones as the harrow may have thrown up.

Used in the spring, on winter grain, or on mowing land or
pastures, the roller corrects the " heaving " effect of the winter's
frosts, settles the plants back into their places, and compresses
fine soil closely around their roots.   It, at the same time, presses
loose stones into the ground, and prepares a smooth surface for
the mowing machine, or reaper.

Of course this implement, like all others which are intended
to make the soil smoother or finer, should be carefully kept off
from the land when it is so wet that, instead of crumbling under
the treatment, it becomes only more closely compacted.   There

is, however, no objection to its use, but almost always an advantage in the dryest weather of summer. As the roller is used only during a very small part of the year, it is far more likely to *rust* out than to *wear* out. It should, therefore, be carefully housed when not needed in the field, and it will be much easier to work if occasionally greased.

THE HARROW.

This ancient, time-honored, and unsatisfactory tool—only a better-than-nothing affair, at best—must retain its hold on the affections of those who like it, and command the toleration of those who use it without liking it—on the principle that (to reverse an old saw) handsome *does* that handsome *is*.

A harrow tooth, (especially if made of iron and well sharpened,) if furnished with a suitable handle, would be the best sort of tool with which to pack the earth around newly set fence-posts. It is impossible to drop it into the ground, or to drag it in a vertical position over the ground, without packing the earth below its point. The earth in a fence-hole that has been packed in with a sharp crowbar may be made *solid* to within two inches of the surface, too solid for any plant to thrive in, although the *immediate surface* may be fine and soft as a flower-bed.

Of course, it would take a good many harrowings to pack the lower soil to any thing like this degree, but every time a sharp-toothed iron harrow is drawn across it, it exercises a *tendency* in this direction, and although I use it myself, for want of a substitute, and know nothing else that will entirely take its place, I hope that some efficient substitute may yet be found, and I should have much faith in the success of an experiment with teeth shaped like those of the steam grubber, which have square, case-hardened, chisel-like ends.

The sorts of harrows in use are numerous, and are generally familiar to all. A very good one has a single square frame, with about twenty teeth. This, in a rather heavy soil, is enough for a single light team. For more general use, it would

be best to purchase Geddes' folding *A* harrow, or the double square
Scotch harrow, for stiffer soil. This may be taken apart, and only
one side used.

There have recently come into use two new forms of harrow which
have much to commend them. The first is Thomas's Smoothing
Harrow, which has teeth of ⅝ steel rods, *sloping backward*, so as
to effect only a smoothing of the surface of the ground. It is a
capital tool to destroy very young weeds and to give a fine tilth to
the seed bed. Used immediately before the planting of corn, and
again as soon as the rows are well indicated by the young sprouts,
the cost of the crop will be very much reduced. The second is the
"chain" harrow, an English invention, but now made in this
country. It is made up of triangular sections of cast iron, connected
with wrought-iron links, so as to be very flexible. It drops into
every depression and rides over every hump so as to scratch the
whole ground thoroughly.

In using the pointed-tooth harrow, where it is desirable to cut up
the soil very thoroughly, at a considerable outlay of power on the
part of the team, I find it a good practice to stand with the feet
wide apart on the harrow, throwing the weight first on one side and
then on the other. This gives a swaying movement to the implement, which tears up the soil very thoroughly.

Shares' harrow (Fig. 62) is a great improvement over the
common harrow for general use. I have used it for ten years
with excellent effect, and confidently recommend it—especially for
harrowing sod-furrows. It is thus described by the manufacturers :—

"The advantages of this harrow lie principally in the con-
"struction of the teeth or colters, which are broad, thin blades
"of cast iron, inclining forward so as to prevent their clogging
"with roots, grass, stones, etc., as well as to cut the sods and
"force an easy entrance into any kind of soil. The mould-
"board is attached to, and forms the lower or back end of the
"colter, the lower edge of which is continued a short distance
"below the covering portion of the tooth, and forms the point.

" This serves to elevate the teeth over stumps, stones, and other
" impediments, and also gives them durability. In preparing land
" which ordinarily needs plowing several times for root crops or

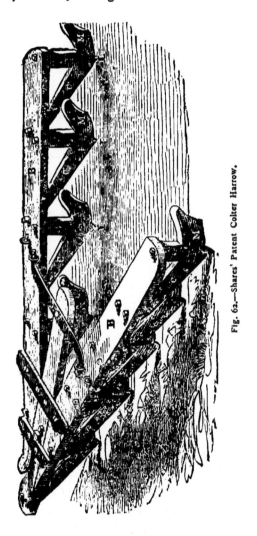

Fig. 62.—Shares' Patent Colter Harrow.

" grain, by the use of this harrow, it is only necessary to plow
" once, and it will, by its lifting, pulverizing process, prepare and
" finish the ground more thoroughly and satisfactorily than can be
" done with the usual styles of harrows, and in less time.

"This harrow is six feet in width when expanded, but when "closed for transportation is less than two feet. It is seven feet "long, and weighs one hundred and fifty-five pounds."

THE CULTIVATOR.

There are various modifications of this tool. The teeth may be made of various forms. Sometimes the common harrow teeth are substituted, and sometimes shovel-shaped teeth. It is a good improvement to use, in the place of the hindmost teeth on the arms, a pair of the small *shares* of the horse-hoe, shown in Fig. 63. The cultivator is used in working between the rows of corn, roots, etc., and is very much better for this purpose than the plow.

In the large corn-fields of the West, a great deal of hard work is saved by the use of a sulky cultivator, on which the driver rides. These are sometimes made wide enough to cultivate two rows at once, and drawn by two horses. It is stated, however, that the cultivation done by this tool is far less complete than is desirable, and that it is less popular than when first introduced.

For the simple purpose of *cultivating* the ground between rows of plants, without reference to the killing of weeds, there is no implement to be compared to the smallest sized subsoil plow of the form shown in Fig. 58, which may easily be drawn by one horse to a depth of from five to eight inches, and which leaves the soil lighter and more exposed to the air than any of the so-named cultivators. If the rows are more than two feet apart, the subsoiler should be run twice in each space, but not so close to the plants as to disturb them in their position, as this would cause the breaking off of important feeding roots, while the tool itself might cut off some of the more important side roots.

In fact, in cultivating hoed crops, it is prudent to act on the theory, that after they have attained one-half their growth, their roots occupy the whole space between the rows, and after this, to confine the cultivator to the most shallow work that will break the crust of the ground, and kill such weeds as may still be growing.

In the early stages of growth, cultivate as deeply as possible—late in the season, only an inch or two.

THE HORSE-HOE.

A modification of the cultivator, and, for most uses, an improvement on it, is the *horse-hoe*, (Fig. 63,) which has a sharp

Fig. 63.—Horse-Hoe.

tooth in front for a steering pivot; a small plow-snaped tooth at each side, which may be made to run very close to the row, as it throws the earth *from* it; and a broad V-shaped, knifelike blade at the rear, ending in a rising comb. The knife edge cuts off all weeds about an inch below the surface, and has sufficient bend to throw back, toward the row, the earth that the wing plow draws from it—leaving it very loose and fine.

The *intention* of the rising comb at the back is to leave the weeds on the surface, allowing the earth to fall through the spaces. I never could see that this part of the programme was carried out; but, notwithstanding this, it is a capital tool, and, with the small subsoiler for the earlier work, is all that could be desired for small-sized fields.

Holbrook's horse-hoe (Fig. 64) is a strong, simple, well-made tool, which is better for hard or rough land than the one described above, and for all work it is a good tool.

Fig. 64.—Holbrook's No. 1 Horse-Hoe.

THE MULLER.

This is a tool much used in Rhode Island, which I have never seen elsewhere, but which is worthy of general adoption. Its local name is the *muller*. Its construction is very simple, (as

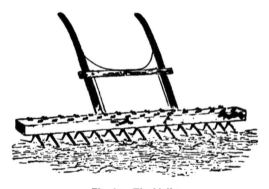

Fig. 65.—The Muller.

shown in Fig. 65,) and it is made at the wagon shops throughout the State. Its teeth are about six inches long, and the front and back teeth alternate along the bar, so that every inch of the ground is pulverized. By bearing on the front or back row of teeth, (by lifting or bearing down on the handles,) slight inequalities in the surface may be made smooth.

The muller is drawn by a single horse, the traces being attached near the ends of the bar. It is more properly a harrow than a cultivator, as it is too wide to be used between rows, although a shorter tool of the same construction, with a steering rest behind, would answer very well for this purpose.

Whatever kind of horse-hoe or cultivator we may use, they will usually be found profitable, in proportion to the frequency and the depth of their use ;—the only qualification of this statement being, that their vigorous use should cease after the side roots of the crop have spread so as to occupy all or nearly all of the ground between the rows.

CHAPTER VIII.

MANURES.

So long as men are cultivating a soil whose virgin fertility responds to their demands with unfailing generosity, so long as the tickling hoe brings the brightest harvest smile, it is useless to talk to them about manure. Indeed, it would not *pay* under such circumstances to use manure, and we have no right to expect any thing to be done in farming that does not pay.

The East has been, and the West now is (very largely) in the hands of farmers who found, or who find, that their fields produce large crops, year after year, without the cost and labor of manuring. Manure would not increase their yield at all in proportion to the outlay. That the soil is being made less valuable for posterity, its occupants cannot be convinced. Their particular locality is an exception to the inexorable rule; it always is,—and they do not always live long enough to be convinced to the contrary. After all, why need they be convinced? It would be better for posterity that they should prevent the soil from growing poor; but posterity, when its time shall come, will be amply repaid for making it rich again, and will have, by reason of a more dense population, better facilities for doing so. In the abstract, it is a sad thing to see the power of production diminishing under cultivation; but we have no just right to blame those who are the cause of the decrease. They are entitled to their use of the land, and if they leave it less fertile than they found it, they, at the same time, in America at least, leave it tamed, peopled, and better fitted for habitation. What they destroy on the one hand, they more than build up on the other.

The farmers of the West deal with wide areas and large herds.

Their pioneer life has its hardships, and its compensations; and I very much doubt the justness of most of the criticisms, which we, who have different necessities, are so free to bestow upon them. Assuredly, our intense system of cultivation, which is necessarily confined to small farms, would fail if attempted on the frontier. We may well afford to let them follow the path that their circumstances have marked out for them, for, after all, it is but the thin surface of the land that they injure, and while they will destroy it for the sort of farming that they pursue, they will hardly touch the stores from which a better system of agriculture will draw the means for its renewed and more permanent fertility.

The foregoing applies only to those who occupy lands of " inexhaustible fertility "—while they remain such. Later in the history of these lands, we begin to hear of "insects," "blight," " wet seasons," " dry seasons," " weeds," and all the long list of scourges which beset the path of all farmers, but which become grave, only when the bountiful productiveness of the soil grows weak and unable to overcome their devastating influence. There is a long period between the eras of " inexhaustible fertility" and " absolute exhaustion," during which the *science* of farming should come to the rescue, and save that which the unaided *art* of farming threatens with destruction. Then we need to study the question of *manure*,—then, true farming begins. Let me not be understood as undervaluing the intelligent management of his affairs, which marks the character of the frontier farmer, or his usefulness in the world. I mean, only, that he is rather a manipulator of what the earth gives him most freely, than a skillful stimulator of her power to give; and even this difference is far more marked with reference to the question of manures, than to any other branch of farming;—generally it is not apparent when we come to the breeding of animals.

Lying between the frontiermen and the farmers of the Atlantic slope, come those who cultivate the garden States east of, and bordering upon the Mississippi River. There seems to be no reason why they should be regarded in this connection as forming a distinct class by themselves. In so far as they are still independent of the necessity of adding manure to their soil, they belong to one class;—when the waning fertility of their land has compelled them to seek its aid, to the other.

When the demand for manure comes, (as it must, inevitably, come in time, to all farms that are not occasionally inundated,) the rules for its application, and the principles of its action must apply to all alike. Of course one soil may be best improved by one manure, another soil by a different manure, but—other things being equal—in all localities, North and South, East and West, the operation of manure and the necessity for its use are based on the same laws, and are regulated by the relation between the plant and the soil on which it grows.

By "manure" we mean all substances which are applied artificially to the soil to increase its ability to produce vegetable growth.

As all manures do not act in the same manner, they are sometimes classified as follows:—

1. NUTRITIVE: those whose own ingredients being taken up by the roots of plants, go to form a part of their structures.

2. SOLVENT: those which give to water a greater power to dissolve the plant food already contained by the soil.

3. ABSORBENT: those which add to the power of the soil to absorb the fertilizing parts of other manures, of the water of rains, and of the atmosphere circulating within it.

4. MECHANICAL: those which improve the mechanical character of the soil;—such as clay on sandy soil, and sand or peat on heavy clays, and such as disintegrate the particles of the soil, and make it finer.

Probably no manure acts in any one of these capacities alone. For instance, common salt not only gives up its own ingredients to plants, but being dissolved in the water in the soil, it gives this water greater power to dissolve other plant food from the surfaces of the particles of earth, or from other manures added to it. It is, therefore, to be regarded as both a nutritive and a solvent manure.

Farm-yard manure, the universal fertilizer, is a direct source of most valuable plant food; it produces, in its decomposition, ammonia and other substances, which, while they feed the crop, add greatly to the solvent power of water; as it rots down, its coarser parts are changed into compounds which are very active absorbers or fixers of ammonia; and, by reason of its fibrous texture, it loosens heavy clays, and binds together blowy sands, while its decomposition produces heat which warms the soil, and its power of absorbing moisture from the air keeps it moist.

The action of all manures is so complex, and, in some respects, so imperfectly understood, that it is not easy to classify them by any system that is free from objection, and as this is a book of practice rather than of principles, it will be best to consider the different common fertilizers in order, leaving the question of their classification to more purely scientific essays. The first in order, in the agriculture of all countries where domestic animals are largely kept, is, of course,

FARM-YARD MANURE.

This consists of the undigested parts of food; of those constituents of the animal's body which, being expended in the vital processes, are discarded in the urine and dung; and of the straw, etc., used for litter. The first two of these constituents always bear a direct relation to the food, and their relative value may be more nearly estimated. The third, the litter, is very variable in kind and in quantity, according as we use much or little of straw, corn-stalks, leaves, peat, sea-weed, beach-sand, etc., etc.

Except when peat, sand, etc., are used, stable manure contains nothing but what has already formed a part of plants, and it contains *every ingredient that plants require for their growth*. This, however, states but one half of the question. The other half —and a very important one it is—is as follows: a given quantity of farm-yard manure does *not* contain all that is needed to produce the same *quantity* of vegetable matter that constituted the food and litter of the animals by which it was produced.

A part of their food has passed into the air in the carbonic acid that they constantly throw off in respiration; this the new plant must get again from the air. A part has been resolved into water, and has been thrown off from the lungs or skin, or has evaporated in the escaping moisture of the manure; this must be taken by the new plant from the water of its sap. Another part has been sold away in milk, wool, flesh, and bone; and this, (the part which demands the attention of the farmer,) the new plant must take from the soil.

If the crop of a field is fed to milch cows, and 100 lbs. of phosphoric acid is sold away in the product, the manure *must* contain 100 lbs. less of this necessary ingredient than the food did, and if the whole of the manure is returned to the field, it still gets back 100 lbs. less than it gave. The next crop must contain less phosphoric acid,—and so be smaller,—or it must take a fresh supply from the soil. In time, the quantity in the soil, however large it may have been at the outset, must be reduced so low that the crop can take up, during its limited period of growth, only a part of what it requires, and its quantity must shrink in proportion to the decreasing supply.

It may be in ten years, or it may be in a hundred, but the day must inevitably come, when the constant removal of more than is returned will lessen the ability of the soil to produce.

This is the theory of the exhaustion of the soil, and it is based on a law so simple, and yet so inexorable, that no man can deny its existence, or reasonably hope to escape the penalty of its infraction. The recuperative power of the soil is very great, and we have many means for amending or postponing the injury of excessive cropping; but the use of green crops, fallows, thorough and deep cultivation, exposure to frost, and the whole array of processes through which we are provided relief, are only so many means for more complete exhaustion in the end.

To what extent it is advisable to increase the immediate fertility of the soil, without the use of manure, must be decided by each man according to his circumstances. Any process by which this may be accomplished is a process of discounting future fertility. No farm from which more of the earthy constituents of plants is sold off than is brought back, can be perfectly manured by using only the excrement of the animals feeding upon it.

These earthy constituents have a very different value in different localities. In Central Illinois—where, as a correspondent of the *Country Gentleman* recently wrote. "Corn is the crop, every time"—they must still be of very little value. On the island of Rhode Island, where it pays to buy coarse stable manure at six dollars per cord, and to expend a day's labor of a man and four oxen in hauling it to the farm, they are of very great value. In Illinois, where there is still a superabundance of them in the soil, their value will increase as the stock on hand becomes reduced by future crops. In Rhode Island, where, probably, as much is now returned as is taken away, their marketable value is likely to be reduced by the more complete development of the supply already contained in the soil.

The question is, after all, a purely commercial one. So long as the soil, aided only by the manures made on the farm, yields paying crops, and purchased manures would not increase the product sufficiently to return their cost, it is of course to be recommended, that the whole attention of the farmer be given to the careful husbanding of his home-made supply. When it becomes profitable to buy manure, (or, which amounts to the same thing, to buy food for the sake of the manure it will make,) that made on the farm should be still more vigilantly protected against loss, and the cheapest means of supplying the deficiency must be sought.

So long as the yield, with no manure, is large enough to satisfy the ambition of the farmer, even farm-yard manure will not be used at all. This is a misfortune, of course, but there is no help for it, and there is nothing to be gained by talking about it.

Within the past twenty years, the question of the use and application of farm-yard manure has been a good deal discussed, and some new ideas on the subject have been developed.

The most complete practical investigations were made by Dr. Voelcker, Professor of Chemistry in the Royal Agricultural College, Circencester, (England,) whose report was published in the "Journal of the Royal Agricultural Society," (vol. xvii.,) and republished in the "Second Report of the New England Agricultural Society." *

The examination extended over a period of more than a year, and included an investigation of the constituents of as uniform a sample as could be prepared of the manure of horses, cows, and pigs, as ordinarily combined in the farm-yard, in its fresh state; after long exposure to the weather; after fermentation in the open air; and after fermentation under a tight shed.

Careful analyses were made of each lot, at intervals during the whole time, and the results were carefully summed up and considered with reference to their bearing on the treatment of manure in practice.

I give the conclusions arrived at, partly in Dr. Voelcker's own words, and partly in a more condensed form :—

1. "Perfectly fresh farm-yard manure contains but a small proportion of free ammonia."

2. The nitrogen of *fresh* dung is mainly insoluble.

3. The soluble parts of the manure are much the most valuable. Therefore, it is important to save the urine, and to keep manure protected from the rain, so that its soluble parts may not be washed out.

4. Farm-yard manure, even in its fresh state, contains soluble phosphate of lime.

5. The urine of the animals above-named does not contain any considerable amount of phosphate of lime, but this is largely contained in the drainings of dung-heaps, which are more valuable than urine.

6. "The most effectual manner of preventing loss in fertilizing "matters is to cart the manure directly on the field, whenever cir-"cumstances allow this to be done."

7. "On all soils with a moderate proportion of clay, no fear "need be entertained of valuable fertilizing substances becoming "wasted if the manure cannot be plowed in at once. Fresh, and "even well-rotted dung, contains very little free ammonia; and

* "On the composition of farm-yard manure, and the changes which it undergoes on keeping under different circumstances."

" since active fermentation, and, with it, the further evolution of
" free ammonia, is stopped by spreading out the manure on the
" field, valuable volatile manuring matters cannot escape into the
" air by adopting this plan.

" As all soils, with a moderate proportion of clay, possess, in
" a remarkable degree, the power of absorbing and retaining
" manuring matters, none of the saline and soluble constituents
" are wasted, even by a heavy fall of rain. It may, indeed, be
" questioned whether it is more advisable to plow in the manure
" at once, or to let it lie for some time on the surface, and to
" give the rain full opportunity to wash it into the soil."

" It appears to me as a matter of the greatest importance to
" regulate the application of manure to our fields so that its con-
" stituents may become properly diluted, and uniformly distributed
" among a large mass of the soil. By plowing in the manure at
" once, it appears to me this desirable end cannot be reached so
" perfectly as by allowing the rain to wash in gradually the manure
" evenly spread on the surface of the field. * * * * * * I am
" much inclined to recommend, as a general rule, carting the
" manure on the field, spreading it at once, and waiting for a favor-
" able opportunity to plow it in. In the case of clay soils, I have
" no hesitation to say the manure may be spread even six months
" before it is plowed in, without losing any appreciable quantity
" of manuring matters. * * * * * * On light, sandy
" soils, I would suggest to manure with well-fermented dung
" shortly before the crop intended to be grown is sown."

8. " Well-rotten dung contains, likewise, little free ammonia,
" but a very much larger proportion of soluble organic and saline
" mineral matters than fresh manure."

9. " Rotten dung is richer in nitrogen than fresh."

10. " Weight for weight, rotten dung is more valuable than
" fresh."

11 and 12. During fermentation, dung gives off organic
matter in a gaseous form, but, if properly regulated, there is
no great loss of nitrogen.

13. During fermentation of dung, organic acids are always

formed, and gypsum is developed, and these fix the ammonia as fast as it is generated.

14. "During the fermentation of dung, the phosphate of lime which it contains is much more soluble than in fresh manure."

15. Ammonia is given off in the heated interior of the fermenting heap, but it is arrested by the organic acids and the gypsum in the colder external layers.

16. While ammonia is not given off from the surface of well-compressed heaps, it is wasted in appreciable quantities, when they are turned over.

17. "No advantage appears to result from carrying on the fer "mentation of dung too far, but every disadvantage."

18. "Farm-yard manure becomes deteriorated in value when "kept in heaps exposed to the weather—the more the longer it is "kept."

19. The loss from manure-heaps kept exposed to the weather is not so much due to the evaporation of ammonia as to the washing out, by rains, of the soluble ammoniacal salts and other soluble fertilizing parts.

20. "If rain is excluded from dung-heaps, or little rain falls at "a time, the loss in ammonia is trifling, and no saline matters, of "course, are removed; but if much rain falls, especially if it "descends in heavy showers upon the dung-heap, a serious loss in "ammonia, soluble organic matters, phosphate of lime, and salts "of potash is incurred, and the manure becomes rapidly deterio-"rated in value, while, at the same time, it is diminished in weight."

21. "Well-rotten dung is more readily affected by the deteri-"orating influence of rain than fresh manure."

22. "Practically speaking, all the essentially valuable manuring "constituents are preserved by keeping farm-yard manure under "cover."

23. If there is a very large amount of litter in the dung, water must be added to it, by pumping or by rain, to enable it to ferment actively.

24. "The worst method of making manure is to produce it "by animals kept in open yards, since a large proportion of valu-

"able fertilizing matter is wasted in a short time; and, after a
"lapse of twelve months, at least two-thirds of the substance of
"the manure is wasted, and only one-third, inferior in quality to
"an equal weight of fresh dung, is left behind."

Dr. Voelcker continued his investigations, especially as to the
character of drainings of dung-heaps, and published a second valuable paper in the "Journal of the Royal Agricultural Society" of
the next year (vol. xviii.) The following are among the conclusions there arrived at :—

"1. It will be seen that these drainings contain a good deal of
"ammonia, which should not be allowed to run to waste.

"2. They also contain phosphate of lime, a constituent not
"present in the urine of animals. The fermentation of the dung-
"heap thus brings a portion of the phosphates contained in manure
"into a soluble state, and enables them to be washed out by any
"watery liquid that may come in contact with them.

"3. Drainings of dung-heaps are rich in alkaline salts, especially
"in the more valuable salts of potash."

"4. By allowing the washings of dung-heaps to run to waste,
"not only ammonia is lost, but also much soluble organic matter,
"salts of potash, and other inorganic substances, which enter into
"the composition of our crops, and which are necessary to their
"growth."

The foregoing statements convey a sufficiently clear idea of the
changes that result from the fermentation of manure, to enable
us to understand the importance of protecting it very carefully
against the action of rains, until it is finally applied to the land.

They furnish, furthermore, the most convincing proof that a
very large majority of American farmers manage the manure of
their stables in the most wasteful and extravagant manner possible.
Many, even of those who attach great value to manure, and purchase large quantities of grain, mainly that the dung-heap may be
made richer, allow the most valuable parts of their entire store to
be stolen away by the drip of their barn-roofs.

Dr. Voelcker's analysis of fresh farm-yard manure, which is
given below, is generally accepted as the best and the most com-

plete that has yet been made, and as representing, probably, a fair average of the composition of the manure of a farm on which are kept the usual variety of stock.   It is as follows :—

COMPOSITION OF FRESH FARM-YARD MANURE, (COMPOSED OF HORSE, PIG, AND COW DUNG,) ABOUT FOURTEEN DAYS OLD.

Detailed Composition of Manure in Natural State.

Water..		66.17
* S luble organic matter.................................		2.48
Soluble inorganic matter (ash) :—		
Soluble silica, (silicic acid)...........................	.237	
Phosphate of lime......................................	.299	
Lime	.066	
Magnesia...	.011	
Potash...	.573	
Soda	.051	
Chloride of sodium....................................	.030	
Sulphuric acid..................................	.055	
Carbonic acid and loss................................	.218	
	———	1.54
† Insoluble organic matter.............................		25.76
Insoluble inorganic matter (ash) :—		
Soluble silica } silicic acid {	.967	
Insoluble silica, } {	.561	
Oxide of iron, and alumina, with phosphates...............	.596	
(Containing phosphoric acid .... .178)		
(Equal to bone earth............................. .386)		
Lime	1.120	
Magnesia..	.143	
Potash...............................:.............	.099	
Soda..	.019	
Sulphuric acid.'......................................	.061	
Carbonic acid and loss................................	.484	
	———	4.05
		100.00

Whole manure contains ammonia in a free state................		.034
" " " " in form of salts........... ...		.088

* Containing nitrogen...	.149	
Equal to ammonia...		.181
† Containing nitrogen	.494	
Equal to ammonia...		.599

According to this analysis, a ton of manure, (2,000 lbs.,) contains, in addition to 1,323 lbs. of water and 515 lbs of insoluble organic matter, (woody fiber, etc.,) the following quantities of the more valuable manuring ingredients :—

Ammonia	15.60 lbs.
Soluble phosphoric acid	3.64 "
Insoluble " "	3.56 "
Potash	13.44 "
Total	36.24 "

As stable manure in towns is usually sold by the cord, I have caused a well-trodden cart-load of good livery-stable manure, (in which hogs had been constantly working, but which contains the usual proportion of straw,) to be carefully weighed, and I find a cord of this manure to weigh 7,080 lbs.

Taking 7,000 lbs., (or 3 1-2 tons,) as the standard weight of one cord (128 cubic feet) of manure, we find it to contain, according to the foregoing analysis, about the following quantities :—

Water	4,632 lbs.
Insoluble organic matter, (woody fiber, &c.)	1,803 "
Ammonia	55 "
Soluble phosphoric acid	13 "
Insoluble " "	12 "
Potash	47 "
Total of the more valuable parts	127 "

This seems, at first sight, to be an exceedingly small proportion of the more valuable fertilizing ingredients ; yet, if we estimate them at their market price, we shall find that they alone are sufficient to give great value to the manure.

In Judd's "Agricultural Annual" for 1868, (p. 40,) we find the following :—

" From a comparison of the cheapest available sources of the " most valuable ingredients in manures, we give the following as " not far from fair prices by which to estimate fertilizers (it is

" well, in making these estimates, to fall a little below, than to go
" above the real value) :—

" Ammonia, 20 cents per pound.

" Phosphoric acid, (insoluble,) 5 cents per pound.

" Phosphoric acid, (soluble,) 14 cents per pound.

" Potash, 5 cents per pound."

Estimated at these rates, and supposing Dr. Voelcker's analysis
to be of an average sample of manure, the value per cord would
be :—

Ammonia,	55 lbs. at 20c......................	$11 00
Soluble phosphoric acid,	13 " " 14c......................	1 82
Insoluble " "	12 " " 5c......................	60
Potash,	47 " " 5c......................	2 35
		$15 77

Of course the only real dependence to be placed on this calculation is confined to the question of *comparative* value, when considering the relative advantages of different manures.   Still, it
shows, unmistakably, that in all localities where manures are used
at all, that made on the farm is very much too valuable to be kept
under the eaves of a barn, or in a yard that will not protect it from
being washed away by the rain.

It is difficult to believe that these four constituents of average
farm-yard manure are worth so much as the above estimate, especially when we consider that the value of the lime, sulphuric acid,
salt, and soda, of the very large amount of carbonaceous matter,
and all the *mechanical* effect of such manure, (greater than that of
any other,) are amply sufficient to repay all of the labor of handling
and of a long haul.

Yet, is it not, after all, this very remarkable money value which
has so strengthened the opposition of " practice " to " science ?"
The " good old stuff " has always been upheld by farmers as the
great manure,—almost the only one that is worth using.   Those
who first commenced the advocacy of more scientific cultivation
were led away by the glittering promises of chemical analysis
of the soil and the plant, and believed that it would be possible

to do away with the use of the more bulky manures, and to accomplish the ·best results by the use of concentrated chemical compounds.

The truth is now known to lie between these two extreme opinions, and all fertilizers are to be regarded as belonging to the same system. The same ingredients are of the same value in all,—if only their condition is such as to render them equally easy of assimilation,—for the *nutrition* of plants ; the same salts have the same *solvent* action ; the same materials have the same *absorbent* power, as affecting the soluble and volatile elements of plant-food ; and they have the same *mechanical* effect on the soil. All manures, therefore, whether organic or mineral, are to be measured by the same rule, and their value must be estimated according to their ability to perform the various offices of manure.

So measured, farm-yard manure is very much the best, in proportion to its price, of all that we buy in the market. The old practice is justified by theory, and theory is sustained by practice.

Probably Dr. Voelcker's analysis would not exactly apply to any other sample of farm-yard manure that could be produced. Some would be richer and others poorer. The variations result from the kind and quantity of food and litter used; the condition of the animal, and the use that is made of its products and of its labor.

The full-grown horse or ox, standing all day in the stable, neither increasing nor decreasing in size, and fed just enough to supply the natural wastes of the body, produces manure which contains a full equivalent of the nitrogen and earthy matter of its food.

If used on the road, so much of the elements of the food as are contained in the manure dropped away from home is lost. If growing, by the development of bone and muscle, a part of the nitrogen and earthy constituents of the food is kept in the body, and there is so much less in the manure.

The manure of a pregnant animal does not contain those parts of the food that are taken up by the growth of the fetus.

The milch cow turns a portion of her food into milk and voids so much less in the manure.

The fleece of a sheep contains much that would be valuable in the dung-heap.

The manure of poultry is less valuable in proportion to the quantity of the food that is contained in the eggs laid.

In short, every product of the animals of the farm, whether it be labor, meat, bone, milk, eggs, wool, or progeny, takes away from the value of the manure, and in proportion as these are sold away, in just that proportion will the manure of the farm be less valuable.

Probably the least amount of fertilizing matter is removed where only butter is sold;—next in order would be the fattening of full-grown animals.

As the more valuable part of manure consists of unassimilated food, of course its composition must depend directly on the character of the food.

Grain, which is rich in nitrogen and the phosphates, yields manure relatively rich in these substances.

Cotton-seed meal, and oil (linseed) meal, being the residuum after the pressing out of the oil from seeds—none of the nitrogen nor of the phosphates having accompanied the oil—make richer manure than other grains.

Hay makes better manure than straw. These differences will be more precisely shown from the analysis of the different sorts of food, in another chapter.

Of course, it is not to be expected that the farmer will watch the character of his cattle food and the condition of his animals for the purpose of ascertaining, minutely, the quality of his dung-heaps. He should, however, keep a very close watch over the exports and imports of his farm, and be careful that the balance of trade is not against him.

If he sells away 100 lbs. of potash, he should buy back, in grain, or green sand marl, or wood ashes, or stable manure, or in some way, another 100 lbs. to take its place;—and so with all of the more valuable earthy constituents of produce sold. If this is not done, there will follow—now or later—a deterioration of the soil. If it will not pay to replace the lost matter now, of course it will not be done; but when the soil is once so reduced as to need manure to enable it to bring paying crops, this process must be commenced, unless by a resort to clover, fallows, etc., the land can be, for a time, brought back to a state of fertility. In this case, the imperative need of fertilizers will be postponed—not rendered forever unnecessary.

So much for the quantity and value of the manure of the stable, —which will be increased or diminished according to the quantity, and quality of the food consumed,—and the purposes for which animals are kept. The next question is, how to take care of that which we have.

By the force of old usage, we speak of all of the manures of the stable as "yard-manure." The farm-yard, or barn-yard, however, as Dr. Voelcker has told us, and as a very little reasoning will demonstrate, is, under the ordinary circumstances of yards, the worst possible place to keep or to make manure. If the yard be so shaped that no drop of its liquid, even in the heaviest rains, can escape from it, and if the ground be covered a foot deep with swamp-muck, or with a mixture of clay and sand, the loss will be very much modified; will sometimes be reduced to insignificance. Ordinarily, it is any thing but insignificant. In ninety-nine out of every hundred barn-yards in America, the manure is subjected to an evaporation of volatile ammonia, and to a washing away of fertilizing soluble parts that must vastly reduce its value.

When we come to speak of "barn cellar" manure, or "shed manure," we shall have changed our practices for the better.

The best place of all in which to store manure, until it can be carted on to the land, is in a tight cellar immediately under the animals by which it is made, where it will absorb all of their urine, and will be protected from freezing, from the drying effect of winds, and from the action of rains. No labor of handling and forking over is required, save what will be done by the hogs that fatten upon the undigested food, while they mix and compost the mass better than any number of forkings would do it.

Manure kept in this way need never be touched, nor even

looked at, until the time comes to throw it into the wagons to be hauled out. If the floor of the cellar is a tight clay soil, and if there be no escape for the liquid portion of the manure by surface-draining, there will have been no appreciable loss.

When a cellar cannot be made, a shed will be found to be a very good substitute. It should be so tight as to exclude all rain, and its floor so arranged that none of the drainings of the manure can flow away—should be low enough to receive all of the urine of the stable.

To keep manure in this way will require much more labor than to drop it directly into a cellar, and the saturation of the whole mass with the urine will be far less complete and uniform ; but it will entail much less loss—very much less—than is inevitable under entire exposure to the weather, in heaps, or spread in the barn-yard.

Under certain circumstances, the best storage place for the manure of the stable is the field where it is to be used. If the land is so situated, and if the soil contains a fair amount of clay, and is in such condition that the water of heavy rains will wash the soluble parts of the manure, not off from, but into, the ground, the surface of the field is the best place for it. We can in no other way distribute the nutritive parts of the manure among the particles of the soil so thoroughly as by allowing them to be washed in among them by falling rains. The only loss sustained in this practice will be by a very slight evaporation of ammonia—very slight, because the formation of volatile ammonia will almost entirely cease when the manure is so spread as to become too cold for rapid decomposition. The soluble ammoniacal salts, and the soluble earthy parts, will be washed into the soil, of which the clay and decomposed organic matter have a very strong absorption action, and which will hold all fertilizing matter that may coat its particles—very much as the fiber of cloth holds the coloring matter of dye stuffs. To continue the comparison, the coating of the particles of soil is not a "fast color," but is removed by the water of the sap in the roots of plants, and is appropriated to their use.

The recommendation to spread stable manure directly upon the land as soon as it is made, or as soon as it can be hauled out, applies only to such soils as are in a condition to receive and to retain its soluble parts. On steep hill-sides, very leachy sands, and over-wet clays, the practice would often, no doubt, result in loss.

When the ground is locked fast with frost, the manure would run away with the water, that, unable to gain entrance, would flow over the surface in times of heavy rain. In the case of thin sandy soils, there is danger that it will be washed down too deeply to have its best effect. On steeply sloping land, of course, the water of heavy rains would flow off over the surface, and some of the manure would go with it.

To state the case simply, wherever and whenever the water of rains and melting snows can find its way *into* the soil, the best way to use the manure of the stable is to spread it broadcast over the surface—except on very light sandy soils. Where the inclination is too steep,—where, from springs or want of drainage, the water would be kept out of the soil and would flow away over the surface of the ground, such use would, probably, be about the worst.

Where the snow lies so deep as to prevent the freezing of the ground, and where, as it melts in spring, it will all, or nearly all, soak into the soil, it is a good plan to spread the manure upon the snow; but it is a very bad plan to do this, when, from the frozen condition of the ground, or from its rapid inclination, the melting snow would run away over the surface.

The principle upon which the advantage and disadvantage of the practice depends is, that the manure will go with the water in which it is dissolved. If it goes into a soil containing a fair proportion of clay or organic matter, it will be distributed in the best places and in the most complete manner; if it runs away over the surface, it will be lost.

Coarse, unfermented manure should be spread upon the land before plowing, and turned well into the soil, where its decomposition will be more rapid than if harrowed into the dry surface, while its best *mechanical* effect will be more completely and more lastingly exerted.

In the case of thoroughly rotted manure, although there are

good arguments in favor of plowing it in, I am inclined to very strongly recommend that it be spread upon the furrow,—*after* rolling, if the roller is used at all ; if not, after once harrowing,— and then be thoroughly worked into the surface with the cultivator, Shares' harrow, or common harrow. So treated, it will lie where the earliest roots of the crop will feel its effect, and its constituents will be more evenly distributed by rains than if it were more deeply covered.

I have lingered over this branch of my subject, and have given it what may seem to be an undue share of attention ; but the universal applicability and usefulness of manure made by the domestic animals, together with its almost universal production, give greater importance to the methods of its preservation and use than attaches to any other fertilizer.

There remains, still, one question connected with the manure of the farm that is of some consequence. That is, as to the relative value of the excrements of different animals. The broad statement of the case is, that the quality of the manure depends on the food, and not on the animal by which it is consumed ; that is, no matter what animal it may be to which we feed a bushel of corn, if he is of mature age, not increasing in any of his parts, be he horse, ox, sheep, or hog, he will return, in his manure, the full equivalent of the nitrogen and earthy parts of his food. In proportion as parts of his food are taken to make bone, flesh, wool, etc., the manure will be of less value ; but the bones of a horse do not differ materially from those of other animals, nor does his muscle. The difference of fertilizing power must be attributed, *mainly*, to a difference of food. Still, the completeness of digestion varies somewhat, in the various species, and this has an effect on the character of the manure—more, however, on the *rapidity* than on the *amount* of its action.

There is not very much to be said as to the use to be made of the different manures, when well rotted, save with reference to that of the pig-sty, which should never be used, no matter how thoroughly decomposed it may be, for any of the *brassica* tribe, (cabbage, cauliflower, ruta-baga, or any of the smooth-leaved turnips,) as it is quite likely to cause the disease known as "club-foot," or " finger and toe."

POULTRY MANURE.

The droppings of poultry deserve especial consideration, as the richest, most concentrated, and most active of all manures produced on the farm.

This superiority arises from two causes. Fowls live on the most concentrated, the richest food—mainly seeds and insects, and they void their solid and liquid excrement together, or rather, the urine is solid, combined with the evacuations of the bowels, or dung, and the whole is of uniform quality and of great richness. Under the best circumstances, (when dry,) it is often nearly equal to Peruvian guano, which is worth $85 per ton.

It has been stated that on land that is naturally good, but exhausted by cultivation, the excrement of a given number of fowls will produce enough *extra* corn to feed them for a whole year.

As a very large part of the manure of birds is already soluble, it is very much reduced in value by exposure to the rain ; while, if it accumulates in too large quantities,—remaining damp,—its decomposition is very rapid, and very exhausting, inasmuch as it does not, like coarse stable manure, contain a large amount of carbonaceous matter, capable of assuming an absorbent form on its decay. When ammonia is formed by the decomposition of this manure, it is much more free to escape than when formed in a heap of the droppings of the stable.

The best, most simple, and most practicable way to protect poultry manure against loss is to have a floor of loose earth in the roosting-house, under the perches, and to spade in the droppings every few days. This will entirely prevent the escape of the fertilizing gases, as well as of all offensive effluvia, and the whole depth of the spaded earth will become as rich, in time, as the droppings themselves.

The empire of Japan, with an area about equal to that of some of our smaller States, has a population, probably, equal to that of the whole United States. For thousands of years, its small hand-tilled fields, without the importation of a grain of food from any foreign source, have supported its teeming millions in comfort and plenty. Shut off, until within a few years, from commercial intercourse with the nations of the West, this remarkable people have, like the Chinese, maintained themselves in sober and industrious prosperity, while they have achieved a civilization, different from ours, it is true, and to be measured by a different standard, but which has, far more successfully than that of America or of Europe, compassed the comfortable subsistence of all classes of a dense population.

The secret of their ability to accomplish what the agriculture of our more favored race has failed to secure, is to be found in the fact that the rule of their life and of their industry has always been *to allow no element of the fertility of their soil to go to waste.* Prohibited by their religion from eating flesh, milk, butter, or cheese, and with farms so small as to forbid the use of draught animals, almost their only source of manure is found in the vegetable food and the fish which they themselves consume.

Human excrement, which we name only in an undertone, and which, when we consider it at all, we generally hurry into the nearest stream of water, is to them the foundation-stone of subsistence. It is their chief prop in all of their cultivation. Their methods of collecting, preserving, and applying it are any thing but delicate, but they are safe and sure, and without them, or their equivalent, Japan would long ago have gone the way of ancient Rome.

Disregarding the lessons of the past, (and of the present, as shown in the East,) the British Empire is now preserving itself from annihilation only by the commerce which brings bread and manure from all parts of the world to supply the enormous waste that swallows up nearly every atom of the food of its population.

Equally disregarding the same lessons, we, with a newer soil, and a more remote necessity for economy, so long as the crops of our fields bring present money, are heedless of future want for ourselves or for posterity.

In the "American Agricultural Annual" for 1868, there was published an article of mine on "Sewers and Earth Closets, and their Relation to Agriculture," from which article the following is extracted :—

"The average population of New York City—including its "temporary visitors—is, probably, not less than 1,000,000. This "population consumes food equivalent to at least 30,000,000 "bushels of corn in a year. Except the small proportion that is "stored up in the bodies of the growing young, which is fully off-"set by that contained in the bodies of the dead, the constituents "of the food are returned to the air by the lungs and skin, or are "voided as excrement. That which goes to the air was originally "taken from the air by vegetation, and will be so taken again—"here is no waste. The excrement contains all that was furnished "by the mineral elements of the soil on which the food was pro-"duced. This all passes into the sewers, and is washed into the "sea. Its loss, to the present generation, is complete.

" In the present half-developed condition of the world, there is "no help for this. The first duty in all towns is to remove from "the vicinity of habitations all matters which by their decomposi-"tion would tend to produce disease. The question of health is, "of course, of the first importance, and that of economy must fol-"low it ;—but it should follow closely, and perfect civilization "must await its solution.

" Thirty million bushels of corn contain, among other minerals, "nearly seven thousand tons of phosphoric acid, and this amount "is annually lost in the wasted night-soil of New York City.*

* " Other mineral constituents of food—important ones, too—are washed away in even " greater quantities through the same channels ; but this element is the best for illustra-" tion, because its effect in manure is the most striking, even so small a dressing as " twenty pounds per acre producing a marked effect on all cereal crops. Ammonia, too, " which is so important that it is usual in England to estimate the value of manure in " exact proportion to its supply of this element, is largely yielded by human excrement."

12

"Practically, the human excrement of the whole country is
"nearly all so disposed of as to be lost to the soil. The present
"population of the United States is not far from 35,000,000. On
"the basis of the above calculation, their annual food contains
"over 200,000 tons of phosphoric acid, being about the amount
"contained in 900,000 tons of bones, which, at the price of the
"best flour of bone, (for manure,) would be worth over $50,000,000.
"It would be a moderate estimate to say that the other constitu-
"ents of food found in night-soil are of least equal value with the
"other constituents of the bone, and to assume $50,000,000 as
"the money value of the wasted night-soil of the United States.

"In another view, the importance of this waste cannot be es-
"timated in money. Money values apply rather to the products
"of labor and to the exchange of these products. The waste of
"fertilizing matter reaches farther than the destruction or exchange
"of products ;—it lessens the ability to produce.

"If mill-streams were failing year by year, and steam were
"yearly losing force, and the ability of men to labor were yearly
"growing less, the doom of our prosperity would not be more
"plainly written than if the slow but certain impoverishment of
"our soil were sure to continue.

"Fortunately, it will not continue always. So long as there are
"virgin soils this side of the Pacific, which our people can ravage
"at will, thoughtless earth-robbers will move West and till them.
"But the good time is coming, when (as now in China and in
"Japan) men must accept the fact that the soil is not a warehouse
"to be plundered—only a factory to be worked. Then they
"will save their raw material, instead of wasting it, and aided by
"nature's wonderful loom, will weave, over and over again, the
"fabric by which we live and prosper. Men will build up as fast
"as men destroy, old matters will be reproduced in new forms,
"and as the decaying forests feed the growing wood, so will all
"consumed food yield food again.

"The stupendous sewers which have just been completed in
"London, at a cost of $20,000,000, and which challenge admira-
"tion, as monuments of engineering achievement, are a great

" blessing to that filth-accursed town, and in the absence of any
" thing better, they might, with advantage, be imitated elsewhere.
" They have had an excellent effect on the health of the popula-
" tion, by removing a prolific cause of typhoid fever and other
" fatal diseases. As affording needed relief from malaria, they are
" of immense importance. Still, they are a great (although neces-
" sary) evil, inasmuch as they wash into the sea the manurial
" product of 3,000,000 people, to supply whom with food requires
" the importation of immense quantities of grain and manure.

" The wheat-market of one-half the world is regulated by the
" demand in England. She draws food from the Black Sea, and
" from California; she uses most of the guano of the Pacific
" islands; she even ransacks the battle-fields of Europe for human
" bones, from which to make fresh bones for her people; and, in
" spite of all this, her food is scarce and high, and bread-riots
" break out in her towns.

" An earnest effort is now being made to use the matters dis-
" charged through these sewers for the fertilizing of the lands
" toward the eastern coast. For this purpose it is intended to
" build a sewer forty miles long, and nine and a half feet in
" diameter, which, with the incidental expenses of its construction
" and management, will cost about $10,000,000. The Sewage
" Company have a farm at Barking, on which they have ex-
" perimented very successfully, one acre of their irrigated mead-
" ows having produced nine tons of Italian rye grass in twenty-
" two days, and fifty tons during the past season up to August
" 15, with a prospect that the yield for the whole season will be
." at least seventy tons from a single acre.

" The system of sewage irrigation has earnest adherents, and
" equally earnest opposers. It does seem a pity, that for every
" pound of excrement given to the land, three or four hundred
" pounds of water must go with it, and it is probable that such
" highly diluted manure can be used with advantage only on grass
" crops. It is further asserted, that as the best results can be
" obtained only by the application of from 6,000 to 10,000 tons
" of the liquid per acre, the cost of the process must prevent its

"general adoption. However, the scheme is about to be thor-
"oughly tested, and it is to be hoped that its success will be such
"as to secure a return to the soil of a vast amount of valuable
"matter, which, hitherto, has been worse than thrown away.

"The many attempts that have been made to extract the fer-
"tilizing parts of the sewage from the deluge of water with
"which they are diluted, have entirely failed of their object. If,
"as now seems probable, the best and cheapest way to remove
"waste matters from large towns is by dilution in large quantities
"of water, the efforts of agriculturists must be directed to the
"best means of making use of the mixture."

*   *   *   *   *   *   *

"So much for the night-soil of large cities. The health of the
"community demands that it be removed, and the prosperity of
"the country demands that it be not wasted. To fulfill these two
"requirements should be the aim of sanitarians and political
"economists.

"But a comparatively small part of the population of the
"United States live in large cities,—a far larger number live in
"small towns and in the country. For their uses the regularly
"organized systems of sewerage are not available. Yet they
"greatly need some radical improvement in their privy accommo-
"dations. Except in those comparatively rare cases in which
"water-works are introduced into houses, the arrangements for
"this purpose are almost always offensive and wasteful; and not
"unfrequently detrimental to health, and indecent in their character
"and tendency.

"The problem of improvement is an exceedingly difficult one.
"While, by an enlightened control, the inhabitants of cities can
"be compelled to conform to certain requirements, those who
"live in villages and on farms are subject only to a much more
"lax discipline, which stops far short of the minuteness of the
"Mosaic law regulating personal habits. If they adopt improve-
"ments,—especially of the sort under consideration,—it will be
"because they find it for their own pecuniary interest, or very
"decidedly for their convenience to do so. No question of

" national economy will move them, and they have not generally
" been educated to the importance of a strict observance of the
" laws of health,—not always of those of decency."

In continuation of the same subject, I publish herewith an article recently furnished to the *New York Evening Post:*

THE EARTH CLOSET AND ITS POSSIBILITIES.

In the *Journal of the London Society of Arts,* for May 16, 1863, there is published a series of tables which had been submitted by Dr. Tudichum, concerning the commercial value of the constituents of human excrement. The most curious are those relating to the composition of urine. He says: " Taking into " account that there are many thousand persons who come to " London during the day, but sleep without (and are not enumerated " as living within) the metropolitan districts, and deposit their fluid " excretion in town; also many thousands of casual visitors; taking " further into account the rapid increase of London, we are justified, " I think, in assuming that the population of London excretes an " amount of urine and valuable ingredients equal to that of two " million adults or middle-aged males."

Table XIX. gives the amount and value of the fluid voidings of the population of London, which, calculated as 2,000,000 adults, makes per day :—

Urine, 650,000 gallons, or 2,901 tons, 176 gallons.
Ammonia from urea, 36 tons at £60 per ton; value, £2,160.
Ammonia from its salts,
Ammonia from uric acid,
Ammonia from creatinine,   } 2.9 tons.
Ammonia from other nitrogenous matters, } val. £174.
Phosphoric acid, 6.2 tons—£86 16s.
Sulphuric acid, 4 tons—£37 6s.
Chloride of sodium, 26 tons—£122 16s.
Potash, 7.3 tons—£233 12s.
Lime and magnesia, 1,714 lbs.—17s. 10d.
Total urine, 2,901 tons, 176 gallons. And in this:
Total solids, 84 tons, or one ton of solids in 34 5 tons of urine.
Total value, £2,832.

Table XX. computes the annual amount and value of the urine voided in London, making the total amount of urine 1,052,151 tons, and the total solids contained therein, being 1 in 34, 30, 735 tons, worth £34 per ton.

Table XXI. gives the annual value of the fluid voidings of the population of London as follows :—

SUMMARY.

	From urea	£788,400
	" ammoniacal salts	27,930
Ammonia.	" uric acid	9,648
	" creatinine	15,108
	" other nitrogenized matters	12,000
Phosphoric acid		31,805
Sulphuric		13,614
Chloride of sodium		44,972
Potash		86,700
Lime and magnesia		325
Total		£1,030,502

Value of one ton of urine rather less than £1.   Value of annual urine of one adult male rather less than 10 shillings.

By this computation the value of the liquid excrement of the people of the United States would amount to at least $50,000,000 per annum. The value of the solid excrement would be somewhat less than this. Of course, very much of this value would be wasted if the most perfect system that our ingenuity could devise were adopted for every community of sufficient size to come under any sanitary or economic discipline. But the amount which might be saved is of sufficient magnitude to make the subject one of the most important that we can consider.

It may be objected that Dr. Tudichum's standard of value is too high. Some writers place it at a higher figure, others at a lower, and it is extremely difficult, if not impossible, to make an exact estimate ; at the same time, the experience of the world, ever since agricultural operations and opinions began to be recorded, shows that human excrement, and especially human urine, is of the utmost value as a manure.

Its economical application has enabled the most populous

countries of the world to sustain themselves without the aid of importation, and its waste has brought destruction upon the most prosperous empires.   History affords no example of an exception to the rule that the careful use of human excrement as manure insures prosperity, and that its waste entails destruction.

At a recent meeting of the Farmers' Club of the American Institute, a paper on " Earth Closets " was presented by Mr. A. Crandall, in which occurs the following paragraph : " Wasted " excrement," says Liebig, " hastened the decay of Roman agricul- " ture, and there ensued a condition the most calamitous and fright- " ful.   When the cloacæ of the Seven-Hilled City had absorbed " the well-being of the Roman peasant, Italy was put in, and then " Sicily and Sardinia and Africa."   Not one of these countries has regained its lost greatness and prosperity.

Longer ago than twice the age of Rome, China was a pros- perous, industrious, and in many respects a cultivated country. From that day to this, every particle of human excrement has been almost religiously returned to the soil.   Yet, to-day, with about one-third of the world's population living exclusively upon her productions, she has less abject poverty than has any other country in the world except Japan, where the same practices pre- vail.

It is difficult to read history in the short chapter that our own country presents, yet the washing of towns into rivers, and of rivers into the sea, is even here telling an unmistakable tale. That myth, " virgin land of inexhaustible fertility," is traveling yearly westward.   Once it was found in the Mohawk Valley, then on the Genesee Flats, then the Western Reserve of Ohio and the Miami and Sciota bottoms, then the wonderful prairies of Illinois, then the States bordering the Mississippi River on the West ; and now, from the very last of these, comes the cry, which has trav- eled toward them by steady steps from the Mohawk valley, of the disastrous effect of midge and rust and Hessian fly, and dry sea- sons and wet seasons, and the endless list of calamities which we rarely hear of save on lands of waning fertility.

By a better system of agriculture, with the aid of underdraining, subsoil plowing, cattle feeding, and rotation of crops, we are fighting the fiend of exhaustion with much success. We are ransacking the remote corners of our soil's pores for plant food which is no longer yielded spontaneously, and, in many cases, we seem to be regaining the original productiveness. But by-and-by, perhaps a hundred years, and, perhaps, five hundred years hence, we may have exhausted even this hidden fertility of the soil, for there is nothing more certain than that the material which we take from the land and deposit in mid-ocean will never return to the land by any natural process. And until we learn to carefully save and faithfully return to the soil the rejected elements of our food, we shall continue to follow, whether apparently or not, the road which Rome has traveled before us.

It is in consideration of the foregoing facts that we are inclined to attach great importance to the possibilities of the earth closet. So long as the use of human excrement is degradingly offensive, neither American farmers nor American citizens will willingly subject themselves to the annoyance of doing any thing with it, save to get it out of the way by the shortest practicable course. If there are sewers to carry it into rivers, or into the ocean, that is all that our highest civilization asks. If there are no sewers, then kindly holes in the ground serve to remove it from sight. We accustom ourselves to its odors, and give it no further thought until necessity compels us to pay for its surreptitious removal by night. Its money value is nothing; the supply is precarious, and the offensiveness of the removal more than offsets for its value as manure. So long as this state of affairs continues, we cannot expect much attention to be given to the subject.

The earth closet has now been so long in use that its value is fully demonstrated. Wherever a water-closet might be undesirable, there an earth closet will be found an unobjectionable, an economical and, from a sanitary point of view, a safe substitute, requiring less attention than a coal stove. It destroys by oxidation much of the organic matter of the fœces committed to its care,—wasting probably the larger part of its ammonia. But it holds fast to the mineral elements,—those which were originally furnished by the soil,—and the decomposition of the organic matter within the pores of its earth, develops new plant-food hitherto dormant therein.

In concluding these remarks, it need only be stated, in general terms, that whatever process is adopted for the economical saving, and the proper application of night-soil as manure, its use must inevitably be attended with the best results, not only on the individual farms to which it is applied, but as most favorably affecting the agriculture of the whole country; and probably it will be found that the use of dry earth in some form, and by means of whatever appliances may be within the most convenient reach of the farmer, will afford very much the most economical and satisfactory solution of the problem.

MINERAL MANURES.

By reference to remarks in preceding chapters, concerning the composition of plants and their uses in the animal economy, it will be remembered that certain portions of them, which constitute the ash left after the burning of any vegetable matter, are of a mineral character and origin; that is to say, they exist in a state of nature, always and only as constituents of the soil or of the rocks from which the soil is originally formed;—and while they are absolutely necessary to the growth of plants, they can be taken up only by the roots from the soil; for they never exist, except as dust, in the air.

While these mineral or earthy constituents constitute but a very small proportion of the plant, and of the animal which gets the substance of its body from the digestion of plants eaten, they are absolutely indispensable to all organic growth; and their importance in agriculture is by no means to be measured by the extent to which they are used. The amount of potash required in the formation of the integral parts of a blade of wheat, is so small as to escape any but the most careful scrutiny. Yet it is absolutely impossible to produce a blade of wheat without furnishing the necessary supply of this apparently insignificant element. The same is true, in a greater or less degree, of all the mineral parts of plant-food.

The analysis of the ashes of all agricultural plants shows that they contain the following substances :—

Potash,	Soda,	Lime,
Magnesia,	Sulphuric acid,	Phosphoric acid, and
Silicic acid,	Oxide of iron,	Chlorine.

Of these the following are always found in abundant quantity in every even tolerably fertile soil,—probably in every soil that it will pay to attempt to cultivate :—

Soda,	Sulphuric acid,	Chlorine, and usually
Oxide of iron,	Silicic acid,	Magnesia.

These, then, need never be taken into consideration in any case where the only object is the supply of the materials which the plant requires.

With the other elements, however, the case is quite different, and

Phosphoric acid,	Lime, and occasionally
Potash,	Magnesia,

require the utmost care on the part of the farmer, and a constant vigilance to prevent their waste, and to restore always at least so much of them as is taken away by the crops.*

The analysis of any tolerably fertile wheat soil will show that it contains, within a foot of the surface, an amount of phosphoric acid sufficient to supply the needs of probably a hundred times as many bushels of wheat as could be grown upon it in a hundred

---

* Probably the analysis of every cultivatable soil in the world would show the presence of a large proportion of lime ; and the rule which requires the use of lime as manure is by no means a definite one. Whether the lime supplied acts only as a plant-food, or whether its chief benefit depends on its action in developing plant-food already contained in the crude soil, is not absolutely known. Probably, however, the latter proposition is the true one, inasmuch as we find that soils which are formed almost exclusively by the crumbling of limestone rocks are quite as much (and often more) benefited by the application of very small quantities of burned lime, as are those in which analysis shows only a trifling proportion of lime ; therefore the above is to be understood as being such a statement of the case as seems most necessary for practical purposes, although not in all respects scientifically correct.

years without the use of manure. Of this phosphoric acid, how-ever, a very large proportion is contained in the interior of pebbles and coarse particles, or is in such a state of combination as not to be available; for plants can take up by their roots only such matters as are exposed on the surface of the particles of soil, and of these even, only such as are sufficiently soluble to yield to the absorptive influence of the moisture which is contained in and about the feeding surfaces of the roots, and the same is true of every other element of plant-food in the soil. Therefore, neither the actual amount of material in the soil, as shown by analysis, nor even the amount which could be dissolved by a strong acid from the surfaces of the particles, is the exact measure of the amount which that soil may be able to supply to the crop ; and, in the absence of absolute knowledge on the subject, all that can be considered as strictly demonstrated is :—

That the amount of mineral plant-food contained in any soil, in such a position, and in such a condition as to solubility, as to be able to supply the demand of roots, is always limited,—limited, indeed, to such a degree that no soil in the world, which does not receive extraneous supplies by means of inundation or irrigation, can, even through the life-time of a single man, be made to produce maximum crops of any given plant, without the return of some form of manure, either by the feeding of the crop to animals pasturing on the ground, by the death and decomposition of the stems and leaves of the plants, or by the return of animal manure or of some form of mineral manure, which will make up the waste.

Practice has demonstrated, even this early in the history of our country, that in order to cultivate any land, year after year and generation after generation, with success, it is necessary that manures be added to the soil ; and more careful practice and investigation have shown that the most economical return of manure is such as will supply in the cheapest form the leading mineral elements that have been removed by the crops sold ;—or, rather, the leading ones of those which we have stated above to be necessary in artificial application.

In nine cases out of ten, that which is most needed, and whose return produces the best result, is undoubtedly phosphoric acid. Such lands, however, as have been long devoted to the cultivation of tobacco, potatoes, etc., most need additions of potash ; and in almost all cases it will be found advantageous to apply both potash and phosphoric acid. It should be borne in mind that we are now speaking only of the requirement of manure for the actual feeding of plants. The solvent action of certain substances makes it frequently profitable to apply fertilizers whose constituents belong to the list given above of matters which the soil always supplies in sufficient quantity. This subject will be discussed hereafter.

Phosphoric acid being, then, the most important mineral element of foreign as well as of home-made manures, it will be well for us to examine the sources from which it may be most cheaply and most advantageously procured, and the best method for its application to the soil.

The bones of animals consist, when thoroughly dried, of about two-thirds earthy matter and one-third organic or combustible matter. The earthy part is almost entirely phosphate of lime, which is also called bone earth, and this consists of about forty-six per cent. of phosphoric acid and about fifty-four per cent. of lime. Bones, therefore, are the most common and most prolific source of the phosphoric acid used in agriculture ; although it is also a very important element of Peruvian guano, and still more largely of what are called phosphatic guanos, and of the phosphatic deposits recently discovered near Charleston, South Carolina.

The manner in which phosphate of lime is used as a manure affects in very great degree its efficiency, and consequently the economy of the application. To state the case in a single sentence, the finer the particles of the manure the more active and the more valuable it will be. In order to attain the greatest degree of fineness, it is found best to manufacture it into what is called superphosphate of lime ;—that is, a compound containing more phosphoric acid and less lime than the simple phosphate does.

The chemistry of the phosphates of lime has been very clearly set forth by Professor S. W. Johnson in his report on manures, made to the Agricultural Society of Connecticut, and it may be worth while to reproduce here, in a very brief form, the principal features of this portion of the report.

A single atom of phosphate of lime contains one atom of phosphoric acid and three atoms of lime. Any process which will remove from the compound two atoms of the lime, leaving the whole amount of phosphoric acid, will convert it into superphosphate of lime, which is very much more soluble than is the original or basic phosphate; and it is the custom in the manufacture of superphosphate of lime to apply such an amount of sulphuric acid as will remove these two atoms of lime, the result being a compound containing superphosphate of lime and sulphate of lime or gypsum; and when no other matters are added to increase the rapidity of the action of the manure, this is the composition of the pure superphosphate of lime of commerce. It contains very much more lime and sulphuric acid than phosphoric acid, but the latter is in such a state of solubility as will allow it to be carried by rains very readily into the soil, and if applied while plants are actually growing, it may be taken up by them without delay.

Ordinarily, however, when superphosphate of lime is applied to the soil, it immediately hunts out particles containing potash or lime or magnesia or soda, with which its unsatisfied phosphoric acid may again combine; and it is not likely that the true superphosphate ever remains for any considerable length of time as an element of the soil; and the question may readily arise, why is it worth while to resort to such an expensive and troublesome process to reduce the phosphate of lime to the superphosphate, when we are almost certain that within a short time after it is applied to the soil it will have returned again to the condition of the comparatively insoluble phosphate? The reason why this is worth while is to be sought only in the degree of fineness to which the article is reduced by the chemical changes through which it has passed.

Professor O. N. Rood, of the Troy University, at the request

of Professor Johnson, measured under the microscope the size of
the particles of the finest bone-dust, and of the phosphate of lime
which had passed through the process described above. He found
that the smallest particles of bone-dust would not average less
than one one-hundredth of an inch in diameter, while the particles
of the prepared phosphate measured only one twenty-three-thou-
sandth of an inch in diameter. If, as is probably the case, the
degree of solubility of both is the same, the amount of surface
which the finer article exposes to the solvent action of water is
so infinitely greater than that of the former, that the total amount
which may be dissolved by the action of a given amount of water
in a given time must be almost inestimably greater; and we
find in practice that the finest phosphate of lime that it is possible to produce by the burning of bone, is very much less rapid
in its action than is that which results from the chemical processes
in use in the manufacture of commercial superphosphate.

Probably it makes but little difference what sort of phosphate
of lime is used in the manufacture of a superphosphate,—whether
the original substance be the earthy matter of bones, the phosphatic deposits of South Carolina, or what is known as Colum-
bian guano; for, probably, the chemical action in the use of each
will be the same, and the same quality of superphosphate, and of
the phosphate which is formed on the application of this to the
soil, will result.

Many directions are given for the manufacture of superphos-
phates on the farm by the decomposition and preparation of bones.
The best of these is, perhaps, the following, which is given by
Dr. James R. Nichols, in his " Chemistry of the Farm and the
Sea ":—

" Take a common sound molasses cask ; divide in the middle
" with a saw ; into one-half of this place half a barrel of *finely-*
" ground bone, and moisten it with two buckets of water, using
" a hoe in mixing. Have ready a carboy of vitriol, and a stone
" pitcher holding one gallon. Turn out this full of the acid, and
" gradually add it to the bone, constantly stirring. As soon as
" effervescence subsides, fill it (the pitcher) again with acid, and

"add as before ; allow it to remain over night, and in the morning
:" repeat the operation, adding two more gallons of acid. When
" the mass is quiet, add about two gallons more of water, and
" then gradually mix the remaining half-barrel of bone, and allow
" it to rest. The next day it may be spread upon a floor, where
" it will dry speedily if the weather is warm ; a barrel of good
" loam may be mixed with it in drying. It may be beaten fine
" with a mallet or ground in a plaster mill. If several casks are
" used, two men can prepare a ton of excellent superphosphate
" after this method in a day's time. * * * * * Much less
"acid is used in this formula than is demanded to accomplish the
" perfect decomposition of the bones ; but it is important to guard
" against the possibility of any free sulphuric acid in the mass."

Dr. Nichols also gives the following recipe for preparing bones
for use without reducing them to the condition of a superphosphate ; and bones applied to the soil, with the addition of the
other materials of the compound, cannot fail to constitute an
excellent manure :—

" Take 100 pounds of bones beaten into as small fragments
" as possible; pack them in a tight cask or box with 100 pounds
" of good wood-ashes. Mix with the ashes before packing 25
" pounds of slaked lime, and 12 pounds of sal soda, powdered
" fine. It will require about 20 gallons of water to saturate the
" mass, and more may be added from time to time to maintain
" moisture. In two or three weeks the bones will be broken
" down completely, and the whole may be turned out upon a
" floor and mixed with two bushels of dry peat or good soil, and
" after drying, it is fit for use."

Whether it will pay the farmer to manufacture superphosphate
of lime, or to reduce coarse bones according to the process described above, must depend upon the amount of labor at his command and upon the extent to which he can profitably apply his
labor to other farm work during the winter season. Probably, if
he has muck which he might be hauling to his barn, or any other
profitable work for his hands, it will be better to purchase such
superphosphate as he may require in the general market ;—for the

material required in this domestic manufacture will be somewhat
expensive, and the process more or less troublesome ; while there
is no doubt that, except in the most remote regions, good superphosphate may be procured at a cost, delivered on the farm, that
will be amply justified by the result of its application to the crops.
In purchasing, however, a farmer runs a considerable risk of
being swindled ; for nothing is easier than to add to any commercial fertilizer such an amount of sand, sifted ashes, or other
worthless material, as will very much reduce its value. Still,
even the most unscrupulous dealer in fertilizers will probably
have the wit to supply a genuine article to any customer whom
it seems unsafe to cheat ; and if the farmer will purchase directly
from the manufacturer, and with the stipulation that every package of the fertilizer shall analyze up to a given standard, the
chances are that the adulterated article will be reserved for
shipment to some other person ; and I am confident at the same
time that there are manufacturers who conduct their business on
strictly honest principles, and who will always send a genuine
article.

The superphosphates of lime which are sold in the American
market, contain, generally, a considerable proportion of ammonia,
which adds to their value for use in connection with the stable
manure of the farm ; but probably, where there is an *abundant*
supply of stable manure, it would be cheapest to invest the whole
amount of purchase-money in the mineral matters, as it is these
which it is, beyond all question, the most important to procure
from external sources.

Concerning the method of application of superphosphate of
lime, two opinions prevail. One is, that it is better to spread it,
if possible, with the use of a broadcast sower evenly over the
whole surface of the land, so that no part of the soil may fail
to receive a certain amount. And the other is, that it is preferable to compost it with stable manure, which, undoubtedly,
adds to its efficiency, but is subject to the objection that as stable
manure is always more or less lumpy, and is necessarily spread by
hand. its distribution when applied in the field is less uniform than

it is desirable that it should be. In either case the manure should be spread broadcast over the whole. surface, and not applied directly to the hill or furrow, for the reason that phosphoric acid is most necessary in the development of the *seed* of the plant, and generally during the latter stages of its growth, at a time when the roots are supposed to occupy every part of the soil, and when many of them, at least, would have passed beyond the narrow limits of the hill or furrow.

The application of phosphoric acid is not most profitable when made most strictly in accordance with the generally accepted scientific theories concerning its use by plants; for it is shown by long experience that it is not so active a manure for wheat as ammonia is, although wheat contains, in the ashes of its seed, about 50 per cent. of phosphoric acid ; and that it is a most valuable stimulant for turnips, although the ashes of these contain only about 7 per cent. Possibly the reason for this apparent discrepancy between theory and practice is to be found in the fact that during the early stages of growth, when the plant is acquiring its ability to make use of the materials already contained in the soil, the phosphoric acid is more necessary to the turnip than to the wheat ; whereas, the wheat, by the time it requires a considerable proportion of phosphoric acid, is in a condition to take up an amount which could not be made use of by the young turnip plant.

We often hear farmers make a distinction between manures which act quickly, and those which are lasting ; and in ordinary practice, the preference is almost invariably given to the "lasting" manure. This idea is not founded, in my opinion, upon reason ; for it may be stated, as a general principle, that manures are lasting only in proportion as they are "lazy." For example : Twenty dollars' worth of whole bones, spread upon an acre of land, would not produce a very marked effect upon the crop immediately following the application ; while twenty dollars' worth of fine bone-dust would probably produce an excellent, and an equal value of a good superphosphate—a capital result. On the other hand, the effect of the whole bones would be perceptible on

13

the crops of a life-time; that of the fine bones would probably disappear or grow greatly less after five or ten years ; and that of the superphosphate would probably not be very marked after two or three years. It is the old story of "the nimble sixpence and the slow shilling." In either case the material applied to the soil produces a given amount of effect on vegetation ; that in the superphosphate being developed within two or three years, results in a few large crops which are immediately available, and the extra money which they produce may be in part applied to the renewal of the manure ; the whole bones, on the other hand, produce the same amount of growth, only during a long series of years, while the interest on their cost, and the interest on the value and on the cost of cultivating the land, are constantly running on. The chance for profit is very much greater in the case in which large immediate returns give through the current year a greater amount of increase or profit above the necessary expenses and loss of interest.

Farmers also speak of superphosphate of lime, Peruvian guano, and other intense manures as being exhausting ; and there is no doubt that in the experience of many districts, as, for instance, those parts of Maryland where, during a few years, the yield of wheat was raised to a very high figure by the use of Peruvian guano, and where it was found that, after these few years, guano failed to produce a beneficial result, they have a good apparent reason for their opinion. Any manures which do not supply all that the plant requires, or all at least of such elements as the soil can furnish in only a limited degree, are *exhausting* manures. For instance, there may be in the soil a certain amount of phosphoric acid available for the uses of plants, and in the ordinary course of growth without manure a sufficient addition to this supply may be made available by natural chemical processes to constantly furnish fair average crops, that is, to furnish the phosphoric acid required by such crops as grow in the natural condition of the land, of which the capacity may be kept at a low point owing to a deficiency of potash, for instance.

Now, if we apply any manure (such as wood ashes) which supplies potash in considerable quantity, the result will be the production of as large a crop as, in view of the composition and circumstances of the soil, it is possible for potash to produce, and the crops may be doubled or quadrupled, as the result of the application of the potash alone. But they, at the same time, remove from the soil double or quadruple the quantity of phosphoric acid that was required by the smaller crop; and the result is, that while the manure has by no means had the effect of exhausting the soil, but has rather added to its valuable ingredients, the crops produced in consequence of the use of that manure have exhausted the soil of some ingredient which the manure did *not* supply, namely, phosphoric acid.

In the case cited above—that of the production of large crops of wheat by the aid of Peruvian guano in Maryland—it is probable that the ammonia of the guano increased so largely the production of wheat, that the soil was robbed, in the course of a few years, of elements which the guano did not supply in sufficient quantity; and, these elements being once removed, no amount of any *other* constituent would suffice for the growth of plants to which *they* are absolutely requisite.

Therefore, in the use of either superphosphate of lime, or of bones or bone-dust, the principal available ingredient supplied being phosphoric acid (and perhaps ammonia), the soil may, as a consequence of the greater production, be robbed of potash, or some other element, to such an extent as to be permanently injured. It is wrong, however, in this case to blame the manure for the result. We should rather blame ourselves for having pursued such a system of cultivation as has taken away elements of the soil's fertility, trusting to some *other* element to supply its place.

To use a homely illustration of our meaning, we will take the case of a merchant tailor who receives a large accession to his stock in the form of woolen cloth, and has not the means of increasing, materially, the quantity of his other supplies. If stimulated by this addition to his stock, he takes an army contract for overcoats, and employs a sufficient number of hands, under contract for the season, to make them, the result will probably be that he will run out of buttons and grogram, and be obliged to throw up his contract, and to expend the last dollar of his substance in compounding with his hands, with whom he is not able to keep his engagements. It would be as just to blame the cloth for ruining the tailor as it is to blame Peruvian guano for exhausting the land. It is very well to have a large amount of the purely stimulating elements of manure, but, unless the farmer keeps a sharp eye to the "buttons and grogram," he will wish that he had never seen any thing but the "good old stuff" of the barnyard, and had been content with the ordinary retail trade on which he was making a comfortable living.

But, on the other hand, it is as easy for him to procure what is necessary to keep up the balance of his stock in trade as it would be for the tailor; and he would make a grave mistake, if, by reason of any bugbear of exhaustion, he neglected to use every available fertilizer which, by any means, might add to the bulk and value of his productions.

Concerning the importance of phosphoric acid, so much has been said, incidentally, in treating of the use of night-soil and stable manure, that it is not worth while to give more space to its consideration here.

It is a capital manure in whatever form it may offer itself; and it is, furthermore, the manure of which all grain and meat producing farms stand in the greatest need. Its importance to the agriculture of the country may be safely assumed to exceed that of all the other elements of imported or of home-made fertilizers— that is, if we take into consideration, not the results of a few years, but the prosperity of the country for generations.

Potash.—Second in importance among the earthy ingredients of plants stands the article which is familiar to every one as "potash." This is known to us all as the chief constituent of the lye which results from the leaching of wood ashes; and, even as we find it to a greater or less extent in the ashes of all wood burned for fuel, so in the laboratory the chemist finds it as a more or less important constituent of every crop grown on the farm. Its proportion as an element of the ashes of plants is by no means slight, as will be shown by the following table giving the amount of potash removed from the soil by various crops :—*

10 bushels of wheat	3 lbs.
1,200 lbs. of wheat straw	9 "
10 bushels of rye	2½ "
1,600 lbs. of rye straw	11 "
10 bushels of corn	2¾ "
1 ton of corn stalks	8 "
10 bushels of oats	1¾ "
1,700 lbs. of oat straw	12 "
10 bushels of beans	5¼ "
1,100 lbs. of bean straw	36 "
1 ton of turnips	7 "
700 lbs. of turnip tops	5 "
1 ton of potatoes	28 "
1 ton of red clover	31 "
1 ton of meadow hay	18 "
1 ton of cabbage	5 "

Assuming the production of a farm to be 500 bushels of wheat, 100 bushels of rye, 10 tons of turnips, 40 bushels of potatoes, 10 tons of clover hay, and 20 tons of meadow hay, and assuming the production of the grain to require the proportion of straw stated above, the amount of potash taken from the soil in a single year would be about 2,500 lbs., being the amount contained in over 1,000 bushels of unleached oak wood ashes, and worth, according to Professor Johnson's estimate, about $100.

This is not an unusually large estimate for the production of any good farm ; and the amount of potash removed is more than the amount returned in the form of purchased manure in any twenty years to an average farm in New England.

The sources from which potash may be most advantageously obtained by the farmer are wood ashes—leached or unleached—green sand marl, sea-weed, and swamp muck.

The most universally accessible source, in any new country like this, is, of course, wood ashes. And such as have not been

* Small fractions are disregarded, as it is only desired in this connection to show general results.

·leached are very much the most valuable, especially so far as their amount of potash is concerned, as the leaching has for its object only the removal of this ingredient.   At the same time, the value of hard-wood ashes for the production of potash is often too high to allow of their use as a manure ; and the chief supply of farmers within easy carriage of leaching establishments, is in the application of leached ashes, which still contain a considerable amount of potash that the imperfect leaching has not withdrawn from them, owing to a low degree of solubility, but that is perfectly available to the roots of plants.   The value of leached ashes (along the New England coast usually about 28 cents per bushel) is fixed solely by an agricultural demand, and may be taken as a fair price for the article as a manure ; although, of course, its entire value is not represented by its content of potash, as it yields, also, an appreciable amount of phosphoric acid, and possibly some readily available silicic acid.

In regions where lime is burned with wood fuel, the ashes (unleached) are sold as a manure, but the large amount of lime that becomes mixed with them considerably lessens their value as a fertilizer, while its uncertain proportion makes it difficult to determine what their actual value is.   Ordinarily, within reach of the limekilns of Maine, they are estimated to be worth about the same as leached ashes ; but there is always room for guessing in making the purchase—they may be worth sometimes more and sometimes less.

The green sand marl of New Jersey, which has been developed within the past twenty or thirty years, has had the effect of regenerating a very large tract of the South Jersey country which was considered almost valueless for agricultural purposes, and of doing much toward raising the entire State to the very first rank as an agricultural region—for, probably, there is no district in the country which, in proportion to the selling value of the land, and to the population employed in agriculture, yields, year by year, so large an amount of money as does that which lies within easy hauling distance of the marl-pits stretching from the Atlantic Ocean to the Delaware River ; and there is reason to believe that the barren lands which comprise almost the whole of New Jersey south of a line drawn from New York to Philadelphia may be profitably brought, by the use of marl, to a state of the highest fertility,—to a condition in which they will even rival the prairie lands of the West. The soil is light and easily worked, but is of so poor a character that the whole country is covered with a stunted vegetation, and is known as the "Barrens." Much attention has been drawn to this region by the profuse advertising of the Vineland tract, and by the efforts which are being made to draw population to other settlements between Vineland and Sandy Hook.

In the autumn of 1867, I visited the farm of the New Jersey Agricultural College at New Brunswick, and Professor Cook, the State geologist, and President of the Agricultural College, showed me a tract of heavy clay land upon which he had experimented with the use of marl. Three pieces of land, in all respects the same, and each measuring one quarter of an acre, were set apart for the experiment. The first received a dressing of 100 pounds of the best flour of bone; the second received nothing; and the third an application of green sand marl, costing, delivered on the ground, the same amount as the 100 pounds of bone dust. There were no means for accurately weighing the crop, but by a careful estimate, the result was as follows: The tract manured with bone dust produced at the rate of 54 cocks of hay to the acre; that which received no manure produced at the rate of 36 cocks; and that which was manured with green sand marl produced at the rate of 85 cocks. The following table of analysis will show the composition of green sand marl:—*

Protoxide of iron	15·5
Alumina	6·9
Lime	5·3
Magnesia	1·6
Potash	4·8
Soluble silica	32·4
Insoluble silica and sand	19·8

* Elements of Agriculture. G. E. Waring, Jr. Page 240.

This is an average of three analyses copied from Professor George H. Cook's report of the geology of New Jersey. According to this estimate, one ton (2,000 lbs.) of green sand marl contains—

Lime..	106 lbs.
Magnesia	32 "
Potash..	96 "
Soluble silicic acid................................	648 "
Sulphuric acid	12 "
Phosphoric acid...................................	26 "

(Equal to phosphate of lime, 56½ lbs.)

It will be seen by this analysis that the amount of phosphoric acid contained is sufficient to add very much to the effect of the marl, but its content of potash is so great as to account for its chief value, and all regions which are within reach of the marl-beds, even by the aid of a cheap water carriage, may be greatly benefited by the use of the material, which is found in comparatively inexhaustible supply. It is to be recommended, however, that its first introduction be only in an experimental way, as it is not equally efficient on all soils. As a source of potash anywhere along the Atlantic coast, it will probably be found an economical fertilizer. In the fall of 1867, I purchased a cargo of about 140 tons of marl, which cost, delivered on the wharf at Newport, $3.60 a ton; and used it in various ways in my market-garden and at Ogden Farm.

In the garden its effect was, in every case, very decided, especially on one tract of three-quarters of an acre of Jersey Wakefield cabbage. The land was manured very heavily, of course, with stable manure, but no more so than is customary in garden cultivation—no more heavily than my cabbage fields had previously been manured. After the plants had been set out, a single handful of a compost of equal parts of green sand marl and clear horse manure was put on the surface about the plants, and I attribute chiefly to the influence of the marl thus applied the fact that the crop thus produced was the finest that had ever been seen in the neighborhood, and better than any I have ever seen anywhere else.

At Ogden Farm, however, where most of the marl was used, I have thus far in no instance seen any decided benefit resulting. But this fact should by no means condemn the marl, for the reason that the land, not then having even been drained, was so excessively wet during the entire season that no manure could have fair play.

The only noticeable advantage resulting from its use was to be found in the spontaneous growth of a very thick mat of white clover in an old meadow. Whether the draining of the farm which is now completed will have the effect of demonstrating the value of the marl remains to be seen. It is my opinion that it will, since not even fish guano and other active manures were able during this wet season to produce a marked result on any part of the farm.

It is hardly fair to confine our account of *sea-weed* to the simple consideration of the potash which it furnishes, since its most valuable constituent is probably nitrogen—producing ammonia, and it contains other earthy elements in perceptible quantity. But its chief value as a *permanent* fertilizer is no doubt due to the potash which results from its decomposition.

The use of sea-weed, however, is confined to such limited localities, and is so thoroughly well understood by all farmers residing near the sea-coast, that it is hardly worth while in a practical treatise of this sort to devote much space to its consideration. Certainly nothing that we could say could possibly increase the enthusiastic devotion to its "getting" which actuates all sea-board farmers.

I once asked a neighbor, who is remarkably "well-to-do" in the world, how he could make up his mind to get up at 3 o'clock on cold winter mornings, and go with his team to a beach, four miles distant, to haul home sea-weed ; and to find his chief winter amusement, even in the coldest weather, in working in the surf, remarking that it did not seem to me that, to a man situated as he was, the sea-weed was worth the trouble. His reply was as follows : " There's more than sea-weed in it—the devil's in it,— " and I don't know how it is, but I had rather sit up all night to " get sea-weed than to go out early in the morning duck-shooting." Indeed, in many sea-board neighborhoods feuds and lawsuits, generations old, are based solely on contests and jealousies concerning " sea-weed rights ;" and the fertility of the grass lands to which sea-weed is habitually applied is sufficiently great to establish its value.

Swamp muck being, so far as its organic matter is concerned, entirely the result of the decomposition of vegetable matter, its ashes, of course, are rich in various earthy ingredients of vegetation. Professor S. W. Johnson publishes a table, giving the average of the analyses of 26 specimens of muck or peat, and in the ashes of these there is an average amount of potash equal to $\frac{89}{100}$ of one per cent. And when we consider the average amount of ash, including the earthy deposits which are added to peat in its formation, and the very large quantities that are used on farms on which it is used at all, we see that the total amount of potash to be derived from this source is by no means insignificant, and that it constitutes an important element of the value of muck as a manure.

Lime.—This material, although forming an important part of the ashes of plants, is to be more properly considered, in its application as a manure, under the head of " mechanical manures," and will, accordingly, be treated hereafter.

SPECIAL FERTILIZERS.

It would be hardly prudent in any work of the character of this to describe the various special fertilizers, under their different names and according to the reputation of their manufacturers. There are many different brands of phosphate of lime, all of which, if made strictly according to the recipe by which they profess to be compounded, should be valuable manures. But the farmer in purchasing them should be guided by other considerations than those of *general* value. The probity of the manufacturer, and the care with which his subordinates carry out his instructions, have so much to do with the value of the product of any establishment, that purchases from each should be made according to more information than it would be safe or proper to give in this book.

Peruvian guano, when purchased from the regular agents of the Peruvian government, or from any thoroughly honest dealer, may be depended on as an extremely valuable manure for certain purposes, but it must always be used with great judgment and discretion. Its valuable constituents are so perfectly prepared for the uses of vegetation, that even so small a dressing as 100 pounds per acre, evenly spread over the land, produces such a marked effect on early vegetation as to give nearly all crops a start so rapid that they are enabled to take up with great vigor from the soil itself such plant-nutriment as it may be able to offer. Probably, even in addition to its influence as an easily assimilated food, it acts as a solvent of certain elements of the soil, and makes them much more readily available. The result is, in many cases, that a soil, which, in its natural condition, would furnish the mineral food for only a small crop, will, with this slight assistance, furnish the mineral matter required for a very much larger crop, the mineral matter taken up being many times greater than that contained in the guano. Herein lies, probably, the only secret of what is called the "exhausting" influence of Peruvian guano, for up to this point (the raising of the crop) no injury has been done. The final result of the cultivation must depend on the judgment and care of the farmer. If, elated by the excessive production or tempted by an exceptionally high price of the crop in market, he sells off from his farm all that has been produced by the aid of the guano, the land must inevitably suffer in consequence; but if the crop be consumed on the farm, or in any manner so made use of that its mineral ingredients are returned to the soil on which it grew, it will be found that the effect of the guano has been permanently beneficial.

In improving waste land with the aid of a stock of cattle to consume the crops raised, there is no other agent so valuable as Peruvian guano; for the cultivation of hired land, or land which has been bought at a low rate for a specific purpose, the crops being sold away, nothing is more injurious.

This manure is as powerful and almost as dangerous as gunpowder. It may be made to produce the best permanent results, and to add more than almost any thing else can to the prosperity of the farmer. But unless managed with care and prudence he might almost as well blow up his whole concern, for certain impoverishment of the land, and probably of the farmer too, will result from such a system of robbery as Peruvian guano makes possible and strongly tempts us to.

Fish guano is subject to all of the recommendations, and to all of the strictures which have been applied in the case of Peruvian guano. It is the refuse of fish-oil works, which have been established within a few years, along our eastern coast, where the menhaden, or moss-bunker, is subjected to hydraulic pressure for the extraction of its oil. The refuse, which is ground more or less fine, is sold for manure, and, containing all of the bones and all of the nitrogenous elements of the fish, has a very highly stimulating effect, and is, undoubtedly, a capital fertilizer when used with discretion. Several manufacturers of superphosphate of lime add fish guano to their products in order to give them a more rapid action. It is a question, however, whether they do not get so high a price for the guano added as to make their fertilizers too expensive for use. Unfortunately, also, there are no means by which they may be restrained from adding sand, ashes, and other worthless material to the mass, and so swindle their purchasers to an unlimited extent. Such fertilizers should be purchased only by careful chemical analysis, their price being regulated according to the value of their useful constituents.

SOLVENT MANURES.

It is hardly possible—indeed, it is quite impossible—to separate into a class by themselves those manures whose action is due to their power of rendering the earthy ingredients of the soil more soluble, or in any way more available to the roots of plants ; for it happens in almost every instance that the solvent effect is produced by the action of materials which also come under the head of *nutrient* manures.

If there is any single fertilizer which is a solvent, and only a solvent, it is common salt. This contains, it is true, only elements (chlorine and sodium) which are found in the ashes of nearly all cultivated plants, and which are more or less important to their growth ; but the amount of either of these that is absolutely requisite to the perfection of the growth of any crop is so slight, and the quantity of each that is to be found in every cultivated soil is so great, that it would be fair to assume that crops can always obtain from the natural source all of either chlorine or sodium that they require. The marked action which generally follows the use of small dressings of salt—say from 5 to 8 bushels per acre—and the exceptional action in those cases where it seems to be almost as active as Peruvian guano itself, indicate that it exerts an influence on vegetation which can by no means be ascribed to its supply of food directly to the plant. The manner in which it is supposed to act as a dissolving agent is very well described in the following quotation from Liebig's last work :—*

" When the exhaustion of a field is not caused by the absolute " deficiency of food elements, when even a more than adequate " supply of all the needful nutriment is there, but not in the pro- " per form, and where consequently fallowing will again render " the crop remunerative, the farmer has means at his disposal to " assist the action of the natural agencies, whereby the conversion " of the food into the state of physical combination is effected, " and thus to shorten the fallowing season, or even, in many in- " stances, to make it altogether superfluous.

" We have seen that the diffusion of earthy phosphates through " the soil is effected exclusively by water, which, if containing a " certain amount of carbonic acid, dissolves these earthy salts.

* The Natural Laws of Husbandry. J. Von Liebig, Munich, March, 1863.

" Now there are certain salts, such as chloride of sodium, (com-
" mon salt,) nitrate of soda, and salts of ammonia, which experi-
" ence has proved to exercise, under certain conditions, a favorable
" action upon the productiveness of a field.

" These salts, even in their most dilute solutions, possess, like
" carbonic acid, the remarkable power of dissolving phosphate of
" lime and phosphate of magnesia ; and when such solutions are
" filtered through arable soil, they behave just like the solution of
" these phosphates in carbonic acid water.   The earth extracts
" from these salt solutions the dissolved earthy phosphates, and
" combines with the latter.

" Upon arable soil mixed with earthy phosphates in excess,
" these salt solutions act in the same way as upon earthy phos-
" phates in the unmixed state, that is, they dissolve a certain pro-
" portion of the phosphates.

" Nitrate of soda, and chloride of sodium suffer, by the action
" of arable soil, a similar decomposition to that of the salts of
" potash.   Soda is absorbed by the soil, and in its stead lime or
" magnesia enters into solution in combination with the acid.

" If we compare the action of arable soil upon salts of potash
" and salts of soda, we find that the soil has far less attraction for
" soda than for potash ; so that the same volume of earth which
" will suffice to remove all the potash from a solution will, in a
" solution of chloride of sodium or nitrate of soda of the same
" alkaline strength, leave undecomposed three-fourths of the dis-
" solved chloride of sodium, and half of the nitrate of soda.

" If, therefore, a field exhausted by culture, which contains
" earthy phosphate scattered here and there, is manured with
" nitrate of soda or chloride of sodium, and by the action of rain
" a dilute solution of these salts is formed, a portion of them will
" remain undecomposed in the ground, and must in the moist
" soil exert an influence, weak in itself, but sure to tell in the
" long run.

" Like carbonic acid generated by the putrefaction of vegetable
" and animal substances, and dissolving in water, these salt
" solutions become charged with earthy phosphates in all places

" where these occur. Now when these phosphates diffused
" through the fluid come into contact with particles of the arable
" soil not already saturated with them, they are thereby withdrawn
" from the solution, and the nitrate of soda or chloride of sodium
" remaining in solution again acquires the power of repeatedly ex-
" erting the same dissolving and diffusing action upon phosphates
" which are not already fixed in the soil by physical attraction,
" until these salts are finally carried down by rain-water to the
" deeper layers of the soil, or are totally decomposed."

*   *   *   *   *   *   *

" Of nitric acid, it is generally assumed that it may, like am-
" monia, serve to sustain the body of the plant. Thus, chloride
" of sodium and the nitrates act in two distinct ways, one direct,
" by serving as food for the plant ; one indirect, by rendering the
" phosphates available for the purposes of nutrition.

" The salts of ammonia act upon earthy phosphates in the same
" way as the salts just mentioned, but with this distinction, that
" their power of dissolving phosphate is far greater ; a solution of
" sulphate of ammonia will dissolve twice as much bone-earth as
" a solution of an equal quantity of chloride of sodium.

" However, as regards the phosphates in the soil, the action of
" the salts of ammonia can hardly be more powerful than that of
" chloride of sodium or nitrate of soda, since the salts of ammonia
" are decomposed by the soil much more speedily, and often even
" immediately ; so that, as a general rule, no solution of such a
" salt can be said to be actually moving about in the soil. But as
" a certain volume of earth, however small, is required to decom-
" pose a given quantity of salts of ammonia, the action of those
" salts upon this small volume of earth must be all the more
" powerful. While, then, the action of salts of ammonia is barely
" perceptible in the somewhat deeper layers of the arable surface
" soil, that which they exercise on the uppermost layers is so
" much the stronger. Feichtinger observed that solutions of salts
" of ammonia decompose many silicates, even feldspar, and take up
" potash from the latter. Thus, by their contact with the arable
" soil, they not only enrich it with ammonia, but they effect, even

" in its minutest particles, a thorough transposition of the nutritive
" substances required by plants."

The above quotation describes the action of all those elements
of manure which come under the head of solvents, and precludes
the necessity of a further discussion of the subject by my less
skillful pen.

ABSORBENT MANURES.

There are no manures applied to the soil which probably depend
entirely for their beneficial action upon their ability to absorb
fertilizing gases from the atmosphere, or fertilizing solutions from
other sources ; and it need only be stated, in general terms, that
clay and decomposed organic matter, and, less conspicuously,
charcoal dust and plaster, in addition to their other modes of action,
have, to a considerable extent this accessory power ; and, whether in
compost with animal manures or as direct applications to the surface of the soil, they are worthy of the farmer's careful attention
and preservation.   In this respect it will be enough to follow the
recognized rule, that, in agriculture, every thing which can in any
way add to the fertility of the land should be secured, from whatever source, and nothing whatever should be allowed to go to
waste.

MECHANICAL MANURES.

Interlacing, also, in almost every part, with the feeding and
solvent action of special fertilizers, and of the results of the decomposition of organic manures, we find another effect which can
hardly in any single instance be set down as the sole source of the
benefit of any manurial application, and which is known as *mechanical*.   Probably the effect of the application of sea-sand, especially such as by exposure to rain has been washed clean of its small
amount of salt, is to be ascribed pretty nearly, if not altogether,
to its purely mechanical effect in loosening the rigidity of clays,
and in rendering heavy soils lighter, and it may, perhaps, be set
down as a simply mechanical manure.

But there is scarcely any thing which we apply to the land that does not owe very much of its fertilizing influence to its mechanical action. For instance, stable manure, when plowed into the soil, by its decomposition elevates its temperature, by its fibrous texture separates its particles, and by the power of its organic matter to absorb moisture prevents very light soils from becoming too dry, while, from its loosening action, it hastens the drying of heavy wet lands. Nearly all manures, also, of which the constituents have a chemical action on the particles of the soil have the effect of breaking down the coarser clods or larger particles, and lessening or increasing their adhesion, and of roughening their particles, giving them greater ability to absorb moisture and greater ability to transmit excessive moisture to or through the sub-soil below.

It would require more space and consideration than is consistent with the plan of this book to enter very largely into the discussion of this branch of the subject. But any farmer who will give himself the trouble to consider the different points enumerated above, and to watch the effect on the mechanical condition of the soil of almost every manure that he applies, will see that this mechanical action constitutes no mean part of the influence that manures exert on vegetation.

Lime, however, an element which exists in almost all soils in considerable quantity, almost invariably in sufficient quantity to supply the lime required for the simple formation of the ashy part of plants, is found to be in many districts the most powerful agent for the amelioration of the condition of the soil, and for the permanent increase of its fertility. It is a singular fact that precisely such soils as are formed by the decomposition of limestone rocks, and which, as a necessary consequence, contain a very large percentage of lime, are the very ones which are most benefited by the application of caustic or slacked lime. In these cases it is undoubtedly true that the action of the lime as a solvent and as a mechanical manure must account for its beneficial effect.

From an article entitled, " Lime on Hill Pastures," contributed by Prof. Johnson to the first number of *Hearth and Home*, I quote

14

the following, which sets forth more clearly than any thing that I have hitherto met, one of the chief reasons why lime often produces an action that justifies the high estimation in which practical farmers hold its application on heavy clays or wet hill lands :—

"I well remember the former condition of your hill-side "at Edgewood, which, as you mention, has been restored from "great poverty, and mainly by lime alone. The present beauty "of that slope is but another evidence of the truth of an asser- "tion that has passed into a maxim in agriculture, namely : ' Lime "has reclaimed more waste land than all other applications put "together.'

"The pasture, which once, no doubt, was comparatively pro- "ductive, probably came to be mossy and worthless by a slow "change in its chemical constitution, analogous to what occurs "in the formation of hardpan in ochrous soils, in the setting of "hydraulic cement, and, generally, in the process of rock making "that has gone on in all ages, and still proceeds, whereby sand "and gravels are changed to freestone, and conglomerate clays are "indurated into slates, and shell-mud is cemented into limestone."

*　　*　　*　　*　　*　　*　　*

"If I rightly remember, the slope has some springs upon it, "and a drain or two has been made to assist them to a speedy "outflow. This oozing of water which, perhaps, made the "ground mossy when covered by the original forest, was not "enough, I suppose, to prevent good pasturage coming in so soon "as the wood was cleared off, for the decay of the leaf-mould "would have left the surface-soil porous and readily able to free "itself from excess of water. The springs, however, have al- "ways tended to stagnation, and when the soil, through oxida- "tion of its mould and much cattle treading, became more com- "pact, the free flow of water was checked, and the stopping of "the springs reacted powerfully upon the soil to increase the "evil.

"If I should venture a surmise as to the nature of the indura- "tion, it would be that oxide of iron and the acids resulting from "a peaty decomposition of vegetable matter—humates, ulmates,

" geates, or whatever chemists choose to name them—have done
" the mischief. The soils of this neighborhood are, for the most
" part, decidedly, often highly ferruginous, and the very sandstone
" that crops out here and there in the vicinity of New Haven
" is, to all appearance, a sandy gravel, cemented by oxide of iron.
" The hillside at Edgewood, before your renovation began, was
" in the early stages of becoming a *moor*, such as, in humid cli-
" mates, occupy immense stretches of country, producing noth-
" ing but moss and heather. Were Edgewood situated in the
" north of Ireland, or Scotland, or in Labrador, the hill-side, left
" to itself, would in all probability soon be covered with plat
" moss, and the heather-bell would make it as poetical as it
" would be useless. The heat and dryness of our summer have
" prevented this combination of beauty and worthlessness, and
" made it simply an ordinary old mossy pasture, until, for a mar-
" vel, it became a feature of Edgewood.

" These little-known humates of iron are poison to all the
" nutritious grasses. As they accumulated, the proper pasturage
" died out, the soil became more and more moist or springy, be-
" cause of its induration on the one hand, and still more so, on
" the other, by reason of the water-loving vegetation increasing
" upon it.

" In our climate sufficient drainage alone would surely cure
" this evil ; but to drain a hill-side so abrupt as that of Edgewood
" would seem absurd. Yet it is not absurd to squeeze a sponge,
" and the soil was a sponge that would not let the water flow out
" of it even on a slope of twenty-five degrees, more or less. By
" drainage the land would be reclaimed, the incipient rock would
" be broken up, the sponge would pass by insensible degrees into
" proper soil, the waters would escape, and then the mosses, that
" live in wet but perish in tilth, would give place to better herbage,
" and the harsh, sharp-edged sedge would be supplanted by the
" true grasses.

" In drainage, *it is the air, and especially its oxygen, which cuts to*
" *pieces the cement that threatens the life of the soil.* The air car-
" ries away in its invisible embrace the moisture—takes position

" among the particles of earth, consumes away the humus, com-
" bines with the black and styptic iron protoxide, burning it to red
" and innocuous peroxide, literally as well as figuratively warms
" the soil, and sets up those inorganic activities that must always
" precede and prepare for the sway of organic life.

" Lime has long been known as a substitute for drainage.
" Even level-lying clays have been made friable and dry by heavy
" liming. In the Ober-Lausitz, (Germany,) in the north of Eng-
" land and Scotland, this effect has been abundantly seen. Lord
" Kames noticed, seventy years ago, that some soils are rendered
" so loose by overdoses of lime as to retain no water. This is
" especially the case with their moorish soils and reclaimed peat.
" Such land becomes puffy and hollow to the tread when limed too
" copiously. If soil or pulverized rocks, like porphyry and
" basalt, are mixed with one per cent. of quicklime, or two per
" cent. of carbonate of lime, (air-slacked lime,) then moistened
" with water and set aside for some months in a closed bottle, it
" will be seen by the eye that a very perceptible change of bulk
" has taken place in the mixture. The rock or soil becomes
" more voluminous and more porous by this treatment.

" The effect of lime in loosening the soil is partly the result
" of chemical action, whereby particle after particle is detached
" from each grain of firm stone, the volume of the whole in-
" creasing, just as the bulk of an ounce of iron is made more by
" cutting it to filings, or that of a rag of linen by tearing it to
" lint.

" The effect is also in part mechanical, especially in clay,
" whose plastic particles adhere together when the mass is swol-
" len with wet, and, on slow drying, still cohere and harden to
" clods. When clay is limed, the lime, being dissolved in rain,
" is carried wherever the rain penetrates, and coats the fine
" grains of clay as the atoms of a dye fix themselves upon the
" fiber of cloth, so that, when the water wastes, it is not any
" longer adhesive clay settling to a doughy paste, but clay rolled
" in lime, that no more sticks together than bread-dough sticks to
" the pan or fingers dusted with flour. Clays that naturally con-

" tain a few per cent. of lime-carbonate (clay-marls) are friable
" and unplastic, and a copious dressing of lime upon a clay field
" converts it, after a year or two, into a marl with a highly im-
" proved texture."

I have found in my own practice, in the cultivation of heavy
moist land in garden vegetables, that an application of a single
barrel of air-slacked lime per acre, spread with perfect uniformity
by a broadcast sower, resulted in a growth of cabbages and root
crops which I think it would have been impossible for me to
have attained on such soil without it.

As an incidental advantage of the use of lime, I am led by my
own experience to indorse most fully the opinion of Peter Henderson concerning its effect on certain insects which are especially
injurious to vegetation. He claims that the reason why those few
favored market-gardeners who cultivate a little tract on the shores
of Communipaw Bay are able to grow cabbages year after year,
on the same land, is, that this region was used for ages, in the olden
time, as a clam-baking ground by the Indians of New Jersey, and
that the immense number of clam-shells that are found to the
depth of a foot or more in all of the land of that region, exert an
influence on the soil which renders it unfavorable to the " club-
foot " insect. That this effect exists there is no doubt, although
it is not in accordance with our generally-received ideas to suppose that bits of insoluble shells should produce a result at all
similar to that of caustic or even more crumbling carbonate of
lime.

The practice of ages has shown that, both by increasing the
power of the soil to admit of the filtration of water and by rendering more available its hidden stores of plant food, an application
of lime to heavy land is productive of the very best immediate
results ; and in this case, as in that of Peruvian guano, the application must be made with care and judgment. It is an old saying
among farmers of certain districts in this country that " lime kills
the land ;" and there is a very old couplet current in England,
which runs as follows :—

" He who limes without manure
  Will leave his farm and family poor."

The fact in this case is, as in that of Peruvian guano, that the application of the single agent stimulates a production which takes from the soil other elements of the ashes of plants than those which the application itself furnishes.

Therefore, while lime is one of the most valuable agents that the farmer can employ, it is only by a careful husbanding of the soil elements these increased crops extract that he will be able to maintain the increased, or even the original fertility of the land.

GREEN CROPS.

After a poor soil has been brought to a condition in which it is possible to produce upon it any considerable amount of vegetation, the road to its entire reclamation is simple and easy.

Probably the most important agent in the production of all fertile soils has been the growth and decomposition of vegetation. In some cases, forests, and in other cases, wild grasses have for ages occupied the land, and by the yearly decomposition of their dying parts—their stems and their leaves—have added, little by little, to the bulk and richness of the earth. By this means not only does the soil receive organic matter which had been drawn chiefly from the atmosphere, but every leaf and every stem rejected by the plant and added to the soil contains potash, lime, phosphoric acid, and other elements of vegetable ashes, which had been slowly withdrawn from the crude soil by the roots of the earlier vegetation—perhaps, in many instances, from considerable depths below the surface. And thus, little by little, perhaps during ten years, and perhaps during a thousand years, a constantly continuing process has brought the soil from a condition in which it would support only the lower orders of plants, or the more vigorous feeding trees, to that in which it is susceptible of supporting plants useful to man.

The practice of manuring by the aid of green crops is an application of the same principle to the requirements of agriculture;

and the success with which this process is availed of for our purposes depends almost entirely upon a proper selection of the plant which is to be used. In America it has come to be an established fact that, wherever clover will grow, it is, all things considered, the best plant for our use ; but the same rules which regulate its adoption and the extent to which we may avail ourselves of its action, govern the cultivation of all other plants for this purpose. Clover is a plant which is capable of germinating and commencing its growth under circumstances of sterility which would be unfavorable to almost all other farm crops. Often, where nothing of value would grow, the application of a few bushels of ground plaster to the acre will be sufficient to stimulate this plant to an active vegetation. Its roots are exceedingly strong, descend to a great depth into the soil, and have an extraordinary power of absorbing matters which, to the roots of other plants, would be entirely unavailable. Its foliage is abundant and fleshy, and, under favorable circumstances, it absorbs ample supplies from the atmosphere. It is asserted, though, perhaps, not quite proven, that clover takes up the free nitrogen of the air. Whether this is true or not, there seems little doubt that it either avails itself of the small quantities of ammonia that come in contact with its leaves, or that it has the peculiar power of extracting ammonia from the soil which would not be yielded to most other crops. Certain it is that both its upper part and its roots contain much more nitrogen than would any other plant with which we are acquainted, grown under similar circumstances. The mineral food which it gets from the soil and subsoil—notably from the latter—and the supplies from the atmosphere, are stored up, not only in the stems and leaves, but, to a very large extent, in the roots also. And when the crop is turned under by the plow, or even when the principal growth having been removed for hay, the roots are killed by the plow, and mixed, as so much dead organic matter, with the soil, their decomposition adds to it, in a readily available form, all of those contents of root and stem by which the growth of future crops is to be benefited. And, in addition to all this, the lower ends of the roots, below where they are cut off by the plow, being deprived of their atmospheric support, die, decompose in their places, and form inviting channels for the penetration of the more delicate roots of wheat and grasses. Even as Peruvian guano stimulates a production which may be made use of as a means for permanently and largely increasing the fertility of the soil, so clover, a little more slowly but much more cheaply, accomplishes the same result. And even as Peruvian guano, when used as a means for obtaining the largest immediate crops for sale, is a most exhausting agent, so clover may become, in the hands of an injudicious cultivator, the surest means for speedy exhaustion. And the same rule applies here as in all other similar cases—that where the results of any fertilizing agent are properly husbanded, the fertility of the land and the wealth of the farmer increase, and that where the immediate results of the fertilizer are turned into money, both the soil and the farmer must ultimately be impoverished.

This subject will be more fully treated in the chapter on Forage Crops

GENERAL CONCLUSIONS.

To sum up, in a few words, all that it has been attempted to teach in this chapter, it may be stated that manures of all kinds should be employed in the light of a comprehensive understanding of their various effects ; and the general principle should be constantly adhered to, that, in the policy of the farm, nothing should be allowed to go to waste, and nothing should be sold without the return of an equivalent, or pretty nearly an equivalent of its mineral value.

If, by the use of lime, Peruvian guano, common salt, or any other manure whose effect exceeds its ability to supply food to the plant, the crop is largely increased, that part of the earthy constituents of the crop which has been supplied by the soil and not by the manure, must be regarded as so much of the original banking capital of the land, which is only to be put in circulation—not to be permanently disposed of. If we sell wheat, the important mineral constituents of the wheat should be purchased and returned to the soil. If we sell milk, or wool, or flesh, the phosphate of lime and potash contained in those products should be returned from some foreign source; and it should be our constant aim to keep the ability of the soil to furnish plant-food continually increasing rather than diminishing.

The greatest care of the farmer should be given to the husbanding of these mineral elements, and while it is, perhaps, on these alone that the permanent fertility of his soil depends, he will find that his true interest requires him to increase, as much as possible, by home manufacture, by purchase, and by absorption from the atmosphere, the amount of ammonia or nitrates on which the extra productiveness of his land must depend. For, although the old " mineral theory " of Liebig is undoubtedly true, it is also true that the amount of ammonia that the soil receives from the atmosphere under natural circumstances may be with advantage increased, both by application in manure and by offering facilities for a still larger absorption from the air.

The careful observance of these rules, coupled, of course, with due attention to the mechanical condition of the soil, especially to its draining, and incidentally to all of those other parts of the farmer's business which help to increase the results of his labor, must inevitably make the cultivation of any land—no matter how poor it may be originally—more and more profitable as years pass on. And it may be stated as a fixed rule, that no system of farming under which land does not, year by year, grow better, can be called good farming; for, however much money soil-robbery may put into the farmer's pocket, it is more than balanced by the deterioration of his original capital and of the fertility on which alone his true prosperity is based.

CHAPTER IX.

ROTATION OF CROPS.

MUCH has been written during the past two thousand years concerning the rotation of crops; yet we are, probably, at this day less certain concerning the various principles upon which the importance of rotation depends than concerning those which govern almost every other branch of agriculture. It is one of those cases in which, while science and practice undoubtedly walk hand in hand, the relation which each bears to the other has never been very definitely defined. In different countries, and in different parts of our own country, different rotations have been adopted; and, in the absence of any good reason for objecting to the local custom, it will be usually the safest guide for the farmer to follow it.

In this country, perhaps the most generally prevailing rotation is the following: First, Indian corn; second, oats; third, wheat; fourth, grasses for mowing; fifth, pasture.

This rotation is subject to the objection that it leaves no place for the root crops, and probably, as a general rule, the scarcity of labor in most parts of the country, and the consequent difficulty of taking proper care of root crops, justifies their omission; but it is very certain that we can never achieve complete success until, by an increase of population or by an increased ability to cultivate these crops by horse-power, we are able to bring them up to their proper position as a part of the rotation—that is, to cultivate as large an area of roots as we do of corn, of oats, or of wheat.

The rotation that I have adopted in my own case, where exceptional circumstances allow me to perform more labor on a

given area than is usual in American agriculture, is the following :
First year, Indian corn; second year, roots; third year, soiling
crops; fourth year, soiling crops during the first half of the season, seeding down to wheat or rye in the autumn ; fifth year,
wheat or rye with clover and timothy ; sixth year, mowing ; the
single year's mowing to be followed by corn again.

It is proper for me to say that, while this rotation has been
adopted after a careful consideration of the practices of different
regions, and of my own circumstances, it has not yet been so
fully tried in practice as to warrant its unqualified recommendation for general use, even where, as at Ogden farm, soiling is to
be adopted to the entire exclusion of pasturing; and it is not
unlikely that, after the fertility of the soil has been sufficiently
increased, the cultivation of corn and even of wheat or rye may
be given up, and their places supplied by crops which, while they
will require somewhat more labor, will produce a larger money
result.

In the London *Gardeners' Chronicle and Agricultural Gazette*,
there is an editorial article on the subject of the rotation of crops,
in which there appears the following very sensible remark :
"Practically, a good rotation should distribute the farm work
" equally, and it should give an opportunity for cleaning the land."
And it is generally advised that the details of the rotation be regulated very much more by the prices of products, and by the farmer's
demand for food for his cattle, than by any arbitrary rule, the two
objects being constantly kept in view, of furnishing, so far as possible, regular employment for men and teams throughout the busy
seasons, and of pursuing such a course as shall supply the land
with the requisite manure at the proper time.

As a matter of general advice, it is to be recommended that the
bulk of the farm manures be applied to such crops (like Indian
corn) as cannot be injured by even the most stimulating application ; that crops which require a settled fertility of the land, but
which are injured by the immediate application of animal manures,
(and this is true of most grain crops,) should follow those to which
the stable manures were originally applied ; that crops which have

but feeble power of sending their roots deep into the soil in search of food (as wheat, for instance) should succeed such crops (like clover and buckwheat) as have this power in an extraordinary degree ; that crops which require clean culture, and the expense of whose cultivation is very much increased by the foulness of the land, should follow crops which leave the land free from weeds, (as roots after grain ;) and that crops which require a large amount of decomposing organic matter in the soil should follow the decomposition of the roots and stubble of grass.

So far as science is able to indicate a guide in this matter, the case is very well laid down in the following quotations from Liebig :—*

" If a given space of a soil (in surface and in depth) contains " only a sufficient quantity of inorganic ingredients for the perfect " development of ten plants, twenty specimens of the same plant, " cultivated on this surface, could only attain half their proper " maturity ; in such a case there must be a difference in the num- " ber of their leaves, in the strength of their stems, and in the " number of their seeds.

" Two plants of the same kind growing in close vicinity must " prove prejudicial to each other, if they find in the soil, or in the " atmosphere surrounding them, less of the means of nourishment " than they require for their perfect development.   There is no " plant more injurious to wheat than wheat itself, none more " hurtful to the potato than another potato.   Hence we actually " find that the cultivated plants on the borders of a field are much " more luxuriant, not only in strength, but in the number and " richness of their seeds or tubers, than plants growing in the " middle of the same field.

" The same results must ensue in exactly a similar manner " when we cultivate on a soil the same plants for successive years, " instead of, as in the former case, growing them too closely to- " gether.   Let us assume that a certain soil contains a quantity of " silicates and of phosphates sufficient for 1,000 crops of wheat,

* Agricultural Chemistry. J. von Liebig. Giessen, 1843.

" then, after 1,000 years, it must become sterile for this plant.
" If we were to remove the surface-soil and bring up the subsoil
" to the surface, making what was formerly surface-soil now the
" subsoil, we would procure a surface much less exhausted than
" the former, and this might suffice to supply a new series of
" crops, but its state of fertility would also have a limit.

" A soil will naturally reach its point of exhaustion sooner the
" less rich it is in the mineral ingredients necessary as food for
" plants. But it is obvious that we can restore the soil to its
" original state of fertility by bringing it back to its former com-
" position ; that is, by returning to it the constituents removed by
" the various crops of plants.

" Two plants may be cultivated side by side, or successively,
" when they require unequal quantities of the same constituents,
" at different times ; they will grow luxuriantly without mutual
" injury, if they require for their development *different* ingredients
" of the soil."

*   *   *   *   *   *   *

" Different genera of plants require for their growth and perfect
" maturity either the same inorganic means of nourishment, although
" in unequal quantities and at different times, or they require dif-
" ferent mineral ingredients. It is owing to the difference of the
" food necessary for the growth of plants, and which must be
" furnished by the soil, that different kinds of plants exert mutual
" injury when growing together, and that others, on the contrary,
" grow together with great luxuriance."

*   *   *   *   *   *   *

" There are certain ashes of plants wholly soluble in water,
" others are only partially soluble, while certain kinds yield only
" traces of soluble ingredients.

" When the parts of the ashes *insoluble* in water are treated
" with an acid, (muriatic acid,) this residue, in the case of many
" plants, is quite soluble in the acids, (as, for instance, the ashes
" of beet, turnips, and potatoes ;) with other plants, only half the
" residue dissolves, the other half resisting the solvent action of

" the acid ; while in the case of certain plants only a third, or
" even less of the residue is taken up by the acid.

" The parts of the ashes soluble in cold water consist entirely
" of *salts with alkaline bases,* (*potash and soda.*) The ingredients
" soluble in acids are *salts of lime and magnesia* ; and the residue
" insoluble in acids consists of *silica.*

" These ingredients being so different in their behavior to water
" and to acids, afford us a means of classifying the cultivated plants
" according to their unequal quantity of these constituents. Thus
" *potash plants* are those the ashes of which contain more than half
" their weight of soluble alkaline salts ; we may designate as *lime*
" *plants* and as *silica plants* those in which lime and silica respect-
" ively predominate. The ingredients thus indicated are those
" which form the distinguishing characteristics of the plants which
" require an abundant supply of them for their growth.

" The *potash plants* include the chenopodia, arrach, wormwood,
" etc. ; and among cultivated plants, the beet, mangel-wurzel,
" turnip, and maize. The *lime plants* comprehend the lichens,
" (containing oxalate of lime,) the cactus, (containing crystallized
" tartrate of lime,) clover, beans, peas, and tobacco. *Silica plants*
" include wheat, oats, rye, and barley.

		Salts of Potash and Soda.	Salts of Lime and Magnesia.	Silica.
Silica Plants.	Oat straw with seeds..........	34·00	4·00	62·00
	Wheat straw	22·00	7·20	61·05
	Barley straw with seeds........	19·00	25·70	55·03
	Rye straw....................	18·65	16·52	63·89
Lime Plants.	Tobacco (Havana).............	24·34	67·44	8·30
	" (Dutch)	23·07	62·23	15·25
	" (grown in an artificial soil)	27·00	59·00	12·00
	Pea Straw....................	27·82	63·74	7·81
	Potato herb	4·20	59·40	36·40
	Meadow clover...............	39·20	56·00	4·90
Potash Plants.	Maize straw..................	71·00	6·50	18·00
	Turnips.....................	81·60	18·40	
	Beet-root	88·00	12·00	
	Potatoes (tubers).............	85·81	14·19	
	Helianthus tuberosus	84·30	15·70	

" This classification, however, is obviously only a very general
" one, and permits division into a great number of subordinate
" classes; particularly with respect to those plants in which the
" alkalies may be replaced by lime and magnesia.   *   *   *

" The potato plant belongs to the *lime plants* as far as regards
" the ingredients of its leaves, but its tubers (which contain only
" traces of lime) belong to the class of *potash plants*. With refer-
" ence to the siliceous plants, this difference of their parts is very
" marked.

" Barley must be viewed as a lime plant, when compared with
" oats or with wheat, in reference to their ingredients soluble in
" muriatic acid; but it would be considered as a siliceous plant, if
" viewed only in reference to its amount of silica. Beet-root
" contains phosphate of magnesia, and only traces of lime, while
" the turnip contains phosphate of lime and only traces of mag-
" nesia.

" When we take into consideration the quantity of ashes, and
" their known composition, we are enabled to calculate with ease,
" not only the particular ingredients removed from a soil, but also
" the degree in which it is exhausted of these by certain species of
" plants belonging to the *potash*, *lime*, or *siliceous plants*. This will
" be rendered obvious by the following examples :—

" A soil, consisting of four Hessian acres, has removed from it by a crop of—

		Salts of potash and soda.		Salts of lime, magnesia, and peroxide of iron.		Silica.
		lbs.	lbs.	lbs.	lbs.	lbs.
Wheat.	In straw........	95·31	130·51	34·75	67·55	260·05
	In corn.........	35·20		32·80		
Peas.	In straw........	150·40	194·42	354·80	371·46	46·60
	In corn.........	44·02		16·68		
Rye.	In straw........	40·73	82·78	36·00	57·82	139·77
	In corn.........	42·05		21·82		
Beet-root without leaves..........		561·00		37·84		
Helianthus tuberosus.............		556·00		104·00		

" The same surface is deprived by these crops of the following quantity of phos-
" phates :—

Peas.	Wheat.	Rye.	Helianthus tuberosus.	Turnips.
117	112·43	77·05	122	37·84

" According to the preceding views, plants must obtain from
" the soil certain constituents, in order to enable them to reach
" perfect maturity—that is, to enable them to bear blossoms and
" fruit. The growth of a plant is very limited in pure water, in
" pure silica, or in a soil from which these ingredients are absent.
" If there be not present in the soil alkalies, lime, and magnesia,
" the stem, leaves, and blossoms of the plants can only be formed
" in proportion to the quantity of these substances existing as a
" provision in the seed. When phosphates are wanting, the seeds
" cannot be formed.

" The more quickly a plant grows, the more rapidly do its leaves
" increase in number and in size, and therefore the supply of
" alkaline bases must be greater in a given time.

" As all plants remove from the soil certain constituents, it is
" quite obvious that none of them can render it either richer or
" more fertile for a plant of another kind. If we convert into
" arable land a soil which has grown for centuries wood, or a
" vegetation which has not changed, and if we spread over this
" soil the ashes of the wood and of the bushes, we have added to
" that contained in the soil a new provision of alkaline bases,
" and of phosphates, which may suffice for a hundred or more
" crops of certain plants. If the soil contains silicates susceptible
" of disintegration, there will also be present in it soluble silicate
" of potash or soda, which is necessary for the rendering mature
" the stem of the siliceous plant ; and, with the phosphates
" already present, we have in such a soil all the conditions neces-
" sary to sustain uninterrupted crops of corn for a series of years.

" If this soil be either deficient or wanting in the silicates, but yet
" contain an abundant quantity of salts of lime and of phosphates,
" we will be enabled to obtain from it, for a number of years, suc-
" cessive crops of tobacco, peas, beans, etc., and wine.

" But, if none of the ingredients furnished to these plants be
" again returned to the soil, a time must come when it can no
" longer furnish these constituents to a new vegetation, when it
" must become completely exhausted, and be at last quite sterile,
" even for weeds.

" This state of sterility will take place earlier for one kind of
" plant than for another, according to the unequal quantity of the
" different ingredients of the soil. If the soil is poor in phos-
" phates, but rich in silicates, it will be exhausted sooner by the
" cultivation of wheat than by that of oats or of barley, because a
" greater quantity of phosphates is removed in the seeds and straw
" of one crop of wheat than would be removed in three or four
" crops of barley or of oats. But if this soil be deficient in lime,
" the barley will grow upon it very imperfectly."

  * * * * * * *

" In a soil rich in alkaline silicates, but containing only a limited
" supply of phosphates, the period of its exhaustion for these salts
" will be delayed if we alternate with the wheat plants, which
" we cut before they have come to seed ; or, what is the same
" thing, with plants that remove from the soil only a small quan-
" tity of phosphates. If we cultivate on this soil peas or beans,
" these plants will leave, after the removal of the crop, a quantity
" of silica in a soluble state sufficient for a succeeding crop of
" wheat ; but they will exhaust the soil of phosphates quite as
" much as wheat itself, because the seeds of both require for their
" maturity nearly an equal quantity of these salts.

" We are enabled to delay the period of exhaustion of a soil of
" phosphates by adopting a rotation, in which potatoes, tobacco,
" or clover, are made to alternate with a white crop. The seeds
" of the plants now named are small, and contain proportionally
" only minute quantities of phosphates ; their roots and leaves,
" also, do not require much of these salts for their maturity. But
" it must be remembered, at the same time, that each of these has
" rendered the soil poorer, by a certain quantity of phosphates.
" By the rotation adopted, we have deferred the period of exhaus-
" tion, and have obtained in the crops a greater weight of sugar,
" starch, etc., but we have not acquired any larger quantity of the
" constituents of the blood, or of the only substances which can be
" considered as properly the nutritious parts of plants. When the
" soil is deficient in salts of lime, tobacco, clover, and peas will
" not flourish ; while under the same conditions the growth of

15

" beet-root or turnips will not be impeded, if the soil, at the same
" time, contain a proper quantity of alkalies.

" When a soil contains silicates not prone to disintegrate, it
" may be able, in its natural state, to liberate by the influence of
" the atmosphere, in three or four years, only as much silica as
" suffices for one crop of wheat.   In this case, such a crop can
" only be grown on it in a three or four years' rotation, assuming
" that the phosphates necessary for the formation of the seeds
" exist in the soil in sufficient quantity.   But we can shorten this
" period by working well the soil, and by increasing its surface,
" so as to make it more accessible to the action of the air and
" moisture, in order to disintegrate the soil, and to procure a greater
" provision of soluble silicates.   The decomposition of the sili-
" cates may also be accelerated by the use of burnt lime ; but it is
" certain that, although all these means may enable us to insure
" rich crops for a certain period, they induce, at the same time,
" an earlier exhaustion of the soil, and impair its natural state of
" fertility.

     *   *   *   *   *   *   *

" It follows, then, from the preceding observations, that the
" advantage of the alternate system of husbandry consists in the
" fact that the cultivated plants abstract from the soil unequal
" quantities of certain nutritious matters.

" A fertile soil must contain in sufficient quantity, and in a
" form adapted for assimilation, all the inorganic materials indis-
" pensable for the growth of plants.

" A field artificially prepared for culture contains a certain
" amount of these ingredients, and also of ammoniacal salts and
" decaying vegetable matter.   The system of rotation adopted on
" such a field is, that a potash plant (turnips or potatoes) is suc-
" ceeded by a silica plant, and the latter is followed by a lime
" plant.   All these plants require phosphates and alkalies—the
" potash plant requiring the largest quantity of the latter and the
" smallest quantity of the former.   The silica plants require, in
" addition to the soluble silica left by the potash plants, a consid-
" erable amount of phosphates ; and the succeeding lime plants

" (peas or clover) are capable of exhausting the soil of this impor-
" tant ingredient to such an extent that there is only sufficient
" left to enable a crop of oats or of rye to form their seeds.

" The number of crops which may be obtained from the soil
" depends upon the quantity of the phosphates, of the alkalies, or
" of lime, and the salts of magnesia existing in it.

" The existing provision may suffice for two successive crops
" of a potash or of a lime plant, or for three or four more crops of
" a silica plant, or it may suffice for five or seven crops of all
" taken together; but after this time all mineral substances re-
" moved from the field, in the form of fruits, herbs, or straw,
" must again be returned to it ; the equilibrium must be restored,
" if we desire to retain the field in its original state of fertility.

" This is effected by means of MANURE."

Since these views were published, further investigation of the
subject has so far modified the opinions of scientific men, that
Liebig's statements (concerning silica especially) are no longer
accepted as correct in all their details. His general principles, on
the other hand, have only been more fully demonstrated to be
correct, and the deductions that he draws from them, so far as the
practice of farming is concerned, bear with undiminished force.

To continue the quotation from this author's works, I take
from his " Modern Agriculture"* the following :—

" Innumerable facts have taught the practical farmer that, in
" many cases, the successful cultivation of an after-crop on a field
" depends upon the nature of the preceding crop, and that it is by
" no means a matter of indifference in what succession or rotation
" he grows his crops. The previous cultivation of some under-
" ground crop, or some plant with extensive root ramifications,
" will tend to make the soil more favorable for the subsequent
" growth of a cereal. The latter will, in such cases, thrive better,
" and it will do so without the use (or with the sparing application)
" of manure, and will yield a more abundant crop. But as re-
" gards *succeeding* harvests, there has been in reality no *saving* of

* " Modern Agriculture." J. Von Liebig. Munich, 1859.

" manure, nor has the field *increased* in the conditions of its fer-
" tility. There has been no augmentation in the gross amount of
" the elements of food in the soil, but simply an increase of the
" *available effective portion* of these elements, and an acceleration
" of the results in a given time.

" The physical and chemical *condition* of the fields has been
" improved, but the chemical *store* has been reduced ; *all plants,*
" *without exception, exhaust the soil, each of them in its own way, of*
" *the conditions for their reproduction.*

" There are fields that will yield without manuring for six,
" twelve, fifty, or a hundred years successively, crops of cereals,
" potatoes, vetches, clover, or any other plants, and the whole
" produce can be carried away from the land ; but the inevitable
" result is at last the same, the soil loses its fertility.

" In the produce of his field, the farmer sells in reality his
" land ; he sells in his crops certain elements of the atmosphere
" that are constantly being replaced from that inexhaustible store,
" and certain constituents of the soil that are his property, and
" which have served to form, out of the atmospheric elements,
" the body of the plant, of which they themselves also constitute
" component parts.   In altogether alienating the crops of his
" fields, he deprives the land of the conditions for their reproduc-
" tion.   A system of farming based upon such principles justly
" deserves to be branded as a system of spoliation.   Had all of
" the constituents of the soil carried off from the field in the
" produce sold, been, year after year, or rotation after rotation,
" completely restored to the land, the latter would have preserved
" its fertility to the fullest extent ; the gain of the farmer would,
" indeed, have been reduced by the repurchase of the alienated
" constituents of the soil, but it would thereby have been rendered
" permanent.

" The constituents of the soil are the farmer's capital, the
" elements of food supplied by the atmosphere the interest of this
" capital ; by means of the former he produces the latter.   In
" selling the produce of his farm he alienates a portion of his
" capital and the interest ; in returning to the land the constituents

" of the soil removed in the crops he simply restores his capital
" to his field.

" Every system of farming based on the spoliation of the land
" leads to poverty. The country in Europe which, in its time,
" most abounded in gold and silver was, nevertheless, the poorest.
" All the treasures of Mexico and Peru brought to Spain by the
" richly laden silver fleets melted away in the hands of the nation,
" because the Spaniards had forgotten, or no longer practiced, the
" art of making the money return to them which they had put
" into circulation in commerce to supply their wants; because
" they did not know how to produce articles of exchange required
" by other nations who were in possession of their money. There
" is no other way of maintaining the wealth of a nation.

" It is not the land in itself that constitutes the farmer's wealth,
" but it is in the constituents of the soil, which serve for the
" nutrition of plants, that this wealth truly consists. By means of
" these constituents alone, he is enabled to produce the conditions
" indispensable to man for the preservation of the temperature of
" his body, and of his ability to work. Rational *Agriculture*, in
" contradistinction to the spoliation system of farming, is based
" upon the principle of restitution ; by giving back to his fields
" the conditions of their fertility the farmer insures the perma-
" nence of the latter.

" The deplorable effects of the spoliation system of farming are
" nowhere more strikingly evident than in America, where the
" early colonists in Canada, in the State of New York, in Pennsyl-
" vania, Virginia, Maryland, etc., found tracts of land, which for
" many years, by simply plowing and sowing, yielded a succession
" of abundant wheat and tobacco harvests. No falling off in the
" weight or quality of the crops reminded the farmer of the ne-
" cessity of restoring to the land the constituents of the soil
" carried away in the produce.

" We all know what has become of these fields. In less than
" two generations, though originally so teeming with fertility, they
" were turned into deserts, and, in many districts, brought to such
" a state of absolute exhaustion that, even now, after having lain

" fallow more than a hundred years, they will not yield a remuner-
" ative crop of a cereal plant."

While the case with reference to the regions of America, to
which allusion is made, is perhaps too strongly stated, the principle
on which those statements are made is entirely correct, and there
can be no greater fallacy than to suppose, as many of our farmers
do, that a well-selected rotation of crops furnishes a sure means
for constantly increasing the fertility of the land.   While one crop
may prepare the soil for the growth of another, and while
during the growth of one crop certain elements which another
would require are developed by natural agencies acting within the
soil, the effect of all cropping—that is, of the removal of vegetation from the land on which it grows—is to lessen the supply of
mineral ingredients in the soil ; and the longer we may be enabled
to carry on such a process the more complete will be the exhaustion of the land in the long run.

Certain excellent writers in America and in other countries are
devoting a great deal of attention to the question of renovating the
soil by the growth of clover; and, so far as the present result of
the practice is concerned, they have every thing their own way ;
that is to say, it is an almost invariable result of the growth of this
plant that the increased fertility which its advocates promise is
sure to follow.   By reference to the subject of " Green Crops "
in the preceding chapter, it will be seen that the power of certain
plants to prepare for the uses of other plants certain elements of the
soil not previously fitted for assimilation by them is very great.
And it is this action on which the confidence in clover culture is
based ; and it may be set down as a fact, that any land on which,
by the aid of plaster or any other fertilizer, even a tolerable crop
of clover may be grown may be, without the application of any
other manure, brought, generally within a short time, to a high
state of fertility.

But there is one feature of the case which these writers over-
look, or the existence of which they persistently deny ; that is,
that so far as the earthy constituents of vegetation are concerned,
the effect of the clover is simply to develop matters already

existing in the soil, and the removal of these matters by other crops, which are sold away, must inevitably lessen the total amount of them contained in the soil.

The fact that within a few years, or even within a few generations, their supply may not be reduced to so low a point as to prevent the cultivation of valuable crops is no argument in favor of a blind dependence upon them. As surely as two and two make four, and two taken from four leave only two to be taken again, just so surely will it, sooner or later, be found that from a given, (limited,) quantity of phosphoric acid in the soil, a yearly quantity cannot be taken without reducing the amount that is left. And if, by the growth of clover, we succeed in hunting out the last hiding-place of an atom of phosphoric acid, and placing it within the reach of a crop of wheat that is to be sold, we shall render the ultimate exhaustion of the soil complete; whereas, by a judicious return of what is taken away, we might make most valuable and repeated use of the soil's constituents. If we depend upon it alone and return nothing but what it contains, we shall finally reach a point where not even clover, where no crop can be grown, and from which it will be impossible to regain fertility without the expenditure of more money than the land would be worth.

I should be glad if I could add to the completeness of this book by specifying certain rotations as being the best to adopt under certain circumstances, and I have tried hard in an examination of the rotations followed in different regions to do this. But the result of my investigations has been simply to convince me that there are so many circumstances of soil, climate, locality, market, home supply, and need of selling crops in order to get money for special uses, and, after all, so much to be left to the fancy or whim of the farmer, that it is not safe to do more than to state general principles, which bear equally on all cases, and, in view of which, each cultivator should select for himself, after due consideration, the system of cultivation that it will be best for him to adhere to.

This selection, however, should not be made without such con-

sideration, for it costs a good deal of trouble to arrange a farm
for a systematic course of rotation, and the trouble will be equally
great, if not even greater, in changing the system after it has once
been decided upon.

If the system of soiling be adopted, either entirely or mainly, it
will be better, where it is practicable, to do away completely with
all interior fences, and to divide the land into so many parts as
there are crops to be grown, the crops of each to follow in the
course of the rotation.   But where pasture forms a considerable
element fences will be necessary, and it should then be the study
of the farmer to make them conform as nearly as possible to the
requirements of his rotation, and, also, to the necessity, which
may be greater or less in different cases, of having more than one
field for pasture.

It has been advocated by Prof. Ville and others, that, under
certain circumstances, where there is a ready sale for particular
crops, the system of rotation should be dispensed with, and that
only such crops should be grown as will find a ready market.
There is no doubt that, within certain limits, this course may be
followed with advantage ; but it is not a safe one to recommend
for any thing like general adoption, and it is only where the crop
grown is such as to keep the soil in a high state of fertility, or
where special fertilizers can be secured with special ease, that it
will be found at all practicable.   Indeed, there is no case, so far
as my experience extends, except, perhaps, with the cultivation of
onions and permanent grasses, where purely agricultural crops
can be so well grown without rotation as with it.   And, in addition to this, the advantage of having work for a given force of
men and teams during the whole season is a very great one, and
this is rarely compatible with the requirements of any special cultivation.

In certain favored districts, such as the blue-grass region of
Kentucky, it is best to keep the land in grass as long as possible—
indeed, sometimes it may be kept permanently in grass ; but on
average farms it will *pay* better, and, consequently, it will *be* better,
to constantly vary the crop to which any field is devoted.

I cannot better close this chapter than by quoting (almost entire) an article on the " Rotation of Crops," furnished to the New York *Tribune*, by the Hon. George Geddes, of Syracuse, N. Y.

Although he attaches less importance to the cultivation of root crops than seems to me just, his remarks are so sensible and so practical that they should be carefully read by all farmers :—

" The idea of preserving the fertility of land, and at the same " time greatly increasing the aggregate of crops produced, by a ju- " dicious *rotation*, is quite modern.

" In England great attention is paid to rotation, and many " elaborate experiments have been made and reported in the agri- " cultural works of that country, showing its importance and its " influence in increasing the agricultural productions of the king- " dom.

" English writers have marked out with much care various " systems of rotation of crops, giving the proper place to each, in " view of the food it demands of the soil, and its power to appro- " priate the food that may be derived from the different stages of " decomposition of the various manures used.

" The only useful lesson we American farmers can derive from " all this English knowledge is the proof that a proper rotation does " preserve the fertility of the soil, and greatly increase its products, " when the aggregate is considered.

" The climate of England is so unlike ours that we must strike " out for ourselves in laying down our plans of rotation. We have " a climate that matures in its perfection the most valuable cereal, " all things considered, that a beneficent Providence has given to " man—that England cannot produce in the open air at all—I " refer to maize or Indian corn, a native of our own country, and " adapted, in its different varieties, to nearly every part of the " United States.

" Admirers of English systems of agriculture have long urged " on the American farmers extensive cultivation of root crops. " Though constantly urged thereto, the practical Yankee has " gone on raising his Indian corn, well knowing that, as a leading " crop, it was, beyond all comparison, of more value, in view of its

" cost, than any root crop, for his own food, or for food for his cat-
" tle, sheep, and horses.   Near cities, root crops will be culti-
" vated ; but far away from markets, where land is comparatively
" cheap, the wise farmer will only produce roots for special purposes,
" such as feed for ewes having lambs in early spring, or as a condi-
" ment for some pet animal.   For special reasons, a farmer of my
" acquaintance has his lambs yeaned in December and January, to
" the number of two or three hundred.   This man raises about
" eight acres of roots to feed with his dry hay to the mothers of
" these lambs, and by the time grass comes the next spring these
" lambs weigh fifty, sixty, or even more pounds each.   This man
" can afford to do as he does, but his case is a very peculiar one.

" The stalks of an acre of corn are generally considered by
" farmers in Central New York to be worth as much as an acre
" of hay to feed their stock in winter.   The stalks should pay
" for the whole cost of the corn crop up to husking.   The acre
" of grain should average not less than 2,500 pounds when dry.
" One pound of corn will feed a fattening sheep one day, and
" eight pounds will feed a fattening steer a day, the proper quan-
" tity of hay or other forage being given in each case.

" The Illinois farmer is quite as likely to continue to raise great
" fields of Indian corn, and go on feeding it in his wasteful way,
" and totally neglect raising roots to feed his cattle, as the Eng-
" lishman in Canada is to follow up his traditions and feed roots
" during his hyperborean winters.   At any rate, all exhortations
" to the Western corn-raisers on this point are useless, for he
" thinks he knows what he is about—and he does.

" With these preliminary remarks we will discuss the question
" of rotation, counting Indian corn in, and root crops out.

"OUR ROTATION.

" *First Year.*—The land having been well seeded with tim-
" othy grass and medium red clover, the first crop taken is hay.

"CLOVER-SEED CROP.

"As soon as the hay has been removed from the ground, the
"clover starts a new growth; and as gypsum is applied and warm
"rains come, by the middle of the month of September there will
"ordinarily be a fine crop of seed matured and ready to cut.
"This seed crop has varied with us from one to seven bushels to
"the acre. It is not the custom here to cut this seed crop close
"to the ground, but to leave a very considerable proportion
"standing. We do not wish to get much more than the heads,
"preferring to leave most of the stalks on the ground. Of
"course, in doing this, we do not get all the seed.

"In the seed crop the timothy shows but little, but it has
"helped make a good sod, and was of considerable value in the
"hay crop. The crop of hay should not average, for a series of
"years, less than two tons to the acre, weighed the next winter,
"and the seed crop should average three bushels to the acre.

"This is the way we manage the first year of our rotation,
"taking two valuable crops.

"*Second Year.*—This year is devoted to pasture, with the ex-
"pectation that each acre will abundantly feed one cow in an
"ordinary season.

"Gypsum, sown about the first day of May on this pasture,
"brings forward the white clover, which abounds, *self-sown*, in
"our pastures; and the timothy and natural grasses will make a
"dense sod several inches thick, and the red clover roots will get
"to their greatest depth and size, such of them as are left.

"*Third Year—Indian Corn.*—About the tenth day of May plow
"the land in the most perfect manner possible, and deep enough
"to bring on top of the reversed sod a sufficient supply of soil
"that is not held too firmly together by the grass roots to allow
"of harrowing and marking without disturbing the sod. The
"roots of the red clover will be either cut off by the plow or
"drawn out by it. Six or seven inclines will be about the least
"depth to give the plowing.

" Indian corn is a gross feeder, and will send its roots through
" the sod and down below it to a great depth, unless the subsoil
" is so hard they cannot penetrate it. As the grass roots decay
" they furnish food to this wonderful plant. I say wonderful,
" for in about one hundred days an immense crop of stalks, and
" perhaps 3,000 pounds of the richest grain (second only in its
" fattening powers to flaxseed) will be produced.

" When the crop is sufficiently ripened, it should be cut near
" the ground, and put in 'stooks' to cure; and no cattle should
" be allowed to tramp over the field in the late autumn or early
" winter, to make tracks in and puddle the soil. In warm cli-
" mates, where the larger varieties of corn are raised, this process
" of harvesting cannot be adopted, and on sandy or other loose
" soils it is not so important to keep cattle off the field.

"*Fourth Year.*—*Barley* or *oats* are sown on the corn-stubble,
" the ground being plowed but once, but that one plowing being
" done perfectly, after the ground has properly dried in the spring,
" cutting narrow, deep furrows.

" Some farmers entertain the opinion that barley is the best
" crop to precede wheat. If the ground is clean, that is, free
" from Canada thistles and other bad weeds, it is; but if the
" ground is not in first-rate condition in this respect, oats are
" better.

" Barley must be sown early to warrant the expectation of a
" good crop. Oats should be sown two weeks or so later than
" barley. By sowing an oat crop late, time is given for the
" thistles and other foul stuff to commence growing, and make
" quite a show above the ground before the plowing; then a
" perfect plowing does much for their extirpation, and the warm
" weather, that at that time of the season may be reasonably
" expected, will force the oat crop forward, and give it greatly
" the start of the weeds, and thus the crop will out-top and keep
" under these pests. Another consideration is the character of
" the soil, in deciding whether barley or oats shall be selected for
" the crop of the fourth year. Barley delights in a clay soil, and
" but rarely does well on a quick sandy soil.

"Whichever of the crops may be selected, the treatment of
" the land after harvest is the same. The stubble being raked
" clean as possible from all the grain ; if the land is not clear of
" weeds plow it, shallow, say four inches, at once, and harrow, so
" as to insure the growth of all the grain left on the ground, and
" the bringing to the surface the roots of weeds. At this season
" of the year the sun is usually hot and the weather dry ; and six
" weeks of summer fallowing in August and the forepart of Sep-
" tember, properly managed, will do much toward freeing the
" land from even couch (quick) grass, especially if the roots are
" gathered by a strong steel-toothed horse-rake, and then drawn
" off the field and destroyed.

" If the land is free from foul stuff, the best course is to turn
" on the stubble sheep or young cattle, and let them pick off
" what they can, until near the time for sowing wheat, and then
" plow once perfectly, and harrow for the next crop, which will
" be wheat.

"*Fifth. Year.*—In the fall of the fourth year wheat was sown,
" and with it, by a device connected with the drill, six quarts of
" timothy-seed. In the spring of the fifth year red clover is to be
" sown. When the wheat is harvested, the ground should be all
" covered with clover and timothy, which are to make the
" meadow or hay crop of the first year of the next rotation.

" This is the first five-year rotation as practiced by the best
" farmers of my acquaintance when no circumstances cause a
" modification—such, for instance, as the failure of clover-seed to
" take and grow well, or, perhaps, an uncommon demand in the
" market for some one crop.

" Our farmers expect, as the proceeds of this five-year rotation,
" from each acre two tons of hay, three bushels of clover-seed,
" the pasturage of one cow for a season, fifty bushels of corn,
" and the forage produced by the corn crop, forty bushels of
" barley, or fifty bushels of oats, as the case may be, and twenty
" to twenty-five bushels of wheat.

" If the ground has previously been well tilled, and is not
" infested with foul weeds, each grain crop is raised by one plow-

" ing. Land free from stone and all other obstructions, and that
" has been previously properly managed, can be perfectly cul-
" tivated by one plowing, that is, the furrow can be turned over
" and pulverized, if the right plow is used, and the right man has
" the holding of it.

" MODIFICATIONS OF OUR ROTATIONS.

" To carry out strictly the five-year rotation, we have to sup-
" pose the farm to be divided into five equal parts, and that the
" owner will find it to his interest to raise crops in just the pro-
" portion laid down. As has been already suggested, for various
" reasons, this is not always so, and thus modifications are from
" year to year made. Some of them will now be stated.

" The yield of grass the first year after the wheat has been
" taken off is much greater than it is the second year; that is, a
" larger crop of hay can be cut the first year; there is more
" clover this year than afterward. The convenience of the
" farmer often causes him to pasture the first year, until late in
" August, and then by one perfect plowing turn all the clover
" that he can and sow wheat. By just this process we have pro-
" duced crops of wheat at the least cost per bushel of any we
" have raised. A case occurs to me in which we treated a
" twenty-acre field in this way, and got thirty-three bushels to
" the acre. This was the cheapest wheat to us of any ever
" raised on the farm.

" The next year this land went into barley, followed by wheat,
" when it was again seeded to grass.

" It has, in some few instances, happened that wheat has been
" sown on wheat stubble, thus taking two wheat crops in suc-
" cession, sowing grass seed on the second crop. But this can
" be justified only on land in high condition.

" Various other modifications, that will readily suggest them-
" selves to the minds of grain-raising farmers, become necessary
" or very convenient. But the leading point is constantly kept
" in view. Fill the ground with clover-roots and the roots of

" grasses as often as practicable, and then kill them with the
" plow, and convert their decomposed substances into grain.

" The grass crop is the basis of all improvement, where it can
" be made to grow well.

" AT WHAT TIME IN THE ROTATION SHOULD THE BARN-YARD MANURE BE APPLIED?

" For many years I have been trying to learn the best methods
" of taking care of and using barn-yard manure, and now I am
" ready to confess my lack of knowledge in regard to this impor-
" tant matter.

" Farmers that raise much grain, and keep a proper stock of
" sheep or cows to consume their coarse fodder, or, if not *con-*
" *sume* it, to *trample it under foot* during the winter, and get it in
" condition to be applied to the land, make immense quantities of
" manure that costs them much labor to handle, and it is always
" a matter of great interest to them to learn the best methods of
" doing this work. I do not propose to enter into the discussion
" of this topic now, but will state the practice most approved
" here.

" Sheep are the best farm stock to manufacture manure.
" Properly wintered, under sheds that can be closed against
" storms, having small yards connected with them, sheep will
" trample much straw under foot, and will dispose in like manner
" of the coarser part of the corn-stalks so well, that twice or
" three times during the winter the manure can be drawn on
" sleds from the sheds and yards, and spread on the snow that
" then covers the pastures and ground designed for the next year's
" crop of corn. The manure must be quite fine to justify its
" being put on the ground designed for corn. Spread on pastures,
" a bad flavor is given to the grass next year ; but, aside from this
" objection, I know of no place where it does so much good. A
" pasture treated in the winter to raw unfermented manure will
" be so strong in grass, and the soil will become so rich, that,
" whether plowed the next summer for wheat, or after being one

"year grazed, and then put into corn, the maximum yield
"may be reasonably expected. This winter manuring costs the
"least of all methods, and probably saves the most of the value
"of the manure of any known to me.

"But the barn-yards of a productive grain farm will be covered
"in the spring a foot or two deep with the butts of corn-stalks,
"straw, and manure from cows, young cattle, etc., that will be
"so coarse that it requires reducing in bulk by fermentation.
"This matter is pitched into large piles in the yard, from time to
"time sprinkled with gypsum, and about the first of July the
"sides of the piles cut down and cast on the top, to promote the
"decay of the part of the manure that has been so exposed to the
"air that fermentation has been very slight.

"Thus treated, this coarse manure will be so reduced that by the
"time wheat is to be sown in the fall it can be drawn out and
"scattered on the *top* of the wheat ground immediately before
"harrowing and drilling in the seed. Selecting that part of the
"wheat ground that most requires help, we top-dress it with this
"rotted manure, not mixing it with the soil more than the harrow
"and drill buries it, with a very slight covering.

"This last-described method of handling barn-yard manure is
"vastly more expensive than the one first given; but, all things
"considered, I know of no better way to take care of the coarser
"parts of it.

"In this very summary statement of our methods of using
"barn-yard manure, I have avoided arguing the controverted
"points that are involved—some of them may come up for con-
"sideration at a future time.

"ROTATION OF CROPS INVOLVES MIXED AGRICULTURE.

"There are sections of country where rotation of crops and a
"system of mixed agriculture is impracticable. And there are
"districts where the plow cannot be used at all. But a very
"large proportion of this country is in all respects well adapted
"to the production of a great variety of crops, and to the sup-
"port, at the same time, of large flocks of sheep, or herds of cattle.

" Wherever mixed agriculture is practicable, it results in vastly
" increasing the grand total of the yield of the fruits of the earth.

" That strange tendency of the American mind to run to
" extremes in every thing appears among the farmers as strongly as
" anywhere else. If fine wool happens to be profitable to raise, a
" fever takes hold of the owners of flocks, which soon becomes a
" mania. Individuals become noted as breeders. Some fancy
" name becomes famous, and the sheep of certain men rise in price,
" first to hundreds, soon to thousands of dollars each, until a single
" animal has been sold for the price of a farm adequate to the sup-
" port, when managed by a rational man, of an ordinary family.

" This sheep fever in due time results in over-production of wool ;
" low prices follow ; men begin to rub their eyes, as though waking
" from some strange dream, and the bubble bursts. A reaction
" follows ; good sheep are slaughtered by the thousand, saving only
" their pelts and tallow, and the business of wool-raising, as a regu-
" lar branch of farming, is as unduly depressed as at the time of the
" popular insanity it was unduly elevated.

" A few men have made money ; many men have lost money ;
" but there has been one real gain. Sheep have been greatly
" improved, and the knowledge of the best manner of managing
" flocks has been very much extended.

" FARM STOCK, WITH GRAIN-RAISING, IS NECESSARILY CON-
NECTED WITH A PROPER ROTATION.

" In the rotation suggested in this paper, one-fifth of the farm
" is pasture, besides the pasturage derived in the early spring from
" ground that is to be plowed for corn, and that which is derived
" from the fields from which wheat has been harvested. The
" wheat stubbles will, without injuring the grass, give a large
" amount of pasture—at a time when usually most desired—that
" will be fresh, and much liked by the farm stock.

" A grain farm, under a proper rotation, will carry through the
" summer a large stock, and produce none the less grain, if we
" take a period of, say ten years, into account. This farm stock,
" in the winter, will work the corn-stalks and straw into manure.

16

" In fact, the stock is a necessity to the grain farmer in the
" winter. Before the grain-raisers of central and western New
" York understood this thing, the straw from their grain was a
" great incumbrance, and much of it was burned up immediately
" after the grain was thrashed, in the fields where it grew.

" To sum this matter up, a proper farm stock, over and above
" the teams, cows, etc., necessary to meet the wants of the farm,
" can be supported on a grain farm with very little cost, except
" the care and attention required.

" It may be said that the straw, corn-stalks, etc., might be sold
" for money. Near large towns this may be true, but it is not
" true away from such markets. But it should not be sold off the
" farm unless the owner of the farm intends to sell the soil within
" a few years. The barn-yard manure made by cattle and sheep,
" by trampling this coarse forage under foot, is an important
" matter in that system that looks to making a farm self-sustaining
" and self-improving.

" A well-managed grain farm should sell grain, clover-seed,
" meat, wool, cheese, and butter—but not hay, corn-stalks, or
" straw, until it has become so fertile by its own self-sustaining
" and creative powers, that too much straw is produced in the
" grain crops. Then, perhaps, it will do to sell a little hay—
" when it brings a large price.

" Such persons as have done me the honor of reading my com-
" munications lately published in *The Tribune*, will have learned
" that I believe in a farm sustaining itself, and that with very
" little aid from outside, it should be, by judicious cultivation,
" carried to the very highest point of production that the climate
" will allow. I fully recognize the inherent differences in soils,
" and their adaptability to special crops, and I do not say that the
" exact methods I have pointed out are applicable everywhere.
" But I have no sympathy whatever with that school of writers
" who appear to think that the world is going to ruin by reason
" of the deterioration of the farming lands.

" There is a period in new countries in which bad farming is
" almost universal; then comes the necessity of reform, and

" reform becomes the order of the day. So far as I know, farm-
" ing is now improving in all the older sections of the country,
" except, perhaps, in the neighborhood of cities. The temptation
" to raise hay and sell it at high prices, in a great city, leads to the
" worst farming that has come under my notice. Whenever I
" hear a farmer say that he pays fifty or sixty dollars an acre for
" manure to put on his fields, and then learn that this manure is
" mostly straw that has become stained a little in some city stable,
" fifty or more miles from where it is applied as manure, I am
" quite apt to tell that farmer that his money has been badly laid
" out, and that, in a proper system of mixed husbandry, and with
"a proper rotation of crops, he would have saved this expense."

CHAPTER X.

THE principal grain crops of America are Indian Corn, Wheat, Rye, Oats, Barley, and Buckwheat. The chief of these is the king of the cereals,

INDIAN CORN.

This is by far the most important product of American agriculture, and it feeds more human beings than any other grain except rice. It takes, in a great measure, the place of the turnip crop of England, and, both as a source of food and as a means for placing the soil in a good condition for the cultivation of other crops, it is the very backbone of our system of farming.

Its range of cultivation is almost co-extensive with the boundaries of the nation, as it grows to perfection from the great lakes to the Gulf of Mexico.

The *varieties* of corn are numerous. In fact, they are constantly increasing in consequence of the ease with which the plant hybridizes;—two sorts growing in the same field usually producing many crosses, having each more or less of the qualities of one or the other of the original sorts. There seems to be two distinct classes of corn, one peculiar to the North, and the other to the South.

The Northern corn, of which the Dutton is the type, has a round, smooth seed, which is entirely coated with a hard, horny substance. This contains less starch and more oil and gluten than does the Southern, or gourd-seed corn, in which the starch occupies the center of the grain quite to its upper end;—the oil and gluten which exist in smaller proportion than in Northern corn, being confined mainly to the sides of the grain. As the grain of this variety ripens, and the starch shrinks, the top of the kernel falls in, producing a dent or depression.

As a general principle, it may be stated that the Southern corn is less nutritious than the Northern varieties.

CULTIVATION.

Corn delights in a soil filled with decaying organic matter of both animal and vegetable origin. It also requires for its perfect growth that the soil be *warm*, sufficiently *moist, loose in its texture*, and, above all, *not too wet*.

As the plant is peculiarly suited to tropical climates,—and requires, at some time during its growth, an intense heat,—it should not be planted until all danger of frost has passed, nor until the soil has become thoroughly warmed. In the latitude of New York the seed should not be put in before the tenth of May, and,—on land that is perfectly adapted for its growth,—it is as well to defer planting until early in June. Put in at this time, the seed will germinate very rapidly, and the growth will proceed without the check that often results from the cold storms of May. It takes longer to recover from a serious checking of the growth than to make a good growth later in the season. The chief advantages of early planting are, that the work is out of the way, and that, in exceptional seasons, the crop will arrive a few days earlier at maturity. This is not always,—perhaps not generally —the case, and in this latitude it is considered quite safe to postpone planting until June.

The *moisture* that the soil requires is rather the natural dampness of freshly-stirred land than the drenching wet of heavy rains. If the soil is loose and friable, so that the air can circulate among its cooler shaded particles, enough water will be condensed from this air to fully supply the crop, and if corn, growing on good land, could be well hoed every day, it would not require a single drop of rain during the whole period of its growth. On the other hand, if the soil is stiff and compact, and is not hoed or cultivated

more than two or three times during the season, it will suffer
materially for want of water, even though the soil is wet one-half
the time ;—because during the other half, it will be baked dry and
hard, excluding the air by whose circulation alone, in time of
drought, can a sufficient supply of water be deposited in the soil.

Looseness of texture in the soil is important, not only as affording
access to air, but also because it allows of the free and wide-
spread ramification of the smaller feeding roots. These would
not penetrate a solid clod of even the richest earth, while, if the
same clod were finely pulverized, every part of it would be penetrated by corn roots, and the plant food contained in it would
become available. Therefore, it is best that the soil should be of
a sort not apt to bake, and that it should be made as fine as possible before planting, and kept as fine as possible as long as the size
of the crop will allow it to be worked.

Drainage is more important than any other item in the preparation of land for corn, unless the soil is already naturally drained.
Stagnant water in the soil—and upon it—is absolutely fatal to success, and whatever care we may take might almost as well be thrown
away if we allow the want of proper under-draining to keep the
soil sometimes too cold, sometimes too dry, and always too stiff
and compact. That the want of draining will produce all of these
unfavorable conditions, no one need be told who has had an
opportunity to see how they all gradually vanish when wet land is
thoroughly under-drained.

The manner in which the corn crop of much of our best corn-
growing region has been this year (1869) destroyed by excessive
wet, the farmers of Central Illinois do not need to be told.

In view of the foregoing principles, I submit the following as
a good course to pursue in the commencement of a rotation, of
which corn is the first crop.

(Other plans may be as good—under certain circumstances they
may be even better—but, so far as it is possible to lay down general rules, I believe that this is, on the whole, the best ; and I am
confident that all who follow it will be satisfied with the result.)

It is assumed that the land on which it is prepared to grow corn next year is now in grass, and that the hurry of the summer work is past.

1. The first step is to haul out manure—commencing in August, if possible—and spread it broadcast on the land. The more heavily it is applied the better,—for *corn cannot be over-fed.* The sooner the manure is spread on the land, after it has been dropped, the better—for in no other place is it subjected to so little loss, and its effect, early in the fall, or in the spring, commences from the moment of its application. I am satisfied that the best practice will be to use as much manure as can possibly be spared, and to get it on the land as early as practicable after the hay is removed.

It stimulates the growth of a luxuriant sod, which it also enriches by its own decomposition; and this sod, with its roots immensely increased in number, in size, and in succulence, is the best supply of food for corn that it is possible to secure. The grass may be eaten off in both fall and spring, but not too closely, and especially the spring feeding should be very slight, if not entirely given up. The chief object is to secure a luxuriant crop of *roots.* So early in the season the grass does not amount to much as a green crop, but the extent to which the growth of the roots may be increased is very great, and these—together with the constituents of the manure absorbed by the soil are of the utmost importance.

2. A few days before it is intended to plant, (the fewer the better,) with ample teams, and implements in good order, the land should be plowed to a depth of not less than *four* inches, and not more than *seven* inches—the object being to keep the mass of roots near to the surface, only turning up enough *earth* to secure good "covering." The furrow should be laid flat, and no grass should be allowed to show on the surface. The surface plow should be followed by a subsoil plow, drawn by a good team and loosening the bottom of the furrow as deeply as possible,—for, although we ought to keep the organic matter in the soil near to the surface, we should at the same time open a passage by which

the deeper roots of the corn can go down below the reach of
drought.

3. As soon as the plowing is finished, the land should be heavily
rolled and dressed with not less than 200 lbs. of Peruvian guano,
300 lbs. of cotton-seed meal, or some equally stimulating manure,
and thoroughly harrowed—preferably with Shares harrow. This
implement should run lengthwise over the furrows, and the operation should be continued until a fine covering not less than two
inches deep is secured.

4. Before the soil has had time to become dry, it should be
marked out and planted, either in " drills " or in " hills." If the
latter plan is adopted, it will be necessary to wait until the whole
field is made ready, so that it may be marked both ways.   If the
planting is in drills, it may be commenced as soon as a single land
—or a few furrows can be harrowed.   The more rapidly the
planting can be made to follow the plowing, the less time will be
allowed for the starting of weeds.

The hill system of planting, as it allows the crop to be cultivated by horse-power, in both directions, is much cheaper, and in
the absence of an abundant supply of labor, it is undoubtedly the
best ; but if the help can be procured for the extra work of planting in drills, and for the greater amount of hoeing that will be
necessary when the cultivator can be worked in but one direction,
the extra production of grain,—and especially of fodder—will
amply repay it.   In drill planting, it will be easier (and equally
good) to drop three seeds in a place, at intervals of two feet, than
to drop single seeds at intervals of eight inches, and the hoeing
of the crop will take much less time.

The seed should not be covered more than one inch deep.
This will be enough to protect it against too much drying, and it
is important that it be within the influence of the sun's heat.
After the planting is finished, it will be well to give the whole
field a light rolling to compact the earth about the seed, and to
make the surface so even as to render the subsequent work of
cultivation lighter.

As soon as the rows can be distinctly seen, the work of cultivation should be commenced. It is easier to prevent the growth of weeds than to kill them after they are grown. If the corn is planted in " hills " the horse cultivator may be run both ways, and thus reduce the handwork to the lowest point. If in " drills," the hoeing should be done with great care—all grass and weeds being thoroughly cleaned out from the rows. This first hoeing should be finished when the crop is not more than six inches high, and the second cultivation should be given before weeds have time to make any considerable headway. A third hoeing, which is erroneously neglected in many instances, should be completed before the crop is so large as to be injured by the working of the horse, and the whiffletree used at this time should be as short as possible.

It is now pretty well settled that " hilling " corn is an injurious practice. It undoubtedly had its origin in the custom of the Indians, who had no other means of giving the plant a bed of fine soil to grow in than by scraping it from the surface with their hoes, and piling it up about the stems. Probably it was continued longer than it otherwise would have been, from the belief that the " brace shoots " that are thrown out above the soil are *roots*,—which they are not. They are intended to hold the stalk in its position, and they do this much more thoroughly than any system of hilling can possibly do, and by being covered with earth they lose their power to act as braces.

A little earth should be drawn about the stem of the plant at the first hoeing,—raising the soil, say an inch or so,—as there is danger that a little earth will be drawn away by the cultivator at the second working, and this would leave the true roots too little protected against the drying influence of sun and wind. If the soil is thoroughly loose and clean all about and between the plants when they are about two feet high, the crop should be " laid by " until harvest. The less it is disturbed after this the better it will be. If it is desired to raise turnips on the land, they should be sown broadcast after the last hoeing, before the earth is beaten down by rain. One pound of turnip-seed per acre is an ample allowance, and the best way to sow it is with a " French " mustard jar, or a broad-mouthed bottle, with a tin cover pierced with large holes. The jar should not be more than half full, and a little practice will soon indicate the extent to which the holes should be covered by the fingers as the seed is flirted out in walking across the field.

The turnip seed,—or enough of it,—will be planted by the first rain, and the plants will be well established by the time the corn is cut up, after which they will make fair-sized roots. The Strap Leaf Red Top is the best American variety for this use.

Whether it is wise to raise this stolen crop of turnips depends on the circumstances of the case. They will, if properly managed (properly planted, that is), yield an abundant supply of valuable food for the early winter, but they are so hard upon the land that they will probably cost all they will be worth. If roots can be as well grown on ground of their own, the corn-field should not be charged with their production,—for they will inevitably use up manure that should remain for the second crop of the rotation.

Harvesting.—Corn should never be "topped." The little that will be gained in fodder, will be more than lost in the grain, which in its maturing assimilates some of the contents of the juices of the whole plant,—above as well as below.

As soon as the kernels are glazed,—as soon as the thumb nail cannot be easily pressed through its skin,—the stalks should be cut up near the ground, and bound in "stooks" to cure. The earlier it is so cut the better will be the fodder, and after the glazing is complete the grain will mature as rapidly and as perfectly on the severed stalk as though it was still in communication with the root.

Late in the fall the ears should be husked and stored in cribs and the stalks tied in bundles for stacking. They will keep much better if the stacks are thatched with rye straw—to exclude rain; and in no case should the diameter of the stack be more than twice the length of the bundles;—that is, it should be built around a pole, and each bundle should reach from this to the outside of the stack. The tops should lie toward the center, and the butts outward.   If it is attempted to store corn-stalks in barns or in very large stacks, they will almost invariably decay, owing to the large amount of water they contain, which it is impossible to dry out by any amount of exposure.

Storing the grain.—Corn cribs are such a simple affair that it would not have occurred to me at all to describe their construction did I not frequently receive applications for plans by which to erect them.   The fundamental principle for the arrangement of the crib is to give the freest possible admission to air, and to keep out rats and mice.   Of course there are many considerations of convenience, which it is best to study, and the mode of construction must depend very much on the amount of grain to be stored.

For a Northern farm, where from 500 to 1,000 bushels of shelled corn are to be kept, (double that bulk of ears,) the plan shown in Fig. 66 will be found effective.   It is 10 feet high

Fig. 66.

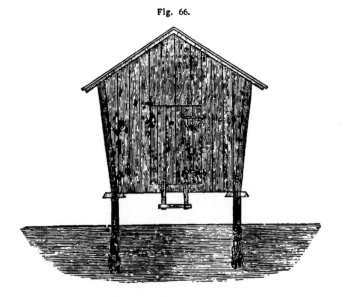

at the sills, 12 feet wide, the plate 7 feet high from the floor to the eaves, and as long as the requirements of the farm make necessary.   It has a passage-way 4 feet wide from the door at the end to within 4 feet of the rear end where there is a bin

4 feet square for shelled corn. The plan of the floor is shown
in Fig. 67. The building should stand on posts 2½ feet above
the ground, these being capped by inverted tins made in the
shape of ordinary milk-pans, but without the wire in the rim,

Fig. 67.

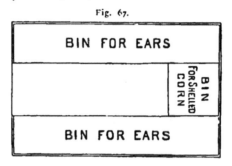

BIN FOR EARS

BIN
FOR SHELLED
CORN

BIN FOR EARS

—which, for this purpose, is unnecessary. This arrangement
will effectually prevent the access of rats,—especially if the
approach to the doorway is an iron stirrup or wagon step let
down from the sill and not coming nearer than within 18 inches
of the ground.

The sides of the crib should be made of vertical slats not more
than three inches wide, and placed at intervals of at least one inch
so as to admit of a free circulation of air; for the same reason the
partitions between the passage way, in the middle of the crib and
the bins, and the floor under the bins, should be made of slats.
The entrances from the passage way to the bins, on either side,
should be only wide enough to admit of the passing of baskets, and
they may be closed, as the corn is put in, by loose boards cut to
fit a groove, into which they are dropped from the top. The
roof should project enough to shed water clear of the sides, which,
for further protection against wet, have a pitch outward of one
foot on each side.

In such a crib, the bins will be 3 feet wide at the bottom, 4
feet at the top (a mean width of 3½ feet), and 7 feet high, which
will give a section of 24½ square feet. Six and a half (6½) feet in
length of such a bin will hold 100 bushels of ears—round measure;
about 1,000 bushels being held by both sides of a crib 30 feet
long.

In writing about the cultivation of wheat, it is but just for me to say that I never raised a bushel of wheat in my life, and that what I have to say on the subject is the purest " book-farming ;" it is the result of study only, and is, of course, not to be considered so reliable as are those parts of this book which relate to matters in which I have had the advantage of personal experience.

The production of wheat seems, from the custom of the whole world, to belong, properly, to the two extremes of farming, the most careless and inconsiderate, and the most complete and well directed. In the wide interval that covers the good, bad, and indifferent agriculture lying between these two extremes, wheat is, to say the least of it, not the most important crop.

On such virgin · soils as are better adapted to the growth of wheat than of corn, there is no crop that is at once so easily raised, and so valuable when raised ; and for a few years after the first breaking up (sometimes for many years). " *Wheat* is the crop every time." In many newly settled countries, 40 bushels of wheat to the acre have been common, and fine crops have been raised for successive years on the same ground. Sooner or later, however, the constant cultivation of this single crop begins to tell on the land, and the yield falls off, while the constitution of the plant suffers more and more from the unfavorable condition of the soil, and the door is opened for the attack of rust, weevil, and blight, which add to the risk and help to reduce the result.

The best wheat lands, treated as they almost invariably (and necessarily) are by new settlers, commence at 40 bushels per acre ; and after two or three years they begin to grow smaller and smaller ;—35—30—20—15—12—sometimes even 8 bushels per acre, marking the steadily decreasing return until the cultivation is abandoned. Usually, every reason but the right one is given for this decrease. Climate, the removal of forests, the proximity of the sea, or of mountains, bugs, blight, " bad luck," winter killing, too much snow, or too little—hundreds of plausible reasons are given why wheat ceases to grow. The right reason is almost

never hit upon, and but few farmers seem to know, what is absolutely the fact, that wheat ceases to grow well, to produce largely,
and to withstand the vicissitudes of the weather and the attacks
of insects when,—and because,—those parts of the ashes of the
grain which are most essential to its perfection are no longer
supplied by the soil in sufficient quantities, and where, from injudicious plowing and harrowing, (especially from plowing in wet
weather), the land has been brought to a condition unfavorable to
its growth.

Wheat requires for its best growth a soil that is compact rather
than loose, and that has been made rich by previous cultivation
with manure, rather than by the application of heavy dressings of
fresh manure during the immediate preparation for the crop.
Peruvian guano, nitrate of soda, super-phosphate of lime,—any
manure in fact which is not subject to an active fermentation,—may,
with advantage, be harrowed in after plowing, or applied as a top
dressing after planting ; but, as a rule, it is better to apply the
manure to a previous crop, thus giving it time to become thoroughly
decomposed before the wheat is sown.

The *universal fertilizer* for wheat, one which is nearly always
accessible, and always effective, is *clover.* If this is sown in the
spring, with barley or oats, allowed to grow without being closely
fed off in the fall, top-dressed with plaster the second spring, cut
once in June and again in August, it will have accumulated in
the soil an enormous quantity of long, deeply-reaching tap-roots,
which,—with the leaves that will have fallen during growth,—
constitute the best manure for the wheat crop ; for, in addition to
the fertilizing effect of the decaying roots, (rich with nutriment
drawn from the lower soil and from the atmosphere,) every fiber
that reaches down into the subsoil, opens the way for the more
delicate roots of the wheat to penetrate in search of food, and, by
its own decomposition, helps to prepare the soil by which it is
immediately surrounded for easy assimilation.

The *mechanical* effect of the plowing down of a strong clover
sod, is very great. It warms the soil, and makes it easy for the

wheat roots to penetrate every part of it. In fact, in so far as it is a question of manuring, it may be safely assumed that if we can secure a good growth of clover, we need have no uneasiness about the wheat.

While compact clay soils (what are known as *strong* soils) are the best for wheat, it is of the utmost importance that they be *well drained*. There is no crop that is grown by American farmers that is more impatient of undue moisture than wheat is ; and it may be considered that every argument that has been advanced in support of tile-draining, applies with redoubled force to the draining of land intended for wheat.

There is now an active discussion going on throughout the wheat-growing world concerning the quantity of seed to be sown per acre. The doctrines of heavy seeding and light seeding have each their earnest advocates, but, as a conclusion drawn from a careful reading of the arguments in favor of each plan, I think the weight of reason and the weight of evidence are both on the side of the thin seeding. One bushel of wheat per acre, planted so carefully as to give a fair proportion of seed to each square foot of land, will give an ample stand,— completely occupying the ground, and returning the largest yield of grain. Of course the seed should be planted at a uniform depth and with great regularity.

It has recently been stated that a field of wheat planted with selected grain, one kernel in a place, rows a foot apart both ways, yielded 159 bushels per acre. This is a marvelous story, and it is not unlikely that the land on which the experiment was tried was in an exceptional state of fertility, nor is it impossible that the truth has been largely overstated. However, it may be assumed as a fact, that a field of wheat planted as above described, with the largest and finest kernels only, has been made to produce much more largely than has ever a field sown in the ordinary way. The quantity of seed used in this planting would not be more than four quarts ; while a single bushel, evenly sown over the whole surface, would give one kernel to each three inches square ; in the case under consideration there was only one kernel to each twelve inches square.

The quantity of seed that it is most judicious to use depends very much on the quality of the land. The richer the land, the larger the growth of the individual plant, and, consequently, the fewer the plants required to occupy the land. Wheat multiplies itself very largely, by sprouting at the crown ; and under the best circumstances, a single seed may result in a stool of from fifty to seventy shoots, each bearing a perfect head of well-filled grain. This process of multiplication is called " tillering." It can only take place under favorable conditions. The too close prox-imity of other plants, and the checking of the root growth by stagnant water, or by an unfavorable subsoil, will arrest it ;—so that a field which has not been too heavily seeded can never bear too many shoots,—no matter how rich it is,—nor can it bear a full crop unless both the mechanical and the chemical condition of the soil are such as to conduce to a sufficient continuation of the tillering process.

WINTER WHEAT.

The great drawback in the raising of *winter wheat* is found in the liability of the plant to be killed by frost. As winter wheat is a perfectly " hardy " plant, this winter killing is never the result of the direct action of the frost on the plant itself, but rather on the soil. If wheat is deeply rooted, a single hard freezing of the soil, by its lifting effect, actually breaks the upper part of the plant from its lower roots, and so greatly injures it. The worst effects are produced, however, by the repeated freezing and thaw-ing of the soil. Thus : a hard frost lifts up the soil, (and carries the plant with it,) then comes a warm sun which thaws the upper soil and allows it to fall back to a lower level, leaving the crown of the plant out of the ground ; the next frost takes a fresh hold on the plant and raises it again ; another thaw leaves it still higher ; and thus the process goes on until the crown is so far above the ground as to be exposed to the action of the weather, entirely unprotected by the soil in which it properly belongs, and the plant is killed.

As this winter killing is largely due to an excess of moisture in the soil, it is very much modified by under-draining ; but not entirely prevented. A top-dressing with sea-weed, stable manure containing a great deal of straw or other suitable material, will be of great service ; but there is nothing so good as a complete covering of snow throughout the winter. This, of course, is a matter of climate, and is entirely beyond the farmer's control. In cold regions, where snow does not lie throughout the winter, and where top-dressing is not practicable, the seed should be sown as late as the first of October, and covered not more than half an inch deep. Planted in this way, the roots will nearly all be in the immediate surface, and there will be less danger from freezing than where the seed is covered several inches deep.

SPRING WHEAT.

Spring wheat is somewhat less productive and less valuable (because making a less attractive flour) than winter wheat, but in regions where the latter is apt to be winter killed, it is the safer variety to grow. It should be planted as early as possible in the spring, and is said to grow best in a somewhat lighter soil than winter wheat.

Wheat, from its great importance, has received much and most careful attention from scientific men and from practical farmers. There is an immense number of varieties cultivated ; valuable experiments have been made with all conceivable sorts of manures ; the diseases to which the plant is subject have been made the subject of especial study and investigation ; the insects by which the crop is sometimes almost swept away have been carefully examined, and their habits clearly described ; and almost innumerable implements for planting, manuring, weeding, harvesting, thrashing, and cleaning have been invented and put in use. To enter satisfactorily into these details, in this limited space, would be

17

impossible, and the reader is referred to the various works on
the subject which are to be obtained from agricultural booksellers.

In considering all that I have myself read on the subject, the
following points strike me as being especially worthy of the attention of all wheat growers:—

I. The land may, with advantage, be made as rich as possible,
—the application of fresh stable manure in the immediate preparation of the crop being avoided.

II. It should be—either naturally or artificially—thoroughly
well drained.

III. The seed should be selected with care, and of the sort
that is most likely to succeed in the climate and soil of the locality.

IV. The seed should always be drilled rather than sown broadcast.

V. The ridges made by the drill should not be leveled by the
harrow or roller until after the ground has settled in the spring.

VI. The amount of seed should be from one bushel, or even
less, on very rich land, to two bushels on the least rich on which
it will pay to grow wheat.

VII. Wherever sufficient help can be obtained, it will probably
pay to hoe the crop early in the spring,—and it will certainly pay
to remove all weeds growing among it.

VIII. The crop should be cut from ten days to two weeks
before the grain is thoroughly ripe.

By proper attention to these requirements, I believe that the
wheat crop of the United States may be increased from its
present average of about 12 bushels per acre (or less) to the 28
bushels (or thereabout) which is the average in Great Britain. I
also believe that much of the so-called worn-out land of New
England may be made to produce profitable crops of wheat. The
freight on 30 bushels of wheat from a farm in Minnesota to the
city of New York is more than the interest on the total value of
an acre of good land in New England, and New England is supplied with its breadstuffs very largely from the far West.

RYE.

More hardy and better suited to land of inferior quality than wheat, rye may be considered the great bread crop of northern countries in which wheat cannot easily be grown. It makes a nutritious, though dark-colored, bread, and its bran is more valuable than the bran of wheat as a food for domestic animals.

Ordinarily, the cultivation of rye is much more careless than is that of wheat, probably for the reason that a paying crop can be much more easily grown. But if it received in all respects the same attention, there is no doubt that the result in money would be almost, if not quite, equally good, for while the yield of grain is increased in proportion to the care bestowed, the straw which, under the best circumstances, yields very largely, is, when hand-thrashed, of great value, being worth now, in the Eastern markets, about $35 per ton.

Rye is much better able than wheat is, to withstand rough treatment in winter. In fact, except upon very wet land, it is rarely winter-killed to any great extent. It grows best on rather light land, and may, with advantage, be sown early in September, though, if the autumn is long and warm, it will grow so large as to make it advisable to feed it down before winter sets in.

A well-established field of rye is the first field on the farm to turn green in the spring, and it is frequently sown to be used exclusively for spring pasture, being plowed under as a green crop after the grass is well started.

As a soiling crop, rye is, by reason of its earliness, very important, and it will be further considered in this connection, in the chapter on soiling.

OATS.

The cultivation of oats is so universal and so well understood, that it is hardly necessary to say more here on the subject than that they should be sown at the earliest practicable moment after the frost is out of the ground ; that they do much better when drilled than when sown broadcast, and that they are better adapted to light than to heavy lands. They are an exhausting crop, but for some years they have borne so high a price that their cultivation is sufficiently profitable to enable us to buy manure to repair the damage. Perhaps it is not exactly correct to attribute their injurious effect entirely to the exhaustion of the land, as some of the injury that they cause is no doubt due to the fact that their roots bind the soil together in clods which it is difficult to reduce.

Oat straw is more valuable than any other for fodder for domestic animals. If the crop is harvested as it should be, before the grain is fully mature, the straw will be but little inferior to common hay, especially if fed in connection with roots.

BARLEY.

Barley may be sown somewhat later than oats, and it is best suited to rather heavier soil than these prefer. On any soil, however, that is in good condition, provided it is sufficiently drained, it is, at the usual prices, a profitable crop, though the straw is less valuable for feeding purposes than is that of either oats or wheat.

BUCKWHEAT.

I can say but little concerning this crop, save that it will grow better than almost any other will on poor, thin, light soils ; that it should not be sown in the latitude of New York before the 10th of July, and that it must be harvested before the frost.

Planted early in the season, it makes a luxuriant growth of stem, but produces but little grain. It is sometimes so planted to be plowed in as a green crop on land intended for wheat or rye, but it is much less valuable for this purpose than is clover, its only advantage being that much less time is required for its production.

It is especially important, as a green crop, on foul land, as it fully occupies the ground to the exclusion of every thing else, and as three crops may be grown and plowed under during a single season, poor, weedy land may sometimes be more cheaply reclaimed by its aid than in any other way.

Buckwheat is considerably grown by farmers who produce milk for sale to the large cities, for the sake of its bran. Having the grain ground at home, they sell the flour, and feed the bran to their cows, adding very much to the quantity, and taking no little from the quality of their milk.

CHAPTER XI.

ROOT CROPS.

IT would not be an extravagant statement to say that the cultivation of root crops is not known in America; for, notwithstanding the fact that it is usual to see one or two acres of turnips or carrots on a farm, the cultivation of these crops to the extent to which they are grown in Europe almost never occurs in America. The reasons for this are obvious, and are based chiefly upon the high price of farm labor, and upon the fact that, except in certain limited regions, women and children rarely work in the field.

The growth of turnips and mangels forms one of the leading items of the cultivation of nearly all English farms, and a very large part of the work is done by women and children, frequently working in gangs under a contractor, and moving from one part of the country to another, as their services may be required. It will be a long time before farmers in this country will be able to make any thing like the important use of these crops to which they have attained in more thickly settled regions;—for where a farm of from fifty to two hundred acres is operated entirely by two or three hands, they have quite enough to do to attend to the cultivation of the corn crop and the harvesting of the hay, both of which occur at the time when the most labor is required in the root fields.

This state of affairs, however, while it is often an argument against the growth of very large areas of roots, by no means militates against the cultivation of such smaller patches as it may be within the power of the farmer to properly attend to. On good land, in a good state of preparation, and with skillful management, the amount of food produced is very much greater, in proportion to the labor and expense attending the cultivation, than can be obtained in any other way ; and when we consider the great value of roots for the winter feeding of animals, and the incidental value of their tops for fall feeding, it may be safely stated, that, even where the amount of help on the farm is in small proportion to its area and the requirement for other work, it would really pay the farmer better to concentrate his efforts and his manure upon a smaller surface, and let the rest of the farm run into natural pasture. However, I am not disposed to recommend this or any other revolution in the farming of the United States ;—for, in the first place, the recommendation would be disregarded ; and, in the second place, it is very questionable whether revolutions in agriculture, except such as are brought about in a slow and natural way, would be of any permanent value. . Our farms are now suited in size and in general arrangement to the ideas and to the capacities of our farmers ; and, as fast as these ideas and capacities change, or range themselves in accordance with higher requirements, just so rapidly will the farms themselves conform to the altered conditions. And an effort to bring about a rapid general change in favor of any given new system would probably be attended with quite as much disadvantage as benefit. Holding this view, I propose only to state some of the results which it is possible to attain by means of root culture, and to give directions for the cultivation of the different crops. The extent to which, and the manner in which, the growth of roots shall be adopted on any given farm, must rest entirely with the judgment of the farmer himself. He will, if he is a good farmer, do exactly that which promises the best compensation for his capital and his labor. Successful root culture requires that the land be in the best possible condition. Many a field will produce large crops of corn, and of other grain, on which it would be folly to attempt to raise roots in any considerable quantity. The land must be rich, well and deeply cultivated, thoroughly well drained, and free from stones ; and it had better be exposed rather to the morning than to the afternoon sun. On such a field it is hardly possible that the proper amount of labor, judiciously directed, should fail to produce most profitable results. But if the land is only half-rich; if, in wet weather, it is too moist, and in dry weather too hard-baked; if it is filled with the seeds of troublesome weeds, or with the roots of quack-grass, or if its exposure is a cold and unfavorable one, it may be fairly assumed that the labor and manure expended in an effort to raise root crops will bring but a meager and unsatisfactory return. While the cultivation of roots is a necessary accompaniment of high farming,—with poor farming, at least so far as the root land is concerned, they can hardly fail to produce a large crop of disappointment to the grower. It is possible to produce on an acre of land two thousand bushels of mangels, or fifteen hundred bushels of turnips. It is hardly possible to produce such a crop as this without deriving a large amount of profit from the operation; for it can only be done under such circumstances as will give the greatest possible effect to the amount of manure used for the crop, and to the labor that its care involves. It is easy on ordinary soils, ordinarily manured and not very carefully attended, to raise three hundred bushels of beets and from one hundred and fifty to two hundred bushels of turnips. Probably under no circumstances would there be a profit attending the growth of such a crop. It will be readily seen, then, that the adoption of root culture on a large scale implies a willingness to resort to such careful modes of cultivation, and such effective means of fertilizing, as will suffice for very much larger crops than are now common on American farms. In favorable seasons, and under the most favorable circumstances, mangels should yield a thousand bushels to the acre, and rutabaga turnips not less than from six to eight hundred, and such crops should pay very well.

It is frequently the case,—indeed, it is very common through the sea-board regions of New England and New Jersey, that the demand for roots for the general market is so active and reliable, that it will pay to go to greater expense, and submit to greater inconvenience, for the sake of growing root crops, than would be possible, or at least profitable, in a purely agricultural region.

For instance, rutabaga turnips are now (January, 1869) selling in the New York market for $2.50 per barrel, which is very nearly $1.00 a bushel. These turnips probably yield to their producers, after deducting the cost of transportation, commissions, etc., 75 cents a bushel; and, at this price, even the small crops of the unfavorable season of 1868 must have been generally profitable. It is hardly necessary to tell a farmer, however, that, except as a condiment with other food, being fed in very small quantities, roots are worth for feeding nothing like 75 cents a bushel. By reference to tables, showing the theoretical and experimental value of different sorts of food, it will be seen that the amount of roots necessary to be fed, in order to produce the same effect as a given weight of hay, is very large; and, if we were to take only this table as a basis for our estimate of the value of roots in feeding, it would seem questionable whether it would pay to raise them at all, except under the very best circumstances. It is not true, however, that in the feeding of farm stock the importance of roots can be exactly measured by this standard. In addition to their nutritive elements, they have the very great advantage of being a fresh and succulent food, that may be easily kept throughout the whole season, and the effect of which, on the animal organization, is similar to that of salad, celery, and other green vegetables, used on our own tables during the winter season. They keep the system in a more healthy and better lubricated condition, and greatly stimulate the growth and thrift of young stock. Where they are largely fed, all animals, both old and young, come out in the spring of the year in much better condition than if kept only on dry food, however rich it may be. The value of roots in their influence on the manure that results from their consumption, is also very great, and should constitute a considerable element of any estimate of their value. The roots which it is most advantageous to grow for use on the farm are the following :—

| Common Turnips, | Carrots, |
| Rutabaga Turnips, | Mangels. |

Parsnips are sometimes grown, and they yield largely ; but the labor required in digging them is often an argument against their cultivation, except on very light lands.

Except for the growth of common turnips, which may generally be raised as a " stolen crop," or on land lying fallow late in the season, the field on which it is proposed to raise roots of whatever kind should, first of all, be most thoroughly underdrained. If it is of a light texture and is underlaid with a soil through which the water of rains will percolate freely, and if it receives no ooze-water from land lying above it, the natural drainage is sufficient ;—but wherever this is not the case ; wherever, either early in the spring or late in the fall, the surface of the land, when plowed, appears damp and soggy when other land is dry; or wherever, during seasons of excessive drought, it cracks into hard clods, it is useless to attempt to raise paying crops of these vegetables unless a thorough system of underdraining with tiles or stones or brush or some other material is first carried into effect. The land being properly drained or naturally sufficiently dry, it should receive the most careful and thorough attention. If the use of the land can be spared, at least one season should be exclusively devoted to the preparation for the growth of the roots. Clover, buckwheat, or some other green crop should be grown to be plowed in in the fall. Probably the best course would be to manure the land quite heavily with stable manure in August or early in September, and then to plow it up deeply and thoroughly, burying, at as great a depth as possible, the green crop and the manure that has been applied to the surface of the land ; and then to run a subsoil plow in the bottom of each furrow as deeply as it can be done with the force at command, thus loosening the earth that has been indurated by the treading of teams and by the sole of the plow during years of previous cultivation. This plowing being done, the surface should be left exposed in the furrow to the action of the frosts of winter and the fall and spring rains. The fall plowing having been done not later than September, the roots and stems of the green crop will be sufficiently rotted not to interfere with subsequent cultivation ; and, as early as possible in the spring, the land should be rolled and the harrow (preferably Shares' harrow) should be run lengthwise of the furrow, at least once, and, if necessary, two or three times. The ground should then be cross-plowed, and again rolled and harrowed. After this, it should receive a copious top-dressing of stable manure, or not less than five hundred pounds per acre of a thoroughly good superphosphate of lime or of Peruvian guano ;—and this manure, whatever its kind, should be only lightly harrowed by a single operation, and then left undisturbed until after a heavy rain, when a second harrowing and rolling will prepare the ground for the reception of the seed.

The operations detailed above will have the effect of loosening the soil to a great depth, of giving it a good supply of organic matter, and of thoroughly enriching it with the different elements of plant food that the coming crop will require ; while its surface will be so freed from clods and other inequalities as to place it in the best condition for the rapid germination of the delicate seeds with which it is to be sown. Except as to the character of the special commercial fertilizer to be applied, the operations, as far as detailed, are suited to the growth of rutabagas, carrots, or mangels, but subsequent operations must depend on the variety of root that it is intended to grow.

RUTABAGA TURNIPS.

What is called in England the Swedish turnip, is known here as the rutabaga, or white French turnip. It is distinct from the common turnip, being more like the cabbage in many of its characteristics. Its German name is "cabbage-turnip." It is subject to the same diseases as cabbage,—notably to the club-foot, —is consumed in its early stages by the skipping-beetle, and grows to its greatest perfection under circumstances which are best adapted to the growth of cabbage, which it cannot successfully follow or be followed by, except in very rare cases,—and it has the same advantage that it may be easily and safely transplanted.

While the rutabaga contains a not very large quantity of phosphoric acid, it is more specifically benefited than is almost any other plant by the use of bone-dust, superphosphate of lime, or any other fertilizer in which phosphoric acid is the leading ingredient ; and, singularly, while it does contain a very large amount of nitrogen, its growth is often rather injured than benefited by the excessive use of ammoniacal manures.   For this reason it will always be found prudent to mix the stable manure used so thoroughly with the soil that its more active stimulating effect may be modified by its combination with earth ; and, in all cases to use bone-dust or superphosphate of lime, and not Peruvian guano, which, although it contains a good deal of phosphoric acid, is a highly stimulating ammoniacal manure.   It is a very general belief, which has been borne out in my own experience and which I believe to be well founded, that, both in the case of cabbages and of rutabagas, the manure of swine is injurious from its tendency, real or supposed, to increase the formation of "clump roots," or what in turnips is known as " fingers and toes." As a special fertilizer for rutabagas, nothing that I have ever tried has been so effective as a liberal application of New Jersey green-sand marl ; and I have always imagined that I obtained very beneficial results from the even sowing of air-slacked lime, applied by means of a broadcast sower, immediately before planting the seeds or setting out the plants.   Peter Henderson asserts, that lime is a sure agent in preventing the clump-foot disease ; whether this is the case or not, the effect of a light application of lime is, in many ways, so beneficial that its use is strongly to be recommended, wherever it can be obtained.

It is the almost universal custom in England, where roots are very largely grown, to raise turnips, and mangels as well, on raised ridges or back-furrows ; and the facts that in this way we increase the depth of soil directly under the plant, and that horse cultivation during the early stages of growth is easier, are arguments in favor of the custom.   Generally, however, flat cultivation for all crops, being the most natural, is considered the most advisable ; and the question whether to ridge or not to ridge should be decided, perhaps, with reference to the character of the land. If it is either very stony or very " cloddy," or if, for any reason, it is not of uniform fineness, it will be well to throw it into ridges, even if the ridges be afterward raked off or flattened down by rolling a barrel over them. By some means they should be so depressed that there will be no danger of the elevated bank of earth becoming too dry during the heat of summer.

Rutabagas are grown both by planting the seed in place, and by raising young plants in a seed-bed for subsequent transplanting. The almost universal system is to sow the seed where the plants are to grow, transplanting only as may be necessary to fill up vacant spaces. All things considered, this system is probably the most advisable, although an experienced farmer of my acquaintance, who has experimented carefully during the past three years, asserts that he finds the growth of his transplanted roots to be so much greater as to amply compensate for the trouble. From my own experiments in this direction, not only with this crop but with several others, I am strongly inclined to believe that the labor of the whole season is less under the transplanting than under the seed-planting method, for the reason that with turnips and mangels the early growth is so slow, and the small plants so delicate, that the cleaning of the ground for the first and second times requires very careful hand-work, which adds greatly to the cost of cultivation. As the transplanting takes place much later in the season than the sowing, we have ample time for at least three light cultivations by horse power, which will destroy the started germs of a very large portion of the weeds, that, under the planting system, would have to be removed by the hoe. The manner in which transplanting should be done is referred to more at length under the head of mangels. For turnips, the process requires only such modification as their smaller size and greater delicacy render obviously necessary.

The ground being in thoroughly good condition, and in all respects suited for the production of a large crop, the most important consideration is the distance at which the rows are to be placed, and the distance in the rows to which the plants are to be thinned out. The temptation is always to plant at too narrow intervals. The rows should never be nearer together than twenty-seven inches, and even thirty would probably produce better results. This gives ample room for thorough cultivation by horse-power, reducing the amount of hand-work to only the cultivation of the rows themselves. The roots are thinned out at distances varying from six to fifteen inches. Six inches is very much too close, and fifteen inches may be a little wider than necessary. It is believed, however, that a larger weight of roots from a given area of land will be produced if the plants stand at intervals of twelve inches than if nearer together. At this distance, and with thirty inches between the rows, the entire surface of the ground will be covered by the leaves, and each plant will have, not only ample feeding-ground for its roots, but ample room for the largest development. If the land is thoroughly well pulverized, and enriched with perfect uniformity, at these distances every root should be perfect.

When the crop is to be transplanted, the seed should be sown in a thoroughly prepared seed-bed, about the middle of May. The young plants should be dusted with soot, ashes, road dust, or air-slacked lime, or with some other powder that will drive away the skipping-beetle, which often causes serious loss. The rows need not be more than twelve inches asunder, and the plants may stand quite thickly in the row, at intervals of not more one-half inch or one inch. The plants for an acre may, in this way, be raised upon a few square rods of ground; although, for fear of accidents, it is always best to be liberal in this respect. The amount of seed sown for the transplanting of an acre should be not less than three-quarters of a pound; and, if there is the least danger that the seed may not be of uniformly good quality, it will be poor economy not to use at least twice this quantity. The seed-bed should be kept thoroughly clean, free from weeds, and well pulverized; and, if the weather is dry, should be occasionally watered, in order that the plants may be as strong and firm as possible at transplanting time. They should be set out in place, not later than the middle of July, if the crop is intended for consumption on the farm. But the first of August will be early enough, if it is intended for the market. In this latter case the seed-bed need not be planted before June first. If, between the time of planting the seed and setting out the plants in the field, the weather is such that they threaten to grow to too large a size, they should be retransplanted, and their growth in this way checked. Every transplanting of turnips, or any thing else that bears transplanting at all, has the effect of increasing the bushiness of the root, and, ultimately, the stamina of the plant. Perhaps it would pay to sow the seed as early as the first of May, and to transplant twice between that time and the first of August. These earlier transplantings are accomplished with very little work, as they are done by the process known as heeling in. A narrow furrow being made with the end of a spade, and the plants set almost touching each other against one side of the furrow, the earth is returned and pressed closely against them with the foot. Each transplanting will check the growth of the leaves for a week or ten days, and during this time the severed roots will establish themselves by making several strong branches. When transplanted again, these branches will branch again, and when the plant is finally put into its place in the field, its feeding roots will be much more numerous than if grown directly from the seed.

When the seed is sown directly in the field, the amount required for an acre is about one pound; and it should be distributed by a drill-barrow,—Emery's and Holbrook's being probably the best. The proper time for field planting is not very well defined. For the production of large roots for home consumption, possibly the middle of June would not be too early for sowing;—for market, however, from the seventh to the tenth of July is quite early enough. If the seed germinates well, there will be at least twenty times as many plants produced as are to be left after the final thinning. Therefore, any slight attack of the skipping-beetle may be disregarded; but the field should be closely watched, and if in any place its ravages threaten to become serious, the plants should be carefully dusted. As soon as the plants have grown to a sufficient size to mark the rows, the intervals between them should be very lightly scarified by the horse-hoe, although no sign of a weed may have shown itself. In fact, the more frequently the ground is disturbed, and the more thoroughly the growth of weeds is nipped in the bud, the cheaper and more complete will be the season's cultivation. It will, indeed, be found profitable, if so much as from five to ten acres of roots are grown, to keep a horse-hoe going constantly whenever the land is sufficiently dry. When the turnips have produced one or two rough leaves, the sides of the rows should be lightly hoed by hand immediately after the passage of the horse-hoe. This will destroy all weeds except those starting directly in the line of the turnips ; and when the leaves of these are three or four inches long, the singling out should be carefully done, leaving the strongest plants at intervals of from ten to fourteen inches, and thoroughly cleaning all of the intervening ground. The effect of this thinning on the appearance of the field is always such as to leave a very poor promise of a crop, but within a few days the plants, which have been deprived of the support of their neighbors, will gain strength, assume a more stocky form, and commence their real growth. From this time on, until the roots have a diameter of about an inch, the hoeing by both horse and hand power cannot be too frequent or thorough for profit. The best of all horse cultivators, so far as my experience goes, is the light one-horse steel subsoil plow, which can be run in well-cultivated land to a depth of six or eight inches, and which produces such a thorough disturbance of the mass of soil as it is difficult to accomplish in any other way, while it is easily drawn, and is not apt to throw dirt on to the leaves of the crop. If I were obliged to discard all but one of my horse-hoeing implements, I should retain this one for all work, including the horse-hoeing of corn. After having attained the diameter of an inch, and being by this time thoroughly cleaned, the crop had better be left to itself, unless the land is unusually weedy ;—for the development of the roots of the turnips so completely fills the soil, that even its very surface is occupied by fibers, whose destruction would be injurious. The crop may now be safely " laid by," and left to take care of itself until harvest time. If it is not now doing well, no effort of the farmer can help it. His care should have been applied during the previous autumn and spring, and during the earlier growth of the plants. Nature will now do all that can be done, and, under favorable circumstances, all that can be desired.

In cultivation by transplanting, very much of this labor may be dispensed with. Soon after the plants are set out they should receive one thorough horse cultivation and hand-hoeing, but they will soon so far occupy the ground, that, except the use of the subsoil plow, there is no room, and, indeed, no necessity, for further cultivation.

The turnip has the one great advantage, that its harvesting may be postponed until nearly all other farm work is closed for the season. I have learned by ample experience that even the severest freezing, provided the crop is not locked in the ground for the winter, is rather beneficial than injurious. During the autumn of 1867, my turnips were left out until after the thermometer had marked 12 degrees Fahrenheit, yet they were excellent for the table, and kept perfectly until late in the spring. If left, however, all winter in the ground, in the latitude of New York or of Philadelphia, they would undoubtedly be destroyed by frequent freezing and thawing. Even the leaves will bear severe frost without injury. The only precautions that it is necessary to take are, not to touch either tops or roots until the frost is thoroughly withdrawn, and to be very careful not to postpone the harvesting so late that they cannot be removed, free from frost, before winter finally sets in. The harvesting is easy and simple, and requires no directions, beyond the statement that the tops and the tap-roots should be cut off, but that the turnip generally should not be "trimmed" until it is required for use; as each abrasion of the surface establishes a weak point at which decay first attacks it, and the less cutting it receives before being stored away, the better its chances for remaining sound until wanted. At this season of the year, the leaves will bear stacking in considerable heaps without fermentation, and may be relied on as a source of valuable fodder for some weeks.

During the harvesting of the crop, the roots may be thrown together in heaps of from ten to twenty bushels, and covered with a few leaves or a little earth, which will prevent their being attacked by frost, until they can be finally put away for the winter.

CARROTS

These are an exceedingly valuable root for the farmer, and have the advantage over turnips, that they impart no unpleasant flavor to milk and butter, and that they add somewhat to its richness and color. For horses, they are especially good food, and, when administered with oats and hay, have the effect of facilitating their complete digestion. Carrots cannot be transplanted, and the seed must be sown where they are to grow. As they form very much less top than turnips do, the rows may be put much closer together, although, unless hand labor can be obtained to advantage, it will be necessary to make the distance sufficient for the use of the horse-hoe. The seed is exceedingly slow in its germination, and the crop is a perplexing one during the first two or three weeks of its growth, as many weeds, unless great care is taken, will push beyond it and obliterate the rows. A common fault in the cultivation of carrots is to plant the seed too early in the season. Put in the ground early in May, as is a quite common custom, the seed lies dormant, often for nearly a month, during the whole of which time weeds are growing and work is accumulating, at the busiest season of the year; while the plants, after they do come up, are so feeble that their early growth is exceedingly slow. Certainly, the labor of cultivation will be much less, and the amount of the crop probably quite as great, if the seed is not planted till the tenth of June, the preceding weeks having been industriously employed in the destruction by horse-power of the early sprouting weeds. It will ordinarily be found that a crop planted at this time, will very soon catch up with one that was put in the ground a month earlier; while the cost of its cultivation will not be one-fourth so much. As soon as the rag-leaf of the plant is fairly shown, the crop should be thinned out, as, owing to the length of the root, if it is left much later than this, there is danger that it will be broken off at the crown and that a subsequent growth will ensue, requiring the operation to be repeated. The distance at which the plants should be left in the rows should not be less than six inches, and probably even more than this would give a larger crop. During the whole of the months of June and July, the carrot field should be very closely attended to, and should be kept thoroughly clean, as during all this time the growth of the plant is slow, and the effect upon it of the growth of weeds is almost disastrous. After this it will require less work, but at no time should it be allowed to become absolutely weedy.

Carrots must be harvested before any severe freezing of the ground takes place, and the roots should be immediately protected against the action of even a slight frost, as any freezing, after they are taken up, greatly increases their tendency to decay. Properly harvested and well secured for the winter, however, they keep perfectly well until spring. The yield of the crop will, of course, depend very much on the character of the land, and the care with which it has been cultivated. Probably no one thing, however, affects the result so much as the perfection of the thinning. In Rhode Island, where large quantities of carrots are grown as a "stolen crop" between onions, and where the seed is merely dropped between the rows of onions, sometimes a dozen in a place, no thinning ever being done, two or three hundred bushels is considered a large crop. In 1819, my father raised a crop on very stony and naturally poor land, in Westchester County, New York, thinning the plants to intervals of from six to eight inches in the rows; and received from the Westchester County Agricultural Society, in 1820, the silver cup awarded for the largest crop of carrots, on proof of a yield of over one thousand bushels to the acre. In the description of the manner in which the crop was raised, published in the Memoirs of the Board of Agriculture of the State of New York, 1823, there appears no evidence of any especially favorable circumstances beyond the perfect natural drainage of the ground. The land was stony, would produce only thirty bushels of corn to the acre with the same amount of manure used for the carrots, and was by no means such as would be selected as best adapted for the growth of this crop. The large crop obtained was the result mainly of very careful and very thorough management. In those days of low prices the total cost of the cultivation and harvesting was only $30 per acre—about three cents a bushel for the roots produced. Of course, so cheap a result could not now be obtained, and it is not likely that it ever can be again ; though when we consider the relative value of the crop, as compared with that of others requiring more or less labor, any yield nearly so large as this must be obtained at a cheap rate.

As they require considerable more labor and are not quite so easily kept in winter, carrots are not so valuable to the farmer as either rutabagas or mangels. A small quantity should always be raised as giving an excellent variety in feeding ; but the main crop should be of the other roots, unless there is some reliable local demand for carrots, as there sometimes is, for feeding livery and private horses. Whenever so high a price as 30 cents a bushel can be relied on, and especially where women and children can be hired to do the weeding and thinning, for a portion of the crop, (on shares,) or for moderate daily wages, it will pay exceedingly well to raise carrots. They may be raised, year after year, on the same land ; and, if the crop is kept thoroughly cleaned throughout the season, the work of weeding will be yearly less and less.

Carrots are grown very largely in certain districts of New England as a second crop among onions, and probably a great deal of the accumulated capital of the farmers of the island of Rhode Island has been derived from this double cultivation. Latterly, the injury of the onion crop by the maggot has greatly lessened the extent of their growth, and the consequent production of carrots. The custom in Rhode Island is, to plant the onions at regular intervals in narrow rows, planting a few carrot seeds between each two plants of every row. After the onion crop is taken off the carrot has all the time that it requires to make a handsome growth ; but, owing to the fact that the carrots grow in bunches together and are not thinned, and that the land is generally only cultivated to a slight depth, the produce is much less than it is where they have a proper depth of soil, and stand singly so that each plant may grow to its full size. One carrot, two inches in diameter at the top and fifteen inches long, contains a great deal more substance than do four carrots an inch in diameter and only five inches long.

The variety of carrot that it is best to raise, taking into view both its quality for feeding and the effect of its coloring matter on the product of the dairy, is the Long Orange. The White Belgian produces more largely, but is inferior for use; while the Crecy, the Horn, and the Altringham, though richer and excellent for the table, yield less.

MANGEL-WURZELS.

The mangel is the king of the root crops. The yield per acre is larger, under favorable circumstances, than that of any other root; the quality is much better than that of the common turnip, and quite as good as that of carrots or rutabagas. It is only exceeded in richness by the potato and the Jerusalem artichoke. The amount that it is possible to produce from an acre of land has probably never been definitely ascertained, for there has never been an acre grown on which all of the plants were so large and perfect as individual plants frequently are.

If I had land exactly suited to the cultivation of this root, and were so circumstanced that I could give it as much manure as it could make profitable use of, and could give the land and the plants in all respects the fullest opportunity to do their best, the limit of my modest ambition would be two thousand bushels per acre, or fifty tons of roots.

To descend from the possible to the actual, instances are numerous of the production of from ten to thirteen hundred bushels per acre; and there is no crop that is grown which, in proportion to the amount of labor required for its production, is so profitable as this. Three hundred and forty-one pounds of mangels are

equal in feeding value to one hundred pounds of the best meadow
hay, and eight and a half tons from an acre of land have the same
actual nutritive value, as proven by experiment, as have two and
a half tons of hay, which is a remarkably good yield from an acre
of excellent grass land, laid down with much expense, and its
crop harvested and stored with care. Of course the labor required
for the production of the mangel crop is larger, area for area, than
is required for the hay crop,—very much larger,—but it bears no
proportion to its excessive superiority in feeding value.

There are two varieties of mangel that are grown quite largely,
and it is still questionable which, if either, is superior to the other.
These are the Long Red, and the Yellow or Orange Globe,—
the former growing chiefly out of the ground, often to a length of
eighteen or twenty inches, and sometimes even more, and having
a circumference nearly equal to its length. The Yellow Globe
is almost a perfect sphere, and has been grown to a diameter of
thirteen inches.

The crop requires the whole growing season for its perfection,
and the seed should be sown as early in spring as the danger of
late frosts will allow. Fresh seed germinates readily, and it probably would not be safe to plant, in the latitude of New York,
much earlier than the 10th of May. The preparation of the land
should be the perfection of all that has been described in the early
part of this chapter. Depth of thorough cultivation, completeness
of drainage, and the richest possible manuring, are all necessary to
the best results. The crop may be grown either on the flat or on
ridges. The rows should be at least thirty inches apart (many
consider three feet none too much), and the plants should stand
twelve, or, better, fifteen inches asunder in the rows. The distance between the rows, and the intervals between the plants,
should be regulated according to the richness of the ground. It
is desirable that during the latter part of the season the entire surface should be covered by the leaves of the crop, and especially
desirable that these leaves should not crowd each other by reason
of too narrow intervals.

Mangels may be grown by planting the seed where the crop is

to stand, or by transplanting. After several years of experiment, I am induced to recommend the system of transplanting. The plants may be grown in the seed-bed to a considerable size ;—in fact, it is better not to remove them until the roots are, on the average, as thick as one's thumb, or even an inch in diameter. This will bring the removal to so late a period that the ground on which they are to grow may be thoroughly cultivated and cleaned of weeds, so that a single hand-hoeing, one horse-hoeing, and one thorough cultivation between the rows with the one-horse steel sub-soil plow will be all that the plant requires. If the seed is sown in place, it should be sown thickly by a seed-drill, say at the rate of six pounds to the acre ; for, in view of the occasional defective germination of the seed, it is best to secure one's self against the possibility of loss from this source,—the cost of the extra seed being a slight insurance as compared with the general result. The rows should be kept thoroughly clean, and the plants slightly thinned out, that is, so that only one shall stand within the space of an inch. As soon as the fleshy leaf commences to show itself, and at about the third hoeing, the rows should be thinned to the intervals recommended above, and every weed, however small, should be carefully taken out. After this time about the same cultivation will be required that is necessary for the transplanted crop. In transplanting, the following plan will be found safe, economical, and satisfactory. The land having been put in a good state of preparation and thoroughly cleared of weeds, scarify the surface with a cultivator, and pass a roller over it to crush such lumps as may remain, and then rake the field by hand with common wooden hay-rakes. The first operation is the marking of the lines, and I have found that this may be cheaply and rapidly done by the use of a cord (common tarred spun yarn is as good as any thing), long enough to reach from one side of the field to the other. Let one man hold each end of the line, standing at opposite sides of the field and near to one side, drawing the line perfectly straight, laying it in the position intended for the first row, and securing the ends by stakes pressed into the ground. Let them now walk toward each other, placing the whole length of

the foot upon the line at each step. When they reach the middle
they return rapidly to the end, and, each being provided with a
gauge marking the distance, move the line to its second position
and walk over it as before,—proceeding in this manner until the
whole field, or so much of it as can be planted in one day, is
marked out. The indentation made in the ground by the line
under the foot will be clear and sufficient for the purpose. This
plan has the advantage of being nearly as rapid as marking out by
the plow, and of making perfectly straight lines at absolutely uniform distances. The whole cost of the operation detailed need
not exceed two dollars per acre, including the scarifying, rolling,
and raking;—and the straightness of the rows and the finely com-
minuted condition of the ground will amply compensate for this
in subsequent cultivation; while the appearance of the crop will
be much more satisfactory than if the lines were not perfectly
straight.

Transplanting is regarded by those who are not accustomed to
it as a great bugbear; and the objection that is most frequently
raised to this system of cultivating roots is based on the cost of
the operation. Until a little experience is gained, the objection
has some value; but as soon as one is accustomed to the use of
the dibber, it will be found that the labor of setting out an acre of
plants is less than that of weeding a sowed crop the first time,
or of thinning out in the second hoeing; while the effect of
the transplanting on the roots is most beneficial, and the crop
produced will be enough larger than is possible by the other process to fully repay the cost.

In transplanting not only mangels, but turnips, cabbages, and,
indeed, all plants, the work can in no way be done so rapidly and
so well as by the use of the dibber, which is a stick about a foot
long and an inch in diameter, having an iron-shod point. This
tool may be made by any blacksmith, and should find a place on
all farms where roots are grown. It is universally used by the
market gardeners in the vicinity of New York; and the rapidity
with which its work is accomplished in the hands of a skillful
man is truly remarkable. My foreman, who has had ten years'

experience in market gardening, can, with a boy to drop them, set out nine thousand plants in a day, and it is rarely that a single plant fails.

The field being ready, the plants should now be drawn from the seed-bed, the largest being selected first. The crown of the plant being held in the hand, the leaves should be cut off about six inches above the crown, and the point of the tap-root a little below the swelling. The plants should be stacked up so that the leaves will all lie in one direction, and should be covered from the rays of the sun. Each planter should be preceded by a boy carrying a basket of plants, which he drops down across the line with the tops toward the left hand of the planter, who follows him. The latter, bending his back for his day's work, picks up the plant with his left hand, makes a hole with the dibber, sets the root in about half an inch below the crown, and by a peculiar twisting thrust of the dibber compacts the earth about the root. If there are men enough, one should be detailed to follow each two or three planters, pressing lightly with his foot over the hole left by the dibber, so as to compact the earth still more around the newly-set plant, and the operation is done. It is better, of course, to select cloudy or damp weather for this work; and it should never be performed during a drought, if there is a hope of rain within a week. The cutting off of the leaves, as it very much reduces the evaporation of water by the plant, enables it to remain nearly dormant until its newly-formed roots have taken hold upon the soil. For ten days or two weeks after transplanting, but little evidence of growth can be seen; but from that time on the growth is rapid and uniform; so that, if the land is in good condition and the plants all good, there will be an equality of appearance over the whole field that cannot be equaled by the most successful cultivation by means of seed planting. If the dryness of the ground is very great, and it is not deemed advisable to wait for a rain, the following operation will be found beneficial: Take equal parts of garden loam and cow-dung, mixing, if convenient, a little guano or superphosphate of lime with the mass, and make it into a semi-fluid paste with water. Into this dip each handful of roots, as they are trimmed, on being first taken from the bed. So treated, mangels, cabbages, and, probably, rutabagas, can be set out even in the dryest weather with success; and in any case this addition of a rich fertilizer at the point at which the new roots are to seek their first food will be found advantageous.

The process of growth of the mangel, and probably of all root crops, is about as follows:—

During the early stages the energies of the plant are devoted chiefly to the forming of leaves; and, even after these have attained sufficient size to absorb atmospheric matter, the growth is confined chiefly to their extension. Later in the season, by the transformation of the contents of the cells of the leaves, these contents, again becoming soluble, pass down and increase the bulk of the root. Thus we see at harvest time that a large proportion of the leaves of the crop have withered and fallen away. It is the erroneous custom, in many districts, to forestall this withering by stripping them off, and using them for cattle food. It is hardly necessary to say that this custom results in great detriment to the crop, as the roots are thus robbed of a large part of the matter which it is the design of nature to store in them for winter use or for the next season's seed-growing. The crop should be left entirely untouched after the leaves have covered the ground until harvest time, which should be before any frost severe enough to seriously affect the roots themselves. Early frosts have but slight effect, even on the leaves, and so long as the ground is well shaded from the morning sun, a slight freezing of the roots does no harm, as the frost will be withdrawn by the gradually increasing heat of the air, before the cuticle is struck by the direct rays of the sun.

In harvesting mangels, the leaves should be twisted or torn off by hand, and not cut off by a knife,—it having been found that cutting induces early decay. As the root grows chiefly above ground, and is rather smoothly rounded even under the surface of the earth, it is not necessary to trim off the rootlets, which are of but very little amount. As the roots are stripped they should be laid on the row, or, at most, each three rows should be laid on the line of the middle one, the leaves being deposited in the intervening spaces. They should be left in this situation until they become thoroughly dry, a slight wilting being beneficial. While turnips and carrots may be thrown together in heaps, or even thrown into carts, mangels require to be handled in the most careful and delicate way, for a slight abrasion of the skin hastens decay. They should be laid with care into baskets, and emptied thence with equal care into carts, from which they should be subsequently removed by hand, and not dumped. As the work of this season is generally pressing, and as it is not well to put roots into warm winter quarters until the weather becomes permanently colder, it is a good plan to stack mangels in the field, in heaps containing from ten to twenty bushels, covering them first with leaves and then with a little earth, to secure them against frost ; but before the weather becomes cold enough to penetrate this thin covering they should be removed to the cellar, or stowed away in pits or banks where they may be safely left even until May. Mangels, as well as other roots, may be stored in the field in either of two ways. One plan is, to build them up compactly in heaps about five feet wide, and as long as the quantity to be stored makes necessary. They should be drawn together to a ridge at the top, and at intervals of about ten feet along this ridge trusses of straw should be built in, projecting about two feet above it. The whole heap should then be covered about six inches thick with straw, (long straw running up and down the sides is best,) and later, the whole should be covered a foot thick with earth, leaving only the trusses sticking out, for ventilation. The earth should be taken from a trench dug completely around the heap, and a sufficient drain should lead away from this. Probably it would be best to so regulate the size of the heaps, that when one is opened its entire contents can be put into the root-cellar at once. If this is not done, the end of the heap that is left when a part of the roots are removed must be covered as above directed.

The other plan, which we think preferable to the foregoing, is to store the roots in a trench in the ground, three feet deep and four feet wide. Commence by building up a tier of roots entirely across one end of the trench, and extending back two feet from the end, sprinkling a little fine earth or sand among the layers to exclude the air. After this tier is built to the top, commence a second one, six inches from the first; and, as you build up, fill the space between the two with earth. Proceed in this manner, laying up successive tiers, until the trench is filled. Then cover the whole with a thin layer of straw, to be increased gradually in thickness as the weather becomes colder. After the first six inches of straw are put on, there is more to be feared from too great heat than from frost; although, after the winter has fairly set in, the covering (being beaten down by rain and snow) should be at least ten or twelve inches thick. Roots stored in this way may be taken out as wanted, (one tier at a time,) and usually keep better than in over-ground ridges. Of course the ground must be naturally dry at all seasons, for the whole depth of the trench, or it must be artificially drained.

The same caution against too rapid covering should be used in the case of the ridge system, and in no case should corn-stalks be used for covering, as these are very apt to decay and communicate decay to the roots.

PARSNIPS.

Parsnips can hardly be regarded in this country as a farm crop; for, while they are excellent for feeding and their productiveness is bountiful, the labor of digging the crop is serious, and, either in the autumn or in the spring, is likely to interfere with other operations. At the same time, these roots possess the great advantage of remaining in the ground where they are grown without protection during the severest winter, coming out in perfect condition at any time before their second season's growth has commenced in the spring. They should be planted, and cultivated in all respects, as has been directed for carrots,—save that the intervals between the plants in the rows should not be less than eight inches.

CHAPTER XII.

FORAGE CROPS.

In its widest sense, the term *forage crops* applies to all herbaceous plants which are used as food for domestic animals. Such grasses, however, as are chiefly grown for hay, are so familiar to all farmers, that in a book of the character of this they may well give place to other matters about which information is now more generally sought, and I shall confine my attention mainly to such plants as are grown for green fodder,—whether for a complete system of "soiling," or for an occasional feed where pastures are not reliable.

The great crops for these purposes in this country, are: Indian Corn; Sorghum, or Chinese Sugar-Cane; Clover; Oats; Rye; and Millet.

"Sowed Corn" is familiar to all good farmers, and all who have grown it under favorable circumstances, will concede that it produces much more food on a given area than any other grass that we have, unless it be its *congener*, Chinese sugar-cane, or sorghum. It has the drawback of not being very early, and of not withstanding the early autumn frosts; it must be planted late enough to avoid the late frosts of spring, and it must be harvested before the weather becomes severe in the fall. But, during the intense heats of summer, it grows (on rich and well-drained land) as nothing else will, affording, during August and September, a most luxuriant supply of the very best food for all animals not kept for work. Even swine will thrive on it as they will on hardly any thing else, and for milch cows it is unequaled by any thing with which we are acquainted.

It is supposed by some who have little experience in the matter that green corn fodder lessens the flow of milk and reduces the quantity of butter. To this opinion I am able to oppose my own experience of the past summer (1869) in the management of a herd of Jersey cows. The quantity of milk was not definitely ascertained, but it was easy to see that the corn increased the flow much more than any other feed. During the months of June and July, the weekly average of butter was $44 \frac{44}{100}$ lbs., —the animals being copiously supplied with the best of clover, and with green oats. During August and September, when we fed, practically, nothing except green corn fodder, the average per week was $57 \frac{56}{100}$ lbs. of butter, of even a finer quality and a better flavor.

But few farmers, even of those who are in the yearly habit of planting a little sowed corn, know what the crop is capable of. They usually prepare a small corner of a field on which they sow the seed *broadcast*, and harrow it in. For want of air and light, and from the compactness of the surface, the growth has a pale and sickly look, and the produce is very much less than it should be.

The land intended for this use should be the richest and best prepared on the whole farm, and the seed should be put in *in drills at least three feet apart*, so that they may be thoroughly worked out with the cultivator, or horse-hoe, at least three times during the early growth, and so that there may be an abundant circulation of air, as well as a free access of light. It is a common mistake, when the corn is planted in drills, to put in so little seed that the stalks grow so large and strong that they will be rejected by the cattle, only the leaves being consumed. There should be at least forty grains to the foot of row. This will take from four bushels to six bushels of seed to the acre, but the result will fully justify the outlay, as the corn standing so close in the row will grow *fine* and thick, and when it is fed out the whole stalk will be consumed.

The variety planted is important. The hard, Northern varieties of corn, which do not produce a luxuriant growth of stalk and leaf, are not nearly so good as the *gourd-seed* varieties, and of these the large, white, Southern corn is much better than the yellow corn of the West.

There is no doubt that sweet corn is better for forage than any other variety, as even the stalk contains much more sugar ; but the seed is costly, and is sometimes not to be obtained at any price, while " white Southern " is always to be had in abundant supply, and it is—in the absence of sweet corn—good enough to satisfy any reasonable man.

My crop of this variety, during the past season,—planted as above described,—grew to a height of six feet, and occupied the whole area,—the leaves interlacing between the rows,—as completely as a heavy crop of any grass would do. I had no means of measuring the precise quantity grown, but I am confident that it would have made eight tons per acre, *dry weight*, while so far as I could judge from its effect when fed green, as compared with green grass, it would have been fully equal to eight tons of the best hay. When at its full growth, a half rod of it was ample for the daily support of a cow in full milk, while young stock and swine flourished on it as well as they possibly could have done on any other feed.

The most profitable time to cut corn fodder, whether for green feeding or for curing, is when one half of the plants are in full tassel. At this stage the nutritive constituents are the most evenly distributed throughout all parts of the plants.

The best means of curing fodder corn is a question that has long occupied the attention of thoughtful farmers, but as yet no satisfactory result has been attained. It seems almost impossible to thoroughly dry a heavy crop on the ground on which it is grown. I have tried many experiments, and the best one I have thus far been able to hit upon has been to spread it as evenly as possible during the hottest days of September, occasionally turning it by hand. Even after two weeks of such exposure it contains too much water for safe storing, while the effect of dews and rains must be very injurious. Unless some means of drying it rapidly and cheaply by artificial heat can be devised, I see no hope of being able to store it properly for winter use.   It may now be made dry enough to be put up in small stacks, (butts outward,) but this is far less satisfactory than it would be to store it securely in a tight barn or a well-thatched, large stack.

The main crop should be planted at the usual time of planting corn for grain, but, so far as it is desired to secure a succession of fodder during the pasturing season, it may be advisable to plant at intervals until the middle of July.

When no suitable implement is available, the planting may be rapidly done by hand, but I have found a grain drill, with all but the middle one and outer two teeth removed, (the hopper being arranged to deliver only to these teeth,) a perfect tool for the purpose, planting three rows at a time as fast as a team can walk, and planting them very evenly.   After planting, it is well to pass over the ground with a heavy roller, and as soon as the rows can be distinguished the cultivator should be set at work,—keeping the ground always loose and light, until the corn is so thick that a horse cannot pass through it without material injury.

SORGHUM (or Chinese sugar-cane) is very similar to Indian corn, and, as it contains more saccharine matter, it may be, in those parts of the country in which it thrives, even better as a green fodder ; but, as I have had no experience with its growth for this purpose, I cannot speak positively about it.

From the greater amount of sugar it contains, it would probably be more likely to sour in curing.

CLOVER.—After Indian corn, there is no forage crop to compare with red clover, and if we take into account its effect on the land, it should be placed at the very head of the list, for, while Indian corn requires rich land and ample manuring, clover is the most fertilizing crop that is grown, and may justly be called the poor man's manure.

We constantly meet in agricultural writings the statement that clover benefits the land because it derives most of its constituents from the atmosphere.   This is an absurd reason, because every

plant that is grown has precisely the same peculiarity, and there
is, practically, no difference among all of our crops as to the proportions in which they take their constituents from the soil and
from the atmosphere. The whole reason for the fertilizing effect
of clover has never been satisfactorily set forth, and science seems
to be thus far at fault in its investigations on this subject. Some
things, however, are definitely known which help to account for
the manurial value of this crop.

Clover is a very strongly tap-rooted plant, striking its feeders deep
into the earth and finding nutriment where the more delicate roots
of cereal plants would be unable to go. The proportion which the
roots bear to the top is very large, and on the removal of the crop
these are all left to decompose and add their elements to the soil.
Not only does the soil in this way receive a large amount of fertilizing matter taken from the atmosphere or developed in the subsoil, but the very mechanical structure of the root causes a fertile
channel to be left, reaching into the lower soil, and easily traversed
by the roots of succeeding plants, while the carbonaceous matter
that remains after the decomposition of the clover root increases
the porosity of the soil and adds very much to its ability to retain
moisture.

Lands that have been exhausted by long-continued cropping,
without manure, if they can be made to produce even a small crop
of clover, may be, by its persistent growth, rapidly and cheaply
restored to the highest fertility. Not only will the growth of
clover restore the carbonaceous matter that repeated cultivation
has *burned* out of the ground, but its vigorous and deeply penetrat-
ing roots extract valuable constituents from the stubborn subsoil, and these, disseminated through the entire root, remain, on its
death and decay, easily available for the uses of succeeding crops.

Thus much concerning the effect of this crop is easily compre-
hended, but there are other facts with regard to it that are not so
readily explained. For instance, it is amply proven that when
the second crop is fed off on the land, the manure that it makes
being deposited upon it, the effect on the succeeding crop is less
favorable than when this second growth is allowed to ripen into

19

seed, and the whole is harvested and removed from the land. This branch of the question is thoroughly discussed in a paper by Dr. Voelcker, which is published herewith; but it seems probable after all,—so great is the manurial influence of clover,—that it must actually absorb and appropriate into its own substance the nitrogen of the atmosphere, though there is no proof, and as yet no means of proving that this process actually takes place.

The paper of Dr. Voelcker referred to above, is copied entire from the " Journal of the Royal Agricultural Society of England."

(This paper is so thoroughly scientific and valuable, and is so logically arranged from beginning to end, that it would be unfair to its author to attempt any condensation of it. Every farmer who cares to consider the reasons for what he does, who realizes the importance of understanding nature's modes of operations, will find its careful perusal to be of the greatest value. Those who, from lack of information or lack of time, desire only to know the conclusions to which it leads, will find them conclusively stated in the summary with which it closes.)

"ON THE CAUSES OF THE BENEFITS OF CLOVER AS A PREPARATORY CROP FOR WHEAT. BY DR. AUGUSTUS VOELCKER.

" Agricultural chemists inform us that, in order to maintain the productive powers of the land unimpaired, we must restore to it the phosphoric acid, potash, nitrogen, and other substances which enter into the composition of our farm crops; the constant removal of organic and inorganic soil-constituents by the crops usually sold off the farm, leading, as is well known, to the more or less rapid deterioration and gradual exhaustion of the land. Even the best wheat soils of this and other countries become more and more impoverished, and sustain a loss of wheat-yielding power, when corn crops are grown in too rapid succession without manure. Hence the universal practice of manuring, and that, also, of consuming oil-cake, corn, and similar purchased food on land naturally poor, or partially exhausted by previous cropping.

" While, however, it holds good, as a general rule, that no soil can be cropped for any length of time without gradually becoming more and more infertile, if no manure be applied to it, or if the fertilizing elements removed by the crops grown thereon be not, by some means or other, restored, it is nevertheless a fact that after a heavy crop of clover carried off as hay, the land, far from being less fertile than before, is peculiarly well adapted, even without the addition of manure, to bear a good crop of wheat in the following year, provided the season be favorable to its growth. This fact, indeed, is so well known that many farmers justly regard the growth of clover as one of the best preparatory operations which the land can undergo in order to its producing an abundant crop of wheat in the following year. It has further been noticed that clover mown twice leaves the land in a better condition as regards its wheat-producing capabilities, than when mown once for hay, and the second crop fed off on the land by sheep; for notwithstanding that in the latter instance the fertilizing elements in the clover crop are in part restored in the sheep excrements, yet, contrary to expectation, this partial restoration of the elements of fertility to the land has not the effect of producing more or better wheat in the following year than is reaped on land from off which the whole clover crop has been carried, and to which no manure whatever has been applied.

"Again, in the opinion of several good practical agriculturists with whom I have conversed on the subject, land, whereon clover has been grown for seed in the preceding year, yields a better crop of wheat than it does when the clover is mown twice for hay, or even only once, and afterward fed off by sheep. Most crops left for seed, I need hardly observe, exhaust the land far more than they do when they are cut down at an earlier stage of their growth; hence the binding clauses in most farm leases which compel the tenant not to grow corn crops more frequently nor to a greater extent than stipulated. However, in the case of clover grown for seed, we have, according to the testimony of trustworthy witnesses, an exception to a law generally applicable to most other crops.

"Whatever may be the true explanation of the apparent anomalies connected with the growth and chemical history of the clover plant, the facts just mentioned having been noticed, not once or twice only, or by a solitary observer, but repeatedly, and by numbers of intelligent farmers, are certainly entitled to credit; and little wisdom, as it strikes me, is displayed by calling them into question, because they happen to contradict the prevailing theory, according to which a soil is said to become more or less impoverished in proportion to the large or small amount of organic and mineral soil-constituents carried off in the produce.

"Agricultural experiences contradicting prevailing and, it may

be, generally current theories, are, unless I am much mistaken, of
far more common occurrence than may be known to those who
are either naturally unobservant or unacquainted with many of the
details of farming operations.   Indeed, an interesting and instruc-
tive treatise might be written on the apparent anomalies in agriculture, and a collection of trustworthy facts of the kind alluded
to would afford valuable hints to intelligent farmers, and suggest
matter for inquiry to chemists and others engaged in scientific
pursuits.

"To me it seems inconsistent with the exercise of common
sense, and opposed alike to the whole tenor of a well-regulated
mind and the progress of scientific agriculture, to discuss agricultural matters in the dogmatic spirit too often so painfully observable when people meet together for the discussion of subjects
relating to farm practice ; but still more painful is the spirit which
pervades the writings of certain scientific men who are bold
enough, from isolated or even a number of analogous facts, to
frame general and invariable laws, in accordance with which they
propose to regulate the profession of agriculture.   That there are
certain fixed laws which determine the growth of the meanest herb
and the mightiest forest tree, no one can gainsay, but it may well
be doubted whether our corn or forage crops would remain as
flourishing as they at present are, if, in preference to some pretty
theory, the farmers of England suddenly threw aside their past
experience, and endeavored to grow corn in accordance with a
mathematical formula which men may fancy they have discovered,
and by which they may suppose the development of our corn-
crops to be governed.   Even great men, by taking too general, or,
as it is often erringly termed, a comprehensive view of agricultural
matters, sometimes totally misrepresent the very law they are
endeavoring to establish.

"The patient investigation of many of these details, with which
those only are perfectly familiar whose daily occupation is in the
field or in the feeding-stall, is, however, often rewarded by success.   Mysteries which puzzle the minds of intelligent farmers
are cleared up, the influences which modify a general rule or practice in farming operations are clearly recognized, and by degrees
principles are established, which, assigning the benefits or disadvantages of a certain course of proceeding to their real cause,
must ever tend to confirm the experienced in good practice,
and afford valuable hints in guiding those inexperienced in farm
management.

"In the course of a long residence in a purely agricultural district, I have often been struck with the remarkably healthy appearance and good yield of wheat on land from which a heavy crop of clover hay was obtained in the preceding year. I have likewise had frequent opportunities of observing that, as a rule, wheat grown on part of a field whereon clover has been twice mown for hay is better than the produce of that on the part of the same field on which the clover has been mown only once for hay, and afterward fed off by sheep. These observations, extending over a number of years, led me to inquire into the reasons why clover is specially well fitted to prepare land for wheat, and in the paper which I have now the pleasure of laying before the readers of the *Journal*, I shall endeavor, as the result of my experiments on the subject, to give an intelligible explanation of the fact that clover is so excellent a preparatory crop for wheat as it is practically known to be.

" By those taking a superficial view of the subject, it may be suggested that any injury likely to be caused by the removal of a certain amount of fertilizing matter is altogether insignificant, and more than compensated for by the benefit which results from the abundant growth of clover roots and the physical improvement in the soil which takes place in their decomposition. Looking, however, more closely into the matter, it will be found that, in a good crop of clover hay, a very considerable amount of both mineral and organic substances is carried off the land, and that if the total amount of such constituents in a crop had to be regarded exclusively as the measure for determining the relative degrees in which different farm-crops exhaust the land, clover would have to be described as about the most exhausting crop in the entire rotation.

" Clover-hay, on an average, and in round numbers, contains in 100 parts :—

Water	17·0
*Nitrogenous substances (flesh-forming matters)	15·6
Non-nitrogenous compounds	59·9
Mineral matter (ash)	7·5
	100·0

* Containing nitrogen .... 2·5

" The mineral portion or ash in 100 parts of clover-hay consists of—

Phosphoric acid	7·5
Sulphuric acid	4·3
Carbonic acid	18·0
Silica	3·0

Lime.. 30·0
Magnesia... 8·5
Potash... 20·0
Soda, chloride of sodium, oxide of iron, sand, loss, etc.......... 8·7
                                                          ———
                                                          100·0

"Let us suppose the land to have yielded 4 tons of clover-hay per acre. According to the preceding data we find that such a crop includes 224 lbs. of nitrogen, equal to 272 lbs. of ammonia, and 672 lbs. of mineral matter or ash constituents.

"In 672 lbs. of clover-ash we find—

Phosphoric acid .... 51½ lbs.
Sulphuric acid .... 29 "
Carbonic acid .... 121 "
Silica... 20 "
Lime.. 201 "
Magnesia.. 57 "
Potash.. 134½ "
Soda, chloride of sodium, oxide of iron, sand, etc.......... 58 "
                                                        ———
                                                        672 lbs.

"Four tons of clover-hay, the produce of one acre, thus contain a large amount of nitrogen, and remove from the soil an enormous quantity of mineral matters, abounding in lime and potash, and containing, also, a good deal of phosphoric acid.

"Leaving, for a moment, the question untouched, whether the nitrogen contained in the clover is derived from the soil or from the atmosphere, or partly from the one and partly from the other, no question can arise as to the original source from which the mineral matter in the clover-produce is derived. In relation, therefore, to the ash-constituents, clover must be regarded as one of the most exhausting crops usually cultivated in this country. This appears strikingly to be the case when we compare the preceding figures with the quantity of mineral matters which an average crop of wheat removes from an acre of land.

"The grain and straw of wheat contain, in round numbers, in 100 parts :—

	Grain of Wheat.		Straw.
Water..................................	15·0	....	16·0
*Nitrogenous substances (flesh-forming matters).	11·1	....	4·0
Non-nitrogenous substances.............	72·2	....	74·9
Mineral matter (ash)...................	1·7	....	5·1
		....	
	100·0	....	100·0
* Containing nitrogen.......	1·78	.....	·64

" The ash of wheat contains in 100 parts :—

	Grain.		Straw.
Phosphoric acid	50·0	....	5·0
Sulphuric acid	0·5	....	2·7
Carbonic acid	....	....	...
Silica	2·5	....	67·0
Lime	3·5	....	5·5
Magnesia	11·5	....	2·0
Potash	30·0	....	13·0
Soda, chloride of sodium, oxide of iron, sand, etc	2·0	....	4·8
	100·0	....	100·0

" The mean produce of wheat per acre may be estimated at 25 bushels, which, at 60 lbs. per bushel, gives 1,500 lbs. ; and as the weight of the straw is generally twice that of the grain, its produce will be 3,000 lbs. According, therefore, to the preceding data, there will be carried away from the soil :—

In 1,500 lbs. of the grain .. 25 lbs. of mineral food (in round numbers).
In 3,000 lbs. of the straw .. 150 " " "

Total......... 175 lbs.

" On the average of the analyses, it will be found that the composition of these 175 lbs. is as follows :—

	In the Grain.		In the Straw.		Total.
Phosphoric acid	12·5 lbs.	....	7·5 lbs.	....	20.0 lbs.
Sulphuric acid	0·1 "	....	4·0 "	....	4·1 "
Carbonic acid	....	....	....	....	....
Silica	0·6 "	....	100·5 "	....	101·1 "
Lime	0·9 "	....	8·2 "	....	9·1 "
Magnesia	2·9 "	....	3·0 "	....	5·9 "
Potash	7·5 "	....	19·5 "	....	27·0 "
Soda, chloride of sodium, oxide of iron, sand, etc.	0·5 "	....	7·3 "	....	7·8 "
	25 lbs.	....	150 lbs.	....	175 lbs

" The total quantity of ash-constituents carried off the land in an average crop of wheat thus amounts to only 175 lbs. per acre, while a good crop of clover removes as much as 672 lbs.

" Nearly two-thirds of the total amount of mineral in the grain and straw of one acre of wheat consists of silica, of which there is an ample supply in almost every soil. The restoration of silica, therefore, need not trouble us in any way, especially as there is not a single instance on record proving that silica, even in a soluble condition, has ever been applied to land with the slightest advantage to corn or grass crops, which are rich in silica, and which, for this reason, may be assumed to be particularly grateful for a supply of it in a soluble state. Silica, indeed, if at all capable of producing a beneficial effect, ought to be useful to these crops, either by strengthening the straw or stems of graminaceous plants, or otherwise benefiting them; but after deducting the amount of silica from the total amount of mineral matters in the wheat produce from one acre, only a trifling quantity of other and more valuable fertilizing ash-constituent of plants will be left. On comparing the relative amounts of phosphoric acid and potash in an average crop of wheat and a good crop of clover-hay, it will be seen that 1 acre of clover-hay contains as much phosphoric acid as 2½ acres of wheat, and as much potash as the produce from 5 acres of the same crop. Clover thus unquestionably removes from the land very much more mineral matter than is done by wheat; clover carries off the land at least three times as much of the more valuable mineral constituents as that abstracted by the wheat. Wheat, notwithstanding, succeeds remarkably well after clover.

"Four tons of clover-hay, or the produce of an acre, contain, as already stated, 224 lbs. of nitrogen, or, calculated as ammonia, 272 lbs.

"Assuming the grain of wheat to furnish 1·78 per cent. of nitrogen, and wheat-straw ·64 per cent., and assuming, also, that 1,500 lbs. of corn and 3,000 lbs. of straw represent the average produce per acre, there will be in the grain of wheat per acre 26·7 lbs. of nitrogen, and in the straw 19·2 lbs., or in both together 46 lbs. of nitrogen; in round numbers, equal to about 55 lbs. of ammonia, which is only one-fifth the quantity of nitrogen in the produce of an acre of clover. Wheat, it is well known, is specially benefited by the application of nitrogenous manure, and as clover carries off so large a quantity of nitrogen, it is natural to expect the yield of wheat, after clover, to fall short of what the land might be presumed to produce without manure, before a crop of clover was taken from it. Experience, however, has proved the fallacy of this presumption, for the result is exactly the opposite, inasmuch as a better and heavier crop of wheat is produced than without the intercalation of clover. What, it may be asked is the explanation of this apparent anomaly?

"In taking up this inquiry, I was led to pass in review the celebrated and highly important experiments undertaken by Mr. Lawes and Dr. Gilbert, on the continued growth of wheat on the same soil for a long succession of years, and to examine, likewise, carefully, many points, to which attention is drawn, by the same authors, in their memoirs on the growth of red clover by different manures, and on the Lois Weedon plan of growing wheat. Abundant and most convincing evidence is supplied by these indefatigable experimenters that the wheat-producing powers of a soil are not increased in any sensible degree by the liberal supply of all the mineral matters which enter into the composition of the ash of wheat, and that the abstraction of these mineral matters from the soil, in any much larger proportions than possibly can take place under ordinary cultivation, in nowise affects the yield of wheat, provided there be at the same time a liberal supply of available nitrogen within the soil itself. The amount of the latter therefore, is regarded by Messrs. Lawes and Gilbert as the measure of the increased produce of grain which a soil furnishes.

" In conformity with these views, the farmer, when he wishes to increase the yield of his wheat, finds it to his advantage to have recourse to ammoniacal or other nitrogenous manures, and depends more or less entirely upon the soil for the supply of the necessary mineral or ash-constituents of wheat, having found such a supply to be amply sufficient for his requirements. As far, therefore, as the removal from the soil of a large amount of mineral soil-constituents by the clover crop is concerned, the fact, viewed in the light of the Rothamsted experiments, becomes at once intelligible; for, notwithstanding the abstraction of over 600 lbs. of mineral matter by a crop of clover, the succeeding wheat-crop does not suffer. Inasmuch, however, as we have seen that not only much mineral matter is carried off the land in a crop of clover, but also much nitrogen, we might, in the absence of direct evidence to the contrary, be led to suspect that wheat after clover would not be a good crop; whereas the result is exactly the reverse.

" It is worthy of notice that nitrogenous manures which have such a marked and beneficial effect upon wheat do no good, but, in certain combinations, in some seasons, do positive harm to clover. Thus Messrs. Lawes and Gilbert, in a series of experiments on the growth of red clover by different manures, obtained 14 tons of fresh green produce, equal to about $3\frac{3}{4}$ tons of clover-hay from the unmanured portion of the experimental field; and where sulphates of potash, soda, and magnesia, or sulphate of potash and superphosphate of lime were employed, 17 to 18 tons (equal to from about $4\frac{1}{2}$ to nearly 5 tons of hay) were obtained. When salts of ammonia were added to the mineral manures, the produce of clover-hay was, upon the whole, less than where the mineral manures were used alone. The wheat grown after the clover on the unmanured plot, gave, however, $29\frac{1}{2}$ bushels of corn,

while in the adjoining field, where wheat was grown after wheat
without manure, only 15½ bushels of corn per acre were obtained.
Messrs. Lawes and Gilbert notice especially, that in the clover-
crop of the preceding year very much larger quantities, both of
mineral matters and nitrogen, were taken from the land than were
removed in the unmanured wheat-crop in the same year, in the
adjoining field. Notwithstanding this, the soil from which the
clover had been taken was in a condition to yield 14 bushels more
wheat per acre than that upon which wheat had been previously
grown ; the yield of wheat after clover, in these experiments, being
fully equal to that in another field, where very large quantities of
manure were used.

"Taking all these circumstances into account, is there not presumptive evidence that, notwithstanding the removal of a large
amount of nitrogen in the clover-hay, an abundant store of available nitrogen is left in the soil, and, also, that in its relations
toward nitrogen in the soil, clover differs essentially from wheat?
The results of our experience in the growth of the two crops
appear to indicate, that whereas the growth of the wheat rapidly
exhausts the land of its available nitrogen, that of clover, on the
contrary, tends, somehow or other, to accumulate nitrogen within
the soil itself. If this can be shown to be the case, an intelligible
explanation of the fact that clover is so useful as a preparatory
crop for wheat will be found in the circumstance that, during the
growth of clover, nitrogenous food, for which wheat is particularly
grateful, is either stored up or rendered available in the soil.

"An explanation, however plausible, can hardly be accepted as
correct if based mainly on data which, although highly probable,
are not proved to be based on fact. In chemical inquiries especially, nothing must be taken for granted that has not been proved
by direct experiment. The following questions naturally suggest
themselves in reference to this subject : What is the amount of
nitrogen in soils of different characters ? What is the amount,
more particularly after a good and after an indifferent crop of
clover ? Why is the amount of nitrogen in soils larger after
clover than after wheat and other crops? Is the nitrogen present
in a condition in which it is available and useful to wheat ? and
lastly, Are there any other circumstances, apart from the supply
of nitrogenous matter in the soil, which help to account for the
beneficial effects of clover as a preparatory crop for wheat ?

"In order to throw some light on these questions, and, if possible, to give distinct answers to at least some of them, I, years
ago, when residing at Cirencester, began a series of experiments,

and more recently I have been fortunate enough to obtain the co-operation of Mr. Robert Vallentine, of Leighton Buzzard, who kindly undertook to supply me with materials for my analyses.

"My first experiments were made on a thin calcareous clay soil, resting on oölitic limestone, and producing generally a fair crop of red clover. The clover-field formed the slope of a rather steep hillock, and varied much in depth. At the top of the hill, the soil became very stony at a depth of 4 inches, so that it could only with difficulty be excavated to a depth of 6 inches, when the bare limestone rock made its appearance. At the bottom of the field the soil was much deeper, and the clover stronger than at the upper part. On the brow of the hill, where the clover appeared to be strong, a square yard was measured out; and, at a little distance off, where the clover was very bad, a second square yard was measured; in both plots the soil being taken up to a depth of 6 inches. The soil where the clover was good may be distinguished from the other by being marked as No. 1, and that where it was bad as No. 2.

" Clover-soil No. 1, (good clover.)

" The roots having first been shaken out to free them as much as possible from soil, were then washed once or twice with cold distilled water, and, after having been dried for a little while in the sun, were weighed, when the square yard produced 1 lb. 10½ oz. of cleaned clover-roots in an air-dried state; an acre of land, or 4,840 square yards, accordingly yielded, in a depth of 6 inches, 3·44 tons, or 3½ tons in round numbers, of clover-roots.

" Fully dried in a water-bath, the roots were found to contain altogether 44·67 per cent. of water, and on being burnt in a platinum capsule yielded 6·089 of ash. A portion of the dried, finely powdered, and well-mixed roots was burned with soda-lime in a combustion-tube, and the nitrogen contained in the roots otherwise determined in the usual way. Accordingly, the following is the general composition of the roots from soil No. 1 :—

Water.. 44·675
*Organic matter....................................... 49·236
Mineral matter...................................... 6·089

                                                        ─────────
                                                        100·000

* Containing nitrogen.. 1·297
Equal to ammonia.. 1·575

" Assuming the whole field to have produced 3½ tons of clover-roots per acre, there will be 99·636 lbs., or in round numbers 100 lbs., of nitrogen in the clover-roots from 1 acre ; or about twice as much nitrogen as is present in the average produce of an acre of wheat.

"The soil which had been separated from the roots was passed through a sieve to deprive it of any stones it might contain. It was then partially dried, and the nitrogen in it determined in the usual manner by combustion with soda-lime, when it yielded ·313 per cent. of nitrogen, equal to ·38 of ammonia, in one combustion ; and ·373 per cent. of nitrogen, equal to ·46 of ammonia, in a second determination.

"That the reader may have some idea of the character of this soil, it may be stated that it was further submitted to a general analysis, according to which it was found to have the following composition :—

" *General composition of Soil No.* 1, *(good clover.)*

Moisture	18·73
*Organic matter	9·72
Oxides of iron and alumina	13·24
Carbonate of lime	8·82
Magnesia, alkalies, etc.	1·72
Insoluble siliceous matter (chiefly clay)	47·77
	100·00

* Containing nitrogen	·313
Equal to ammonia	·380

"The second square yard from the brow of the hill where the clover was bad, produced 13 ounces of air-dry and partially clean roots, or 1·75 tons per acre. On analysis they were found to have the following composition :—

" *Clover-roots No.* 2, *(bad clover.)*

Water	55·732
*Organic matter	39·408
Mineral matter (ash)	4·860
	100·000

* Containing nitrogen	·792
Equal to ammonia	·901

"The roots on the spot where the clover was very bad yielded only 31 lbs. of nitrogen per acre, or scarcely one-third of the quantity which was obtained from the roots where the clover was good.

" The soil from the second square yard on analysis was found, when freed from stones by sifting, to contain in 100 parts :—

" *Composition of Soil No. 2, (bad clover.)*

Water	17·24
*Organic matter	9·64
Oxides of iron and alumina	11·89
Carbonate of lime	14·50
Magnesia, alkalies, etc	1·53
Insoluble silicious matter	45·20

100·00

		2d determination.
* Containing nitrogen	·306 ...	·380
Equal to ammonia	·370	·470

" Both portions of the clover soil thus contained about the same percentage of organic matter, and yielded nearly the same amount of nitrogen.

" In addition, however, to the nitrogen in the clover-roots, a good deal of nitrogen, in the shape of root-fibers, decayed leaves, and similar organic matters, was disseminated throughout the fine soil in which it occurred, and from which it could not be separated ; but unfortunately I neglected to weigh the soil from a square yard, and am, therefore, unable to state how much nitrogen per acre was present in the shape of small root-fibers and other organic matters. Approximately, the quantity might be obtained by calculation ; but, as the actual weight of cultivated soils varies greatly, I abstain from making such a calculation, even though it might be done with propriety, as I took care in the following season to weigh the soil of different parts of the same field.

" Before mentioning the details of the experiments made in the next season, I will here give the composition of the ash of the partially cleaned clover-roots :—

" *Composition of Ash of Clover-roots, (partially cleaned.)*

Oxide of iron and alumina	11 73
Lime	18·49
Magnesia	3·03
Potash	6·88
Soda	1·93
Phosphoric acid	3·61
Sulphuric acid	2·24
Soluble silica	19·01
Insoluble siliceous matter	24·83
Carbonic acid, chlorine, and loss	8·25

100·00

"This ash was obtained from clover-roots, which yielded, when perfectly dry, in round numbers, 8 per cent. of ash. Clover-roots washed quite clean, and separated from all soil, yield about 5 per cent. of ash; but it is extremely difficult to clean a large quantity of fibrous roots from all dirt, and the preceding analysis distinctly shows that the ash of the clover-roots analyzed by me was mechanically mixed with a good deal of fine soil, for oxide of iron and alumina and insoluble silicious matter in any quantity are not normal constituents of plant-ashes. Making allowance for soil-contamination, the ash of clover-roots, it will be noticed, contains much lime and potash, as well as an appreciable amount of phosphoric and sulphuric acid. On the decay of the clover-roots, these and other mineral fertilizing matters are left in the surface-soil in a readily available condition, and in considerable proportions when the clover stands well. Although a crop of clover removes much mineral matter from the soil, it must be borne in mind that its roots extract from the land soluble mineral fertilizing matters, which, on the decay of the roots, remain in the land in a prepared and more readily available form than that in which they originally occur. The benefits arising to wheat from the growth of clover may thus be due partly to this preparation and concentration of mineral food in the surface-soil.

"The clover on the hill-side field on the whole turned out a very good crop; and as the plant stood the winter well, and this field was left another season in clover without being plowed up, I availed myself of the opportunity of making, during the following season, a number of experiments similar to those of the preceding year. This time, however, I selected for examination a square yard of soil from a spot on the brow of the hill where the clover was thin and the soil itself stony at a depth of 4 inches; and another plot of one square yard at the bottom of the hill, from a place where the clover was stronger than that on the brow of the hill, and the soil at a depth of 6 inches contained no large stones.

"*Soil No.* 1 (*Clover thin*) *on the brow of the hill.*

"The roots in a square yard, 6 inches deep, when picked out by hand and cleaned as much as possible, weighed, in their natural state, 2 lbs. 11 oz.; and when dried on the top of a water-bath, for the purpose of getting them brittle and fit for reduction into fine powder, 1 lb. 12 oz. 31 grains. In this state they were submitted, as before, to analysis, when they yielded in 100 parts :—

" *Composition of Clover-roots, No.* 1, (*from brow of the hill.*)

Moisture...	4·34
*Organic matter..	26·53
Mineral matter..	69·13
	100·00

* Containing nitrogen...............	·816
Equal to ammonia..............................	·991

" According to these data an acre of land will yield 8 tons 12 cwts. of nearly dry clover-roots, and in this quantity there will be about 66 lbs. of nitrogen.

" The whole of the soil from which the roots had been picked out was passed through a half-inch sieve. The stones left in the sieve weighed 141 lbs. ; the soil which passed through weighing 218 lbs.

" The soil was next dried by artificial heat, when the 218 lbs. became reduced to 185·487 lbs.

" In this partially dried state it contained—

Moisture	4·21
*Organic matter	9·78
†Mineral matter...	86·01
	100·00

* Containing nitrogen...	·391
Equal to ammonia...	·475
† Including phosphoric acid...................................	·264

" I also determined the phosphoric acid in the ash of the clover-roots. Calculated for the roots in a nearly dry state, the phosphoric acid amounts to ·287 per cent.

" An acre of soil, according to the data furnished by the six inches on the spot where the clover was thin, produced the following quantity of nitrogen :—

	Tons.	cwt.	lbs.
In the fine soil.........................	1	11	33
In the clover-roots	0	0	66
Total quantity of nitrogen per acre.....	1	11	99

" The organic matter in an acre of this soil, which cannot be picked out by hand, it will be seen, contains an enormous quantity of nitrogen ; and although probably the greater part of the roots and other remains from the clover crop may not be decomposed so thoroughly as to yield nitrogenous food to the succeeding

wheat-crop, it can scarcely be doubted that a considerable quantity
of nitrogen will become available by the time the wheat is sown,
and that one of the chief reasons why clover benefits the succeeding wheat-crop is to be found in the abundant supply of available
nitrogenous food furnished by the decaying clover-roots and leaves.

" *Clover-soil No. 2 from the bottom of the hill, (good clover.)*

" A square yard of the soil from the bottom of the hill, where
the clover was stronger than on the brow of the hill, produced 2
lbs. 8 oz. of fresh clover-roots, or 1 lb. 11 oz. 47 grains of partially dried roots, 61 lbs. 9 oz. of limestones, and 239·96 lbs. of
nearly dry soil.
" The partially dried roots contained :—

Moisture	5·c6
*Organic matter	31·94
Mineral matter	63·00
	100·00
* Containing nitrogen	·804

" An acre of this soil, 6 inches deep, produced 3 tons 7 cwts.
65 lbs. of clover-roots, containing 61 lbs. of nitrogen—that is,
there was very nearly the same quantity of roots and nitrogen in
them as that furnished in the soil from the brow of the hill.
" The roots, moreover, yielded ·365 per cent. of phosphoric
acid, or, calculated per acre, 27 lbs.
" In the partially dried soil I found—

Moisture	4·70
*Organic matter	10·87
†Mineral matter	84·43
	100·00
* Containing nitrogen	·405
Equal to ammonia	·491
† Including phosphoric acid	·321

" According to these determinations an acre of the soil from the
bottom of the hill contains—

	Tons.	cwts.	lbs.
Nitrogen in the organic matter of the soil ...	2	2	0
" clover-roots " ...	0	0	61
Total amount of nitrogen per acre...	2	2	61

" Compared with the amount of nitrogen in the soil from the brow of the hill, about 11 cwt. more nitrogen was obtained in the soil and roots from the bottom of the hill where the clover was more luxuriant.

" The increased amount of nitrogen occurred in fine root-fibers and other organic matters of the soil, and not in the coarser bits of roots which were picked out by the hand. It may be assumed that the finer particles of organic matter are more readily decomposed than the coarser roots ; and as there was a larger amount of nitrogen in this than in the preceding soil, it may be expected that the land at the bottom of the hill, after the removal of the clover, was in a better agricultural condition for wheat than that on the brow of the hill.

" *Experiments on Clover-soils from Burcott Lodge Farm, Leighton-Buzzard.*

" The soils for the next experiments were kindly supplied to me in 1866, by Mr. Robert Vallentine, of Burcott Lodge, who also sent me some notes respecting the growth and yield of clover, hay, and seed on this soil.

" Foreign seed, at the rate of 12 lbs. per acre, was sown with a crop of wheat which yielded 5 quarters per acre the previous year.

" The first crop of clover was cut down on the 25th of June, 1866, and carried on June 30th. The weather was very warm from the time of cutting till the clover was carted, the thermometer standing at 80° Fahr. every day. The clover was turned in the swathe on the second day after it was cut ; on the fourth day it was turned over and put into small heaps of about 10 lbs. each ; and on the fifth day these were collected into larger cocks and then stacked.

" The best part of an 11-acre field produced nearly 3 tons of clover-hay, sun-dried, per acre ; the whole field yielding on an average 2½ tons per acre. This result was obtained by weighing the stack three months after the clover was carted. The second crop was on 21st of August and carried on the 27th, the weight being nearly 30 cwts. of hay per acre. Thus the two cuttings produced just about 4 tons of clover-hay per acre.

" The 11 acres were divided into two parts. About one-half was mown for hay a second time, and the other part left for seed. The produce of the second half of the 11-acre field was cut on the 8th of October, and carried on the 10th. It yielded in round

20

numbers 3 cwts. of clover-seed per acre, the season being very
unfavorable for clover-seed. The second crop of clover mown
for hay was rather too ripe and just beginning to show seed.

"A square foot of soil, 18 inches deep, was dug from the
second portion of the land which produced the clover-hay and
clover-seed.

" Soil from 11-acre field twice mown for hay.

"The upper 6 inches of soil, 1 foot square, contained all the
main roots of 18 strong plants ; the next 6 inches only small root-
fibers ; and in the third section, a 6-inch slice cut down at a depth
of 12 inches from the surface, no distinct fibers could be found.
The soil was almost completely saturated with rain when it was
dug up on the 13th September, 1866 :—

		lbs.
The upper 6 inches of soil 1 foot square weighed		60
The second 6 " . " "	....	61
The third 6 " " "	....	63

"These three portions of one foot of soil, 18 inches deep, were
dried nearly completely, and weighed again ; when the first 6
inches weighed 51¼ lbs. ; the second 6 inches, 51 lbs. 5 oz. ; and
the third section, 54 lbs. 2 ozs.

"The first 6 inches contained 3 lbs. of silicious stones (flints)
which were rejected in preparing a sample for analysis ; in the
two remaining sections there were no large-sized stones. The
soils were pounded down and passed through a wire sieve.

"The three layers of soil, dried and reduced to powder, were
mixed together, and a prepared average sample, when submitted to
analysis, yielded the following results :—

*Composition of Clover-soil, 18 inches deep, from part of 11-acre
field, twice mown for hay.*

	Organic matter	5·86
	Oxides of iron...................................	6·83
	Alumina..	7·12
Soluble in Hydrochloric Acid.	Carbonate of lime	2·13
	Magnesia	2·01
	Potash	·67
	Soda	·08
	Chloride or sodium.............................	·02
	Phosphoric acid	·18
	Sulphuric acid.................................	·17

	Insoluble siliceous matter....74·61	
	Consisting of—Alumina	4·27
	Lime (in a state of silicate)............	4·07
	Magnesia........................	·46
	Potash.........................	·19
	Soda	·23
	Silica..........................	65·29

99·68

"This soil, it will be seen, contained, in appreciable quantities, not only potash and phosphoric acid, but all the elements of fertility which enter into the composition of good arable land. It may be briefly described as a stiff clay-soil, containing a sufficiency of lime, potash, and phosphoric acid to meet all the requirements of the clover crop. Originally rather unproductive, it has been much improved by deep culture; by being smashed up into rough clods early in autumn, and by being exposed in this state to the crumbling effects of the air, it now yields good corn and forage crops.

"In separate portions of the three layers of soil, the proportions of nitrogen and phosphoric acid contained in each layer of 6 inches were determined and found to be as follows :—

	Soil dried at 212° Fahr.		
	1st 6 inches.	2d 6 inches.	3d 6 inches.
Percentage of phosphoric acid......	·249	·134	·172
Nitrogen	·162	·092	·064
Equal to ammonia	·198	·112	·078

"In the upper 6 inches, as will be seen, the percentage of both phosphoric acid and nitrogen was larger than in the two following layers; while the proportion of nitrogen in the 6 inches of surface soil was much larger than in the next 6 inches; and in the third section, containing no visible particles of root-fibers, only very little nitrogen occurred.

"In their natural state the three layers of soil contained :—

	1st 6 inches.	2d 6 inches.	3d 6 inches.
Moisture	17 16	18·24	16 62
Phosphoric acid..............	·198	·109	·143
Nitrogen	·134	·075	·053
Equal to ammonia...........	·162	·091	·064
	lbs.	lbs.	lbs.
Weight cf 1 foot square of soil..	60	61	63

"Calculated per acre, the absolute weight of 1 acre of this land, 6 inches deep, weighs :—

	lbs.
First 6 inches	2,613,600
Second "	2,637,160
Third "	2,746,280

" No great error, therefore, will be made if we assume in the subsequent calculations that 6 inches of this soil weigh $2\frac{1}{2}$ millions of pounds per acre.

" An acre of land, according to the preceding determinations, contains :—

	1st 6 inches. lbs.		2d 6 inches. lbs.		3d 6 inches. lbs.
Phosphoric acid	4,950	....	2,725	....	3,575
Nitrogen	3,350	....	1,875	....	1,325
Equal to ammonia	4,050	....	2,275	....	1,600

" The proportion of phosphoric acid in 6 inches of surface soil, it will be seen, amounted to about two-tenths per cent. ; a proportion of the whole soil so small that it may appear insufficient for the production of a good corn-crop. However, when calculated to the acre, we find that 6 inches of surface soil, in an acre of land, actually contain over 2 tons of phosphoric acid. An average crop of wheat, assumed to be 25 bushels of grain, at 60 lbs. per bushel, and 3,000 lbs. of straw, removes from the land on which it is grown 20 lbs. of phosphoric acid. The clover-soil, analyzed by me, consequently contains an amount of phosphoric acid in a depth or only 6 inches, which is equal to that present in $247\frac{1}{2}$ average crops of wheat ; or supposing that, by good cultiva tion and in favorable seasons, the average yield of wheat could be doubled, and 50 bushels of grain at 60 lbs. a bushel and 6,000 lbs. of straw could be raised, 124 of such heavy wheat-crops would contain no more phosphoric acid than actually occurred in 6 inches of this clover-soil per acre.

" The mere presence of such an amount of phosphoric acid in a soil, however, by no means proves its sufficiency for the production of so many crops of wheat ; for, in the first place, it cannot be shown that the whole of the phosphoric acid found by analysis occurs in the soil in a readily available combination ; and, in the second place, it is quite certain that the root-fibers of the wheat-plant cannot reach and pick up, so to speak, every particle of phosphoric acid, even supposing it to occur in the soil in a form most conducive to " ready assimilation by the plant."

" The calculation is not given in proof of a conclusion which would be manifestly absurd, but simply as an illustration of the

enormous quantity, in an acre of soil 6 inches deep, of a constituent forming the smaller proportions of the whole weight of an
acre of soil of that limited depth. It shows the existence of a
practically unlimited amount of the most important mineral constituents of plants, and clearly points out the propriety of rendering available to plants the natural resources of the soil in plant-
food ; to draw, in fact, up the mineral wealth of the soil by
thoroughly working the land, and not leaving it unutilized as so
much dead capital.

" The exact determination of phosphoric acid in a soil, it may
be observed in passing, is attended with no difficulty, if certain
precautions, which it is feared are sometimes neglected by chemists,
be taken. I will, therefore, give a brief outline of the plan—commonly known to chemists as the molybdic acid plan of determining phosphoric acid—which yields accurate results.

" Not less than 100 grains, or better, 200 grains, of the dried
and finely-powdered soil are digested for an hour, or thereabouts,
with 3 or 4 ounces of moderately strong nitric acid. The acid
solution is then passed through a filter, and together with the washings from the insoluble portion of the soil left on the filter, is
evaporated to a small bulk ; thus getting rid of the greater part of
the acid employed for effecting the solution. During evaporation
a large excess of molybdate of ammonia is added to the solution,
care being taken to keep it strongly acid.

" If there be much phosphoric acid in the soil, a bright yellow
precipitate, consisting of molybdic and phosphoric acid, makes its
appearance at once ; if traces only be present, the yellow precipitate appears only on the concentration of the liquid, after the
great excess of nitric acid has been been expelled by evaporation.
The yellow precipitate containing the whole of the phosphoric
acid present in the soil, molybdic acid, together with a little silica,
and frequently some oxide of iron, is thrown on a filter and washed
with a solution of molybdate of ammonia rendered strongly acid
by nitric acid, until a drop of the washings passing through the filter
ceases to show a reaction of iron with yellow prussiate of potash
solution. It is then dissolved on the filter in an excess of ammonia, and the ammoniacal liquid precipitated with an ammoniacal
solution of sulphate of magnesia, which throws down the phosphoric acid as phosphate of magnesia and ammonia. After standing at rest for about 12 hours, the magnesia precipitate is collected
on a small filter and washed clean with strong ammonia water.
Together with the phosphoric acid, traces of silica, and generally
also traces of oxide of iron, are thrown down with the magnesia pre-

cipitate. In order to separate these impurities the precipitate is dissolved in a few drops of hydrochloric acid, and the acid solution carefully evaporated to complete dryness. The hard, dried residue is again made acid with muriatic acid, a little water is then added, and the liquid passed through a small filter, on which are left insoluble traces of the silica originally thrown down with magnesia. A few drops of citric acid having been added to the acid solution, with a view of keeping any traces of iron in solution, strong ammonia is finally added, which throws down a second time phosphate of magnesia and ammonia, now free from silica and oxide of iron. The precipitate is collected, washed with ammonia water, dried, burned in a platinum crucible or capsule, weighed, and the phosphoric acid calculated from the weight of the tri-basic phosphate of magnesia left on burning.

" Following this plan and the precautions here indicated, the smallest amount of phosphoric acid in a soil can be determined with great precision. If the magnesia precipitate be not redissolved and freed from silica, as pointed out, a higher percentage of phosphoric acid necessarily is obtained than the actual quantity which the soil contains.

" *Clover-roots.*—The roots from 1 square foot of soil were cleaned as much as possible, dried completely at 212°, and in that state weighed 240 grains. An acre consequently contained 1,493½ lbs. of dried clover-roots.

The clover-roots contained :—

	Dried at 212° Fahr.
*Organic matter	81·33
†Mineral matter (ash)	18 67
	100·00

* Yielding nitrogen	1·635
Equal to ammonia	1·985
† Including insoluble silicious matter (clay and sand)	11·67

" Accordingly, the clover-roots in an acre of land furnished 24½ lbs. of nitrogen. We have thus :—

	lbs. of Nitrogen.
In the 6 inches of surface soil	3,350
In large clover-roots	24½
In second 6 inches of soil	1,875
Total amount of nitrogen in 1 acre of soil 12 inches deep.	5,249½
Equal to ammonia	6,374½

or, in round numbers, 2 tons 6 cwts. of nitrogen per acre, an enormous quantity, which must have a powerful influence in encouraging the luxuriant development of the succeeding wheat-crop, although only a fraction of the total amount of nitrogen in the clover-remains may become sufficiently decomposed in time to be available to the young wheat-plants.

" *Clover-soil from part of* 11-*acre field of Burcott Lodge Farm, Leighton-Buzzard, once mown for hay, and left afterward for seed.*

" Produce 2½ tons of clover-hay and 3 cwts. of seed per acre.
" This soil was obtained within a distance of 5 yards from the part of the field where the soil was dug up after the two cuttings of hay. After the seed there was some difficulty in finding a square foot containing the same number of large clover-roots as that on the part of the field twice mown ; however, at last, in the beginning of November, a square foot containing exactly 18 strong roots was found and dug up to a depth of 18 inches. The soil dug after the seed was much drier than that dug after the two cuttings of hay :—

				lbs.
The upper, 6 inches deep, 1 foot square, weighed				56
The next, " " "				58
The third, " " "				60

" After drying by exposure to hot air, the three layers of soil weighed :—

			lbs.
The upper 6 inches 1 foot square			49¾
The next " "			50½
The third " "			51¼

"Equal portions of the dried soil from each 6-inch section were mixed together and reduced to a fine powder. An average sample thus prepared, on analysis was found to have the following composition :—

Composition of Clover-soil once mown for hay, and afterward left for seed.

Dried at 212° Fahr.

Soluble in Hydrochloric Acid.	Organic matter	....	5·34
	Oxides of iron	....	6·07
	Alumina	....	4·51
	Carbonate of lime	....	7·51
	Magnesia	....	1·27
	Potash	....	·52
	Soda	....	·16
	Chloride of sodium	....	·03
	Phosphoric acid	....	·15
	Sulphuric acid	....	·19

Insoluble in Acid.	Insoluble silicious matter........ 73·84		
	Consisting of—Alumina	....	4·14
	Lime (in a state of silicate)	....	2·69
	Magnesia	....	·68
	Potash	....	·24
	Soda	....	·21
	Silica	....	65·88

99·59

" This soil, it will be seen, in general character resembles the preceding sample ; it contains a good deal of potash and phosphoric acid, and may be presumed to be well suited to the growth of clover. It contains more carbonate of lime, and is somewhat lighter than the sample from the part of the field twice mown for hay, and may be termed heavy calcareous clay.

" An acre of this land, 18 inches deep, weighed, when nearly dry :—

lbs.

Surface 6 inches	2,407,900
Next "	2,444,200
Third "	2,480,500

" Or in round numbers, every 6 inches of soil weighed per acre 2½ millions of pounds, which agrees tolerably well with the actual weight per acre of the preceding soil.

" The amount of phosphoric acid and nitrogen in each 6-inch layer was determined separately as before, when the following results were obtained :—

	In Dried Soil.		
	1st 6 inches.	2d 6 inches.	3d 6 inches.
Percentage of phosphoric acid ...	·159	·166	·140
Nitrogen	·189	·134	·089
Equal to ammonia	·229	·162	·108

" An acre, according to these determinations, contains in the three separate sections :—

	1st 6 inches. lbs.		2d 6 inches. lbs.		3d 6 inches. lbs.
Phosphoric acid	3,975	....	4,150	....	3,500
Nitrogen	4,725	....	3,350	....	2,225
Equal to ammonia	5,725	....	4,050	....	2,700

" Here again, as might naturally be expected, the proportion of nitrogen is largest in the surface where all the decaying leaves dropped during the growth of the clover for seed are found, and wherein root-fibers are more abundant than in the lower strata. The first 6 inches of soil, it will be seen, contained, in round numbers, $2\frac{1}{2}$ tons of nitrogen per acre, that is, considerably more than was found in the same section of the soil where the clover was mown twice for hay ; showing plainly that during the ripening of the clover-seed the surface is much enriched by the nitrogenous matter in the dropping leaves of the clover-plant.

" *Clover-roots.*—The roots from 1 square foot of this soil, freed as much as possible from adhering soil, were dried at 212°, and when weighed and reduced to a fine powder, gave, on analysis, the following results :—

```
*Organic matter ........................................... 64·76
†Mineral matters .......................................... 35·24
                                                         _____
                                                          100·00
```

```
* Containing nitrogen .......................................... 1·702
  Equal to ammonia ... ...................................... 2·066
† Including clay and sand (insoluble silicious matter). ............ 26·04
```

" A square foot of this soil produced 582 grains of dried clover-roots, consequently an acre yielded 3,622 lbs. of roots, or more than twice the weight of roots obtained from the soil of the same field where the clover was twice mown for hay.

" In round numbers, the 3,622 lbs. of clover-roots from the land mown once, and afterward left for seed, contained $51\frac{1}{2}$ lbs. of nitrogen.

" The roots from the soil after clover-seed, it will be noticed, were not so clean as the preceding sample, nevertheless, they yielded more nitrogen. In 64·76 of organic matter we have here 1·702 of nitrogen, whereas in the case of the roots from the part of the field where the clover was twice mown for hay, we have 81·33 parts—that is, much more organic matter, and 1·635, or rather less of nitrogen. It is evident therefore, that the organic matter in the soil after clover-seed occurs in a more advanced stage of decomposition than found in the clover-roots from the part of the field twice mown. In the manure in which the decay of such and similar organic remains proceeds, much of the non-nitrogenous or carbonaceous matters, of which these remains chiefly, though not entirely, consist, is transformed into gaseous carbonic acid, and what remains behind becomes richer in nitrogen and mineral matters. A parallel case, showing the dissipation of carbonaceous matter, and the increase in the percentage of nitrogen and mineral matter in what is left behind, is presented to us in fresh and rotten dung ; in long or fresh dung the percentage of organic matter, consisting chiefly of very imperfectly undecomposed straw, being larger, and that of nitrogen and mineral matter smaller, than in well-rotted dung.

" The roots from the field after clover-seed, it will be borne in mind, were dug up in November, while those obtained from the land twice mown, were dug up in September ; the former, therefore, may be expected to be in a more advanced state of decay than the latter, and richer in nitrogen.

" In an acre of soil after clover-seed, we have—

	lbs.
Nitrogen in first 6 inches of soil.	4,725
Nitrogen in roots	51½
Nitrogen in second 6 inches of soil.	3,350
Total amount of nitrogen per acre in 12 inches	8,126½
Equal to ammonia.	9.867

or, in round numbers, 3 tons and 12½ cwts. of nitrogen per acre, equal to 4 tons 8 cwts. of ammonia.

" This is a very much larger amount of nitrogen than occurred in the other soil, and shows plainly that the total amount of nitrogen accumulates, especially in the surface soil, when clover is grown for seeds ; thus explaining intelligibly, as it appears to me, why wheat, as stated by many practical men, succeeds better on land where clover is grown for seed than where it is mown for hay.

" All the three layers of the soil after clover-seed are richer in nitrogen than the same sections of the soil where the clover was twice mown, as will be seen by the following comparative statement of results :—

	I. Clover-soil twice Mown.			II. Clover-soil once Mown, and then left for Seed.		
	Upper 6 inches.	Second 6 inches.	Third 6 inches.	Upper 6 inches.	Next 6 inches.	Lowest 6 inches.
Percentage of nitrogen in dried soil	·168	·092	·064	·189	·134	·c89
Equal to ammonia.......	·198	·112	·078	·229	·162	·108

" This difference in the amount of accumulated nitrogen in clover-land appears still more strikingly on comparing the total amounts of nitrogen per acre in the different sections of the two portions of the 11-acre fields :—

Percentage of nitrogen per acre :—

	1st 6 inches. lbs.		2d 6 inches. lbs.		3d 6 inches. lbs.
* I. In soil, clover twice over ...	3,350	....	1,875	....	1,325
† II. In soil, clover once mown and seeded afterward	4,725	....	3,350	....	2,225

Equal to ammonia :—

* I. Clover twice mown	4,050	......	2,275	......	1,600
† II. Clover seeded....................	5,725	......	4,050	......	2,700
* I. Nitrogen in roots of clover twice mown..............	24½				
† II. Nitrogen in clover, once mown and grown for seed afterward.	51½				
I. Weight of dry roots per acre from Soil I..............	1,493¼				
II. Weight of dry roots per acre from Soil II.............	3,622				
* Total amount of nitrogen in 1 acre, 12 inches deep, of Soil I	5,249½				
† Total amount of nitrogen in 1 acre, 12 inches deep, of Soil II	8,126½				
* Equal to ammonia	6,374¼				
† Equal to ammonia..................	9,867				
Excess of nitrogen in an acre of soil, 12 inches deep, calculated as ammonia in part of field mown once and then seeded.	3,492½				

" It will be seen that not only was the amount of large clover roots greater in the part where clover was grown for seed, but that likewise the different ayers of soil were in every instance richer in nitrogen after clover-seed than after clover mown twice for hay ; or as it may be expressed : In 1 lb. of ammonia there were 3,492° of ammonia in the land where clover-seed was grown than where other clover was made entirely into hay ; or the former part of the same field produced rather more than half the total quantity of nitrogen yielded by the latter.

" Reasons are given in the beginning of this paper which it is hoped will have convinced the reader that the fertility of land is not so much measured by the amount of ash-constituents of plants which it contains, as by the amount of nitrogen which, together with an excess of such ash-constituents, it contains in an available form. It has been shown, likewise, that the removal from the soil of a large amount of mineral matter in a good clover crop, in conformity with many direct field experiments, is not likely, in any degree, to affect the wheat crop, and that the yield of wheat on soils under ordinary cultivation, according to the experience of many farmers, and the direct and numerous experiments of Messrs. Lawes and Gilbert, rises or falls, other circumstances being equal, with the supply of available nitrogenous food which is given to the wheat. This being the case, we cannot doubt that the benefits arising from the growth of clover to the succeeding wheat are mainly due to the fact that an immense amount of nitrogenous food accumulates in the soil during the growth of clover.

" This accumulation of nitrogenous plant-food, specially useful to cereal crops, is, as shown in the preceding experiments, much greater when clover is grown for seed than when it is made into hay. This affords an intelligible explanation of a fact long observed by good practical men, although denied by others who decline to accept their experience as resting on trustworthy evidence, because, as they say, land cannot become more fertile when a crop is grown upon it for seed which is carried off, than when that crop is cut down and the produce consumed on the land. The chemical points brought forward in the course of this inquiry show plainly that mere speculations as to what can take place in a soil and what not, do not much advance the true theory of certain agricultural practices. It is only by carefully investigating subjects like the one under consideration that positive proofs are given showing the correctness of intelligent observers in the fields. Many years ago I made a great many experiments relative to the chemistry of farm-yard manure, and then showed, among other particulars, that manure, spread at once on the land, need not there and then be plowed in, inasmuch as neither a broiling sun nor a sweeping and drying wind will cause the slightest loss of ammonia, and that, therefore, the old-fashioned farmer,who carts his manure on the land as soon as he can, and spreads it at once, but who plows it in at his convenience, acts in perfect accordance with correct chemical principles involved in the management of farm-yard manure. On the present occasion my main object has been to show, not merely by reasoning on the subject, but by actual experiments, that the larger the amounts of nitrogen, potash, soda, lime, phosphoric acid, etc., which are removed from the land in a clover crop, the better it is, nevertheless, made thereby for pro-ducing in the succeeding year an abundant crop of wheat, other circumstances being favorable to its growth.

"Indeed no kind of manure can be compared, in point of effi-cacy for wheat, to the manuring which the land gets in a really good crop of clover. The farmer who wishes to derive the full benefit from his clover-lay, should plow it up for wheat as soon as possible in the autumn, and leave it in a rough state as long as is admissible, in order that the air may find free access into the land, and the organic remains left in so much abundance in a good crop of clover be changed into plant-food; more especially, in other words, in order that the crude nitrogenous organic matter in the clover-roots and decaying leaves may have time to become transformed into ammoniacal compounds, and these, in the course of time, into nitrates, which I am strongly inclined to think is the form in which nitrogen is assimilated, *par excellence*, by cereal crops, and in which, at all events, it is more efficacious than in any other state of combination wherein it may be used as a fertilizer.

"When the clover-lay is plowed up early, the decay of the clover is sufficiently advanced by the time the young wheat-plant stands in need of readily available nitrogenous food, and this, being uniformly distributed through the whole of the cultivated soil, is ready to benefit every single plant. This equal and abundant dis-tribution of food, peculiarly valuable to cereals, is a great advan-tage, and speaks strongly in favor of clover as a preparatory crop for wheat.

"Nitrate of soda, an excellent spring top-dressing for wheat and cereals in general, in some seasons fails to produce as good an effect as in others. In very dry springs the rain-fall is not suffi-cient to wash it properly into the soil and to distribute it equally, and in very wet seasons it is apt to be washed either into the drains or into a stratum of the soil not accessible to the roots of the young wheat. As, therefore, the character of the approaching season cannot usually be predicted, the application of nitrate of soda to wheat is always attended with more or less uncertainty.

" The case is different when a good crop of clover-hay has been obtained from the land on which wheat is intended to be grown afterward. An enormous quantity of nitrogenous organic matter, as we have seen, is left in the land after the removal of the clover crop ; and these remains gradually decay and furnish ammonia, which at first, and during the colder months of the year, is retained by the well-known absorbing properties which all good wheat-soils possess. In spring, when warmer weather sets in, and the wheat begins to make a push, these ammonia compounds in the soil are by degrees oxidized into nitrates ; and as this change into food, peculiarly favorable to young cereal plants, proceeds slowly but steadily, we have in the soil itself, after clover, a source from which nitrates are continuously produced ; so that it does not much affect the final yield of wheat, whether heavy rains remove some or all of the nitrate present in the soil. The clover-remains thus afford a more continuous source from which nitrates are produced, and greater certainty for a good crop of wheat than when recourse is had to nitrogenous top-dressings in the spring.

" The remarks respecting the formation of nitrates in soils upon which clover has been grown, it should be stated, do not emanate from mere speculations, but are based on actual observations.

" I have not only been able to show the existence of nitrates in clover-soils, but have made a number of actual determinations of the amount of nitric acid in different layers of soils on which clover had been grown ; but as this paper has grown already to greater dimensions than perhaps desirable, I reserve any further remarks on the important subject of nitrification in soils for a future communication.

" *Summary.*

" The following are some of the chief points of interest which I have endeavored fully to develop in the preceding pages :—

" 1. A good crop of clover removes from the soil more potash, phosphoric acid, lime, and other mineral matters, which enter into the composition of the ashes of our cultivated crops, than any other crop usually grown in this country.

" 2. There is fully three times as much nitrogen in a crop of clover as in the average produce of the grain and straw of wheat per acre.

" 3. Notwithstanding the large amount of nitrogenous matter

and of ash-constituents of plants in the product of an acre, clover is an excellent preparatory crop for wheat.

" 4. During the growth of clover a large amount of nitrogenous matter accumulates in the soil.

" 5. This accumulation, which is greatest in the surface-soil, is due to decaying leaves dropped during the growth of clover, and to an abundance of roots, containing, when dry, from $1\frac{3}{4}$ to 2 per cent. of nitrogen.

" 6. The clover-roots are stronger and more numerous, and more leaves fall on the ground when clover is grown for seed, than when it is mown for hay; in consequence, more nitrogen is left after clover-seed than after hay, which accounts for wheat yielding a better crop after clover-seed than after hay.

" 7. The development of roots being checked when the produce, in a green condition, is fed off by sheep, in all probability leaves still less nitrogenous matter in the soil than when clover is allowed to get riper and is mown for hay; thus, no doubt, accounting for the observation made by practical men that, notwithstanding the return of the produce in the sheep-excrements, wheat is generally stronger and yields better, after clover mown for hay, than when the clover is fed off green by sheep.

" 8. The nitrogenous matters in the clover-remains on their gradual decay are finally transformed into nitrates, thus affording a continuous source of food on which cereal crops specially delight to grow.

" 9. There is strong presumptive evidence that the nitrogen which exists in the air in the shape of ammonia and nitric acid, and descends in these combinations with the rain which falls on the ground, satisfies, under ordinary circumstances, the requirements of the clover crop. This crop causes a large accumulation of nitrogenous matters, which are gradually changed in the soil into nitrates. The atmosphere thus furnishes nitrogenous food to the succeeding wheat indirectly, and, so to say, gratis.

" 10. Clover not only provides abundance of nitrogenous food, but delivers this food in a readily available form (as nitrates) more gradually and continuously, and consequently with more certainty of a good result, than such food can be applied to the land in the shape of nitrogenous spring top-dressing.

"LABORATORY, 11 SALISBURY SQUARE,

FLEET STREET, E. C., *July*, 1868."

In addition to the foregoing, I extract the following from a paper written by the Hon. Geo. Geddes for the New York *Tri-*

bune. Mr. Geddes is one of the most skillful and enlightened
farmers in the country. He says :—

"At a meeting of the New York State Agricultural Society,
"many years ago, I was awarded the first premium for the best
"cultivated farm in competition that year,—1845. The com-
"mittee that made the award said that I did not use enough
"manure. My four hundred to five hundred loads from the
"barns and stables drawn out each year, and my fourteen tons of
"gypsum, and all the ashes made on the premises, they said was
"too little for the farm. A discussion followed the reading of
"the report, and I tried to show that I did do all that true
"economy dictated in the way of making barn-yard manure ;
"that gypsum and clover furnished the means of increasing fer-
"tility, at less cost than drawing leaves from the woods, muck
"from the swamps, and making expensive compost heaps. In
"the years that followed, my friend, the author of this last edi-
"tion of the book I have been noticing, has had not a little laugh
"at my expense, growing out of my views on the manure ques-
"tion. In several of the meetings for discussion of our State
"Agricultural Society, manure has been the subject before us,
"and for all these years, I have insisted that a farm should,
"unless situated in the immediate vicinity of some village or city,
"be so managed that its fertility should constantly increase, with-
"out going off of it for manure, with the exception of gypsum,
"and perhaps salt. In my report ' on the agriculture and indus-
"try of the county of Onondaga,' made in 1860, I said much of
"the use of red clover as a fertilizer, and doubtless astonished
"many of my readers by some things in that report. In turn I
"was not a little astonished at some of the comments made on
"my statements. A very eminent writer on agricultural matters,
"living in New Hampshire, said over his own name, in an agri-
"cultural paper, that he had never before heard of plowing in a
"crop of clover for manure, and that where he lived the farmers
"preferred to make hay, rather than manure, of clover.

"In Mr. Allen's reference to what I said on this question, he
"makes me say that the farmers in this vicinity ' would not draw
"*barn manure* a mile, if it were given to them.' I do not complain
"of this, for perhaps, I have in some discussion said this ; but I
"was speaking of barn manure, or rather *yard* manure as it is
"made here, where, as Mr. Allen says, ' we raise wheat
"largely as well as other cereals.' In doing this, we raise a great
"deal of straw and corn-stalks. The straw and corn-stalks

" are fed to our farm stock with great profusion. After every
" heavy snow-storm of winter our barn-yards are covered deeply
" with straw to be trodden under foot by the cattle ; the lead-
" ing object being to get this straw wet and broken up, so that as
" soon as the frost has gone out in the spring, the whole mass
" can be flung into piles to rot, and become so reduced in bulk
" that, by once turning a part of it, in midsummer, we can get
" it into shape to draw on our wheat lands, or pastures, in the
" fall. Now, what is this barn-yard manure, as it is left when
" the cattle are turned to pasture in the spring ? A great mass of
" straw, and butts of corn-stalks, having a very small per cent. of
" the dung of the cattle,—filling the yards two or more feet deep,
" and saturated with water. What sensible farmer would go one
" mile from home and draw this stuff to his farm, pile it, cut it
" down, and repile it, and in the fall find it reduced perhaps four-
" fifths in bulk, and then again load it, and draw it on his fields, to
" fill them with the seeds of foul weeds, when fifteen pounds of
" clover-seed, that would cost perhaps two dollars, and a bushel
" of gypsum, would manure an acre of land far better than
" would fifty loads of this barn-yard manure, as it was found in
" the spring ?
  " Where cattle are stall-fed, and given all the grain they will
" eat, and in cases like this, the whole thing is changed. Manure
" from such sources, perhaps, would bear even here transportation
" for many miles. One load of the dung of high-fed horses would
" be worth many loads of the strawy contents of a wheat-grower's
" barn-yard.
  " But a few words in regard to the Ohio farmer that our author
" found wasting his hog manure, by allowing it to run into a con-
" venient brook. There may have been, and probably was, much
" water to a little manure in this case, and like city sewage, the
" manure might after all have been so diluted as to have been worth
" much less than would at first have been supposed. At any rate,
" we have seen all through this country the streams made foul and
" unhealthy to the fish in them, and to the people along them,
" by the drainage of the hog-pens of distilleries. In a case near
" me, no man but a raiser of fruit-trees could be found, who
" was willing to provide water-tight wagon boxes and draw on
" his nursery the very much diluted manure of a large establish-
" ment of this kind, and within a few days I have seen the brook
" that runs by it used to conduct the manure to Onondaga
" Lake.
  " But to return to the clover. It is sometimes said, that it is
21

"a great waste of a hay crop, and a great loss of time, to manure
"with clover. Let us examine this point a little.

"A farmer has a fine meadow, consisting of the clover that
"has grown from fifteen pounds of seed—not of the large 'pea-
"vine' kind, but of the smaller variety of red clover—and from
"five quarts of timothy seed, sown on each acre, which has been
"treated to a dressing of gypsum (commonly, but very improperly
"called plaster). This meadow is cut for hay, as soon as the
"clover is in full bloom. A crop of two tons to the acre, of
"this *best of hay*, should be secured. Another dressing of gypsum
"is then sown, and unless the season is uncommonly dry, up
"starts the clover, and generally by the first day of October,
"in this latitude, there will be a crop of clover-seed averaging
"three bushels to the acre, that should pay, over and above
"all expense for labor, fifteen dollars. The timothy grass
"will in this second crop make very little show, and if the clover-
"seed is cut, as it should be, so high as to leave a large part of
"the stalks on the ground, there will be enough left to about fill
"the furrow, if plowed that autumn. The next year a crop of
"barley sown on the inverted sod, should give the highest yield
"for that grain. One plowing turns up this decayed sod and
"clover, and a crop of wheat should give its best yield. Clover
"and timothy seed sown on that wheat, enables the farmer to
"repeat the process.

"I have supposed the land to be in good condition to begin
"with, and many years' experience justifies me in saying that
"it will be richer after these crops—four of them, in three
"years—have been taken off than it was before. But on this
"point, I propose, presently, to introduce a witness, whose testi-
"mony will have more weight than any thing I can say. I now
"ask what time has been lost, and what has been sacrificed in the
"way of a hay crop, or any thing else, and what has been the cost
"of filling the ground with clover-roots, and the furrow with
"clover-tops?

"But perhaps the owner of the land desires to do more in the
"way of increasing fertility than I have thus far supposed. Let
"him plow under, if he can find a plow that will do it, the
"second crop of clover, and not cut his crop of seed. The crop
"of hay will pay full interest on the land for one year, and the
"barley and wheat crops will do the same in their seasons.
"What grain-raiser can draw from his own barn-yard so much
"manure as this clover makes, for the cost of the clover and
"timothy seed, and of the gypsum, and the sowing? But does

" the clover add to the land the fertilizing properties desired in
" the necessary quantities to replace all that is taken off by the
" crops named, and leave a satisfactory balance in bank to go to
" new account?"

*   *   *   *   *   *   *

Here follow copious extracts from Dr. Voelcker's paper, quoted
from above.

Mr. Geddes concludes as follows :—

" About the time this great agricultural chemist, who perhaps
" stands at the head of his profession, was delivering the lecture
" from which I have been making quotations, before the Royal
" Agricultural Society of England, I was writing articles for the
" readers of the *Tribune*, urging the use of clover as a manure,— using
" my own and my neighbors' experience from which to draw my facts.
" I am not a little pleased at finding that this great chemist has got
" out of his laboratory and gone into the field for his facts, and then
" carried his facts, so obtained, into the laboratory, and given a
" scientific explanation of them. His language is vastly stronger
" than any I have ever used in favor of clover as compared with
" other manures. His comparison of clover with Peruvian guano
" goes further than I have ever gone, even in the heat of debate,
" in an agricultural club meeting.

" In addition to the advantages growing out of the use of clover
" as a manure that have been stated by the learned professor, I
" wish to call attention to the important fact that, as the clover
" grows evenly all over the ground, it will, in its decomposition,
" reach with its fertilizing powers every square inch of land. No
" reasonable expenditure of labor will so break up and distribute
" barn-yard manure that every part of the surface of the soil will
" be reached.

" All grain-growers that have extensively used clover as a
" fertilizer have thereby enormously increased the quantity of
" barn-yard manure made on their farms ; and it certainly should be
" comforting to that class of men who still believe that additional
" value is imparted to vegetable matter by drawing it from the
" field to the barn, and passing it through the bodies of farm stock,
" and then drawing it back to the field, to learn that by raising
" large crops of clover, and turning a part of them into the ground,
" it will certainly follow that the barn-yard manure will be greatly
" increased in quantity by the increased yields of straw and corn-
" stalks produced by the clover.

" The men who do the most at manuring with clover by no

"means underrate the value of other manures, but they do
"fall into the custom of laying out the least possible amount of
"labor that they can on the contents of their barn-yards, and get
"them back into the soil.   The manure cart is apt to be emptied
"on some field near the barn, and the 'back end of the back
"field,' to use the expression of one of my volunteer correspon-
"dents, never is visited by it.

   " No other class of farmers (I do not mean gardeners) with
"whom I am acquainted manure as highly as the men who make
"the freest use of clover the leading principle of their farm man-
"agement.

   "FAIRMOUNT, N. Y. *Oct.* 23, 1869."

   While on this subject of the fertilizing effect of clover, I desire
to record my belief, that, theoretically considered, clover *may*
become a means for the more complete exhaustion of the soil in
the end.   Fertility depends for one of its chief supports upon
mineral matters, of which even the best soils contain comparatively but a very small proportion.   These are absolutely necessary to the growth of all agricultural plants.

   Clover can *create* none of them.   Its only ability is to develop
and make more readily available that which the soil already contains, and, while a soil which has been so completely exhausted to
the depth of its shallow plowing, that it will produce neither
wheat nor corn, nor grass, may, by the aid of clover, have so much
of the fertilizing minerals of its subsoil brought into action as
to become more fertile than before, it may, by persistent plun-
dering,—by constantly taking off and bringing nothing back,—be
made so poor, (subsoil and all,) that not even clover will grow.
In this condition the land is called " clover sick," and to restore
it from this impoverishment, nothing will suffice but long-continued exposure to the atmosphere, by frequent plowing, or the
addition of enormous quantities of manure.   Judiciously managed, clover culture may be made the means of restoring the
most exhausted soils to more than their virgin fertility, and of
keeping their productiveness always at the top mark ; but employed
without judgment, it must in time (perhaps a very long time)
effect an absolute impoverishment.

It seems hardly necessary, in a book of directions for practical farmers, to tell how clover is grown ; but as the crop is not universally grown, the information may be of value to some of my readers.

Clover is never (so far as I know) grown alone. It is benefited during its earliest growth by being sheltered from the sun and wind, and it takes a better hold of the ground when sown with oats or barley, or other spring grain, or among the standing plants of wheat or rye. The seed is sown broadcast on the surface as early as possible in the spring, (even on the snow in March,) or immediately after the harrowing in of spring grain. It is sufficiently covered by subsequent rains. Indeed, it seems hardly to require covering at all, and it takes root in the compact soil of a wheat-field, which has been beaten hard by the rains of a whole winter.

After the grain has been mowed, the clover (with a moderate amount of rain) grows vigorously, and will, on rich land, attain a height of a foot or more. Under such circumstances, it should be fed down sufficiently to allow the free access of the sun and air to the soil, that the roots may become well established and the growth stocky. In this condition, it will much better withstand the vicissitudes of an open winter, which is its greatest enemy.

In latitudes where the snow lies on the ground throughout the season, there is no trouble from winter-killing, but when this protection is not to be depended on, it is well to top-dress the plants with sea-weed, strawy manure, or other rubbish. For manure, clover asks little else than ground plaster, or gypsum, and of this so small a quantity as a single bushel per acre will suffice, if it be sown evenly (on the plants rather than on the ground) when the leaves are wet with dew or with a misty rain.

The amount of seed used on an acre is from one peck to four pecks, and I am by no means certain that the larger amount is not the more profitable,—costly though clover-seed is.

Under the " soiling " system, and indeed on all farms where the highest cultivation is the rule, it will be found best to crop the clover but a single year, cutting three times during the summer,

except so much as it may be desired to save for seed. On rich
land, such as is adapted for soiling, an amount of clover may be
cut which would, if cured, make four or six tons of hay, and
there would be left in the soil a mass of roots, that, with liberal
manuring, would be an excellent preparation for corn, or any
other crop desired.

A good field of clover is one of the very earliest ready to cut
for fodder, and after the third clip has been taken off, the soil will
afford a capital bite for young stock late into the fall.

For hay, the crop should be allowed to stand until two-thirds
of the plants are in full bloom, and after cutting, it should be cured
(in the cock) with the least possible amount of rough handling, as
the leaves will be dry while the stems are yet quite green, and
will be likely to be broken off and lost if much handled.

From what has been said, it will be seen that clover is to be
regarded as the "sheet-anchor" of American agriculture, and
especially of the system of soiling. It enriches the land, and nour-
ishes the herd as no other crop can. As a forage crop *simply*, it
is later than winter rye, and less productive (probably less nutritious) than Indian corn ; but its value as a fertilizer so far compensates for its shortcomings in these directions, that it should
always play an important part in all cases where green fodder is
used.

As a hay crop, clover is excellent for cows, but less valuable
than the grasses for horses. In my own practice I shall depend
on it almost exclusively for *hay* for my dairy cows.

Oats are not very much grown as a green forage crop, as it
is generally considered more profitable to ripen the grain for market ; but whenever " soiling " is practiced,—and soiling is the only
method yet devised that will, in the future, enable New England
to keep dairy animals in competition with the richer lands at the
west,—oats will be found of the greatest importance as filling
the gap between early rye, and the grasses and Indian corn.
When grass has become too ripe and hard for the best use of
milking animals, the oat-field is in its best estate, and will furnish

an excellent fodder, which is greatly relished by all stock, and which, up to the time of the hardening of its stem, is admirably suited to the production of milk.

The only specific directions for its cultivation are to put the seed into the ground at the earliest practicable moment in the spring, and to sow thickly. An early start (on land that is not too wet) seems to be even more important than richness of soil. And (unlike this crop when grown for grain) the land *cannot be too rich*, as it should all be removed before it is sufficiently matured to lodge. As soon as the crop has fairly blossomed,—if there is a bit of corn or clover that can be cut for the stock,—the oats should all come down. At this stage, (as is the case with all cereals,) the nutritive constituents of the plant are the most uniformly distributed throughout all parts of its structure, and probably it contains (straw and all) very nearly all that it will at any time contain. At all events, any slight disadvantage that may result from cutting the crop before it has ceased to receive nutriment from its roots, will be more than compensated for by the fact that even the butts of the straw will be sweet and nutritious, and will be consumed without waste. Cut at this stage of growth, and properly cured, oats will be little, if any, inferior to the best hay.

A good growth of oats, from rich and well-cultivated land, will make from two and a half to three tons of hay, equal to average meadow hay. It is easily cured, and keeps perfectly. Therefore there is nothing risked in sowing much more than will probably be needed for green feeding. It *may* be very convenient to have it, so as to avoid cutting the corn too early, and if it is not needed green, it is worth all it costs as hay.

RYE is the great lengthener of the seasons. Sown early in September, on rich land, using four bushels of seed to the acre, it will often afford a good bite for the stock well into the winter, if only the severe frosts hold off, and in the spring, almost before the snow is fairly off of the ground, it starts its vigorous growth, and may be cut or pastured fully two weeks before the first grass is ready.

To get the best results for early soiling, the cutting should not be too *early*, but the crop is not injured (only delayed) by cutting or feeding off as often as is desired at any time before the "jointing" takes place, as a new and vigorous growth will follow every cutting.

I am credibly informed that by being cut often enough, rye has been kept in luxuriant condition for five years. I have myself taken two heavy cuttings in one season, and had a crop of ripe grain afterward.

Rye is a good green fodder only when in a comparatively green and immature condition. If left until it blossoms, the lower part of the straw, although it may still be green, is too hard to be readily eaten by cattle.

Still more than oats is rye a safe crop to plant to excess, as when grown on land fit for soiling uses, its production of straw is very large, and rye straw, thrashed by hand, is always marketable at a very high price, usually much higher than the best hay, and the grain is of considerable importance.

MILLET, the remaining forage crop of our list, is one on which I do not feel qualified to give instruction, having never succeeded in producing a satisfactory crop. I am informed by those who have grown it regularly, that it is a valuable adjunct in green soiling. My own conviction is that it cannot compete with Indian corn,—nor can any thing else,—and that, therefore, as it cannot be produced any earlier than this, there is no advantage in growing it.

Allen says:* "It grows to the height of two and a half to four "feet, with a profusion of stalks and leaves which furnish excel- "lent forage for cattle. From eighty to one hundred bushels of "seed per acre have been raised, and with straw equivalent to one "and a half to two tons of hay; but an average crop may be "estimated at about one-third this quantity. Owing to the great "waste during the ripening of the seed, from the shelling of the

* New American Book of the Farm. New York : Orange Judd & Co.

" earliest of it before the last is matured, and the frequent depre-
" dations of birds, which are very fond of it, millet is more profit-
" ably cut when the first seeds have begun to ripen, and harvested
" for fodder. It is cured like hay, and in good land yields from two
" and a half to four tons per acre. All cattle relish it, and
" experience has shown it to be fully equal to good hay.

" Millet requires a dry, rich, and well-pulverized soil. It will
" grow on thin soil, but best repays on the most fertile. It should
" be sown broadcast or in drills from the first of May to the first
" of July. If for hay and sown broadcast, forty quarts per acre
" will be required; if sown in drills for the grain, eight quarts of
" seed will suffice. It will ripen in sixty to seventy-five days
" with favorable weather. When designed for fodder, the nearer
" it can approach to ripening without waste in harvesting, the
" more valuable will be the crop."

It is possible that Mr. Allen is mistaken in this latter statement. It seems to be a well-established fact that all plants of
this character are in their best condition for hay at about the
period of blossoming.

Flint says :* " It is very valuable and nutritious for milch cows,
" both green and when properly cured. The curing should be very
" much like clover, care being taken not to overdry it. For fodder,
" either green or cured, it is cut before ripening. In this state all
" cattle will eat it as readily as green corn, and a less extent will
" feed them. Millet is worthy of a widely-extended cultivation,
" particularly on dairy farms."

If millet has any marked advantage which should bring it into
common use, it lies in its ability to withstand drought,—whether
from the thinness of the soil or the heat of the sun.

---

* Milch Cows and Dairy Farming. Boston: Tilton & Co.

CHAPTER XIII.

LIVE STOCK.

LIVE stock is more or less important to the farmer, according to the circumstances under which his business is carried on. In extensive grain-growing regions, where the policy is simply to raise the largest possible crops, rather by extent of cultivation than by excessive production per acre, and where it is intended either to trust to luck for the fertility of the land or deliberately to exhaust and abandon it, live stock forms no important part of the farm machinery, it being necessary only to keep such teams as are required for plowing, cultivation, and harvesting.

In other extensive regions, where the chief, almost the entire, business of the farmer is confined to the grazing of large flocks and herds on natural pastures, he cares for little else than live stock ; but, at the same time, his animals live almost in a state of nature, require scarcely any attention beyond the annual branding and the annual selection of droves for market, and he needs to know almost nothing concerning their management as understood by skillful husbandmen.

Live stock becomes an important element in the economy of the farm only when our object is to raise fine animals, to raise beef for market, or wool, or dairy products, or poultry, as a means for converting the production of the land into a marketable form. And in these cases its management always is, or always should be, attended by a full appreciation of the value of manure.

> " No manure—no grass,
> No grass—no cattle,
> No cattle—no manure."

This is the circle within which the reasoning of the best modern agriculture constantly revolves. We may make our chief business the growth of large crops, yet, unless we are surrounded by some peculiar circumstances, we cannot hope to continue the profitable growth of large crops without the aid of manure resulting from the feeding of animals. We may make it our chief object to raise fine beef or other animal products for sale, and we may regard every thing else connected with the farm as purely incidental to this ;—yet we shall soon find that the key to our success lies in the fertility of the land, increased by a judicious use of the manure that the animals make.

It is impossible in any mixed husbandry, or in what may more properly be called general husbandry, to disregard for a moment the relation always existing between the three cardinal points of crops, cattle, and dung. If we do away with the cattle and sell our crops, we fall short of dung, and must buy it or its substitute in the market. If we fall short of food, our cattle and our manure-pits both suffer. If we allow our manure to run to waste, or use it with bad economy, both cattle and crops must suffer in the end. Of course there are circumstances in which special facilities for purchasing manure, extraordinarily high prices for grain, or the prevalence of diseases which make it unsafe to keep large stocks of cattle, compel a deviation from the foregoing principle. But, as a principle, it is a fixed one, and any change from its requirements should be adopted only with due consideration and for good and sufficient reasons, which, being generally of a local character, it is not necessary nor desirable to discuss in this connection.

To return to the illustration with which this work commenced, —that of a young man about entering upon the improvement of a farm,—we find that one of the questions which it will be most important for him to decide is, that of the extent to which the raising of live stock should form a part of his plan, and having decided this, to fix upon the direction which his live stock efforts shall take.

The following fields are open to him: the raising of horses, the making of beef, the making of pork, the sale of milk, the manufacture of butter or cheese, the growth of wool, the production of poultry and eggs, and the raising of thoroughbred animals for what is called the fancy market.

Ordinarily he will find it best to select as his main object such a branch of industry as his farm, his buildings, and his market indicate as most desirable; but to couple with this in all cases some collateral branch of stock-keeping, so that, to use a common expression, he may not have his eggs all in one basket; and that he may be able to make one department assist somewhat in the development of the advantages of another. For example, in the manufacture of butter or cheese there should be at least a sufficient herd of swine to consume the refuse products of the dairy;—and in the case of all animals to which grain is fed, it will be found advantageous to have at least enough poultry to pick up the sweepings of the stables and the waste of the thrashing-machine. Again, whatever his business may be, it will be necessary for him to keep working-teams, and if the production of beef promises to be profitable, he will find it advantageous to keep several yokes of oxen, working each pair only sufficiently to stimulate their appetites and keep them in an improving condition; while, if he prefers to use horse-teams, there will be generally a decided advantage in having mares from which one or two colts each year may be expected.

It is, of course, impossible to say, that, as a general rule, any branch of stock-raising is more profitable than any other branch; and it is probably true that over the whole country there is, in ordinary husbandry, not very much difference between any of the leading branches. If there were a decided advantage in favor of any one kind of stock, the difficulty would soon correct itself by reason of the neglect of some other branch, until the price of its products brought it again within the practicable range of profit. All that it is proper for me to do, therefore, is to state briefly the advantages of the different kinds of stock, and some of the rules which should govern their management.

HORSES.

According to the census of 1860, there were 6,249,174 horses in the United States, equal in value to at least one-fourth of the present national debt ; and, in addition to these, there were probably over one million mules (1,151,148 asses and mules). Of course, so far as the more settled parts of the country are concerned, a very large proportion of the horses are in use upon farms ; and their chief value to most farmers consists in their ability to do his work. At the same time, in addition to this and incidental to it, the very large demand for horses for work, and for pleasure-driving in cities and towns, creates such a market for them, among those who are not engaged in their production, that the sale of the increase of farm stock is a great source of agricultural profit ; and wherever a farmer is so circumstanced that he can raise a few colts without inconvenience, he will generally find it advisable to have a large proportion of mares among his working teams.

The breeding of horses in this country has generally been carried on in a most careless and haphazard way. Any broken-down, spavined, heavy old mare, that ought to be knocked on the head,—that certainly would not, for general use, be worth keeping,—is usually considered good enough to get colts from. And this accounts for the fact that all persons who are familiar with the horses raised in this country consider it advantageous to buy rather old animals, with the idea that if they have passed their seventh or eighth year without developing a congenital disease, they may be depended on for a fair amount of service ;—and the immense number of five and six year old horses that go blind or lame, or get broken-winded, is a very severe comment on the ordinary policy of farmers in raising horses.

The rule that " like begets like " holds in no case with greater force than in the breeding of horses ; and we may, with the same reason, expect healthy children from scrofulous and consumptive parents, as sound colts from unsound mothers.

There are many imperfections, to which horse-flesh is subject,

that do not interfere with the production of sound progeny; as
the accidental loss of an eye, for instance, which is a blemish,
but which is not real unsoundness, and is not likely, after inflammation has subsided and after the animal's attention has ceased to
be drawn to that part, to produce any unsoundness in the eyes
of the colt. And the same is true of several kinds of lameness
which result from purely accidental causes, from bad shoeing, etc.
In no case would it be prudent to breed from a mare while she is
actually suffering from the effects of any accident or ill-treatment;
but after the wound has healed and she has settled down to the
even tenor of her way, there is no reason why such accidental
imperfections should be perpetuated. As a general rule, it may
be stated that the mare that is best suited to the farmer's purposes
as a team animal, is precisely the one from which he may most
reasonably expect to get good colts; and the same rule that should
guide him in the purchase of a mare for work should also guide
him in the matter of breeding.

In Stonehenge's "British Rural Sports," the following directions are given concerning the choice of a brood mare, the portion which relates chiefly to the breeding of race-horses being
excluded from the quotation :—

"In choosing the brood mare, four things must be considered :
"first, her blood; secondly, her frame; thirdly, her state of
"health; and fourthly, her temper.

      *   *   *   *   *   *   *

"In frame, the mare should be so formed as to be capable of
"carrying and well nursing her offspring; that is, she should be
"what is called 'roomy.' There is a formation of the hips which
"is particularly unfit for breeding purposes, and yet which is some-
"times carefully selected, because it is considered elegant; this is
"the level and straight hip, in which the tail is set on very high,
"and the end of the haunch-bone is nearly on a level with the pro-
"jection of the hip-bone. * * * By examining her [a well-
"formed mare's] pelvis, it will be seen that the haunch-bone forms
"a considerable angle with the sacrum, and that, as a consequence,
"there is plenty of room, not only for carrying the foal, but for

" allowing it to pass into the world. Both of these points are
" important, the former evidently so, and the latter no less so on
" consideration, because if the foal is injured in the birth, either of
" necessity or from ignorance or carelessness, it will often fail to
" recover its powers, and will remain permanently injured. The
" pelvis, then, should be wide and deep, that is to say, it should be
" large and roomy ; and there should also be a little more than the
" average length from the hip to the shoulder, so as to give plenty
" of bed for the foal ; as well as a good depth of back-ribs, which
" are necessary in order to support this increased length.   *   *
" Beyond this roomy frame, necessary as the eggshell of the foal,
" the mare only requires such a shape and make as are well adapted
" for the particular purpose she is intended for.   *   *   *

    "In health, the brood mare should be as near perfection as the
" artificial state of this animal will allow ; at all events, it is the
" most important point of all, and in every case the mare should
" be very carefully examined, with a view to discover what devia-
" tions from a natural state have been entailed upon her by her own
" labors, and what she has inherited from her ancestors.   Indepen-
" dently of the consequences of accidents, all deviations from a
" state of health in the mare may be considered as more or less
" transmitted to her, because, in a thoroughly sound constitution,
" no ordinary treatment such as training consists of will produce
" disease, and it is only hereditary predisposition which, under this
" process, entails its appearance.   Still there are positive, compara-
" tive, and superlative degrees of objectionable diseases incidental
" to the brood mare, which should be accepted or refused accord-
" ingly.   All accidental defects, such as broken knees, dislocated
" hips, or even breaks down, may be passed over ; the latter, how-
" ever, only when the stock from which the mare is descended are
" famous for standing their work without this frailty of sinew and
" ligament.   Spavins, ring-bones, large splints, side-bones, and, in
" fact, all bony enlargements, are constitutional defects, and will
" be almost sure to be perpetuated, more or less, according to the
" degree in which they exist in the particular case.   Curby hocks
" are also hereditary, and should be avoided ; though many a one

" much bent at the junction of the *os calcis* with the *astragalus* is
" not at all liable to curbs. It is the defective condition of the
" ligaments there, not the angular junction, which leads to curbs ;
" and the breeder should carefully investigate the individual case
" before accepting or rejecting a mare with suspicious hocks. Bad
" feet, whether from contraction or from too flat and thin a sole,
" should also be avoided ; but when they have obviously arisen
" from bad shoeing, the defect may be passed over. Such are the
" chief varieties of unsoundness in the leg which require circum-
" spection ; the good points, which, on the other hand, are to be
" looked for are those considered desirable in all horses that are
" subjected to the shocks of the gallop. *   *   *   * Such are
" the general considerations bearing upon soundness of limb. That
" of. the wind is no less important. Broken-winded mares seldom
" breed, and they are therefore out of the question, if for no other
" reason ; but no one would risk the recurrence of this disease,
" even if he could get such a mare stinted. Roaring is a much
" vexed question, which is by no means theoretically settled among
" our chief veterinary authorities, nor practically by our breeders.
" Every year, however, it becomes more and more frequent and
" important, and the risk of reproduction is too great for any person
" willfully to run by breeding from a roarer. As far as I can learn,
" it appears to be much more hereditary on the side of the mare
" than on that of the horse ; and not even the offer of a virago
" should tempt me to use her as a brood mare. There are so many
" different conditions which produce what is called roaring, that it
" is difficult to form any opinion which shall apply to all cases. In
" some instances, where it has arisen from neglected strangles, or
" from a simple inflammation of the larynx, the result of cold, it will
" probably never reappear ; but when the genuine ideopathic roaring
" has made its appearance, apparently depending upon a disease of
" the nerves of the larynx, it is ten to one that the produce will
" suffer in the same way. Blindness, again, may or may not be
" hereditary, but in all cases it should be viewed with suspicion as
" great as that due to roaring. Simple cataract without inflam-
" mation undoubtedly runs in families ; and when a horse or

" mare has both eyes suffering from this disease, without any
" other derangement of the eye, I should eschew them care-
" fully. When blindness is the result of violent inflammation
" brought on by bad management, or by influenza, or any other
" similar cause, the eye itself is more or less disorganized; and
" though this itself is objectionable, as showing a weakness of the
" organ, it is not so bad as the regular cataract. Such are the chief
" absolute defects, or deviations, from health in the mare; to which
" may be added a general delicacy of constitution, which can only
" be guessed from the amount of flesh which she carries while suck-
" ling or on poor 'keep,' or from her appearance on examination
" by an experienced hand, using his eyes as well. The firm, full
" muscle, the bright and lively eye, the healthy-looking coat at all
" seasons, rough though it may be in the winter, proclaim the
" hardiness of constitution which is wanted, but which often coex-
" ists with infirm legs and feet. Indeed, sometimes the very
" best topped animals have the worst legs and feet, chiefly owing
" to the extra weight they and their ancestors also have had to
" carry. Crib-biting is sometimes a habit acquired from idleness,
" as also is wind-sucking; but if not caused by indigestion, it often
" leads to it, and is very commonly caught by the offspring. It is
" true that it may be prevented by a strap; but it is not a desirable
" accomplishment in the mare, though of less importance than
" those to which I have already alluded, if not accompanied by
" absolute loss of health, as indicated by emaciation, or the state of
" the skin.

" Lastly, the temper is of the utmost importance, by which
" must be understood not that gentleness at grass which may lead
" the breeder's family to pet the mare, but such a temper as will
" serve for the purposes of her rider, and will answer to the
" stimulus of the voice, whip, or spur. A craven or a rogue is
" not to be thought of as the 'mother of a family;' and if a mare
" belongs to a breed which is remarkable for refusing to answer
" the call of the rider, she should be consigned to any task rather
" than the stud-farm. Neither should a mare be used for this
" purpose which had been too irritable to train, unless she hap-

22

"pened to be an exceptional case; but if of an irritable family,
"she would be worse even than a roarer, or a blind one.   These
"are defects which are apparent in the colt or filly, but the
"irritability which interferes with training often leads to the
"expenditure of large sums on the faith of private trials, which
"are lost from the failure in public, owing to this defect of
"nervous system."

The mare described in the foregoing quotation is a thoroughbred race-horse, intended only, or chiefly, for fast running; but
any farmer who has an eye for horse-flesh, and who will take the
pains to examine the form and constitution of the best mares
working in his neighbors' teams, will find that, in its general particulars, it applies very well to them.   Of course, it is not to be
recommended that farmers, who intend that their team mares shall
be used for breeding, should purchase only such mares as come
up to this description; but merely that in purchasing, with an incidental view to breeding, or, indeed, in purchasing for work
alone, there will be a decided advantage in following, as closely
as circumstances and prices will allow, the standard herein laid
down.   Very careful attention in breeding should also be paid
to the different forms of unsoundness and bad conformation described.

It being assumed that the mares from which we are to breed are
sound and of good temper and form,—or, at least, that they are
not decidedly ill-formed, and that they have no hereditary disease
or imperfection,—the great remaining question for the farmer
relates to the selection of a stallion.   And herein I am decidedly of the opinion that the common practice of our agricultural
neighborhoods is a faulty one.   Horse-breeding has so long been
almost a science, that several things connected with it have been
determined with a good deal of accuracy; and one of these is, that
the preponderance of "blood"* should be on the side of the sire.

* By "blood" is meant that strain which has descended in direct line from the animals imported, more than a century ago, into England, from Barbary, Arabia, and Tur-
key; and which has there been developed, through a long course of training, into a race
of greater speed and endurance than even the Arabian horse himself possesse

The passion for raising fast trotters,—a passion which has been stimulated by very high prices, and which is likely to continue and to increase,—has led to a quite general adoption of the practice of breeding to fast-trotting stallions. And there is no doubt that this practice frequently results in the production of fast trotters; often enough, perhaps, to make it a tempting lottery,—but a lottery it certainly is, for while the few fast trotters produced are of exceptional value, a large majority of the " get " have decided defects, which reduce them below the average of good horses. Even in raising horses for the trotting turf, I should adhere in my own practice very strictly to the rule which has been established by the origin of the trotting-horse himself,—that is, to get the largest amount of blood on the side of the sire.

Almost without exception, every really distinguished trotting horse in the country traces back, largely on the side of the sire, to the thoroughbred English race-horse, which is the only source of what is now known among English and American breeders as " blood;" and while the high, free action which fast trotting requires has been introduced very considerably through cold-blooded mares, and occasionally through cold-blooded horses, it is only by a combination of this action with the best qualities of " blood" that the best results may be confidently sought. Therefore, the opinion is a very well-established one, that, in all systematic breeding, whether for the turf or for any other purposes, whatever the mare may be, the sire *should* be a thoroughbred horse; and in making this statement I by no means confine it to the production of horses for fast work or for pleasure-driving, for I believe that for every use, except, possibly, the slow draft of very heavy loads or city trucks, it is more economical for the teamster and for the farmer himself to have a large admixture of thorough-blood in the stock.

As a case in point, I would state that I recently employed a neighbor to do some plowing for me; his team consisted of a pair of oxen and a horse on the lead. The horse was of only average size, but I observed from a distance that there was a

spring and an agility in his movements that are uncommon in the
region, and on examination, I found that he was obviously doing
quite one-half of the work.   At the end of a long day he had the
same vigor and activity with which he commenced in the morning, and there was an intelligent, quick movement of the ears,
and a spring in his step, that one rarely sees in a farm-horse.
On inquiry, I found that he was twenty-eight years of age, had
been owned by the same man and employed in the same work
twenty-four years, had never missed a day, and had never let pass
an opportunity to do as much work as lay in his power.   He was
fat and sleek, and I should have judged him, from his general appearance, to be not more than seven or eight years old.   It turned
out that he was the progeny of a common farm mare, of good form,
by a thoroughbred race-horse, that had been brought into the
country for a single season, and so few mares were sent to him,
that it was not found profitable to keep him here.

On the Madison Avenue line of omnibuses in New York City,
it has always been the rule to buy horses with the largest possible
proportion of thorough-blood.   I should say that, at the time
when I noticed the teams of this line, the horses of the whole
stable would average more than half-bred, many of them probably
seven-eighths; and during the heavy snows of winter, this line
always makes better time than any other, and the proportion of
loss among their teams is much less, while the average number of years of service of each horse is much greater than on
any other line in the city, the others paying no regard to blood,
but purchasing any animals that are sound, and, apparently, of
strong frame.

Several years ago I rode almost daily—sometimes from fifty to
sixty miles in a day—a thoroughbred English mare, weighing less
than eight hundred pounds, and, although rather a heavy-weight
myself, I have never found another horse, even of much greater
size, that would carry me so far in a day, so many days in succession, and with so little apparent distress, as this mare would.

In the army, in the spring and summer of 1864, I rode a horse
captured from a rebel officer, and learned that he was probably

thoroughbred, and that he had been used for racing. He was a rather leggy animal, very tall, but as thin as a shingle, and by no means such a horse as most farmers would have selected to carry a man through a long day's ride. Yet, on the occasion of the battle of Tishamingo Creek, I rode him from four o'clock on Monday morning until half-past ten on Wednesday morning, and during the whole time, was certainly not more than two hours out of the saddle ; and much of the time I was riding furiously, and necessarily without the slightest regard to what became of my horse. The command comprised about 4,000 cavalry, and I am satisfied, from an examination of the troops as they returned, that there were not five horses in the whole army that had suffered so little from their work as mine had. He had the same springy gait, as he came neighing into his stable, that he had when he first started out from Monday's camp.

These instances, and many others that have come under my own observation, fully confirm me in the opinion that what is lost in size and apparent strength is more than made up by the endurance and activity which have given rise to the proverb— "blood will tell."

In his directions for the choice of a stallion for breeding, Frank Forrester says :—*

"Now, as to what constitutes value or excellence in all horses. "It is indisputably quickness of working ; power to move or carry "weight, and ability to endure for a length of time ; to travel for a " distance with the least decrease of pace ; to come again to work " day after day, week after week, and year after year, with undi- " minished vigor. And it is scarcely needful to say, that, under all " ordinary circumstances, these conditions are only compatible with "the highest form and highest physical health of the animal. " Malformation must necessarily detract from speed and power ; " hereditary disease or constitutional derangement must necessarily " detract from all powers whatsoever. Under usual circumstances, "it would hardly be necessary to undertake to show that quickness "of working, or, in other words, speed, is necessary to a high de-

* Herbert's Hints to Horsekeepers. O. Judd & Co., N. Y.

"gree of excellence in a horse of any stamp or style, and not one
" iota less for the animal which draws the load, or breaks the glebe,
" than for the riding-horse or the pleasure-traveler before light
" vehicles.   But it has of late become the fashion with some parties
" to undervalue the advantages of speed, and to deny its utility for
" other purposes than for those of mere amusement; and as a
" corollary from this assumption, to disparage the effect and deny
" the advantage of blood, by which is meant descent, through the
" American or English race-horse, from the Oriental blood of the
" desert, whether Arabian, Barb, Turk, Persian, or Syrian, or a
" combination of two or more, or all of the five.

    " The horse which can plow an acre while another is plowing
" half an acre, or that which can carry a load of passengers ten miles
" while another is going five, independent of all considerations of
" amusement, taste, or what is generally called fancy, is absolutely
" worth twice as much to his owner as the other.

    " Now the question for the breeder is simply this :   By what
" means is this result to be obtained ?   The reply is, by getting the
" greatest possible amount of pure blood compatible with size,
" weight, and power, according to the purpose for which he intends
" to raise stock, into the animal bred.   For not only is it not true
" that speed alone is the only good thing derivable from blood, but
" something very nearly the reverse is true.   It is very nearly the
" *least* good thing.   That which the blood-horse does possess is a
" degree of strength in his bones, sinews, and frame at large, utterly
" out of proportion to the size or apparent strength of that frame.
" The texture, the form, and the symmetry of the bones,—all, in
" the same bulk and volume,—possess double, or nearer fourfold,
" the elements of resistance and endurance in the blood-horse that
" they do in the cold-blooded cart-horse.   The difference in the
" form and texture of the sinews and muscles, and in the inferior
" tendency to form flabby, useless flesh, is still more in favor of the
" blood-horse.   Beyond this, the internal anatomical construction
" of his respiratory organs, of his arterial and venous system, of his
" nervous system, — in a word, of his constitution generally,—is cal-
" culated to give him what he possesses, greater vital power, greater

" recuperatory power, greater physical power, in proportion to his
" bulk and weight, than any other known animal, added to greater
" quickness of movement, and to greater courage, greater endurance
" of labor, hardship, suffering,—in a word, greater (what is called
" vulgarly) game or pluck than will be found in any other of the
" horse family.

" But it is not to be said, or supposed, that all blood-horses
" will give these qualities in an equal degree, for there is as much
" or more choice in the blood-horse than in any other of the family.
" Since, as in the blood of the thoroughbred horse, all faults, all
" vices, all diseases are directly hereditary, as well as all virtues, all
" soundness, all good qualities, it is more necessary to look, in the
" blood-horse, to his antecedents, his history, his performances, and,
" above all, to his shape, temper, soundness, and constitution, than
" it is in any other of the horse family.

" To breed from a small horse with the hope of getting a large
" colt ; from a long-backed, leggy horse, with the hope of getting a
" short, compact, powerful one ; from a broken-winded, or blind,
" or flat-footed, or spavined, or ring-boned, or navicular-joint-dis-
" eased horse, with the hope of getting a sound one ; from a vicious
" horse, a cowardly horse,—what is technically called a dunghill,—
" with the hope of getting a kind-tempered and brave one ; all or
" any of these would be the height of folly. The blood sire (and
" the blood should always be on the sire's side) should be, for the
" farmer-breeder's purposes, of medium height, say fifteen and a half
" hands high, short-backed, well ribbed up, short in the saddle-place,
" long below. He should have high withers, broad loins, broad
" chest, a straight rump,—the converse of what is often seen in
" trotters, and known as the *goose rump* ; a high and muscular, but
" not beefy crest ; a lean, bony, well-set-on head ; a clear, bright,
" smallish, well-placed eye ; broad nostrils and small ears. His
" fore-legs should be as long and as muscular as possible above the
" knee, and his hind-legs above the hock, and as lean, short, and
" bony as possible below those joints. The bones cannot by any
" means be too flat, too clear of excrescences, or *too large*. The
" sinews should be clear, straight, firm, and hard to the touch.

" From such a horse, where the breeder can find one, and from a
" well-chosen mare (she may be a little larger, more bony, more
" roomy, and in every way coarser than the horse, to the advantage
" of the stock), sound, healthy, and well-limbed, he may be certain,
" accidents and contingencies set aside, of raising an animal that
" will be creditable to him as a scientific stock-breeder, and profit-
" able to him in a pecuniary sense.

" The great point then to be aimed at is, the combining in the
" same animal the maximum of speed compatible with sufficient size,
" bone, strength, and solid power to carry heavy weights or draw
" large loads, and at the same time to secure the stock from the
" probability, if not certainty, of inheriting structural deformity or
" constitutional disease from either of the parents. The first point
" is only to be attained, first, by breeding as much as possible to
" pure blood of the right kind ; and, second, by breeding what is
" technically called among sportsmen and breeders, *up*, not *down :*
" that is to say, by breeding the mare to a male of superior (not
" inferior) blood to herself,—except where it is desired to breed
" like to like, as Canadian to Canadian, or Norman to Norman,
" for the purpose of perpetuating a pure strain of any particular
" variety, which may be useful for the production of brood
" mares."

It is frequently objected by farmers that they cannot afford to
pay forty or fifty dollars for the service of a thoroughbred stallion,
when they can get that of a good common horse for ten or fifteen.
To this objection the only proper reply is, that they cannot afford
to take the service of the common horse as a gift. The cost of
the service of the stallion is a very small part of the cost of raising
a horse. The care and attention that the mare should receive
during pregnancy, the risks of foaling, and the feed of the
mother and colt during lactation, as well as the growth and training of the colt for four or five years, are the same in every case ;
and it may be safely assumed, as an average rule, that while the
thoroughbred colt may cost from twenty-five to fifty dollars more
than the common-bred one, the vigor of his constitution during
his growth, and the extra value of his appearance and his ability

to perform when ready for market, will be worth from one to several hundred dollars more. If it will pay to raise horses at all, and this is a question which must be decided by each man for himself, it will certainly pay, in every case, to raise the best horses that it is possible to produce.

If blood-horses were only valuable for pleasure-driving and for racing, the case would be quite different; but they are more valuable for road-work, for farm-work, for horse-cars and omnibuses, and for all of the uses to which horses are ordinarily put, than are any others; so that there is no risk in making the experiment, while there is always a chance of securing an animal of extraordinary value.

The mare and the stallion having been coupled, the work of horse-raising is only fairly commenced. The success with which it is carried on will depend upon the skill and attention with which every detail is attended to, from this time until the weaning, and, indeed, until the training of the colt is accomplished. It should be remembered that the mare has now, not only to make up the wastes of her own frame, but to carry on the growth of a fœtus, weighing at birth probably two hundred pounds; and she should be allowed such a quantity of nutritious food as will secure the best development of the foal, and as shall keep her in the best condition for delivery, and for the supply of milk to her offspring. She should never be overworked, and she should never be allowed to remain entirely idle; for exercise and good grooming are as important to the mother as they are to the colt himself. During the latter months of pregnancy, when the mare may be too heavy for use on the road, she should be allowed a free range in the fields, or at least a roomy loose box in which she may take the necessary amount of exercise; and she should never be harassed or teazed, or in any way annoyed.

After the birth, if it is necessary to work her, as it generally is on farms, the foal should not be allowed to run by her side, nor to draw her milk while she is overheated. Nor should she be so excessively worked that she cannot furnish him always, after having had time to cool off, with an abundant supply of healthy milk.   It is not usually the custom among farmers to feed grain to breeding-mares, nor to young colts; but there is no period in the life of a horse when a little grain judiciously given will produce so good an effect on his form, his spirit, and his constitution, as during the six months before and the six months after his foaling; and, very early during his colthood, he should receive, first an occasional handful, and then a regular daily feeding of the best oats.

As it has been well-demonstrated, in the care of all live stock, that a clean and open condition of the skin is conducive to health and to economical feeding, so it will be found that no labor on the farm is more profitably expended than that which is devoted to a a daily thorough grooming of even the very young colt.   Both before weaning, and after, the young animal should be treated in such a manner as his future usefulness and his future need for strength make necessary.   He should be well fed, well groomed, constantly handled, and petted and talked to, and should have sufficient exercise, and, during the first five years, no excessive work; and should be, even in his infancy, accustomed to harness and wheels and saddles, and all the other accompaniments of his future service.

By following these rules we may hope, without any perceptible additional expense, to raise an animal that will be, other things being equal, many times more valuable than the poor, half-starved, and neglected "shag" that farmers generally bring to market. Any fair horse is worth one hundred and fifty dollars in the New York market, although he may have been neglected from the day of his conception until the day of his sale to the drover, but very often the same animal, if he had received the care herein recommended, would have been eagerly bought for from five hundred to one thousand dollars on the farm; and the whole extra amount of the price will have been gained by the inexpensive means of a litt'e extra care, and by the proper selection rather than by the increased quantity or value of the food.   If, in addition to all this care and attention, we have taken pains at the outset to put the right blood into the brute's veins, we may feel confident, not only that he will be purchased at a high price, but that the purchaser will always feel satisfied with his bargain.

Much has been said and written in this country about the Percheron horses, and surely any one who will visit the animals imported by the Massachusetts Agricultural Society, and now standing at Mr. Motley's farm at Jamaica Plain, will realize the fact that only one-half of the story has been told. They are large, magnificent animals, of immense weight and power, and yet with an activity that it is surprising to see in such a mass of flesh. Of course, being large, they are large feeders, and " Orleans," who weighs fifteen hundred pounds, would undoubtedly consume as much as an average pair of farm-horses ; but, on the other hand, he would probably draw a heavier load than the pair would, and would draw it the same distance in less time.

It is supposed that these horses originated in a cross of the old horse of Normandy with the blood of the desert, originally introduced into Spain by the Moors, and in the conflicts between Spain and France, brought into connection with the blood of Normandy. Certainly these horses, in their heads and in their action, show many of the characteristics of the Arabian horse, and for heavy teams, especially for city truck-work, it would be difficult to conceive of better animals. Frank Forrester recommends, and the recommendation seems to be a good one, that mares of this breed be crossed with the thoroughbred English race-horse ;—certainly, for farm teams or for carriage use, a combination of the size and lofty action of the one, with the quickness, determination, and endurance of the other, must produce the most satisfactory results. I cannot better conclude these remarks on horse-breeding than by giving Frank Forrester's summary :—

" *First*. Size, symmetry, and soundness are mostly to be " regarded in the mare ;—blood from the sire, beauty from the dam, " is the golden rule. *Second*. She should have a roomy frame, hips "somewhat sloping, a little more than the average length, wide- " chested, deep in the girth, quarters strong and well let down, " hocks wide apart, wide and deep in the pelvis. *Third*. In tem- "per she should be gentle, courageous, free from all irritability

"and viciousness. *Fourth.* Previous to putting her to the horse,
"she should be brought into the most perfect state of health, not
"overfed, or loaded with fat, or in a pampered state, but by judi-
"cious exercise and an abundance of nutritious food and proper
"grooming, she should be in the very best condition. *Fifth.*
"During gestation she should have generous and nourishing,
"but not heating diet. For the first three or four months she
"may be worked moderately, and even to within a few weeks
"of her foaling she may do light work with advantage to her
"system."

The treatment of farm teams is a matter of great consequence to
the farmer; for the same principle which requires that the driver
of the steam-engine should keep every part of his machine well
oiled and in good adjustment, and that he should keep his boiler
well supplied with fuel and with water, should actuate the farmer
in keeping this most valuable and really expensive assistant to his
labors in efficient condition by careful grooming, judicious feeding,
and attentive oversight.

Very much of the value and availability of the horse depends on
the quality and quantity of his food, and on the manner in which it is
given to him. Too much food at one time, too little at another,
food of improper kinds or in a bad state of preparation, is the
foundation of one-half the ills that horse-flesh is heir to. There
is no worse economy than the stinting of food, or the administering of bad food because it is cheap. Also, there is no more
wasteful practice than the giving of too rich and expensive food.
Neither is there any greater source of loss in connection with the
keeping of farm-horses, than the neglect to which they are systematically subjected. The horse, even in the rudest state, is of a
somewhat delicate organization. His powers are very great,—
greater than is generally supposed;—but in order to their development and to their long endurance, it is necessary that he be fed
with the greatest care and with an ever-watchful judgment.
Probably the capital invested in farm-horses in the United States
would go twice as far; that is, the animals would last in a useful

condition twice as long, if they were thoroughly well fed and cared for.

At the National Horse Show at Springfield, several years ago, Mr. Lewis B. Brown, of New York, exhibited a four-in-hand team, which trotted around the course in about three minutes. The united ages of the four horses amounted to more than one hundred years, and even the oldest of them remained useful for a long time after that. Indeed, Mr. Brown told me that he did not consider it of much importance that a horse should be less than twenty years old. Yet, as we look over the farms of even our best farming districts, how few useful teams do we find that are more than fourteen or fifteen years old. Deducting the years of their colthood, we see that the period of their possible usefulness is reduced fully one-half by careless and injudicious treatment, and especially by stingy or indiscreet feeding. To go over the whole range of directions for feeding, from the time when the mare is first got with foal, until the foal is worn out by years of service, would require more space than can here be spared. Concerning farm-horses, the following directions from Herbert's " Hints " will be found useful :—

" With regard to mere farm-horses, it is, usually, the habit to " feed them entirely on hay, or cut straw, with now and then a " mash, giving them little or no oats or corn. It is certain, how- " ever, that this is a mistake. That the value of the work which " the horse can do, and of the horse himself, arising from his im- " proved condition and increased endurance, will be materially " raised, while the actual cost of his keep will not be very materially " increased by the diminution of the quantity of the cheaper " and less nutritious food given to him, and the addition of a " smaller or larger portion of the more nutritive grain, which fur- " nishes stamina and strength in a degree greatly in excess of its " own increased value, may be assumed as facts.

" Slow-working horses do not, of course, require so much nutri- " ment of a high quality, as those which are called on to do quick " work, and perform long distances; but, as a rule, all animals " which have to do hard work, and much of it, must necessarily

" be so kept as to have hard flesh ; and they cannot be so kept
" unless they are fed on hard grain."

To show the manner in which horses are kept by the New
York omnibus proprietors, the following is extracted from a report
offered to the Farmers' Club of the American Institute, and published in the transactions of the Institute for 1855 :—

STAGE LINE.	Number of animals.	Miles of daily travel.	Pounds of cut hay daily fed.	Pounds of corn-meal daily.	Pounds of salt per month.	Increase of meal for recent severe term of traveling.
Red Bird Stage Line..........................	116	17	14	18	1½	3½
Spring Street Stage Line..................	105	21	14	20	4	3½
Seventh Avenue do.	227	22	10	18½	1	2½
Sixth Avenue. ∫ Horses	117	17	10	14	2	...
Railroad. ₍ Mules	211	17	10	7	2	...
New York Consolidated Stage Company...........	335	21	8	17	2.9	2½
Washington Stables, 6 livery horses...............	..	..	12	7.*	..	..

" It is the object of the stage proprietors to get all the work
" out of their teams possible, without injury to the animals.
" Where the routes are shorter, the horses consequently make
" more trips, so that the different amounts and proportions of
" food consumed are not so apparent when the comparison is
" made between the different lines, as when it is made also with the
" railroad and livery horses. The stage-horses consume most,
" and the livery horses least.

" The stage-horses are fed on cut hay and corn-meal wet, and
" mixed in the proportion of about one pound of hay to two
" pounds of meal, a ratio adopted rather for mechanical than
" physiological reasons, as this is all the meal that can be made to
" adhere to the hay. The animals eat this mixture from a deep
" manger. The New York Consolidated Stage Company use a

* And six quarts of oats at noon.

" very small quantity of salt. They think it causes horses to
" urinate too freely. They find horses do not eat so much when
" worked too hard. The large horses eat more than the small
" ones. Prefer a horse of one thousand to one thousand one hun-
" dred pounds weight. If too small, they get poor, and cannot
" draw a stage ; if too large, they ruin their feet, and their shoul-
" ders grow stiff and shrink. The principal objection to large
" horses, is not so much the increased amount of food required,
" as the fact that they are soon used up by wear. They would pre-
" fer for feed, a mixture of half corn and half oats, if it were not
" more expensive. Horses do not keep fat so well on oats alone,
" if at hard labor, as on corn-meal, or a mixture of the two.

" Straw is the best for bedding. If salt hay is used, horses eat
" it, as not more than a bag of two hundred pounds of salt is used
" in three months. Glaubers-salt is allowed occasionally as a laxa-
" tive in the spring of the year, and the animals eat it voraciously.
" If corn is too new, it is mixed with an equal weight of rye-bran,
" which prevents scouring. Jersey yellow corn is best, and horses
" like it best. The hay is all cut, mixed with meal, and fed moist.
" No difference is made between day and night work. The travel
" is continuous, except in warm weather, when it is sometimes
" divided, and an interval of rest allowed. In cold weather the
" horses are watered four times a day in the stable, and not at all
" on the road. In warm weather, four times a day in the stables,
" and are allowed a sip on the middle of the route.

" The amount that the company exact from each horse is all that
" he can do. In the worst of traveling they fed four hundred and
" fifty bags per week of meal, of one hundred pounds each. They
" now feed four hundred. The horses are not allowed to drink
" when warm; if allowed to do so, it founders them. In warm
" weather a bed of sawdust is prepared for them to roll in.
" Number of horses, three hundred and thirty-five. Speed varies,
" but is about four miles an hour. Horses eat more in cold
" weather than in warm, but the difference cannot be exactly
" determined."

Proper stabling and grooming are hardly less important to the

economical keeping and to the long-sustained usefulness of the
horse than proper feeding. The horse is always kept in a more or
less artificial condition. His food is generally much richer than
that which he would obtain in a state of nature, and the amount
of steady exercise which is required of him is very much greater.
It has been found by long experience that his artificial condition
requires equally artificial treatment; but, so far as farm-horses are
concerned, the accompaniments of warm clothing, bandaging the
legs, and habitual sweating, may be dispensed with. The regular,
thorough, daily grooming, however, and such housing as is necessary to prevent undue exposure to cold or to drafts, are as important with farm teams as with those kept for fast work. The
amount of food consumed will be less, and the ability to perform
work will be greater, if the animals are every day thoroughly well
curried and brushed. The horse's legs and pasterns in particular,
and the setting on of the mane, should be efficiently cleansed and
rubbed; and he should be kept in all respects in a cleanly, tidy,
cheerful, and healthy condition.

Horses, properly kept and regularly worked, are but little liable
to disease, and where the team force of the farm is neither too
small nor too great, their work is performed at an economical rate;
but where they are either overworked or allowed to stand long
idle, they are exceedingly expensive and hazardous property.
Properly kept, properly managed, and properly used, horses are,
in the main, much cheaper than oxen, because they perform their
work with so much greater celerity; but, in the ramshackle stable
system that prevails on a majority of farms, oxen, which are too
slow and too stupid to be easily abused, and which will keep in
condition on less nutritious food, are generally most esteemed.
One important effect of their selection, however, in place of
horses, is a great waste of the labor of the farm-hands. The
difference between plowing an acre a day or an acre and a half,
between traveling ten miles or fifteen in the same number of
hours, is one of those differences which are constantly under-
mining our calculations for profit. Good and profitable farming
necessarily implies brisk and active work on the part of every man

connected with it; and it is only with the aid of two horses, kept in the best condition, performing their work with alacrity, and stimulating their attendants to activity, that we may hope to accomplish the best results. But all this involves much more care in feeding and grooming than farmers are disposed to give to their teams. If I were writing a book of directions for hand-to-mouth farmers, I should advise them to have no horses upon their farms, but to poke along through life in a slow and slipshod way, with comfortable and lazy cattle and comfortable and lazy farm hands. As, however, my object is to introduce an improvement in every branch of agriculture, and to increase the activity and economy with which every operation is performed, I do not hesitate to recommend, that, for all *regular* farm-work, horses, or, still better, large mules, be employed. For the extra work of a large farm, especially where the fattening of beef cattle is one of the objects, a few pairs of oxen, to be worked moderately from time to time will be found economical. Under all other circumstances I should be disposed to discard them.

NEAT CATTLE.

In 1860 there were in the United States 23,419,378 neat cattle,—old and young, working oxen, and milch cows,—and these were all, or almost all, owned by farmers and graziers. Their immense number indicates the magnitude of their importance to the farmer; and, indeed, it is rare to find any farm, large or small, upon which the feeding of the bovine race is not a very large element of the business. So far as their treatment in this book is concerned, however, it has been thought better to devote to its discussion several distinct chapters, namely, "Soiling and Pasturing," "The Dairy," and "Winter Management and Feeding." We will pass, therefore, to the consideration of

SHEEP AND WOOL GROWING.

Sheep husbandry seems to be, just now, under a cloud. Probably there are not nearly so many sheep now in the country as there were ten years ago.

23

Common mutton is and has been for some time very low, and the low price to which wool has fallen, owing to the extra production that high war prices induced, has made the prospect very gloomy. As a consequence, hundreds and thousands of sheep have been slaughtered for their pelts, and sheep-farmers are, in many parts of the country, turning their attention to other branches of industry.

At the same time, the markets are very poorly supplied with *good* mutton, and really fine carcasses are in demand at paying prices. Whether wool-growing will become profitable is largely a question of tariff, and of the extension of woolen manufacture, and this is too much a matter of speculation for a sound opinion to be given.

All that it is safe to say is, that well-fattened mutton of the larger breeds is sure to remain, as it now is, sufficiently in demand at high prices to leave a good margin of profit for the farmer;—as much, probably, as in the feeding of beef cattle. Early lambs, also,—wherever the cost of transportation to the larger markets does not interfere,—may be produced at a good profit, under careful management.

There is no branch of husbandry in which more depends on *close attention to details* than in the raising of sheep, and no one who is not experienced in their management should undertake the business without first making a special study of the subject, which it would be impossible to treat fairly in a limited space. Any attempt to condense the necessary instructions, so as to bring them within the limits of the plan of this work, would surely be unsatisfactory. The reader is referred to Randall's excellent treatise on Sheep Husbandry.

SWINE.

Swine hold an exceedingly important place in agriculture,—the stock of swine in the United States in 1860 having numbered 30,354,213.

So far as the agriculture of the more improved parts of the country is concerned, swine have three important uses: *First,*

the consumption of grain, roots, etc., which would otherwise be
unsalable at remunerative rates ; *second*, the consumption of refuse,
which, but for them, would be wasted ; *third*, the production and
preparation of manure. In all cases, where manure is used at
all, the last of these is one of the most important of their advantages. In those almost mythically large grain-fields of the West,
where the crop is said to be harvested mainly by droves of cattle
whose gleaners are herds of swine, it is not to be expected,—
perhaps it is hardly possible,—that much system should be introduced. It is one of those cases where unavoidable waste can only
be mitigated, and where the amount lost is considerably less than
would be the cost of more systematic harvesting. On the small
farms of the poorer regions of New England, where nearly every
crop requires its yearly application of manure, the services of
swine become important, chiefly in the manipulation and increase
of this article. In the wide range of districts lying between these
two extremes, they are more or less important according to the system of cultivation pursued. The extent to which it is profitable
to feed swine solely for the production of pork, and the value to
be attached to their influence on the dung-heap, must be regulated
according to the circumstances of each district, and almost of
each farmer. All that can be done in this connection is to state
a few well-known facts concerning their care, treatment, and
varieties.

On butter-farms, where there is a large quantity of skimmed
milk that it is not considered worth while to make into cheese,
almost the only means for disposing of this valuable material is to
feed it to swine. And it should be the care of the farmer to
regulate the number kept as closely as possible by the quantity of
milk that can be supplied to them, unless his circumstances would
justify his feeding them largely with grain, or purchased food,
which is not always the case.

Where the supply of skimmed milk is depended upon as the
chief food of these animals, it will be better to keep breeding
sows, coming in at different times, so that, for as large a part of
the year as possible, there may be young pigs to be fed, as these

convert the milk more rapidly into flesh than do older animals. Generally, in well-settled neighborhoods, and in the vicinity of towns, the price paid for weaning-pigs is much greater in proportion to their weight than that paid for fat hogs.

If it is considered profitable, owing to the low price of grain, or the probable high price of pork, to feed grain, it will be found better in all cases to steam this, or otherwise to cook it. If it is previously ground the profit will be still greater. Especially if it is not to be steamed or cooked, all except nubbins and waste grain should be finely ground, and soaked in water before feeding. The question of steaming, which is a very important one, is discussed at length under its proper head. It may be stated, in general terms, that there will be an economy of fully one-third of the food, if it is properly cooked before being given to the animals. If there are no facilities for cooking or steaming, it will be a good plan to mix the meal with hot water, and to leave it a few hours in a covered barrel, or other closed vessel, before feeding it.

POULTRY.

There is a good deal more to be said about poultry, which it would be of advantage for every farmer to hear, than I can properly take room for in this connection. Ideas as to the best manner of keeping poultry vary so much that it is only on a careful consideration of the farmer's local circumstances that it will be safe to make a decision as to the kinds to be raised, the size of the flocks, and the manner in which they are to be kept. It has long been believed, and perhaps it is true, that it is impossible to keep a thousand hens with the same proportional profit that one may obtain from a flock of a dozen or twenty. But there is a large class of poultry-fanciers who discard this idea, and think that if the same amount of freedom were given to the larger flock, the degree of profit would be the same. This is, to a certain extent, demonstrated by the experience of Mr. Warren Leland, of the Metropolitan Hotel in New York, who, at his farm near Rye, on the New York and New Haven Railroad, keeps several thousand fowls and large flocks of ducks and turkeys with very great success. His profits, and the quite uniform results of several years, indicate that with his circumstances one may raise an almost unlimited amount of poultry. But many farmers would find it inconvenient to carry on the business on Mr. Leland's system. He gives to it a large area of woodland and meadow, with various exposure, and a good stream of running water, and exercises but little restraint over his birds. They go where and when they please, roost in trees or in a warm stone houseas they please, and hatch their broods in prepared boxes or in natural nooks as they please. His proportional loss is very small ; the number of eggs he obtains is probably pretty nearly as large in degree as it would be with a small flock, and his success with early and late chickens is enough to satisfy any breeder. Of course, even in this very natural system, the fowls are by no means left in an unguided state of nature ; for a skillful person devotes his whole time to their feeding and supervision, and to great care with reference to sitting hens. The feeding is liberal but not wasteful, and the poultry-raising is an important branch of the business of the farm rather than a mere incident.

Many years ago, in Western New York, an aged couple supported themselves by the production of eggs on a' place of about four acres. They kept a thousand laying hens and no cocks. The whole place was surrounded by a high fence, and was divided into two plots, the fowls being kept in one of the plots of two acres during the whole of one season, while corn was being raised on the other ; and the land was kept for several years in this uniform rotation of poultry and Indian corn. The eggs were sold by contract throughout the season for eleven cents a dozen, and the annual income varied but little from a thousand dollars. In the autumn the fowls were slaughtered and sent to market, and a fresh lot of early pullets was bought early in the next season. This man believed, on comparing the production of corn on his own land with that of the neighborhood, that the manure of the poultry increased the crop to such an extent that the extra product was sufficient for the entire season's feeding. Probably this is the rose-colored side of the story, and there may have been drawbacks with which I am not acquainted, but my information as above given was received from a perfectly reliable source.

In a little book recently published,* a very elaborate description is given of a system which is now being adopted in England for raising poultry, mainly under glass and in large establishments, and on thoroughly well-organized business principles. The detail is curious, and it will be agreeable to know that the results are satisfactory; but it is yet too uncertain to be adopted here except as an experiment. In Mr. Flint's preface, however, there is given a plan for keeping poultry in confinement, which will probably answer very well, and which is at least worthy of careful trial with some of the large Asiatic breeds which are less inclined to roam, and need, probably, less active exercise than our old-fashioned fowls.

"Build coops," says Mr. Flint, "of lath or thin boards, about "ten feet long, four feet wide, and two feet high,—four feet in "length at one end to be a tight house, or coop of boards, with "floor and feeding conveniences, water, etc.,—the latticed portion "to be bottomless. Arrange handles at each end, so that two men "could lift and move the whole; set these coops upon grass ground, "and move them their length or width daily, thus affording a fresh "grass run. Twelve chickens should do well in each. As soon "as they can be distinguished, separate the cocks from the pullets, "and *never* allow them together, except for breeding purposes, after- "ward. As soon as the cocks are marketable, sell them, reserving "only the best individuals as breeders, with little, if any, regard to "consanguinity. Keep an unlimited supply of cracked corn before "them until they are large enough to eat it whole, when it may be "given them uncracked. This, with grass, is their main diet. "Give also some variety with a little animal food. The pullets "should begin to lay early in October, when they should have "a plenty of fish-waste, and lime in some form, in addition to "the grain. In twelve months from the time they begin to lay

---

* Geyelin's Poultry Breeding, with a preface by Charles L. Flint. Boston: 1867.

" they should produce one hundred and fifty eggs each, and, if
" properly cared for, they might do more. As soon as the hens
" stop laying and begin to moult, kill and sell them. The white
" Leghorns are always ready for the table.

" I do not know that this movable coop has been tried on a
" large scale; but there seems to be no reason why it should not
" prove successful. Grass will grow wonderfully under it; and
" this could be used either for soiling or for hay. Some other
" conveniences would, of course, be necessary in winter.

" A coop of the above-mentioned size would accommodate twelve
" laying hens; and four of them with forty-eight hens, would
" probably do better than the same number in the inclosure plan,
" and avoid the necessary investment for fences and repairs.
" Some say poultry in such confinement, when *all* their wants are
" supplied, will pay better than when running at liberty, either in
" growth, fat, or eggs; and it is probably true.

" Now, if one coop will succeed, or if one inclosure like that
" described will succeed, what conceivable reason is there why
" any number should not? We all know that success in any
" thing depends as much upon details as upon plan; without
" attention to either, failure is certain; with only one, success
" can be but partial."

As with every thing else on the farm, the profit of poultry-
raising must be sought largely in some extra production,—either
extra size, extra early maturity, early laying, fine varieties, or
extra preparation for market,—in short, whatever may enable
one to get " fancy prices." Very early in the spring, or late in
the winter, before our neighbors' fowls have commenced to lay,
if we can stimulate ours to the plentiful production of eggs, we
can sell them for twice or three times the later price, while the
cost of the stimulant is inconsiderable. For early laying two
things are necessary : *first*, very early pullets of the spring before ;
second, warm and sunny quarters. If to these we add stimulating
food,—a little pepper, a little chopped roots or cabbage,—and
especially if we cook the grain, we may hope to get in February
eggs for which we should otherwise be obliged to wait until April

or May. Probably it would be most profitable to sell out all but the breeding stock of old fowls every fall, and to retain from our own early broods, or to purchase from our neighbors, well-grown pullets that were hatched not later than the middle of April. Under the proper treatment, these birds will commence to lay plentifully about Christmas, and will give many eggs before common flocks commence laying at all.

As the best means for explaining my idea of what a poultry-house should be, I add the following description of the house that I have recently built at Ogden Farm.

Its north wall is a well-laid stone fence, five feet high, well-pointed with cement on both sides. The rear plate of the roof is laid in cement on the top of this wall, and the openings between the sides and the wall are closed with cement. The height of the plate in front is eight feet; the batter, or slope of the front, two feet. The length of the house is twenty-five feet. The door is in one end. The sashes are made like those used in greenhouses, with only longitudinal bars, the glass being lapped one pane over another, with no putty at the lap. The width between the bars is ten inches. The sashes are let in at the outside of the upright joists supporting the roof; the joists project about four inches inside of the inner face of the sashes; and, stretched along these at a distance of about five inches from the glass, is a netting, (made of very light galvanized wire,) which cost less than $10,—the entire cost of the house being about $75. The nests are placed (in a row running the whole length of the house) immediately under the windows. The perches (four in number) are raised only two feet from the ground, and run the entire length of the building, occupying the rear half of the house.

Both ends and the roof of the house are lined with lathing, the space between which and the outer wall is filled with straw for cold weather. The ventilator at the top of the house can be opened or closed as the temperature may require. The nests are " secret," but so arranged that they may be entirely opened and swept out at pleasure. The perches are placed near the ground, in order that heavy birds may not injure themselves in flying down ; and they are all movable so that they may be taken out and exposed if necessary to the sun and rain for freshening, and so that the ground beneath the perches may be easily removed, the principle of the earth closet being adopted for the preservation of the manure,—it being the rule to mix the droppings about twice a week with loose dry earth, either by spading or raking. In summer time the sashes can be removed, and the house will have the effect simply of a well-built shed open only to the south.

As I have only just constructed this house, I cannot speak with the authority of experience concerning it, but I see no reason why it may not be as effective as it is simple and economical.

Concerning the breed of fowls which it is most profitable to keep, opinions vary so much that it would be well for each man to experiment for himself. After a careful consideration of all that has been said on the subject during the past few years by writers for agricultural papers, and after a considerable observation of different flocks, I have decided upon a cross between the Brahma Pootra and the Gray Dorking, breeding only from Brahma hens and Dorking cocks. The progeny of these birds are quite good layers, and arrive early at maturity, growing to a good size ; while the quiet disposition that they inherit from their mothers, and the domestic habits that these teach them, especially adapt them for confined localities. When fattened for market, they are of good size and particularly good appearance.

Among the pure breeds, all things considered, especially when they must be confined within narrow limits, I think that the Brahmas are the best of those with which we are familiar ; although the French breeds of Houdan and Crèvecœur, which are being actively brought into notice, have, it is claimed, some advantages over even these. I have no personal experience with them beyond an admiration of their fine proportions and beautiful plumage, which form attractive features of all modern poultry shows.

Among turkeys, the Bronze variety probably holds the highest place ; and among ducks, I prefer the Rouen.

In feeding poultry, quite as much advantage will be derived from the cooking or steaming of grain, as follows from the adoption of the practice with any other stock of the farm.

Poultry yards, except for temporary use at planting time, are decidedly objectionable ; and, in a rather extensive experience in market-gardening, I have concluded that at no time during the year do fowls do so much harm as good in the garden. In large fields the good that they do in consuming insects, much more than compensates for their slight injury to the crops ; but, of course, in small house-gardens, where a few square yards of freshly set plants cannot be spared, the injury that they do is proportionately much greater, and for a little while they had better be kept out of the garden.

CHAPTER XIV.

SOILING AND PASTURING.

THERE is one improvement in agricultural operations which, although it originated many years ago, and although, in certain parts of Europe, and in a very few instances in this country, it is in constant and successful use, has made far less progress in winning public favor among farmers than it was at first supposed that it would. The practice referred to is that of feeding cattle during the summer season entirely in the stall or in the yard, sowing special crops for forage, and regularly cutting this and hauling it to the feeding-place.

The reason for the limited adoption of the system of soiling is to be sought in the scarcity and consequent high price of farm labor, and also in the large size of average American farms, as compared with the average working force employed upon them. Not only is it found expensive and annoying to a farmer, who is short of help, to attend daily, and several times a day, to the feeding of cattle; but there are so many fields on our farms, as generally arranged, which are either too large or too remote from the homestead for proper cultivation, that the only resource is to make use of their crops by pasturing. As a general rule, too, these fields are too poor and in too low a state of cultivation to produce enough fodder to make soiling advisable.

A great deal has been said in deprecation of these circumstances, and it is commonly recommended that farmers employ more labor, that they bring their fields to a higher state of cultivation, and that they do many other things which the best agriculture renders desirable. But I am not disposed to join the popular cry. We must take

facts in this world as we find them, and we can hope to improve
our circumstances only very gradually.   If a farmer has 200 acres
of land, and only two or three hired hands, it would be folly for him
to attempt to make any better use of the crops of his grass-fields
than by grazing his animals upon them.   And if a man so circumstanced were to adopt the system of soiling, he would necessarily
neglect other very important parts of his business, and would find
that the system results in loss rather than in profit.   If he could
judiciously sell one-half of his domain, probably he would find it to
his advantage in many ways to do so.   But there is a feeling about
the ownership of broad acres which will generally undo any argument in favor of their reduction.   If a farmer finds it practicable
to add largely to his working force, and if he has the skill and
executive power to manage the increased force successfully, there
is no doubt that he might derive great advantage from the adoption
of soiling.   But unfortunately, a very large proportion of American
farmers would find it impossible either to employ or to house a
largely increased force of farm-hands ; and a great many of them
would never succeed in controlling a larger number of men than
could follow themselves in any given piece of work.   To all such,
then, the only wise recommendation is, that they adhere to their old
practices, merely watching carefully for every opportunity for
adopting the new ones when circumstances shall allow them to
do so.

For those who own small farms, and who, from their proximity
to thickly settled neighborhoods, or by reason of any special circumstances, may be able to employ profitably an increased number of men, it has been amply proven, by experience in this country
and in Europe, that their surest road to the most successful agriculture lies in the practice of soiling all of their live stock which cannot
be fed upon the waste corners of the farm.   It may be stated, as a
general principle, that any land which will properly pasture
throughout the season one cow to two acres, will, at least after a
year or two of preparation, produce enough if its crops are mowed
and carried to the barn, to support two cows to one acre.   And
this has reference only to the growing of ordinary forage crops,

such as clover, rye, oats, and sowed corn. Where labor is still cheaper and the land is worked to a still higher degree, it is possible to do even much more than this. But it should be a sufficient argument to say that the ability of a given area of land to support animal life may be, by soiling, increased fourfold.

This increased ability to supply food is, after all, only one of the many important advantages that soiling offers. The better condition of the animals, and the far larger quantity of disposable manure, together with the yearly improving condition of the land itself, both in texture and in richness, are hardly less important.

In an essay read before the Massachusetts Agricultural Society in 1819, by Josiah Quincy, several points with reference to the soiling of cattle were very clearly set forth. This essay, and another on the same subject, have recently been republished. * Mr. Quincy enumerates the following as the chief advantages of soiling :—

" 1st, The saving of land.
" 2d, The saving of fencing.
" 3d, The economizing of food.
" 4th, The better condition and greater comfort of the cattle.
" 5th, The greater product of milk.
" 6th, The attainment of manure,"
and, I might add—

7th, The improvement of the condition of the soil.

Concerning *the saving of land,* the fact alluded to above, that four times as many cattle, or even more, may be kept by soiling as by pasturing, is sufficiently conclusive. Strictly speaking, there is hardly a limit to the production that is possible under the highest cultivation, but probably under the circumstances of ordinary farming the quadrupled production is all that could be hoped for. And surely this is sufficient to induce any one who can conveniently do so to keep his stock in this manner.

The *saving of fencing,* which was discussed at length in the chap-

* Essays on the Soiling of Cattle, etc. By Josiah Quincy. Boston : 1866.

ter on " Fences," is a matter of great consequence ; for the large
amount of money, or what is equal to money—time and labor,
expended in building and repairing the interior fences of the farm,
is often appalling ; while the loss by reasoning of the shortening
of the plow furrow, and the ground occupied by the fence and
headland, and the excessive growth of noxious weeds on both sides
of the fence, are serious arguments in favor of any practice by
which fences may be entirely done away with or their extent
reduced.

The *economizing of food* is an economizing of the very elements
of all agricultural success, for the first object of all farming is the
production of food for men and animals ; and it seems worse than
waste to have any valuable thing that the farm produces destroyed
without return.

Quincy says, " There are six ways by which beasts destroy the
" article destined for their food,—1st, By eating ; 2d, By walk-
" ing ; 3d, By dunging ; 4th, By staling ; 5th, By lying down ;
" 6th, By breathing on it.   Of these six, the first only is useful.
" All the rest are wasteful.

" By pasturing, the five last modes are exercised without any
" check or compensation.   By keeping in the house, they may be
" all prevented totally by great care, and almost totally by very
" general and common attention."

Of course, it is not to be inferred from this that animals avail
themselves of only one-fifth of the food produced by the field on
which they are pastured.   But any farmer will at once admit that
the amount destroyed in the various ways referred to is very great ;
and it is probably even greater in rich pastures than in poor ones,
for the reason that after an animal has once filled itself it seems to
devote a large part of the remaining hours of the day to the
destruction of luxuriant food for which it has no immediate use.
Whether the amount wasted is small or great, the waste may be
almost entirely prevented by cutting and hauling to some other
place than the surface of the field on which the crop grows.   In
soiling, especially in stalls, the amount of food administered may
be exactly adjusted to the needs of the animals.   They may

receive at each feeding exactly the quantity that they will entirely consume, and all beyond this may be reserved for future use ; while the small amount of rejected herbage will be ordinarily only so much as will be consumed with advantage by swine.

With regard to *the better condition and greater comfort of the cattle*, there is a sentimental idea that the advantage lies on the side of the pasturing ; and the most prevalent argument advanced in this connection is, that it is the *natural* way for animals to obtain their food. That it is natural is undoubtedly true ; and, for animals in a state of nature, grazing, being the only means of subsistence possible, is, of course, the best means. But when we withdraw animals entirely from a state of nature, and reduce them, or elevate them, to such an artificial condition as shall cause them best to subserve our ends, there is no reason why unnatural means may not be with advantage adopted, provided they result in no detriment to the animals' health, comfort, or condition The amount of exercise required to maintain the health of any domestic animal is not great, and if we observe the conduct of cows at pasture we shall see that under the most favorable circumstances they take only so much exercise as is necessary to enable them to fill their stomachs with the choicest grasses within their reach, and that, being filled, they invariably remain quiet until, after rumination is completed, they need food again. On poor pastures, where a half-starved cow is obliged to walk nearly the whole day to pick up a scanty subsistence, there is no doubt that one of the principal causes of her poor condition is to be sought in the fact that she has been obliged to take more than the proper amount of exercise.

Ample experience, the world over, has clearly demonstrated the fact, that, with proper facilities for exercising in the yard, cattle, fed regularly with nutritious food only in their stalls, are in better condition, and live longer in good health, than do those who are exposed to the vicissitudes of the weather, and to the more precarious subsistence that natural herbage usually affords. Mr. Quincy refers to the assertion of a writer on soiling, to the effect that, during his experience with a large herd, kept for several years in this way, "he never had an animal essentially sick, had never one die, and had never one miscarry."

The product of milk, as is very ably stated by Mr. Quincy, is greater throughout the whole season than under the system of pasturing, although there is no doubt that during the few weeks that follow the first turning out of hay-fed animals on to luxuriant and tempting pastures, the production of the field-fed cows is larger than that of the stall-fed ones ; but this excess very soon dwindles to an equality, and then falls below the soiling point. The early ripening of meadow-grasses, renders them soon less nutritious and less tempting ; and especially the pinching effect of long-continued drought reduces the average yield of pastures during the whole season considerably below what it would be, if, from the first opening of spring until the closing in of winter, there were never a day when the food was not ample and regularly administered. In pasturing we must either have so small a stock as not to be able to make full use of the growth of the early summer, or, if we are able to consume that entirely, must see our larger herds suffer for the want of abundant food during the season of less luxuriant growth.

The *attainment of manure*, which is so greatly facilitated by the soiling system, may be regarded as second in importance only to the saving of land. Indeed, it is to this effect of soiling that what is technically known as "high farming" looks for its greatest support. Of course, with a given amount of food, animals make a given amount of dung, and whether they eat that food in the fields or in the house makes no difference in this regard. But in the field the dung is dropped with great irregularity, and principally on those parts which, from shelter, shade, dryness during wet weather, or other causes, are chiefly selected by the animals for their resting-places. So far as the dropping of manure during the feeding-time of the animals is concerned, more will fall upon the rich land than upon the poor ; and it is impossible, in any ordinary system of pasturing, to secure any thing like an even distribution of the voidings of the stock. In addition to this, a very large proportion of the value of the manure, especially of cows, is wasted by evaporation, and by becoming the food of myriads of insects. The urine at each voiding falls only upon a limited surface, and there is nothing like a proper distribution of its fertilizing elements over the whole soil. It is doubtful, also, whether this deposit of manure upon the surface of the land, during the hottest season of the year, is the most economical. And even if there were no waste, and no concentration of the manure on certain parts of the field to the deprivation of other parts, the fact that the application is not under the control of the farmer, and that, as a rule, the land pastured this year is not most in need of this year's manure, would be sufficient to re-enforce whatever argument may be advanced against the custom. To have a large quantity of manure made under cover, and kept under such circumstances as to suffer very little, if any, waste, is of an importance which all farmers will readily acknowledge ; and the ability to control the application of this manure at will is of great consequence. I know, from my own experience in the stall-feeding of animals, that the amount of manure made in this way is enough to amaze any farmer who is not familiar with the practice. And not only is the quantity of the manure itself increased, but, by adding to it muck, dry earth, or other similar refuse, its valuable parts may be distributed throughout a still greater mass of material, enabling us to spread it more evenly over the ground.

In all well-arranged soiling-barns the manure is received in a cellar under the animals, or in well-covered sheds behind them, both of which are protected against the draining away or waste of the manure. Therefore in this respect there is absolutely no waste, and it is a source of great satisfaction to the farmer to feel that he has the fertilizing capital of the whole farm completely under his control, and that he is able to apply it in such quantities as he deems best to the fields on which it will do the most good.

The following quotation from Mr. Quincy's first essay will illustrate the truth of the foregoing statements :—

" The twenty head consumed the product of

24

<pre>
2 1-2 acres, road-sides and orchard
3   "   mowing-land.
3 1-4 "   Indian corn cut as fodder.
2   "   late and light barley.
3   "   oats.
2   "   late-sown Indian corn after a pea-crop.
  1-4 "   buckwheat.
1   "   millet, buckwheat, and oats.
_____
17   acres.
</pre>

"This is the whole land which was cut over for soiling, with "the exception of the after-feed on the mowing land, and the tops "of carrots and turnips. In comparing this result with the for- "mer practice of my farm, I apprehend the following statement to "be just :—

"I offset the keeping from the 11th of September to the 20th "of November against the old manner of letting the cattle run at "large during the autumn months on the mowing-land to its great "injury, by poaching and close feeding. If this should not be "deemed sufficient, I then make no estimate of the difference "between keeping fifteen head of cattle, the old stock, and twenty "head of cattle, my present stock. After these allowances and off- "sets (which no man can doubt are sufficiently liberal), then I state "that my experiment has resulted in relation to land, in this, that I "have kept the *same amount of stock, by soiling, on seventeen acres of* "*land, which had always previously required fifty acres.* The result "is, in my opinion, even in this respect, greater than what is here "stated. This, however, is sufficient to exhibit the greatness of "the economy of this mode, so far as relates to land.

"With respect to saving of fencing, the previous condition of "my farm was this. I had, at the lowest estimate, five miles of "interior fence, (equal to sixteen hundred rods,) which, at one dol- "lar the rod, was equal, in original cost, to sixteen hundred dol- "lars, and annually, for repairs and refitting, cost sixty dollars. "*I have now not one rod of interior fence.* Of course, this saving is "great, distinct, and undeniable.

"In relation to manures, the effect of soiling is not less apparent "and unquestionable. The exact amount of summer product I

" have not attempted to ascertain; but I am satisfied, that, every
" thing considered, it is not less than one buck-load per month per
" head; or, on twenty head of cattle, one hundred and twenty
" loads for the six soiling months. In this estimate, I take into
" consideration the advantage resulting from the urine saved by
" means of loam, sand, or some imbibing recipient, prepared to
" absorb it.

" It remains to show that the cost of raising the food, cutting
" it, and distributing it to the cattle, is compensated by these
" savings. Upon this point, my own experience has satisfied me
" that the value of the manure alone is an ample compensation for
" all this expense; leaving the saving of land, of food, and of
" fencing-stuff, as well as the better condition of the cattle, as a
" clear gain from the system. As an evidence of this I state my
" expenses for labor in conducting the soiling process.

" During the month of June, I hired a man to do every thing
" appertaining to the soiling process—that is, cutting the food,
" delivering it, taking care of the cattle in the day-time—for
" fifteen dollars the month, he finding himself. In this arrange-
" ment, it was estimated that I availed myself of half his labor.
" At the end of the month I had the manure measured; and I
" found that the manure collected in my receptacle, (which was a
" cellar under the barn,) and not including that which had been
" made during the four hours each day in the yard, amounted to
" fifteen loads,—a quantity of manure which I could not have
" placed on my farm for thirty dollars; and which I could have
" sold there for twenty dollars, upon the condition it should be
" carried away. It cost me, as above stated, fifteen dollars in the
" labor of the attendant.

" During the remaining five months, I added another man, be-
" cause I found that a great economy in vegetable food would
" result from cutting it into pieces by a cutting-knife, and mixing
" with it about one-third of cut salt hay or straw. This was
" done; and I kept an accurate account of all the labor of cutting
" the food in the field, bringing it into the barn, cutting it up there,
" cutting salt hay or straw to mix with it, mixing this food, and

" delivering it to the cattle; and found that it amounted to one
" hundred and forty-eight days' labor. This, estimated at a dollar
" the day, is one hundred and forty-eight dollars; to which adding
" fifteen dollars paid for labor in the month of June, the whole
" expense was one hundred and sixty-three dollars.

" The manure, at the end of the soiling season, certainly
" equaled one hundred and twenty loads; and could not have
" been bought and brought there for three hundred dollars. Let
" it be estimated at only two hundred dollars in value. No man
" can question, I think, the correctness of my assertion, that the
" value of the manure obtained is a clear compensation for this
" amount of labor; and this including all the expense of labor con-
" nected with soiling.

" It remains to be shown in what manner the whole process
" ought to be conducted by any one who may originally attempt
" it, and also *how far* it is applicable to the farming condition of
" New England, and what species of farmers would find their
" account in attempting it.

" As to the manner in which the soiling process ought to be
" conducted, besides that general care and personal superintendence
" (at least occasionally, and by way of oversight) which is essential
" to success in this as in every other business in life, three general
" objects ought to claim the attention of every farmer or other
" person who undertakes this process.

" 1. Provision against seasons of extraordinary drought, or
" deficiency of general crop from any other natural accident.

" 2. Succession of succulent food during the whole soiling sea-
" son, and facility of its attainment.

" 3. Preparation relative to care of the stock, and increase of
" manure,—the particular objects of the soiling process."

Concerning the crops to be raised for soiling, it is not possible
to give such specific directions as will be applicable to all parts of
the country, nor even to the circumstances of different farms in
the same district. In many instances, the luxurious growth of
meadows and clover-fields, together with the cuttings at the sides
of lanes and on the ground about the house, etc., will be a very

important item of the supply of food. In others, it will be found best to depend almost entirely upon crops raised exclusively for this purpose. The principle, under all circumstances, is the same, and it is a very simple one, namely,—to get the largest possible quantity of nutritious, succulent food from the smallest possible area of land, and to constantly re-invigorate the land with the excessive quantity of manure resulting from the feeding of its crops ; so that, year by year, its productiveness may be increased, and that it may yearly carry a larger number of animals.

As an illustration, rather than as a series of directions, I give herewith the system which was adopted in 1869 for the soiling of about thirty animals, old and young, at Ogden Farm. As the land had but recently come into my possession, after years of leasing and skinning, and as it is now very far from being in proper condition for the best results of soiling, I make no reference to the quantity of land sowed to each crop, as prudence required me to make this very much larger than on any average farm would have been desirable. I simply took care to provide for the production of more than could possibly be required, adopting the practice of cutting and curing for winter use whatever might be left standing on one field when its successor was ready for the scythe. I have already seen enough to convince me that within a very few years I shall be able to feed a full-grown animal abundantly from the produce of a single half-acre during the whole season from May 15 to November 15 ; and it seems evident that the increased production from one year to the next will be in constantly growing proportion, the fertility of the land being improved, not only in the ratio of the amount of manure applied, but also according to the number of cultivations and the absence of the injurious effect of the feet of animals pasturing upon it.

The preparation consists in the sowing of winter rye early in September. In exceptional seasons this rye may, with advantage, be mowed over late in November, but ordinarily it had better be left untouched. Early in the winter, when the ground is so frozen that it will bear the treading of teams, it should be top-dressed with rather coarse stable manure, which serves not only as a direct fertilizer, but as a mulch to protect the crop from the injurious effect of too frequent freezing and thawing, and of violent winds.

In the autumn, before the ground becomes too wet, a considerable area is plowed up and made ready for spring planting. As early in the spring as it is possible to go on to this land with teams, without injuring its texture, it is once lightly harrowed, then sowed with oats, and these thoroughly harrowed in,—the land, however, not being rolled, as the clods will afford a certain protection against late frosts and high, cold winds. This sowing should always be made early in April, or, if the weather will admit, even in March. The commencement of its growth, however, may always be dated, in the latitude of New York, from about the 10th or 15th of April. The only object in getting the seed in before this time is to get the work out of the way, and to insure its being planted in ample season for the earliest growing weather.

About the first of May another tract, which had been plowed in the fall, is prepared in precisely the same manner and sown with oats. About the middle of May, or as soon as the plants are strong enough to bear the treatment, these two fields, if the land is dry and in good condition, should be neatly rolled down.

It will be well, also, to make another sowing of oats or barley as late as the middle of May, but from the tenth of May until the first of August sowed corn should be put in, on a separate piece about every two weeks. That first planted will be large enough to cut late in July or early in August, and throughout the whole of August and September, and often far into October, corn may be relied upon as the chief soiling-crop, and both the quantity per acre and the value of the material as food, make it almost the best of all soiling-crops.

In addition to the foregoing, a considerable area of grass or clover should be well manured and kept in all respects in the best condition ; and the hay crop being early taken off, the aftermath should be stimulated to the greatest possible extent. For, in exceptional seasons, or as the result of circumstances which cannot be foreseen, it might become necessary to depend very largely upon our best grass to help out deficient crops upon the soiling ground. Of course, the better the condition of the land, and the longer it has been used for soiling, the less will be the liability of such requirement.

In favorable seasons, the soiling commences about the 15th of May, at which time rye, sown upon good land, will be high enough for cutting to be advantageously commenced, and it should be commenced some time before the crop heads out. Feeding from this crop may be continued until the grain is pretty well formed, but it should not be continued after the straw begins to grow hard and yellow. That portion of the rye which was cut off, after heading out, will produce nothing more, but that which was first cut will have shot up again, and will generally be ready for a second cutting by the time the whole field has been gone over. Matters should be so arranged that the rye will last until the early part of June, when, unless the area of rye is very large, the reliance for two or three weeks must be upon clover and grass which have been top-dressed for a heavy crop.

Late in June, the earliest sown oats will begin to be fit for the scythe, and cutting upon them, and again upon the second and third sowings, may be continued until the straw commences to grow hard. They should form the chief reliance until about the first of August, when the sowed corn will be large enough for cutting. With this, as with the rye, that cut in an early stage of its growth will shoot up again and give a good second crop. By the aid of these second and third cuttings, the corn should be able to furnish all that will be required, until the danger of frost makes it necessary to cut it up for curing. After this, for a short time, the second growth, or aftermath, of the mowing lands, may be resorted to; and when the grass begins to lose condition, and even far into December, the leaves of carrots, mangel-wurzels, and rutabagas, will form a valuable addition to the food; and they and imperfectly developed cabbages may be used to usher in the slowly commencing feeding of hay and dried soiling crops. If the leaves, cabbages, etc., are properly protected at this cool season of the year, they may be kept fresh and succulent pretty nearly until

Christmas time, and if roots and cabbages have been raised in sufficient quantity to furnish an important supply of food in this way, the roots and cabbages themselves will after that furnish an ample supply of fresh vegetable food.

The prevailing argument against the soiling system, and one which naturally has great weight with nearly all farmers, is founded upon the scarcity and high price of labor. Scarcity, if the scarcity exist to such an extent as to withdraw the article from the market, is an argument to which there is no reply; but if it is only sufficient to create a high price, there is very much to be said on the other side of the question. If a farmer is so circumstanced that he can, even for high wages, always be sure of hiring additional help, and if his domestic arrangements are such that he can increase his force without abusing his family, there are few good farms, with properly arranged buildings, upon which soiling will not pay a handsome profit. Probably in feeding twenty cows the extra labor of planting, cutting, and feeding, and hauling out and spreading manure, would require, during six months of the year, the services of one man and one yoke of oxen. This may be set down as a permanent increase of the expenses of the farm, and in average regions it would probably amount to $400 each year. The abundant pasturage of twenty cows would require forty acres of good land, worth say $150 per acre, or $6,000. In soiling they would require but ten acres of land, worth $1,500, leaving to be charged to the pasturage system a capital sum of $4,500, upon which the interest, at seven per cent., would be $315. The product of manure would probably be at the rate of one two-horse load per month for each cow, or 120 loads. It is not easy to fix the value of this manure, as it must, of course, vary in different localities. In Rhode Island it would be worth three dollars a load, and in all of the older settled portions of New England, especially in the neighborhood of good markets, it would probably be worth pretty nearly that amount. As we proceed farther west, the value of the manure will decrease until it finally reaches the zero point. However, as it is quite certain that soiling will not be adopted except where manure has a high value, it will be fair to assume that the quantity of manure specified above will be worth $250;—and if we allow $65 as the value of the manure dropped upon the pasture under the pasturing system, we shall have, in the two items of interest and manure, $500 return for $400 expended in labor, leaving a profit of twenty-five per cent.

This is not, in itself, a particularly brilliant showing; for, under many circumstances, the simple item of contingencies would not unfrequently consume the entire profit;—but the following facts are to be considered: *first*, the man and team employed for the soiling work will render valuable assistance at harvest time, and whenever the work of the farm is hurried, and will regularly do a considerable amount of outside work; *second*, the condition of the animals will be much better than when they are pastured in the field; *third*, the product of milk will be larger; *fourth*, the chances that butter, cheese, or milk will have their taste affected by wild onion and other high-flavored weeds will be reduced; *fifth*, the time wasted, and the derangement of farm-work encountered in driving cattle to and from the pasture will be entirely obviated; *sixth*, the fertility of the farm will be immensely increased.

The first five of the advantages enumerated may be set down as incidental benefits, which will be sufficient to offset the contingencies which, in their turn, may offset the 25 per cent. profit on the expense. But the last, the question of increased fertility, while it is an element to which it is impossible to attach a money value, is of far greater importance than all of the others combined. Indeed, I have not the least hesitation in saying, that the fertility of any average land devoted exclusively to the soiling of cattle, and receiving all of the manure produced by them during the soiling season, will be doubled in five years, and the value of the land will be doubled as well. Whether it would double again in the next five years is by no means certain, but that it would, at the end of twenty years, be permanently worth for cultivation four times its original price is unquestionable. The frequent cultivation, usually twice in the season and sometimes three times, the immense amount of the very best of all farm manures applied yearly to the soil, and the almost entire absence of the treading of animals, this being confined entirely to the seasons of working, will obviously add almost incalculably to the fertility of any soil not already in the condition of a garden. Land which this year will soil twenty head of cattle, should, five years hence, soil at least thirty under the same general treatment; while it will have been raised to such a condition of fertility that it may be repeatedly cropped with grain with the certainty of the very best results.

Without greatly increasing and greatly modifying the labor of cultivation, it will be difficult to make use of the entire accumulated fertility of land that has been used for soiling for a number of years. It would be better, therefore, to use the practice as a means of increasing the fertility of different parts of the farm consecutively, and thereby putting them in a condition for the production of larger and more profitable crops of grain or of grass.

The arrangements necessary for soiling may be very simple. They should, however, in all cases comprise easy facilities for distributing the food, perfect shelter for the manure, shade and good ventilation for the animals themselves, convenient appliances for watering, and, above all, ample exercising grounds. It is impossible to keep animals in a state of the highest health if they are constantly tied in their stalls; and there should be in connection with the barn or shed, a good, dry, partly shaded, and large yard, into which the animals may be turned whenever the weather is favorable, and where it will generally be found advantageous to allow them to remain three or four hours every day; the custom being, usually, to turn them out at eight in the morning, bringing them in at ten for their second feed, turning them out again at three after their third feed, and bringing them in again for the fourth feed at five, another liberal feed following during or after the evening milking.

Opinions vary somewhat as to the condition in which it is best to administer the food. Some give it to the animals when it is freshly cut and full of juice, while others prefer to let it wilt for a few hours before being taken into the barn. My own opinion is that the fresh feeding is the most natural, and productive of the best results, although the excessive succulence of the food may at first have a loosening effect upon the bowels of the animals, which will render it necessary to give them one feed each day of dry hay or dried soiling fodder. In practice, there will always be more cut than can be fed at once, and in this way the stock will receive enough wilted food to modify the laxative tendency of that which has been given to them fresh. By reference to the plan and description of the barn and yards at Ogden Farm, it will be seen that all of these requirements have there been provided for; and in any case in which it is deemed advisable to construct a large and rather expensive barn the soiling facilities may probably be attained as cheaply in the regular stalls as in any other way; but if a special shed is to be erected, as an addition to already existing farm buildings, it will be sufficient to make a drive-way in front of the stalls, through which the carts can be directly led, the grass being thrown on the ground at the sides of the alley. The chief objection to sheds built directly upon the ground, even where the site is very well drained, lies in the fact that it is difficult to remove the large amount of manure without either exposing it to the weather or rendering the shed untidy and inconvenient.

To end this chapter in the spirit in which it was commenced, it may be well to restate the opinion, that while soiling offers immense advantages to the owners of small farms, near to good markets, and in localities where extra labor can be obtained without difficulty, it must work its way slowly to the favor of those who are not so circumstanced; and, taking a larger view of its influence on the general agriculture of the country, it is not so likely that it will be widely adopted upon large farms as it is that it will make farmers content with small ones, and that it will hasten the happy day when American farmers generally shall realize the fact that the road to their best prosperity lies, not through broad fields covered by their parchments, but through deep furrows in their well-enriched land; and when their accumulated capital will be invested neither in bank-stocks nor on bond and mortgage, nor yet in more land, but in such improvements on that already owned as shall double its value and quadruple its profits.

CHAPTER XV.

I SHALL offer no apology for taking the material of this chapter almost exclusively from the writings of others. The question of the diseases of domestic animals is one of such great importance that it has received a good share of the attention of able men for many years. Old and barbarous practices, which entailed more suffering than benefit upon the poor brutes, are being rapidly given up, and, under the light afforded by considerate and thoughtful men, the treatment of even the most severe cases is at least much more humane than it formerly was, and, in proportion to its humanity, is undoubtedly more successful.

Unfortunately, as in the case of the treatment of the diseases of the human race, nearly all recipes and instructions are more or less empirical, the administering of medicines belonging, as yet, by no means to the list of "exact sciences." The most that can be said in favor of the directions of veterinary surgeons is, that they have, especially during the last twenty years, devoted an untiring energy and sound judgment to an investigation of the causes of disease and of the effects of remedies ; and that they have, as a consequence, rejected many things that were formerly considered of absolute necessity, and have substituted simple remedies for severe ones.

It has now come to be a recognized fact with veterinary surgeons, livery-stable keepers, and intelligent farmers, that the sovereign remedy for external injuries, and for all strains, bruises, irritations, and cutaneous affections, is *water*. Applied hot or cold, as the occasion may require, and accompanied by the necessary bandaging, blanketing, and fomentations, it is fast driving the firing-iron and the blister, with the inexpressible suffering that they have caused, out of the stable and the shed. With regard to internal remedies and medicines, the scientific and practical worlds are yet apparently far from having reached a point entirely satisfactory even to themselves. But the tendency is undoubtedly in favor of a greater dependence on the natural restorative agencies of diet, fresh air, and suitable temperature. Old-fashioned grooms still have their mysterious secrets concerning the composition of " balls," and their peculiar ways of crowding them down the throats of patient and long-suffering horses ; and the empire of balls and drenches, though happily weakened in its foundations, has by no means given up its sway over the uneducated minds of those to whom the care of our domestic animals is chiefly intrusted. Specifics for loosening the bowels, producing silkiness of coat, brightness of the eye, and briskness of temper,—all more or less injurious,—are still much in use. Happily, however, the number is yearly increasing of those who are disposed to send all of these remedies after the vanishing firing-iron and blister, believing that the same effect on the bowels, the skin, the eye, and the temperament may be produced almost as readily, and certainly with less danger, by a judicious change in the character of the food. A soft, moist, warm diet, such as steamed hay or a hot bran-mash, will, except in such obstinate cases as ought not to be allowed under ordinary circumstances to arise, produce all the relaxation of the bowels that it is desirable to effect ; and in obstinate cases of constipation a copious injection of tepid water, repeated as often as may be necessary, cannot fail to produce the desired result, if any thing will do it.

Especially in the case of horses, the constant winter diet, almost the whole year's diet indeed, consisting, as it usually does, simply of hay and oats in their raw state, is very liable to produce derangements of the digestive organs ; and it has been the custom to remedy the evil by the use of violent cathartic medicines. A particular attention to the changing of the food at times,—the occasional or even regular feeding of carrots, at least the occasional cutting and moistening of food, and its more or less perfect steaming,—the occasional introduction of bran mashes into the weekly regimen,—will give that variety that the permanent health of the animal requires; and the necessity for administering medicines will be very largely avoided.

Without by any means wishing to enter the lists in the contest between allopathy and homeopathy, I cannot refrain from saying that my own experience, which has been but slight, and my observation, which has been considerable, both lead me to believe that, so far as it is necessary to administer medicines at all to domestic animals, the seemingly insignificant doses of the homeopathic practitioner are more rapidly effective, and far less injurious in their permanent results, than are the old prescriptions. And if there is any real foundation at all for the rapid and general establishment of homeopathy throughout the world, it is only reasonable that in the treatment of domestic animals its effect should be more certain and more active than in the treatment of our own diseases, for the reason that the diet of the brute world is so simple and inoffensive that there is little danger, either of a counteracting of the effect of the medicine, or of the creation of such a condition of the system as will require the vigorous action of large doses.

HORSES.

Several works on veterinary homeopathy have been published, which contain sufficiently full and sufficiently simple instructions for the administering of the remedies in those cases in which the character of the disease can be determined. In preparing for the press, several years ago, the book known as Herbert's "Hints to Horsekeepers," I compiled a chapter on veterinary homeopathy, which is as applicable at the present day as at the time when it was written. This chapter was made up chiefly from material found in Schæfer's "New Manual of Veterinary Homeopathic Medicine," and the "Hand-Book of Veterinary Homeopathy" by John Rush. The instructions of this chapter were intended only for the use of horsemen, but the same principle applies throughout the whole list of domestic animals, and specific directions for the medication of all are included in the principal works upon the system, several of which may be obtained through any bookseller. The following extracts are made from the chapter above referred to :—*

" The remedies being in a liquid form, the best means of ad-
" ministering them to the horse is to put six drops on a small
" piece of bread, or on a wafer of flour paste, and to raise the
" horse's head a little, ' press down the tongue to one side, and
" pull it out as far as may be, and then place the wafer as far back
" as possible ; after which the mouth is held closed with the hand,
" in order to compel the animal to swallow the wafer.' Schæfer
" says : In some cases the dose has to be repeated ; but all use-
" less and improper repetition should be avoided. If no change
" of any kind should take place after the first dose, this is a sure
" sign that the medicine has been improperly selected, and that
" a second dose of the same remedy would not do any more good
" than the former has done. In this case we have to review the
" symptoms a second time, and to select a different remedy.
" If the first dose should produce a favorable change in the
" symptoms of the disease, and this change should again be fol-
" lowed by an aggravation, it is proper to give a second dose of
" the same remedy. If the symptoms should become aggravated
" after the first dose, we should not all at once resort to a differ-
" ent remedy ; for this aggravation might be what we have termed
" homeopathic aggravation, which would soon be followed by a
" favorable reaction. In all very acute diseases that run a rapid
" course, and, after one, two, or four weeks, terminate in death
" or recovery, such as glanders, pleura pneumonia, etc., the dose
" should be repeated every five, ten, or fifteen minutes.

" In such dangerous maladies, the first dose is often followed
" by a visible improvement, which soon ceases, however ; this is
" the time to repeat the dose, and a second dose may then be emi-

* Herbert's Hints to Horsekeepers.   Orange Judd & Co., New York.

" nently useful. In chronic diseases that run a long course, the
" medicine may be repeated every day, or every two, three, or
" four days. In such cases the rule is, likewise, not to interfere
" with an incipient improvement by giving another dose of the same
" or some other remedy.

" If the improvement stops, the medicine may be repeated, and
" if no improvement at all should set in after a reasonable lapse
" of time, another medicine may be chosen. Among the class of
" chronic diseases we number all nervous and mental diseases,
" lingering fevers, etc. An improper remedy does not produce
" any *very injurious* effects ; for a homeopathic remedy only
" acts upon a disease to which the medicine is really homeo-
" pathic : otherwise, the smallness of the dose is such that the
" medicine cannot possibly affect the organism. All that we have
" to do is, to give another remedy, and endeavor to avoid mistakes
" for the future. Homeopathic remedies may be applied exter-
" nally in the case of burns and other injuries. We use princi-
" pally arnica, symphytum, and urtica-ureus, from twenty to
" thirty drops in a half-pint of water, and this mixture to be
" applied to the part according to directions.

" *A proper diet* in the case of sick domestic animals is of great
" importance. All applications, quack medicines, etc., that might
" interfere with the regular treatment, have to be avoided. In-
" jections of water mixed with a little salt or soap are allowable.
" The usual feed may be continued. * * * Half an hour,
" at least, should elapse between the feeding and the taking of
" the medicine.

" On the treatment of the sick animal, Rush says :—

" *Treatment of a sick animal.*—As soon as an animal is discov-
" ered to be unwell, let it be immediately placed in a house by
" itself ; this is necessary both for the welfare of the sick animal
" and for the safety of the others. The house that the animal is
" placed in ought to be warm, well lighted and ventilated, and,
" above all, kept scrupulously clean. Let the person who attends
" to the wants of the animal be very cautious to approach in a
" quiet manner, never make any unnecessary noise, or do any

" thing that would tend to irritate the animal when in a state of
" health.

" *With regard to diet.*—In acute diseases no food whatever
" ought to be given until improvement has taken place, and even
" then only in a sparing manner ; the articles of diet most suitable
" are bran, oats, hay, carrots, Swede turnips, and green food,
" either grass or clover.

" The bran may be given either dry or wetted, whichever way
" the animal prefers it.

" Oats may be given mixed with the bran, either raw and
" crushed, or whole and boiled.

" It is necessary to keep the animal without food or water half
" an hour before and after administering the medicine.

" *Repetition of the dose.*—In acute diseases it is necessary to
" repeat the dose every *five, ten, fifteen*, or *twenty* minutes.

" In less acute diseases every *two, four, six,* or *eight* hours.

" In chronic diseases once in *twenty-four* hours is sufficient."

The following are the directions given for the treatment of a few
of the more simple diseases of horses, and they are included here
rather by way of illustration than as a part of a complete system,
which, of course, it would be impossible within such narrow limits
to give :—

" GREASE.

" REMEDIES.—*Thuja occidentalis, Secale cornutum, Arsenicum,*
" *Mercurius vivus,* and *Sulphur.*

" *Thuja occidentalis,* both internally and externally, if there are
" bluish or brownish excrescences, which bleed on the least touch,
" and there is a discharge of fetid ichor.

" DOSE.—Six drops three times a day ; at the same time the
" parts may be bathed with the strong tincture night and morning.

" *Secale cornutum* and *Arsenicum* may be used in alternation, if
" there is a watery swelling or dark-looking ulcers, with fetid dis-
" charge.

" DOSE.—The same as directed for *Thuja occidentalis*, internally.

25

" *Mercurius vivus* when there are numerous small ulcers that
" discharge a thick matter, and bleed when touched.

" Dose.—Six or eight drops twice a day.

" It is necessary to give a dose of *Sulphur* once a week during
" the treatment, and keep the legs clean by washing them with
" warm water.

" FOUNDER.

" Remedies.—*Aconite, Bryonia, Veratrum, Arsenicum,* and *Rhus
" toxicodendron.*

" *Aconite,* if there is inflammation, the animal stands as if rooted
" to one spot, the breathing is hurried and interrupted, the breath
" is hot and the pulse accelerated.

" Dose.—Six drops every one, two, or three hours.

" *Bryonia,* complete stiffness of the limbs, with swelling of the
" joints.

" Dose.—Six drops every two hours.

" *Veratrum,* if it is brought on by violent exercise.

" Dose.—The same as directed for *Bryonia.*

" *Arsenicum,* if it is caused by bad or heating food, or after a
" cold drink when overheated.

" Dose.—The same as directed for *Aconite.*

" *Rhus toxicodendron,* if there is much pain in the feet, and the
animal is very stiff in his movements.

" Dose.—Six drops or eight globules three times a day ; at the
" same time the limbs may be bathed with a solution of *Rhus,*
" externally, twice a day.   *   *   *   *

"INFLAMMATION OF THE BRAIN.

" Remedies.—*Aconite, Belladonna, Veratram,* and *Opium.*

" *Aconite,* in the very commencement of this disease, if the
" pulse is accelerated, fever, congestion toward the brain, rapid
" breathing, and trembling of the whole body.

" Dose.—Six drops every twenty minutes until several doses
" have been taken, or the more violent symptoms subdued, after
" which the next remedy should be taken into consideration.

" *Belladonna*, if the animal has a wild, staring, fixed look, dashes
" furiously and unconsciously about, which is indicative of violent
" congestion of the brain.

" DOSE.—Six drops put upon the tongue every fifteen or thirty
" minutes, until the violence of the attack is subdued.

" *Veratrum*, if the legs and ears are icy cold, with convulsive
" trembling of the whole body, or where there is a reeling, stag-
" gering motion, and the animal plunges violently and falls down
" head foremost.

" DOSE.—The same as directed for *Belladonna*.

" *Opium*, if after the paroxysm the animal remains motionless,
" with fixed, staring eyes, the tongue of a black or leaden color.

" DOSE.—Six drops every half, one, or two hours, according to
" circumstances.

" CATARRH, OR COMMON COLD.

" REMEDIES.—*Aconite, Nux vomica, Dulcamara, Rhus toxico-
" dendron, Bryonia, Arsenicum, Mercurius vivus,* and *Pulsatilla.*

" *Aconite* will be useful in the beginning of the disease, if there
" is fever and heat of the body, restlessness, short, hurried breath-
" ing, violent thirst, urine fiery red, and the discharge from the
" nose impeded.

" DOSE.—Six drops or six globules every three hours until
" better

" *Nux vomica*, if during the prevalence of northeasterly winds,
" and if the mouth is dry, tongue coated white, an offensive earthy
" odor emitted from the mouth, and a thin watery or thick bloody
" discharge from the nose.

" DOSE.—Six drops or six globules twice a day.

" *Dulcamara*, if the attack was brought on from exposure to
" wet, and the animal is dull and drowsy, the tongue coated with
" a thick sticking phlegm.

" DOSE.—The same as directed for *Nux vomica*.

" *Rhus toxicodendron*, if short dry cough, great accumulation of
" mucus in the nose, without being able to discharge it, obstructed
" respiration, frequent sneezing and restlessness.

" Dose.—Four drops or six globules three times a day.

" *Bryonia*, if there is difficulty in breathing, dry spasmodic
" cough, swelling of the nose, profuse coryza, or crusts of hardened
" mucus in the nose.

" Dose.—The same as directed for *Rhus toxicodendron*.

" *Arsenicum*, if the discharge from the nose continues too long,
" is acrid and corroding to the nostrils, dry cough, sneezing, with
" discharge of watery mucus from the nose.

" Dose.—Six drops twice a day.

" *Mercurius vivus*, in the first stage of the disease, if there is
" swelling of the nose, profuse coryza with much sneezing.

" Dose.—Six drops or six globules three times a day.

" *Pulsatilla*, if the cough is loose, discharge of greenish fetid
" matter from the nose.

" Dose.—The same as directed for *Mercurius vivus*.

" COUGH

" Remedies.—*Dulcamara, Nux vomica, Squilla, Bryonia, Amo-*
" *nium muriaticum, Drosera, Pulsatilla,* and *Lycopodium*.

" *Dulcamara*, if it follows cold, especially if the cold comes on
" from wet, and there is a discharge from the nose.

" Dose.—Four or six drops three or four times a day until
" better.

" *Nux vomica*, if the cough is dry, and the cough comes on
" when first leaving the stable.

" Dose.—The same as directed for *Dulcamara*.

" *Squilla*, if the animal makes a groaning noise before coughing,
" and the whole body shakes from coughing.

" Dose.—Four drops or six globules two or three times a day.

" *Bryonia*, if the cough is of several weeks' standing, and worse
" from motion.

" Dose.—Six drops night and morning.

" *Ammonium muriaticum*, if the horse appears to be choked or
" about to vomit, loss of flesh, the skin sticks to the ribs.

" Dose.—Four drops every three hours until improvement is
" manifest.

" *Drosera*, if the cough is of long standing, worse at night when
" the animal lies down.

" Dose.—Six drops night and morning.

" *Pulsatilla*, if the animal is timid and easily frightened, or if
" with the cough there is a bad smelling discharge from the
" nostrils.

" Dose.—Four drops or six globules every three hours.

" *Lycopodium*, if the cough is excited or worse after drinking,
" and comes on in fits, coughing a great many times in rapid
" succession.

" Dose.—Six drops three times a day.

" Attention ought to be paid to diet in this disease ; no inferior
" food should be given, such as the animal must eat a large
" quantity of to keep itself alive ; but whatever is given should
" be good, and that moistened with *cold* water ; carrots are very
" good, either raw or boiled.   *   *   *   *   *

" COLIC, OR GRIPES.

" REMEDIES.—*Aconite, Arsenicum, Nux vomica, Opium, Cham-*
" *omilla, Colchicum, Cantharis, Hyoscyamus,* and *Colocynth.*

" *Aconite*, in the commencement, if there is dryness of the mouth,
" the ears are either hot or cold, breath hot, pulse accelerated.

" Dose.—Four drops or six globules every fifteen or thirty
" minutes, according to the urgency of the case ; if no relief is ob-
" tained after the third dose, proceed then with the next remedy.

" *Arsenicum*, if the disease depends on indigestion, food of bad
" quality, drinking cold water when heated, or if it is caused by
" a constipated state of the bowels, in which case it is considered
" to be specific.

" Dose.—Six drops every half, one, or two hours.

" I have succeeded in curing a great number of cases with these
" two medicines ; I generally, after giving two or three doses of
" *Aconite*, give *Arsenicum* and *Aconite* alternately.

" *Nux vomica* is useful for colic from constipation, when the
" animal walks slowly round, and then lies or falls down suddenly,
" bloated appearance of one or both flanks.

" Dose.—The same as directed for *Arsenicum*.

" *Opium*, if *Nux vomica* fails to remove the constipation, or if
" the excrements are very dry, hard, and dark colored, nearly
" black, and the animal lies stretched out as if dead.

" Dose.—Four drops or six globules every one, two, or three
" hours, according to the urgency of the case.

" *Chamomilla*, if the bowels are relaxed, the animal is very rest-
" less, frequently lying down and getting up ; an attack of pain
" soon followed by an evacuation, swelling of the abdomen, ex-
" tremities cold, especially the ears.

" Dose.—Six drops every one or two hours, according to the
" severity of the case, until better.

" *Colchicum*, if the disease is caused by green food, and there is
" flatulent distention of the abdomen, protrusion of the rectum, the
" animal strikes at his belly with his hinder feet.

" Dose.—The same as directed for *Chamomilla*.

" *Cantharis*, if there is a troublesome retention of urine, and the
" animal often places himself in position to pass urine, but only
" succeeds in passing a few drops ; if this remedy does not relieve,
" give *Hyoscyamus*.

" Dose.—The same as directed for *Chamomilla*.

  * * * * * * *

" INFLAMMATION OF THE BOWELS.

" Remedies.—*Aconite, Arsenicum, Rhus toxicodendron, Colocyn-
" this, Nux vomica, Cantharis*, and *Arnica*.

" *Aconite* is the chief remedy to be depended upon in this dis-
" ease, and should be frequently administered till a calm is estab-
" lished, which generally takes place in about an hour.

" Dose.—Six drops, or eight globules every ten or fifteen
" minutes, until relieved.

" *Arsenicum*, if after the use of *Aconite* some symptoms still
" remain, especially if the disease has been produced by green
" food, or by drinking cold water when heated.

" Dose.—Six drops every half, one, or two hours, or at longer
" intervals if the disease is not very violent.

" *Rhus toxicodendron*, if the extremities are alternately hot and
" cold, with sweating of the belly, and a frequent discharge of
" urine.

" DOSE.—The same as directed for *Arsenicum*.

" *Colocynthis*, if *Arsenicum* does not remove all the symptoms,
" especially if it is accompanied with colic, and there are bloody
" evacuations.

" DOSE.—Six drops, or eight globules every half or one hour.

" *Nux vomica*, or *Opium*, if after the disease is cured there
" remains a constipated state of the bowels.

" DOSE.—Six drops night and morning.

" *Cantharis*, or *Hyoscyamus*, if there is retention of urine.

" *Arnica* will be useful in very obstinate cases ; if the discharges
" are very fetid, frequently small stools consisting only of slime.

" DOSE.—Six drops every one or two hours until better."

Similar treatment is equally applicable in the case of sick cows,
sheep, and swine.

In the treatment of the diseases of domestic animals by what is
known as the allopathic system, or by the old system of farriery,
and, indeed, in all cases, if the ailment is serious, it is best, whenever
possible, to obtain the services of a really competent veterinary
surgeon. Unfortunately, there are few such in the country, and the
local horse and cattle doctors to be found in almost every farming
neighborhood are a sorry substitute for them. Oftentimes, it is
true, long experience and good natural judgment has enabled them
to understand pretty well the common complaints to which stock
is subject, and they are frequently quite successful in their treatment ; but in the majority of cases it is doubtful whether they do
not really do more harm than good.

In Herbert's " Hints to Horsekeepers," there is a chapter
concerning " Simple Remedies for Simple Ailments," which, so
far as it has been possible to condense, within the limits of a few
pages, practical directions in this matter, is probably the best com-
pendium now within reach. The writer says,—

" It is not too much to say, that more than onehalf the ail ments

" of horses arise, in the first instance, from bad management,—or,
" to speak more correctly, from absence of all management, from
" an improper system of feeding, from ill-constructed, unventilated,
" filthy stabling, from injudicious driving, and neglect of cleaning.
" When disease has arisen, it is immediately aggravated, and, per-
" haps, rendered ultimately fatal, either by want of medical aid, or,
" what is far more frequent as well as far more prejudicial, igno-
" rant, improper, and often violent treatment, either on a wrong
" diagnosis of the affection, or on a still more wrong system of
" relieving it. Over-medicining and vulgarly quacking slightly
" ailing horses is the bane of half the private stables in cities, and
" of nearly all the farm stables in the country ; and one or the
" other, or both combined, cause the ruin of half the horses which
" ' go to the bad ' every year.

" There is no quack on earth equal to an ignorant, opinionated
" groom ; and every one, nowadays, holds himself a groom, who is
" trusted with the care of a horse, even if he do not know how to
" clean him properly, or to feed him so as not to interfere with his
" working hours. Every one of these wretched fellows, who has
" no more idea of a horse's structure or of his constitution than he
" has of the model of a ship or the economy of an empire, is sure
" to have a thousand infallible remedies for every possible disease,
" the names of which he does not know, nor their causes, origin,
" or operation ; and which, if he did know their names, he is
" entirely incapable of distinguishing one from the other. These
" remedies he applies at haphazard, wholly in the dark as to their
" effect on the system in general, or on the particular disease, and,
" of course, nine times out of ten he applies them wrongfully, and
" aggravates fiftyfold the injury he affects to be able to relieve.

" These are the fellows who are constantly administering purga-
" tive balls, diuretic balls, cordial balls on their own hook, without
" advice, orders, or possible reason—and such balls, tool some of
" them scarcely less fatal than a cannon-ball—who are continually
" drugging their horses with niter in their food, under an idea that
" it is cooling to the system, and that it makes the coat sleek and
" silky, never suspecting that it is a violent diuretic ; that its ope-

" ration on the kidneys is irritating and exhausting in the extreme,
" and that the only way in which it cools the animal's system is
" that it reduces his strength, and acts as a serious drain on his
" constitution. These, lastly, are the fellows who are constantly
" applying *hot oils*, fiery irritants and stimulants to wounds, strains,
" bruises, or contusions, which, in themselves, produce violent
" inflammation ; and to which, requiring, as they do, the exhibition
" of mild and soothing remedies, cold lotions, or warm fomenta-
" tions, the application of these stimulating volatile essences is
" much what it would be to administer brandy and cayenne to a
" man with a brain fever.

" It should, therefore, be a positive rule in every stable, whether
" for pleasure or farm purposes, that not a dram of medicine is
" ever to be administered without the express orders of the
" master. Even if a horsekeeper be so fortunate as to possess a
" really intelligent, superior servant, who has served his apprentice-
" ship in a good stable, and has learned a good deal about horses,
" he should still insist on being invariably consulted before medi-
" cine is administered."

In all serious cases, of course, the best medical aid that it is
possible to procure should be at once called in ; but in all cases
the owner should, as far as possible, exercise his own judgment as
to the extent to which the directions given are to be followed,
unless the practitioner is a regularly educated veterinary surgeon.
Concerning purgatives, Herbert writes as follows :—

" We are very decided opponents of purgatives in general, and
" have been gratified by observing that the recent cause of veteri-
" nary practice, both in France and England, is tending to the
" entire abandonment of the old system ; according to which,
" every horse, whether any thing ailed him or not, was put through
" two annual courses of purgation, each of three doses, in the
" spring and fall, besides having to bolt a diuretic ball fortnightly,
" or oftener, according to the whim of the groom, when his kidneys
" no more required stimulation than his hocks did blistering.

" A horse of ordinary size contains, on an average, from twenty
" to twenty-four quarts of blood, and the loss to him of four quarts

" is not so much as a pound or pint to a human being. In cases
" of acute inflammation, a horse may be bled eight or ten quarts
" at a time, or until he lies down, with advantage ; and if the
" symptoms do not abate, may be bled again at intervals of an
" hour or two, to an extent which a person, ignorant how rapidly
" blood is made, would suppose must drain the animal of his life.
" Purgatives, in our opinion, on the other hand, should be very
" cautiously administered ; *never* when there is any inflammation
" of the lungs or bowels ; very rarely when there is any *internal*
" inflammation ; and when given, should never, or hardly ever, in
" our judgment, exceed five drams of new Barbadoes aloes. Injec-
" tions, diet, and mashes are vastly superior, for general practice,
" to acute purgatives, horses being extremely liable to super-pur-
" gation, and many valuable animals being lost in consequence of it
" yearly.

     " The first branch of the subject on which we propose to treat,
" is the early application of remedies to horses suddenly seized
" with violent and acute diseases, anticipatory to the calling in of
" regular medical assistance. It is highly necessary that this should
" be done as soon as the horse is known to be seized, and the
" nature of his seizure is fully ascertained, since, in several of the
" diseases to which the horse is most liable, the increase of the
" malady is so rapid that, if early steps be not taken to relieve the
" sufferer, the evil becomes so firmly seated that the remedy, if
" long delayed, comes too late, and an animal is lost, which, by
" timely assistance, might have easily been preserved. These
" ailments, especially, are of common occurrence with the horse,
" of highly dangerous character, and so rapid in their development
" and increase, that if steps be not taken for their relief almost
" immediately after their commencement, all treatment will be
" useless ;—these are spasmodic colic, inflammation of the bowels,
" and inflammation of the lungs."

     Mr. Youatt, in his excellent work on the horse, says of colic,—
     " There is often not the slightest warning. The horse begins
" to shift his posture, look round at his flanks, paw violently, strike
" his belly with his feet, lie down, roll, and that frequently on his

" back. In a few minutes the pain seems to cease, the horse
" shakes himself and begins to feed ; but on a sudden the spasm
" returns more violently, every indication of pain is increased, he
" heaves at the flanks, breaks out in a profuse perspiration, and
" throws himself more violently about. In the space of an hour
" or two either the spasms begin to relax and the remissions are
" longer in duration, or the torture is augmented at every paroxysm,
" the intervals of ease are fewer and less marked, and inflam-
" mation and death supervene."

Youatt also gives the following tabular statement of the symptoms by which colic and inflammation of the bowels may be distinguished from each other :—

"COLIC.	INFLAMMATION OF THE BOWELS.
" Sudden in its attack, and without any warning.	Gradual in its approach, with previous indications of fever.
" Pulse rarely much quickened in the early period of the disease, and during the intervals of ease, but evidently fuller.	Pulse very much quickened, but small, and often scarcely to be felt.
" Legs and ears of natural temperature.	Legs and ears cold.
" Relief obtained from rubbing the belly.	Belly exceedingly painful and tender to the touch.
" Relief obtained from motion.	Pain evidently increased by motion.
" Intervals of rest and ease.	Constant pain.
" Strength scarcely affected.	Great and evident weakness."

With reference to colic, inflammation of the bowels, and inflammation of the lungs, Herbert says,—

" COLIC is usually produced by sudden cold, often the result
" of drinking cold water when heated ; sometimes by exposure to
" cold wind in a draft, when heated ; sometimes by overfeeding
" on green meat or new corn. The causes of inflammation of
" the bowels are somewhat similar, though not identical. Horses
" used to high feeding and warm stabling, which, after sharp exer-
" cise and being for some hours without food, are exposed to cold
" wind, or are allowed to drink freely of cold water, or are
" drenched with rain, or have their legs and belly washed with cold
" water, are almost sure to be attacked with inflammation of the

" bowels. An overfed or overfat horse, which is subjected to
" severe and long-continued exertion, if his lungs be weak, will
" be attacked, probably the same night, by inflammation of the
" lungs ; if the lungs be sound, the attack will be on his bowels
" the following day.

" The diagnosis being made, and the disease being fully estab-
" lished to be spasmodic colic, and not inflammation, the treat-
" ment should be as follows : Give at once, in a drench, by a
" horn or bottle, three ounces of spirits of turpentine, and an
" ounce of laudanum in a pint of warm ale, the effect of which
" will often be instantaneous. If these ingredients cannot be
" quickly obtained, a drench of hot ale with ginger, a wine-glass-
" ful of gin, and a teaspoonful of black pepper, with, if possible,
" the laudanum added, will succeed as a substitute. If the par-
" oxysm returns, or if relief of a decided kind do not take place
" within half an hour, from four to six quarts of blood may be
" taken, with advantage, in order to prevent inflammation. The
" dose of turpentine should be repeated, and clysters of warm
" water, with an ounce of finely-powdered Barbadoes aloes dis-
" solved in them, should be injected, at intervals, until the counter-
" irritation puts a stop to the spasms. For the injections, a com-
" mon wooden pipe with an ox-bladder will answer, although the
" patent syringe is far better. The pipe should be greased and
" introduced gently and tenderly, great care being had not to alarm
" or startle the animal. The operation and effect of the medicines
" will be promoted by gentle friction of the belly with a brush
" or hot flannel cloth, and by walking the horse or trotting him
" very gently about ; but all violence, or violent motions, must
" be avoided, as tending to produce inflammation. These reme-
" dies, which can be procured with ease in any village, almost in
" any house, will almost to a certainty remove the disease.
" When relief is obtained, the horse's clothes should be changed,
" which will be found to be saturated with sweat ; he should be
" slightly cleaned ; warmly and dryly littered down, if possible,
" in a loose box, and should be fed for two or three days on warm
" bran mashes, and suffered to drink warm water only. It is

" evident that the above treatment, which is stimulating, would be
" probably fatal, as it would aggravate all the worst features, in a
" case of inflammation, which must be treated, as near as possi-
" ble, on the opposite plan—that is, antiphlogistically.

" INFLAMMATION OF THE BOWELS.—The first step, in decided
" cases where the extremities are cold and the pulse very quick and
" very feeble—observe here that fifty-five is very quick, indicating
" considerable fever, and seventy-five perilously quick—is to take
" eight or ten quarts of blood as soon as the malady appears, for
" there is no other malady that so quickly runs its course. If this
" do not relieve the pain and render the pulse more moderate, and
" fuller, and rounder, four or five quarts more may be taken with-
" out any regard to the weakness of the animal. That weakness
" is a part of the disease, and when the inflammation is subdued by
" the loss of blood, the weakness will disappear. We have said
" that most of the acute diseases of the horse and the man are
" closely similar, and their treatment analogous. In acute inflam-
" mation of the bowels there is an exception. The human prac-
" titioner properly uses strong purgatives in cases of acute inflam-
" mation of the bowels. The irritability of the horse's bowels will
" not allow their exhibition. The most that can be done is to throw
" up copious injections—they can hardly be too copious—of thin
" gruel, in which half a pound of Epsom salts, or half an ounce of
" Barbadoes aloes, has been dissolved. The horse should be en-
" couraged to drink freely of warm, thin gruel, and he should have
" a draught every six hours of warm water, with from one to two
" drams—never more—of aloes dissolved in it. Above all, the
" whole belly should be blistered as quickly as possible after the
" nature of the disease is fully ascertained, with tincture of can-
" tharides well rubbed in. The legs should be well bandaged, to
" restore the circulation ; and the horse should be warmly clothed,
" but the stable kept cool ; no hay or oats must be allowed during
" the attack, but merely bran-mashes and green meat ; of the latter,
" especially, as much as he will eat. As the horse recovers, a little
" oats may be given, a handful or two at a time, twice or thrice a
" day, but not more ; and they should be increased sparingly and

"gradually. Clysters of gruel should be continued for two or three
" days, and hand-rubbing and bandaging, to restore the circulation.
" There is another kind of inflammation of the bowels, which
" attacks the inner or mucous membrane, and is produced by super-
" purgation, and the exhibition of improper medicine in improper
" quantities. Its characteristics are incessant purging, laborious
" breathing, pulse quick and small, but less so than in the other
" form of disease; and above all, the mouth is hot, and the legs
" and ears warm. In this disease no food must be allowed, least of
" all laxative food, such as mashes or green meat; but draughts
" and clysters of gruel, thin starch and arrow-root may be given
" frequently. If the pain and purging do not pass away within
" twelve hours, astringents must be given. The best form is
" powdered chalk, 1 ounce; catechu, ¼ of an ounce; opium, 2
" scruples, in gruel, repeated every six hours till the purging be-
" gins to subside, when the doses should be gradually decreased
" and discontinued. Bleeding is not generally necessary, unless
" the inflammation and fever are excessive. The horse should
" be kept warm, and his legs rubbed and bandaged as directed
" in the former type of the disease.

" INFLAMMATION OF THE LUNGS.—This disease, which, in a
" state of nature, is almost unknown to the horse, is one to which
" in his domesticated state he is most liable, and which is most
" fatal to him. It requires immediate and most active treatment.
" It is sometimes sudden in its attack, but is generally preceded
" by fever. The pulse is not always much quickened in the first
" instance, but is indistinct and depressed. The extremities are
" painfully cold; the lining membrane of the nostrils becomes
" intensely red; the breathing is quick, hurried, and seems to be
" interrupted by pain, or mechanical obstruction. The horse
" stands stiffly, with his legs far apart, so as to distend his chest
" to the utmost, and is singularly unwilling to move, or to lie
" down, persisting in standing up, day after day, and night after
" night; and if at last compelled by fatigue to lie down, rises again
" after a moment's repose. The pulse soon becomes irregular,
" indistinct, and at last almost imperceptible. The legs and ears

" assume a clay-like, clammy coldness,—the coldness of death.
" The lining of the nostril turns purple ; the teeth are violently
" ground ; the horse persists in standing until he can stand no
" longer, when he staggers, drops, and soon dies.

" For this disease the only remedy that can be depended upon
" is the lancet. The horse must be bled, not according to quan-
" tity, not only till the pulse begins to rise, but until it begins to
" flutter or stop, and the animal begins to faint. The operator
" should watch this effect, with his finger on the pulse, while the
" bleeding is in process. At the end of six hours, if the horse
" still persist in standing and the laborious breathing still continue,
" the bleeding should be repeated to the same extent. This will
" generally succeed in conquering the strength of the disease.
" If a third bleeding be necessary, as is sometimes the case, it
" must not be carried beyond four or five quarts, lest not only
" the disease, but the recuperative power be subdued. After
" this, if the symptoms return, successive bleedings to the extent
" of two or three quarts should be used, to prevent the re-estab-
" lishment of the disease. The instrument for bleeding should
" be a broad-shouldered thumb-lancet, and the stream of blood
" should be full and strong. Some of the blood from each bleed-
" ing should be set aside in a glass tumbler, and suffered to grow
" cold, in order to note the thickness of the buff-colored, adhesive
" coat which will appear on the top of it, and which indicates the
" degree of inflammation at the time the blood was drawn. We
" have seen it occupy above one-half the depth of the tumbler.
" As the condition of the blood improves, and the symptoms of
" the animal decrease, the bleeding may be gradually discon-
" tinued.

" The whole of the horse's chest and sides, up as far as to the
" elbows, should now be thoroughly blistered, the hair having
" been previously closely shaved, with an ointment of one part of
" Spanish flies, four of lard, and one of rosin, well rubbed in. In
" making the ointment, the rosin and lard should be melted
" together, and the flies then added.

" A horse with inflammation of the lungs must never be

" actively purged ; the bowels and lungs act so strongly in sym-
" pathy, that inflammation of the former would surely supervene,
" and prove fatal.   The horse must be back-raked, and clystered
" with warm gruel, containing eight ounces of Epsom salts.
" Castor oil must never be given ; it is a most dangerous medi-
" cine to the horse.   Doses of niter, digitalis, and tartar emetic,
" in the proportion of three ounces of the first, one of the second,
" and one and a half of the third, may be given, morning and
" evening, until the animal begins to amend, when the dose may
" be reduced to one-half.   The horse must be warmly clothed,
" but kept in a cool box.   As he recovers, his skin should be
" gently rubbed with a brush, if it do not irritate him ; but his
" legs *must* be constantly and thoroughly hand-rubbed and ban-
" daged.   He should not be coaxed to eat, but may have a little
" hay to amuse him, cold mashes and green meat, but on no
" account a particle of oats.   Eight-and-forty hours generally
" decides the question of death or life.   But in case of recovery,
" it is necessary long to watch for a relapse, which is of frequent,
" one might say of general, occurrence.   It is to be met at once
" by the same energetic treatment.   And now, one word to the
" owner of a horse which has had one bad attack of inflammation,
" either of the lungs or of the bowels.   Get rid of him as soon
" as possible !   It is ten to one that he will have another, and
" another, and, as in the former instance, end by becoming
" broken-winded,—in the latter by being useless, from a nearly
" chronic state of the disease."

*   *   *   *   *   *   *

" COMMON COUGH is generally subdued without much diffi-
" culty, though it often becomes of most serious consequence
" if neglected.   It is accompanied by a heightened pulse ; a slight
" discharge from the nose and eyes, a rough coat, and a dimin-
" ished appetite, being its symptoms.   The horse should be kept
" warm, fed on mashes, and should have a dose or two of medi-
" cine.   If the cough be very obstinate, bleeding may be necessary."

The following further directions by the same author contain
valuable information for all owners of horses :—

" In giving medicine, if balls be used, they should never
" weigh above an ounce and a half, or be above an inch in
" diameter, and three in length. The horse should be lashed in
" the stall, the tongue should be drawn gently out with the left
" hand on the off side of the mouth, and fixed there, not by con-
" tinuing to pull at it, but by pressing the fingers against the side
" of the lower jaw. The ball is then taken between the tips of
" the fingers of the right hand, the arm being bared and passed
" rapidly up the mouth, as near the palate as possible, until it
" reaches the root of the tongue, when it is delivered with a
" slight jerk, the hand is withdrawn, and the tongue being re-
" leased, the ball is forced down into the œsophagus. Its passage
" should be watched down the left side of the throat, and if it do
" not pass immediately, a slight tap under the chin will easily
" cause the horse to swallow it. The only safe purgative for a
" horse is Barbadoes aloes; or the flour of the Croton bean, for
" some peculiar purposes, but its drastic nature renders it unde-
" sirable as a general aperient. When aloes are used, care should
" be taken to have them new, as they speedily lose their power,
" and they should be freshly mixed. Very mild doses only should
" be used; four or five drams are amply sufficient, if the horse
" has been prepared, as he should be, by being fed, for two days at
" least, entirely on mashes, which will cause a small dose to have
" a beneficial effect, equal to double the quantity administered to a
" horse not duly prepared for it. The immense doses of eight,
" nine, ten, and even twelve drams, which were formerly in vogue,
" and which are still favored by grooms, hostlers, and carters, are
" utterly exploded; and it is well known that eight or nine good
" fluid evacuations are all that can be desired, and far safer than
" twice the number.

" Four and a half drams of Barbadoes aloes, with olive or lin-
" seed oil and molasses, sufficient to form a mass in the proportion
" of eight of the aloes to one of the oil and three of the molasses,
" is the best general ball, though often four drams given after a
" sufficiency of mashes or green food, will accomplish all that is
" needed or desirable. Castor oil is a most dangerous and uncer-

26

" tain medicine. Linseed oil is not much better. Olive oil is
" safe, but weak. Epsom salt is inefficient, except in enormous
" doses, and is then dangerous. It is, however, excellent, given
" in clysters of weak gruel, which, by the way, except where
" very searching and thorough purging is required, as in cases of
" mange or grease, is by far the safest, most agreeable, and mild-
" est way of purging the horse, and evacuating his bowels.
" Where, however, his intestines are overloaded with fat, where
" he shows signs of surfeit, or where it is necessary to prepare
" him to undergo some great change of system, as from a long
" run at grass to a hot stable, or *vice versa*, a mild course of two
" or three doses of physic, with a clear interval of a week between
" the setting of one dose and the giving of another, is necessary,
" and cannot be properly dispensed with.

" COSTIVENESS.—Ordinary cases can generally be conquered
" without medicine, by diet, such as hop or bran mashes, green
" meat, and carrots ; but where it is obstinate, the rectum should
" be cleared of dry fæces by passing the naked arm, well greased,
" up the anus ; and the bowels should be then thoroughly evacu-
" ated by clysters of thin gruel, with half an ounce of Barbadoes
" aloes, or half a pound of Epsom salts dissolved in it. If the
" patent syringe be used, the injection will reach the colon and
" cœcum, and dispose them also to evacuate their contents."

   *   *   *   *   *   *   *

" STRANGLES, or colt-distemper, is a disease which shows itself
" in all young horses, and from which, when they have once
" passed through its ordeal, they have no more to fear. It is pre-
" ceded by some derangement of circulation, quickening of the
" pulse, some fever, cough, and sore throat. The parts around
" the throat swell, the maxillary glands are swollen and tender,
" and sometimes the parotids also. The animal refuses to drink,
" and often declines his food. There is a flow of saliva from the
" mouth, and a semi-purulent discharge from the nose. The
" jaws, throat, and glands of the neck should be poulticed with
" steaming mashes, the skin stimulated by means of a liquid blis-
" ter, and the head steamed in order to promote suppuration. As

" soon as fluctuation can be perceived, the swelling should be
" lanced, and a rowel introduced, to keep the abscess open and
" the discharge flowing for a few days. The animal should have
" walking exercise, and be treated with green food until the
" symptoms abate, when he will require liberal and generous food
" to recruit his strength.

" WORMS are sometimes troublesome to a horse, but in a far
" less degree than is generally supposed. Botts have long since
" been proved to be perfectly harmless while they are within the
" stomach,—all the stories of their eating through its coats being
" pure *myths*, although they are very often troublesome after they
" have passed out of the œsophagus and rectum, and begin to
" adhere to the orifice of the anus. Common purgatives will
" often bring away vast numbers of the long, white worm, *teres*
" *lumbricus*, which occasionally, when existing in great numbers,
" consume too large a proportion of the animal's food, and pro-
" duce a tight skin, a tucked-up belly, and a rough coat. Calo-
" mel should never be given, as it too frequently is, for the
" removal of these worms, which will readily yield to balls of two
" drams of tartar emetic, one scruple of ginger, with molasses and
" linseed oil *quantum suff.*, given alternate mornings, half an
" hour before feeding time. The smaller worm, *ascaris*, which
" often causes serious irritation about the fundament, is best re-
" moved by injecting a quart of linseed oil, or an ounce of aloes
" dissolved in warm water, which is a most effectual remedy.

" DISEASES OF THE BLADDER are many, serious, and often
" mistreated. They require, however, so much skill and so ac-
" curate a diagnosis, that none but a regular practitioner should
" pretend to treat them. Simple difficulty of staling can generally
" be relieved by cleansing the sheath with the hand, and giving
" gentle doses of niter. These are most of the simpler diseases
" which may be simply and successfully treated at home, and with
" which every horsekeeper ought to be at least superficially and
" generally acquainted. We shall touch upon the subjects of ac-
" cidents, strains, simple lameness, contusions, and the like, which
" can often be perfectly cured by cold lotions, or simple warm

" fomentations, without any further or more difficult process,
" though ignorant persons make much of them, as if their cure
" proved marvelous skill and required magnificent appliances.

" Before proceeding to the consideration of simple accidents and
" their treatment, we shall devote a few words to an affection of
" the feet, or, to speak more correctly, heels, which, although not
" exactly an accident, is not a natural disease, but arises from filth,
" neglect, cold, wet, and the omission to clean and dry the feet
" and legs of the horse, after work and exposure to weather. It
" has been rightly called the disgrace, as it is the bane, of inferior
" stables both in the city and the country, but more commonly in
" the latter, where, to pay any attention to the legs and feet of a
" farm-horse, is an almost unheard-of act of chivalric Quixotism.
" This is the ailment known in England as the 'grease,' in the
" United States, generally, as the 'scratches.' It is perfectly easy
" to be prevented, and easy to be cured if taken in the first
" instance; but if neglected and allowed to become virulent, is
" nearly incurable.

" GREASE.—The first appearance of 'grease,' which is caused
" by the feet and heels being left wet after work in muddy soil,
" and exposed to a draft of cold air, is a dry and scurfy state of
" the skin, with redness, heat, and itching. If neglected, the hair
" drops off, the heels swell, the skin assumes a glazed appearance,
" is covered with pustules, cracks open and emits a thin, glairy
" discharge, which soon becomes very offensive. In the last,
" worst, and incurable stage, the leg, half-way to the hock, is
" covered with thick, horny scabs, divided into lozenge-shaped
" lumps by deep cracks, whence issues an extremely offensive
" matter. In this stage the disease is called 'grapy heels,' and is
" scarcely curable. In the first stage all that is necessary is
" frequent washing with tepid water and Castile soap, and the ap-
" plication of a flannel bandage, evenly applied over the whole
" limb, moistened with warm water and allowed to dry on the
" part. An ointment of one dram of sugar of lead in an ounce
" of lard, will supple, soften, and relieve the parts. The cracks
" may be washed with a solution of four ounces of alum in a pint

" of water, which will in most cases suffice. A dose of medicine
" is now desirable, for which the horse should be well prepared by
" the administration of bran-mashes, as before advised, for a couple
" of days; after which, a ball of four or five drams of Barbadoes
" aloes will suffice. An injection will not answer in this case, as
" the object is not to empty the bowels, but to cool the system.
" The horse should be fed on mashes, carrots, and green meat ;
" oats, Indian corn, and high food of all kinds are to be avoided
" as too heating.

" When the disease has reached the second stage, the physick-
" ing must be persevered in for three doses, with the regular
" intervals ; carrot poultices must be applied to the heels. This
" is best done by drawing an old stocking minus the foot, over
" the horse's hoof, confining it around the fetlock joint with a
" loose bandage, and filling it from above with carrots, boiled and
" mashed into a soft pulp. This mass should be applied tolerably
" hot, and repeated daily for three days. When removed, the
" heels should be anointed with an ointment of one part of rosin,
" three parts of lard, melted together, and one part of calamine
" powder added when the first mixture is cooling. The cracks
" should be persistently washed with the alum lotion, and the
" bandage applied whenever the poultices are not on the part.
" The benefit of carrot poultices for all affections where there is
" fever, swelling, and a pustular condition of the skin, cannot be
" over-rated. Stocked legs and capped hocks we have seen com-
" pletely cured by them ; and, on one occasion, at least, we have
" known incipient farcy to give way before their emollient and
" healing influence. Where the 'grease' has degenerated into
" the 'grapes,' the aid of a veterinary surgeon must be invoked;
" but he will rarely succeed, as the ailment is now all but incurable.
" It is, however, only the height of neglect which ever allows the
" ailment to degenerate into this filthy and malignant stage of
" disease."

In the treatment of thrush, or any injury to the sole of the hoof,
perfect cleansing twice a day and a stuffing of the sole inside of
the hoof with a mixture of tar, cow-dung, and soft clay, will

usually effect a cure. Strains and bruises are best treated by simple fomentations of hot water, to which a little vinegar may with advantage be added; and if the strain is in the pastern joint the foot should be placed in a pail full of water, which should be kept by repeated additions as hot as the animal will bear. After the removal of the foot from the pail, the part should be covered with thick bandages of cloth, or wound with straw ropes; and very warm water should be frequently poured upon it.

Farriery includes various operations, such as castration, nicking, bleeding, clipping and singeing, trimming the hair, etc.; and ample directions concerning its processes are given by Herbert, Youatt, Stewart, Spooner, and others. The following are Mr. Youatt's directions for castration :—

"The period at which this operation may be best performed "depends much on the breed and form of the colt, and the pur-"pose for which he is destined. For the common agricultural "horse, the age of four or five months will be the most proper "time, or, at least, before he is weaned. Few horses are lost "when cut at that age. Care, however, should be taken that the "weather is not too hot nor the flies too numerous.

"If the horse is designed either for the carriage or for heavy "draught, the farmer should not think of castrating him until he "is at least a twelvemonth old; and even then the colt should be "carefully examined. If he is thin and spare about the neck and "shoulders, and low in the withers, he will materially improve by "remaining uncut another six months; but if his fore-quarters "are fairly developed at the age of a twelvemonth, the operation "should not be delayed, lest he become heavy and gross before, "and perhaps has begun too decidedly to have a will of his own. "No specific age, then, can be fixed; but the castration should "be performed rather late in the spring or early in the autumn, "when the air is temperate, and particularly when the weather "is dry.

"No preparation is necessary for the sucking colt, but it may "be prudent to bleed and to physic one of more advanced age. "In the majority of cases, no after-treatment will be necessary,

" except that the animal should be sheltered from intense heat,
" and more particularly from wet."

Concerning the practices of docking and nicking, which, until
recently, were almost universal, Herbert says :—

" These barbarous methods of depriving the horse of his natural
" form and appearance, in order to make him conform to the
" fashion of the time, are, fortunately, very fast going into disuse.
" If the tail of the horse were given to him for no good purpose,
" and if it were not a design of nature that he should have the
" power of moving it forcibly to his sides, there might be some
" excuse for cutting it off, within a few inches of his body, or for
" separating the muscles at its sides to lessen this power ; but that
" this is not the case, must be acknowledged by all who have seen
" how a horse, whose tail has been abridged by ' docking,' or
" weakened by nicking, is annoyed by flies.

" If a horse has a trick of throwing dirt on his rider's clothing,
" this may be prevented by cutting off the *hair* of the tail, below
" the end of the bones, as is the custom with hunters in England,
" where the hair is cut squarely off about eight or ten inches
" above the hocks.

" No apology is offered for not giving in this work a description
" of these two operations ; they are so barbarous and so senseless,
" that they are going very rapidly out of fashion, and it is to be
" hoped that they will ere long have become obsolete, as has the
" cropping of the ears, formerly so common in England.

" A more humane way of setting up the horse's tail, to
" give him a more stylish appearance, is by simply weighting it,
" for a few hours each day, in the stall, until it attains the desired
" elevation. This is done by having two pulleys at the top of the
" stall, one at each side, through which are passed two ropes,
" which come together and are fastened to the tail, the ropes hav-
" ing at their other ends weights, (bags of sand or of shot are very
" good for the purpose,) which must be light at first, and may be
" increased from day to day. The weighting should be continued
" until the tail has taken a permanent position as desired. It is
" true that this method requires a somewhat longer time than that

" of cutting the muscles, but while it is being done the horse is
" never off his work, and he suffers infinitely less pain.

" The method of nicking or pricking, as usually performed in
" this country, is not quite so cruel or so hazardous as the cutting
" of the muscles ; it is thus described in Stewart's ' Stable Book ':—

" 'The tail has four cords, two upper and two lower. The
" upper ones raise the tail, the lower ones depress it, and these
" last alone are to be cut. Take a sharp penknife with a long
" slender blade ; insert the blade between the bone and un-
" der cord, two inches from the body ; place the thumb of the
" hand holding the knife against the under part of the tail, and
" opposite the blade. Then press the blade toward the thumb
" against the cord, and cut the cord off, but do not let the knife
" cut through the skin. The cord is firm, and it will easily be
" known when it is cut off. The thumb will tell when to desist
" that the skin may not be cut. Sever the cord twice on each
" side in the same manner. Let the cuts be two inches apart.
" The cord is nearly destitute of sensation ; yet, when the tail is
" pricked in the old manner, the wound to the skin and flesh is
" severe, and much fever is induced, and it takes a long time to
" heal. But with this method the horse's tail will not bleed, nor
" will it be sore, under ordinary circumstances, more than three
" days ; and he will be pulleyed and his tail made in one-half of
" the time required by the old method.'"

In this connection it is important to give some attention to the
question of shoeing horses ; a department of farriery in which the
world has received much assistance from the little work of Mr.
Miles.* He illustrates the construction of the foot by the following cuts, (Figs. 68 to 70,) which, with their accompanying
description and the following extracts from his work, will be
readily understood :—

" The hoof is divided into horny crust or wall, sole, and frog.

" The horny crust is secreted by the numerous blood-vessels,
" that soft, protruding band which encircles the upper edge of the

* Miles on the Horse's Foot. O. Judd & Co., New York.

" hoof, immediately beneath the termination of the hair ; and is
" divided into toe, quarters, heels, and bars.   Its texture is in-
" sensible, but elastic throughout its whole extent ; and, yielding
" to the weight of the horse, allows the horny sole to descend,

Fig. 68.

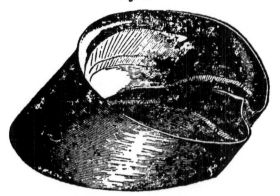

" whereby much inconvenient concussion of the internal parts of
" the foot is avoided.   But if a large portion of the circumference
" of the foot be fettered by iron and nails, it is obvious that that
" portion, at least, cannot expand as before ; and the beautiful and

Fig. 69.

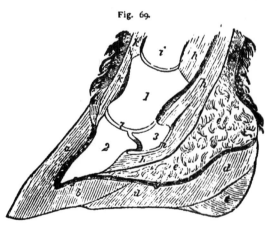

" efficient apparatus for effecting this necessary elasticity, being
" no longer allowed to act by reason of these restraints, becomes
" altered in structure : and the continued operation of the same
" causes, in the end, circumscribes the elasticity to those parts

" alone where no nails have been driven,—giving rise to a train
" of consequences destructive to the soundness of the foot, and
" fatal to the usefulness of the horse.

" The toe of the forefoot is the thickest and strongest portion
" of the hoof, and is in consequence less expansive than any other
" part, and therefore better calculated to resist the effect of the
" nails and shoe. The thickness of the horn gradually diminishes
" toward the quarters and heels, particularly on the inner side of
" the foot, whereby the power of yielding and expanding to the
" weight of the horse is proportionably increased, clearly indicat-
" ing that those parts cannot be nailed to an unyielding bar of iron,

Fig. 70.

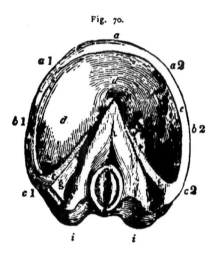

" without a most mischievous interference with the natural func-
" tions of the foot.   In the hind-foot, the greatest thickness of
" horn will be found at the quarters and heels, and not, as in the
" forefoot, at the toe.   This difference in the thickness of horn
" is beautifully adapted·to the inequality of the weight which each
" has to sustain, the force with which it is applied, and the por-
" tions of the hoof upon which it falls.   The toe of the forefoot
" encounters the combined force and weight of the forehand and
" body, and consequently, in a state of nature, is exposed to con-
" siderable wear and tear, and calls for greater strength and sub-
" stance of horn than is needed by any portion of the hind-

" foot, where the duty of supporting the hinder parts alone is
" distributed over the quarters and heels of both sides of the foot.

" The bars are continuations of the wall, reflected at the heels
" toward the center of the foot, where they meet in a point, leav-
" ing a triangular space between them for the frog.

" The whole inner surface of the horny crust, from the center
" of the toe to the point where the bars meet, is everywhere lined
" with innumerable narrow, thin, and projecting horny plates,
" which extend in a slanting direction from the upper edge of the
" wall to the line of junction between it and the sole, and possess
" great elasticity. These projecting plates are the means of greatly
" extending the surface of attachment of the hoof to the coffin-
" bone, which is likewise covered by a similar arrangement of pro-
" jecting plates, but of a highly vascular and sensitive character ;
" and these, dovetailing with the horny projections above named,
" constitute a union combining strength and elasticity in a won-
" derful degree.

" The horny sole covers the whole inferior surface of the foot,
" excepting the frog. In a well-formed foot it presents an arched
" appearance and possesses considerable elasticity, by virtue of
" which it ascends and descends, as the weight above is either sud-
" denly removed from it or forcibly applied to it. This descending
" property of the sole calls for our special consideration in direct-
" ing the form of the shoe ; for, if the shoe be so formed that the
" horny sole rests upon it, it cannot descend lower; and the sen-
" sible sole above, becoming squeezed between the edges of the
" coffin-bone and the horn, produces inflammation, and perhaps
" abscess. The effect of this squeezing of the sensible sole is
" most commonly witnessed at the angle of the inner heel, where
" the descending heel of the coffin-bone, forcibly pressing the vas-
" cular sole upon the horny sole, ruptures a small blood-vessel,
" and produces what is called a corn, but which is, in fact, a bruise.

" The horny frog occupies the greater part of the triangular
" space between the bars, and extends from the hindermost part
" of the foot to the center of the sole, just over the point where
" the bars meet ; but is united to them only at their upper edge :

"the sides remain unattached and separate, and form the channels
"called the 'Commissures.'"

The principles on which Miles bases his directions for shoeing
are, that, as at every step of the horse the crust or wall of the
hoof expands and contracts, this alternate movement being necessary to the natural performance of the act, the shoeing should be
so done as in nowise to prevent it; that, as the bars of the hoof
are naturally intended to receive a very large proportion of the
burden in the stepping of the horse, the shoe should be broad at
the heel and should rest well upon them, they not having been cut
away, as is the too frequent custom, so as not to touch it; that,
as the sole of the hoof inside of the wall is much subject to injury
if constantly pressed, the inner surface of the shoe should be so
beveled off as to allow it to be easily cleaned out and to render it
little likely that pebble-stones or other matters will lodge inside of
it; and that the shoeing should be so done that there will be little
danger of the hoof working forward off of the shoe.

Mr. Miles' system of shoeing, which is only a modification of
the commonest practices, requires that the hoof be exactly fitted by
the shoe, and that no effort be made to fit it to an improperly
shaped shoe, the assumption being that nature understands, better
than the blacksmith does, what is necessary in this respect. The
manner in which the shoe supports the wall and bars of the hoof
is shown in Fig. 71.   The shoe itself, with its beveled upper
surface, the projecting point in front to prevent the hoof from slip-
ping forward, and the broad heel, are shown in Fig. 72.   It will
be seen that this shoe has but six nail-holes, only two of which
are upon the inside, and none of which reach farther back than
the center of the hoof.   This is the chief improvement that Mr.
Miles introduced, and it has come into quite general use among
all good horsemen.   So far from the security of the shoe being
lessened by this apparent insufficiency of nailing, it is found in
practice that it is actually increased.   I have had my own horses
(some of them saddle-horses, doing hard work over rough, moun-
tainous roads) shod in strict accordance with this principle, for
more than ten years past; and the shoes have almost invariably

remained in their places until the growth of the hoof, or the wearing out of the iron, required them to be renewed or removed.

When the nailing is continued around on the inside as far as

Fig. 71.

the center of the hoof, and on the outside still farther to the rear, the shoe acts as an iron clamp to prevent the expansion of the hoof, and the effort toward expansion being constantly exercised

Fig. 72.

at every step that the horse takes, the nails become loosened in the wall, and the shoe is much more likely to be cast. With the smaller number of nails, all of them being placed in that part of the hoof where the movement in expansion and contraction is very slight, that part of the hoof which is required to make the greatest movement is left free to move over the shoe; and the natural action of the parts is preserved, so far as, in the artificial condition, it is possible that it should be.   Concerning the paring of the hoof in shoeing, Youatt says :—

"The act of paring is a work of much more labor than the proprietor of the horse often imagines.   The smith, except he is overlooked, will frequently give himself as little trouble about it as he can; and that portion of horn which, in the unshod foot, would be worn away by contact with the ground, is suffered to accumulate month after month, until the elasticity of the sole is destroyed, and it can no longer descend, and its other functions are impeded, and foundation is laid for corn, and contraction, and navicular disease, and inflammation.   That portion of horn should be left on the foot which will defend the internal parts from being bruised, and yet suffer the external sole to descend.   How is this to be ascertained?   The strong pressure of the thumb of the smith will be the best guide.   The buttress, that most destructive of all instruments, being, except on very particular occasions, banished from every respectable forge, the smith sets to work with his drawing-knife and removes the growth of horn, until the sole will yield, although in the slightest possible degree, to the strong pressure of his thumb.   The proper thickness of horn will then remain.

"The quantity of horn to be removed, in order to leave the proper degree of thickness, will vary with different feet.   From the strong foot, a great deal must be taken.   From the concave foot the horn may be removed, until the sole will yield to a moderate pressure.   From the flat foot, little need be pared; while the pumiced foot should be deprived of nothing but the ragged parts.

"The crust should be reduced to a perfect level all round, but left a little higher than the sole, or the sole will be bruised by its pressure on the edge of the seating.

"The heels will require considerable attention.   From the stress which is thrown on the inner heel, and from the weakness of the quarter there, the horn usually wears away considerably faster than it would on the outer one; and if an equal portion of horn were pared from it, it would be left lower than the outer heel.   The smith should therefore accommodate his paring to the comparative wear of the heel, and be exceedingly careful to leave them precisely level."

Miles recommends that the frog of the hoof be left entirely to itself, and never touched with the knife at all, for the reason that, as fast as the superfluous horn is formed, it will be removed by a natural shelling, and its raggedness can do no harm.   Within a few months after the paring of the frog has ceased, it will have the character of the frog of a horse at pasture, which is always, when in a state of health, sound and smooth.

THE GOODENOUGH SYSTEM OF HORSESHOEING.

The Goodenough system has now had a sufficient trial to establish its claim to general favor. It has been adopted, after critical tests, for the U. S. Cavalry service, and for some of the largest and best-managed omnibus and street-railroad companies in New York and Boston. It is now being favorably introduced in Europe. Its purpose is simply to protect the *rim* of the hoof from becoming broken and worn, to raise the *sole* of the foot from the ground sufficiently to save it from bruising, and *to allow the back part of the frog to rest on the ground, and to relieve the shock of the step* by the "buffer"-like action for which Nature intended it. The process is a simple one, any good shoeing-smith being able to apply it with no stock beyond a supply of "Goodenough" shoes. Where these shoes cannot be procured, it will answer a good purpose to use narrow "tips," drawn down quite thin at the rear, so as to allow the frog to come to the ground. The cutting of the foot should be simply what is needed to compensate for the loss of natural wear. The frog should not be cut *at all*, and the corn-points inside the bars should be pared down barely enough to make sure that they are below the bearing of the shoe.

As to the need for applying to a veterinary surgeon, except for accidents, it may be said that with a clean skin and abundance of pure air, protection against cold drafts, and suitable food administered regularly and in proper quantity, it will be but rarely that horses of good constitution will require any further remedy than the curry-comb, the bran-bin, and warm water afford.

HORNED CATTLE.

In the treatment of dairy stock and other horned cattle, the extent to which it becomes necessary to resort to medical or surgical treatment, except for very simple ailments, will be, in a great degree, in proportion to the observance or neglect of the fundamental principles of breeding and management. Long-continued in-and-in breeding, or the breeding from sires and dams tainted with hereditary diseases, or weakened by neglect or ill-treatment, will inevitably result in the deterioration of the stock ; and medical treatment will become more and more necessary, while such injurious breeding is continued. Deprivation of pure air, pure water, comfortable quarters, good and varied food, will also almost inevitably introduce troublesome and expensive diseases.

The same may be said in this case as has just been said of the treatment of horses, that is, that simple remedies sensibly applied, the calling in of skillful medical assistants whenever medical assistance is required, and the keeping of the animal under all circumstances in the healthiest possible condition, will generally effect the desired cure, so that blistering and bleeding and purging need almost never be resorted to, and should never be adopted without sound advice.

Flint gives the following directions for the treatment of several of the more prevalent complaints :—

"GARGET is an inflammation of the internal substance of the "udder.   One or more of the teats, or whole sections of the udder "become enlarged and thickened, hot, tender, and painful.   The "milk coagulates and thickens in the bag and causes inflammation "where it is deposited, which is accompanied by fever.   It most "commonly occurs in young cows after calving, especially when "in too high condition.   The secretion of milk is very much "lessened, and in very bad cases, stopped altogether.   Sometimes "the milk is thick, and mixed with blood.   Often, also, in severe "cases, the hind extremities, as the hip-joint, hock, or fetlock, are "swollen and inflamed to such an extent that the animal cannot "rise.   The simplest remedy, in mild cases, is to put the calf to "its mother several times a day.   This will remove the flow of "milk, and often dispel the congestion.

"Sometimes the udder is so much swollen that the cow will not "permit the calf to suck.   If the fever increases, the appetite "declines, and rumination ceases.   In this stage of the complaint "the advice of a scientific veterinary practitioner is required.   A "dose of purging medicine, and frequent washing of the udder in "*mild* cases, are usually successful.   The physic should consist "of Epsom salts one pound, ginger half an ounce, nitrate of po- "tassa half an ounce, dissolved in a quart of boiling water ; then "add a gill of molasses, and give to the cow lukewarm.   Diet mod- "erate : that is, on bran ; or, if in summer, green food.   There

" are various medicines for the different forms and stages of garget,
" which, if the above medicine fails, can be properly prescribed
" only by a skillful veterinary practitioner.

" It is important that the udder should be frequently examined,
" as matter may be forming which should be immediately released.
" Various causes are assigned for this disease, such as exposure to
" cold and wet, or the want of proper care and attention in partu-
" rition."

[In addition to the foregoing, or, indeed, before any medicine is
used, it is strongly to be recommended that copious and frequent
spongings with cool water be thoroughly tried, as many cases of
apparently obdurate character have yielded completely to this
simple treatment.]

      *   *   *   *   *   *   *

" PUERPERAL OR MILK FEVER.—Calving is often attended with
" feverish excitement. The change of powerful action from the
" womb to the udder causes much constitutional disturbance and
" local inflammation. A cow is subject to nervousness in such
" circumstances, which sometimes extends to the whole system,
" and causes puerperal fever. This complaint is called *dropping*
" after calving, because it succeeds that process. The prominent
" symptom is a loss of power over the motion of the hind extremi-
" ties, and inability to stand ; sometimes loss of sensibility in
" these parts, so that a deep puncture with a pin or other sharp
" instrument is unfelt.

" This disease is much to be dreaded by the farmer, on account
" of the high state of excitement and the local inflammation.
" Either from neglect or ignorance, the malady is not discovered
" until the manageable symptoms have passed, and extreme
" debility has appeared. The animal is often first seen lying
" down, unable to rise ; prostration of the strength and violent
" fever are brought on by inflammation of the womb. But soon
" a general inflammatory action succeeds, rapid and violent, with
" complete prostration of all the vital forces, bidding defiance to
" the best-selected remedies.

27

"Cows in very high condition, and cattle removed from low
"keeping to high feeding, are the most liable to puerperal fever.
"It occurs most frequently during the hot weather of summer,
"and then it is most dangerous. When it occurs in winter, cows
"sometimes recover. In hot weather they usually die.

"Milk fever may be induced by the hot drinks often given after
"calving. A young cow at her first calving is rarely attacked
"with it. Great milkers are most commonly subject to it ; but
"all cows have generally more or less fever at calving. A little
"addition to it, by improper treatment or neglect, will prevent
"the secretion of milk ; and thus the milk, being thrown back
"into the system, will increase the inflammation.

"This disease sometimes shows itself in the short space of two
"or three hours after calving, but often not under two or three
"days. If four or five days have passed, the cow may generally
"be considered safe. The earliest symptoms of this disease are
"as follows :—

"The animal is restless, frequently shifting her position ; occa-
"sionally pawing and heaving at the flanks. Muzzle hot and
"dry, the mouth open, and tongue out at one side ; countenance
"wild ; eyes staring. She moans often, and soon becomes very
"irritable. Delirium follows ; she grates her teeth, foams at the
"mouth, tosses her head about, and frequently injures herself.
"From the first the udder is hot, enlarged, and tender ; and if
"this swelling is attended by a suspension of milk, the cause is
"clear. As the case is inflammatory, its treatment must be in
"accordance ; and it is usually subdued without much difficulty.
"Mr. Youatt says : ' The animal should be bled, and the quantity
"regulated by the impression made upon the circulation,—from
"six to ten quarts often before the desired effect is produced.'
"He wrote at a time when bleeding was adopted as the universal
"cure, and before the general reasoning and treatment of diseases
"of the human system was applied to similar diseases of animals.
"The cases are very rare, indeed, where the physician of the pres-
"ent day finds it necessary to bleed in diseases of the human
"subject ; and they are equally rare, I apprehend, where it is

" really necessary or judicious to bleed for the diseases of animals.
" A more humane and equally effectual course will be the fol-
" lowing :—

" A pound to one and a half pounds of Epsom or Glauber's
" salts, according to the size and condition of the animal, should
" be given, dissolved in a quart of boiling water ; and when dis-
" solved, add pulverized red pepper, a quarter of an ounce, car-
" away, do., do., ginger, do., do. ; mix, and add a gill of molasses,
" and give lukewarm. If this medicine does not act on the
" bowels, the quantity of ginger, capsicum, and caraway, must be
" doubled. The insensible stomach must be roused. When
" purging in an early stage is begun, the fever will more readily
" subside. After the operation of the medicine, sedatives may be
" given, if necessary.

" The digestive function first fails, when the secondary or low
" state of fever comes on. The food undischarged ferments ; the
" stomach and intestines are inflated with gas, and swell rapidly.
" The nervous system is also attacked, and the poor beast stag-
" gers. The hind extremities show the weakness ; the cow falls,
" and cannot rise ; her head is turned on one side, where it rests ;
" her limbs are palsied. The treatment in this stage must depend
" on the existence and degree of fever. The pulse will be the
" only true guide. If it is weak, wavering, and irregular, we must
" avoid depleting, purgative agents. The blood flows through the
" arteries, impelled by the action of the heart, and its pulsations
" can be very distinctly felt by pressing the finger upon almost
" any of these arteries that is not too thickly covered by fat
" or the cellular tissues of the skin, especially where it can
" be pressed upon some hard or bony substance beneath it. The
" most convenient place is directly at the back part of the lower
" jaw, where a large artery passes over the edge of the jaw-bone
" to ramify on the face. The natural pulse of a full-grown ox,
" will vary from about forty-eight to fifty-five beats a minute ;
" that of a cow is rather quicker, especially near the time of calv-
" ing ; and that of a calf is quicker than that of a cow. But a
" very much quicker rate than that indicated will show a feverish

" state, or inflammation; and a much slower pulsation indicates
" debility of some kind."

*   *   *   *   *   *   *

" No powerful medicines should be used without discretion; for
" in the milder forms of the disease, as the simple palsy of the
" hinder extremities, the treatment, though of a similar character,
" should be less powerful, and every effort should be made for the
" comfort of the cow, by providing a thick bed of straw, and rais-
" ing the fore-quarters to assist the efforts of nature, while all filth
" should be promptly and carefully removed.   She may be covered
" with a warm cloth, and warm gruel should be frequently offered
" to her, and light mashes.   An attempt should be made several
" times a day to bring milk from the teats.   The return of milk
" is an indication of speedy recovery.

" Milch cows in too high condition appear to have a constitu-
" tional tendency to this complaint, and one attack of it predisposes
" them to another.

" SIMPLE FEVER.—This may be considered as increased arterial
" action, with or without any local affection; or it may be the
" consequence of the sympathy of the system with the morbid
" condition of some particular part.   The first is pure or idiopathic
" fever; the other, symptomatic fever.   Pure fever is of frequent
" occurrence in cattle.   Symptoms as follows: muzzle dry; ru-
" mination slow or entirely suspended; respiration slightly accel-
" erated; the horn at the root hot, and its other extremity
" frequently cold; pulse quick; bowels constipated; coat staring,
" and the cow is usually seen separated from the rest of the herd.
" In slight attacks a cathartic of salts, sulphur, and ginger is
" sufficient.   But if the common fever is neglected, or improperly
" treated, it may assume, after a time, a local determination, as
" pleurisy, or inflammation of the lungs or bowels.   In such cases
" the above remedy would be insufficient, and a veterinary surgeon,
" to manage the case, would be necessary.   Symptomatic fever is
" more dangerous, and is commonly the result of injury, the
" neighboring parts sympathizing with the injured part.   Cattle
" become unwell, are stinted in their feed, have a dose of physic,

" and in a few days are well; still, a fever may terminate in some
" local affection. But in both cases pure fever is the primary
" disease.

" A more dangerous form of fever is that known as SYMPTOM-
" ATIC. As we have said, cattle are not only subject to fever of
" common intensity, but to symptomatic fever, and thousands die
" annually from its effects. But the young and the most thriving
" are its victims. There are few premonitory symptoms of
" symptomatic fever. It often appears without any previous indi-
" cations of illness. The animal stands with her neck extended,
" her eyes protruding and red, muzzle dry, nostrils expanded,
" breath hot, base of the horn hot, mouth open, pulse full,
" breathing quick. She is often moaning; rumination and appe-
" tite are suspended; she soon becomes more uneasy; changes her
" position often. Unless these symptoms are speedily removed,
" she dies in a few hours. The name of the ailment, inflam-
" matory or symptomatic fever, shows the treatment necessary,
" which must commence with purging. Salts here, as in most
" inflammatory diseases, are the most reliable. From a pound to
" a pound and a half, with ginger and sulphur, is a dose, dissolved
" in warm water or thin gruel. If this does not operate in twelve
" hours, give half the dose, and repeat once in twelve hours, until
" the bowels are freed. After the operation of the medicine the
" animal is relieved. Then sedative medicines may be given.
" Sal ammoniac, one dram; powdered niter, two drams, should
" be administered in thin gruel, two or three times a day, if
" required.

" TYPHUS FEVER, common in some countries, is little known
" here among cattle.

" TYPHOID FEVER sometimes follows intense inflammatory
" action, and is considered the second stage of it. This form of
" fever is usually attended with diarrhea. It is a debilitating com-
" plaint, and is sometimes followed by diseases known as black
" tongue, black leg, or quarter-evil. The cause of typhoid fever
" is involved in obscurity. It may be proper to say that copious
" drinks of oatmeal gruel, with tincture of red pepper, a diet

" of bran, warmth to the body, and pure air, are great essentials in
" the treatment of this disease.

" The barbarous practices of boring the horns, cutting the tail,
" and others equally absurd, should at once and forever be dis-
" carded by every farmer and dairyman.   Alternate heat or cold-
" ness of the horn is only a symptom of this and other fevers, and
" has nothing to do with their cause.   The horns are not diseased
" any further than a determination of blood to the head causes
" a sympathetic heat, while an unnatural distribution of blood,
" from exposure or other cause, may make them cold.

" In all cases of this kind, if any thing is done, it should be an
" effort to assist nature to regulate the animal system, by rousing
" the digestive organs to their natural action, by a light food, or,
" if necessary, a mild purgative medicine, followed by light stimu-
" lants.

" The principal purgative medicines in use for neat cattle are
" Epsom salts, linseed oil, and sulphur.   A pound of salts will
" ordinarily be sufficient to purge a full-grown cow.

" A slight purgative drink is often very useful for cows soon
" after calving, particularly if feverish, and in cases of over-feed-
" ing, when the animal will often appear dull and feverish ; but
" when the surfeiting is attended by loss of appetite, it can gen-
" erally be cured by withholding food at first, and then feeding
" but slightly till the system is renovated by dieting."

*   *   *   *   *   *   *

" The Hoove, or Hove, is brought on by a derangement of
" the digestive organs, occasioned by over-feeding on green and
" luxuriant clover, or other luxuriant food.   It is simply the dis-
" tention of the first stomach by carbonic acid gas.   In later stages,
" after fermentation of the contents of the stomach has com-
" menced, hydrogen gas is also found.   The green food being
" gathered very greedily after the animal has been kept on dry and
" perhaps unpalatable hay, is not sent forward so rapidly as it is
" received, and remains to overload and clog the stomach, till this
" organ ceases or loses the power to act upon it.   Here it becomes
" moist and heated, begins to ferment, and produces a gas which

" distends the paunch of the animal, which often swells up enor-
" mously. The cow is in great pain, breathing with difficulty, as
" if nearly suffocating. Then the body grows cold, and, unless
" relief is at hand, the cow dies.

" Prevention is both cheaper and safer than cure ; but if by
" neglect, or want of proper precaution, the animal is found in
" this suffering condition, relief must be afforded as soon as possi-
" ble, or the result will be fatal.

" A hollow flexible tube, introduced into the gullet, will some-
" times afford a temporary relief till other means can be had, by
" allowing a part of the gas to escape ; but the cause is not
" removed either by this means or by puncturing the paunch,
" which is often dangerous."

     *   *   *   *   *   *   *

" If the case has assumed an alarming character, the flexible
" tube, or probang, may be introduced, and afterward take three
" drams either of the chloride of lime or the chloride of soda,
" dissolve in a pint of water, and pour it down the throat. Lime-
" water, potash, and sulphuric ether, are often used with effect.

" In desperate cases it may be found necessary to make an in-
" cision through the paunch ; but the chloride of lime will, in most
" cases, give relief at once, by neutralizing the gas.

" CHOKING is often produced by feeding on roots, particularly
" round and uncut roots, like the potato. The animal slavers at
" the mouth, tries to raise the obstruction from the throat, often
" groans, and appears to be in great pain. Then the belly begins
" to swell, from the amount of gases in the paunch.

" The obstruction, if not too large, can sometimes be thrust
" forward by introducing a flexible rod, or tube, into the throat.
" This method, if adopted, should be attended with great care
" and patience, or the tender parts will be injured. If the ob-
" struction is low down, and a tube is to be inserted, a pint of
" olive or linseed oil first turned down the throat will so lubricate
" the parts as to aid the operation, and the power applied must be
" steady. If the gullet is torn by the carelessness of the operator,
" or the roughness of the instrument, a rupture generally results

"in serious consequences.   A hollow tube is best, and if the ob-
"ject is passed on into the paunch, the tube should remain a short
"time, to permit the gas to escape.   In case the animal is very
"badly swelled, the dose of chloride of lime, or ammonia, should
"be given, as for the hoove, after the obstruction is removed.

"Care should be taken, after the obstruction is removed, to
"allow no solid food for some days."

*Foul in the Foot, Red-Water, Hoose, Inflammation of the Glands,
Inflammation of the Lungs, Diarrhea, Dysentery, Mange, Lice,
Warbles, Loss of Cud, Constipation,* and *Diseases of Calves,* are
treated at length in Mr. Flint's work.

Abortion, which seems to assume almost the character of a contagious disease in many dairy districts, has thus far baffled every
attempt, either to detect its cause, or prevent its recurrence ; but
it is to be hoped that Dr. Dalton's Commission of the New York
State Agricultural Society will be able, as the result of their labors,
to throw some light on the question.

Happily it is not necessary in an American work to discuss the
dreaded question of the Rinderpest, which has, within the past few
years, decimated the herds of Europe.   It seems to have been
finally removed from all of those countries into which its appearance introduced so much suffering; and it is to be hoped that it
will be many years before even so slight danger of the infection
of American cattle as we have just passed will recur.

The Texas cattle disease, which has recently shown itself
in American herds, does not promise, under the vigorous treatment that it has received, to become a nationally serious question.
But it behooves all farmers to attend carefully to the facts with
which its development is attended, and to join unflinchingly in
any attempt to prevent its extension, wherever it gets a foothold.

SHEEP.

On the subject of the diseases of sheep, Dr. Henry S. Randall,* the most voluminous and the most practical American
writer upon sheep-raising, wool-growing, etc., says,—

* The Practical Shepherd.   D. D. T. Moore.   Rochester, N. Y., 1864.

" Many of the diseases of sheep which are described as com-
" paratively common in Europe, are unknown in the United
" States ; and this remark applies particularly to those which have
" proved most destructive in the former.

" I have owned sheep the entire period of my life,—a little over
" half a century,—my flock numbering at alternating periods from
" hundreds to thousands. I have for considerably more than half
" of this period been constantly concerned in their practical man-
" agement, and a deeply interested observer of them. For more
" than twenty years I have been engaged in a constant and exten-
" sive correspondence in respect to sheep and their diseases, with
" flock-masters in various portions of the United States, and have
" been in the frequent habit of inspecting flocks of every size and
" description, and I never yet have witnessed or had satisfactory
" proof brought home to me of the existence of a single case of
" hydatid, water on the brain, palsy, rot, small-pox, malignant in-
" flammatory fever, (*La Maladie de Sologne*,) blain or inflammation
" of the cellular tissue about the tongue, enteritis or inflammation
" of the coats of the intestines, acute dropsy or red-water, acute
" inflammation of the lungs, or of a whole host of other formidable
" maladies described by every European writer on the diseases of
" sheep. I do not aver that they never occur in the United States,
" but the above facts would seem to show their occurrence must
" at least be very rare, or confined to localities where they are not
" recognized.

" To correct or confirm my own impressions on this subject,
" I addressed letters a few months since, to a large number of
" highly intelligent and experienced flock-masters residing in
" various States, and in situations differing widely in respect to
" climate, soil, elevation, etc.; asking them what diseases sheep
" were subject to in their respective regions, and what remedies
" were most successfully employed for their cure. The spirit
" and substance of nearly all the replies are contained in the fol-
" lowing extract from a letter of my off-hand friend, Mr. Theodore
" C. Peters, of Darien, New York :—

" ' You ask me for our sheep diseases and for the remedies.

" After years of experience I discarded all medicines, except those
" to cure hoof-rot and scab ; and I finally cured those diseases
" cheaper by selling the sheep.   An ounce of prevention is worth
" a pound of cure.   If sheep are well kept, summer and winter,
" not over-crowded in pastures, and kept under dry and well-ven-
" tilated covers in winter, and housed when the cold fall rains
" come on, there will be no necessity for remedies of any kind.
" If not so handled, all the remedies in the world won't help them,
" and the sooner a careless, shiftless man loses his sheep, the
" better.   They are out of their misery and are not spreading
" contagious diseases among the neighboring flocks.'

" When to the two maladies above named, (hoof-rot and scab,)
" are added a very fatal but infrequent one in the spring, ordinarily
" termed grub-in-the-head, catarrh or cold, colic, parturient fever,
" (the last quite rare and mostly confined to English sheep,) and
" the few minor diseases of sheep or lambs—we have almost the
" entire list with which the American sheep-farmer is familiar.
" All the diseases named do not, in my opinion, cut off annually
" two per cent. of well-fed and really well-managed *grown* sheep !
" Nothing is more common than for years to pass by in the small
" flocks of our careful breeders, with scarcely a solitary instance
" of disease in them.   I have not space to offer any conjectures
" as to the causes of an immunity from disease so remarkable in
" comparison with the condition of England, France, and Ger-
" many, in the same particular.

" LOW TYPE OF AMERICAN SHEEP DISEASES.—A discrim-
" inating English veterinary writer, Mr. Spooner, has remarked
" that owing to its greatly weaker muscular and vascular structure,
" the diseases of the sheep are much less likely to take an inflam-
" matory type than those of the horse, (and, he might have added,
" the ox,) and that the character of its maladies is generally that of
" debility.   Mr. Spooner wrote with his eye on the mutton sheep
" of England—constantly forced forward by the most nutritious
" food, in order to attain early maturity and excessive fatness.
" Still more strongly then do his remarks apply to the ordinarily
" fed wool-producing sheep of the United States.   I long ago

" remarked that the depletory treatment by bleeding and cathartics,
" resorted to in so many of the diseases of sheep in England, is
" inapplicable and dangerous here. The American sheep, which
" has been kept in the common way, sinks from the outset, or
" after a mere transient flash of inflammatory action ; and in any
" stage of its maladies active depletion is likely to lead to fatal
" prostration.

" It is not purposed here to enter upon any explanation of the
" anatomy of the sheep, further than is necessary to give a general
" view of the principal internal structures which determine the
" form, discharge some of the principal animal functions, and
" become the seats or subjects of disease. And in treating of
" maladies, I shall aim to adapt both the language and the
" prescriptions to the degree of knowledge already possessed
" on the subject by ordinary practical men, instead of learned
" veterinarians."

Dr. Randall's list of troublesome diseases is, therefore, as
follows :—

Hoof-rot,	Scab,
Grub-in-the-head,	Catarrh, and
Colic,	Parturient Fever.

Hoof-rot is thus described :—

" The horny covering of the sheep's foot extends up, gradually
" thinning out, some way between the toes or division of the
" hoof—and above these horny walls the cleft is lined with skin.
" Where the points of the toes are spread apart, this skin is shown
" in front covered with soft, short hair. The heels can be sep-
" arated only to a little distance, and the skin that is in the cleft
" above them is naked. In a healthy foot it is as firm, sound,
" smooth, and dry, as the skin between a man's fingers, which,
" indeed, it not a little resembles; on a mere superficial inspection.
" It is equally destitute of any appearance of redness, or of fever-
" ish heat.

" The first symptom of hoof-rot, uniformly, in my experience,
" is a disappearance of this smooth, dry, colorless condition of the
" naked skin at the top of the cleft over the heels, and of its cool-

"ness. It is a little moist, a little red, and the skin has a slightly
"chafed or eroded appearance—sometimes being a very little
"corrugated, as if the parts had been subjected to the action of
"moisture. And, on placing the fingers over the heels, it will be
"found that the natural coolness of the parts has given place to a
"degree of heat. The inflammation thenceforth increases pretty
"rapidly. The part first attacked becomes sore. The moisture
"—the ichorous discharge—is increased. A raw ulcer of some
"extent is soon established. It is extended down to the upper
"portion of the inner walls of the hoof, giving them a whitened
"and ulcerous appearance. Those thin walls become disorgan-
"ized, and the ulceration penetrates between the fleshy sole and
"the bottom of the hoof. On applying some force, or on
"shaving away the horn, it will be found that the connection
"between the horny and fleshy sole is severed, perhaps half-way
"from the heel to the toe, and half-way from the inner to the
"outer wall of the hoof. The hoof is thickened with great
"rapidity at the heel by an unnatural deposition of horn. The
"crack or cavity between it and the fleshy sole very soon exudes
"a highly fetid matter, which begins to have a purulent appear-
"ance. The extent of the separation increases by the disorgani-
"zation of the surrounding structures ; the ulceration penetrates
"throughout the entire extent of the sole ; it begins to form
"sinuses in the body of the fleshy sole; the purulent discharge
"becomes more profuse ; the horny sole is gradually disorganized,
"and finally the outer walls and points of the toes alone remain.
"The fleshy sole is now a black, swollen mass of corruption, of
"the texture of a sponge saturated with bloody pus, and every
"cavity is filled with crawling, squirming maggots. The horny
"toe disappears ; the thin, shortened side-walls merely adhere at
"the coronet ; they yield to the disorganization ; and nothing is
"left but a shapeless mass of spongy ulcer and maggots. At-
"tempts to cure this disease, the state of the weather, and other
"incidental circumstances, cause some variations from the above
"line of symptoms. When the first attack occurs in hot weather,
"the progress of the malady is much more rapid and violent.

" The fly sometimes deposits its eggs in the ulcer, and maggots
" appear almost before—sometimes actually before—there are any
" cavities formed, into which they can penetrate. The early ap-
" pearance of maggots greatly accelerates the process of disorgani-
" zation in the structures.

" The forefeet are usually first attacked, sometimes both of
" them simultaneously, but more generally only one of them.
" The animal at first manifests but little constitutional disturb-
" ance. It eats as is its wont. When the disease has partly run
" its course in one foot, the other forefoot is likely to be attacked,
" and presently the hind ones. When a foot becomes considera-
" bly disorganized, it is held up by the animal. When another
" one reaches the same state, the miserable sufferer seeks its food
" on its knees; and if forced to rise and walk, its strange, hob-
" bling gait betrays the intense agony it endures on bringing its
" ulcerated feet in contact with the ground. There is a bare spot
" on the under side of the brisket, of the size of the palm of a
" man's hand, but perhaps a little longer, which looks red and
" inflamed. There is a degree of general fever, and the appetite
" is dull. The animal rapidly loses condition, but retains consid-
" erable strength. Nowhere else do sheep seem to me to exhibit
" such tenacity of life. After the disappearance of the bottom
" of the hoof, the maggot speedily closes the scene. Where the
" rotten foot is brought in contact with the side in lying down,
" the filthy, ulcerous matter adheres to and saturates the short
" wool of the shorn sheep; and maggots also are either carried
" there by the foot, or they are speedily generated by the fly. A
" black crust soon forms and raises a little higher round the spot.
" It is the decomposition of the surrounding structures,—wool,
" skin, and muscle,—and innumerable maggots are at work below,
" burrowing into the living tissues, and eating up the miserable
" animal alive. The black, festering mass rapidly extends, and
" the cavities of the body will soon be penetrated, if the poor
" sufferer is not sooner relieved of its tortures by death.

" The offensive odor of the ulcerated feet, almost from the
" beginning of the disease, is so peculiar that it is strictly pathog-

"nomonic.   I have always believed that I could, by the sense of
"smell alone, in the most absolute darkness, decide on the pres-
"ence of hoof-rot with unerring certainty.   And I had about as
"lief trust my fingers as my eyes to establish the same point,
"from the hour of the first attack, if no other disease of the foot
"is present.   But the heat which invariably marks the earliest
"presence of hoof-rot, might arise from any other cause which
"produced a local inflammation of the same parts.

"When the malady has been well kept under during the first
"summer of its attack, but not entirely eradicated, it will almost
"or entirely disappear as cold weather approaches, and not mani-
"fest itself again until the warm weather of the succeeding sum-
"mer.   It then assumes a mitigated form ; the sheep are not
"rapidly and simultaneously attacked ; there seems to be less
"inflammatory action in the diseased parts, and less constitutional
"disturbance ; and the course of the disease is less malignant,
"more tardy, and it more readily yields to treatment.   If well
"kept under the second summer, it is still milder the third.   A
"sheep will occasionally be seen to limp, but its condition will
"scarcely be affected, and dangerous symptoms will rarely super-
"vene.   One or two applications of remedies made during the
"summer will now suffice to keep the disease under, and a little
"vigor in the treatment will entirely extinguish it.

"With all its fearful array of symptoms, can the hoof-rot be
"cured in its first attack on a flock ?   The worst case can be
"promptly cured, as I know by repeated experiments.   Take a
"single sheep, put it by itself, and administer the remedies daily,
"after the English fashion, or as I shall presently prescribe, and
"there is not an ovine disease which more surely yields to treat-
"ment.   But, as already remarked, in this country where sheep
"are so cheap and labor in the summer months so dear, it would
"be out of the question for an extensive flock-master to attempt
"to keep each sheep by itself, or to make a daily application of
"remedies.   There is not a flock-master within my knowledge
"who has ever pretended to apply his remedies oftener than once
"a week, or regularly as often as that, and not one in ten makes

" any separation between the diseased and healthy sheep of a flock
" into which the malady has been once introduced. The conse-
" quence necessarily is, that though a cure is effected of the sheep
" then diseased, it has infected or inoculated others, and these in
" turn scatter the contagion before they are cured. There is not
" a particle of doubt, nay, I know, by repeated observation, that
" a sheep once entirely cured may again contract the disease, and
" thus the malady perform a perpetual circuit in the flock. For-
" tunately, however, the susceptibility to contract the disease
" diminishes, according to my observation, with every succeeding
" attack; and fortunately also, as already stated, succeeding
" attacks, other things being equal, become less and less virulent."

In order to reach the seat of the disease, it is necessary that
the horn of the hoof be entirely removed over those parts where
the difficulty is located. This work is done by the aid of sharp,
thin knives and strong toe-nippers, which, with the manner of
using them, are described in Dr. Randall's work, and he continues:—

" *And on the effectual performance of this, all else depends.* If the
" disease is in the first stage—*i. e.*, if there is merely an erosion
" and ulceration of the cuticle and flesh in the cleft above the
" walls of the hoof, no paring is necessary. But if ulceration has
" established itself between the hoof and the fleshy sole, the ul-
" cerated parts, be they more or less extensive, *must be entirely de-*
" *nuded of their horny covering, cost what it may of time and care.* It
" is better not to wound the sole so as to cause it to bleed freely, as
" the running blood will wash off the subsequent application ; but
" no fear of wounding the sole must prevent a full compliance
" with the rule above laid down. At worst, the blood can soon
" be stanched, however freely it flows, by a few touches of a
" caustic—say butter of antimony.

" If the foot is in the third stage,—a mass of rottenness and
" filled with maggots,—the maggots should first be killed by spirits
" of turpentine, or a solution of corrosive sublimate, or other
" equally efficient application. It can be most conveniently used
" from a bottle having a quill through the cork. By continuing

" to remove the dead maggots with a stick, and to expose and kill
" the deeper-lodged ones, all can be extirpated. Every particle
" of loose horn should then be removed, though it take the entire
" hoof,—and it frequently does take the entire hoof at an ad-
" vanced stage of the disease. The foot should be cleansed, if
" necessary, with a solution of chloride of lime, in the proportion
" of a pound of the chloride to a gallon of water. If this is not
" at hand, plunging the foot repeatedly in water, just short of
" scalding hot, will answer the purpose."

Quite a number of remedies are given as being, or having been,
in successful operation in different parts of this country and in
Europe.

" The most common and popular remedy now used in Central
" New York is: 1 lb. blue vitriol; ¼ lb. (with some, ½ lb.) ver-
" digris; 1 pint of linseed oil; 1 quart of tar. The vitriol and
" verdigris are pulverized very fine, and many persons, before add-
" ing the tar, grind the mixture through a paint-mill. Some use
" a decoction of tobacco boiled until thick, in the place of oil."

* * * * * * *

" Any of these remedies, and fifty more that might be com-
" pounded, simply by combining caustics, stimulants, etc., in
" different forms and proportions, will prove sufficient for the ex-
" tirpation of hoof-rot, *with proper preparatory and subsequent*
" *treatment*. On these last, beyond all question, principally de-
" pends the comparative success of the applications.

" *First*. No external remedy can succeed in this malady unless
" it comes in contact with all the diseased parts of the foot; for if
" such part, however small, is unreached, the unhealthy and ul-
" cerous action is perpetuated in it, and it gradually spreads over
" and again involves the surrounding tissues. Therefore every
" portion of the diseased flesh must be denuded of horn, filth,
" dead tissue, pus, and every other substance which can prevent
" the application from actually *touching* it, and producing its
" characteristic effects on it.

" *Second*. The application must be kept in contact with the dis-
" eased surfaces long enough to exert its proper remedial influence.

" If removed, by any means, before this is accomplished, it must
" necessarily proportionably fail in its effects.

" The preparation of the foot, then, requires no mean skill.
" The tools must be sharp, the movements of the operator careful
" and deliberate. As he shaves down near the quick, he must
" cut thinner and thinner, and with more and more care, or else
" he will either fail to remove the horn exactly far enough, or he
" will cut into the fleshy sole and cause a rapid flow of blood. I
" have already remarked that the blood can be stanched by caus-
" tics—but they coagulate it on the surface in a mass which
" requires removal before the application of remedies, and in the
" process of its removal the blood is very frequently set flowing
" again, and this sometimes several times follows the application
" of the caustic."

*   *   *   *   *   *   *

" The separation of the sheep, poulticing, inclosing of the foot,
" etc., I believe to be unnecessary—but the feet must be well
" prepared, and the sheep must be kept out of the rain, or grass
" wetted by rain or dew, for twenty-four or thirty-six hours after-
" ward—the longer the better. *Without this the most careful prepa-*
" *ration of the foot and the best remedies cannot be made effectual.*
" *   *   *   * The best place to put sheep after applying
" remedies to their feet, is on the naked floors of stables—scatter-
" ing them over as much surface as practicable, so that there
" shall be as little accumulation of manure as possible under foot.
" Straw, especially if fresh littered down, absorbs or rubs off the
" moist substances which have been applied to their feet. The
" *bottoms* of the feet are soon thus cleaned off. A boy should go
" round with a shovel, until night, taking up the dung as fast as
" dropped. The sheep should be kept in the stables over the
" first night, and not let out the next day until the dew is off the
" grass ; then they should be turned on the most closely cropped
" grass on the farm. It well pays for the trouble to put them in
" the stables the second night before the dew falls, and to keep
" them, as before, until it is dried off the next day.

" I have never found that for moderate cases of hoof-rot—the

28

" worst ones which are allowed to occur in well-managed flocks—
" that there is, in reality, any possible beneficial addition to mere
" blue vitriol, as a remedy, if it is applied in the most effective
" way.   Twice I have cured a diseased *flock* by one application
" of it,—and I never heard of it being done in any other way, or,
" indeed, on any other occasion."

SCAB is a disease of the skin like the itch in the human race, or
the mange in horses.   It is caused by a minute insect known to
entomologists as the *Acarus.*   Dr. Randall does not think that the
disease originates spontaneously in the United States, and its
prevalence here is confined chiefly to long-wooled sheep.

" It spreads from individual to individual, and from flock to
" flock, not only by means of direct contact, but by the acari left
" on posts, stones, and other substances against which diseased sheep
" have rubbed themselves.   Healthy sheep are therefore liable to
" contract the malady if turned on pastures previously occupied
" by scabby sheep, though some considerable time may have
" elapsed since the departure of the latter.

" The sheep laboring under the scab is exceedingly restless.   It
" rubs itself with violence against trees, stones, fences, etc.   It
" scratches itself with its feet, and bites its sores, and tears off its
" wool with its teeth.   As the pustules are broken, their matter
" escapes and forms scabs covering red, inflamed sores.   The
" sores constantly extend, increasing the misery of the tortured
" animal.   If unrelieved, it pines away and soon perishes."

Having detected the appearance of scab in a newly purchased
flock of sheep, Dr. Randall adopted the following treatment :—

" The sheep had been shorn, and their backs were covered with
" scabs and sores.   They evidently had the scab.   I had a large
" potash kettle sunk partly in the ground as an extempore vat,
" and an unweighed quantity of tobacco put to boiling in several
" other kettles.   The only care was to have enough of the decoc-
" tion, as it was rapidly wasted, and to have it strong enough.   A
" little spirits of turpentine was occasionally thrown on the decoc-
" tion, say, to every third or fourth sheep dipped.   It was neces-
" sary to use it sparingly, as, not mixing with the fluid and floating

" on the surface, too much of it otherwise came in contact with
" the sheep. Not attending to this at first, two or three of the
" sheep were thrown into great agony, and appeared to be on the
" point of dying. I had each sheep caught and its scabs scoured
" off by two men, who rubbed them with stiff shoe-brushes dipped
" in a suds of tobacco-water and soft soap. The two men then
" dipped the sheep all over in the large kettle of tobacco-water,
" rubbing and kneading the sore spots with their hands while im-
" mersed in the fluid. The decoction was so strong that many of
" the sheep appeared to be sickened either by immersion or by its
" fumes ; and one of the men who dipped, though a tobacco-
" chewer, vomited, and became so sick that his place had to be
" supplied by another. The effect on the sheep was almost magi-
" cal. The sores rapidly healed, the sheep gained in condition,
" the new wool immediately started, and I never had a more per-
" fectly healthy flock on my farm."

Randall also gives several other methods of treatment which are
in vogue in England, some of which are better adapted than is the
tobacco-water for use with sheep carrying long fleeces.

The GRUB-IN-THE-HEAD is the grub of the gadfly of the sheep,
(*Œstrus ovis.*) The egg is deposited within the nostrils of the
sheep, where it is immediately hatched by the warmth and moisture ; and the larvæ crawl up the nose to the sinuses, where they
attach themselves to the membrane and remain until the next
year, feeding upon the mucus. Randall thinks that many of the
ills that sheep flesh is heir to are erroneously attributed to the
effect of this grub, concerning which he says :—

" I have had a singularly limited experience with any diseases
" which could reasonably be attributed to the presence of these
" parasites, and therefore do not feel myself at all well qualified to
" judge of their actual effects on the sheep. That want of expe-
" rience is a strong proof of itself that resulting maladies are not
" as frequent by any means as is popularly supposed. And know-
" ing, as I do, that other and wholly dissimilar diseases are habitu-
" ally termed 'grub-in-the-head,' I can entertain no doubt that the
" extent of the injuries thus inflicted is enormously exaggerated.

" Influenced by these latter considerations, and by the strong
" counter-testimony of such really able veterinarians as Messrs.
" Clark and Youatt, and the silence on the subject of Mr.
" Spooner and some other modern writers, I was formerly led
" to doubt whether the larvæ of the *Œstrus ovis* ever did
" more in the sheep's head than effect a degree of temporary
" irritation of the lining membranes, which might produce serious
" inconvenience when acting in concert with the inflammation
" already established by catarrhal or other cerebral affections, but
" which never caused death. Again reminding the reader that I
" speak from a very limited personal knowledge of the disease, I
" feel it due to frankness to say that my opinions have undergone
" some change. The testimony of intelligent men has satisfied
" me that the irritation and ultimate inflammation of the mucous
" lining of the head, produced by the tentacula of the worm and
" by its constant feeding on the secretions, if not even on the
" substance of the membrane itself, in certain stages of the dis-
" ease, are sufficient in some cases to cause death. I should not
" expect a sheep in high condition and apparent health to die sud-
" denly from this cause without previous symptoms of disease, and
" under circumstances resembling those of apoplexy. I should
" not expect the powerful nervous disturbances of epilepsy. But
" if the sheep began to fall off rapidly in condition a little before
" the opening of spring, without any other traceable cause—if it
" wandered round with irregular movements, twisting about its
" head occasionally as if it was suffering pain—and especially if
" the mucus discharged from the nose was tinged with blood—I
" should *suspect* 'grub-in-the-head,' and administer remedies or
" antidotes on that hypothesis. And, after the death of patients,
" I should, as carefully as practicable, examine not only the
" sinuses of the head, but also the entire nasal cavities, to ascer-
" tain whether there were any traces of the supposed destructive
" action of the larvæ.

" Some farmers protect their sheep measurably from the attacks
" of the *Œstrus ovis*, by plowing a furrow or two in different por-
" tions of their pastures. The sheep thrust their noses into this

" on the approach of the fly. Others smear their noses with tar,
" or cause them to smear themselves, by sprinkling their salt over
" tar. Those fish oils which repel the attacks of flies might be
" resorted to. Blacklock suggested the dislodgment of the larvæ
" from the head by blowing tobacco smoke up the nostrils—as it
" is said to be effectual. It is blown from the tail of a pipe, the
" bowl being covered with cloth. Tobacco-water is sometimes
" injected with a syringe for the same purpose. The last should
" be prevented from entering the throat in any considerable
" quantity."

*　　*　　*　　*　　*　　*　　*

" CATARRH.—Catarrh is an inflammation of the mucous mem-
" brane which lines the nasal passages—and it sometimes extends
" to the larynx and pharynx. In the first instance—where the
" lining of the nasal passages is alone and not very violently
" affected—it is merely accompanied by an increased discharge of
" mucus, and is rarely attended with much danger. In this form
" it is usually termed snuffles, and high-bred English mutton
" sheep, in this country, are apt to manifest more or less of it,
" after every sudden change of weather. When the inflammation
" extends to the mucous lining of the larynx and pharynx, some
" degree of fever usually supervenes, accompanied by cough, and
" some loss of appetite. At this point the English veterinarians
" usually recommend bleeding and purging. Catarrh rarely attacks
" the American fine-wooled sheep with sufficient violence, in sum-
" mer, to require the exhibition of remedies. I early found that
" depletion, in catarrh, in our severe winter months, rapidly pro-
" duced that fatal prostration from which it is next to impossible
" to recover the sheep—entirely impossible without bestowing an
" amount of time and care on it costing far more than the price of
" any ordinary sheep.

" The best course is to prevent the disease by judicious pre-
" cautions. With that amount of attention which every prudent
" flock-master should bestow on his sheep, the hardy American
" merino is little subject to it. Good, comfortable, but well-
" ventilated shelters, constantly accessible to the sheep in winter,

" with a proper supply of food regularly administered, is usually a
" sufficient safeguard ; and after some years of experience, during
" which I have tried a variety of experiments on this disease, I
" resort to no other remedies—in other words, I do nothing for
" those occasional cases of ordinary catarrh which arise in my
" flock ; and they never prove fatal."

    *   *   *   *   *   *   *

    " COLIC OR STRETCHES.—The cause of this disease is generally
" costiveness. The paroxysms recur at intervals. During the
" continuance of them the sheep stretches itself incessantly, and
" often twists about its head as if in severe pain. It lies down
" and rises frequently. The termination is occasionally fatal,
" unless the bowels are promptly opened by medicine. An ounce
" of Epsom salts dissolved in warm water, with a dram of ginger
" and a teaspoonful of peppermint, should be administered to
" a sheep, and half as much to a lamb. Three very excellent
" practical shepherds write me—the first, that ' he gives Epsom
" salts successfully for stretches ;' the second, that he ' uses a
" decoction of thoroughwort or boneset—that warm tea is also
" good ;' the third, that he ' employs castor-oil, and if the case is
" obstinate, a moderate dose of aloes.' Attacks of this disease
" become habitual to some sheep. It can always be prevented by
" giving green feed daily, or even once or twice a week."

    Dr. Randall states that he has never seen a case of parturient
or puerperal fever, and believes that it is exclusively confined to
English sheep. As English sheep have been largely introduced
into this country, the following statement concerning it, taken
from the *Journal of the Royal Agricultural Society* will be valuable :—

    " *Symptoms.*—The most early symptom that marks the com-
" mencement of this disease—first the ewe suddenly leaves her
" food, twitches both hind legs and ears, and returns again to her
" food ; during the next two or three days she eats but little,
" appears dull and stupid ; after this time there is a degree of
" general weakness, loss of appetite and giddiness, and a discharge
" of dark color from the vagina ; while the flock is driven from

" fold to fold the affected sheep loiters behind and staggers in her
" gait, the head is carried downward, and the eyelids partly closed.
" If parturition takes place during this stage of the disease, and the
" animal is kept warm and carefully nursed, recovery will fre-
" quently take place in two or three days ; if, on the contrary, no
" relief is afforded, symptoms of a typhoid character present them-
" selves ;   the animal is found in one corner of the fold, the head
" down, and extremely uneasy, the body is frequently struck with
" the hind feet, a dark colored fetid discharge continues to flow
" from the vagina, and there is great prostration of strength.   A
" pair of lambs are now often expelled in a high state of putrefac-
" tion, and the ewe down and unable to rise, the head is crouching
" upon the ground, and there is extreme insensibility ; the skin
" may be punctured and the finger placed under the eyelids
" without giving any evidence of pain ; the animal now rapidly
" sinks and dies, often in three or four days from the commence-
" ment of the attack.   Ewes that recover, suffer afterward for
" some time great weakness, and many parts of the body become
" denuded of wool.

   " *Treatment.* — The ewe immediately noticed ill should be
" removed from the flock to a warm fold apart from all other
" sheep, and be fed with oatmeal gruel, bruised oats, and cut hay,
" with a little linseed cake.   If in two or three days the patient
" continues ill, is dull and weak, a dark colored fetid discharge
" from the vagina, and apparently uneasy, an attempt to remove
" the lambs should be made.   The lambs in a great majority of
" cases at this period are dead, and their decomposition, (that is,
" giving off putrid matter,) is a frequent cause of giddiness and
" stupor in the ewe.   If the *os uteri* (the entrance into the uterus)
" is not sufficiently dilated to admit the hand of the operator, the
" vaginal cavity and *os uteri* should be smeared every three hours
" with the extract of belladonna, and medicine as follows given :—

Calomel............................ ....8. grains
Extract hyoscyamus....................................1 dram
Oatmeal gruel.......................................8 ounces

" mix, and give two table-spoonfuls twice a day.

Epsom salts...8 ounces
Niter..½ ounce
Carbonate of soda....................................2 ounces
Water...1 pint

" mix, and give two wine-glassfuls at the same time the former
" mixture is given. Let both mixtures be kept in separate bottles,
" and well shaken before given. The bowels being operated
" upon, omit both former prescriptions and give the following :—

Niter...½ ounce
Carbonate of soda....................................1 ounce
Camphor...1 dram
Water...8 ounces

" A wine-glassful to be given twice a day.

" Feed the ewe principally upon gruel and milk, or linseed
" porridge. Parturition having taken place, the uterus should be
" injected with a solution of chloride of lime, in the proportion
" of a dram to a pint of warm water, and repeated twice a day
" while any fetid discharge from the vagina remains."

" *Prevention.*—The most important feature connected with our
" subject is the prevention of the disease, for it most interests the
" breeder in a pecuniary point of view. I would recommend as
" most important during the last five or six weeks' gestation, regu-
" lar and nutritious feeding, *regular exercise*, dry and extensive
" folding. If turnips be the article of food, let there be given in
" addition a few oats, linseed cake, with hay and straw chaff; let
" a well-sheltered and dry fold be arranged at a short distance
" from where the ewes are fed during the day, wherein to lodge
" for the night ; *the driving to and from these folds will give exer-
" cise, a circumstance tending much to promote health in the pregnant
" ewe ;* if the system of heath or pasture feeding is practiced, night
" folding is then equally necessary. The night fold in common
" use—that formed by building straw and stubble walls, with
" sheds attached, the front of which has a southern aspect—
" answers admirably. Further explaining the comforts of the
" pregnant ewe, I will add, in the words of the poet,—

> " ' First with assiduous care from winter keep,
> Well foddered in the stalls, thy tender sheep;
> Then spread with straw the bedding of thy fold,
> With fern beneath to 'fend the bitter cold,' "

The following letter to Dr. Randall is based on the experience of one of the earliest and most successful breeders of English sheep in America :—

"THORNDALE, WASHINGTON HOLLOW, N. Y., April 13, 1863.

"DEAR SIR :—* * The puerperal fever has been known in "this neighborhood since I first came here, though only to a lim- "ited extent during the last two seasons. * * * The disease "more generally affects middle-aged ewes, and ewes producing or "carrying twins. It does not select those lowest in flesh; hence "the farmers, as a class, are unwilling to believe that feed can "remedy it. It generally shows itself from four or five to ten "days before lambing. * * * The treatment which my shep- "herd has followed, and with good success,—saving sixteen out "of twenty sick, in 1859,—has been to separate the sick ewe at "once from the flock and give a dose of two ounces Epsom salts, "two to three ounces molasses, one dram of niter, mixed with a "pint of warm linseed gruel. The object is to open the bowels, "and should the above not operate in eight or ten hours, it should "be repeated. After that, the niter and molasses are given night "and morning in an ordinary quart bottle of gruel, until there is "an abatement of the fever, when the niter is discontinued. Fre- "quently, in fact, generally, after they have been down three or "four days,—if they live so long,—the brown discharge which has "been noticed passing from the vagina, becomes putrid, showing "that the fœtus is dead. In such cases a small quantity of bella- "donna—applied dry on the end of the finger—is applied to the "mouth of the womb every hour until it is sufficiently relaxed to "allow of the removal of the decaying mass. After that has "has been done, the womb is thoroughly syringed with warm "water, to which milk is sometimes added. The ewe's position "is made as comfortable as possible, and always changed once or "twice a day. Where the ewe brings forth her young alive she

" recovers more rapidly.   The remedies and treatment, as you
" will see, are perfectly simple, and easily tried by any flock
" owner.   The great secret of success, with it, as with a large
" majority of diseases, I believe, is good nursing.   * * * Since
" my flock have received a small quantity of grain, say half a pint
" per head daily, before lambing, they have been quite free from
" any signs of that trouble.   As an illustration that a small quan-
" tity of feed is a preventive, a flock belonging to one of my friends
" was divided, upon going into winter-quarters, into two lots,—
" one of sixty old ewes, the other of thirty two-year old ewes.
" The former received a very small quantity of corn daily—the
" latter only hay.   His loss from the former lot was two—from
" the latter, fourteen head; though the younger ones generally
" escaped.   * * *

" Yours faithfully,   SAM'L THORNE."

SWINE.

The following statement concerning swine, by Dr. Finlay
Dun, of the Edinburgh Veterinary College, to the *Journal of the
Royal Agricultural Society of England,** advances an idea that is not
in accordance with the views of most American farmers.   He
says :—

" Pigs, when carefully managed, are hardy and little liable to
" disease.   Wild breeds in both the Old and New Worlds are
" remarkably healthy ; but it must be recollected that they con-
" stantly breathe pure fresh air, have regular exercise, feed mod-
" erately on roots and fruits, and carefully avoid all kinds of filth ;
" for they are naturally a very cleanly race, and indulge in wal-
" lowing in the mire, not from any love of filth, as is generally
" supposed, but, like the elephant, rhinoceros, and other pachy-
" dermata, for the purpose of protecting their skins from the attacks
" of insects.   In a state of domestication, however, their condition
" is usually very different.   They are cooped up in narrow, damp,
" and dirty sties, and constrained to inhale all kinds of noxious va-

---

* Journal of the Royal Agricultural Society of England, Volume XVI, page 37.

" pors, and to eat coarse, innutritious, and unsuitable food. We can-
" not, then, be surprised that under such circumstances they should
" not only become the victims of disease from which in their nat-
" ural state they are free, but should also transmit to their progeny a
" weakened and morbidly predisposed constitution. But we believe
" that much of the hereditary disease of pigs is due to another
" cause than that just indicated, viz.: breeding in and in. * * *
" In several cases which have come under our own observation,
" it has induced total ruin of the entire stock. At first it merely
" rendered the animals somewhat smaller and finer than before,
" and improved rather than injured their fattening properties.
" Very soon, however, it caused a marked diminution in size and
" vigor, and engendered a disposition to various forms of scrofu-
" lous disease, and to rickets, tabes mesenterica, and pulmonary
" consumption. Many of the boars became sterile, and the sows
" barren or liable to abortion. In every succeeding litter the pigs
" became fewer in number and more and more delicate and diffi-
" cult to rear. Many were born dead, others without tails, ears,
" or eyes; and all kinds of monstrosities were frequent. * * *
" The occurrence of such effects should induce the breeder of
" swine, and indeed of all animals, to practice breeding in and in
" with much caution, to adopt it only occasionally and with strong
" and healthy animals, and to recollect that though it may im-
" prove the symmetry and fattening capabilities of stock, it does
" so at the sacrifice of their general vigor and disease-resisting
" powers."

Dr. Dun states with reference to epilepsy, with which pigs are
often suddenly attacked, that the inherited tendency may be mitigated by keeping the animals clean, warm, and comfortable, and
supplied with a sufficiency of good, digestible, and somewhat laxative food.

" To eradicate it the stock must receive an infusion of new
" blood; and this is especially necessary, as epilepsy in pigs
" depends in most cases on continued breeding in-and-in."

There sometimes appears among pigs an hereditary predisposition to lung diseases, indicated by a narrow chest, and a lanky and

thriftless appearance, their great liability to suffer from coughs
being readily excited by exposure to cold or wet, or by changes
of food.

" Pigs, from their susceptibility to cold, are often attacked by
" *rheumatism,* especially in its more chronic forms. This is a
" constitutional disease depending on the presence in the blood of
" some poisonous materials, probably analogous to those found
" within the gouty joints of men. Like other constitutional dis-
" eases, it is accompanied by certain local symptoms. In pigs, it
" chiefly affects the fibrous serous tissues of the larger joints, gives
" evidence of local inflammation, and general fever, progresses
" with slow and lingering steps, and does not, like ordinary inflam-
" mation, terminate in suppuration and gangrene. It most com-
" monly occurs among young pigs, and usually owes its origin to
" lying in a wet cold bed. It always produces alteration of
" structure in the parts affected, which predisposes the individual
" to subsequent attacks, and tends to reappear in the progeny,
" rendering them also specially predisposed to the complaint.

" *Scrofula* is more common in pigs than in any other of the
" domestic animals. It sometimes carries off whole litters before
" they are many weeks old.   *   *   *   Consumption exhibits the
" same symptoms as in other animals—gradually increasing ema-
" ciation ; imperfect digestion and assimilation ; disturbed respira-
" tion, with a frequent short cough ; weakened and unusually
" accelerated circulation ; diarrhœa of a most intractable kind,
" often merging into dysentery ; and general prostration of the
" vital powers.   *   *   *

" *Scrofulous Tumors* are sometimes met with among pigs. * * *
" They are produced by the fusion of degenerated lymph, incapa-
" ble of perfect organization, and mixed up with tuberculous mat-
" ter.   *   *   *   These local symptoms are often accompanied
" by some of the usual constitutional symptoms of scrofula, as im-
" pairment of digestion and assimilation.   *   *   In conclusion,
" we may repeat, that many of the most common, and some of
" the most serious, diseases of sheep and pigs, are hereditary, and
" that they spring from certain vices of structure or disproportion

" of parts, either of a local or general nature. They are propagated
" alike, whether occurring in the male or female parent, but
" always most certainly and in the most aggravated form when
" occurring in both. Defects and diseases that have already been
" transmitted through several generations are impressed on the
" progeny in a most decided, permanent, and irremediable form;
" but those acquired during the life-time of an individual also
" sometimes become hereditary, especially when of a constitu-
" tional nature, and accompanied by any considerable alteration
" of structure or function, or by a debilitated and deteriorated state
" of health. Indeed, debility, however produced, is almost cer-
" tain to be hereditary; and hence all breeding animals should be
" in a strong and vigorous condition, especially at the period of
" sexual congress."

It is hardly necessary to say that the principles laid down in the
foregoing extracts from Dr. Dun's essay apply with almost equal
force to the breeding of all animals,—to the extent, at least, of
suggesting that in all cases the utmost care should be taken to
prevent the propagation of constitutional defects, whether hereditary in the parents or acquired by them as a consequence of
improper circumstances of living.

Mr. Allen says:*

" Mortifying as the fact may be to human pride, it is neverthe-
" less certain, that the internal arrangements—the viscera, digestive
" organs, omnivorous propensities, and the general physiological
" structure—of the hog and the bear more nearly resemble man
" than any other animal. Many of their diseases may therefore
" be expected to be a modification of those of the human species,
" and require a similar treatment.

" To pulmonary affections, colds, coughs, and measles, swine
" are peculiarly liable, and, as with most other evils, prevention
" of disease in swine is more easy and economical than cure. A
" dry, warm bed, free from winds or storms, and suitable food, will
" most effectually prevent any injuries, or fatal attacks. The hog

---

* Domestic Animals R. L. Allen. O. Judd & Co., New York.

" has little external covering to protect him against cold.   Nature
" has provided this immediately within the skin, in the deep layer of
" fat which surrounds the full, plump hog.   Fat is one of the best
" non-conductors of heat, and the pig which is well fed bids defi-
" ance to the intense cold, which would produce great suffering
" and consequent disease in the ill-conditioned animal.   By the
" observance of a proper medium between too much fat or lean
" for the store or breeding swine, and providing them with com-
" fortable beds and proper feed, nearly all disease will be avoided.

" For *cough and inflammation of the lungs*, bleeding should be
" immediately resorted to, after which give gentle purges of castor
" oil, or Epsom salts ; and this should be followed with a dose of
" antimonial powders—two grains, mixed with half a dram of niter.

" For *costiveness* or loss of appetite, sulphur is an excellent
" remedy, given in a light mess.

" *Itch* may be cured by anointing with equal parts of lard and
" brimstone.   Rubbing-posts, and a running stream to wallow in,
" are preventives.

" The *kidney worm* is frequently fatal ; and always produces
" weakness of the loins and hind legs, usually followed by entire
" prostration.   A pig thus far gone is hardly worth the trouble of
" recovering, even where practicable.

" *Preventives* are, general thrift, a range in a good pasture, and
" a dose of half a pint of wood-ashes every week or fortnight in
" their food.   A small quantity of saltpeter, spirits of turpentine,
" or tar, will effect the same object.   When attacked, apply spir-
" its of turpentine to the loins, and administer calomel carefully ;
" or give half a tablespoonful of copperas daily for one or two
" weeks.

" *Blind staggers* is generally confined to pigs, and manifests
" itself in foaming at the mouth, rearing on their hind legs, champ-
" ing and grinding their teeth, and apparent blindness.   The
" proper remedies are bleeding and purging freely, and these fre-
" quently fail.   Many nostrums have been suggested, but few are
" of any utility.   It is important to keep the issues on the inside
" of the fore-legs, just below the knee, thoroughly cleansed.

"The tails of young pigs frequently *drop* or *rot off*, which is "attended with no further disadvantage to the animal than the "loss of the member. The *remedies* are, to give a little brimstone "or sulphur in the food of the dam; or rub oil or grease daily on "the affected parts. It may be detected by a roughness or scab-"biness at the point where separation is likely to occur.

"*Bleeding.*—The most convenient mode is from an artery just "above the knee, on the inside of the fore-arm. It may be drawn "more copiously from the roof of the mouth. The flow of blood "may usually be stopped by applying a sponge or cloth with cold "water.

"The diseases of swine, though not numerous, are formidable, "and many of them soon become fatal. They have not been the "subject of particular scientific study, and most of the remedies "applied are rather the result of casual or hap-hazard suggestion "than of well-digested inference from long-continued and accu-"rate observation."

The cardinal principles of successful pig raising are, to breed only from sound and healthy parents of remote relationship, to keep the animals in dry, warm, and cleanly quarters, to feed regularly sufficiently and with varying food, and to remove as early as possible any diseased or weakly animal from the herd.

POULTRY.

It is rare to take up an agricultural paper without coming across a recipe for the treatment of some one of the diseases to which poultry is subject; and in almost all cases the recommendations given claim to be based on the successful experience of the writers. Probably there is no branch of the comprehensive subject of the treatment of the diseases to which farm stock is liable, on which so much has been written, and in which so much uncertainty still exists. It would be easy to write an interesting chapter for this book on the subject of the different ailments of poultry, and the different recommendations for their treatment. As the most comprehensive and lucid statement concerning the management of the more important diseases is given in Saunders' *Domestic Poultry*,* I can hardly do better within my narrow limits than to copy it entire :—

"Among the diseases of fowls, nothing is so fatal to the bird, "or so vexatious to the fancier, as the Roup. Very close ob- "servation and experience have taught me the first premonitory "symptom is a peculiar breathing. The fowl appears in perfect "health for the time, but it will be seen that the skin hanging "from the lower beak, and to which the wattle is attached, is "inflated and emptied at every breath—such a bird should always "be removed.

"The disease may be caused, first, by cold, damp weather and "easterly winds, when fowls of weakly habit and bad constitution "will often sicken, but healthy, strong birds will not. Again, if "by any accidental cause they are long without food and water, "and then have an unlimited quantity of drink and whole corn "given to them, they gorge themselves, and ill-health is the con- "sequence ; but confinement is the chief cause, and above all, "being shut up in tainted coops. Nothing is so difficult as to "keep fowls healthy in confinement in large cities ; two days "will often suffice to change the bright, bold cock into the spirit- "less, drooping, roupy fowl, carrying contagion wherever he goes.

"But all roup does not come from cities ; often in the spring "of the year the cocks fight, and it is necessary to take one "away ; search is made for something to put him in, and a rab- "bit-hutch or open basket is found, wherein he is confined and "often irregularly supplied with food, till pity for his altered "condition causes him to be let out ; but he has become roupy, "and the whole yard suffers. I dwell at length on this, because "of all disorders it is the worst, and because, although a cure may "seem to be effected, yet at moulting, or any time when out of "condition, the fowl will be more or less affected with it again. "One thing is here deserving of notice. The result of the atten- "tion paid to poultry of late years has been to improve the health "and constitution of the birds. Roup is not nearly so common

* New York : O. Judd & Co. 1867.

" as it was, nor is it so difficult of cure. It went on unnoticed, for-
" merly, till it had become chronic, and it would not be difficult to
" name yards that have now a good reputation, but which, a few
" years since, never had a healthy fowl. It is now treated at the
" outset, if seen, but the improved management in most places ren-
" ders it of rare occurrence. The cold which precedes it may
" often be cured by feeding twice a day with stale crusts of bread
" soaked in strong ale. There must be provided warm, dry hous-
" ing, cleanliness, nutritive and somewhat stimulating food, and
" medicine. In my own case I generally give as medicine some
" tincture of iron in the water pans, and some stimulants. The
" suspected fowl should be removed directly, and if there be
" plenty without it, and if it be not of any breed that makes its pres-
" ervation a matter of moment, it should be killed. There is very
" little doubt of a cure if taken in the first stage ; but, if the eye-
" lids be swollen, the nostrils closed, the breathing difficult, and
" the discharge fetid and continual, it will be a long time before
" the bird is well. In this stage it may be termed the consumption
" of fowls, and with them, as in human beings, most cases are
" beyond cure. However I may differ from some eminent and
" talented amateurs, I do not hesitate to say it is contagious in a
" high degree. Where fowls are wasting without apparent dis-
" order, a teaspoonful of cod-liver oil per day will be found a most
" efficacious remedy.

" I will next mention a disease common to chickens at an early
" age—I mean the gapes. These are caused by numerous small
" worms in the throat. The best way I know of getting rid of
" them is, to take a hen's tail-feather, strip it to within an inch of
" the end, put it down the chicken's windpipe, twist it sharply
" round several times, and draw it quickly out ; the worms will
" be found entangled in the feathers. When this is not effectual
" in removing them, if the tip of the feather be dipped in turpen-
" tine it will kill them, but it must be put down the windpipe, not
" the gullet. I have always thought these were got from impure
" water, and I have been informed by a gentleman who inquires
" closely into those things, that having placed some of the worms

29

" taken from the throat of a chicken, and some from the bottom
" of a water-butt, where rain-water had stood a long time, under
" a microscope, he found them identical.   I have never met with
" gapes where fowls had a running stream to drink at.   Camphor
" is perhaps the best cure for gapes, and if some is constantly
" kept in the water they drink, they take it readily.   This has
" been *most successful.*   There is also another description of
" gapes, arising probably from internal fever ; I have found meal
" mixed with milk and salts a good remedy.   They are sometimes
" caused by a hard substance at the tip of the tongue ; in this case,
" remove it sharply with the thumb-nail, and let it bleed freely.
" A gentleman mentioned this to me who had met with it in an
" old French writing on poultry.

    " Sometimes a fowl will droop suddenly, after being in perfect
" health ; if caught directly, it will be found it has eaten some-
" thing that has hardened in the crop ; pour plenty of warm water
" down the throat, and loosen the food till it is soft ; then give a
" tablespoonful of castor-oil, or about as much jalap as will lie on
" a ten-cent piece, mixed in butter ; make a pill of it and slide it
" into the crop ; the fowl will be well in the morning.

    " Cayenne pepper or chalk, or both mixed with meal, are con-
" venient and good remedies for scouring.

    " When fowls are restless, dissatisfied, and continually scratch-
" ing, it is often caused by lice ; these can be got rid of by sup-
" plying their houses or haunts with plenty of ashes, especially
" wood ashes, in which they may dust themselves, and the dust-
" bath is rendered more effectual by adding some sulphur to the
" dust.   It must be borne in mind, all birds must have the bath ;
" some use water, some dust ; but both from the same instinctive
" knowledge of its necessity.   Where a shallow stream of water
" runs across a gravel road, it will be found full of small birds
" washing ; where a bank is dry, and well exposed to the sun,
" birds of all kinds will be found burying themselves in the dust.

    " Sometimes fowls appear cramped, they have difficulty in
" standing upright, and rest on their knees ; in large, young
" birds, especially cocks, this is merely the effect of weakness

" from fast growth, and the difficulty their long, weak legs have
" in carrying their bodies. But if it lasts after they are getting
" age, then it must be seen to. If their resting-place has a
" wooden, stone, or brick floor, this is probably the cause ; if this
" is not so, stimulating food, such as I have described for other
" diseases, must be given.

" Fowls, like human beings, are subject to atmospherical influ-
" ence ; and if healthy fowls seem suddenly attacked with illness
" that cannot be explained, a copious meal of bread steeped in ale
" will often prove a speedy and effectual remedy. For adults,
" nothing will restore strength sooner than eggs, boiled hard,
" and chopped fine. If these remedies are not successful, then
" the constitution is at fault, and good, healthy cocks must be
" sought to replace those whose progeny is faulty.

" ' Prevention is better than cure.' The cause of many diseases
" is to be found in enfeebled and bad constitutions ; and these are
" the consequences of in-and-in breeding. The introduction of
" fresh blood is absolutely necessary every second year, and even
" every year is better. Many fanciers who breed for feather, fear
" to do so lest false colors should appear, but they should recollect
" that one of the first symptoms of degeneracy is a foul feather ;
" for instance, the Sebright bantam loses lacing, and becomes
" patched, the Spanish fowls throw white feathers, and pigeons
" practice numberless freaks. An experiment was once tried
" which will illustrate this. A pair of black pigeons was put in
" a large loft, and allowed to breed without any introduction of
" fresh blood. They were well and carefully fed. At the end of
" two years an account of them was taken. They had greatly
" multiplied, but only one-third of the number were black, and the
" others had become spotted with white, then patched, and then
" quite white ; while the latter had not only lost the characteristics
" of the breed from which they descended, but were weak and
" deformed in every possible way. The introduction of fresh
" blood prevents all this ; and the breeder for prizes, or whoever
" wishes to have the best of the sort he keeps, should never let
" a fowl escape him if it possesses the qualities he seeks.

" Such are not always to be had when wanted, and the best
" strains we have, of every sort, have been got up by this plan.
" There is one thing worthy of remark; none of our fowls
" imported from warmer climates are subject to roup, as Spanish,
" Cochins, Brahmas, and Malays. But those from a damp
" country, like Holland, seem to have seeds of it always in
" them. The following tonic is highly recommended by Mr.
" John Douglas of the Wolsely Aviaries, England, to prevent
" roup and gapes in chickens and old fowls :—' One pound of
" sulphate of iron, one ounce of sulphuric acid, dissolved in a jug
" with hot water, then let it stand twenty-four hours, and add one
" gallon of spring water ; when fit for use, one teaspoonful to a
" pint of water given every other day to chickens and once a
" week to old fowls, will make roup and gapes entirely a stranger
" to your yards.' This may be true if perfect cleanliness is main-
" tained, and the fowls are in other respects well-treated."

There are other works on poultry in which the question of
diseases is more fully treated, and from which much sound advice
may be obtained, but in reading these, as in considering the instructions given in agricultural papers, the farmer should exercise
a full share of discreet judgment, and hesitate to adopt any
severe remedy which does not commend itself as rational.

Making Capons.—The excellence of the flesh of the capon has
been known for ages, and the price of these birds in the poultry
markets of the world, is always very much higher than is that of
other poultry. It is hardly astonishing that their production is so
limited, when we consider the fact that the castration of the cock
is a much more delicate operation, and is more likely to be
attended with fatal results, than is that of other animals. An
idea prevails, though I can hardly think it a just one, that caponizing is an especially cruel process. Castration is unquestionably
in all cases attended with pain ; but it is extremely doubtful
whether it produces more pain in the case of the bird than of the
quadruped. The greediness with which the removed parts are
eaten by the animal himself, while still bound to the table, would
indicate that the pain of the operation is not very depressing.

The following account of the manner in which capons are made in France was prepared many years ago, for private circulation, by a gentleman in Philadelphia who had great skill in the art and whose success was admirable. I am enabled by personal experience to say that if the directions are strictly adhered to there is very little risk of the loss of life, and, so far as I have been able to observe, no more suffering than attends the castration of calves and pigs. The instruments referred to can be obtained from surgical-instrument makers. With these before him, the reader will readily understand the directions.

" DIRECTIONS FOR MAKING CAPONS.

" Fowls intended to be cut, must be kept at least twenty-four " hours without food, otherwise the entrails will fill the cavity of " the belly, and render it almost impossible to complete the opera- "tion ; besides, when they have been starved the proper length of " time, they are less liable to bleed.

" The chicken is taken at any age, from five days old until it be- " gins to crow, or even after. Lay the fowl on its left side on the " floor, draw the wings back, and keep it firm by resting the right " foot on its legs, and the other foot or knee on its wings. (The " table with the apparatus does away with the necessity of this stoop- " ing position.) Be careful that the head of the fowl is not held " down, or even touched during the operation, as it would be sure " to cause it to bleed. Pluck the feathers off from its right side near " the hip joint, in a line between that and the shoulder joint ; the " space uncovered should be a little more than an inch square. " Make an incision between the *last two ribs*, having first drawn the " part backward, so when left to itself it will cover the wound in the " flesh. In some fowls the thigh is so far forward that it covers " the last two ribs ; in which case, care must be taken to draw the " flesh of the thigh well, so as not to cut through it, or else it " would lame the fowl, and perhaps cause its death in a few days " after the operation, by inflaming.

" The ribs are to be kept open by the hooks—the opening must " be enlarged each way by the knife, if necessary, until the tes-

" ticles, which are attached to the backbone, are entirely exposed
" to view, together with the intestines in contact with them.
" The testicles are inclosed in a thin skin, connecting them with
" the back and sides—this must be laid hold of with the pliers,
" and then torn away with the pointed instrument ; doing it first
" on the upper testicle, then on the lower. (The lower testicle
" will generally be found a little behind the other—that is, a little
" nearer the rump.)   Next introduce the loop, (which is made of
" a horse hair or a fiber of cocoanut ;) it must be put around the
" testicle which is uppermost, in doing which the spoon is ser-
" viceable to raise up the testicle and push the loop under it, so
" that it shall be brought to act upon the part which holds the
" testicle to the back ; then tear it off by pushing the tube toward
" the rump of the fowl, at the same time drawing the loop.   Then
" scoop it and the blood out with the spoon, and perform the
" same operation on the other testicle.   Take away the hooks,
" draw the skin over and close the wound ; stick the feathers that
" you pulled off before, on the wound, and let the bird go.

" *Remarks.*—If the operation be performed without sufficient
" skill, many of the fowls will prove not to be capons ; these may
" be killed for use as soon as the head begins to grow large and
" get red, and they begin to chase the hens.   The real capon will
" make itself known by the head remaining small, and the comb
" small and withered ; the feathers of the neck or mane will also
" get longer, and the tail will be handsomer and longer : they
" should be kept to the age of fifteen or eighteen months, which
" will bring them in the spring and summer, when poultry is
" scarce and brings a high price.   Take care, however, not to
" kill them near moulting time, as all poultry then is very inferior.
" The operation fails, principally, by bursting the testicle, so that
" the skin which incloses the soft matter, remains in the bird and
" the testicle grows again.

" Birds of five or six months are less liable to have the testicles
" burst in the operation than younger fowls, but they are more
" apt to bleed to death than those of from two to four months old.

" A skillful operator will always choose fowls of from two to

" three months ;—he will prefer also, to take off the lower testi-
" cle first, as then the blood will not prevent him from proceeding
" with the other ; whereas, when the upper one is taken off the
" first, if there should be any bleeding, he has to wait before he
" can take off the lower testicle.

" The large vein that supplies the entrails with blood passes in
" the neighborhood of the testicles ; there is danger that a young
" beginner may pierce it with the pointed instrument in taking off
" the skin of the *lower* testicle, in which case the chicken would
" die instantly, for all the blood in its body would issue out.
" There are one or two smaller veins which must be avoided,
" which is very easy, as they are not difficult to see, If properly
" managed, no blood ever appears until the testicle is taken off ; so
" that should any appear before that, the operator will know that
" he has done something wrong.

" If a chicken die, it is during the operation, by bleeding, (of
" course it is as proper for use as if it bled to death by having its
" throat cut ;) they very seldom die after, unless they have re-
" ceived some internal injury, or the flesh of the thigh has been
" cut through, from not being drawn back from off the last two
" ribs, where the incision is made ; all of which are apt to be the
" case with young practitioners.

" If the testicles be found to be large, the bamboo tube should
" be used, and it should have a strong cocoanut string in it,—for
" small ones the silver tube with a horse hair in it, is best.

" When a chicken has been cut, it is necessary before letting
" it run, to put a permanent mark upon it ; otherwise it would
" be impossible to distinguish it from others not cut. I have been
" accustomed to cut off the outside or the inside toe of the left
" foot,—by this means I can distinguish them at a distance.
" Another mode is to cut off the comb, then shave off the spurs
" close to the leg, and stick them upon the bleeding head, where
" they will grow and become ornamental in the shape of a pair of
" horns. This last mode is perhaps the best, but it is not so
" simple and ready as the first. Whichever mode is adopted, the
" fowl should be marked before performing the operation, because

" the loss of blood occasioned by cutting off the comb or a toe,
" makes the fowl less likely to bleed internally during the
" operation.   It is very common, soon after the operation, for the
" chicken to get wind in the side, when the wound is healing, be-
" tween the flesh and the skin ; it must be relieved by making a
" small incision in the skin, which will let the wind escape.

" Those fowls make the finest capons which are hatched early
" in the spring ; they can be cut before the hot weather comes,
" which is a great advantage.

" Never attempt to cut a full-grown cock ; it is a useless
" and cruel piece of curiosity.   I have never known one to live.
" The first efforts at acquiring this art should be made on dead
" subjects ; this will save the infliction of much cruelty.   Be not
" discouraged with the first difficulties; with practice they will
" disappear ; every season you will find yourself more expert,
" until the cutting of a dozen fowls before breakfast will be a
" small matter.

" It may be well to give a warning against becoming dissatisfied
" with the tools.   A raw hand, when he meets with difficulties, is
" apt to think the tools are in fault, and sets about to improve
" them and invent others ; but it is only himself that lacks skill,
" which practice alone can give.   I have spent money, besides
" wasting my time in this foolish notion, but have always found
" that the old, original tools, which came from China, and where
" this mode of operating was invented, are the best.

" Take care that the tools are not abused by ignorant persons
" attempting to use them ; they will last a person's life-time if
" properly used ; but if put out or order, none but a surgical-
" instrument maker can repair them properly."

In all cases where sufficient attention is given to the raising of
poultry to make their preparation for the market an important
item of business, there can be no question that much profit would
result from an adoption of the system of caponizing ; but, done in
a hap-hazard way, no especial care being given to the preparation
of the birds for sale, and to the establishment of a reputation in the
market, it would probably not be worth while to attempt it at all.

CHAPTER XVI.

THE DAIRY.

OF all the means by which farmers convert the productions of the soil into merchantable products the dairy is the most scientific and systematic. At the same time, if its various operations are conducted with care and on sound business principles, it is by far the most profitable, and conduces more than any other to the proper maintenance of the fertility of the soil.

Dairy farming includes the preparation for market of the three great staples,—milk, cheese, and butter.

Farmers living within easy reach (and in these days two hundred miles of railroad are easy) of a large market for milk, have generally found that, in view of the less care required, the most profitable course to pursue is to sell the entire product of milk to the wholesale dealers. Were this course pursued for many years in succession, without the purchase of food from exterior sources, the result would be injurious to almost any land. But since it is universally found to be profitable to purchase brewers' grains, bran, linseed meal, cotton-seed meal, or other concentrated food, it is probable that the amount of phosphates and of ammonia restored to the farm in the purchased food, compensates for the loss of mineral matter in the milk sold. For the future,—for that day when the constant removal of more earthy plant constituents than are restored in the purchased food shall have materially lessened the productiveness of the land,—there is no doubt that means of restoration will be found that do not now exist in an available form, or that such as do now exist will be more largely made use of, and that when the addition of large quantities of phosphoric acid, potash, etc., become necessary to fertility they can be obtained by farmers at paying rates.

To take an extremely theoretical view of the selling of milk, it may be said that we act on the principle that " sufficient unto the day is the evil thereof." Practically, I am inclined to think that, while the future deterioration of the soil is pretty certain, all of the circumstances of the case being considered, this system is not injudicious. So long as by the feeding of purchased food, and by the careful use of the manure produced, the fertility of the land may be kept at a satisfactory point, farmers, as a rule, will not, and perhaps it is not necessary that they should, spend large sums in the purchase of special fertilizers ; because, when they become really necessary, they are morally certain to be purchased and to be applied with judgment. Therefore, the most careful and economical foresight need not be greatly alarmed by the present waste of capital. Or, to state the case in a few words, so long as farming will pay without the purchase of foreign manures, so long will they be dispensed with ; when farming will only pay with their assistance they are sure to be purchased ; consequently, while in an operation of my own I should carefully eschew any system which removed from the soil in any single year more mineral matter than the purchased food of that year returned to it, I am fully aware that most farmers situated, as they often are, remote from the sources of these fertilizers, either will not or cannot adhere to this rule ; and while I believe that either they or their descendants will suffer to a certain extent from their course, I do not believe that the inconvenience will be very great, or that the ultimate profit of their operations will be disastrously reduced. This question of the removal of phosphates and potash is the only grave objection to the selling of milk. Setting that aside, we see ample reason why all farmers, who are so situated that their milk can be conveniently sold, day by day, should prefer this means of converting it into money ; for it is desirable to avoid the perplexing cares of the buttery and cheese-room when possible ; and ordinarily the price obtained for the milk is pretty nearly as great as would be obtained for the various products of milk if manufactured at home.

To show, however, that the " mineral theory " offers a grave objection to the sale of milk, it is only necessary to state the teachings of the following :—

Analysis of Milk by Haidlen.

Water	873·
Butter	30·
Caseine	48·2
Milk Sugar	43·9
Phosphate of Lime	2·31
Magnesia	·42
Iron	·07
Chloride of Potassium	1·44
Sodium and Soda	·66
	1,000·00

One hundred gallons of milk weigh about 1,000 pounds ; therefore, each hundred gallons remove from the farm 2·31 pounds of phosphate of lime, and 1·44 pounds of chloride of potassium. For our present purposes the other constituents of the milk may be disregarded, as being less in quantity and comparatively unimportant. Ten cows of good average quality will produce perhaps 5,000 gallons of milk per annum, and the sale of their milk will remove from the farm 115·5 pounds of phosphate of lime, and 72 pounds of chloride of potassium.

It is true that these amounts seem trifling, when compared with the immense quantities of both of these elements that all fertile soils contain ; but it must not be forgotten that of the very large content of mineral food developed by a searching analysis of the soil, only a slight proportion is yearly made available for the uses of the plant, and that the whole quantity removed is taken from this available stock. If the restoration by natural processes is sufficiently active to make up for the removal, and in many cases no doubt it would be, practical farming need take no cognizance of the loss. But on lands where yearly manuring is necessary for the production of satisfactory crops, there is no doubt that even this slight removal would in many instances tend, sooner or later, to the impoverishment of the land. As before stated, however, the threatened impoverishment is now so remote, and the means

of recuperation so certain, that the question whether to sell milk
or to manufacture it on the farm should be decided mainly in the
light of the question of profit and loss.

For a milk dairy, pure and simple, such cows should be selected
as are known to give an excessively large yield of milk.   For sale
in the market the question of quality is of little consequence, as,
especially when sold to wholesale dealers, there would be no difference in price resulting from superior richness.   Quantity is the
only point to be looked to, and to gain this we should not only
select large milkers, but should feed them on such food as, while
it would properly sustain all of the functions of their bodies, would
stimulate the production of the greatest possible flow of milk.

For the manufacture of butter and cheese, however, we should
be influenced by far different considerations.   Not only should we
select such cows as are known to produce milk rich in the constituents that our butter or cheese requires, but we should feed
them on such food as will increase the production of these richer
constituents to the greatest extent that is possible without injury
to the animals' health.

BREEDS OF DAIRY CATTLE.

The short-horns, while they are the largest of all the bovine
races, are sometimes the greatest milkers.   Certain families,
that have long been grown for beef purposes only, produce so
little milk that it is sometimes difficult to give calves a fair headway by feeding them on the milk of their dams alone.   Other
families again, which are known as great milkers, give larger yields
than almost any other breed with which we are familiar, and they
have the great advantage that, when their usefulness for milking is
ended, they may be rapidly fattened to a great size and sold to the
butcher at high prices.

Dutch cattle, which are supposed to have entered largely
into the formation of the short-horn breed, are very large
milkers, and probably the milking qualities of the short-horns are
inherited from this side of their ancestry.   The pure race (many
of which have been recently imported into this country, although

they are by no means generally disseminated, nor yet within the reach of common farmers) promises to the milk producer perhaps as good results as can be obtained from the consumption of his crops by the aid of any other. The black and white cattle which are so common along the banks of the Hudson River, and in other parts of the States of New York and New Jersey which were originally settled from Holland, are mainly Dutch in their origin ; and they are to this day, as a rule, great milkers and excellent cows.

Devons and Herefords, although most valuable for the production of beef and as working oxen, are less conspicuous than some of the other breeds as good dairy cattle.

The Ayrshire is, *par excellence*, the milkman's cow. She is rather small, perfectly formed, well developed in every point that tends to the production of large quantities of milk, and of that delicacy of organization which invariably accompanies the production of rich milk ; and whether the business be the sale of milk or the manufacture of cheese, she leads the list of the pure breeds, while for butter she is hardly, if at all, inferior to any other in the quantity produced. Were it required that we should lose from our dairy farms all but one breed of our cattle, the Ayrshire should by all means be the one retained ; for, although a large eater, she converts her food into milk more completely than does any other animal.

The Jersey (often miscalled the Alderney) is, essentially, a butter cow. The quantity of milk given is very much less than that of the Ayrshires, Short-horns, and Dutch cattle, and the production of a large quantity of milk is by many breeders of Jerseys considered by no means an advantage. The proportion of cream contained in the milk, the richness of the cream itself, and the completeness with which the butter-forming elements of the food are converted, mark the Jersey as the most profitable, and in all respects the most satisfactory animal for butter farms. While the average production of cream from the milk of ordinary cows is about 12 1-2 per cent., that of the Jersey's produces generally about 20, and sometimes even 25 per cent.,—

the cream at the same time producing more ounces of butter to the quart.

An experiment was recently tried, with a view to testing this question, with three pure-bred Jersey cows, three grades, (one one-half, one three-quarters, and one seven-eighths Jersey,) and three native animals. All were in about equally good condition, having run about the same average length of time since calving, and all were fed in precisely the same manner. It was found that while it required eleven quarts of the milk of the "native" cows to make a pound of butter, and eight and a quarter quarts of the milk of the grades, a pound of much better butter was made from six and one-third quarts of the milk of the Jerseys. The difference in the amount of food was considerable,—that of the pure Jerseys being the least of all. The number of quarts of milk, of course, was much less in the case of the Jerseys than of the grades, and in the case of the grades than of the " natives ;" but the general result established the fact that a given quantity of butter was produced by the Jersey cattle by the consumption of less food than the others required. Being smaller animals, less was required to maintain their ordinary vital functions. There recently came to my notice the case of a pure Jersey cow that, during her prime, for eight weeks in succession produced sixteen pounds of butter per week. The late Mr. John T. Norton, of Farmington, Connecticut, keeping quite a large herd of pure Jersey cows, found that they yielded a yearly average of somewhat more than two hundred pounds of butter each. While these animals are noted for the production of large quantities of rich butter, they are comparatively valueless for the cheese dairy, and still more so for the selling of milk.

These pure breeds are in the main the originators of the dairy animals of the United States ; yet there are very few dairies in the whole country that are supplied only with pure stock, the pure breeding being almost exclusively in the hands of those who make the sale of thoroughbred animals, at high prices, a considerable item of their business. But the demand on which their high prices are based is largely for the use of thoroughbred animals in improving the stock of common farms ; and it is fast coming to be understood that, while for ordinary purposes there is not, perhaps, a great advantage in favor of pure breeding, there is a decided advantage in the infusion of a large proportion of the blood of some well-defined race, into the mixed breeds kept for various dairy purposes; and while it is not seldom that we find a common or "native" cow that, both in the production of milk, and cheese, and of butter, is in all respects as good as ordinary specimens of the pure breeds, it is a general truth that the larger the proportion of a thoroughbred strain that we are able to introduce into our common herds, the better will be the general results, and, what is incidentally of great advantage, the more uniform will be their character, and the more will they come under the influence of a regularly established and methodical system of treatment.

It is a well-established principle in cross-breeding, not only with cows, but with all domestic animals, from horses to poultry, that the purity of blood should be on the side of the sire ; and by a proper observance of this principle we may, within two or three generations, bring the general characteristics of our herds to a tolerably close conformity with the thoroughbred standard. The physiological reason for this influence is supposed to be, that, by a long course of careful breeding, certain desirable qualities have become so established in the race,—such a "fixity of type" has been created,—that the pure blood, crossed with animals of less marked peculiarities, has, so to speak, a greater impetus, and exercises a more powerful influence over the progeny. A dozen native cows of varying form, color, and quality, crossed with a pure Devon bull, would produce calves possessing very generally the characteristics of the Devon race ; and after the second or third generation reversals to the common type would be comparatively rare.

Therefore, if it is determined by a farmer that any one of the pure races of dairy animals possesses for his purposes decided advantages, it is within his power, simply by the use of vigorous males of that race, to establish throughout his herd, within a very few years, most, if not all, of the desirable dairy qualities of the pure

breed ; and not unfrequently there will be retained the size, soundness, and adaptability to the climate and soil of the district, which
the common-bred herd possessed in marked degree.   Of course, in
securing the good qualities of two classes of animals, there is always
the risk of perpetuating their bad qualities as well ; and attention
should always be given to the avoidance of individual elements of
weakness, on the side of both the sire and the dam, for it is a
well-known fact in breeding that defects are transmitted quite as
surely as are good qualities.

As to the general hardiness of constitution, including good
appetite, cheerful spirits, and ability to withstand the rigors of
inclement seasons, so great is the flexibility of nature that I doubt
if very much is to be said in favor of any particular race or breed.
Treated in the same manner, all of the breeds of dairy cattle, provided, of course, that they are not exposed to undue hardships,
will be found to be about equal in this respect.   It was for a long
time a popular objection to the Jerseys, that their delicacy of conformation and texture unfitted them for use in our more Northern
States.   But the universal success that has attended their establishment in eastern Massachusetts, (in probably the worst climate on
the Atlantic coast,) where they were introduced more than twenty
years ago, and where not only has the original stock been bred
pure, but almost yearly fresh importations have been added to
them, demonstrates the fact that this objection is a purely imaginary one.   Jerseys, although originating in the moderate and
humid climate of the English Channel, support as well the rigors
of our winters as the Ayrshires of Scotland do ; and there is no
doubt that the still more delicate animals of the Azores, with the
aid of judicious care in their first introduction, would compare
favorably with our native animals in their ability to withstand the
effect of the weather.   The immense herds of animals brought
yearly from Texas to pass their winters in the open air in the
cold Northwest, sufficiently establish the soundness of the fore
going opinion.   The Short-horn, a short and fine-haired animal,
which seems especially adapted to the soil and climate of Kentucky,
is nowhere raised in greater perfection than high among the moun-

tains of Berkshire County, Massachusetts ; and the thin-skinned Ayrshires thrive remarkably in every part of the North.

Of course, every good animal, whether of an imported or of the native stock, requires comfortable shelter during the winter season or it must suffer in proportion to its exposure. The scrub races of the poor farming of our cold Northern hills which have through many generations developed into any thing but good animals, might be improved by being brought under better treatment ; and there is no doubt that any good native or foreign animal, subjected to the treatment under which these have been bred, would soon deteriorate into a scrub, or would die in the early effort. Dairy animals all require a certain protection and care ; but it is doubtful whether that which is suited to those that are apparently the most hardy, is not equally applicable to those of more delicate appearance. It may be said, with reference to all breeds of dairy cattle, that they are, to a very large extent, an artificial production. The effect of their long domestication, the constant object having been to procure as large an amount as possible of milk, cheese, and butter, has been to stimulate to a great extent a single characteristic, which, in a state of nature, is only so far developed as the nutrition of the calf renders necessary. In the wild state the cow gives but little milk at any time, and none at all during the greater part of the year. The effect of domestication has been to very greatly increase both the quantity and duration of the yield, so that now the chief energies of the animal's organization are devoted simply to the production of milk. And in all of our operations, both of breeding and feeding, the object of still further developing this quality should be kept constantly in mind. In addition to the control over the character of our herds that the simple element of " blood " gives us, a very important influence is also exercised by the circumstances under which they are kept, and especially by the abundance and quality of their food. It may be set down as a general rule, that the animals of rich countries are large, and those of poor countries are small ; and even a few generations' breeding on a rich farm will considerably increase the size of the smaller races, while in a few

30

generations on poor land the size of the larger breeds will be equally reduced. Thus nature is constantly seeking to bring about a due conformity between the soil and the herds feeding upon it. It would be useless, therefore, to attempt to raise any herd to its highest pitch of excellence, no matter how pure the breed might be, unless at the same time the proportion and quality of food required by the perfect animal of the breed, were regularly supplied. Either we should too greatly increase the tendency to fat and to large development on the one hand, or we should too much reduce these on the other. Having adopted the type that we wish to attain in breeding, it is necessary always to adjust the quality and quantity of the food to its preservation or improvement. By too great an increase of size and tendency to fatten we may reduce the milking qualities ; or by stinted feeding we may so enfeeble the constitution as to destroy the especial quality on which our preference for a given breed has been based. This question of breeding furnishes in itself ample material for a larger book than this, and it would be improper to enter here more fully into its discussion. The few hints already given should suffice to induce any thoughtful farmer to study carefully the principles set forth in more elaborate works on the subject.

THE SELECTION OF MILCH COWS.

In the selection of milch cows care should be given, in the first instance, to those general characteristics of the dairy animal which are permanent in all breeds, and which are the universal indications, the world over, of good milkers. The following statement by Mr. Flint very well covers the more important points of the case :—*

"In order to have no superfluous flesh, the cow should have a "small, clean, and rather long head, tapering toward the muzzle. "A cow with a large, coarse head, will seldom fatten readily, or "give a large quantity of milk. A coarse head increases the pro- "portion of weight of the least valuable parts, while it is a sure

* Milch Cows and Dairy Farming. By Charles L. Flint. Boston : 1867.

" indication that the whole bony structure is too heavy. The mouth
" should be large and broad ; the eye bright and sparkling, but of
" a peculiar placidness of expression, with no indication of wildness,
" but rather a mild and feminine look. These points will indicate
" gentleness of disposition. Such cows seem to like to be milked,
" are fond of being caressed, and often return caresses. The
" horns should be small, short, tapering, yellowish, and glistening.
" The neck should be small, thin, and tapering toward the head,
" but thickening when it approaches the shoulders ; the dewlaps
" small. The fore-quarters should be rather small when com-
" pared with the hind-quarters. The form of the barrel will be
" large, and each rib should project further than the preceding
" one, up to the loins. She should be well-formed across the
" hips and in the rump.

" The spine, or backbone, should be straight and long, rather
" loosely hung, or open along the middle part, the result of the
" distance between the dorsal vertebræ, which sometimes causes a
" slight depression, or sway back. By some good judges this
" mark is regarded as of great importance, especially when the
" bones of the hind-quarters are also rather loosely put together,
" leaving the rump of great width, and the pelvis large, and the
" organs and milk-vessels lodged in the cavities largely developed.
" The skin over the rump should be loose and flexible. This
" point is of great importance ; and as, when the cow is in low
" condition, or very poor, it will appear somewhat harder and
" closer than it otherwise would, some practice and close observ-
" ation are required to judge well of this mark. The skin, indeed,
" all over the body, should be soft and mellow to the touch with
" soft and glossy hair. The tail, if thick at the setting on, should
" taper and be fine below.

" But the udder is of special importance. It should be large in
" proportion to the size of the animal, and the skin thin, with soft,
" loose folds extending well back, capable of great distention when
" filled, but shrinking to a small compass when entirely empty. It
" must be free from lumps in every part, and provided with four
" teats set well apart, and of medium size. Nor are the milk-

" veins less important to be carefully observed. The princ'pal
" ones under the belly should be large and prominent, and extend
" forward to the navel, losing themselves, apparently, in the very
" best milkers, in a large cavity in the flesh, into which the
" end of the finger can be inserted; but when the cow is not
" in full milk, the milk-vein, at other times very prominent, is not
" so distinctly traced; and hence, to judge of its size when the
" cow is dry, or nearly so, this vein may be pressed near its end,
" or at its entrance into the body, when it will immediately fill up
" to its full size. This vein does not carry the milk to the udder,
" as some suppose, but is the channel by which the blood returns;
" and its contents consist of the refuse of the secretion, or what
" has not been taken up in forming milk. There are, also, veins
" in the udder and the perineum, or the space above the udder,
" and between that and the buttocks, which it is of special import-
" ance to observe. These veins should be largely developed, and
" irregular or knotted, especially those of the udder. They are
" largest in great milkers.

" The knotted veins of the perineum, extending from above
" downward in a winding line, are not readily seen in young heif-
" ers, and are very difficult to find in poor cows, or cows of only
" a medium quality. They are easily found in very good milkers,
" and if not at first apparent, they are made so by pressing upon
" them at the base of the perineum, when they swell up, and send
" the blood back toward the vulva. They form a kind of thick
" net-work under the skin of the perineum, raising it up somewhat,
" in some cases near the vulva, in others lower down and nearer to
" the udder. It is important to look for these veins, as they often
" form a very important guide, and by some they would be con-
" sidered as furnishing the surest indications of the milking qual-
" ities of the cow. Their full development almost always indicates
" an abundant secretion of milk; but they are far better developed
" after the cow has had two or three calves, when two or three
" years' milking has given full activity to the milky glands, and
" attracted a large flow of blood. The larger and more promi-
" nent these veins, the better. It is needless to say, that in observ-

" ing them some regard should be had to the condition of the cow,
" the thickness of skin and fat by which they may be surrounded,
" and the general activity and food of the animal.   Food calcu-
" lated to stimulate the greatest flow of milk will naturally increase
" these veins, and give them more than usual prominence."

Flint gives the following description of the characteristics of the
Ayrshire cow :—

    *   *   * " In color, the pure Ayrshires are generally
" red and white, spotted, or mottled, not roan like many of the
" short horns, but often presenting a bright contrast of colors.
" They are sometimes, though rarely, nearly or quite all red, and
" sometimes black and white ; but the favorite color is red and
" white brightly contrasted, and by some, strawberry-color is pre-
" ferred, The head is small, fine, and clean ; the face long and
" narrow at the muzzle, with a sprightly yet generally mild ex-
" pression ; eye small, smart, and lively ; the horns short, fine,
" and slightly twisted upward, set wide apart at the roots ; the
" neck thin ; body enlarging from fore to hind quarters ; the back
" straight and narrow, but broad across the loin ; joints rather
" loose and open ; ribs rather flat ; hind-quarters rather thin ; bone
" fine ; tail long, fine and bushy at the end ; hair generally thin
" and soft ; udder light color and capacious, extending well for-
" ward under the belly ; teats of the cow of medium size, gener-
" ally set regularly and wide apart ; milk-veins prominent and well
" developed. The carcass of the pure-bred Ayrshire is light,
" particularly the fore-quarters, which is considered by good
" judges as an index of great milking-qualities, but the pelvis is
" capacious and wide over the hips."

Concerning the points of the Jersey cow, the following is copied
from the scale of points established by the Royal Jersey Agricultural Society, and is the standard of the best breeding of that island
for many years :—

    *   *   * " The head of the pure Jersey is fine and
" tapering, the cheek small, the throat clean, the muzzle fine,
" and encircled with a light stripe, the nostril high and open ; the
" horns smooth and crumpled, not very thick at the base, taper-

"ing, and tipped with black; ears small and thin, deep orange-
"color inside; eyes full and placid; neck straight and fine; chest
"broad and deep; barrel hooped, broad and deep, well ribbed
"up; back straight from the withers to the hip, and from the
"top of the hip to the setting on of the tail; tail fine, at right
"angles with the back, and hanging down to the hocks; skin
"thin, light color, and mellow, covered with fine soft hair; fore
"legs short, straight, and fine below the knee, arm swelling and
"full above; hind-quarters long and well filled; hind legs short
"and straight below the hocks, with bones rather fine, squarely
"placed, and not too close together; hoofs small; udder full in
"size, in line with the belly, extending well up behind; teats of
"medium size, squarely placed and wide apart, and milk-veins
"very prominent."

Much attention has been paid during a few years past to what
is known as the Milk Mirror or Escutcheon. The relation
between this and the capacity for milk was discovered by
Mr. Guénon, a native of the south of France, whose early life
was passed in the care of a herd of cows. Being a close observer
of nature, an excellent judge of cattle, and a man of great natural
sagacity, he established, after many years of investigation, a system by which he claimed to be able to determine the quantity of
the yield, its duration, and the quality of the milk for the manufacture of butter, by what he called the "Escutcheon."   He
received a gold medal from the Agricultural Society of Bordeaux,
in 1837, as a recognition of the value of his discovery; and
although many of the details of the intricate system established
by him have failed of general adoption, the general principle on
which his system is based is of so much value that it is often
taken as an important criterion in the selection of dairy animals.

The Milk Mirror is the upward-growing hair on the back part
of the udder and the inside of the hind legs.   An examination of
any cow will show that the line where this hair meets the down-
ward-growing hair of the immediately adjacent parts of the body, is
well defined by what is called a "quirl," and the hair included within the quirl and covered by the upward-growing hair is the Milk

Mirror. The shape of the Mirror is very different in different races, and generally assumes one of two or three different forms. For details concerning this subject the reader is referred to well-known publications in which it is set forth. For the purposes of this chapter it will be sufficient to say, in general terms, that, as a general rule, the size of the mirror bears a pretty constant proportion to the amount of the yield of milk ; and while it is true that this indication of great milking qualities, in those cases where it is a reliable indication, accompanies such other general characteristics as of themselves indicate good milkers, at the same time it is one which is so easily studied, that it constitutes perhaps the simplest indication of the general dairy qualities of any individual animal.

The great value of Guénon's system depends on the fact that in *calves* which, neither by the texture of their hides nor the conformation of their bodies, nor, indeed, by any of the general marks on which we depend in the selection of dairy animals, give any indication of their future milking qualities, it is possible by a sole dependence on the character of the escutcheon to predict with considerable certainty their future usefulness for the dairy. Of course, owing to the slight development of the udder, the escutcheon is always very much smaller, even in proportion to the size of the animal, than in the milch cow ; yet the different pro-portions that the escutcheons of two calves bear to their size are an excellent general indication of their future usefulness ; and any farmer who will carefully study this peculiarity of his animals during the various stages of their growth, with the assistance of the plates laid down in Guénon's book (also to be found in Mr. Flint's work), will arrive at a tolerably accurate means of judging of the value of full-grown animals that it is contemplated to purchase, and of the calves that his own herd produces

THE FEEDING AND MANAGEMENT OF DAIRY COWS.

In the chapter on " Winter Feeding and Management " the subject of the treatment of milch cows is considered at length, and a general reference to it will be found in the chapter on " Soiling and Pasturing." It may be well, however, in this connection, to insist on the importance of an exact adaptation of the means used to the end desired to be obtained. The following general principles should never be lost sight of :—

I. To keep the cow always in a thrifty, healthy condition, and with a voracious appetite. The great end of her life, the production of milk, cannot be perfectly accomplished unless she is comfortable and cheerful, and unless she consumes the largest amount of food that it is possible for her to take into her stomach without injury to her health. She should be regarded as an agricultural implement—as a mill, in which we grind up fodder and roots and grain for the purpose of turning out as large a quantity of dairy products as that food is capable of producing. For the same reason that it would be un-profitable to keep an expensive grist-mill running on half-work, so it is unprofitable to keep a cow in such a way that she will turn into milk and butter only a part of the food that her organs are capable of so turning. Up to a certain point every ounce of food given is appropriated for the supply of the natural wastes of the body, and for the production of animal heat. It is only after this universal demand has been supplied that surplus production becomes possible. We will suppose, by way of illustration, that a cow is capable of consuming 100 pounds a day of hay, grain, and roots, and that twenty-five pounds a day would be sufficient to maintain her in good, healthy condition. By drying off her milk we could carry her through the winter in good condition on twenty-five pounds of food per day. But from the consumption of this food we should have gained literally nothing beyond a small quantity of manure. In order to obtain any profit from her keep, it is necessary that she be fed more than this twenty-five pounds a day, and pretty nearly the whole amount in excess of this contributes to the yield of milk and its products. Therefore, the greater the amount of food that we can induce her to con-sume, the greater the proportion of profit resulting from the operation. And herein lies the chief argument against overstock-ing, that is, the keeping of more animals than we can feed in the most liberal manner. For while four cows would, under the foregoing hypothesis, be kept in good condition on 100 pounds of food per day without profit, two cows consuming the same amount would yield a considerable profit, and one cow would yield still more.

2. To adjust the character of the food to the end it is desired to attain. That is to say, if milk is to be sold, the food should be of such a character as to stimulate as much as possible the production of quantity, and, incidentally, to induce the drinking of a large amount of water ; while, if it be the object to make butter, the food should be less watery in its character and much richer in quality—richer chiefly in fat-forming substances ; although even with butter-cows, the fact should be constantly borne in mind that the assimilation by the digestive organs of fat-forming materials, such as sugar, starch, vegetable oils, etc., bears a very close relation to the amount of nitrogenous or flesh-and-cheese-forming matter that the food contains. The principle in this case is, that if a bushel of food contain twenty pounds of starch, this starch will not be assimilated unless accompanied by so much gluten or albumen as must necessarily be taken up by the animal in the digestion of so much starch. The proportion between the nitrogenous food required and that of a fat-forming character, is not constant in all animals, but depends more or less on the extent to which they yield or waste their flesh or fat. Working animals wasting in their economy a large amount of flesh-forming material, would assimilate less starch in proportion to the quantity of this than would milch cows, with whom the production of fat in cream is very great. Experiments on which to base definite directions on this subject are wanting ; and in their absence the farmer must be guided largely by his own observation ; and under the best circumstances he will generally fail to establish the most economical proportion between the two constituents of food ; but there is no doubt that he may, by a proper attention to the principle, add materially to the economy of his operations.

3. To pay attention to the fact that pregnant animals, in addition to the demand which the secretion of milk makes upon their digestive organs, require a certain quantity of food, and food of

the most nutritious character, for the development of the fœtus ; and that they must not be allowed to become so fat, nor to get into such a stimulated and feverish condition as to render the process of parturition dangerous.

4. To so feed the stock that the manure heap shall be made as rich as is consistent with profitable feeding.

The details of the stable work should receive much more attention than farmers usually give them. Above all should every operation be conducted with perfect regularity and system, and in a quiet and orderly manner. Neither boisterous actions, singing, nor unnecessarily loud talking should be allowed to disturb that tranquillity which is more conducive than is any thing else to the successful keeping of milch cows. Not only should all of the utensils used for receiving and carrying milk be kept perfectly sweet and clean, but the stable itself should be kept as clean as a stable can be, should be thoroughly well ventilated, and should be light and cheerful. Food and water should be given by the clock at unvarying hours ; and the hours of milking should be as punctually adhered to as is the dinner hour of the farmer himself.

These details are often regarded by the farmer as minor and unimportant. Minor they undoubtedly are, but their importance is much greater than is commonly supposed. The fact should be considered that proper attention to them adds nothing, or comparatively nothing, to the expenses of the business ; and that even a slight benefit resulting from them is to be passed entirely to the side of profit. But ordinarily the benefit will be by no means slight. Cows fed at irregular hours, spend much of their time in a state of worrying expectancy. Either they eat or drink too little, owing to the short interval that has elapsed, or the sharp edge is taken off of their appetites by too long waiting, while that regular secretion of milk, which ought, in animals of full flow, to accomplish the complete distention of the udder at exactly the time when the milking is to be done, is very much disturbed, and the completeness of the secretion permanently injured by too great distention at one time and too little at another. It is generally stated that it is better that milking should be done

by women than by men or boys; and owing to the greater gentleness of women this is probably true; but by whomsoever the
milking may be done, it should be insisted that under all circumstances the cows shall be treated with the utmost tenderness, and
that they shall not be agitated by loud talking and skylarking.
Perfect decorum and absolute silence should be the rule of the
cow stable; frolicking, music, and story-telling should be reserved,
for some other place.

Bearing in mind the well-known physiological principle that a
perfect development of any organ or any function of the animal
system is only possible in a general condition of perfect health and
normal activity of every organ, much attention should be given to
the condition of the animal's hide. The transmission of animal
moisture and the loose texture of the skin, which indicate perfect health, always conduce to the most complete development
of activity in the various departments of the organism, and to the
best adjustment of the secretion of milk that, under the various
circumstances of food, shelter, and individual capacity, is possible.
At pasture, cows should be afforded either natural or artificial
shelter from the intense rays of the sun, should be undisturbed by
rolicking colts, and unworried by dogs. The feed should be ample—enough to enable them to fill themselves without undue
labor; and there should be comfortable places where, unpestered
by flies, they may chew their cuds in quiet contentment. It is
easy, both in the stable and in the pasture, for every element of
profitable keeping to be harassed out of the best cow; and it is no
less important to keep her in all respects in such condition as to
be able to make the most of what she eats, than it is to give her
food enough.

The question of exercise, especially during the winter season, is
an important one; and, in estimating its advantages, we should
not lose sight of the importance of maintaining an equal temperature. Many of the most successful dairymen in the country keep
their cattle in the stall uninterruptedly, providing water within the
building in order that the animals may have no occasion to go out
into the cold air. I have in my mind now one well-managed

dairy, where nearly fifty pure-bred and high grade Ayrshires are kept, and kept in the most profitable way, in which it is a rule that, from the time of the first tying up in the autumn until the spring pastures are ready for use, no cow shall leave her stall for any purpose, except when it is necessary to take her to the calving pen.   I saw this herd late in the winter, when they had been tied by the neck for four months, and I never saw animals in more perfectly satisfactory condition in all respects.   The most perplexing question attending the proper arrangement of cow stables lies in the apparently contradictory requirements of ventilation and temperature.   Fresh air is indispensably necessary to health ; a tolerable degree of warmth is highly important to profitable feeding ; and while it should be the study of every farmer to supply his animals with a sufficient amount of fresh air, he should endeavor to do this with the least possible reduction of the temperature of the stable.   The different means of ventilation, all of which have much to recommend them, may be selected according to the requirements of individual cases,—due regard being had chiefly to avoiding the creation of drafts of air about the animals. The heat emanating from a full-grown and healthy animal is sufficient to modify the temperature of the air by which she is surrounded, provided this be not too rapidly removed ; and a well-thatched and warm shed, open to the leeward, is not a bad place to keep cows in ordinary weather.   Certainly it is much better than a barn, through the open doors of which a draft of air is constantly sweeping across their backs.   It will be well to have doors or windows opening from the stable toward different points of the compass, being careful to open only such as are not on the side against which the wind is blowing.   The foul air, escaping from the animal's lungs and from the decomposition of the manure, should be carried off through ascending ventilators ; but, as the resulting gases of decomposition and respiration are heavier than the atmosphere, it will be best for these ventilators, supplied with a strong draft at the cap, to have their opening near the floor.   They will, under this arrangement, remove very much less of the accumulated warmth of the stable than if starting from the ceiling.

MILK AND ITS PRODUCTS.

The prime object in keeping dairy cows is to obtain milk. To this end, under ordinary circumstances, every thing else is made to yield. The increase of size, the production of calves, the yielding of good beef, are all either of no importance or of very secondary importance. Every effort in breeding and in feeding is directed toward the production of the largest quantity or the richest quality of milk.

This being the case it is the only wise policy to continue, after the milk has been secreted into the udder, the same care in its drawing and in its preparation for market that have attended the treatment of the animal. Milking should be done quickly, regularly, and thoroughly, the last drop being drawn from the udder at each milking; since nothing tends so much to cause a cow to fall off in her yield as the leaving of even a small quantity of strippings in the udder. As the milk or some part of it is to be used as food, of course every thing connected with the operation of milking should be as cleanly as possible. Not only should the vessel into which the milk is drawn be thoroughly clean, but the udder and teats should, if necessary, be washed, and the hands of the operator should be free of offense. Immediately after milking the pail should be taken at once out of the stable, for even within a short time after the milk has been drawn, it may become tainted by the exhalations from the accumulations of filth which are unavoidable even in the best-regulated stables.

In all cases milk should be strained as soon as possible after it is drawn, should be either cooled or warmed or left at its natural temperature, according to the season, and the uses for which it is intended. For instance,—if to be sent to the milk dealers in cities, it should be immediately put in the cans, these being surrounded by cold water (if possible, by running water) so that the natural heat of the milk may be withdrawn as rapidly and thoroughly as possible. If it is intended for butter making, it should be set away in pans, either at the natural temperature in warm and moderate weather, or in cold weather heated to such a

degree that the rising of the cream will have commenced before
the temperature of the mass is too greatly reduced for the operation
to be carried on with the requisite activity.   In summer time milk
intended for butter should be set away in a cool place, so that it
may be soon reduced to a degree of heat that is not conducive to
rapid souring ; and even in moderate weather, as in spring and
fall, due care should be taken that it does not become too warm.
The heating of milk in winter time is by no means universally
practiced, but where it is practiced, and I speak from my own
experience, it is productive of excellent results.   My custom is
to have a kettle of water put on the stove at milking time, and
raised to the boiling point by the time the milk is brought to
the house.   Into this water the milk pail is placed and allowed to
remain, until a little steam begins to show itself over the surface
of the milk, the mass being gently stirred once or twice during the
heating.   It is then strained directly into pans, and an amount of
cream rises within twenty-four hours which, without the heating,
would have required double that time.   I fancy, too, that the consistency of the cream is rather better, its quantity somewhat greater,
and its color somewhat deeper, while the firmness of the butter
is in no way reduced, nor is the product in any way injured, even
if it is not benefited as I think that it is.   Milk for cheese-making,
however it may be kept immediately after being brought in, should
be artificially raised to the required temperature before the rennet
is added.

As in the case of the selling of milk, no further preparation is
necessary than the early cooling above alluded to, the remainder
of this chapter may be best devoted to the consideration of the
manufacture of butter and cheese.

BUTTER.

Concerning the manufacture of butter much has been written, and much of the lore of local neighborhoods can hardly
be written, consisting as it does of traditional manipulations
which are to be learned much better by experience than
by reading.   Processes in some respects differ almost diamet-

rically. As each may be presumed to think that he has hit upon the plan that is likely to produce the best results, I can hardly do better than to detail here the various processes of my own system of butter-making, which is attended with highly satisfactory results, my butter usually selling for considerably more than the average of the highest market-prices.

The milk-room plays a very important part in the manufacture of butter. It should be airy and cool without being too cold, and should be so arranged that it may be kept at all times scrupulously clean.

The spring-house, in common use in the dairy regions about Philadelphia, and which is almost peculiar to that part of the country, is admirably adapted for the purpose, and although opinions vary as to its necessity for the attainment of the very best results, the results which, in good hands, are obtained with its use, are a strong argument in its favor, and it certainly offers some advantages over the system of dry rooms. A description of one of these spring-houses is included in the following communication that I made in 1868 to the New York *Evening Post*, after a visit to several dairy farms in Chester and Delaware counties :—

" *Philadelphia Butter.*—We took an evening train for the farm " of Mr. S. J. Sharpless, whose herd of pure Jerseys feed on the " rich pastures of Chester County, and arrived in time for the " evening milking. It was a pleasant ending to our journey to " see the fine-skinned and deer-like creatures marching in regular " procession through the long grass to the milking-house, imported " ' Niobe ' swaggering along with her enormous orange-colored " udder, at the head of the troop ; and we were disposed to think " that with such a farm and with such a herd, we too could make " ' Philadelphia ' butter.

" The milking-house is a light, wooden structure, with so many " open doors and windows that it is hardly more than a shed. In " winter it is closed up and used as a stable for young stock. In " size it is about twenty-two feet by thirty-six, with a row of " stanchions on each side, and with mangers in which a little bran

"is put at each milking-time. Each cow has her own place,
"with her name, age, and pedigree over her manger, and she
"always goes to it as though she could read. Their names have
"been put up in the order in which they come from the pasture,
"the 'master' cow entering first and the least plucky last.

"The milking is done by women, the same one always attend-
"ing to each cow, and it is done rapidly and quietly, no unneces-
"sary talking and no skylarking being allowed. We measured
"'Niobe's' yield and found it to be eleven quarts, (she gave nine
"the next morning—making twenty for the two milkings,) not
"bad for a butter-making Jersey cow. The others gave less,—
"the smallest not more than eight quarts at two milkings,—but
"the whole herd of eighteen cows could not have given less than
"two hundred quarts a day, and this of milk that yields over
"twenty per cent. of cream.

"Near by the milking-house is the 'spring-house,' the institu-
"tion of this region, about twenty-four feet long and eighteen feet
"wide, built of stone, with its foundation set deeply in the hill-
"side, and its floor about four feet below the level of the ground
"at the down-hill side. The site is that of a plentiful spring,
"which is allowed to spread over the whole of the inclosed area
"to a depth of about three inches above the floor of oak, laid
"on sand or gravel. At this height there is an over-floor by
"which the water passes to a tank in an open shed at the down-
"hill end of the house. On the floor of the spring-house there
"are raised platforms or walks, to be used in moving about the
"room, but probably three-quarters of the space is occupied by
"the slowly-flowing spring-water. The walls are about ten feet
"high, and at the top, on each side, are long, low windows,
"closed only with wire-cloth, which gives a circulation of air at
"the upper part of the room. The milk is strained into deep
"pans of small diameter, that are kept well painted on the
"outside, and are provided with bails by which they are
"handled. The depth of the milk in the pans is about
"three inches, and they are set directly upon the oak floor,
"the water, which maintains a temperature of fifty-eight degrees

" Fahrenheit, surrounding them to about the height of the
" milk.

" The cream is taken off after twenty-four hours, and is kept
" in deep vessels having a capacity of about twelve gallons.
" These vessels are not covered, and as the room is scarcely
" warmer than the water, the cream is kept at about fifty-eight or
" fifty-nine degrees, until it is put in the churn.

" Having inspected the dairy arrangements, we took our trav-
" elers' appetites to the supper-table, where we were regaled
" with such butter and with such cream as only Jersey cows can
" give, and then we passed a long evening in a discussion of the
" merits of the breed and of its individual members which we had
" examined since our arrival ; and in devising the ways and means
" for making—by the aid of windmills and otherwise—such sub-
" stitutes for the spring-house as our more scantily-watered farms
" might admit of.

" *Churning.*—The next morning we rose at half-past four to
" see the churning and butter-making. The churn is a large
" barrel (bulging only enough to make the hoops drive well) with
" a journal or bearing in the center of each head, so that it may
" be revolved by horse-power. This barrel has stationary short
" arms attached to the inside of the staves, so arranged as to cause
" the greatest disturbance of the milk as it passes through them
" in the turning of the churn. At one side is a large opening
" secured by a cover that is screwed firmly into its place—this is
" the cover or lid of the churn. Near it is a hole less than an inch
" in diameter, for testing the state of the churning and for drawing
" off the buttermilk. This is closed with a wooden plug.

" The churning lasted about an hour, at the end of which time
" it was necessary to add a little cold milk to cause the butter to
" gather. This being secured, and the buttermilk drawn off, cold
" water was twice added, a few turns being given each time to the
" churn, and when the last water was drawn off it came nearly
" free of milkiness. A crank was then put on to an arm of the
" churn, the horse-power thrown out of gear, and a gentle rocking
" motion caused the butter to be collected at the lower side, directly

31

" over the small hole—through which the remaining water escaped.
" It was left in this condition about two hours. After breakfast
" we returned to see the working of the butter.

" *Butter-worker.*—In one corner of the spring-house stands the
" butter-worker, a revolving table about three feet in diameter.
" The center of this, for a diameter of twelve inches, is an iron
" wheel with a row of cogs on the upper side of its rim. From
" this rim to the raised outer edge the table (made of wood) slopes
" downward, so that as the buttermilk is worked out it passes into
" a shallow groove and is carried away through a pipe which dis-
" charges into a pail standing below. Over the sloping part of
" the table there works a corrugated wooden roller, revolving on
" a shaft that is supported over the center of the table, and has a
" small cog-wheel that works in the cogged rim of the center
" wheel, and causes the table to revolve under the roller, as this
" is turned by a crank at its outer end. Of course the roller is
" larger at one end than at the other, so as to conform to the slope
" of the table, and its corrugations are very deep, not less than
" two inches at the larger end. Supported at each end of the
" roller, and on both sides, are beveled blocks, which, as the
" table revolves, force the butter from each end toward the center
" of the slope. About twenty pounds of butter is now put on the
" table, and the roller is turned, each corrugation carrying through
" a long, narrow roll, which is immediately followed by another
" and another, until the whole table is covered. The roller does
" not quite touch the table, and there is thus no actual crushing of
" the particles. The beveled blocks slightly bend these rolls
" and crowd them toward the center of the sloping part, so that
" when they reach the roller again they are broken in fresh places,
" and by a few revolutions are thoroughly worked in every part.

" *Final Processes.*—Then follows a process that was new to all
" of us—the ' wiping ' of the butter. The dairy-maid (in this
" instance a lusty young man) turning the roller backward, with
" the left hand, so that the butter comes through at the right hand
" side, presses upon every part of it a cloth which has been wrung
" dry in the cold spring water, and which he frequently washes

" and wrings out. This is continued until not a particle of water
" is to be seen in the butter as it comes from the roller, to which
" it now begins to adhere. If there is any secret in the making
" of Philadelphia butter, this is it ; and it has much to do with its
" uniform waxiness of texture, whether hard or soft.

" After this, the butter is salted (an ounce of salt to three
" pounds of butter)—still, by the aid of the machine, and any
" lurking atom of moisture is in this way prevented from becom-
" ing a cause of rancidity.

" When the salt is thoroughly worked through the whole mass,
" the butter is removed to a large table, where it is weighed out
" and put up into pound-prints.

" The working, wiping, and salting of over one hundred pounds
" of butter occupied about an hour, and before 10 A. M. the entire
" churning, beautifully printed, as fragrant as the newest hay, and
" as yellow as pure gold, such butter as only Jersey cream will
" make, was deposited in large tin trays and set in the water to
" harden. The next morning it was wrapped in damp cloths, each
" pound by itself, put in a tin case, each layer having its own
" wooden shelf, with two compartments of pounded ice to keep
" it cool, and, surrounded by a well-coopered and securely-locked
" cedar tub, was sent to the Continental Hotel, where we found
" it, on our return, as delicious as when it left the farm.

" It is very difficult to describe any process in which so much
" depends on the judgment of the operator, and the writer hardly
" hopes for more than that this will stimulate others who are inter-
" ested in the subject, to examine for themselves the dairy opera-
" tions of this interesting and beautiful region.

" One of the strongest impressions that we had thus far received
" was, that much of the excellence of the butter was due to the
" use of the spring-house, but our next visit (on the recommenda-
" tion of a friend who gave us the names of the most noted of the
" fancy-price dairies) was to a farm where the milk is kept in a
" deep vault, arranged very much like a spring-house, but without
" water. The proprietor of this farm, a man of long experience
" and of excellent reputation as a butter-maker, has satisfied him-

" self, by a long trial of both systems, that the dry room is the
" best.   He attributes the advantage to greater dryness of the air,
" but as, with a free circulation against the cold stone the walls
" were covered with moisture, he had gained very little in this
" respect, even supposing, which is doubtful, that dryness would
" be a gain.

" The thermometer on the wall of his vault was not more than
" one degree higher than that of the spring-house, and our impres-
" sion was that a low and uniform temperature, however attained,
" is the important consideration.   In the dairy that we were now
" visiting there were no shelves, and no provision was made for a
" circulation of air around the pans, as is considered important in
" the dairies of our own region.   In the vault, as in the spring-
" house, the pans, which are equally deep and have even a greater
" depth of milk (over four inches) were placed directly upon the
" floor.   In this dairy the milk was allowed to stand thirty-six
" hours before being skimmed.   The butter is worked and
" salted in the same way, and is equally good in its texture, and
" of very fine flavor.   The color, however, it being thought
" desirable to bring it up to ' Alderney ' standard, was secured by
" the use of *annotto*, which is used winter and summer to secure
" uniformity of coloring.   A solution of the annotto is made by
" boiling it in water, and the extract is mixed with the cream in
" the churn.   On this farm we saw some fine specimens of the cel-
" ebrated Chester white swine, which are bred in their perfection
" in this region, and are sold at very high prices.   They are sent
" by express, at a tender age, to all parts of the country.

" From here we went to another farm in the vicinity of West-
" chester, which bears an equally high reputation for its butter, and
" where the spring-house has been abandoned, and the cream is kept
" as previously described, in a dry vault.   In the manufacture of
" the butter, the same processes obtain, and the same good result
" is secured.   In all of the instances described a very high price,
" much above that of the common market, is obtained."

My own milk-house at Ogden Farm, where it was impossible
to secure the advantages of a living spring, has been so constructed

ás to secure the advantage of cold water forced from a constant well, about 1000 feet away, by a self-regulating windmill. This is the same well and mill by which the barn is supplied, as before described. When the flow is not needed at the barn, it is diverted to the milk-house, where it is received in a mason-work tank 3 ft. deep, 2 ft. wide and 10 ft. long. The overflow of this tank runs to a duck-pond near the house.

After due experimenting with other systems of setting milk, and after a careful examination of the "large-pan" system, I have settled on the use of deep cans,—8 inches in diameter and 20 inches deep,— filled with milk to within about 3 inches of the top. These cans are ballasted by a heavy "iron-clad" bottom, so that they will float upright. They are placed in the tank, where they float with the surface of the milk an inch or more below the level of the water. This secures a sufficiently rapid reduction of the temperature of the milk to that of the water, which is in our case about 54°, but which would be better to be much lower,—even 40°.

At a temperature of 54° the milk remains sweet until all the cream has risen.

The cream is taken off with a skimming-dipper. It is from 2 inches to 4 inches deep, according to the season.

The churning is done in a "Bullard" churn, which is an oblong box attached to an oscillating table, having a fly-wheel attached to it to regulate its motion. There are no cleats or paddles in this box; the milk is thrown with a "swash" from end to end. We consider it the best of the many churns we have tried, and have had it in use for some years.

The above system is radically different from the one with which we began our operations ten years ago,—shallow pans and a dasher churn,—and it has commended itself as a great improvement. We have found by careful and repeated trials that we make at least as much butter,—we think rather more; that the quality is decidedly better; and especially that it is more uniform throughout the year.

The butter is washed in the churn and is quickly worked on a white-oak table. Two persons do the working; one chops the butter well over with a two-handled oak worker, and the other pats the surface, as it is being chopped, with a damp sponge (wrung out of cold water), to remove the exuding water and buttermilk. The mass is repeatedly turned and reworked, and at each turning the table is sponged off.

Salt is then added, at the rate of one ounce to each three pounds of butter, and the salted mass is put into a tin pail and floated in the water vat to cool. This small quantity of salt can be safely used only when the butter is to be used fresh. Our deliveries are made twice a week. In the case of butter to be packed and sold in bulk, for shipping much more salt will be needed. It must, however, be borne in mind that salt injures—or over-rides—the delicate natural flavor of butter. It is to be used only in such quantity as will give it the necessary keeping quality.

After a few hours it is taken out, worked (not too much) and sponged, and then made up into half-pound pats for market. Each pat is wrapped in a square of damp cloth and put into the delivery-boxes,—ice being used in summer.

The *extra work* of making and shipping we estimate at one cent per pound. The extra price is considerable. For all that we can supply at all regularly we get *one dollar* per pound. On about 1000 lbs. of the yearly supply we pay 12½ per cent. commission to our city agent. In June we often have a large surplus, which we must sell at any price we can get. In one year we have sold over 5900 lbs., and received for it, *in cash*, over $4400. In winter we color the butter by the process recommended by Whitman & Burrill, of Little Falls, N. Y. This color is an alkaline extract of the pigment of annattoine, which is the dried coloring-matter of annatto. The quantity used is very slight,—only about one tablespoonful of the extract being used for five quarts of cream. It is put into the cream before churning. The amount which attaches to the butter is infinitesimal. Annatto itself is not only not objectionable; it is a wholesome condiment largely used in Brazil for coloring and flavoring dishes,—very much as we use tomato. Care must be taken not to color too deeply. The tint grows more intense with time. If a good "grass-color" is given to the fresh butter, it will, after standing a day or two, become much too deep an orange shade.

In the *American Agricultural Annual* for 1868, there appears an article from the pen of Prof. S. W. Johnson, of Yale College, on the subject of "Milk and Butter,"* from which the subjoined quotations are made. Prof. Johnson's article is based chiefly on researches made at the Experiment Station of the Royal Agricultural Academy of Sweden, in Stockholm :—

"*Composition of milk.*—Analyses were made of the mixed milk " of fifteen cows, (five Ayrshire, five Pembrokeshire, and five " Swedish cows,) which were highly fed and milked at $6\frac{1}{2}$–$7\frac{1}{2}$ " A. M., and $5\frac{1}{2}$–$6\frac{1}{2}$ P. M. These analyses, extending throughout "a whole year, gave the following average result :—

Fat, (butter,)	4·05
Albuminoids, (caseine, etc.,)	3·32
Sugar of milk	4·71
Ash	0·73
	12·81

Dry matter	12·81
Water	87·19
	100·00

" The fluctuations during the entire period were remarkably " small. The lowest percentage of water observed was 85·92, " and the highest was 88·35. In but four instances did the water " fall below 86·6, and in but four did it rise above 88. The com- " position of the milk of uniformly well-fed cows is therefore very " uniform, and scarcely varied throughout the year, whatever may " be the changes in temperature, weather, etc.

" *Morning and Evening Milk* exhibit a constant though slight " difference in composition, which, in general, consists simply in " containing *a half per cent. more fat at night than in the morning.* " *In the morning milk this fat is replaced by almost precisely the same* " *quantity of water.*

" Further investigations showed that the proportion of fat is " influenced somewhat by the time that passes between the milk- " ings—is, in fact, less the longer this time. Thus, milk taken " after an interval of

* American Agricultural Annual, 1863. Orange Judd & Co., New York.

10 hours, contained........................ 4·36 per cent. of fat.
11   "   "   .... 4·31 "   "
12   "   "   .... 3·97 "   "
13   "   "   .... ·· 3·97 "   "
14   "   "   .... 3·51 "   "

" Taking into account the greater quantity of milk obtained in
" the morning, the absolute amount of fat yielded by the cow is
" rather more at morning than at night.

" *Average Composition of the Products obtained from Milk in mak-*
" *ing Butter.*—In making butter, 100 parts of milk yield, on the
" average, in round numbers the following proportions of cream,
" butter, etc., provided the cream rises in a cool apartment, so that
" no sensible evaporation of water takes place :—

Buttermilk .... 6·0
Butter .... 4·0 ⎫ Calculated
Water removed from butter by salting .... 0·1 ⎭ without salt.
                                              _____
                                               10·1

Cream... 10
Skimmed Milk.................................... 90
                                              _____
                                               100

" The average percentage composition of these products is
" given in the subjoined table :—

	New milk.	Skimmed milk.	Cream.	Buttermilk.	Butter.[†]	Brine.[‡]
Fat.................	4·00	0·55	35·00	1·67	85·00	0·00
Albuminoids*.........	3·25	3·37	2·20	3·33	0·51	0·39
Milk sugar...........	4·50	4·66	3·05	4·61	0·70	3·84
Ash........	0·75	0·78	0·50	0·77	0·12	0·86
Water..............	87·50	90·64	59·25	89·62	13·67	94·91
Total.............	100·00	100·00	100·00	100·00	100·00	100·00

" *When is Milk or Cream ready for Churning ?*—It is well
" known that it is very difficult, if not impossible, to bring butter
" speedily from fresh milk, or from the thin cream that gathers
" upon milk kept *cold* for twenty-four hours. It has been supposed

* Caseine and albumen.   † Unsalted.
‡ Brine that separates on working after salting; salt not included.

" that milk should *sour* before butter can be made. This is an
" error, numberless trials having shown that sweet milk and
" sweet cream yield butter, as much and as easily as sour cream,
" provided they have stood for some time at medium temperatures.
" It is well known that the fat of milk exists in minute globules,
" which are inclosed in a delicate membrane. It was natural to
" suppose that in fresh milk this membrane prevents the cohesion
" of the fatty matters, and that when, by standing, the milk or
" cream becomes capable of yielding butter after a short churn-
" ing, it is because the membrane has disappeared or become ex-
" tremely thin. Experiments show, in fact, that those solvents
" which readily take up fat, as ether, for example, dissolve from
" sweet milk more in proportion to the length of time it has stood
" at a medium temperature.

" Readiness for churning depends chiefly upon the *time that has*
" *elapsed since milking*, and the *temperature to which it has been*
" *exposed* in the pans. The colder it is, the longer it must be
" kept. At medium temperature, 60°–70° F., it becomes suita-
" ble for the churn within twenty-four hours, or before the cream
" has entirely risen. Access of air appears to hasten the process.

" The souring of the milk or cream has, directly, little to do
" with preparing them for the churn. Its influence is, however,
" otherwise felt, as it causes the caseine to pass beyond that gelati-
" nous condition in which the latter is inclined to foam strongly
" at low temperatures, and by enveloping the fat-globules hinders
" their uniting together. On churning cream that is *very sour*, the
" caseine separates in a fine granular state, which does not inter-
" fere with the 'gathering' of the butter. Even the tenacious,
" flocky mass that appears on gently heating the sweet whey
" from Chester cheese, may be churned without difficulty after
" becoming strongly sour.

" Cream churned when *slightly* sour, as is the custom in the
" Holstein dairies, yields butter of a peculiar and fine aroma.
" Butter made from very sour cream is destitute of this aroma,
" and has the taste which the Holstein butter acquires after keep-
" ing some time.

" The circumstances that influence the rapidity of souring are
" chiefly *temperature* and *access of air*.   When milk sours, it is
" because of the formation of lactic acid from the milk sugar.   This
" chemical change is the result of the growth of a microscopic vege-
" table organism, which, according to Hallier's late investigations,
" is of the same origin as common yeast.   Like common yeast, this
" plant requires oxygen for its development.   This it gathers from
" the air, if the air have access; but in comparative absence of air, as
" when growing in milk, it decomposes the latter (its sugar) and the
" lactic acid is a chief result of this metamorphosis.   If milk which
" by short exposure to the air has had the microscopic germs of the
" ferment plant sown in it, be then excluded from the air as much
" as possible, the ferment, in its growth, is necessitated to decom-
" pose the milk sugar, and hence the milk rapidly sours.   On the
" other hand, exposure to the air supplies the ferment partly with
" free oxygen, and the milk remains sweet for a longer period.
" Such is the theory of the change.   Müller's experiments confirm
" this view by demonstrating that free exposure to the air, or, bet-
" ter, a supply of pure oxygen gas, retards the souring of milk ;
" while confinement from the air, or replacing it with pure nitro-
" gen, hastens this change.   That low temperatures should prevent
" souring, is in analogy with all we know, both of ordinary chemi-
" cal change and of changes that depend upon vital operations."
*   *   *   *   *   *   *

" *Aeration of the cream during churning* is of little importance.
" Neither chemically nor mechanically does a stream of air favor
" the separation of the butter in any perceptible degree.   On the
" contrary, cream that is cold and slightly sour, is thereby con-
" verted into a mass of froth, from which it is exceedingly difficult
" to make butter."
*   *   *   *   *   *   *

" *Washing Butter.*—To prepare butter for keeping without
" danger of rancidity and loss of its agreeable flavor, great pains
" are needful to remove the buttermilk as completely as possible.
" This is very imperfectly accomplished by simply working or
" kneading.   As the analysis before quoted shows, salting removes

" but little besides water and small quantities of sugar. Caseine,
" which appears to spoil the butter for keeping, is scarcely dimin-
" ished by these means. Washing with water is indispensable
" for its removal.

" In Holland and parts of Holstein it is the custom to mix the
" cream with a considerable amount of water in churning. The
" butter is thus washed as it 'comes.' In Holland it is usual to
" wash the butter copiously with water besides. The finished
" article is more remarkable for its keeping qualities than for fine-
" ness of flavor when new.

" The Holstein butter, which is made without washing, has at
" first a more delicious aroma, but appears not to keep so well as
" washed butter."

*   *   *   *   *   *   *

" *Salting*.—Immediately after churning the mass consists of a
" mixture of butter with more or less cream. In case very rich
" cream (from milk kept warm) is employed, as much as one-third
" of the mass may be cream. The process of working completes
" the union of the still unadhering fat globules, and has, besides,
" the object of removing the buttermilk as much as possible.
" The buttermilk, the presence of which is objectionable in new
" butter by impairing the taste, and which speedily occasions
" rancidity in butter that is kept, cannot be properly removed by
" working alone. Washing, as already described, aids materially
" in the disposing of the buttermilk, but there is a limit to its use,
" since, if applied too copiously, the fine flavor is impaired.
" After working and washing, there remains in the butter a quan-
" tity of buttermilk, or water, which must be removed if the butter
" is to admit of preservation for any considerable time.

" To accomplish this as far as possible, salting is employed.
" The best butter-makers, after kneading out the buttermilk as
" far as practicable, avoiding too much working so as not to
" injure the consistence or ' grain ' of the butter, mix with it about
" three per cent. of salt, which is worked in layers, and then
" leave the whole twelve to twenty-four hours. At the expira-
" tion of this time, the butter is again worked, and still another

"interval of standing, with a subsequent working, is allowed in
"case the butter is intended for long keeping. Finally, when put
"down, additional salt (one-half per cent.) is mixed at the time
"of packing into the tubs or crocks.

"The action of the salt is *osmotic*. It attracts water from the
"buttermilk that it comes in contact with, and also takes up the
"milk-sugar. It thus effects a partial separation of the con-
"stituents of the buttermilk. At the same time it penetrates the
"latter and converts it into a strong brine, which renders decom-
"position and rancidity *difficult* or *impossible*. Sugar has the same
"effect as salt, but is more costly, and no better in any respect.

"Independently of its effect as a condiment, salt has two dis-
"tinct offices to serve in butter-making, viz.: 1st, to remove
"buttermilk as far as possible from the pores of the butter; and
"2d, to render innocuous what cannot be thus extracted.

"It hardly need be stated that the salt must be as pure as pos-
"sible. It must be perfectly white, must dissolve completely in
"water to a clear liquid, untroubled by any turbidity, without
"froth or sediment, must be absolutely odorless, of a pure salt
"taste, without bitterness, and in a moderately dry room must
"remain free from perceptible moisture."

Concerning the very important question of the kind of salt to
be used, the following quotation, taken from the same article, will
be found useful :—

"As regards the purity of different kinds of salt, some of those
"in use in this country deserve notice here. The Turk's Island
"salt has a repute not justified by any facts. As commonly sold
"in the coarse state, it is extremely dirty and impure. Much of
"the fine table salt commonly sold in New England, in Connecti-
"cut, at least, is also impure, and not fit for dairy use. The purest
"salt made in this or any country that the writer is acquaint-
"ed with, came some years ago from Syracuse, New York,
"where the ingenious processes of Dr. Goessman were then
"employed. If, as we suppose, the same processes are in use
"now, the 'Onondaga Factory Filled Salt' must take a rank
"second to none as regards purity and freedom from deleterious

" ingredients, especially the chlorides of calcium and magnesium.
" This rank, we believe, it has assumed in the estimation of all
" who have given it a fair trial. The brand ' Onondaga Factory
" Filled Dairy Salt ' corresponds closely with Dr Müller's de-
" scription of the best salt for removing buttermilk. It is seen
" by the microscope to consist very largely of their shallow,
" hopper-shaped crystals, or thin lamina, probably resulting from
" the fracture of such crystals. In dimensions the crystals are
" perhaps a trifle finer than Dr. Müller recommends. By sifting
" on meshes of one-thirtieth of an inch, the coarser parts would
" leave nothing to be desired in working butter, and the finer
" portion would be perfectly adapted for its putting down."

It cannot be too strongly impressed on the mind of the dairyman that his success in the manufacture of butter for market will
depend on scrupulous cleanliness in every operation, more even
than upon the quality of the milk which his cattle yield. Every
pail, pan, stick, and cloth used in any part of the whole operation,
should be thoroughly washed in boiling hot water, perfectly dried,
and as often as possible exposed to the sun and air. The least
neglect in this particular will inevitably result in such a tainting
of the cream or butter as must unavoidably affect its quality, and
in still greater degree the reputation of his dairy in the market.
A little expenditure of time and labor in attention to these details
will be better rewarded than will any other equal outlay in the
whole course of the business.

The golden rule of agriculture,—that whatever is worth doing
at all is worth doing well, applies with greater force to the operations of the butter dairy than to those of any other department of
farming. Probably a neat and attractive mould for putting up
butter for table use is worth, in the long run, fully five cents for
every pound of butter made ; and in like manner the wrapping of
the prints in cloths, and the sending them to market in the most
carefully prepared condition, adds also to the value of the product ;—and it is in many cases to these little details, which conduce to the securing of fancy prices, that we must look for almost
the sole profit of butter-making. During periods when butter is

cheap, and feed and labor are high, probably the average market-
price will be hardly more than enough to pay the expenses of
cultivation and manufacture; while the slightly, and indeed often
the considerably higher prices that extra care enables us to realize,
will throw the balance very satisfactorily to the right side of the
sheet.

In putting up butter for distant markets, much attention should
be paid to the style of the package. Oak pails, such as are used by
farmers in the vicinity of New York, holding from ten to twenty
pounds of butter, always command a better price for their contents
than do tubs containing butter of the same quality. It has been
recently discovered by dairymen, even as far west as Ohio, that by
using the form of tub that has long been in use in Orange
County, New York, and by branding the cover "Orange County," or "Goshen," they can secure a sufficiently larger price
for the same quality of butter to defray the expenses of shipment
and sale. Of course these practices are not to be recommended,
and it is a subject of regret that those who purchase butter in the
large markets, care so much more for its appearance than for its
quality. But the fact certainly exists that this high value is attached to the simple matter of looks, and he would be an unwise
man who would refuse to avail himself of the suggestion hereby
given, not to the extent, of course, of adopting a false brand, but
by giving in some manner the most attractive appearance possible
to the product of his dairy, and by establishing as soon as possible,
a reputation for his own packages.

Butter for immediate use is often sent, to even distant markets
which are within easy reach, in what is called a cooler-tub.
This tub, the hinged top of which may be firmly secured by the
locking of a bar which passes over it, is entirely filled by a tin
vessel of which each end is cut off with tin partitions, leaving
spaces in which to place pounded ice. The center space is occupied by thin, wooden platforms, laid upon projections on the side
of the tin vessel, which serve to separate the layers of prints or
balls, and prevent their being bruised. The tub is usually made
of sufficient size to hold sixty pounds of butter. In using a tub

of this sort it is found that after it has made a trip of four or five hours in the hottest weather there is still ice remaining in the compartments ; and, with the aid of the wet cloths about the prints, butter is delivered at all times in the hardest possible condition.

In packing down butter for winter use, equally careful attention should be paid to all the details of its manufacture, but the intervals between the churnings should be as long as it is possible to make them without allowing the cream to sour, for the reason that large churnings of butter packed away at one time keep better, and make a more uniform appearance throughout the package, than where smaller quantities are put in in thinner layers. Each layer, after being thoroughly pressed into its place, should be covered with a light sprinkling of the best quality of salt, and the surface should always be covered with a damp cloth sprinkled also with salt.

CHEESE.

The manufacture of cheese in this country is very rapidly being concentrated into a wholesale business by means of the factory system, it being generally found that in the wholesale operation there is sufficient economy to enable the manufacturers to pay to the farmer a higher price for his milk than it would yield if manufactured at home. The further fact exists, that cheese so manufactured according to a regular system, large quantities being made at the same time, is generally of better quality than it is possible to attain in smaller workings. So strikingly true is this, that in England, American factory-made cheeses are taking the precedence of all others, except the peculiar fancy brands, such as Stilton, Chedder, etc. ; and here as well as there it is a recognized fact that the factory-made cheeses are generally superior to any others. The best exposition that has yet been made of the factory system, is to be found in the *American Agricultural Annual* for 1868, before quoted from, in treating of butter-making, in which there is an article entitled, "Factory Dairy Practice," by Gardner B. Weeks, secretary of the American Dairymen's

Association. As being valuable to farmers who may contemplate the organization of cheese-making companies, the entire article is well worthy of perusal. For the purpose of making this description as complete as possible the following extracts from it are here made :—

" The original price paid for making cheese was one cent per " pound, (cured,) and the patrons of the factory were charged, in " addition, with their proportion of the expenses for boxes, bandage, " coloring, rennets, salt, etc. During the war, however, this price " rose in many cases to one cent and a half per pound, and justly " too. At present the usual charge is one cent and a quarter per " pound. In many cases the patrons pay two cents per pound for " making and for the materials.

" A factory of 300 cows requires the labor of one man and two " women.

" One of from 400 to 500 cows will need two men and two " women.

" One of 600 to 750 cows will require three men and two " women.

" The wages paid to cheese-makers vary from eight to thirty " dollars a week, and board—according to the experience and " reputation of the maker, the size of the dairy, and other circum- " stances. The average price paid does not vary much from two " dollars per day, and board. The other ' help' need not " be experienced hands, but should at least be active and intelli- " gent.

" Very often factories are let to a competent cheese-maker, " or other person, who engage to furnish the necessary help for " making and curing the cheese for a stipulated price per pound. " Usually this price is about three-fifths of a cent per pound, " (cured.)

" *Site for a Factory.—Requirements.*—The first requisite is a " spring furnishing good water and abundance of it, and so situated " that the necessary fall may be obtained. Good water is that " which stands in the summer at from 42° to 54° Fahrenheit. A " spring which furnishes water of such a quality, sufficient to fill a

" two-inch pipe under a good head, will supply a factory of 600
" to 800 cows.

" *The Manufacturing or Vat-room* should be so situated that the
" water from the spring may be readily conducted into the vats,
" and wherever else needed ; and also so placed with reference to
" the road that teams may have easy access to the delivery
" window. The sills should be laid on stone piers, and raised so
" that the water may constantly stand underneath the entire floor
" without wetting the sills. The object of this is to catch the
" drippings of whey and water from the floor. This water should
" be frequently drawn of and immediately replaced, thus convey-
" ing away all matter that might become foul. Cleanliness and
" sweetness of premises and apparatus are absolutely imperative,
" if a high degree of excellence in the cheese is aimed at.

" The weight upon the floor of the vat-room is sometimes very
" great, consequently the timbers and flooring should be strong.
" As water is used abundantly about this room, it is well to have
" the floor so laid that all water will converge to some point or
" points, and be easily swept away. It should, besides, be light
" and cheerful, and be well arranged for complete and constant
" change of air by a ventilator in the roof.

" *Size.*—For two or three vats, and other necessary appliances,
" a room will be required about 24 × 28. Four vats will need a
" space about 30 × 30, or 26 × 34. Height of posts about 10 feet.

" *Press-Room.*—This should be immediately contiguous to the
" vat-room, and on the same level. The size will depend upon
" the number of presses required. In most cases it is best to
" have the building wide enough to contain two rows of presses,
" with ample room for the curd-sink to pass between them. A
" room 14 × 30 would easily accommodate 24 to 28 presses. It
" should also be flooded underneath at all times. There is here
" so much weight upon the floor that it is recommended that
" planks be used underneath the press frames. In many factories
" the vat-room is made large to accommodate the presses.

" *The Curing-House*, by far the largest of the buildings required,
" should always be situated on firm, dry ground, where pure air,

32

" and none other, will surround the cheese. If, with these re-
" quisites, it can also be placed on the same level with the press-
" room, and adjacent to it, the arrangement cannot be improved.
" The cheese-house, for a dairy of 500 to 650 cows, should be
" about 28 x 100 feet, and two stories high. If a basement room
" can be had in addition, it is very desirable for use in spring and
" autumn, when fires are needed ; and even in the warmer part of
" the season it is immensely better to put cheese in an under-
" ground room, than in the upper story beneath the heated roof.

" Four windows on each side in each story will be sufficient,
" and the arrangement should be such that when these are opened
" for ventilation, the wind will not strike directly upon the cheese.
" Holes should be cut in the various floors, and at frequent inter-
" vals, and through these a current of air will constantly be pass-
" ing, and ventilation by the windows need seldom be resorted to.
" In the roof of the curing-house there should be at least two
" large ventilators.

" A building 26 feet wide will accommodate five lengths of
" tables or ranges, each table holding two rows of cheeses of 16
" inches diameter ; and there will be ample space left for the
" necessary alleys. To avoid in some measure the inroads of
" of mice and other vermin, it is better to have passages next the
" sides of the building, instead of putting tables there.

" *Boiler-room and Ice-house.*—In most cases the former, and in
" many the latter, will be required ; but it is not essential to de-
" scribe them here. Easy access and convenience will guide in
" their location. The boiler-room should be large enough to hold
" at least two or three days' supply of wood. And if it contain
" also a small work-bench, with tools, vise, etc., it will be much
" resorted to."

After describing at length and with good illustrations the
different utensils used in cheese factories, the following directions
for manufacture are given :—

" The evening's milk, on being received, should be about equally
" divided among the vats in use. Cold water is kept constantly
" passing around the vats, and the milk should be carefully stirred

"at frequent intervals, until a temperature of 68°, or lower, has
"been reached. In many factories, the lack of water in warm
"weather necessitates the use of ice in cooling the evening's milk.
"It is usually put directly into the milk. Of course, 'necessity
"knows no law' in such exigencies, but where it is possible to
"avoid the use of ice, it had better be done. Its use has never
"been claimed as an advantage, and very many of our best cheese-
"makers believe that strictly fine cheese cannot be made from milk
"thus treated. In some of the Massachusetts cheese factories,
"and in an occasional one in New York, and elsewhere, milk is
"received but once daily—in the morning. Only in cases where
"each patron is provided with an abundance of good, cool water,
"proper vessels for keeping the milk in small quantities, and
"exercises unusual care, can this be done with safety. In the
"majority of factories, early and late in the season, milk is re-
"ceived in the morning only; but as the warm nights of May
"come on, trouble is experienced, unless this course is changed.
"The practice of adding salt to the milk on sultry evenings, is
"recommended by some, but its utility has never been demon-
"strated. (In cases where the water used in cooling milk is
"deficient in quantity, or possesses too high a temperature, it is
"sometimes necessary to make cheese at night, and again in the
"morning. In both cases the animal heat should be removed
"from the milk before the rennet is added.)

"In the morning, the night's milk will be found so cool, that
"when the morning's milk is added to the vats, the temperature
"of the whole mass will stand at about 65°.

"*Treatment of the Cream.*—The cream which rises upon the
"night's milk is treated in two ways. It is either stirred thor-
"oughly into the milk while cold and before the addition of any
"warm milk, or it is carefully skimmed off, diluted with warm
"water, and passed through the strainer into the vat again. In
"either case, the loss of cream is small.

"*Setting the Curd.*—Before any thing else is done in the morn-
"ing, the exact condition of the milk in each vat should be ascer-
"tained. If all is right,—well. If one vat of milk seems

"inclined to 'change,' or sour, fill that vat first, work it first,
"and get it first to press. In such case, too, it is well to add
"only so much morning's milk as the limited capacity of the
"other vats renders imperative. The vat being filled, apply the
"steam at once. Stir frequently and deeply, and pass into the
"small strainer all specks and flies that may appear upon the
"surface.

" In the cooler portions of the season, the heat should be shut
"off when the temperature of the milk is from 85° to 88°. In
"the summer, it should not be carried higher than 80° to 82°.
"The coloring is now added, and when this is thoroughly stirred
"in, the rennet should be put in. The milk should now be left
"entirely at rest, to facilitate coagulation.

" On cold days the vat must be carefully covered over, either
"by cloths or a wooden frame, prepared for that purpose. In
"about fifteen minutes' time let the milk be carefully examined to
"see if the action of the rennet has begun. In most cases, the
"hand will decide this matter; if not, a tin cup is nearly filled
"with hot water, and set into the milk for a few moments. If,
"on removing this, a mucous gathering be formed upon the bot-
"tom and sides of the cup, all is going on right. If both tests
"are unsatisfactory, they are to be repeated after ten minutes
"longer. If now there are no signs of coagulation, the hand is
"passed down into the milk to the bottom of the vat, and if there
"is no thickening there, more rennet is added at once. The
"'setting' of the milk is one of the nicest operations of cheese-
"making, and requires experience and judgment.

" *Treatment of the Curd in the Vat.*—The curd, when ready for
"cutting, will break with a clean fracture over the finger when
"tested. In some factories the use of the knife is not at all re-
"sorted to, the breaking of the curd being done entirely by hand.
"In most instances, however, the knife is used. At first the
"curd is cut lengthwise; then allowed to stand for a few minutes,
"when it is cut across. The knife is passed quickly but carefully
"through the curd, and care must be taken to have the bottom
"reached by the blades.

"The curd remains entirely at rest for twenty minutes, in "order that the whey may separate and rise to the surface. If "the vat is too full for working with comfort, a portion of the "whey is now dipped off. Just here, practice differs somewhat. "Many cheese-makers apply the heat now, and use the knife no "more until increased warmth has hardened the curd to some ex- "tent. In other cases, in what is known as the 'coarse curd sys- "tem,' the curd is cut scarcely at all, being left in flakes as large as "the palm of the hand, and nearly as thick. We will confine our "remarks, however, to a description of the medium curd plan. "After there has been a free separation and rising of the whey, "the agitator is used in carefully turning over the curd, and in "bringing to the surface the larger particles from the bottom. "Then follows the knife with a steady, even motion, going to the "center of the vat only. Two or three times passing around the "vat will bring the particles of curd to the desired size, i. e., about "the size of chestnuts, or a little larger. If, however, the curd "be in a bad condition, and inclined to sour, it is cut finer. Just "before the cutting is done, the heat is again turned on, and "gradually the temperature of the entire mass is increased to 88° "or 90°. It should be gently stirred to avoid packing or lumping, "and to render an evenness of heat more secure. Cheese-makers "who favor strictly fine curds, use the knife freely during this "operation of heating, and bring the curd to the fineness of wheat "kernels.

"The heat being now shut off, the gentle agitation of the curd "is continued for about ten minutes, or until all disposition of the "curd to pack is past. After remaining at rest for fifteen minutes, "in order that the finer particles of curd may settle to the bottom, "the tin strainer is placed in one corner of the vat, and by means "of the siphon the whey is drawn off until the mass of curd be- "gins to appear above the surface. It is now again carefully brok- "en up and separated, and the heat is once more applied and con- "tinued until the thermometer indicates 96° to 98°. In cold "weather the temperature may be carried to 100° or 102°, but "ordinarily 98° is sufficient. Stirring is continued for about fifteen

"minutes after this, and then the curd is allowed to remain at rest
"until perfected. On cool days it is better to cover the top of
"the vats with cloths to retain the heat.

"Formerly cheese-makers believed that the curd was ready
"for dipping out when sufficiently cooked, whether any change or
"acidity was perceptible in the whey or not. It is now the
"almost universal practice to retain the curd in the vat until the
"whey is slightly sour. It is believed that this acidity has a
"direct beneficial influence upon the texture and flavor of the
"cheese, rendering it less porous and less liable to get into that
"state in warm weather which dealers denominate ' out of flavor.'
"Here, however, is another nice point in cheese-making, to
"determine just how far this acidity may safely proceed, and
"to know precisely when the curd should be removed from the
"whey; for, if permitted to go one step too far, a sour cheese is
"inevitable.

"*Salting.*—A few cheese-makers recommend salting the curd
"in the vat while a small portion of the whey remains. The
"advantage claimed is, that the curd can be more evenly salted
"than in any other way. Salting is generally done in the sink,
"however, after the whey is drained off and the curd is pretty dry
"and cool. The salt is not usually put on all at once, but grad-
"ually, and the curd is well mixed at each salting.

"Ordinarily, the rule for salting is about $2\frac{7}{10}$ pounds of salt
"to 1000 pounds of milk; considerably less than this very early in
"the season, somewhat less in the autumn months, and perhaps a
"little more in very warm weather.

"In Central New York, the Syracuse Factory Filled Salt is
"almost universally used for dairy purposes. Doubtless the Ash-
"ton Salt (from Liverpool) is purer and better, but it is far more
"expensive.

"When *thoroughly cooled*, the curd is dipped into the hoops, and
"pressed about an hour. It is then taken out, carefully bandaged,
"and returned to the press, there to remain until the latter is
"needed again. Perhaps in no point is the ordinary practice in
"cheese factories so radically wrong as in pressing cheese. They

" should always be pressed two days, or more ; but in reality they
" seldom remain in the hoops over twenty hours."

* * * * * * *

" *Treatment of Cheese in the Curing-Room.*—On being brought to
" the cheese-house, the cheeses are placed upon the tables or
" ranges and after standing a few minutes in order to dry, the top
" surfaces should be liberally greased with hot whey-oil. The
" bandage which extends above the edge should be about 1½ inches
" wide, cut down in slits, so that it may, when dry, be oiled and
" neatly plaited down upon the surface. In most factories the
" sides of the cheese are also greased, after each cheese has been
" properly marked and numbered.

" The next day the cheeses are turned and the other surface is
" oiled. The grease first used upon the cheese is colored
" with annotto, so as to present a rich and attractive appearance
" outwardly.

" Ordinarily, cheeses require oiling only two or three times be-
" fore being fit for market. In cold or windy weather, however,
" the surfaces need frequent applications, or they will ' check,'
" (crack on the surface.)

" Until three weeks old, cheese should be turned every day,
" (except Sundays ;) afterward once in two days will answer.
" The temperature of the curing-house is most favorable if about
" 70° to 75° ; if warmer ventilate thoroughly ; if much cooler,
" employ artificial heat, or the new cheese will become bitter.

" Wind, blowing upon the cheese, will ' check ' the surface ;
" the sun, shining directly upon them, will heat and soften them
" too much.

" Cheeses insufficiently cooked or lightly salted, or those into
" which cold curd has been put, will, in warm weather, huff or
" swell up in spots upon the surface. In such cases the confined
" air and gas which produces the trouble must be frequently let
" out, and the hole thus opened carefully closed to avoid injury
" from flies.

" Sour cheese will check or crack despite all efforts, but extra
" attention and frequent oiling and turning will be beneficial.

"Cracks or blemishes upon the surface of the cheese, caused
"either by sourness, accident, flies, or mice, should be carefully
"filled up with a bit of cured cheese, and a piece of thin manilla
"paper put over the spot to keep out the flies.   Flies are a source
"of serious trouble during a portion of the season, and unless the
"cheeses are most assiduously watched, considerable injury will be
"done.   When the mites have secured a lodgment in the cheese,
"they can be brought to the surface by placing a cloth or paper
"over the orifice so as to entirely exclude the air.   In some cases, if
"they are very numerous and have been at work for several days,
"the knife must be freely used, and the affected portion cut away.
"Then refill with cured cheese.   Cayenne pepper put into the
"grease, is thought to be a protection against the depredations of
"flies.   And alcohol, in which red-pepper pods have been soaked
"for some days, applied to the surface of checked cheese, will
"keep off flies for a time.   Some persons put beeswax into the
"grease, believing that this better prepares the surface of cheese
"to resist the attacks of flies.

"It is to the curing-room that the cheeses are brought for per-
"fecting and ripening, and it is here they are inspected by the pur-
"chaser.   Any blemish or imperfection will here be brought to
"light.   It is true that if cheeses are not properly made, no
"amount of care in this department can atone for this deficiency.
"It is also true that cheese, to which justice has been done in
"the manufacture, may be very much injured and depreciated by
"want of judicious care and attention while curing.

"Nicety in small things will pay ; not alone in the satisfaction
"of admiring them, but in dollars and cents."

Concerning the manufacture of cheese in domestic dairies, very
complete directions are given in Flint's "Milch Cows and Dairy
Farming," to which the reader is referred, as it would be difficult
to condense within the narrow limits of this chapter, so much as
would be necessary for the practical information of cheese-
makers.

The principle upon which the manufacture of cheese is based

is, that the caseine of milk, (that is its cheesy part,) is held in solution in the liquid only in the presence of an alkali there existing. Any acid that will neutralize this alkali, deprives it of the power of causing the solution of the caseine, which is thereupon rejected by the water and forms the curd. All acids produce this effect, although many of them, of course, are, for various reasons, not suited to the requirements of cheese-making. Milk is curdled by the action of the lactic acid that forms in the natural process of its souring. Flint states that in some of the northern countries of Europe a little butterwort (*Singuicula vulgaris*) is sometimes mixed with the cow's food, causing the milk to coagulate without the addition of an acid within a few hours after being drawn. In the almost universal dairy practice of the world, rennet (the prepared stomach of the calf) is used to produce coagulation.

The richness of cheese depends very much upon the quantity of cream that it contains, but not a little, also, on the mode of manufacture. Sometimes the cream of the night's milk is added to the morning's milk, and the latter made into cheese ; sometimes the whole milk of each milking is curdled ; sometimes only skim-milk or buttermilk is used, producing a cheese which, although lacking in richness, and somewhat also in flavor, is a highly nutritious food. As an instance of the effect of the mode of manufacture upon the cheese-dairy, it may be stated that the very popular Gruyère cheese (Schweitzer-kaese) which seems to be rich and is certainly very high flavored, is made from skim-milk.

Mr. Flint quotes the following from a report made to the New York State Agricultural Society, by A. L. Fish, of Herkimer County, whose cows averaged 775 pounds of cheese each in the year 1845. It is a simple statement of the practical operations of a successful dairyman.

" The evening's and morning's milk is commonly used to make " one cheese. The evening's is strained into a tub or pans, and " cooled to prevent souring. The proper mode of cooling is to " strain the milk into the tin tub set in a wooden vat, described in " the dairy house, and cool by filling the wooden vat with ice-

" water from the ice-house, or ice in small lumps, and water from
" the pump. The little cream that rises over night is taken off
" in the morning, and kept till the morning and evening milk are put
" together, and the cream is warmed to receive the rennet. It is
" mixed with about twice its quantity of new milk, and warm
" water added to raise its temperature to ninety-eight degrees; stir
" it till perfectly limpid, put in rennet enough to curdle the milk
" in forty minutes, and mix it with the mass of milk by thorough
" stirring; the milk having been previously raised to eighty-eight
" or ninety degrees, by passing steam from the steam generator to
" the water in the wooden vat. In case no double vat is to be
" had, the milk may be safely heated to the right temperature, by
" setting a tin pail of hot water into the milk in the tubs. It may
" be cooled in like manner by filling the pail with ice-water, or
" cold spring-water, where ice is not to be had. It is not safe to
" heat milk in a kettle exposed directly to the fire, as a *slight*
" scorching will communicate its *taint* to the whole cheese and
" spoil it. If milk is curdled below eighty-four degrees, the cream
" is more liable to work off with the whey. An extreme of heat
" will have a like effect.

" The curdling heat is varied with the temperature of the air,
" or the liability of the milk to cool after adding rennet. The
" thermometer is the only safe guide in determining the tem-
" perature; for, if the dairyman depends upon the sensation of the
" hand, a great liability to error will render the operation uncer-
" tain. If, for instance, the hands have previously been immersed
" in cold water, the milk will feel warmer than it really is; if, on
" the contrary, they have recently been in warm water, the milk
" will feel colder than it really is. To satisfy the reader how
" much this circumstance alone will affect the sensation of the
" hand, let him immerse one hand in warm water, and at the same
" time keep the other in a vessel of cold water, for a few
" moments; then pour the water in the two dishes together, and
" immerse both hands in the mixture. The hand that was previ-
" ously in the warm water will feel *cold*, and the other quite warm,
" showing that the sense of feeling is not a test of temperature

" worthy of being relied upon. A fine cloth spread over the tub
" wh.le the milk is curdling, will prevent the surface from being
" cooled by circulation of air. *No jarring of the milk*, by walking
" upon a springy floor, or otherwise, should be allowed while it is
" curdling, as it will prevent a *perfect cohesion* of the particles.

" When milk is curdled so as to appear like a solid, it is divided
" into small particles to aid the separation of the whey from the
" curd. This is often *too speedily done*, to facilitate the work, but
" at a sacrifice of *quality* and *quantity*."

He also publishes the following statement of a lady in Massachusetts, whose cheeses received the first premium at the Franklin
County fair, in 1857, for their richness, fineness, and delicacy of
flavor :—

" My cheese is made from one day's milk of twenty-nine cows.
" I strain the night's milk into a tub, skim it in the morning, and
" melt the cream in the morning's milk. I warm the night's milk,
" so that with the morning's milk, when mixed together, it will
" be at the temperature of ninety-six degrees ; then add rennet
" sufficient to turn it in thirty minutes. Let it stand about half
" or three quarters of. an hour ; then cross it off and let it stand
" about thirty minutes, working upon it very carefully with a skim-
" mer. When the curd begins to settle, dip off the whey, and
" heat it up and pour it on again at the temperature of one hun-
" dred and two degrees. After draining off and cutting up, add a
" teacup of salt to fourteen pounds.

" The process of making sage cheese is the same as the other,
" except adding the juice of the sage in a small quantity of milk."

The manufacture of the celebrated Cheddar, Gloucester, Dun-
lop, Dutch, and Parmesan cheeses, is described with some fullness
in Mr. Flint's book, that of the Dutch or Gouda cheese being
more curious than any of the others. There is also contained in
the same work a very interesting and fully illustrated account of
the Holland dairy system, which may be read with advantage by
all American farmers, since there is no country in the world in
which the various processes of the manufacture of butter and
cheese are carried out with so much precision, and with such

scrupulous attention to that cleanliness on which complete success
in all dairy operations must inevitably depend.

This chapter cannot be more appropriately closed than by introducing the following extracts from Mr. Flint's "Letter to a
Dairy Woman" :—

"I need not remind you that any addition, however small, to
"the market value of each pound of butter or cheese, will largely
"increase the annual income of your establishment.   Nor need I
"remind you that these articles are generally the last of either the
"luxuries or the necessaries of life in which city customers are
"willing to economize.   They must and will have a good article,
"and are ready to pay for it in proportion to its goodness ; or, if
"they desire to economize in butter, it will be in the quantity
"rather than the quality.

"Poor butter is a drug in the market.   Nobody wants it, and
"the dealer often finds it difficult to get it off his hands, when a
"delicate and finely flavored article attracts attention and secures
"a ready sale.   Some say that poor butter will do for cooking.
"But a good steak or mutton-chop is too expensive to allow any
"one to spoil it by the use of a poor quality of butter ; and good
"pastry-cooks will tell you that cakes and pies cannot be made
"without good sweet butter, and plenty of it.   These dishes rel-
"ish too well, when properly cooked with nice butter, for any one
"to tolerate the use of poor butter in them.

"I have dwelt on the necessity of extreme cleanliness in all the
"operations of the dairy ; and this is the basis and fundamental
"principle of your business.   I would not suppose, for a moment,
"that you are lacking in this respect.   The enormous quantities
"of disgusting, streaky, and tallow-like butter that are daily thrust
"upon the seaboard markets must be due to the carelessness
"and negligence of heedless men, to exposure to sun and rain,
"to bad packing, and to delays in transportation.   Many of these
"evils you may not be able to remove, since you cannot follow
"the article to the market, and see that it arrives safely and
"untainted.   But you can take greater pains, perhaps, in some
"of the preliminary processes of making, and produce an article

" that will not be so liable to injure from keeping and transporta-
" tion; and then, if fault is to be found, it does not rest with you.

  " I will not suggest the possibility that your ideas of cleanliness
" and neatness, may be at fault ; and that what may seem an excess
" of nicety and scrubbing to you, may appear to be almost slov-
"enliness to some others, whose butter receives the highest price
" in the market, and always finds the readiest sale."   *   *   *
" Dutch dairy-women give all the utensils of the dairy, from the
" pails to the firkins and the casks, infinite attention, and are also
" extremely careful that no infectious odor rises from the surround-
"ings.   I think you will see that it is a physical impossibility that
" any taint can affect the atmosphere or the utensils of such a
" dairy, and that many of the details of their practice may be
" worthy of imitation in our American dairies.

  " And here allow me to suggest that, though we may not approve
" of the general management in any particular section, or any
" particular dairy, it is rare that there is not something in the
" practice of that section that is really valuable and worthy of
" imitation."

       *   *   *   *   *   *   *

  " Under ordinarily favorable circumstances, from twelve to
" eighteen hours will be sufficient to raise the cream, and I do not
" believe it should stand over twenty-four hours under any circum-
" stances.   This, I am aware, is very different from the general
" practice over the country.   But, if you will make the experi-
" ment in the most careful manner, setting the pans in a good, airy
" place, and not upon the cellar bottom, I think you will soon
" agree with me that all you get, after twelve or eighteen hours,
" under the best circumstances, or at most after twenty-four hours,
" will detract from the quality and injure the fine and delicate
" aroma and agreeable taste of the butter to a greater extent than
" you are aware of.   The cream which rises from milk set on the
" cellar bottom acquires an acrid taste, and can neither produce
" butter of so fine a quality or so agreeable to the palate, as that
" which rises from milk set on shelves from six to eight feet high,
" around which there is a full and free circulation of pure air.

" The latter is sweeter, and appears in much larger quantities in
" the same time, than the former.

" If, therefore, you devote your attention to the making of
" butter to sell fresh in the market, and desire to obtain a repu-
" tation which shall aid and secure the quickest sale and the high-
" est price, you will use cream that rises first, and that does not
" stand too long on the milk. You will churn it properly and
" patiently, and not with too great haste. You will work it so
" thoroughly and completely, with the butter-worker and the
" sponge and cloth, as to remove every particle of buttermilk,
" never allowing your own or any other hands to touch it. You
" will keep it at a proper temperature when making, and after it
" is made, by the judicious use of ice, and avoid exposing it to
" the bad odors of a musty cellar. You will discard the use of
" artificial coloring or flavoring matter, and take the utmost care
" in every process of making. You will stamp your butter taste-
" fully with some mould which can be recognized in the market
" as yours ; as, for instance, your initials or some form or figure,
" which will most please the eye and the taste of the customer.
" You will send it in boxes so perfectly prepared and cleansed as to
" impart no taste of wood to the butter. If all things receive due
" attention, my word for it, the initials or form which you adopt,
" will be inquired after, and you will always find a ready and a
" willing purchaser, at the highest market-price.

" But if you are differently situated, and it becomes necessary
" to pack and sell as firkin-butter, let me suggest the necessity
" of an equal degree of nicety and care in preparation, and that
" you insist, as one of your rights, that the article be packed in the
" best of oak-wood firkins, thoroughly prepared after the manner of
" the Dutch. A greater attention to these points would make the
" butter thus packed worth several cents a pound more when it
" arrives in the market, than it ordinarily is. Indeed, the man-
" ner in which it not unfrequently comes to market is a disgrace
" to those who packed it ; and it cannot be that such specimens
" were ever put up by the hands of a dairywoman. I have often
" seen what was brought for butter, opened so marbled, streaked,

" and rancid, that it was scarcely fit to use on the wheels of a
" carriage.

" If you adopt the course which I have recommended in regard
" to skimming, you will have a large quantity of sweet skimmed-
" milk, far better than it would be if allowed to stand thirty-six or
" forty-eight hours, as is the custom with many. This is too
" valuable to waste, and it is my opinion that you can use it to far
" greater profit than to allow it to be fed to swine. There can be
" no question, I think, that cheese-making should be carried on at
" the same time with the making of butter, in small and medium
" sized dairies. Some of the best cheese of Holland is made of
" sweet skim-milk. The reputation of Parmesan—a skim-milk
" cheese of Italy—is world-wide, and it commands a high price
" and ready sale. By cheese-making you can turn the skim-milk
" to a very profitable account, if it is sweet and good. You will
" find, if you adopt this system, that your butter will be improved,
" and that, without any great amount of extra labor, you will
" make a large quantity of very good cheese, and thus add largely
" to the profit of your establishment, and to the comfort and pros-
" perity of your family.

" But, if you devote all your attention to the making of cheese,
" whether it is to be sold green, or as soon as ripe, or packed for
" exportation, I need not say that the same neatness is required as
" in the making of butter. You will find many suggestions in
" the preceeding pages which I trust will prove to be valuable
" and applicable to your circumstances. There is a general com-
" plaint among the dealers in cheese that it is difficult to get a
" superior article. This state of things ought not to exist. I
" hope the time is not far distant when a more general attention
" will be paid to the details of manufacture, and let me remind
" you that those who take the first steps in improvement will reap
" the greatest advantages."

CHAPTER XVII.

THE WINTER FEEDING AND MANAGEMENT OF LIVE STOCK.

THE objects in keeping animals on a farm are :—

1. To convert vegetable products into animal products.
2. To make manure.
3. To secure the necessary motive power for the operations of the farm.

All of these are items of the farm's *business*, and viewed in this light, the domestic animals bear the same relation to his operations, that the steam-engine, the carding-machine, and the loom do to the owner of a cotton-mill.

They are a part of the machinery by which he accomplishes his ends, and they should, in a purely practical point of view, be regarded as such. They should be kept in sound condition, and in good running order, and made to perform their part of the work, day by day, in the best and most economical manner. In proportion to the completeness with which this is done,—in proportion, that is, to the intelligence and constant watchfulness with which they are kept up to the mark, and made to perform their full share of the work,—will they be profitable or unprofitable.

If the mill owner keeps his engine running with full power, consuming its maximum amount of fuel, and then supplies his looms with barely enough cotton for the profit on the cloth made to pay his operatives, he will be out of pocket by the full cost of running his engine, of the wear and tear of his machinery, and of the interest on the value of his mill. Before he can actually make money, he must supply enough raw material to increase his production to an amount that will *more than cover all* outlays.

The extent to which he does this must decide the degree to which he is to be considered a successful manufacturer.

The farmer's case is a precisely parallel one, as I shall endeavor to prove—for he cannot be considered a *practical farmer* in the best sense of the term, unless he makes every animal on his farm do its full proportion of the money making of the business—for money making is the chief aim of his life and occupation.

The grain-grower—pure and simple—has much less occasion for the constant exercise of skill than the stock-raiser. He has only to produce his crops, to sell them, and to keep his soil in condition for his requirements. The stock-raiser has all this to attend to, and, in addition, he must constantly regard the manifold needs of his animals, forcing them to consume the largest possible amount of food, and to yield the utmost possible return for the food and care bestowed upon them.

His success depends on an early and earnest appreciation of the fact that only to the degree to which he causes his animals to consume more food than is required to support their frames, and to carry on the various vital functions, will there be a profit resulting from their keep. A certain amount of food is required to supply the animal's respiration, and the natural waste of its body. If only this amount is given, the food consumed will be a total loss, except for the value of the manure that it produces, while the interest and insurance on the animal itself, the time expended in its care, and all the buildings and appliances of the farm that its keeping makes necessary, will be lost.

Not only must the feeding be so managed as to contribute the material from which profit is to be made, but due attention should be given to the items of (1) cleanliness, (2) regularity, (3) temperature, (4) exercise, (5) fresh water, (6) pure air.

1. *Cleanliness* is of the utmost importance. It is impossible for any of the domestic animals to do their best unless their skins are free from dirt, and in a fresh and healthy condition. It is of the utmost importance that they be not allowed to accumulate a winter coat of clotted manure; and it is at least very desirable that they be daily thoroughly carded or brushed from head to foot, whenever sufficient labor can be commanded. Better keep fewer animals well groomed than to allow the herd to remain in a condi-

33

tion in which it cannot make the best use of the expensive food it consumes.

2. *Regularity*, especially in feeding and watering, is very important. Animals will always thrive best when the hours of feeding are regularly established, so that they will come with full appetite to each meal. In establishments where feeding is done by the clock, the animals will lie quietly down until very nearly the time for feeding. As the hour approaches they will get up up, eager and expectant, ready to attack their rations with good appetite. If they are fed sometimes at long, sometimes at short intervals, they will eat less, will chew the cud less contentedly, and will be generally restless and uneasy, expecting something to be given them whenever a man enters the stables, and when food is given them, eating it much more daintily.

3. *Temperature.*—Probably the first use that the animal organism makes of food consumed is to appropriate it to maintaining the proper temperature of the body. Heat is, to a certain extent, constantly given off in respiration : air thrown out from the lungs is always warmer than when taken in. The additional heat is manufactured in the system, by the union of certain elements of the food with the oxygen of the air inhaled. There is very little difference in the temperature of the air breathed out in cold weather and in warm, in cold stables and in warm ones. If the air of the stable is at 50°, and is exhaled at 90°, it has taken 40° of heat from the system ; while if it was taken in at zero, it would have taken 90° from the system. Probably this illustration is not scientifically exact, but it sufficiently exhibits the principle. The extra amount of heat required to raise the breath to the standard temperature is produced by the consumption of parts of the food, which, if not so wasted, might have gone to form fat or butter ; hence we see the importance of protecting our stock from undue exposure to the cold. The animal is surrounded by warm air, that is to say, the spaces in its hairy covering are filled with air of which the temperature is elevated by the escape of heat from the body. When this air is once sufficiently warmed, the animal's coat preventing its rapid change or circulation, it loses its heat but

slowly, but if a draft of air or a gale of wind is allowed to agitate this blanket, its warm air is carried away and the body constantly parts with more heat, in order to warm the colder fresh supply. The heat used in this way is formed by the oxidation of elements of the food in precisely the same manner as in the case of respiration ; consequently, the more we protect our animals against the rapid circulation of cold air, the more we reduce this waste of the heat-producing elements which it is our object to convert into fat.

While, therefore, fresh air should be regularly supplied, all unnecessary loss of heat should be avoided.

4. *Exercise.*—It is difficult to determine what amount of exercise different animals require. Messrs. S. & D. Wells, of Wethersfield, Connecticut, (who have a valuable herd of Ayrshire cattle, which they manage very judiciously,) tie their cows in winter quarters early in November, and they never untie them again, except for calving, until the spring pastures are ready for turning out. Some of their animals remain fastened by the neck nearly six months at a time, yet they come out in spring in superb condition, apparently not at all injured by their long repose. It may be in deference to an idea that systematic exercise is generally given to dairy cattle, but without having any positive reason for doing so, I prefer that my own animals should be loose in the yard for a few hours on every pleasant day during the winter. Such a course certainly does no harm, and it constitutes a sort of return to a natural condition, which seems to me very desirable.

Horses, certainly, and probably sheep also, are benefited by regular exercise whenever the weather is not too cold.

5. *Fresh Water.*—By this I do not mean *cold* water, for probably it would be better in summer, and certainly it would be better in winter, that the water should not be cold enough to produce a chill. It is most important to provide water that is free from organic impurities, and untainted by the drainings of barn-yard and dung heaps. It would be better, if it can be so arranged, that suitable water should be always within reach of the cattle. There need be no fear of their abusing their privilege and drinking im-

moderately, and we should guard against the possibility of their wants being occasionally forgotten.

6. *Pure Air.*—Hardly second in importance even to nutritious food is an abundant supply of pure air, at all times and seasons. Animals kept in ill-ventilated stables, in which the air is impregnated with the carbonic acid from the breath, and ammonia from the droppings, can neither make the best use of the food that is given them, nor preserve their bodies in rugged health.

It is impossible that there should not be always, even in the best-regulated stables, more or less ammonia and more or less offensive odor. All that we can do is to overcome the ill-effect of these, by providing an abundant supply of pure air from out of doors to dilute and dissipate them.

While this supply of fresh air is a matter of absolute necessity, it is hardly less important to guard against strong currents blowing directly across the animals, especially in cold weather. There are many ways in which stables may be ventilated without subjecting their inmates to draughts. Those plans are the best which cause the vitiated air to escape from near the floor and admit fresh air from above, but at such distance from the animals that its current will be diffused before it reaches them.

As far as the economy of the stable is concerned, farm stock may be classified as follows :—

1. Growing stock.
2. Fattening stock.
3. Milking stock.
4. Working stock.

According to the class to which an animal belongs, must its food and its exercise be regulated.

1. Growing animals have not only to support the ordinary wastes of animal life, but to lay up in all of their parts the material that contributes to the growth of their bodies. This requires the greatest diversity of nutritious elements in the food. If a colt is fed only on roots, he will become pot-bellied, lean, and defective in his bony structure. In proportion as we supply him with food

containing more nitrogen and phosphates, will his bones grow large and his muscles more full. If fed largely upon pea and bean meal, his growth will be much accelerated and his vigor increased. Oats, which are very strongly nutritious, accomplish the same effect to a less degree, while owing to the bulkiness of the woody fiber of the husk, their effect on the digestive organs is better, though of course no grain should be used as the exclusive food of any animal. All such nutritious forage should be accompanied with enough hay or straw to form bulk, and keep the digestive organs sufficiently distended. Indian corn, which contains a large amount of oil and starch, (fattening materials,) is not nearly so well adapted as oats, peas, and beans to the needs of growing animals.

2. Fattening stock has the least amount of waste of bone and muscle to make up, since it takes but little exercise and does no work. Our sole object is to keep the animal in a state of robust health, so that it consume and properly digest a large amount of food, and at the same time store up, in the adipose tissue, a large proportion of fat. Such animals should receive sufficient hay or straw for the proper distention of the intestines, and as much fat-forming food as they are capable of thoroughly digesting. With such animals roots may be largely fed, the quantity of coarse fodder being proportionately reduced, and Indian corn meal or oil meal, may be largely used with advantage.

3. With milking cows, one object should be to reduce the amount of exercise to the least that will keep them in a state of health; to avoid all accumulation of fat, and to stimulate to the utmost the secretion of milk. This is best accomplished by the use of rich and well-cured hay, roots, and bran.

4. Working animals are constantly wearing out their bones and muscles, while their vigorous exercise causes them to consume more of their food in respiration than do animals in a state of rest. Their requirements approximate to those of growing young stock, the chief difference being, that instead of supplying material to be accumulated in the bones and muscles, we supply the waste that these have undergone in the performance of labor.

These are the general principles on which the feeding of animals depends. At the first glance they seem to suggest a simple set of rules by which the most skillful feeding should be guided. But as we analyze them more closely and see how the result is influenced by a variety of considerations, especially by the peculiar temperament of the individual animal, the whole question becomes involved in an intricacy that is thus far beyond our full comprehension, and we soon learn that no rules and no theories on the subject are of much practical value. Certain general principles are to be borne always in mind, and we should avoid their direct violation, but beyond this we must seek our only help in individual experience and close observation.

These general principles are, so far as they can be simply stated, the following :—

1. Food contains both fat-forming (or heat-producing) and muscle-and-bone-forming materials.

2. The proportions of these elements are different in different kinds of food.

3. We should give a larger proportion of one or of the other, according to the condition and requirements of the animal. That is: a fattening animal should have an excess of the fat-forming elements, and a growing or a working animal should have an excess of the muscle-and-bone-forming elements.

4. Animals subjected to excessive cold have use for more heat-producing (or fat-forming) material than have those which are kept warmly housed, or which live in a warmer climate.

5. Work, especially *fast* work, develops bone and muscle, and gives the system a tendency to appropriate food to this development rather than to the accumulation of fat, which the more rapid and full respiration that work induces causes the fat-forming parts of the food to be consumed in the production of heat, which is supposed to be the representative of work. Idleness, on the other hand, lessens the muscular development, and induces the production of fat.

6. The animal system is susceptible—so far as the performance of its functions is concerned—of considerable cultivation. That

is : by careful attention to the development of any peculiarity, generation after generation, it may be increased and intensified, and it will be transmitted from father to son with more or less certainty, according to the prominence it has attained. The " thorough-bred " horse (the English race-horse) is the fleetest of the horse family, and has wonderful power of endurance—owing, largely, to the excessive development of his lungs and blood-vessels, and to the arrangement of these latter ; the peculiarities are so much a part of the nature of this horse, that they are not only observable in all thorough-bred horses and mares, but, to a great extent, in the progeny of thorough-bred sires with common dams. The Short-horn has a tendency to lay on fat that has been developed (and fixed as the leading characteristic of the herd) by many generations of breeding for a specific purpose. The Jersey cow is a butter producer—and nothing else—because, for generations, she has been kept only for butter-making. It would be possible to start with a herd of fat Short-horns and in time to make them lean butter producers ; or to breed a herd of Jerseys to the size and amplitude of the Short-horn.

7. Our success in any branch of stock-raising or feeding will depend, very much, on the skill with which we adapt our food and our management to the special characteristics of the particular breed of animals we keep. Nothing should be done that has a tendency to divert the animal's organic activities from the channel in which they have learned to flow :—for instance, we must not work the bulls of our dairy breeds of cattle, for work will develop the breathing apparatus, and increased breathing will consume, in the production of heat, fat-forming material which should have gone to the increase of cream. This is only a single illustration of a universal principle, which I can here treat only thus meagerly. It underlies the whole question of the domestication of the animals which have become useful to man, and may be roundly stated thus : —The difference between our domestic animals and their wild ancestors is a difference of development ; and this development is entirely within the control of the farmer. He may allow his flocks and herds to retrograde

toward the wild type ; he may develop still further their useful
qualities ; or he may give prominence to some feature that is now
inconspicuous.

The really practical farmer should bear the foregoing in mind,
and he would be greatly benefited by making himself familiar
with all that is known of the " physiology " of farm animals.   At
the same time, no amount of theoretical knowledge (book-farming)
can take the place of practical skill and observation.   One must
know, not only the general rules of the stable, and what is the
best food and the best management for the different results aimed
at, but the temperaments, habits, and peculiarities of different
individuals of the herd.

This sort of " stable wisdom " only a man of tact, vigilance,
and close observation can attain to.   Tempered by such knowledge as may be readily gathered from books, it is the corner-stone
of the farmer's fortune.   He must—in his breeding and in his
feeding—try to develop, to the utmost, the most desirable qualities of each animal under his care.   Beginning with a good father
and a good mother,—whether it be a question of a horse or only of
a chicken,—and ending with the best possible treatment throughout its life, he should make each animal an object of special
study and strive to adapt it as perfectly as he can to the service
he intends it for,—closely observing its peculiar temperament.
In this way will he get from each animal the greatest profit it is
capable of returning.

The principles which govern the use of nutriment by all kinds
of farm stock being the same, I cannot better illustrate the
practice that is to be recommended for all, than by the following
quotation from Mr. Flint's work :—*

" *Keep the cows constantly in good condition*, ought, therefore, to
" be the motto of every dairy farmer, posted up over the barn-
" door, and over the stalls, and over the milk-room, and repeated
" to the boys whenever there is danger of forgetting it.   It is the
" great secret of success, and the difference between success and

* Milch Cows and Dairy Farming.

" failure turns upon it. Cows in milk require more food in pro-
" portion to their size and weight than either oxen or young cattle.

" In order to keep cows in milk well and economically, reg-
" ularity is next in importance to a full supply of wholesome
" and nutritious food. The healthy animal stomach is a very nice
" chronometer, and it is of the utmost importance to observe
" regular hours in feeding, cleaning, and milking. This is a point,
" also, in which very many farmers are at fault—feeding when-
" ever it happens to be convenient. The cattle are thus kept in
" a restless condition, constantly expecting food when the keeper
" enters the barn, while, if regular hours are strictly adhered to,
" they know exactly when they are to be fed, and they rest quietly
" till the time arrives. Go into a well-regulated dairy establish-
" ment an hour before the time of feeding, and scarcely an animal
" will rise to its feet ; while, if it happens to be the hour of
" feeding, the whole herd will be likely to rise and seize their food
" with an avidity and relish not to be mistaken.

" With respect to the exact routine to be pursued, no rule
" could be prescribed which would apply to all cases ; and each
" individual must be governed much by circumstances, both in
" respect to the particular kinds of feed at different seasons of the
" year, and the system of feeding. I have found in my own
" practice, and in the practice of the most successful dairymen,
" that, in order to encourage the largest secretion of milk in stalled
" cows, one of the best courses is, to feed in the morning, either
" at the time of milking—which I prefer—or immediately after,
" with cut feed, consisting of hay, oats, millet, or corn-stalks,
" mixed with shorts, and Indian, linseed, or cotton-seed meal,
" thoroughly moistened with water. If in winter, hot or warm
" water is far better than cold. If given at milking-time, the
" cows will generally give down the milk more readily. The
" stalls and mangers ought always to be well cleaned out first.

" Roots and long hay may be given during the day ; and at the
" evening milking, or directly after, another generous meal of cut
" feed, well moistened and mixed, as in the morning. No very
" concentrated food, like grains alone or oil-cakes, should, it seems

"to me, be fed early in the morning on an empty stomach, though
"it is sanctioned by the practice in the London milk-dairies.
"The processes of digestion go on best when the stomach is
"sufficiently distended; and for this purpose the bulk of food is
"almost as important as the nutritive qualities. The flavor of
"some roots, as cabbages and turnips, is more apt to be imparted
"to the flesh and milk when fed on an empty stomach than
"otherwise. After the cows have been milked, and have finished
"their cut feed, they are carded and curried down, in well-
"managed dairies, and then either watered in the stall, which in
"very cold or stormy weather is far preferable, or turned out to
"water in the yard. When they are out, if they are let out at
"all, the stables are put in order; and, after tying them up, they
"are fed with long hay, and left to themselves till the time of
"next feeding. This may consist of roots, such as cabbages,
"beets, carrots, or turnips sliced, or of potatoes, a peck, or, if the
"cows are very large, a half-bushel each, and cut feed again at
"the evening milking, as in the morning, after which water in the
"stall, if possible.

"The less cows are exposed to the cold of winter, the better.
"They eat less, thrive better, and give more milk, when kept
"housed all the time, than when exposed to the cold. Caird
"mentions a case where a herd of cows, which had been usually
"supplied from troughs and pipes in the stalls, were, on account
"of an obstruction in the pipes, obliged to be turned out twice a
"day to be watered in the yard. The quantity of milk instantly
"decreased, and in three days the falling off became very con-
"siderable. After the pipes were mended, and the cows again
"watered as before, in their stalls, the flow of milk returned.

"This, however, will be governed much by the weather; for in
"very mild, warm days it may be judicious not only to let them
"out, but to allow them to remain out for a short time, to ex-
"ercise.

"Any one can arrange the hour for the several processes named
"above, to suit himself; but, when once fixed, let it be rigidly
"and regularly followed. If the regular and full feeding be

" neglected for even a day, the yield of milk will immediately
" decline, and it will be very difficult to restore it.   It may safely
" be asserted, as the result of many trials and long practice, that
" a larger flow of milk follows a complete system of regularity in
" this respect than from a higher feeding where this system is not
" adhered to.

   " One prime object which the dairyman should keep constantly
" in view is, to maintain the animal in a sound and healthy con-
" dition.   Without this, no profit can be expected from a milch
" cow for any considerable length of time ; and, with a view to
" this, there should be an occasional change of food.   But, in
" making changes, great care is required to supply an equal amount
" of nourishment, or the cow falls off in flesh, and eventually in
" milk.   We should therefore bear in mind that the food con-
" sumed goes not alone to the secretion of milk, but also to the
" growth and maintenance of the bony structure, the flesh, the
" blood, the fat, the skin, and the hair, and in exhalations from
" the body."

   So much of the value of any food depends on the condition in
which, and the circumstances under which it is fed, that it is
impossible to make a comparison which shall at all times hold
good ; but the following tables from Boussingault, giving as it
does the results of a number of carefully conducted experiments,
will be found valuable :—

TABLE, *showing the comparative difference between good hay and the
   articles mentioned below, as food for stock—being the mean of
   experiment and theory.*

100 lbs. of hay are equal to	100 lbs. of hay are equal to
275 lbs. green Indian corn.	54 lbs. rye.
442 " rye straw.	46 " wheat.
360 " wheat "	59 " oats.
164 " oat "	45 " peas and beans mixed.
180 " barley "	64 " buckwheat.
153 " pea "	57 " Indian corn.
200 " buckwheat straw.	68 " acorns.
201 " raw potatoes.	105 " wheat bran.
175 " boiled "	109 " rye
339 " mangel-wurzel.	167 " wheat, pea, and oat chaff.
504 " turnips.	179 " rye and barley, mixed.
300 " carrots.	

NUTRITIVE EQUIVALENTS. (PRACTICAL AND THEORETICAL.)

ARTICLES OF FOOD.	Water in 100 parts.	Boussingault: Nitrogen in 100 parts of dried substance.	Boussingault: Nitrogen in 100 parts of undried substance.	Boussingault: Nutritive equivalent.	Fresenius: Relative proportion of nitrogen to non-nitrogenized substances.	Fresenius: Nutritive equivalent.	Block.	Petri.	Meyer.	Thaër.	Pabst.	Schweitz.	Schweitzer.
English Hay	11.0	1.34	1.15	100	......	100	100	100	100	100	100	100	100
Lucerne	16.6	1.66	1.38	83	......	...	...	90	...	90	100	100	...
Red Clover-hay	10.1	1.70	1.54	75	1 to 6.08	77.9	100	90	...	90	100	100	...
Red Clover (green)	76.0	....	.64	311	......	...	410	...	150	450	425	...	267
Rye-straw	18.7	.30	.24	479	1 to 24.40	527 7-12	200	500	150	666	350	400	200
Oat-straw	21.0	.36	.30	381	1 to 12.50	445 5-12	200	200	...	190	200	400	...
Carrot-leaves (tops)	70.9	2.94	.85	115	......	...	...	...	...	...	...	...	...
Swedish Turnips	91.0	1.83	.17	676	1 to 7.26	391 1-1	...	300	150	300	250	200	...
Mangel-Wurzel	...	1.43	.18	669	......	...	366	400	...	400	250	333	333
White Silician Beet	85.6	2.40	.30	382	1 to 7.84	542.1	366	250	225	...	...	...	...
Carrots	87.6	1.50	.36	319	1 to 9.00	330 5-12	216	200	150	300	250	270	300
Potatoes	75.9	1.18	.10	383	......	...	400	54	50	200	200	200	200
Potatoes kept in pits	74.8	....	....	...	......	...	...	54	48	...	...	...	...
Beans	7.9	5.50	5.11	23	1 to 2.8	14 5-12	30	52	...	71	40	Boussin-gault 59	30
Peas	8.6	4.20	3.84	27	1 to 2.14	14 1-3	30	54	...	66	40	...	30
Indian Corn	18.0	2.00	1.64	70	1 to 6.55	...	.	52	...	...	...	...	...
Buckwheat	12.5	2.40	2.10	55	1 to 6.05	93 5-12	33	51	55	76	...	...	...
Barley	13.2	2.02	1.76	65	1 to 4.25	58 11-12	34	71	...	86	50	...	15
Oats	12.4	2.22	1.92	60	1 to 4.08	58 1-16	31	55	51	71	60	...	...
Rye	11.5	2.27	2.00	58	1 to 4.42	58 5-6	27	52	46	64	50	...	...
Wheat	12.5	2.11	2.09	55	1 to 2.42	18 5-6	41	108	...	...	42	...	...
Oil-cake (Linseed)	13.4	6.00	5.20	22	......	...	...	...	...	...	...	...	...

STEAMING FOOD.

I have now (1870) steamed all of the hay and most of the grain that has been fed out at Ogden Farm, and I do not hesitate to recommend the practice to all who are so circumstanced that they can do the work systematically.

For want of space I will simply detail our *modus operandi*, and others will be able, readily, to make such modifications as may be necessary to meet the requirements of their own cases.

We have about fifty head of stock, and I find that—averaging them all, old and young—it costs not more than fifteen cents per day to feed them, including the cost of grain, labor, fuel, wear and tear of machinery, etc. Kept in good condition, as they are, this is low enough.

By referring to the plans of the Ogden Farm barn, the reader will be able to understand the following description of the arrangement of the machinery and fixtures. The engine (six-horse power) and the boiler (ten-horse) stand in a lean-to shed on the north side of the barn, (back of the ox-stalls.) The "counter-shaft," by which the power is communicated, is at the west end of the feed-room, about seven feet from the floor. One end of this shaft runs out through the north side of the building and is connected with the driving-wheel of the engine by a belt. The cutting-machine stands on the hay floor, with its knife-end toward the feed-room and about four feet distant from it. Power is carried to it by a belt from a pulley on the counter-shaft. The steaming-chamber occupies what was formerly a pair of ox-stalls on the cattle floor. It reaches to the ceiling, and is entered by a hatchway through the floor of the feed-room. It also has a side-door opening on the gangway, through which the feed-car passes. The steam is supplied, under a loosely-laid false bottom, by a pipe leading from the boiler.

We run the engine three or four hours one day in the week— cutting about three tons of long fodder, which usually consists of hay, straw, and corn-stalks in about equal parts. One half of this is put into the chamber on the day of cutting, and the other half is laid away until the next steaming day. We cut and steam on Saturdays, and fire up again, for steaming only, on Wednesdays. The cut fodder is thoroughly wetted, and has the allowance of bran or meal well mixed through it. It is then put through the hatchway into the chamber and trampled down. Three or four times during the filling of the box, the steam is turned on and allowed to flow until it appears at the hatchway. This serves to soften the mass and allow it to pack more closely. When the chamber is quite full, the hatch is closed and keyed down, and a full head of steam is allowed to flow until it blows out *hot* from the slight openings about the hatch and the lower door. This usually takes from an hour and a half to two hours,—generally in the evening. The steam is then turned off and the mass is allowed to cook itself, by the accumulated heat, until morning, when any mustiness or mouldiness of the long fodder is destroyed, and the whole is permeated with the flavor and odor of the bran or meal mixed with it.

The above-described operation is very simple, and only requires precaution on two points :—

1. The steaming-box or chamber must have a weak point at which the steam may find its way out without straining the permanent parts. This will usually supply itself in a little imperfection of fitting about the doors.

2. The fodder must be well moistened before it is put into the chamber, for *dry hay will not cook.*

My chamber, which has a capacity of about 425 cubic feet, holds, if packed full, enough food to supply my whole stock for rather more than four days. It is made with matched spruce flooring nailed on both sides of 6-inch joists, and to the under side of the floor-joists above. The spaces above and on the four sides are packed full with sawdust. The floor is covered with galvanized iron, with soldered joints, turned up a little at the sides. On the bottom 3 × 4 joists are laid, and on these there are loose strips of board about six inches wide, laid with half-inch spaces between them. The steam is admitted below this loose bottom and rises through its spaces.

As to the *profit* of steaming, I am not prepared by definite figures to assert that the usual estimate is correct, that one-third of the food is saved, though, after two seasons' careful observation, I fully believe it. This I am sure of: that corn-stalks that have moulded in the stack, musty oats which have been cut green and badly cured, and smoky hay,—nearly the whole of which would be rejected if fed uncooked,—are eaten with avidity and with evident benefit to the stock.

On the score of health and condition, this system is all that could be desired. In only two or three instances have cases of "scouring" occurred, and these were immediately remedied by the substitution of long hay for a few days. I question whether there is any advantage in cooking roots. There is a freshness about these in their raw state that is perhaps beneficial,—and is surely very acceptable to stock.

It would be an easy (and a pleasant) task to write a book as large as this one on the single subject of this chapter. To enter with any thing like fullness into details in this limited space, would be impossible, and I have preferred to devote the few pages that could be spared for the purpose rather to general principles than to minute instructions. What I have chiefly tried to accomplish has been to so state a few of the leading points, that my readers should be induced to seek fuller information in works devoted especially to physiological questions, and to the economy of the stable.

It is proper to say that, so far as our own practice is concerned, we have steamed less and less every year since we began to have good early cut hay from our own land. We still use it for corn-fodder and for purchased hay which is not of the best quality. For all such material as this the process is decidedly profitable; for the preparation of *first-rate* hay it is not needed. Really good hay is good enough.

CHAPTER XVIII.

USEFUL TABLES FOR FARMERS.

THE following tables, collected from various sources, contain information to which it will be especially "handy" for every farmer and gardener to have easy access. Of course, much of their contents it would be impossible for me to verify by actual experience, but they are all taken from standard authorities, and are universally accepted as correct.

TABLE, *showing the square feet and the feet square of the fractions of an acre.*

Fractions of an acre.	Square feet.	Feet square.	Fractions of an acre.	Square feet.	Feet square.
1/16	2722½	52¼	½	21780	147⅗
⅛	5445	73¾	1	43560	208⅗
¼	10890	104⅓	2	87120	295⅕
⅓	14520	120½			

TABLE, *showing the number of hills or plants on an acre of land, for any distance apart, from* 10 *inches to* 6 *feet—the lateral and longitudinal distances being unequal.*

	10 in.	12 in.	15 in.	18 in.	20 in.	2 ft.	2½ ft.	3 ft.	3½ ft.	4 ft.	4½ ft.	5 ft.	5½ ft.	6 ft.
10 in	62726													
12 "	52272	43560												
15 "	41817	34848	27878											
18 "	34848	29040	23232	19360										
20 "	31363	26136	20908	17424	15681									
2 feet	26135	21780	17424	14520	13068	10890								
2½ "	20908	17424	13939	11616	10454	8712	6969							
3 "	17424	14520	11616	9680	8712	7260	5808	4840						
3½ "	14935	12446	9953	8297	7467	6223	4976	4148	3565					
4 "	13068	10890	8712	7260	6534	5445	4356	3630	3111	2722				
4½ "	11616	9680	7744	6453	5808	4840	3872	3226	2767	2420	2151			
5 "	10454	8712	6969	5808	5227	4356	3484	2904	2489	2178	1936	1742		
5½ "	9504	7920	6336	5280	4752	3960	3168	2640	2263	1980	1760	1584	1440	
6 "	8712	7260	5808	4840	4356	3630	2904	2420	2074	1865	1613	1452	1320	1210

TABLE, *showing the number of plants, hills, or trees contained in an acre at equal distances apart, from 3 inches up to 66 feet.*

Distance apart.	No. of plants.	Distance apart.	No. of plants.
3 inches by 3 inches	696,960	6 feet by 6 feet	1,210
4 " by 4 "	392,040	6½ " by 6½ "	1,031
6 " by 6 "	174,240	7 " by 7 "	881
9 " by 9 "	77,440	8 " by 8 "	680
1 foot by 1 foot	43,560	9 " by 9 "	537
1½ feet by 1½ feet	19,360	10 " by 10 "	435
2 feet by 1 foot	21,780	11 " by 11 "	360
2 " by 2 feet	10,890	12 " by 12 "	302
2½ " by 2½ "	6,960	13 " by 13 "	257
3 " by 1 foot	14,520	14 " by 14 "	222
3 " by 2 feet	7,260	15 " by 15 "	193
3 " by 3 "	4,840	16 " by 16 "	170
3½ " by 3½ "	3,555	16½ " by 16½ "	160
4 " by 1 foot	10,890	17 " by 17 "	150
4 " by 2 feet	5,445	18 " by 18 "	134
4 " by 3 "	3,630	19 " by 19 "	120
4 " by 4 "	2,722	20 " by 20 "	108
4½ " by 4½ "	2,151	25 " by 25 "	69
5 " by 1 foot	8,712	30 " by 30 "	48
5 " by 2 feet	4,356	33 " by 33 "	40
5 " by 3 "	2,904	40 " by 40 "	27
5 " by 4 "	2,178	50 " by 50 "	17
5 " by 5 "	1,742	60 " by 60 "	12
5½ " by 5½ "	1,417	66 " by 66 "	10

TABLE, *showing the quantity of garden seeds required to plant a given space.*

Designation.	Space and quantity of seeds.
Asparagus	1 oz. produces 1000 plants. and requires a bed 12 feet square.
" Roots.	1000 plant a bed 4 feet wide 225 feet long.
Eng. Dwarf Beans	1 quart plants from 100 to 150 feet of row.
French "	1 " " 250 or 350 feet of row.
Beans, pole, large	1 " " 100 hills.
" " small	1 " " 300 " or 250 feet of row.
Beets	10 lbs. to the acre ; 1 oz. plants 150 feet of row.
Broccoli and Kale	1 oz. plants 2500 plants. and requires 40 square feet of ground.
Cabbage	Early sorts same as broccoli, and require 60 square feet of ground.
Cauliflower	The same as cabbage.
Carrot	1 oz. to 150 of row.
Celery	1 oz. gives 7000 plants, and requires 8 square feet of ground.
Cucumber	1 oz. for 150 hills.
Cress	1 oz. sows a bed 16 feet square.
Egg Plant	1 oz. gives 2000 plants.
Endive	1 oz. " 3000 " and requires 80 feet of ground.
Leek	1 oz. " 2000 " and " 60 " "
Lettuce	1 oz. " 7000 " and " seed bed of 120 feet.
Melon	1 oz. for 120 hills.
Nasturtium	1 oz. sows 25 feet of row.
Onion	1 oz. " 200 " "
Okra	1 oz. " 200 " "
Parsley	1 oz. " 200 " "
Parsnip	1 oz. " 250 " "
Peppers	1 oz. gives 2500 plants.
Peas	1 quart sows 120 feet of row.
Pumpkin	1 oz. to 50 hills.
Radish	1 oz. to 100 feet.
Salsify	1 oz. to 150 " of row.
Spinage	1 oz. to 200 " "
Squash	1 oz. to 75 hills.
Tomato	1 oz. gives 2500 plants, requiring seed bed of 80 feet.
Turnip	1 oz. to 2000 feet.
Water Melon	1 oz. to 50 hills.

TABLE, *showing the quantity of seed required to the acre.*

Designation.	Quantity of seed.	Designation.	Quantity of seed.
Wheat	1½ to 2 bush.	Broom Corn	1 to 1½ bush.
Barley	1½ to 2½ "	Potatoes	5 to 10 "
Oats	2 to 4 "	Timothy	12 to 24 quarts.
Rye	1 to 2 "	Mustard	8 to 20 "
Buckwheat	½ to 1½ "	Herd Grass	12 to 16 "
Millet	1 to 1½ "	Flat Turnip	2 to 3 lbs.
Corn	½ to 1 "	Red Clover	10 to 16 "
Beans	1 to 2 "	White Clover	3 to 4 "
Peas	2½ to 3½ "	Blue Grass	10 to 15 "
Hemp	1 to 1½ "	Orchard Grass	20 to 30 "
Flax	½ to 2 "	Carrots	4 to 5 "
Rice	2 to 2½ "	Parsnips	6 to 8 "

TABLE, *showing the quantity per acre when planted in rows or drills.*

Broom Corn	1 to 1½ bush.	Onions	4 to 5 lbs.
Beans	1½ to 2 "	Carrots	2 to 2½ "
Peas	1½ to 2 "	Parsnips	4 to 5 "
		Beets	4 to 6 "

TABLE, *showing the number of seeds in one pound, and weight per bushel.*

NAME.	No. of Seeds per lb.	No. lbs. per bush.
Wheat	10,500	58 to 64
Barley	15,400	48 to 56
Oats	20,000	38 to 42
Rye	23,000	56 to 60
Vetches	8,300	60 to 63
Lentils	8,200	58 to 60
Beans	600 to 1,300	60 to 65
Peas	1800 to 2,000	60 to 65
Flax seed	108,000	50 to 60
Turnip seed	155,000	50 to 56
Rape seed	118,000	50 to 56
Mustard (white)	75,000	57
Cabbage seed	128,000	52
Mangel-wurzel	24,600	20 to 24
Parsnip seed	97,000	14
Carrot seed	257,000	9
Lucern seed	205,000	58 to 60
Clover (red)	249,600	60 to 63
" (white)	686,400	59 to 62
Rye-grass (perennial)	334,000	20 to 28
" (Italian)	272,000	13 to 18
Sweet vernal grass	923,000	8

TABLE, *showing the number of rails, stakes, and riders required for each 10 rods of fence.*

Length of rail.	Deflection from right line.	Length of panel.	Number of panels.	Number of rails for each 10 rods.			Number of stakes.	Number of riders. (Single.)
Feet.	Feet.	Feet.	Feet.	5 rails high.	6 rails high.	7 rails high.		
12	6	8	20½	103	123	144	42	21
14	7	10	16½	83	99	116	34	17
16½	8	12	13¾	69	84	95	28	14

TABLE, *showing the number of rails and posts required for each* 10 *rods of post and rail fence.*

Length of rail.	Length of panel.	Number of panels.	Number of posts.	Number of rails for each 10 rods.			
Feet.	Feet.			5 rails high.	6 rails high.	7 rails high.	8 rails high.
10	8	20½	21	103	123	144	165
12	10	16½	17	83	99	116	131
14	12	13¾	14	69	84	95	109
16½	14½	11½	12	57	69	81	93

TABLE, *showing the number of loads of manure and the number of heaps to each load required to each acre, the heaps at given distances apart.*

Distance of heaps apart, in yards.	NUMBER OF HEAPS IN A LOAD.									
	1	2	3	4	5	6	7	8	9	10
3	538	269	179	134	108	89½	77	67	60	54
3½	395	168	132	99	79	66	56½	49½	44	39½
4	203	151	101	75½	60½	50½	43½	37¾	33½	30¼
4½	239	120	79½	60	47¾	39¾	34½	30	26½	24
5	194	97	64½	48½	38¾	32½	27¾	24¼	21½	19½
5½	160	80	53½	40	32	26¾	22¾	20	17¾	16
6	131	67	44¾	33½	27	22½	19¼	16¾	15	13½
6½	115	57½	38¼	28¾	23	19	16¼	14¼	12¾	11½
7	99	49½	33	24¾	19¾	16½	14	12¼	11	10
7½	86	43	28¾	21½	17¼	14½	12½	10¾	9½	8½
8	75½	37¾	25¼	19	15¾	12½	10¾	9½	8½	7½
8½	67	33½	22¼	16¾	13½	11¼	9½	8½	7½	6½
9	60	30	20	15	12	10	8½	7½	6½	6
9½	53½	26¾	18	13½	10½	9	7¾	6½	6	5½
10	48½	24½	16¼	12	9½	8	7	6	5½	4½

TABLE, *showing the relative values of decomposed vegetables as manures,
from the inorganic matter they contain.*

Inorganic Matter.
lbs.   lbs.

1 ton	Wheat Straw made into manure returns to the soil....	70 to 360
1 "	Oat	"	"	"	"	"	.... 100 to 180
1 "	Hay	"	"	"	"	"	.... 100 to 200
1 "	Barley	"	"	"	"	"	....100 to 120
1 "	Pea	"	"	"	"	"	....100 to 110
1 "	Bean	"	"	"	"	"	.... 100 to 130
1 "	Rye	"	"	"	"	"	.... 50 to 100
1 "	Dry Potato-tops	"	"	"	"	400
1 "	Dry Turnip-tops	"	"	"	"	370
1 "	Rape Cake	"	"	"	"	120
1 "	Malt Dust	"	"	"	"	180
1 "	Dried Seaweed	"	"	"	"	 560

Johnston.

TABLE, *showing the relative values of decomposed vegetables as manures,
from the nitrogen they contain.*

100 lbs. of farm-yard manure is equal to

130 lbs. Wheat Straw Manure.	80 lbs. Fresh Seaweed	Manure.
150 " Oat " "	20 " Dried "	
180 " Barley "	26 " Bran of Wheat or Corn "	
85 " Bkwheat " "	13 " Malt Dust "	
45 " Pea " "	8 " Rape Cake "	
50 " Wheat Chaff "	250 " Pine Sawdust "	
80 " Green Grass "	180 " Oak " "	
75 " Potato Tops "	15 " Coal Soot "	

Boussingault.

TABLE, *showing the labor one horse is able to perform at different rates
of speed on canals, railroads, and turnpikes. Drawing force, 83½ lbs.*

Speed per hour. Miles.	Duration of day's work—hours.	Useful effect for 1 day in tons, drawn 1 mile.		
		On canal—tons.	On a railroad—tons.	On a turnpike, tons.
2½	11¼	520	115	14
3	8	243	92	12
3½	6	154	82	10
4	4¼	101	72	9
5	2 9/10	52	57	7.3
6	2	30	48	6
7	1¼	19	41	5
8	1¼	11.8	36	4.5
9	9/10	9.	32	4.
10	¼	6.5	28.8	3.6

WEIGHT of the bushel of agricultural produce, etc., as established by law in the United States, Territories, and British Provinces, compared with the most recent enactments.

	California	Canada	Connecticut	Dakota	Delaware	Illinois	Indiana	Iowa	Kansas	Kentucky	Louisiana	Maine	Maryland	Massachusetts	Michigan	Minnesota	Missouri	Nebraska	Nevada	New Brunswick	New Hampshire	New Jersey	New York	Nova Scotia	Ohio	Oregon	Pennsylvania	Rhode Island	Vermont	Washington Ter.	Wisconsin
Apples	50					48		48	48		32			48	48	48	48	48	50	50		48	48	52¼	48	45				45	
Barley	40	48	48	48		48	48	48	48	48		48		48	48	48	48	48	50	50		48	48	52¼	48	46	47		48	45	48
Bran		48				20		20	20	20							20	20													
Broom Corn Seed	40	60				52	50	50	50	52						42	52	52	40	50		50			50	42	48	50	46	42	42
Buckwheat	52	40	55	42			50	52	50	52		48		48	48	42	52	51		56		50	48		50	42	48	50	46	50	42
Carrots							46	46	46						46		46	46													
Castor Beans		40				80	80*	80	80					80	80		80	80							80						
Coal, Mineral				56	56	56	56	56	56	56	56	56		56	56		56	56	52	60	56	56	58	58	56	56	56	50	56	56	56
Corn, Shelled		56		56		56	56	56	56	50					56		56	56			56				60	56	56	56		56	
Corn, in Ear				72		70	68	70	70					70	70		70	70		60					70						
Corn Meal	40		50			48	50			50				50	40			50			50				60						
Cranberries		22				24	25	24							32	28	24	24							25	28				28	28
Dried Apples		33				33	33	33							28	25	33	33							33	28				28	28
Dried Peaches						56		56	56	56					56		56	56				55	58	58	56					56	56
Dried Plums		14		8		14	14	14		14					14		14	14													
Flax Seed		60		60		60	60	56	60	60						60	60	60				64	60		62	60	62		60		60
Grass Seed, Blue															50		60	85							50		62				
Grass Seed, Clover								45							50			60							50						
Grass Seed, Hungarian								45							14																
Grass Seed, Millet		48		42		45	45	45	45	45					14		45	45		40					45				42	40	46
Grass Seed, Orchard						8									14		8	8					44								
Grass Seed, Red Top		44				44	44	44	44	44					44		44	44		40			44	39	44						
Grass Seed, Timothy						80		44																	44						
Hair, Plastering		16				38												10							34						
Hemp Seed																															
Lime, Unslacked																															
Malt																															

* Mined within the State, 70 lbs.; without the State, 80 lbs.   † Foreign,—Barley produced in the Province, 48 lbs.   ‡ Bituminous,—Cannel Coal, 70 lbs.

WEIGHT OF THE BUSHEL OF AGRICULTURAL PRODUCE (continued).

	California.	Canada.	Connecticut.	Dakota.	Delaware.	Illinois.	Indiana.	Iowa.	Kansas.	Kentucky.	Louisiana.	Maine.	Maryland.	Massachusetts.	Michigan.	Minnesota.	Missouri.	Nebraska.	Nevada.	New B'unswick.	New Hampshire.	New Jersey.	New York.	Nova Scotia.	Ohio.	Oregon.	Pennsylvania.	Rhode Island.	Vermont.	Washington Ter.	Wisconsin.
Mangel-Wurzel	12		60	12		32		35	32	11½	32	60		32	32		35	32		35	30	32	32		32	32	32	50	30	35	12
Oats		34	32	32		32	32	32	32	57	32	32		32	32		32	32		32										50	
Onions, Top		60	50			57	48	57	57	57		52			50			50													
Osage-Orange Seed			45																											45	
Parsnips		60	60	60		60	60	60	60					60	60		60	60		50			50		50		50		50	60	
Pears								46										56		56						45					
Peas		60	56	60		60	60	60	60	56		60	56	60	60		60	60	54	56	56		60	56	60	60	56			60	60
Potatoes, Irish		60	60	60	60	60	60	60	60	56	32	60		60	60		60	60		56	60		60				85	60		60	
Potatoes, sweet																				56							70	55			
Ruta Baga	54		60									64																			
Rye		56	56	56		56	56	56	56	56		56	56	56	56		56	56		56	56	56	56	56	56	56	56	56	56	56	56
Salt, Coarse																															
Salt, Fine																															
Salt, Ground								130																							
Sand																															
Sugar Beets																															
Turnips		60	60	60		55	56	60	60	60		60			55			55		56	60		60					50		60	60
Wheat		60	60	60	60	60	60	60	60	60	60	60		60	60	60	60	60		60	60	60	60	60	60	60		55	60	60	
White Beans		60	60									64			60			60			60										

"Salt" in Canada is 56 pounds to the bushel; in Illinois, Indiana, Iowa, Kansas, Kentucky, Missouri, and Nebraska it is 50 pounds to the bushel. In Michigan, "Michigan Salt," is 56 pounds to the bushel. In Massachusetts "Salt" is 70 pounds to the bushel.

Coal in Kentucky is 76 pounds per bushel, *except* Wheeling coal, which is 84, and Kentucky River, which is 78 pounds per bushel, and Adrian Branch, or Cumberland River coal, which is 72 pounds per bushel. Cotton seed is 33 pounds to the bushel in Missouri

Sorghum seed is 30 pounds to the bushel in Iowa and Nebraska. Strained honey is 12 pounds to the gallon in Nebraska

To reduce cubic feet to bushels, struck measure, divide the cubic feet by 56 and multiply by 45.

AVERAGE *composition, per cent. and per ton, of various kinds of agricultural produce, etc.*

	PER CENT.					LBS. PER (LONG) TON.					Value of manure in £ and cts. from 1 ton (2000 lbs.) of food.
	Total dry matter.	Total mineral matter (ash.)	Phosphoric acid reckoned as phosphate of lime.	Potash.	Nitrogen.	Total dry matter.	Total mineral matter (ash.)	Phosphoric acid reckoned as phosphate of lime.	Potash.	Nitrogen.	
1. Linseed cake	88.0	7.00	4.92	1.65	4.75	1,971	156.8	110.2	37.0	106.4	19.72
2. Cotton-seed cake	89.0	8.00	7 00	3.12	6.50	1,994	179.2	156.8	70.0	145.6	27.86
3. Rape cake	89.0	8.00	5.75	1.76	5.00	1,994	179.2	128.8	39.4	112.0	21.01
4. Linseed	90.0	4.00	3.38	1.37	3.80	2,016	89.6	75.7	30 7	85.1	15.65
5. Beans	84.0	3.00	2.20	1.27	4.00	1,882	67.2	49.3	28.4	89.6	15.75
6. Peas	84.0	2.40	1.84	0.96	3.40	1,893	53.8	41.2	21 5	76.2	13.38
7. Tares	84.5	2.00	1.63	0.66	4.20	1,892	44.8	36.5	14.8	94.1	16.75
8. Lentils	88.0	3.00	1.89	0.96	4.30	1,971	67.2	42.3	21.5	96.3	16.51
9. Malt dust	94.0	8.50	5.23	2.12	4.20	2,106	190.4	117.1	47.5	94.1	18.21
10. Locust beans	85.0	1.75	...	....	1.25	1,904	39.2	....	....	28.0	4 81
11. Indian meal	88.0	1.30	1.13	0.35	1.80	1,971	29.1	25.3	7.8	40.3	6.65
12. Wheat	85.0	1.70	1.87	0.50	1.80	1,904	38.1	42.0	11.2	40.3	7.08
13. Barley	84.0	2.20	1.35	0.55	1.65	1,882	49.3	30.2	12.3	37 0	6.32
14. Malt	95 0	2.60	1.60	0.65	1 70	2,128	58.2	35.8	14.6	38 1	6.65
15. Oats	86.0	2 85	1.17	0.50	2.00	1,926	63.8	26.2	11.2	44.8	7.70
16. Fine pollard*	86.0	5.60	6.44	1 46	2.60	1,926	125.4	144.2	32.7	58.2	13.53
17. Coarse pollard†	86.0	6.20	7.52	1 49	2.58	1,926	138.9	168.4	33.4	57.8	14.36
18. Wheat bran	86.0	6.60	7.95	1.45	2.55	1,926	147.8	178.1	32.5	57.1	14.59
19. Clover hay	84.0	7.50	1.25	1.30	2.5.	1,882	168.0	28.0	29 1	56.0	9.64
20. Meadow hay	84.0	6.00	0.88	1.50	1 50	1,882	134.4	19.7	33.6	33.6	6.43
21. Bean straw	82.5	5.55	0.90	1.11	0.90	1,848	124.3	20.2	24.9	20.2	3.87
22. Pea straw	82.0	5.95	0.85	0.89	....	1,837	133.3	19.0	19.9	20.2	3.74
23. Wheat straw	84.0	5.00	0.55	0.65	0.63	1,882	112.0	12 3	14.1	11.2	2.68
24. Barley straw	85.0	4.50	0.37	0.63	0.50	1,904	100.8	8.3	14.1	11.2	2.25
25. Oat straw	83.0	5.50	0 48	0.93	0.60	1,859	123.2	10.7	20.8	13.4	2.90
26. Mangel-wurzel	12.5	1.00	0 09	0.25	0.25	280	22.4	2.0	5.6	5.6	1.07
27. Swedish turnips	11.0	0.68	0.13	0.18	0.22	246	13.4	2.9	4 0	4.6	0 91
28. Common turnips	8.0	0.68	0.11	0.29	0.18	179	15.2	2.5	6 5	4.0	0.86
29. Potatoes	24.0	1.00	0.12	0.41	0.35	537	22.4	7.2	9.6	7.8	1.50
30. Carrots	13.5	0.70	0.13	0.23	0.20	302	15.7	2.9	5.1	4.5	0 80
31. Parsnips	15.0	1.00	0.42	0.36	0.22	336	22.4	9.4	8.1	4.9	1.14

* Middlings, Canielle. † Shipstuff.

TABLE, *showing the proportion of solid matter and water in 100 parts each of the following articles of diet.*

Designation.	Solid Matter.	Water.	Designation.	Solid Matter.	Water.	Designation.	Solid Matter.	Water.
Wheat	87	13	Lean beef	26	74	Carrots	13	87
Peas	87	13	Eggs	26	74	Beets	13	87
Rice	86	14	Veal	25	75	Milk	13	87
Beans	86	14	Potatoes	25	75	Oysters	13	87
Rye	86	14	Pork	24	76	Cabbage	8	92
Corn	86	14	Codfish	21	79	Turnips	7	93
Oatmeal	74	26	Blood	20	80	Water melon	5	95
Wheat bread	51	49	Trout	19	81	Cucumber	3	97
Mutton	29	71	Apples	18	82			
Chicken	27	73	Pears	16	84			

TABLE, *showing at one view when forty weeks (the period of gestation in a cow) will expire, from any day throughout the year.*

Jan.	Oct.	Feb.	Nov.	March.	Dec.	April.	Jan.	May.	Feb.	June.	March.
1	8	1	8	1	6	1	6	1	5	1	8
2	9	2	9	2	7	2	7	2	6	2	9
3	10	3	10	3	8	3	8	3	7	3	10
4	11	4	11	4	9	4	9	4	8	4	11
5	12	5	12	5	10	5	10	5	9	5	12
6	13	6	13	6	11	6	11	6	10	6	13
7	14	7	14	7	12	7	12	7	11	7	14
8	15	8	15	8	13	8	13	8	12	8	15
9	16	9	16	9	14	9	14	9	13	9	16
10	17	10	17	10	15	10	15	10	14	10	17
11	18	11	18	11	16	11	16	11	15	11	18
12	19	12	19	12	17	12	17	12	16	12	19
13	20	13	20	13	18	13	18	13	17	13	20
14	21	14	21	14	19	14	19	14	18	14	21
15	22	15	22	15	20	15	20	15	19	15	22
16	23	16	23	16	21	16	21	16	20	16	23
17	24	17	24	17	22	17	22	17	21	17	24
18	25	18	25	18	23	18	23	18	22	18	25
19	26	19	26	19	24	19	24	19	23	19	26
20	27	20	27	20	25	20	25	20	24	20	27
21	28	21	28	21	26	21	26	21	25	21	28
22	29	22	29	22	27	22	27	22	26	22	29
23	30	23	30	23	28	23	28	23	27	23	30
24	31		Dec.	24	29	24	29	24	28	24	31
	Nov.	24	1	25	30	25	30		March.		April.
25	1	25	2	26	31	26	31	25	1	25	1
26	2	26	3		Jan.		Feb.	26	2	26	2
27	3	27	4	27	1	27	1	27	3	27	3
28	4	28	5	28	2	28	2	28	4	28	4
29	5	29	6	29	3	29	3	29	5	29	5
30	6			30	4	30	4	30	6	30	6
31	7			31	5			31	7		

TABLE, *continued.*

July.	April.	Aug.	May.	Sept.	June.	Oct.	July.	Nov.	Aug.	Dec.	Sept.
1	7	1	8	1	8	1	8	1	8	1	7
2	8	2	9	2	9	2	9	2	9	2	8
3	9	3	10	3	10	3	10	3	10	3	9
4	10	4	11	4	11	4	11	4	11	4	10
5	11	5	12	5	12	5	12	5	12	5	11
6	12	6	13	6	13	6	13	6	13	6	12
7	13	7	14	7	14	7	14	7	14	7	13
8	14	8	15	8	15	8	15	8	15	8	14
9	15	9	16	9	16	9	16	9	16	9	15
10	16	10	17	10	17	10	17	10	17	10	16
11	17	11	18	11	18	11	18	11	18	11	17
12	18	12	19	12	19	12	19	12	19	12	18
13	19	13	20	13	20	13	20	13	20	13	19
14	20	14	21	14	21	14	21	14	21	14	20
15	21	15	22	15	22	15	22	15	22	15	21
16	22	16	23	16	23	16	23	16	23	16	22
17	23	17	24	17	24	17	24	17	24	17	23
18	24	18	25	18	25	18	25	18	25	18	24
19	25	19	26	19	26	19	26	19	26	19	25
20	26	20	27	20	27	20	27	20	27	20	26
21	27	21	28	21	28	21	28	21	28	21	27
22	28	22	29	22	29	22	29	22	29	22	28
23	29	23	30	23	30	23	30	23	30	23	29
24	30	24	31		July.	24	31	24	31	24	30
	May.		June.	24	1		Aug.		Sept.		Oct.
25	1	25	1	25	2	25	1	25	1	25	1
26	2	26	2	26	3	26	2	26	2	26	2
27	3	27	3	27	4	27	3	27	3	27	3
28	4	28	4	28	5	28	4	28	4	28	4
29	5	29	5	29	6	29	5	29	5	29	5
30	6	30	6	30	7	30	6	30	6	30	6
31	7	31	7			31	7			31	7

TABLE, *showing the period of reproduction and gestation of domestic animals.*

Designation.	Proper age for reproduction.	Period of the power of reproduction in years.	Number of females for one male	Period of gestation and incubation.		
				Shortest period, days.	Mean period, days.	Longest period, days.
Mare.........	4 years.	10 to 11	...	322	347	419
Stallion........	5 "	12 to 15	20 to 30	....	....	....
Cow	3 "	10 to 14	....	240	283	321
Bull	3 "	8 to 10	30 to 40	....	....	....
Ewe	2 "	6	......	146	154	161
Ram........ ..	2 "	7	40 to 50	....	....	....
Sow	1 "	6	....	109	115	143
Boar...	1 "	6	6 to 10	....	....	....
She Goat.......	2 "	6	....	150	156	163
He Goat	2 "	5	20 to 40	....	....	....
She Ass.... ...	4 "	10 to 12	..... .	365	380	391
He Ass........	5 "	12 to 15	....	....	....	....
She Buffalo.....	....	8	....	281	308	335
Bitch	2 "	8 to 9	....	55	60	63
Dog..........	2 "	8 to 9	....	....	....	....
She Cat.......	1 "	5 to 6	....	48	50	56
He Cat	1 "	9 to 10	5 to 6	....	....	....
Doe Rabbit	6 months.	5 to 6	....	20	28	35
Buck Rabbit ...	6 "	5 to 6	30	....	....	....
Cock...... ...	6 "	5 to 6	12 to 15	....	....	....
Hen...........	....	3 to 5	....	19	21	24
Turkey........	....	....	....	24	26	30
Duck..........	....	....	....	28	30	32
Goose	....	....	....	27	30	33
Pigeon	....	....	....	16	18	20
Pea Hen.......	....	....	....	25	28	30
Guinea Hen....	....	....	....	20	23	25
Swan..........	....	....	....	40	42	45

TABLE, *showing the price of pork per pound at different prices per bushel for corn.*

Corn per bushel. Cents.	Pork per pound. Cents.	Corn per bushel. Cents.	Pork per pound. Cents.
12½	1.50	38	4.52
15	1.78	40	4.76
17	2.	42	5.
20	2.38	45	5.35
22	2.62	50	5.95
25	2.96	55	6.54
30	3.57	60	7.14
33	3.92	65	7.74
35	4.	70	8.57

TABLE, *showing the contents of circular cisterns in barrels for each foot in depth.*

5 feet	4.66
6 "	6.74
7 "	9.13
8 "	11.93
9 "	15.10
10 "	18.65

TABLE, *showing the contents of circular cisterns from 1 foot to 25 feet in diameter, for each 10 inches in depth.*

Diameter.	Gallons.	Diameter.	Gallons.
1	4.896	7½	271.072
1¼	11.015	8	313.340
2	19.583	8½	353.735
2½	30.545	9	396.573
3	44.064	9½	441.861
3½	59.980	10	489.600
4	78.333	11	592.400
4½	99.116	12	705.
5	122.400	13	827.450
5½	148.546	14	959.613
6	176.253	15	1101.610
6½	206.855	20	1958.421
7	239.906	25	3059.934

ESTIMATING THE WEIGHT OF HAY BY THE MOW OR STACK.

By a careless oversight in the revision of " Courtney's Farmers' and Mechanics' Manual," an error appeared in the first edition, which brought me so many letters from all parts of the country, informing me that five cubic yards of mow hay do *not* weigh one ton, that it may be well to say here that the weight depends very much on coarseness, fineness, dryness, dampness, compactness, quality, time of making, weather during harvest, etc., etc., etc. In view of these changing conditions it is impossible to give any rule that is of much value

Hay in a mow ten feet drop, put in in good order, and not too ripe when cut, *ought* to average one ton to each 525 cubic feet. The compression increases rapidly as the height increases, and a mow of the same hay, fifteen feet drop, would probably turn out a ton to 475 cubic feet if not even to 425 feet. All such guessing, however, is very hazardous, and it is always safer to buy or sell only by actual weight.

Perhaps it would be a safe formula to say, *sell at 400 cubic feet and buy at 600 cubic feet.*

TABLE, *showing the price per cwt. of hay, at given prices per ton.*

Price per ton.	½ hundred.	1 hundred.	2 hundred.	3 hundred.	4 hundred.	5 hundred.	6 hundred.	7 hundred.	8 hundred.	9 hundred.	10 hundred.	11 hundred.
$	cts.	cts.	$ cts.	$ cts.	$ cts.	$ cts.	$ cts.	$ cts.	$ cts.	$ cts.	$ cts.	$ cts.
4	10	20	40	60	80	1.00	1.20	1.40	1 60	1.80	2.00	2.20
5	12	25	50	75	1.00	1.25	1.50	1.75	2 00	2.25	2 50	2.75
6	15	30	60	90	1.20	1 50	1.80	2.10	2.40	2.70	3 00	3.30
7	17	35	70	1.05	1.40	1.75	2.10	2.45	2.80	3.15	3.50	3 85
8	20	40	80	1.20	1.60	2.00	2.40	2.80	3.20	3 60	4.00	4.40
9	22	45	90	1 35	1.80	2.25	2 70	3.15	3.60	4.05	4 50	4.95
10	25	50	1.00	1.50	2.00	2.50	3.00	3.50	4.00	4.50	5.00	5.50
11	27	55	1.10	1.65	2.20	2.75	3.30	3.85	4.40	4.95	5.50	6 00
12	30	60	1.20	1.80	2.40	3.00	3 60	4.20	4.80	5.40	6.00	6.60
13	32	65	1.30	1.95	2.60	3.25	3.90	4.55	5.20	5.85	6.50	7.15
14	35	70	1.40	2 10	2.80	3.50	4.20	4.90	5.60	6.30	7.00	7.70
15	37	75	1.50	2.25	3.00	3.75	4.50	5.25	6.00	6.75	7.50	8.25

INDEX.

539